D0758870

THE
PUSHCART PRIZE, XXV:
BEST OF THE
SMALL PRESSES

25th Anniversary Edition

BEST OF
THE SMALL PRESSES

THE
PUSHCART
PRIZE
2001
XXV

EDITED BY
BILL HENDERSON
WITH THE PUSHCART
PRIZE EDITORS

PUSHCART PRESS
WAINSCOTT, NEW YORK

Note: nominations for this series are invited from any small, independent, literary book press or magazine in the world. Up to six nominations–tear sheets or copies, selected from work published, or about to be published, in the calendar year—are accepted by our December 1 deadline each year. Write to Pushcart Press, P.O. Box 380, Wainscott, N.Y. 11975 for more information.

Acknowledgments

Selections for The Pushcart Prize are reprinted from recent publications with the permission of authors and presses cited. Copyright reverts to authors and presses immediately after publication.

Distributed by W. W. Norton & Co.
500 Fifth Ave., New York, N.Y. 10110

Library of Congress Card Number: 76–58675
ISBN: 1–888889–22–5
        1–888889–27–6 (paperback)
ISSN: 0149–7863

In Memoriam:

STANLEY W. LINDBERG (1939–2000)
PAUL BOWLES (1910–1999)

INTRODUCTION
by BILL HENDERSON

T WENTY-FIVE YEARS AGO, Pushcart Press threw a party for the first *Pushcart Prize* at Manhattan's Gotham Book Mart. All of the 70's literati showed up to sip white wine from plastic glasses and wish us well. I am looking now at photographs from that gathering. In one, I am standing near a young Jon Galassi—now head of Farrar, Straus & Giroux—and poet John Ashbery. In another, Francis Steloff, nearly 100 years old, founder of the store, laughs with Nona Balakian of the *New York Times.* Harold Brodkey had just entered the room behind them. Although the photos don't show it, I am terrified.

What exactly was I doing at the center of all this pleasant uproar? What were my qualifications to edit and publish an annual collection of my betters? None. I'd been fired from my last two publishing jobs, at Doubleday and Putnam. My only novel had been roundly rejected. I hadn't even finished reading *Ulysses* yet.

Somehow, with the help of friends, and copious sauce, I got through the evening in a shaky but not too embarrassing style, and settled into the task ahead—establishing a series that any wise person would have told me was doomed.

I didn't know then that George Plimpton had just been pummeled to a pulp for daring to edit three volumes of the *American Literary Anthology,* very similar to the *Pushcart Prize* idea but sponsored with federal money. Years later, George let me know that because his collection had mentioned a Vaseline jar with some connection to Allen Ginsberg, a fussy, ambitious congressman had threatened to shut down the entire National Endowment for the Arts. When George offered to postpone the Vaseline article, he was crucified by the literary powers of the time. Read about it in his hilarious introduction to *Pushcart Prize X.*

Everybody at that Gotham Book Mart gathering but me knew that PPII would probably never appear. A terrific idea, but who would fund such a venture? A collection of mostly unknown poets, essayists and fictioneers? Worthy, sure. But forget about it.

What those silent critics didn't know, however, was that I had a force behind me—the enthusiasm of 22 Founding Editors who had offered me, an unknown, their unqualified support. I repeat their names with reverence: Anaïs Nin, Buckminster Fuller, Charles Newman, Daniel Halpern, Gordon Lish, Harry Smith, Hugh Fox, Ishmael Reed, Joyce Carol Oates, Len Fulton, Leonard Randolph, Leslie Fiedler, Nona Balakian, Paul Bowles, Paul Engle, Ralph Ellison, Reynolds Price, Rhoda Schwartz, Richard Morris, Ted Wilentz, Tom Montag, William Phillips.

Without their support, no *Pushcart Prize.* They had responded to a two page, single-spaced letter that I had typed and mailed to over 100 literary lights during the summer of '75. These were old-fashioned, authentic letters, typed by the sender on an Olivetti manual from start to finish. No computer involved. You could believe the effort and earnestness because you were holding evidence of it in your hand. Typos, smudges and all.

In that letter, I described my plans for an annual celebration of small press authors and publishers. The idea had come to me over coffee at the Mediterranean Cafe in Berkeley, California, on a brief vacation: "why not a best of the small presses? So little read, so much good out there" I jotted in a notebook. It would be financed entirely by the one other book on Pushcart's list, *The Publish It Yourself Handbook,* published in 1973 on a budget of a few thousand dollars. It had sold 20,000 copies and I planned to sink all profits into the Prize project, and live simply and cheaply—no requests for grants from private, state or federal foundations. I wouldn't allow committees to make my decisions for me, and besides I was too lazy to fill out the required forms.

The response to the letter was quite unexpected. Joyce Carol Oates called early one morning and I mistook her quiet voice for that of a young school girl who had perhaps missed her bus. Paul Bowles air-mailed his immediate and favorable response from his home in Morocco. Ralph Ellison said it sounded like a fine idea to him and go ahead and use his name, but "I'm terribly busy and don't expect me to do any work." In a few weeks, I had my board of Founding Editors, and knew that, in theory at least, the *Pushcart Prize* was welcome.

I spent a good chunk of the budget on a full-page announcement in *Publishers Weekly* (and soon after was fired from my last publishing job). Peter Mayer, Avon's editor-in-chief, spotted the ad and summoned me to his office where I hoped I might be employed in some way. But it wasn't me he was interested in. "What's this Pushcart Prize?" he asked. I explained our plans and left his office with a small paperback offer. Since I had envisioned only an expensive, hardcover edition, Peter's contract was good news: readers without a huge book budget would now be able to afford our collection.

Nine years of paperbacks followed from Avon Books (where Walter Meade offered enthusiastic support), followed by four years from Penguin, four from Simon & Schuster's Touchstone (where André Bernard presided); and since PPXIX, Pushcart's own paperbacks distributed by W.W. Norton & Co., one of the few surviving independent, commercial presses and an organization of people so fine, and fair, and high-minded that I am constantly amazed that they are still in business.

What was the world like 25 years ago—the deep, dark ages when Doubleday, producer of 700 titles a year (remember Doubleday?) was the giant of the industry? Some publishers still printed books with linotype machines! How did any of us survive without the frantic Information Age? Weren't we starved for Info? And think about the creaky pace of things without e-mail and the Internet. Poor us.

Actually, 25 years ago was startlingly like the present. The root of all evil—love of cash—was just as real then as now. The terror that somebody else would get to the latest technology, thus depriving your firm of money and caché, was just as real.

During the early 70's, I was a young, associate editor at Doubleday. I had a cubicle in a bank of other cubicles and a secretary all my own, plus an expense account that I was supposed to blow on lunch with agents. Sometime during my brief stay there, books started to be called "units" and worse, the higher corporate powers were spooked by Marshall McLuhan's dictate "the medium is the message". Books ("units") were finished. Television was all. Immediately Doubleday bought up a few TV stations, trashed its book publisher letterhead and announced itself as "a multi-media corporation". Books be damned. Profit was heading elsewhere, said the popular wisdom.

9

(Shortly after that Nelson Doubleday ditched "multi-media" too. He sold the company and bought the New York Mets baseball team.)

When we learned we were now a "multi-media" outfit, bookish sorts, who revered authors and words, either became cynical (a tell-tale nervous laugh whenever bucks and principle clashed) or, as in my case, we spent lonely boozy lunches at the Blarney Stone, ignoring agents, preparing for the end of books, or at least the titles we loved and wanted to publish.

One mercenary incident remains burned in my mind from those days: The Prudential Insurance Company announced to Doubleday that it would like its corporate biography published for its 75th Birthday, and they hand-picked us to do it, with a handsome fee plus a nice salary for a safe writer. Somehow this proposal landed in my cubicle from the higher-ups. I brought it to our weekly editorial conference and denounced that whole idea as mere corporate vanity publishing and took it for granted that we would assert our dignity and dismiss Prudential with scorn. Immediately I was pounded on by senior editors as a complete idiot. If there had been a dunce cap in the room, it would have been jammed on my head. The hymn to Prudential was published with the Doubleday logo affixed to the spine, and both companies celebrated its happy birthday. We pocketed the payoff. Needless to say, if a novelist or poet had offered to pay for publication, the proposal wouldn't even have made it out of the slush pile.

In short, those times were very much like these times. Money attempting to stomp out value, and value popping up again here and there. Eliot Freemont-Smith, reviewer for the *Village Voice,* quoted in *Pushcart Prize III* (1978), complained "the treatment of writers does, I believe, get more callous every day—in newspapers, magazines and books as well. More and more accountants are taking over publishing. Numbers, leading to the holy bottom line, have always counted, but never to such an exclusionary degree." *Kirkus Reviews,* in lauding *Pushcart Prize IV* (1979), lashed out at commercial publishers for "lapping up the flashy and no-account."

Many critics saw our Prize as one of the cultural doughboys doing valiant battle against evil forces like General Electric and Mattel Toys, who were then poised to snap up a portion of the industry. Little did we know then but it wasn't GE and Barbie Doll we needed to fear. Soon the good book and magazine people themselves, led by MBA's, would begin to consume each other for profit, and then be

10

eaten alive by gargantuan firms based in England and Germany, leaving us today with only a handful of viable commercial houses—all of them, David *and* Goliath, terrified they will be decimated by the e-book and the Internet.

But way back in the gala 70's, writers still mattered to a few. Writers were not mere "content providers" hired to fill in the blanks around magazine ads. People were still called "customers," and not "consumers"—as if we are a nation of Biblical locusts consuming vast fields and laying waste to everything in our path. (Actually, come to think of it, "consumer" is exactly the word we deserve.)

At the head of the *New York Times Book Review* was Harvey Shapiro, a poet, an active, respected poet, for gosh sakes. Harvey was there every year with reviews for our Prize, most of them favorable, and almost single-handedly made sure we would not sink after PPI. Tom Lask, in the daily *Times*, took care to mention us too. *The Philadelphia Inquirer* and the *Times* named us a notable book of the year. The English Speaking Union, an international outfit, called the Prize one of the ten best books of the year. And *Publishers Weekly* in 1979 handed me its Carey Thomas Award for creative publishing. I remember the plaque was so heavy I had to make a very brief acceptance speech lest I drop it on the lunch table at the Algonquin and spoil our dessert.

From Iowa, Founding Editor Paul Engle, called with news that The People's Republic of China, then in the midst of the loosening of cultural regulations, was considering translating and distributing all editions of our Prize. Whatever happened to that notion I have no idea. Deep in some Beijing vault the answer lies on a scrap of decaying paper. Perhaps the Prudential folks nixed it. What glorious paranoia!

In any case, my letters to our Founding Editors in the summer of 1975 had led to a terrific response and much hard work. For some reason, Walden Books, then an immense chain that bestrode the book-retailing world like a behemoth (remember Walden Books?), decided its major stores needed hardcover Pushcarts, two or three copies each. By then I had left Pushcart's original home, a tiny studio in Yonkers, New York, for an even tinier room on New York City's Bleecker Street. Since I had no distributor in those early, pre-Norton days, I asked my mother if I could use her garage in suburban Philadelphia as a warehouse. She agreed and soon, to the amazement of her neighbors, two hundred-plus boxes, each with its own label

11

and invoice, were planted down on her driveway while her unusual son stuffed them with tomes, sealed them, personally licked the stamps and piled the boxes into her Pontiac for trips to the post office.

Months later, when copious returns arrived from Walden at New York's Prince Street post office, I jammed them into #1 mailbags and dragged them to Bleecker Street where my bed rested on said returns.

I realized I was somewhat of a fool but I thought at least "a holy fool" as Ted Hoagland described us small press types in his introduction to PPXVI.

In other introductions to our Prizes in those years, Cynthia Ozick declared, "Henderson's *Pushcart Prize* hears America singing its varied carols . . . a living current that unites." Tess Gallagher remembered her husband Ray Carver's joy in reading small press works aloud to her and how he fell asleep with an anthology (*Best American Short Stories*) under his head as a pillow when his first piece appeared there. And Russell Banks noted, "I would guess that the *Pushcart Prize* is the best-read annual that is published—read and not merely sold and collected on a shelf . . . this is the anthology that the writers read, especially the young writers—perhaps because its the only anthology whose contents have been selected by writers themselves."

All, of course, was not sweetness and light for the last 25 years. In reviewing PPVII, the *Village Voice* reviewer announced that it was boring and filled with typos. About the typos, she was right. Somebody (me) had failed to do a final check on the Index. And then there was the case a few years before that when two poems were stuck together and published as one. I reprinted the entire edition to fix that horror. And by issue #9 some wag at a right wing rag, hollered that I had a secret plan to take over all of New York publishing. I thought this was a rather curious delusion, since that was the year my wife Genie and I had moved a hundred miles from New York and our daughter Lily was born soon after. Then, as now, I work from an 8x8 hut in our backyard, heated with a space heater sparked by an extension cord running from the house.

Also, about that time, the bean counters at Avon had decided Pushcart's paperback revenues were not sufficient to continue Avon's association however "important to our culture", etc. etc. I took the

Prize to Penguin where Peter Mayer was now employed and where we were greeted with open arms and a new paperback contract. Peter was, and is, a legendary publishing independent at Overlook Press with his own shack in Woodstock, New York.

By the mid-eighties Pushcart's annual was recognized as "an institution" or as Anne Tyler put it in the *New York Times Book Review,* "a distinguished annual literary event." Pushcart, of course, has had a hard time passing as an institution since the press is usually near bankruptcy. (Often we have been rescued from such difficulties by Elizabeth and Michael Rea, who seemed to know when a check would be handy). And Pushcart has never considered itself particularly distinguished, or even literary for that matter. Keeping us humble have been the unceasing and opinionated contributions of over 200 contributing editors who annually nominate writers and their particular works that they have loved from the past year's small press publications. For 25 years, their letters have arrived, a generous outpouring of support that has kept me at my desk with a conviction that Pushcart must be doing at least something right to deserve such unequivocal backing.

Maybe those Founding Editors really did know what they were doing when they let a bored, disillusioned, naive refugee from commercial publishing use their names. I thank them.

And a whole lot more people too.

Thanks to Hannah Turner, who for almost the entire history of the project has managed the processing of almost 8,000 nominations every year. Hannah works from her home in Maryland and fills out the names on the nomination forms in calligraphy. What a joy it has been for authors to not only be nominated but to learn about it in Hannah's beautiful handwriting.

Thanks to the thousands of small presses who have sent in nominations over the decades, presses with names like *Bleb, Lame Johnny, Holy Cow!, Mr. Cogito, Crawl Out Your Window, Attaboy, Cat's Pajamas, Cosmic Circus, pulpart forms, Angst World Library, Scree, Paunch, Duck, Happiness Holding Tank, Alternative to Alienation*—and many with names well-known like *Paris Review, Partisan Review, Parnassus: Poetry In Review,* and *Ploughshares* to take but a short dip into the P's. (A complete list of reprinted presses follows).

Thanks also to the authors we have been honored to publish, over 1,000 of them, often early in their vocations: among them Ai, Paul

Auster, Donald Barthleme, Rick Bass, Charles Baxter, Harold Brodkey, Rosellen Brown, Ray Carver, Steve Dixon, Rita Dove, Andre Dubus, Stephen Dunn, Stuart Dybek, Louise Erdrich, Carolyn Forché, Richard Ford, Tess Gallagher, John Gardner, Louise Glück, Mary Gordon, Jorie Graham, Robert Hass, Seamus Heaney, Edward Hirsch, Linda Hogan, John Irving, Ha Jin, Mary Karr, Wally Lamb, Li-Young Lee, Philip Lopate, Alistair MacLeod, Bobbie Ann Mason, Susan Minot, Rick Moody, Tim O'Brien, Mary Oliver, Tom Paine, Jayne Anne Phillips, Francine Prose, Lynne Sharon Schwartz, Charles Simic, Mona Simpson, and Alexander Theroux, to name but a few who appeared in these pages during their early years.

Thanks also to Gail Godwin, Jayne Anne Phillips, George Plimpton, Cynthia Ozick, Frank Conroy, Richard Ford, Tess Gallagher, Russell Banks and Edward Hoagland for writing introductions to these volumes when I ran out of things to say and needed their visions.

Thanks to the Poetry Editors, new for each volume: Lloyd Van Brunt, Naomi Lazard, Lynn Spaulding, Herb Leibowitz, Jon Galassi, Grace Schulman, Carolyn Forché, Gerald Stern, Stanley Plumly, William Stafford, Philip Levine, David Wojahn, Jorie Graham, Robert Hass, Philip Booth, Jay Meek, Sandra McPherson, Laura Jensen, William Heyen, Elizabeth Spires, Marvin Bell, Carolyn Kizer, Christopher Buckley, Chase Twichell, Richard Jackson, Susan Mitchell, Lynn Emanuel, David St. John, Carol Muske, Dennis Schmitz, William Matthews, Patricia Strachan, Heather McHugh, Molly Bendall, Marilyn Chin, Michael Dennis Browne, Kimiko Hahn and, for this edition Billy Collins and Joan Murray.

And thanks to the people who helped with this 25th edition, in particular Tony Brandt, who for over a decade has been diligently reading the essays nominations. Not a syllable of nonsense escapes Tony, so don't even think of parking there. Look for *The Pushcart Book of Essays*, the best essays from a quarter century of Prize volumes, edited by Tony, coming soon.

Also a thanks to my fishing buddy, Jack Driscoll, who once again came into shore to help me edit the fiction nominations. His new novel is *Stardog*, soon to be a major motion picture, I predict. Major.

This year's Pushcart includes more poems than ever, picked by two super novas: Billy Collins and Joan Murray, who have since gone on

long vacations to recover from sampling thousands of poems and try-
ing to reach a final judgment. Both say they wish we could have
found space for dozens more poems.

Billy Collins is one of the few poets in history to have been fea-
tured on the front page of the *New York Times*. The article was about
a publishing squabble between two of his publishers, and the cher-
ished subject of the squabble, Mr. Collins. The *Times* noted that
John Updike is a Collins fan as are Edward Hirsch and Richard
Howard plus millions of ordinary poetry lovers who have heard him
read on National Public Radio and on Garrison Keillor's Prairie
Home Companion. "It can be argued that with his books selling
briskly and his readings packing them in, Mr. Collins is the most pop-
ular poet in America," the article concluded.

Billy, who began publishing in *Flying Faucet Review* and *Oink*, is
now the author of five books of poetry including *Questions About
Angels* (1999) and *Picnic, Lighting* (1998), both published by the
University of Pittsburgh Press. His recognitions include grants from
The Guggenheim Foundation and the National Endowment for the
Arts plus several awards from *Poetry*. In 1992, he was named "A Lit-
erary Lion" by the New York Public Library.

Joan Murray has yet to be featured on page one of the *Times* (their
loss) but she is one of the great forces of nature behind today's poets
and poetry publishing. Joan's books include: *Looking for the Parade*
(W.W. Norton, 1999), winner of the National Poetry Series, and,
Queen of the Mist (Beacon Press, 1999). Her collection, *The Same
Water* was winner of the Wesleyan New Poets Series (1990). She has
been featured in *Best American Poetry* and *The Pushcart Prize*. She
is a founding member of The Lead Pencil Club.

Many more people remain to be thanked in this introduction. In
twenty-five years, Pushcart has gathered more friends than can be
listed in any book. From that first notion of an annual anthology one
quiet morning at Berkeley's Mediterranean, to a summer of letter
typing in 1975, to decades of response from thousands of writers and
editors, *The Pushcart Prize* has been touched by grace and good will.
Flannery O'Connor described the moral basis of great writing as "the
accurate naming of the things of God." Over the years, I have seen
many such accurate namings, and the work has become better and
better, not, as one would suspect in the age of celebrity worship and
electronic din, worse and worse.

Talent abounds. Grace abounds. In evidence: the 74 stunning works from 54 presses that follow. Take it from this "Content Provider." We are not going away. Quite the opposite. God willing, I intend to write my next quarter century update in 2025. But first I have to learn how to count that high in roman numerals.

THE PEOPLE WHO HELPED

FOUNDING EDITORS—*Anaïs Nin (1903–1977) Buckminster Fuller (1895–1983), Charles Newman, Daniel Halpern, Gordon Lish, Harry Smith, Hugh Fox, Ishmael Reed, Joyce Carol Oates, Len Fulton, Leonard Randolph, Leslie Fiedler, Nona Balakian (1918–1991), Paul Bowles (1910–1999), Paul Engle (1908–1991), Ralph Ellison (1914–1994), Reynolds Price, Rhoda Schwartz, Richard Morris, Ted Wilentz, Tom Montag, William Phillips, Poetry editor: H. L. Van Brunt.*

CONTRIBUTING EDITORS FOR THIS EDITION—*Stephen Corey, Forrest Gander, Katayoon Zandvakili, Sharon Solwitz, Lynne McFall, Cathy Song, Antler, Brenda Hillman, Molly Giles, Thomas Kennedy, Christina Zawadiwsky, Tomaz Salamun, Jim Barnes, Janice Eidus, Robert Phillips, Alice Mattison, Elizabeth Spires, Rita Dove, William Olsen, Christopher Howell, Joe Stroud, Gary Fincke, Renée Ashley, Toi Derricotte, Gerry Locklin, Kenneth Gangemi, Andrew Hudgins, Carl Phillips, Christopher Buckley, Rachel Hadas, Gibbons Ruark, Agha Shahid Ali, Arthur Sze, Cyrus Cassells, Martin Espada, Thomas Lux, Claire Davis, Jennifer Atkinson, Tony Ardizzone, Len Roberts, Mark Cox, Marvin Bell, C. E. Poverman, Lynn Emanuel, DeWitt Henry, S.L. Wisenberg, Colum McCann, Tom Filer, Adrienne Su, Maureen Seaton, Steven Stern, Timothy Geiger, Mariko Nagai, Chard deNiord, Marilyn Hacker, Edmund Keeley, Lee Upton, Lance Olsen, Erin McGraw, Gordon Weaver, Colette Inez, Paul Zimmer, Grace Schulman, Edward Hoagland, Sheila Schwartz, Molly Bendall, James Harms, Laura Kasischke, Sylvia Watanabe, Philip Appleman, Emily Fox Gordon, David Romtvedt, Mark Jar-*

MANAGING EDITOR—*Hannah Turner*

AT LARGE—*Monica Hellman*

FICTION EDITORS—*Jack Driscoll, Bill Henderson*

POETRY EDITORS—*Billy Collins, Joan Murray*

ESSAYS EDITOR—*Anthony Brandt*

EDITOR AND PUBLISHER—*Bill Henderson*

CONTENTS

THE
PUSHCART PRIZE, XXV:
BEST OF THE
SMALL PRESSES

THE ANOINTED

fiction by KATHLEEN HILL

from DOUBLETAKE

My harp is turned to mourning.
And my flute to the voice of those who weep.
—Job 30:31

I

In MISS HUGHES'S SEVENTH-GRADE MUSIC CLASS, we were expected to sit without moving finger or foot while she played for us what she called "the music of the anointed." At a moment known only to herself, Miss Hughes opened the album of records ready at her elbow and, tipping her head from side to side, cautiously turned the leaves as if they had been the pages of a precious book. When she had found the 78 she was looking for, she drew it from its jacket and placed it on the spinning turntable. But before lowering the needle she took a moment to see that we were sitting as she had instructed: backs straight, feet on the floor, hands resting on our darkly initialed wooden desktops.

While the record was playing, Miss Hughes's face fell into a mask, her mouth drooping at the corners. A small woman in high heels, she stood at attention, hands clasped at her waist, shiny red nails bright against her knuckles. She wasn't young, but we couldn't see that she was in any way old. The dress she wore was close-fitting. Often it was adorned by a scarf, but not the haphazard affair some of our teachers attempted. Miss Hughes's scarf was chosen with care, a splash of

27

blue or vermilion to enliven a somber day, and was generous enough to allow for a large, elegant loop tied between her breasts.

Most of us had turned twelve that year and were newly assembled at the high school. The spring before we had graduated from one or another of our town's four elementary schools, where we had stooped to water fountains and drawn time charts on brown paper. Now we watched with furtive interest while the juniors and seniors parked their cars with a single deft twist of the steering wheel. This was the grown-up world we had been waiting for, fervently and secretly, but once here most of us knew we had still a long way to travel. Our limbs were ungainly, ridiculous. We twitched in our seats; our elbows and knees, scratched and scabbed, behaved like children's. We knew we couldn't lounge at our lockers with the proper air of unconcern, nor did we suppose we could sit upright and motionless for the duration of the "Hallelujah Chorus" from Handel's *Messiah* or a Beethoven sonata. Yet under Miss Hughes's surveillance, we learned to do so. If the grind of a chair's legs or a sigh reached her ears, Miss Hughes carefully lifted the needle from the spinning record and, staring vaguely into space, showing no sign that she recognized the source of the disturbance, waited until the room was silent before beginning again.

In other classes we doodled in our notebooks, drawing caricatures of our teachers, words streaming from their mouths in balloons. Small pink erasers flew through the air. On the Monday morning following a stormy bout with us on Friday, Mrs. Trevelyan, our math teacher, was tearful. "My weekend was ruined," she told us. "It troubles me very much when we don't get along together. Surely we can do better, can't we? If we make a little effort?" We looked at her with stony eyes. To our social-studies teacher, Miss Guthrie, we were deliberately cruel. Her voice was high, her mouth was tense, and often when she spoke a tiny thread of spittle hung between her lips. If someone answered a question in a strangled voice, mimicking her, she pretended not to notice.

Miss Hughes neither cajoled nor ignored us. Instead she made us her confidants. Music class met on Friday afternoons and through the windows the dusty autumn sunlight fell in long strips across our backs and onto the wooden floor. Behind us, flecked with high points of light, trees lined one end of the playing field. It was hard to tell, turning to look after a record had wound to its end, if the sun were striking to gold a cluster of leaves still green and summery or if a nighttime chill had done it.

The class always followed the same turn: first, Miss Hughes dictated to us what she called "background," pausing long enough for us to take down what she said in the notebooks we kept specially for her class, or for her to write on the blackboard a word we might not know how to spell. *To what class of stringed instruments does the pianoforte belong?* we wrote. *The pianoforte belongs to the dulcimer class of stringed instruments.* Or: *Name several forerunners of the pianoforte. Several forerunners of the pianoforte are the clavichord, the virginal, the harpsichord, the spinet.* If giggles rose involuntarily in our throats at the word "virginal," we managed to suppress them.

Following dictation, which she delivered without comment or explanation, she would ask us to assume our "postures." We had already written down the name of the piece we were about to hear, its composer, and usually some fact having to do with its performance—*on the harpsichord, the third movement of Mozart's Sonata in A Major, otherwise known as the "Turkish March," played by Wanda Landowska.* After she had set the needle on its course, we were for the moment alone with ourselves, a fact we were given to understand by the face wiped clean of all expression she held before us. We were then free to think of whatever we liked: a nightmare we had almost forgotten from the night before; a dog shaking water from its back, the drops flying everywhere like rain; a plan we had made with a friend for the weekend. Or we were free simply to watch the dust floating in the shafts of sunlight, to follow a path the sounds led us up and down.

We marveled that Miss Hughes always knew exactly when to turn and lift the needle, that she knew without looking when the record was almost over. After she had replaced the arm in its clasp, she turned her full attention to us. "You have just heard, boys and girls, in the 'Turkish March,' a great virtuoso performance. What do I mean by 'virtuoso'? A virtuoso performance is one executed by an instrumentalist highly skilled in the practice of his art, one who is able to bring to our ears music that we would otherwise go to our graves without hearing. The first great virtuosi pianists were Liszt and the incomparable Chopin, both of whom you will meet in due course.

"In fact, boys and girls," she said, lowering her voice a little so that we had to lean forward to hear, "we have our own virtuosi pianists,

29

ones who regularly perform close by in New York City, only a half hour's ride away on the train. You have heard the name Artur Rubinstein, perhaps? You have heard the name Myra Hess? These are artists whose work you must do everything in your power to appreciate first-hand. We go to sleep at night, we wake in the morning, we blink twice and our lives are over. But what do we know if we do not attend?"

Miss Hughes suddenly held up her two hands in front of us, red fingernails flashing. "You will see, boys and girls, I have a fine breadth of palm. My fingers are not as long as they might be, but I am able to span more than an octave with ease. Perhaps you do not find that remarkable. But I assure you that for a woman a palm of this breadth is rare. I had once a great desire to become a concert pianist myself. A very great desire. And I had been admitted to study at Juilliard with a teacher of renown. A teacher, Carl Freidburg, who in his youth in Frankfurt had been the student of Clara Schumann. Who had heard Liszt interpret his own compositions. When I went for my audition, when I entered the room where the piano was waiting and Mr. Freidburg was sitting nearby, I was afraid. I do not hide that from you, boys and girls. I was very much afraid. But as soon as I began to play Chopin's Polonaise in A-flat, a piece that requires much busy fingerwork by the left hand and a strong command of chords, I was so carried away by the fire of the music that I forgot the teacher. I forgot the audition. I forgot everything except the fact that I was now the servant of something larger than myself. When I reached the end and looked up—and I was in a bit of a daze, I may tell you—the great teacher's eyes were closed. He bowed his head once, very simply. That was all. I left the room. Soon afterward I received a letter assuring me that he would be proud to have me for his student."

Miss Hughes's face had registered the sweep of feelings she was recounting to us. Her eyes had narrowed with her great desire to be a pianist; entering the audition room, her jaw had grown rigid with fear; and while the great teacher had sat listening to her play, her face had assumed the look we were familiar with, the mask. Now her dark eyes took on a dreamy expression we had not yet seen. She seemed to be looking for words in a place that absorbed all her attention, over our heads, out the window, beyond.

"It was that winter, boys and girls, that my destiny revealed itself to me. If it were not too dramatic to put it this way, I would say that my fate was sealed. Everything I had hoped for, worked for, practicing seven hours each day after I had finished giving lessons—everything was snatched away in a single instant. I will tell you how it happened. Because someday in your own lives you may wake to a new world in which you feel a stranger. And you will know, if by chance you remember our conversation here today, that someone—no, my dear boys and girls, many others, a host of others, have also risen to a dark morning.

"A friend, a friend whom I loved, had asked if I would accompany him on a skiing trip to Vermont. Of course I said yes. Why should I not? We were to spend a day on the slopes. I was a great skier—my father had taught me when I was a child—and I looked forward to this holiday with the greatest excitement. I had been working hard that winter, too hard. It may have been my fatigue that in the end brought about my ruin. Because taking a curve that at any other time I might have managed with ease, my legs shot out from beneath me, and in an attempt to catch myself I let go of my pole and put out my hand, as any good skier knows not to do. Instead of fracturing a leg or a hip, both of which I might easily have spared, I injured my left hand, breaking three fingers that never properly healed."

This time Miss Hughes raised her left hand alone. She must have been about to point out to us the fatally injured fingers when the bell rang and she immediately dropped her arm. "To each of you a pleasant weekend, boys and girls," she said, turning to replace her records in their sleeves.

By class the following Friday we had other things to think about, and perhaps she did as well. We had just listened to Bach's Fugue in G Minor, for the purpose of learning to recognize the sound of the oboe—and the room for once had an air not of enforced constraint but of calm—when Miss Hughes lifted her head and, looking out the window, told us that there was one of us, sitting now in our midst, who listened to music in a manner quite unlike the rest. "He listens as if for his life, boys and girls, and it is in this manner that the music of the anointed was written. For the composer, the sounds struggling in his imagination are a matter of life and death. They are as necessary to him as the air he breathes."

She kept us in no more suspense, but allowed her gaze to rest on a boy who always sat, no matter the classroom, at the end of a row. We had scarcely noticed him at all, those of us who had not gone to elementary school with him. But there he sat—at this moment, blushing. His hair was sandy, his face was freckled, and he wore glasses with clear, faintly pinkish rims. His name was Norman de Carteret, a name that in a room full of Daves and Mikes and Steves we found impossible to pronounce without lifting our eyebrows. During the first week of September, Miss Hughes had asked him how he would like us to say his last name, and he had answered quietly, so quietly we could scarcely hear him, that it was Carteret, pronouncing the last syllable as if it were the first letter of the alphabet. The "de" he swallowed entirely.

"Then," Miss Hughes had said, "your father or his father must have come from France, the country that gave us Rameau, that invaluable spirit who for the first time set down the rules of harmony. The country to which we are indebted as well for Debussy, who accomplished what might have been thought impossible: he permitted us to hear the sound of moonlight."

• • •

I knew something about Norman the others didn't.

My mother had lived in our town as a child and occasionally met on the street someone she would later explain was once a friend of her mother's, dead long ago. Hilda Kelleher was one of these friends, even a cousin of sorts, and lived in a large, brown-shingled Victorian house, not far from the station. A wide porch, in summer strewn with wicker rocking chairs, ran along the front and disappeared around one side. The other end of the house was flanked by tall pines that in winter received the snow. Hilda was of an uncertain age—older than my mother, but maybe not a full generation older. Her hair was dyed bright yellow, and when she smiled her mouth twitched up at one corner uncovering teeth on which lipstick had left traces. Hilda had never married, but there was nothing strange in that. The town was full of old houses in which single women who had grown up in them lived on with their aging mothers, going "to business," teaching in the schools, supplementing their incomes in whatever ways they could. I supposed that they, too, had been girls, just as I was then, walking on summer nights beneath streetlights that threw leafy shadows on the sidewalks, that they, too, had listened to the murmur of voices drifting from screened porches, had heard the clatter of passing trains and dreamed of what would happen to them next. But life had passed them by, that was clear.

Hilda had dealt with the problem of dwindling resources by taking in boarders. An aunt of my mother's, a retired art teacher who, as my mother liked to say, "had no one in the world," was looking for a place to live. One afternoon in late summer, just before school opened, my mother visited Hilda to inquire about arrangements, and I went with her. While they sat talking in rocking chairs on the front porch I discovered around to the side a swing hanging from four chains. It was easy to imagine sitting there on summer nights behind a screen of vines, morning glories closed to the full moon, listening to the cicadas. Swinging back and forth I could hear their voices, my mother's telling Hilda how Aunt Ruth had lived in Mrs. Hollingsworth's house in Tarrytown, how this arrangement would seem familiar to her. I heard Hilda saying how glad she was that a room was available, that we would look at it in a moment. She went on to say that one boarder, who had been with her a year, had moved out of the room into a smaller one that better suited his means. Did my mother know a Mr. de Carteret? He had a son who was going to the high school, she thought, in the fall. The son lived with the mother but came to visit the father on Saturdays. The terrible thing was that when he came the father wouldn't open the door of his room to him.

Her voice sank so low that I got out of the swing and stood along the wall to listen. "The poor child," she said in a loud whisper. "He knocks, and when his father won't let him in he sits outside the door in the hall. Saturday after Saturday he comes to the house and waits outside his father's room and still his father won't see him. Sometimes—oh, the poor child, I wish I knew what to do—he is there all afternoon."

I was back in the swing by the time they called me to look at the vacated room. We followed Hilda up a staircase of wide oak steps and along a hall, passing mahogany doors on either side. At last she threw one open on a room that had a neat bed covered with a white spread, a desk, and a chest of drawers. The afternoon sun was sifting through the pines and falling on the bed. My mother said she couldn't imagine that her aunt wouldn't be happy here; the room seemed to breathe tranquility. We closed the door, then went down the hallway to the staircase and out of the house.

I had been wondering whether or not I should whisper to my closest friends what I had heard Hilda say about Norman, but after Miss Hughes had asked us to notice his perfect attention it seemed to me

I should not. Why not, I couldn't be sure, except it seemed that if he were listening "as if for his life," he had heard something in the music that I hadn't, and I didn't think the others had either. I felt out of my depth. And soon enough, by saying nothing, by keeping to myself what I took to be his secret, I came to feel that some understanding had sprung up between us, that we shared a knowledge hidden from the others.

Then, very soon, our paths crossed.

II

In our old school there had been a classroom filled with books which we called the library. Twice a week we sat in a circle around Miss Kendall, the librarian, while she read to us, turning the book around from time to time to show us the pictures. I knew the books I wanted to read in that library; they were not the history books urged on us by our teachers, or the books about boys running away to sea, or even the large and lavishly illustrated volumes of myths and fairy tales. It was stories about girls I wanted, mostly orphan girls, or at least girls, like Sarah Crewe, whose mothers were dead and who had been left to the care of cruel adults to whom they refused to be grateful—to whom, in moments of passion, they poured out their long-suppressed feelings of outrage.

I had tried to explain all this to the older girl in the high school library who was supposed to show us around, and she had said I might like to read *Jane Eyre*, pointing to shelves lodged in a corner. I should look under the B's, she said, but I ended up nearby, facing shelves where all the books were written by people whose names began with a C. I was stopped by a title: *Lucy Gayheart*, a book about a girl, and perhaps even the kind I had in mind. It was written by Willa Cather, a name I had never heard, and I quickly looked around for a place to read.

This library was much larger than our old one, and instead of a little table where books were set on their ends for display—picture books and books for older children with such titles as *The Story of Electricity* and *Abigail Adams: A Girl of Colonial Days*—here there were unadorned long tables stretching the width of the room, with chairs tucked in on either side. High windows filled one end, and beneath them the librarian sat at her desk, ink pad and rubber date stamps poised at her elbow. I had sat down and opened the dark blue

34

cover of the book to the first page when I looked up and saw Norman de Carteret sitting across the table, poring over an immense open volume. One foot was drawn up to rest on the seat of his chair, and as he read he leaned his face against his knee. It was a book about ships, I could see that; there was a full-scale picture of a sloop, or a schooner, with all its sails unfurled. There was writing on the different parts of the ship and on the sails, too, probably to let you know what they were called. Norman was absorbed, and I began to read.

> In Haverford on the Platte the townspeople still talk of Lucy Gayheart. They do not talk of her a great deal, to be sure; life goes on and we live in the present. But when they do mention her name it is with a gentle glow in the face or the voice, a confidential glance which says: "Yes, you, too, remember?" They still see her as a slight figure always in motion; dancing or skating, or walking swiftly with intense direction, like a bird flying home.

Lucy was one of the vivid creatures I wanted to read about, that was clear, but there was something that seemed not quite right, some note I had not yet heard. The story was already over and she lived on the first page not as a living person but as a memory.

I read on and to my surprise saw that Lucy, like Miss Hughes, wanted to be a pianist. She had been giving lessons to beginners from the time she was in tenth grade and had left Haverford to study music with a teacher in Chicago. Now she had come home for the Christmas holidays and had gone skating with her friends on the Platte. A young man, Harry, had joined them, and at sunset Lucy and he had sat together

> on a bleached cottonwood log, where the black willow thicket behind them made a screen. The interlacing twigs threw off red light like incandescent wires, and the snow underneath was rose-colour. . . . The round red sun was falling like a heavy weight; it touched the horizon line and sent quivering fans of red and gold over the wide country. . . . In an instant the light was gone. . . . Wherever one looked there was nothing but flat country and low hills, all violet and grey.

These words, too, seemed remarkable, because I thought I recognized the place. In our town, if you followed the railroad tracks over the bridge that looked down on Main Street, on past the red-brick factory and Catholic church, you came to a reservoir that in spring was overhung with Japanese cherry trees, their branches weeping pink blossoms into the black water. During the winter months, when the reservoir had frozen over, we skated there. No prairie surrounded the water, only rocks and frozen grass and crouching woods; but the sky loomed wide overhead, and on winter afternoons the red sun was caught for a moment in the drooping silver branches of the cherry trees. I thought I knew how the Platte would look, the sun going down on it, thought I knew how afterward everything would turn ordinary and flat.

Norman was still contemplating the picture of the sailing ship. I could glimpse him sitting there as I lowered my head to continue reading. Now Lucy and Harry were settled in a sleigh that was, I read,

> a tiny moving spot on that still white country settling into shadow and silence. Suddenly Lucy started and struggled under the tight blankets. In the darkening sky she had seen the first star come out; it brought her heart into her throat. That point of silver light spoke to her like a signal, released another kind of life and feeling which did not belong here.

I closed the book, deciding for today to forget *Jane Eyre*. I knew I had never read a book like this one. I had been expecting someone else to come along, or for Lucy and Harry to say something surprising or romantic to each other—something to happen besides the round red sun falling on the prairie and the star speaking to Lucy like a signal. And yet I felt that in this book these were enough. The pages I had read threw open the strange possibility that looking at things, feeling them, were also things that happened to you, just as much as meeting someone or going on a trip. What you thought and felt when you were alone or silently in the presence of someone else also made a story.

I looked up to see that Norman seemed to have fallen asleep on his book. His glasses were standing on their lenses beside him on the table and his face was in his arms. When the bell shrilled through the room, his shoulders twitched and he raised his head from the picture of the boat with all its sails. Looking up, still half asleep, his short-sighted blue eyes came to rest on mine. Another time I might have looked away. But as I, too, was half asleep, entertaining visions of quivering fans of red and gold playing on the prairie, turning over my new thoughts, I realized only after a moment that Norman had smiled at me as if he were still dreaming, as if he had been alone and, suddenly seized by a happy idea, were smiling at himself in a mirror.

III

One Friday afternoon in October we filed into Miss Hughes's class-room to find her standing beside the day's album of records, dressed entirely in white. Her dress, made of soft white wool, fell just below her knees. There was no crimson or purple scarf tied round her neck; instead, a long necklace of pearls hung between her breasts.

"You will be wondering, boys and girls," she said to us as soon as we were seated, "why you find me today dressed as you see. I am in mourning, but a mourning turned to joy. White is the color of sorrow, as it is of radiance. And today I am going to play for you a piece of music that throughout your lives you will return to again and again. If ever you must make a decision, if ever you find yourselves tossing on a stormy sea—and life will not spare you, boys and girls; it spares no one—I beg you to do as I say. Find a spot where no living soul will disturb you, not even your dearest friend, and in the silent reaches of your soul listen to the music you are about to hear. Today we shall have no dictation, because it is my idea that Mozart's Requiem is best introduced without preliminaries. A requiem, you must know, is a prayer for the dead. Today we shall hear the opening section of this great work. One day—we shall see when—I shall play for you an-other."

Miss Hughes lowered the needle to the record that was already in place and spinning on the turntable. For a few moments a mournful sound filled the room, something that seemed to move forward, as if people were walking—a rhythmic, purposeful sound, with an echo for every step—when suddenly, without any warning, a blare of trum-pets and kettle drums broke it all up, a frightening, violent blast that made us jump in our seats. Then, into the clamor, a chorus of men's voices forced their way, low, solemn, moving forward as before, but confident, as if they were sure of what they were saying. We were

37

just getting used to the chorus when high above all the rest floated a single woman's voice, a voice raised high above the world but sliding down to meet it, and so calm, so full of understanding, I could have cried.

Miss Hughes lifted the needle and allowed her face to keep the expression of the mask for a few moments longer than usual. Then she drew a deep breath. "To comment on this music, boys and girls, would be an impertinence. We must let it rest in us where it will. Rest: a word, as it is used in music, to mean the absence of sound, a silence, sometimes short and sometimes long, when we hear only the vibrations of what has come before and prepare for those that will follow. You will understand what I mean if you think of a wave, the kind you see in a Japanese painting, caught in that moment just before it breaks."

The record had remained spinning on the turntable, its black surface crossed by a silver streak of light. Now Miss Hughes bent down, turned the knob, and the record slowly wound to a halt. Then she again stood upright, facing us. "The word 'requiem'—a Latin word you of course already know—might best be translated by several words in English: may he find rest at last, the one who has died. But my own prayer, I shall tell you now, is that we, the living, may find rest within the span of our own lives. I mean that rest we know only when we are most awake to sorrow and to joy, when we find we can no longer tell the difference. Then we are living outside of time, as we are when we are listening to music such as that we have just heard. In such an instance, death is only something that happens to us, like being born or growing old, but is of less consequence than the many deaths we sustain in life. I mean the deaths, my friends, when our dearest hopes are blasted."

Miss Hughes had been speaking slowly, meditatively, choosing her words with care. Her eyes had gone from one of us to the other. Now she assumed the dreamy look we had seen once before. She looked beyond us, through the clear panes of the window, into the distance. "Because, boys and girls, death may come to us in many disguises. You see, I, too, have gone down into the waters.

"I think I have told you already that my great desire in life was to have become a pianist, to play for myself one of the late piano concerti of Chopin, let us say, or of Schubert's impromptus. To that end I was living in Paris, studying with a teacher who was drawing from me all those feelings that I had supposed—young as I was—must re-

38

main outside music, separate from it. I had embraced discipline, and practicing for hours and hours everyday was the only way I knew to approach a sonata or prelude. It was this teacher who showed me that music is composed by a spirit alive to suffering and to joy and must be played by another such spirit. That it was only by bringing every moment of my life to the music that I could hope to draw from it what the composer had put in."

For a moment Miss Hughes seemed to wake from a sleep and looked at us alertly. "As indeed, boys and girls, in this room we must bring every moment of our lives to the music as we listen."

I wondered, while she stared from face to face, if her damaged hand had healed by the time she arrived in Paris, or if all this had taken place sometime before the skiing accident. But I would no more have thought to question whether or not Lucy Gayheart had taken the train back to Chicago the night after she had sat on the log and seen the round red sun falling like a weight into the prairie. The facts, the before and after of events, had their own logic by which, trusting the source, I supposed they must take their place in some pattern hidden from me.

Miss Hughes was playing with her pearls, winding them around her fingers. Again her gaze had retired to a place beyond the window.

"The city of light, boys and girls; that's what you will hear Paris called. But it is also, I will tell you, the city of darkness. If you cross the Pont des Arts one day, you will see the Ile de la Cité, that great barge of an island, drifting up the river—the River Seine, I'm sure you know. And on that island, as you make your way across the bridge, you will see swing slowly into view a spectacle that has greeted the eyes of bewildered humanity for almost eight hundred years, the great square towers of Notre Dame. I say 'slowly,' you will notice, because like the opening of the requiem we have just heard, like Bach's Fugue that stirred our souls a few weeks ago, that's how many of the best things come to us. The catastrophes stop us in our tracks. I know, my friends, because I came to a halt on the bridge that day; I was unable to continue my walk. I had a letter with me that I had only just received and that had thrown me into a state of the most painful confusion."

In the silence that followed these words we could hear the excited cawing of crows on the playing field behind us.

"The letter was from a close friend at home relating the pitiable state into which my father had fallen. A debilitating illness from

39

which he could not recover. The friend, who was old himself, did not ask me to return. But how could I think of anything else? Who would care for my father if I did not? I was all he had in the world, and it was to him that I owed my early life in music, he who had given me my first lessons on the piano. Of course I must return to look after him.

"And yet—and here, my dear boys and girls, I do not seek an answer—how would that be possible? To leave Paris, to leave the city in which I had been so happy! To leave all those feelings I had begun to put into my music! In short, to leave my teacher! It was not to be thought of. I leaned out over the edge of the bridge and looked down into the river flowing beneath. I could not see my way. I tasted the bitter waters of defeat. Oh, I was tempted! Finally, scarcely knowing how I got there, I found myself in my room, and after closing the door and pulling the shutters, I listened to Mozart's Requiem. By the time it had concluded I knew my way."

Miss Hughes, standing immobile in white, continued to gaze out the window. Surely the class would be over in a minute or two, but she didn't seem to recollect our presence. I stealthily turned my head to see sleek black crows lifting out of the trees and lighting back into them, their outspread wings glinting in the afternoon light, the branches with all their yellow leaves tossing up and down.

IV

In the days that followed, I decided that Miss Hughes had been in love with her teacher. She must have been, I thought, because I had now followed Lucy Gayheart to Chicago where she lived alone in a room at the top of a stairs. A room, perhaps, like the room in Paris to which Miss Hughes had stumbled and had drawn shutters on a bright day. Lucy Gayheart was not in love with her teacher, but her teacher had urged her to attend a concert given by a celebrated singer named Clement Sebastian who, although he lived in France, was spending the winter in Chicago. "Yes, a great artist should look like that," she had thought the moment he had walked onto the stage. And then he had sung a Schubert song.

> The song was sung as a religious observance in the classical spirit, a rite more than a prayer. . . . *In your light I stand without fear, O august stars! I salute your eternity.*

. . . Lucy had never heard anything sung with such eleva-
tion of style. In its calmness and serenity there was a kind
of large enlightenment, like daybreak.

I remembered that Lucy had struggled up in Harry's sleigh when
she had seen the first star flashing to her on the wide prairie, and I
thought perhaps this was what Miss Hughes had meant about listen-
ing for your life: what you heard in the music was something exalted
that you already knew, but weren't aware that you did—something
you had blindly felt or heard or seen.

But then, reading on, I learned that Lucy's mood had quickly
changed. There was to be no more serenity and calm. She listened to
Sebastian sing five more Schubert songs, all of them melancholy, and
felt that

there was something profoundly tragic about this man. . . .
She was struggling with something she had never felt be-
fore. A new conception of art? It came closer than that. A
new kind of personality? But it was much more. It was a
discovery about life, a revelation of love as a tragic force,
not a melting mood, of passion that drowns like black wa-
ter.

Although I didn't understand exactly how the music had led to this
discovery, I knew that in this book, called by her name, I was not
reading about Lucy alone. The lines that came next made it clear she
was merely one member of a select company, a company set apart—
as Miss Hughes had set Norman apart—by a destiny determined
from within: "Some peoples' lives are affected by what happens to
their person or their property; but for others fate is what happens to
their feelings and their thoughts—that and nothing more."

V

One Saturday afternoon in late October my mother asked if I would
take Hilda and Aunt Ruth a lemon poppyseed cake she had made for
them. It was not only Aunt Ruth she felt had no one in the world, but
Hilda as well. "Poor souls," she said. "To be all alone like that." I put
the cake, wrapped in wax paper, in the straw basket that hung from
the handlebars of my bike. The leaves were now almost gone from

41

the trees, but the day was clear and warm, like a day in early September. In less than a week it would be Halloween, and although we now thought it childish to go out begging, it was nice to think about walking from house to house, the night with its bare branches stark against a sky filled with spirits riding the air. I was in no rush to arrive at Hilda's because Aunt Ruth made me uneasy. When she came to our house she would give paper and colored pencils to my sisters and me and tell us to let our imaginations run wild. Then she would look at our efforts and to mine she would say, "D minus." Just as she might say the same if one of us carried her a cup of coffee that was not hot enough. But how could you obey a direction to let your imagination run wild? It was like someone wishing you sweet dreams.

By the time Hilda's house came into view I was riding my bike in loops, swerving sharply toward one curb then the other, doubling back. In the middle of the street I made a circle, three times. I knew now it was not so much Aunt Ruth I was afraid of running into; it was Norman de Carteret. Suppose he was sitting in the dark hall outside his father's door? Or suppose I met him coming out of the house as I was going in?

And then, my bike making wider and wider loops both toward and away, going over in my mind what I would say to Norman if we happened to meet, I finally dared to look up and saw him there on the porch at the side of the house, sitting on the swing that hung from the four chains. The morning-glory vines were bare, and he was sitting with his feet against the porch railing, pushing himself back and forth. I could see, too, that when he saw me he flinched and lowered his head to hide his face. But then, as I was about to ride by, pretending I hadn't seen him, he looked up and—as he had done in the library—smiled. I parked my bike at the bottom of the steps, removed the cake from the basket, and went around the corner of the porch to where he was sitting.

"Hi," he said. His brown high-top sneakers were resting on the porch railing. Behind his glasses his blue eyes floated a little.

"Hi," I said. There was a long pause before I thought of something to say. "My aunt lives here."

"I know." His voice was high and childish. "So does my father."

I sat down on the railing not far from his feet, swung my legs up and leaned back against one of the round white pillars. It seemed surprising that Norman spoke of his father. Had he knocked on his door this morning and, like all the other times, been greeted with si-

42

lence? Had he been waiting in the hall for hours, not knowing what to do, and finally come down to sit on the swing?

"Did you come here to see him?" I asked, both fearful and eager that he say more.

"Yes," he answered, looking straight ahead, out between the vines that in August had made a screen from the sun. Now a few shriveled leaves hung in the warm afternoon. Just as at school, Norman was wearing corduroy trousers a little too big for him, and a plaid flannel shirt buttoned at the neck. The sleeves came down almost to his knuckles. "I'm waiting till he wakes up. He told me not to go away. He wants me to wait for him here."

"Oh," I said and came to a stop. His voice had something in it I thought I recognized. It was in Miss Hughes's voice when she stared out the window while the crows were squawking and flapping in the trees. But Miss Hughes, as she stood there with her hands clasped at her waist, seemed to be communing with something only she could see. Norman's face, on the other hand, had lost its dreamy quality: his freckles stood out while he spoke; his eyes looked sharp and aware. He was looking at me as if he had made a point that he expected me to respond to.

Suddenly overcome with anxiety, not knowing what to answer, wanting only to erase the look in his eyes that made me afraid, I started unwrapping the cake. "Want some?" I asked.

"Sure," he said, and when I broke off a large chunk and held it out to him he leaned forward in the swing and took it in a hand I could see was trembling. I broke off another chunk for myself. At first we ate demurely, silently, spilling a few crumbs around us and brushing them away. I would find a way later on, I thought, to explain to my mother about the cake. Then I swallowed a piece that was too big for me and choked and sputtered, and then, on purpose this time, crammed a fistful in my mouth, pretending to frown at him disapprovingly, as if he were the one stuffing his mouth, until suddenly I was aping convulsions, bent double, holding my side, almost falling off the railing. Norman at first looked on, snorting with laughter. Then he, too, snatched a handful of cake and shoved it in his mouth, and soon we were both grabbing for more, exploding in high giggles, looking at each other cross-eyed, holding our sides, pretending to be on the point of collapse, pretending to be falling and dying, until the cake had disappeared, lying around us in half-eaten pieces.

Gradually we subsided, our shoulders stopped shaking, and we could breathe without gasping for air. The afternoon grew quiet around us. We could hear children playing up the block and the sound of someone raking leaves. Inside the house someone began to play the piano, some song from a time before we were born, something the grown-ups had sung when they were young. On the other side of the hedge, the late sun struck a large window into a flaming pool of orange. We avoided each other's eyes as if we had shared a secret we were ashamed of. After a while whoever was playing the piano broke off abruptly in the middle of a song and closed the cover with a bang. The sun slipped from the window, the branches of the trees reached ragged above our heads. When I finally got to my feet, taking leave of Norman without saying a word, it was almost dark.

For a few days afterward I tried falling in love with Norman de Carteret. I passed him in the halls sometimes, and once caught sight of him at his locker, turning his combination lock. But since our afternoon on Hilda's porch we were shy with each other, lowering our eyes when we met. Once, in music class, when Miss Hughes was playing a Brahms quintet for clarinet and strings, I tried to imagine how he might be listening, perhaps in the way Lucy had listened to Sebastian sing the Schubert songs. He was seated behind me, at the end of the row, and when I turned my head very slightly I could see him sitting there, his eyes sharp and aware, as they had been when he talked about his father. But at the end of the class when he walked through the door, his corduroy pants hanging from his hips, I could see he was only a child like myself.

VI

During the following weeks I pursued the story of Lucy Gayheart in fits and starts. I read with a sense of exaltation and impending doom, dipping back from time to time, for reassurance, into the world of Sara Crewe and Anne of Green Gables. There was some new strain in the voice telling the story, something I had not encountered in any other book. It ran along beneath the words like a stream beneath a smooth surface of ice, some undertone murmuring, "This is the way life is, this is the way life is." It was a voice—dispassionate, stern—I listened for with joy, as if it brought news from a country for which I had long been homesick. And yet my nightly dreams told me, too, it was a country where terror and brutality might strike out of a benign blue sky. It seemed not so much that my child life was fading into the past. It was more that my entire future life was rising before me, as if it were already known to me, as if it had already happened long ago and was waiting to be remembered.

Despite my fitful reading, Lucy's story was quickly running its course. She had already become Clement Sebastian's piano accompanist, already fallen in love with him. He was Europe, the wide world, the life of feelings, unabashed and unashamed, not cramped or peevish as in Haverford. He was a singer, an artist. And although he was married, he had fallen in love with Lucy, with her youth, her enthusiasm, perhaps with her rapturous admiration of himself, he who was disillusioned and tired of the world. And so when Harry came to see her in Chicago, to take her to a week of operas and to propose marriage, she told him desperately that she couldn't marry him, that she was in love with someone else.

None of this seemed surprising. The undertone I listened for, I knew, had something to do with desire, with wanting someone who wasn't there. Or maybe someone who was there but whom you couldn't reach out and touch. It had to do with feelings that couldn't be spoken and yet had to be spoken, the space between.

But now Lucy's story was taking an unexpected turn, was moving in directions my daytime self would not have thought possible. In response to what Lucy told him, Harry, in a fit of pique, married a woman lacking in that quick responsiveness he had loved in Lucy, and regretted the marriage immediately. Sebastian left Chicago for a summer concert tour in Europe and met a sudden death. In despair, Lucy returned to Haverford, to a "long blue-and-gold autumn in the Platte valley."

Then January came and "the town and all the country round were the colour of cement." Lucy left the house one afternoon to skate on the river, just as we would soon be skating on our reservoir with its weeping cherry trees. What she didn't know was that the bed had shifted, that what once had been only a narrow arm of the river had become the swift-flowing river itself. She skated straight out onto the ice, large cracks spreading all around her. For a moment she was waist deep in icy water, her arms resting on a block of ice. Then "the ice cake slipped from under her arms and let her down."

I was incredulous. Despite the opening sentences of the book, I thought I hadn't understood and read the passage over and over, looking for some hint, some odd word or phrase, that would change its meaning. And yet, even while searching, even while trying to reassure myself that I must have missed something, I was aware—by some inner quaking that echoed the sound of splintering ice—I had understood very well. Harry is left to take up a life wracked with remorse that only time will soften, and Lucy slips into the regions of the remembered. It was as the undertone running beneath the story had assured all along: Lucy's response to Sebastian's songs, her bleak sense of foreboding, would be fulfilled. An early death—anticipated by the intense life of feelings—had been her destiny, and at the appointed time her death had risen to meet her. This, I supposed, was what people called tragedy.

VII

Because of Haverford whose sidewalks Lucy had walked in the long autumn of her return, the houses and streets of our town looked different, the late gardens of chrysanthemums and Michaelmas daisies, the silver moon rising above them. In the November afternoons we ran up and down the hockey field in back of the school, and even at four o'clock the red bayberries flickered in the twilight. Walking home, thinking of Lucy, I noticed the cracks in the sidewalks, the way the roots of trees had splintered them. Beneath the sidewalks ran a river of fast-flowing roots that could throw slabs of cement into the air, make a graveyard of the smooth planes where we used to roller-skate and sit playing jacks. From the end of one street I could see the train station, its roof black against the orange sky, and could imagine the tracks running over the bridge and past the reservoir into the city. Even now Myra Hess might be practicing the Chopin she would play tonight to a crowd at Carnegie Hall. Perhaps Miss Hughes was sitting on the train that would take her to the concert; perhaps she would return late at night to a room in a big house like Hilda's, a room that looked on pines.

For Thanksgiving my mother invited Hilda and Aunt Ruth, who must not be left alone. Hilda's lipstick, a wan hope, had left traces on her teeth, I took note as she leaned across the table to ask if I had met Norman de Carteret in any of my classes. Before answering I vowed I would not, cost what it might, be trapped as she had been, would not become an old woman in a town where life was one long wait. Hilda went on to recount to the table at large that Mr. de Carteret, who had scarcely stirred from his room for months, had been busy during the last days buying a turkey to cook for his son.

He had bought cranberry sauce and sweet potatoes, she told us, and a bag of walnuts. It was all assembled on the table in the kitchen, and she herself had contributed two bottles of ginger ale. She had helped him put the turkey in the oven several hours before and at this moment it must almost be done. She hoped he wouldn't leave it in so long that it dried out. She hoped, too, that he remembered to turn off the oven once he took it out, because something might catch fire. She wondered if she should telephone him now to warn him but was persuaded by my father that a fire was unlikely.

On Monday we were back in school. I didn't see Norman that day, or the next, or the next, not until Friday, when, passing in the hall, I caught sight of him standing at his locker. He was standing idly there, staring into it in his usual absentminded way, not looking for anything in particular, it seemed. That was in the morning. By lunch a rumor had run through the school like fire through grass. One friend whispered it, and then another. Had I heard? Norman de Carteret's father had killed himself. Yes, it was true. He had drowned himself in the reservoir on Saturday. He'd done it by putting stones in his pockets. Someone's father had been there, had been part of the group that had pulled him from the water on Saturday night. That's why Norman hadn't been in school. All the teachers had been sent a notice, but Norman was in school today. Had I seen him? I had? What did he look like? Was he crying?

I absorbed the news as if it were of someone I knew nothing about, someone I had to strain to place or remember, someone whose name I barely recognized. Norman had again become a stranger, someone wrapped in an appalling story. My exchanges with him had separated me from the group; for a while I had shared his isolation and in drawing near him had drawn closer to my dreaming self, my reading self. Now I wanted nothing more to do with him. I was terrified that recalling our shared silences might draw me into some vortex of catastrophe. My fear was akin to what I had felt when, reaching the end of Lucy's story, I had looked frantically for something to tell me that I had not understood, that the words printed so boldly in black on the white page spelled out a meaning I had not grasped.

All day there had been the promise of snow in the air, and when we filed into Miss Hughes's room a few stray flakes had begun to fall. They were there in the window, the first of the season. Norman was already sitting in his place at the end of a row and the snow was

47

falling behind him. He was sitting bolt upright in his seat, staring straight ahead, the corners of his mouth twisted up into something like a grin. But we only glanced at him, we didn't stare, sitting down as quickly as we could in our own places to get him out of our sight. We were overwhelmed with curiosity but also repelled. It would have been better if he hadn't been there at all, if we could have gone over the story, embellishing it with each retelling, without having to look at him, without having to sit with him in the same room.

Miss Hughes was, as usual, standing in her place beside the phonograph, the album on the table beside her. She was wearing a dark gray dress with a scarf that shimmered blue one moment, green the next. We had not met for two weeks because of the Thanksgiving vacation, but she had told us the last time we had seen her that she would welcome us back by introducing us to that consummate artist, Chopin. Now, rather brusquely, without the preliminary remarks with which she usually asked us "to silently invite our souls in order to prepare for the journey ahead," she asked us to open our notebooks and she began to dictate. "For Chopin," she pronounced, "the keyboard was a lyric instrument. He told his students, 'Everything must be made to sing.' "

For a few moments there were the sounds of papers rustling and of pencil cases coming unzipped. Then we settled to writing down her words.

"Chopin was a romantic in his impulse to render passing moods, but he was a classicist in his search for purity of form. His work is not given to digression. The Preludes are visionary sketches, none of them longer than a page or two. 'In each piece,' Schumann said, 'we find in his own hand, "Frederic Chopin wrote it!" He is the boldest, the proudest poet of his time.' "

We wrote laboriously, stopping as Miss Hughes carefully wrote on the board the words "classicist," "digression," "visionary." She made sure we had written quotation marks around Schumann's words, the exclamation point where it belonged. Out of the corner of my eye I saw that Norman was hunched over his notebook, writing.

Miss Hughes had turned to the album. "Now, boys and girls, we shall listen to one of Chopin's Preludes, the fourth, in E minor. It is very brief."

She drew a record out of its sleeve and placed it on the spinning turntable. After three months' training, we knew to assume our postures, so she had only to glance quickly around the room before lowering the needle. We heard the chords, the chords going deeper and deeper, and I pictured pine trees pointing to the sky at sunset; a darkness was about to overwhelm them, but for the moment they were lit by the setting sun. Everything was disappearing, the chords were telling us; a deep shadow was falling over the side of the mountain, yet the melody was singing of the last golden light thrown up from behind the rim.

"Do you hear it, boys and girls?" Miss Hughes asked us as she lifted the needle from the record. "Do you hear there the voice of desire? Not for one thing or another, not for a person or a place, but desire detached from any object. What we have heard in this fourth Prelude is the voice of longing when it breaks through into the regions of poetry, into the regions of whatever lives closest to us and furthest away."

Miss Hughes's scarf flashed blue then green against her gray dress, against the dark square of the blackboard behind her. Her eyes assumed the dreamy look we had seen before. "It was for this I had hopes of becoming a pianist," she told us, looking out the window. "To coax that voice from the instrument, to allow others to hear it in the way that I did." She was gazing into the snowflakes, it seemed, into the bare, black branches through which they were falling in the waning afternoon. She was watching them spill from the gray sky; in a trance she was following their white tumble. But all at once, as if she, too, were falling from some high place, as if she, too, were whirling through deep silent spaces, she seemed to catch herself. I had turned in my seat to look at the snow but also to catch a glimpse of Norman. He was sitting now with his face buried in his arms, as he had sat that day in the library.

Miss Hughes looked around her sleepily, and for the first time we saw her face, without the prompting of music, assume the mask. For a long moment she stood before us, impassive, mouth pulled down at the corners, eyes closed. When she opened them they rested darkly on Norman's lowered head. She allowed them to remain there a few seconds, taking her time, as if she were inviting us to consider with her which words she might choose.

"Is there anything we can do for you, Norman?" she asked at last.

There was silence in the room. I thought of the snow hitting the ground and wondered whether it had already begun to cover the brown grass beneath the trees, thought of Norman's father lying somewhere in the earth, his body in its coffin perhaps already beginning to rot, his grave still raw and exposed. The snow would hide all that, the dirt piled on top, and if Norman went to look where his father was, he would see an even cover of white.

"Because," Miss Hughes continued, "we would like you to know that you are sitting in the company of friends."

She brooded, frowning, while we sat rigidly in our seats. Then she turned her eyes from Norman to us. "You are perhaps not aware, boys and girls, that Mozart was Chopin's favorite composer. I shall now tell you a story. When Chopin died at the age of thirty-nine, in Paris, his funeral was held at the Madeleine, a church of that city. Afterward he was buried in a cemetery called Père-Lachaise, where you may someday wish to visit his grave. But at his funeral, it was Mozart's Requiem that the gathered mourners were given to hear. I once told you that before long we would listen together to another section of it. Today we shall hear the Lacrimosa. The word means 'full of tears.' "

We waited while she returned the record we had heard to its sleeve and drew out another.

She brooded over us now as a moment ago she had brooded over Norman. "We cannot see into the mysteries of another person's life, dear boys and girls. We have no way of knowing what deaths a soul has sustained before the final one. It is for this reason that we must never presume to judge or to speak in careless ways about lives of which we understand nothing. I tell you this so that you may not forget it. We may honor many things in life. But for someone else's sorrow we must reserve our deepest bow."

Miss Hughes had placed the record on the turntable and now paused before lowering the needle. "You will hear in the music that I am about to play for you a prayer for the dead, a prayer that they may at last find the peace that so often escapes us in life. Because, boys and girls, in praying for the dead we are praying for ourselves in that hour when we, too, far away as that hour might seem to us now, shall join their ranks. But even more—and you will understand me in time—we are honoring the suffering in our own lives, those of us who barely know how we shall survive the day. If you listen closely I know you cannot fail to hear something else: the tale of how our grief, the desire for what we do not have, the desire for what is forever denied us, may at length—when embraced as our destiny—become indistinguishable from our joy. Indistinguishable, you will understand, my dear friends, in that moment when time, as in the most sublime music, has ceased to be.

"When the record comes to an end I ask that you gather your things and silently take your leave. I shall look forward, in a week's time, to the return of your company."

We heard strings draw out one note and then two more, a little higher, the same pattern repeated three times, very sweet, very light, as if we might all float on these blithe strains forever. Into this—not denying but blending—broke a chorus of plaintive voices repeating something twice, voices asking, imploring, like a wind that moans in the night; then quickly gaining strength and conviction, they began an ascent, a climb, in which they mounted higher and higher, at each step becoming bolder, a procession like the first section we had heard weeks before. But now the voices surged as if straining toward something nobody had ever reached, up and up, the procession climbing higher and higher, the kettle drums pounding, the trumpets blaring, the echo falling in the wake of each step, until they could mount no higher and then—with utter simplicity, with utter calm— the voices returned to the point from which they had begun and pronounced their words in an ordinary manner, foot to earth.

When the record had spun to its end, when there was nothing more to listen for, we slowly picked up our books and filed out of the room. At the door I turned to look back and saw Miss Hughes still standing at attention before the phonograph, her hands together in front of her. Norman had not moved; his face was hidden in his arms. It was early December and already the room was filling with shadows, but the snow swirling at the window cast a restless light, the flickering light of water, over Miss Hughes's frozen mask, over Norman bowed at his desk. For the moment Miss Hughes was standing watch. But soon Norman would raise from his arms the face we had not yet seen and that would be his until, in life or in death, he opened his eyes on eternity.

Nominated by Brigit Kelly, Kate Walbert, Doubletake

TOWARD HUMILITY

memoir by BRET LOTT

from FOURTH GENRE

5

ONCE IT'S OVER, you write it all down in second person, so that it doesn't sound like you who's complaining. So it doesn't sound like a complaint.

Because you have been blessed.
You have been blessed.
You have been blessed.
And still you know nothing, and still it all sounds like a complaint.

4

You are on a Lear jet.

It's very nice: plush leather seats for which leg room isn't even a matter, the jet seating only six; burled wood cabinets holding beer and sodas; burled wood drawers hiding bags of chips, boxes of cookies, cans of nuts; copies of three of today's newspapers; a stereo system loaded with CDs.

Your younger son, age thirteen, is with you, invited along with the rest of your family by the publicist for the bookstore chain whose jet this is. When you and your wife and two sons pulled up to the private end of the airport in the town where you live, there on the tarmac had sat a Lear jet, out of which came first the publicist, a young and pretty woman in a beige business suit, followed by the pilots, who introduced themselves with just their first names—Hal and John—and shook hands with each member of your family.

"You're all welcome to come along," the publicist had said, and you'd seen she meant it. But it was an invitation made on the spot, nothing you had planned for. And since your older son, fifteen, has a basketball tournament, and your wife has to drive, it is left to your younger son to come along.

Your younger son, the one who has set his heart and mind and soul upon being a pilot. The one whose room is plastered with posters of jets. The one who has memorized his copy of Jane's Military Aircraft.

"I guess we can get you a toothbrush," you'd said to him, and here had come a smile you knew was the real thing, his eyebrows up, mouth open, deep breaths in and out, in his eyes a joyful disbelief at this good fortune. All in a smile.

Now here you are, above clouds. In a Lear jet, your son in the jump seat—leather, too—behind the cockpit, talking to Hal and John, handing them cans of Diet Coke, the publicist talking to you about who else has ridden in the corporate jet. Tom Wolfe, she tells you. Patricia Cornwell. Jimmy Carter. And a writer who was so arrogant she won't tell you his name.

This is nowhere you'd ever thought you might be. Sure, you may have hoped a book you wrote might someday become a bestseller, but it wasn't a serious hope. More like hoping to win the lottery. A pretty thought, but not a whole lot you could do about it, other than write the best you knew how.

But getting on a list wasn't why you wrote, and here, at 37,000 feet and doing 627 miles an hour over a landscape so far below you, you see, really, nothing, there is in you a kind of guilt, a sense somehow you are doing something you shouldn't be doing.

Riding in a Lear jet to go to a bookstore—four of them in two days—to sign copies of your book.

Your book: published eight years before, out of print for the last two. A book four books ago, one you'd thought dead and gone, the few copies left from the one-and-only hardcover print run available in remainder bins at book warehouses here and there around the country.

A book about your family, based on the life of your grandmother, who raised six children, all of whom were born in a log cabin your grandfather built, the last of those six a Down's Syndrome baby, a

53

daughter born in 1943 and for whom little hope of living was held out by the doctors of the time. It is about your grandmother, and the love she has for that baby, her desire to see her live, and her own desire to fix things for her daughter as best she can, if even at the cost of her other children and, perhaps, her husband.

A book recently anointed by a celebrity talk show host. Not a celebrity, but an icon. Not an icon, but a Force. A person so powerful and influential that simply by announcing the name of your book a month ago, your book has been born again.

Bigger than you had ever imagined it might become. Bigger than you had ever allowed yourself even to dream. Even bigger than that. And bigger.

Guilt, because it seems you're some kind of impostor. Even though it is based on your family, you had to reread the novel for the first time since you last went through it, maybe nine years ago, when it was in galleys, you sick of it by that time to the point where, like all the other books you have published—there are eight in all—you don't read them again. But this one you had to reread so that you could know who these characters were, know the intricate details of their lives so that if someone on the television show were to have asked you a question of an obscure moment in the whole of it all, you would have seemed to them and to the nation—Who would be watching? How many people? As many as have bought the book? And more, of course—to be on close terms with the book, with its people, its social context and historical and spiritual significance.

You wrote it ten years ago.

And yesterday you were on this talk show host's program.

Tom Wolfe, you think. Jimmy Carter, and you realize you are dressed entirely wrong, in your dull green sweater and khaki pants, old leather shoes. Maybe you should have worn a sport coat. Maybe a tie. Definitely better shoes.

You can see the soles of your son's skateboard shoes, worn nearly through at the balls of his feet, him on his knees and as far into the cockpit as he can get. He's got on a pair of cargo shorts, the right rear pocket torn, and a green T-shirt. He'd been lucky enough to wear a polar fleece jacket to the airport this February morning in the sunny South.

This is all wrong.

The publicist continues on about who has ridden in the corporate jet, and you nod, wondering, How did I get here?

All you know is that you wrote this book, and received a phone call the first week in January, a call that came on a very bad day for you, a call that found you out a thousand miles from your home, where you were teaching others how they might learn to write. A job in addition to the daily teaching job you have so that you might make ends meet, and so that your wife wouldn't have to work as many hours as she has in the past.

The Force found you there, on a very bad day, and gave you unbelievable news. And now your book is on the lists.

You think about that day. About how very bad it was, how empty, and hollow, and how even the news that was the biggest news of your life was made small by what happened.

And now the plane begins its initial descent into the metropolis, and your son returns to the seat beside you, still with that incredulous smile, though you have been airborne nearly an hour. Hal and John happily announce you'll be landing in moments, the landscape below hurrying into view—trees, highways, cars, homes. Nothing different from the view out any airplane window you have looked before, but different all the way around.

Everything is different.

The jet settles effortlessly to the ground, taxies to the private end of an airport you've flown into before, the public terminal out your window but far, far away, and you see, there on the tarmac as the jet eases to a stop, a Mercedes limousine.

Yep. A Mercedes.

You look at your shoes, and at your son's. His cargo shorts. This sweater you have on.

"When we were here with Jimmy Carter, the lines were all the way out the store and halfway around the building," the publicist says. "This is going to be fun," she says, and smiles, stands, heads out the door past smiling, nodding Hal and John.

Then John asks, "What would you guys like for dinner?"

You and your son look at each other—he's still smiling, still smiling—and then you look to John, shrug, smile. "Subs?" you say, as if the request might be too much to manage.

"No problem," John says, and both he and Hal nod again.

Here is the store: brick, tall, a presence. A single store in a huge bookstore chain, every store complete with a coffee bar and bakery, a gift shop with coffee mugs and T-shirts and calendars.

And books.

You climb out the limousine before the chauffeur can get around to open your door, because you don't want to make him feel like you're the kind of person who will wait for a door to be opened. Then you and your son, the publicist in the lead, make your way for the front doors.

Inside is a huge poster in a stand, the poster two feet by four feet, advertising your being at this store for a signing. In the center of the poster is your picture, formidable and serious, it seems to you. Too serious. This isn't you, you think. That person staring pensively off the photographer's left shoulder is somebody posing as an author, you think.

There are a few people in the store, and you wonder if the line will form a little later on, once the signing gets underway, and you are ushered by a smiling store manager in a red apron to the signing area.

It's in the middle of the store, and is a table stacked with copies of the anointed book, and with reprints of the earlier three books, and of the four that have come out since the anointed one first appeared all those years ago. Your books, you see, are piled everywhere. Books, and books.

"Look at this!" the manager exclaims, and points like a game show hostess to a rack of paperback books beside you, the Bestseller rack. "You're the number one book," the manager says, and you see the rows of your book, beneath them a placard with #1 printed on it.

You look at your son to see if he's as impressed as you are beginning to be.

He smiles at you, nods at the books, his eyebrows up.

He's impressed.

You take your seat behind the table laden with your books, and see between the stacks that there is a kind of runway that extends out from the front of your table to the other end of the store, a long and empty runway paved with gray-blue carpet. Big, and wide, and empty.

"We'll get you some coffee and cookies, if that's all right," the publicist says to you, then, to your son, "Hot chocolate sound good?" and your son says, "Yes ma'am," and, "Thank you."

You are here. The signing has begun.

But there are no customers.

You wait, while the manager announces over the in-store speakers

56

your presence, fresh from yesterday's appearance on national TV. This drives a couple of people to the runway, and they walk down the long corridor of gray-blue carpet toward you. It seems it takes a long time for them to make it to you, longer even than the flight up here from your hometown, and you smile at these people coming at you: a young man, tall and lanky; a woman your age with glasses and short brown hair.

They are smiling at you.

You know them. Students of yours from the program where you teach a thousand miles from home. They are students of yours, friends, writers. Both of them.

You stand, hug them both, introduce them to your son, to the manager back from the announcement, and to the publicist returning now with that coffee and hot chocolate, those cookies. Then the three of you remark upon the circumstance of your meeting here: they live in the same city, and have been waiting for your appearance at the store; how wonderful and strange that your book has been picked, what a blessing!; when Jimmy Carter came here, the line was out the door and halfway around the building.

You talk, sip at the coffee, don't touch the cookie. There are no other customers, and the manager promises they will come, they will come. She's had phone calls all day asking when you will get here, and if the lines will be too long to wait through.

You talk more, and more. Talk that dwindles to nothing but what is not being said: where are the customers?

Now, finally, fifteen minutes into a two-hour signing, you see an older woman rounding the end of the runway. She has bright orange hair piled high, and wears a tailored blue suit. She's pushing a stroller, and you imagine she is a grandmother out with her grandchild, the child's mother perhaps somewhere in the store right now, searching out children's books while Grandma takes care of the baby.

It's an expensive suit, you can tell as she moves closer, maybe thirty feet away now, and you see too the expensive leather bag she carries with her. The baby is still hidden under blankets, and you smile at the woman as she moves closer, closer, a customer heralding perhaps more customers, maybe even a line out the store and halfway around the building by the time this is all over.

Maybe.

Then here is the woman arriving at the other side of the table, and you see between the stacks she is even older than you believed.

Heavy pancake make-up serves in a way that actually makes her wrinkles bigger, thicker; watery eyes are almost lost in heavy blue eye shadow; penciled-in eyebrows arch high on her forehead.

And you are smiling at this person, this customer, as she slowly bends to the stroller and says in the same moment, "Here's the famous writer, Sophie, the famous writer Mommy wants you to meet," and she lifts from inside the blankets, the woman cooing all the while and making kissing sounds now, a dog.

A rat dog, a pink bow in the thin brown fur between its pointy ears.

"Sophie," the woman says to the dog, "would you mind if Mommy lets the famous writer hold you?" and her arms stretch toward you between the stacks of your books, in her hands this dog with a pink ribbon, and without thinking you reach toward her, and now you are holding Sophie.

The dog whimpers, shivers, licks its lips too quickly, tiny eyes darting again and again away from you to Mommy.

You don't know what to say, only smile, nod, and let your own eyes dart to your students, these friends, who stand with their own smiles, eyes open perhaps a little too wide, and then you glance behind you to the publicist, whose chin is a little too high and whose mouth is open, and to the manager, who stands with her arms crossed against her red apron. She's looking at the gray-blue carpet.

And here is your son. He's standing at the end of this line of people, hands behind his back, watching. He's not smiling, his mouth a straight line, and your eyes meet a moment.

He's watching.

"Sophie would love it," the woman begins, and you turn to her. She's plucked a copy of the anointed book from one of the piles, has opened it to the title page. Those watery eyes are nearly lost in the wrinkles gathering for the force of her smile. "I know Sophie would absolutely love it," she continues, "if you were to sign this copy to her."

You swallow, still smiling. "For Sophie?" you say.

The woman nods, reaches toward you for the dog, and you hand it out to her while she says, "She'll love it. She'd be so very proud."

Here is your book, open and ready to be signed.

You look at your students. Their faces are no different, still smiling. They are looking at you.

You look at the publicist, and the manager. They are both looking at you, too.

And you look to your son. He has his hands at his sides now, his mouth still that thin, straight line. But his eyes have narrowed, looking at you, scrutinizing you in a way that speaks so that only you can hear, This is what happens when you're famous?

These are the exact words you hear from his eyes, narrowed, scrutinizing.

"She would be so very proud," the woman says, and you look to her again, Sophie up to her face now, and licking her cheek, that pancake make-up.

You pull from your shirt pocket your pen.

3

Everyone is here, your living room choked with friends, maybe fifty people in all, all there to watch the show. You and your wife have laid out platters of buffalo wings, fresh vegetables, jalapeño poppers, various cheeses and crackers and dip; there are bowls of chips, a vast array of soft drinks. Cups have been filled with store-bought ice, paper plates and napkins and utensils all spread out.

They are here for the celebration. You, on the Force's talk show, your book the feature.

Kids swirl around the house and out in the yard, their parents laughing and eating and asking what it was like to meet her, to be with her, to talk with her. Some of them tell you, too, that they have finally read your book, and tell you how wonderful your book was.

You've known most of these people for years, and there are moments that come to you while these friends tell you how wonderful your book was when you want to ask them, Why didn't you read it when it came out eight years ago? But you only smile, tell them all the same thing: thank you, thank you, thank you.

You tell them, too, that the Force was incredibly intelligent, disarming, genuine, better read than you yourself are. A genuine, genuine person.

This was what she was like when you met her, when you taped the show for three hours two weeks ago, you and her book club guests—four women, each of whom wrote a letter about the effect of your book on their lives that was convincing enough to get the producers of the show to fly them in, be these book club guests—and there were moments during that whole afternoon when, seated next to her and listening to one or another of the guests, you stole a look at her and told yourself, That's her. That's her. I'm sitting next to her. Moments that startled you with the reality of this all, moments that in the next moment you had to shut down for fear that thinking this way would render you wordless, strike you dumb with celebrity were the conversation to turn abruptly to you.

Then the show begins. Kids still swirl, and your wife has to pull two preschoolers from the computer in the sunroom off the living room, where they are banging two-fisted each on the keyboard, no one other than you and your wife seeming to notice this, everyone watching the television. There are no empty chairs left, no space on the sofa, the carpet in front of the TV spread with people sitting, paper plates in hand heaped with buffalo wings and jalapeño poppers and veggie sticks, and you have no choice but to stand in the back of the room, watching.

Here is what you were warned of: this episode of the book club show—your episode—happens to fall during sweeps month, when ratings are measured so as to figure how much to charge for advertising time, and since the viewership for the monthly show featuring the book and the author always plummets, the producers have decided to spend the first half of the hour with bloopers from past shows. "Forgettable moments," these fragments have been called by the promotional ads leading up to the air date.

This was what you were warned of, two weeks ago when you were through with the taping. Officials from the show told you all this, and you'd nodded, smiling, understanding. What else was there for you to do? Demand equal time with everyone else?

No. You'd nodded, smiled, understood.

Now the Force introduces video clip after video clip of, truly, forgettable moments from past episodes: two people argue over whether the toilet paper is more efficiently utilized if rolled over the top or out from beneath; a woman tells a Viagra joke; the Force marches down the street outside her studio in protest of uncomfortable panty hose.

Your guests look at you.

"I had nothing to do with this," you say, too loud. "It'll be on the last half of the show," you say, too loud again.

They are quiet for a while, then return to ladling dip onto plates, loading up wings and poppers, pouring soda, until, finally, you are introduced, and the book, and there you are for two minutes talking about your grandmother, and your aunt with Down's Syndrome, your voice clear and calm, and you are amazed at how clear and calm you are there on the television, when you had wanted nothing more than to jump from the sofa you were seated on in the studio and do jumping jacks to work off the fear and trembling inside you. Now comes a series of family photos, a montage of images with your voice over it all, calm and smooth, the images on the screen pictures your family has had for years.

Pictures of your grandmother, and of your aunt.

The people you wrote about, whose lives are now here for the world to see, and you realize in this moment that you had nothing to do with this. That these photos—of your grandmother, your aunt, and your grandfather and aunts and uncles and your father too, all these family photos that have existed for years—simply bear testament to the fact they were lives lived out of your hands, and all you had to do was to write them down, getting credit for all those lives led.

You think about that bad day in January. About how this all began, and how all this credit has come to you.

Yet you are still a little steamed about losing the first half of the show, when every other author you've seen featured on the show has gotten most of the program. You are a little steamed, too, about not having some place to sit here in your living room, and about those kids banging on the keyboard. You are a little steamed.

Then the discussion with you and the four women and the Force begins, and you see, along with everyone in your house, and everyone in the country, the world, a discussion that had lasted three hours squelched down to eight minutes, and six or so of those given to a woman who gave up her Down's Syndrome child at birth because of the "life sentence" she saw being handed her. You see in your living room choked with your friends this woman crying over her life, her decision, and see her somehow thank you for your book and the meaning it has given her life.

You knew this would be what was included on the air. You'd known it the moment her voice wavered and cracked that afternoon two weeks ago, there in the studio. You knew it then, and now here it is: this woman, crying over giving up her baby, and thanking you for it.

And you see yourself nod on the air, looking thoughtful.

She makes great TV, you think. This woman who missed the point of your book entirely.

2

You are answering the phones for a while, because of the terrible thing that has happened this bright, cold January day.

"We'll send you a brochure," you say to someone on the other end of the line, no one you know, and as she tells you her address you do not write it down, only sit with your back to the desk, looking out the window onto the late afternoon world outside: snow, sky.

A little after lunch, this day turned very bad, a turn that has led to you here, in the office of the program in which you teach a thousand miles from home, to answer the phone for the administrative director.

She is in the other room, too much in shards to answer the phone, to field the bonehead questions that still come to a program such as this one no matter what bad things happen and when. People still call to ask about the program, about costs and applications, about credits and teachers. About all things.

Earlier today, before you began answering the phone, before lunch, your agent called here, where you are teaching others to write because it seems you know something about writing, to tell you the novel you have just finished writing is awful.

You are here for two weeks, in workshops and seminars, lectures and readings, the students adults who know what is at stake. Though they have lives away from here, just as you have your own, you and they converge on this New England campus from all over the country, the world, twice a year to study the word and all it can mean. They come here to study writing, because they want to write, and some of them become friends to you and to the other writers teaching here, because it is this love of the word that unites you all.

Some of them become your friends.

Your agent said to you this morning, "What happened to this?" She said, "Where was your heart?"

Her call, you'd recognized with her words and tone, had not surprised you. You knew it was coming. You knew the book was dead and gone to hell in a hand basket, had known it for the last month as you'd tried to get to the end of the thing. You knew it had gone to hell in a hand basket even before you missed the deadline last week.

You knew.

The novel: a sequel to the last one you published, early last year. That one had done well, better than any of the others you've published this far. A novel you'd had a tough time trying to get published, seeing as how your books have never done that well. You're a literary author, and publishers know that means you don't sell many books. You're not a bestseller, they know. You write well enough, but you're just not a bestseller, a fact you reconciled yourself to many years ago.

But the first hardcover run of this latest book—a run in the low five figures—sold out in a few months, the publisher electing not to reprint. They'd sold as many as they'd believed they could sell, had also sold it to paperback with another publisher.

Everything was great, with selling out the print run. So great they asked ten months ago if you would write a sequel to it, and you agreed, though it wasn't anything you'd thought much about. Not until you saw how well the book was selling.

Now, here you were, ten months later, teaching people to write on a day cursed with the sad and empty curse of a startlingly blue winter sky. A day in which you have been informed of what you have known all along: this one didn't work.

You know nothing about writing.

But this is not the bad thing. It had seemed bad enough to you, walking across campus to lunch after the phone call, three hours long, from your agent, a phone call in which you both reconnoitered the train wreck before you, pieced out what was salvageable, shrugged over what was lost.

The day seemed bad enough then.

And then.

Then, after lunch, one of the students was found in his room, dead. Not one of the students, but one of your students.

Not one of your students, but a friend.

Some of them become your friends.

You were to have had dinner in town with him tonight, to talk about the novel he is writing, the novel you had been working on with him all last semester, when he was a student of yours and during which time he became a friend. A big, ambitious, strange and haunting novel.

A novel that will go unfinished now.

He was found in his dorm room, sitting at his desk, having gone to

63

his room the night before, students have said, complaining of a headache.

He was found sitting at his desk, reading a copy of one of your books. A novel. A lesser known one, one it seemed no one really cared for.

Your friend was reading it.

He was found at 1:30 on this blue and cursed January afternoon. Now it is 4:00, between that time and this a somber and hushed chaos breaking out all over campus. Everyone here knows everyone here. No one has ever died here before. He was too young. He was your friend.

And now you are answering phones for the administrative director who is in the other room. You told her you wanted to answer the phone to give her time away from the bonehead questions, but you know you offered as a means to keep yourself from falling into shards of your own. You offered, so that you would have something to do, and not have to think of this very bad day, when the loss of your own book, you see, means nothing. A book means nothing.

You have lost a friend. A friend who is here, a thousand miles from home, too. A friend not much older than you, his death a complete and utter surprise. He lives with his mother, you know, where he takes care of her, an invalid, and where he is writing a big, ambitious, strange and haunting novel.

The phone rings. You are looking out the window at the afternoon sky growing dark, the blue gone to an ashen violet, and you turn to the phone, watch it a moment as though its ringing might change how it appears, like in cartoons when the phone jumps from its place and shivers.

It rings, and nothing happens, rings again, and you pick up the receiver, hold it to your ear knowing another bonehead question is on its way.

"May I speak to _____ _____?" a man says, all business, a solid voice that carries authority with it, and you think perhaps this is an official from the college, calling on business. Not a bonehead.

"Hold on," you say, and place the phone down, go to the room next door, where she is sitting, gathering herself.

"Can you take a call?" you ask, and try to smile. "It's for you," you say, and she nods, sniffs, tries at a smile herself. She stands, and you follow her back into her office, her domain, you only a brief tenant this afternoon of a very bad day.

64

She picks up the phone, says, "Hello?" and her eyes go immediately to you. "You were just talking to him," she says, and hands you the phone, trying to smile.

You take the receiver, bring it to your ear, say, "Yes?"

"I'm calling from Chicago," the businessman's voice says to you, "and my boss is working on a project she needs to talk to you about. I need to break her from a meeting. Can you hold?"

A meeting, you think. My boss. What is this about?

You say, "Sure," and now music comes on the line, and you glance up at the director, who is looking at you, wondering too, you can see, what this might be about. You don't live here. You're a thousand miles from home. Who knows you are here, and why?

You shrug at her in answer to her eyes, and then the music stops with a phone connection click, and a voice you think you may recognize says your name, then her own, then shouts, "We're going to have so much fun!"

Who is this? Is this who you think it is? Is this who she says she is? Is this her?

"Is this a joke?" you shout. "Is this for real?" and your eyes quick jump to the director, who sits in a chair across from you, watching you in wonder.

This makes the woman calling—her—laugh, and she assures you this is no joke, this is for real, and that she has chosen a book you have written as her book of the month next month.

It's a book four books ago, a book out of print. A book about your grandmother, her Down's Syndrome daughter, your family.

This isn't happening. It hasn't happened. It will not happen.

But it has happened: you have been chosen. Your book has been anointed.

"This is secret," she says. "You can't tell anyone. We'll announce it in twelve days. But you can't tell anyone."

"Can I tell my wife?" you manage to get out, and she laughs, says you can, but that's all, and she talks a little more, and you talk, and you cannot believe that you are talking to her, you here a thousand miles from home and with a secret larger than any you have ever had lain upon you. Even bigger.

Yet all you can think to say to her is, A friend of mine died today. A friend of mine died. Can I tell you a friend of mine died?

But you do not say it. You merely talk with her, her, about things you won't be able to recall five minutes from now.

And then the phone call is over, and you hang up, look at the administrative director.

She knows who it was, you can tell. She knows, but asks, "Was it her?"

"It's a secret," you say, your words hushed for fear someone else in the office might hear. "You can't tell anyone," you say, and you are standing, and you hug her because she is the closest person to you and you have this secret inside you, and because she is the only other person on the planet to know.

You will call your wife next. You will call her and tell her of this moment, of this delivery. Of this news beyond any news you have ever gotten.

You let go the director, and see she is crying, and you are crying now, too. You are crying, and you are smiling, and you look back to the window, see the ashen violet gone to a purple so deep and so true that you know none of this is happening, none of it. This is what you finally understand is surreal, a word you have heard and used a thousand times. But now it has meaning.

A friend has died. The Force has called. The sky has gone from a cold and indifferent blue to this regal purple. A secret has been bestowed. A novel has been lost. Another gone unfinished.

This is surreal.

You go to the window, lean against the frame, your face close enough to the glass to make out the intricate filaments of ice crystals there.

You want to feel the cold on your cheek, want evidence this is real, all of this day is real. You want evidence.

You listen again to her voice on the phone, the words exchanged. You feel this cold.

A friend has died, and you did not record his passing with the Force.

And now you cry openly, watching the sky out there in its regal color, regal not for anything you have done. Only assigned that value by your eyes on this particular January day. That color has nothing to do with you, exists as it does as a kind of gift whether you are here to see it or not.

What does a book matter?

Still you cry, and do not know if it is out of sorrow or joy, and decide in the next moment it is out of both.

Your newest book is pretty much going to hell. In a hand basket.

Late afternoon, December, and you and your wife are in lawn chairs at the soccer field, watching your younger son play in one of the last games before Christmas.

Christmas. Your deadline for the next novel. The advance you were given, a sum the same as you were paid for your last book, even though it sold out its print run and sold to paperback as well, was spent months ago. Ancient history. Now here's Christmas coming hard at you, the novel going to hell.

Your son, a wing, is out on the field, your wife sitting beside you on your left, your older son a few feet farther to your left and in a lawn chair too, and talking to a schoolmate sitting on the grass beside him. Long shadows fall from across the field toward you, cast by the forest there. Other parents, schoolmates, brothers and sisters are spread across your side of the field, those shadows approaching you all. Maybe thirty or forty people altogether. It's a small school, new and with no field on campus, this one a municipal field at a city park. Lawn chairs is the best anyone can do.

And of course here with you, too, is your book pretty much going to hell, and this fact, its lack of momentum in your head and heart coupled with that looming deadline, might as well be a dead body propped in yet another lawn chair sitting next to you for all its palpable presence in your life. The world knows, it seems to you, that you are flailing.

You are cranky. That's what you would like to think it is. But it is more than that, and you know it, and your wife knows it, and your children do too. You are angry, resentful. You are in the last fifty pages, but the book is leaving you, not like sand through your fingers, but like ground glass swallowed down.

You believed you had something, going in to the writing of it nine months ago. You believed you were headed somewhere.

You thought you knew something: that you could write this book.

So, when you see your son lag behind on a run downfield, you yell at him, "Get on the ball! Run! Get in the game!"

It's too loud, you know, with the first word out of your mouth, and you turn to your wife, say, "Why doesn't he get into the game?" as though to lend your outburst credence. As though to find in her some kind of agreement that it's your son slacking off, when you know too well it's about a book you are writing going down like ground glass.

She looks at you out of the corner of her eye, says nothing.

Your older son gets up from his lawn chair, and moves even farther away with his friend, and you look at him, too. He's got on sunglasses, a ball cap on backwards. He's embarrassed by you, you know.

You would have been, too, were you him.

But the book is dying. It is dying.

You yell, even louder, "Let's GO! Get in the GAME!" and feel your hands in fists on the arms of the lawn chair.

This time your younger son looks over his shoulder, though far downfield, and his eyes meet yours. Then, quickly, they dart away, to others on the sidelines, then to the ground, his back fully to you now, him running and running.

"He's always just hanging back like that," you say to your wife, quieter but, you only now realize, with your teeth clenched. "It's like he's always just watching what's going on." You know your words as you speak them are one more attempt to give your anger, your resentment a clear conscience: you're yelling because of your kid. Not because of you.

And now your wife stands, picks up her lawn chair, moves away, settles her chair a good fifty feet from you.

This is no signal to you of the embarrassment you are. It is nothing cryptic you are meant to decipher. It is her truth and yours both, big and dumb: you are a fool.

And it is because of a book. A stupid book. There are more important things, she is shouting to you in settling her lawn chair that far from you. There are more important things than a book.

You are here in your chair, alone with yourself. And the corpse of your book propped beside you.

You look off to the right, for no good reason but that it's away from those you have embarrassed, and those who know you for the fool you are.

And see there near the sideline, almost to the corner of the field, a blond kid, down on one knee on the sideline, his back to you. He's maybe ten yards away, the sun falling across the field to give his blond hair an extra shimmer to it, turning it almost white.

He's talking to himself, you hear, his voice quiet but there, just there. He's got on a black T-shirt, cargo shorts, skateboard shoes, and though his back is to you, you can see he has in one hand a plastic yellow baseball bat, in the other a plastic Day-Glo orange squirt gun.

He's holding them oddly, you can see, the bat by the thick end, where the ball makes contact, the handle up and perpendicular to the ground, like a flagstaff with no flag; the squirt gun he holds delicately, thumb and first finger at the bottom of the grip, as though it might be too hot.

He's still talking, and you can see the gun and bat moving a little, first the gun, his hand shaking it in sync, you hear, with his words, then the bat, the movement small, like the sound of his voice coming to you across the grass, and over the shouts of players at the far end of the field. Then the gun shakes again, and you see too by the movement of his head that he looks at the gun when he moves it and talks, and looks as well at the bat when he moves it and talks.

What is he doing?

Then he turns, rolls toward you from the knee he is on to sitting flat on the ground. He's facing you now, still holding the bat and gun in this odd way, and you see, now, now, he is a Down's Syndrome boy: almond eyes, thick neck, his mouth open.

He speaks again, looks at the bat, moving it with his words, and you only now realize he is speaking for the bat, that the bat itself is talking, this boy supplying the words, and then the gun answers the bat.

They are talking one to the other: a yellow bat, a Day-Glo squirt gun.

The boy is about your younger son's age, you see, and see too the shimmer of late afternoon sunlight in his hair the same as a few moments before, when his back was to you, and you hadn't known. You hadn't known.

You look at him. Still they talk one to the other, the words nothing you can make out, but there is something beautiful and profound in what you see. Something right and simple and true, and just past your understanding.

It's a kind of peace you see, and can't understand, this moment.

I wrote a book about that, you think. I wrote a book about a Down's Syndrome person, my aunt, and her mother. My grandmother, you think.

That was a good book, you think. That one was a gift, given to you without your even asking.

A gift, you think, and you wonder who this boy is with, who his own family is, who he is a gift to, and just as you wonder this you hear a rise in the crowd.

Parents and children in lawn chairs are growing louder now, clapping, hollering, though nothing as bombastic as what you knew you let out a few minutes before, and you turn to the sound, see your son's team moving and moving before the goal down there, the ball popped to the left and then right, and now you hear from the boy the word, "Go," then louder, "Go! GO!" and you look at him, see him turned to that end of the field now too, see the bat and gun held still, this boy back up on one knee and in profile to you. "GO JOHNNY!" he yells, and you know he has a brother out there.

The gun and bat talk to one another again, while the shadows from the far side of the field grow closer to you all, to everyone, and now you know you knew nothing in writing that book. It was a gift, this story of a mother and daughter, but has it made you a better father to your son? Has it made you a better husband to your wife?

The answer, of course, is no, because here you are, chewing out the world around you because a book is going down like ground glass swallowed.

This is when the boy happens to glance up from the dialog he creates and lives at once, to see you looking at him. Your eyes meet a moment, the talking toys now still, and you say, "Hi." You say it just to be nice to him. You say it because your eyes have met, and he has seen you watching him.

But you say it to try and save yourself.

He looks at you, looks at you, and even before he goes back to the dialog at hand, his friends these toys, you know he won't say a thing.

You are a stranger.

You look beside you. There is no corpse of a book here, not anywhere around. Your wife is gone too, her to your left and away from you, your older son even farther away. And there is your younger son, out on the field and running away from you as best he can. Your son, a teammate to this boy's brother.

There is, you know, only you here with you, and though you wish it were possible, pray it might be possible, there is no way for you to stand and lift your lawn chair and walk fifty feet away from you.

Which is what you want to do. To be away from you, here.

Because you have been blessed.

You have been blessed.
You have been blessed.

0

You have everything to learn.

This will be what keeps you. What points you toward humility: knowing how very little you know, how very far you have to go. As far now, in the second person and once it's all over, as on an afternoon soccer field, shadows growing long.

I know nothing. I know I know nothing.

I have been blessed.

for Jim Ferry

Nominated by David Jauss, Fourth Genre

NINGUNA BRAHMA

by AMUDHA RAJENDRAN

from POET LORE

Two Hindhu boys stand on a platform
inside Victoria Station.

Two hours ago,
they'd brought seven German tourists
to Chandi Chowk, and traded them
to the head goon of the autorickshaw drivers
in exchange for a can of aerosol paint.

In religion class that morning,
Guruji, a short-sighted man,
had taught them the trick of defining God
by listing what he was not.

The class looked at pictures of sail-boats,
looked out the windows at the tamarind trees,
looked into their own palms and said:
Neti, neti, Ninguna Brahma!
Not this, not this, thou God without attributes!

Guruji had qualified the exercise:
It is not to say that God is not in the world.
But he is too grand to be contained within
the known universe. He does not fit inside you.

After class, the two boys had wandered
through the city in an inarticulable rage.

They'd shouted at White girls
dressed in shorts and sari jackets,
and had razzed the Muslim ladies exiting
the halal market with packets of mincemeat,
shouting *Beef-eaters!* and *Invaders!*

until the women had disappeared down the street,
clad in a riot of neon pink and sequins.

The boys had then stood outside
the new fastfood eatery that reminded them
of cathedrals, with its tall arches and steep roof.

They'd paced the parking lot while couples
eating mutton burgers and sipping milkshakes
had watched them with mistrust.

You have cigs?
Sure, yaar.
Terrific. I have the matchbox.
It's true, yaar—in time they will cut up cows and serve
beef openly—in no time we'll be cut up for catsup!
Sure. God cannot fit inside a cow.

Underneath a blaring cluster of loudspeakers,
one boy unravels a strip of gauze lifted from home.

Now, this cloth has a history of it's own—
it had once been his mother's dupatta,
her drape of modesty,
which was worn for twelve years, then retired.

Binding their two heads together,
the boys flare their nostrils and take in quick snorts

of fuschia paint through the cloth.
Three seconds: the snarl of fabric is gone.
Two seconds: comes the stunning moment—
with one spasm, both collapse into fits.

Chai-wallahs hawk tea, and coolies balance suitcases
on their heads—the station is in its own thrall.

Trying to stand, the boys are lost in a light-blear:
pupils dilate, eyes lock,
until the platform becomes a pasture, becomes a field
of brown-beetle cataracts, a blindness
which accompanies the throb of concussion:

here, in India, where cows are yet revered,
this is a kind of prediction—hammer-struck, stumbling,
these boys are heifers in a slaughterhouse.

Only the spray can is attuned to their jerking bodies:
it lies on the tracks, where the gust
from the coming train is like the night winds
that prepare Bombay for monsoon.

The spray can rolls, and its nozzle core rattles:
Neti, neti, it says, *neti, neti, Brahma!*
You do well to make your home outside,
you God without attributes!

Nominated by Edward Hirsch, Poet Lore

PRAIRIE

fiction by SALVATORE SCIBONA

from NEWS FROM THE REPUBLIC OF LETTERS

Rosalie and I are twins. We were born here in Manitoba where our parents had settled after fleeing the war in Kentucky and President Lincoln's Conscription Act of 1863. Our father was a Quaker and so a pacifist and so unwilling "to kill any man for any cause, however righteous," as he told us. When the draft officials in Bowling Green, Kentucky informed him that—as he was sane, thirty-two years old, had all his fingers and sight in both eyes—he must either enlist or pay $200 to a substitute, he persuaded Mother that they should move north. Our mother was not a Quaker, she was Methodist, but all three of her brothers had gone to Tennessee and joined the Confederate army to whip the "miscegenist baboon" (as they called Lincoln), and she had no desire to see her husband and brothers on opposite sides of a war. They intended to return once the war ended, but Father soon found that the prairie so cleared his mind that he could not recall what it was in Kentucky he'd planned on missing, and Mother was so smitten with him, she claimed, that if our father asked her "to move to the south pole and live on penguin eggs" she thought it would be a fine life, if he was there. So he stayed and she stayed with him, and they never left Manitoba. I have never left it either.

We were born on June 3, 1864, the day of the Confederate victory at Cold Harbor in Virginia. Mother told us that she had thought her baby was still another month away and on that day she'd been picking strawberries two miles from the house. When the birth pangs struck, she tried to walk back home but the contractions crippled her, and she lay down in a thicket of poplars and gave birth to Rosalie. I, she had assumed, was the afterbirth. Father found us early that night. Mother had bit off our umbilical cords, cleaned us with her skirts, laid us down in the dry leaves beside her, and passed out.

I have only a few memories from early youth: the shushing sound of Rosalie's boots through unbroken snow, the snap of her leg bone after she fell out of a tree, her cold feet against my knee after I woke from a nightmare. However, when we were eight, Father began to take us with him on his semiannual trips to Winnipeg to trade for the supplies we could not produce on our own, paper for example, and sugar. I remember that first trip clearly.

Rosalie and I had never seen a town, had never traveled further than five miles from home. We hardly slept the night before we left. In the morning, Father hitched Isaiah and Chester, our oxen, to the barley wagon and Mother packed us rye bread, a sack of onions, pemmican and a jar of gooseberry preserves. We headed southeast, Mother stayed home.

The prairie around our farm rolls slightly; wide patches of junipers and poplars interrupt the grasses and line the creek shores. When my sister and I were young, bison herds passed over the prairie around us so regularly that we didn't need to keep cattle or pigs, since bison meat and the pemmican we made from it were so easy to come by. But as we rode toward Winnipeg that October, Rosalie and I sitting on either side of Father at the front of the wagon, the prairie turned dead flat for as far as you could see in all directions, empty of almost anything but short, dry sedges covering the ground. We went a whole day's driving, forty miles, without seeing a tree, and there was no game at all except groundhogs and a pack of wolves we heard. The aurora those nights, with nothing on the ground and no moon even to distract your eyes from it, seemed brighter than it was at home. I had never paid much attention to it before.

Rosalie asked Father why the lights seemed to move sometimes and sometimes to be still, and why they were green and blue one night but almost red the next. He said, "I have no earthly idea, Rosie."

It took us six days to get there. As we entered Winnipeg, a noise rose up around us. It was the ugliest sound I'd ever heard. I thought it might be river rapids, but I couldn't see the river, and it sounded harsher than water rushing; there were shrill noises in it. I covered my ears as we drove past the people walking and talking hurriedly in the street. After about a minute, I realized that I was hearing the sound of many people speaking at once. This was a crowd. Rosalie was leaping in the barley, and laughing.

I also recall a blue storefront in the middle of town. Mother had taught both of us how to read the Bible, and had told us many stories—of children who had disobeyed and been switched, of men who had sinned and been cast out of their towns, and of unrepentant old people who had died and been damned forever. Until our first trip to Winnipeg however, Rosalie and I believed that the Bible was the only story anyone had written down. Imagine our astonishment then, amid all the uncountable wonders and noises of Winnipeg, when we entered that blue building and saw hundreds of books on the walls. Rosalie and I began to trap badgers and raccoons so that we could sell their pelts twice a year in Winnipeg and buy books with the money.

We had learned to read as most children do, I suppose: by saying, in order, the sounds of the letters. After we recognized the words by sight, we continued to read them out loud, as our parents did. As far as I could tell, even reading by ourselves, all of my family spoke the words as we read them. I hadn't imagined that one could read silently until I was seventeen. And I wish I had known that before. Because for all the time I read aloud, regardless of how taken I was with the characters or the scenes of the stories, I still had to endure my own awkward, gruesome voice speaking. Mother and Rosalie had high, liquid reading voices. They often sounded as if they were singing as they read. The words came out so casually, with none of the stutters which ruined my voice, that you'd think they were talking about the weather. So usually Rosalie read our books to me. I would often take over her chores, work twice as long in the field, the barn or our kitchen and she would follow me reading Roman history or English novels or American adventure stories aloud.

While Father and I waded far out in the Assiniboine River, gathering stones with which to build the house where I still live, the house which replaced the windowless sod one that became the granary, Rosalie sat on the shore yelling out *A Tale of Two Cities* over the sound of the current. Father kept stopping her to say, "Go back a piece. I lost you." And, "Is he the scruffy one or the rich one?" By the time she finished it, we were laying the foundation. Father looked up out of the hole in the ground and said, "Go on, Rosie, start over." We heard that book three times while building the house, then Father let her move on to *David Copperfield*.

When we were sixteen, in the summer of 1880, Father began to cough, hard. His lips turned purple. One bright afternoon in late October, while Rosalie was reading *Great Expectations* to him, he died; we buried him under a patch of tamaracks on the hill. Five days later, before dusk, telling us, "Dears, nothing so confirms my faith in the Lord's grace as His sunset, I think I shall go to watching it now," Mother stepped out our front door.

An hour later, I looked on the front porch and Mother was gone. She had been taking long walks by herself along the river the last few days and not eating much so Rosalie and I decided to have supper without her. We ate dried sturgeon, onions and buckwheat cakes. By the time we'd finished washing our dishes outside, it had gotten much colder, begun snowing, and the wind had picked up some; Mother still wasn't home.

Rosalie said, "If we don't start looking now, her tracks might get too snowed over to see." So we filled up our lanterns with bison oil and followed mother's tracks through the mud toward the river. It had rained hard all morning, so the mud was soft and her tracks were clear but our boots were sinking past our ankles and it was slow going. Just as we reached the river, the snow covered over her trail completely and we didn't know which direction to go.

I looked over the river but it was too dark to see anything further than three feet away from our lamps, except for the snow disappearing on the surface of the water. "Why don't you go upstream and I'll go down?" I said to Rosalie, then turned to her, and saw in the lamplight that she had covered her mouth with her hand and was weeping. "Or we can go together and then check back the other way."

She took her hand away from her face and said, "Yes, let's do that."

We doused the lamps so we could see further ahead of us, and walked about four miles upstream but saw only trees, mud, snow and the river, then we turned back downstream. Just before the sky began to grow light again, Rosalie said she saw something move on the other side of the river, but as we got closer to it, we saw that it was a young black bear, and then it ran off. We found Mother's body just after sunrise, washed up on the east shore of the Assiniboine, five miles downstream from the place where we had first reached the river the night before. The snow was still falling when we found her, and it continued to fall the rest of the day.

It took us about three hours to walk back home through the snow. I hitched Isaiah and Chester to the sleigh and put our canoe in the back, then we drove to the river, dropped the canoe into it, and paddled to the other shore where Mother was. Her legs and arms were twisted so I tried to straighten them out but they wouldn't bend. The canoe was too slight to hold the three of us so I paddled Mother back over the river and left Rosalie on the far shore. Then I returned for Rosalie. By the time we had gathered Mother into the sleigh and rode back home, it was dark.

As Isaiah and Chester climbed up the slope toward the stable, Rosalie said, "I have to sleep a little, Julius. I'm tired."

Then I realized that neither of us had eaten or slept since the day before. I was tired but not hungry, and knew I wouldn't be able to sleep. So I said, "You go in and sleep then and I'll get you once I'm done digging," and I went into the barn to get a spade.

"Julius, we can't leave her out here!" she said. Mother lay in the back of the sleigh, partly covered with snow.

"She's already frozen."

"Bring her into the house," she said.

"Sister—"

"Listen to me, Julius," she said, "please bring her inside." So I did.

After I'd cleared the snow away from an open place next to Father, I found that only the top of the ground had frozen and it was still wet underneath, so the earth was soft. But the tamarack roots were hard to get through. Once I'd finished the grave, I went back home to wake Rosalie. She had wrapped Mother in a bison skin, washed Mother's face, braided her hair, and wound it in a bun at her nape.

As we carried Mother up the hill, the wind was fierce. My face was too numb to sting, but the wind had stiffened it, and I could not have moved my lips to sing "Shall We Gather at the River" with Rosalie even if I had wanted to. Once she finished singing, I closed the ground up over Mother. And we went back home and slept for a long time.

So we were alone. As the winter wore on, I grew quieter and quieter. When I poured out my whiskey at night, I began to take care to keep the bottleneck from clinking against the edge of my glass. And outside, where the wind nearly deafened one to all other sounds anyway,

I tried to drive nails into stockade posts with one swing, not out of a desire to conserve my labor, but because all the sounds I made, even breathing, became hideous to me. I hardly spoke at all.

The wind that winter was harsher than any I had experienced. Blizzards followed blizzards. I went outside only rarely, to fish through the ice on the lake two miles north of our house and to keep my eyes open for bison but they had grown scarce by that time. The winter of 1880 to 1881 seems to have killed all the bison left in western Manitoba. After that time, I never saw one again. In the mornings and late afternoons I piled and repiled the snow up along the west and north walls of our house and the stable, to stifle the wind. Even so, during one especially windy and frigid week, I couldn't keep the walls buried for very long before the wind, blowing from the northwest at an angle to the walls, swept the snow away and three of our seven hens froze in the stable.

The summer before, at the bookstore in Winnipeg, Rosalie had discovered a Greek New Testament and a Greek primer, which fascinated her for some reason. She seemed to spend much of that winter studying those books at the desk in front of the window, which looked south and so was shielded from the wind. At breakfast, we had much the same conversation every day.

"That's unbecoming, Julius," Rosalie said. I was picking at my ear with the blunt end of a pencil.

"Beg pardon," I said.

She watched me eat. "Do you want more pemmican?"

"No, this's all right."

"If you want more, Brother, it won't trouble me." She had pulled up the hatch in the floor and started climbing into the cellar.

"It's enough. I'm full."

From the cellar she said, "If I were a girl you were courting and I saw that thing in your ear at my table you wouldn't get any more food from me."

"I don't want more," I said.

"It reflects poorly on one's sister, such behavior from a boy, you know that don't you? They'll think you're a boor, which may be true, but they'll think I had no sense at all, couldn't train you to eat at table."

Later, as I was cutting the second helping of eggs she had made me, my fork squeaked on the plate and I winced. It turned my stomach, that noise. How she failed to notice the sound or just failed to be

80

bothered by it bewildered me. She kept talking and asking my opinion of what she said but every day I had less to reply.

Maybe I got lazy. Talking had always felt like labor to me, like an obligation to respond to other people for whom speaking came easily—people, like Mother and Rosalie, who seemed to enjoy the sounds of their own voices. It satisfied me so much only to listen, not because I had nothing to tell them, but because, before I spoke, I had to steel myself against the revulsion I felt for my voice and that steeling took effort, and maybe I was sick of the effort.

Rosalie begged me to speak to her, and the more she asked the less able I felt to do it. By February I could manage little more than "I reckon not," "yes" and "thank you," and those with tremendous effort and shame. By March I was not speaking at all. Honestly, I do not understand it, even now. I can only say that I hated the sounds of my feet and the sounds of my tools striking their objects and more than all by far, I hated the sound of my voice.

Hated my voice I say, in the past tense, because I no longer remember it. One night during that winter, when Rosalie finished reading the Gospel of Mark to me, I said, "Thank you" because I was so grateful to hear her voice telling the story, grateful to her for abiding my quietness. But the next morning I could not thank her for breakfast nor say good-bye as I left the house. I have not spoken since I thanked her for reading to me that night. Probably my voice has changed much since I last used it when I was sixteen. Even if I wanted to speak now I cannot remember which muscles are used to form spoken words. I may have become a mute out of choice or complacency but by now, I believe, I am as incapable of speech as a dead man.

The thaw came early that spring and three or four acres of the field near the hill were dry enough in April that I could start plowing for seed potatoes and rye. The prairie was green everywhere and the wild strawberries seemed about to bloom already, which worried me because another frost seemed almost inevitable and if they bloomed too early they might get frozen and not bear that year. Still, the day I started plowing was warm, and there was a breeze, and no mosquitoes yet. Rosalie swept the stable and patched its roof with new shakes. When I came in for supper, she had roasted the last of our bison meat and made some rye bread. We finished supper and washed the dishes. I sat down next to the stove with Father's pipe and some willow bark to smoke while Rosalie read a history of the recent war in the United States to me. It was from the second volume of this

81

history that we learned about the battle that had taken place on the day we were born. When she finished, she pinched out the tallow flame between her thumb and first finger and we went to bed.

After a while she said, "Are you awake, Julius?"

I rolled over.

"So tomorrow, I'll wake up and you'll wake up and it will be just like today was, won't it?" I shrugged my shoulders. There was a long silence. I was almost sleeping when she said, "Do you think it will snow again?" I thought about it. "Maybe we should get a dog in Winnipeg, hm?" she said. Her voice was getting louder.

Then she said, "Goddamn it! Will you please say something?"

I did not speak. "Damn you!" She got out of bed and paced in front of the windows. "It's as if you were a stone! As if you were sitting there on the ground and someone picked you up and threw you into the river and now you were under water, but you don't care because you're just going to sit there where you fell just as before. What difference does it make to you? Nothing. Well you're not a stone, Brother. You're not. And I'm not either. You think you can just work all day like before and pretend somebody else is talking to me. But nobody is. I am all alone."

She was screaming, "And you're thinking, To hell with my sister. Then to hell with you!"

I sat up in bed. She walked outside barefoot. I could hear her pacing on the porch and got up and sat at the desk and watched her pacing through the window. I tried to think of something to say and to find the will to say it. Then I couldn't see or hear her anymore. I took a piece of paper out of the drawer and wrote on it, "I am sorry." When I went outside to the front porch, she was sitting on its floor, leaning against the house. I gave her the paper. She looked at it, crumpled it, and threw it onto the grass.

In June, Rosalie moved us into Winnipeg. "I'm asking your opinion about this but I know you won't answer me. If you don't want to go, speak," she said, and laid her hand on the side of my neck. "I don't want to leave either, Brother, but I must have someone to talk to." Eggs snapped in the skillet and the prairie wind spilled in through the open doorway; there were no other sounds in the house. Winnipeg, I thought, would be a crowd of awful sounds. I did not wish to go there. But I did not wish my sister misery either. So I said nothing and we left home.

All we owned of value was Father's deed to our 160 acres of the prairie, our chickens, and Isaiah and Chester. We didn't want to sell the farm, though in 1881, the land boom in Manitoba was near its height and we could have gotten a fair sum for it; so we sold the chickens and our oxen who were old by then and we got only £21 altogether. We lived on that money until Rosalie was hired as the apprentice to the cook of a wealthy Quebecois named Papillon. His house was four stories tall, built from American limestone. It had eight chimneys, fifteen-foot ceilings in all its rooms, seventy-eight windows, a chapel, a kitchen ten times the size of our home on the prairie, five French crystal chandeliers and quarters for fifteen servants in the basement. The Premier of Manitoba was said to have exclaimed one night, after a formal dinner in Papillon's house, that once Papillon died, the King of France might use his house for a second Versailles. Rosalie and I moved into a room, with one ground level window, in the basement.

I had no skills for urban life, and because I did not speak, people assumed, absurdly I have always thought, that I could not hear. In her free hours, Rosalie walked with me around the city to mills, smiths, butchers, and just about anybody, asking them if they had work for her brother who was standing beside her.

"What's he need his sister to ask for?"

"He does not speak, you see, but—"

"Then no I don't," they answered, and we moved on.

Depending on my sister's wages for my food humiliated me, but even so my inactivity was worse. Some days, I walked through town from sun-up until dark, just to keep the sloth from stealing my mind. Twice I tried to ask for work at the railway office, even wrote down my request before I walked in. But as the secretary stood staring at me, my hand froze around the paper in my pocket until finally I ran back outside. I did not understand looking for work, as if it were hidden. On the farm, work was always there, like a great feast whose abundance outstripped the most ravenous appetite, there was always, always more to do. But in Winnipeg I starved for it. And because I was not working, I had no appetite, and I ate almost nothing of what Rosalie brought from Papillon's kitchen. Sometimes a potato in a day. I grew thin.

I woke in darkness one December night. The darkness was pure, more absolute than the blue light of nighttime, because there was no light at all. The perfect blackness was familiar vaguely. I felt Rosalie's back at my side and was suddenly very happy but I didn't know why. Then I realized that we were in our old house, the sod house with no windows, and all that had come after it—the riverstone house Father and I had built and laid the three windows in, Father and Mother's deaths, our move to Winnipeg and so much sadness were all a dream, and here was Rosalie beside me, and the coals in the stove were dying out so I must go outside to get more wood, and there was the door, right over there, and the prairie lay outside it. I leapt from the bed, pulled on my trousers and boots, and as I reached my hand over to the wall where my hat hung from a hook, I didn't feel the hat, but something cold, flat and smooth.

The window. It had snowed that night and the snow had piled up and blocked out the usual dim light from outside. We were in Papillon's house after all.

"Julius?" Rosalie said. I only stood there, with my hand pressed against the cold glass. She didn't say anything for a long time. It was cold and deadly quiet and all I wanted at that moment was to listen to her talking, which she knew. I didn't care what she talked about. She sat up in bed and told me about the recipe for honeyed pheasant; about the recent shooting of the President of the United States by a man who had sought office in his administration; she told me the names of clouds which she had overheard while serving lunch to Papillon's son and his tutor; and about the university student who was teaching her, on Saturday and Tuesday evenings, to read Greek. She talked for a long time, an hour maybe, and finally, just after I had taken my boots and trousers back off and got in bed and just before I fell asleep, she said, "It's so dark now. It reminds me of the old house."

That spring, Papillon and his chief of staff, a short half-Blackfoot named DuPage, were inspecting leaks in the basement walls and came into our room in the afternoon. Rosalie was working in the kitchen, and I sat under the window reading. I stood as they came in.

DuPage was running his fingers down the brown cracks in the wall and saying something in French to Papillon who nodded and rubbed his eyes. Papillon did not seem to notice I was in the room until he turned around and put his glasses on.

"Who is this?" He asked DuPage in English.

"He belongs to your undercook, Monsieur."

"You pay my servants enough to have servants do you, Mr. Du-Page?"

"No. He is her brother I think."

"How do you enjoy living here then, Sir?" Papillon asked me. I looked at my feet.

"Why doesn't he answer me? Do you like my house?"

"He's an idiot, Monsieur, he can't answer." I looked up quickly and glared at DuPage.

"He understands you, apparently," Papillon said to him and looked back at me. "What is your trade, young man?" He waited for me to answer. "I see that you understand me, so either you can't speak," he held out his right hand, "or you have no trade," and held out his left, "which is it?"

By now his voice had changed tone. At first he seemed annoyed to have found me there, but now he was looking at me with a wide-eyed expression I have seen people use when addressing their dogs.

"Which is it?" he said again holding out his hands, and after an uncomfortable silence he folded his hands together and said, "Perhaps it's both."

I nodded.

"His sister is the one who came in from the wild last fall, yes?" he asked DuPage.

"Yes, Monsieur."

"Probably you can hold a plow then, grow things?" he asked me.

I nodded again.

"Delightful." He told me about the twelve acres on the back of his property which he had hired a young man to cultivate with wheat, broccoli and "vegetables, you know." How this young man had recently run off, allegedly to Chicago, in the middle of his planting. I could have his job if I wanted it. By the time he finished, DuPage had left the room. I nodded to him that I would take the job, and then pulled from the desk at my right a piece of brown paper and wrote on it, "I am very grateful to you." And gave it to him. He looked down at the paper then back up at me and whispered conspiratorially, "You can write! You're not an idiot at all then!" But I did not respond to this.

Many years passed.

I often longed for our return home. But in lieu of that, living in Papillon's house and working in his fields suited me as well as any other arrangement I could imagine. I worked alone and outside, as I wanted to. The other servants had never heard me speak and never expected me to, so my silence was never a point of contention with them. Rosalie seemed to reconcile herself to it.

Rosalie continued to study Greek with her tutor, who had graduated university and taken a teaching position at a boys' school in town. His name was Benjamin. Usually he would come to Papillon's house and they would walk back to the school together and use an empty classroom there. If Rosalie was not finished working in the kitchen when he came, he would sit at the desk in our room and he and I would converse, so to speak. Except for Rosalie, Benjamin was the only person I knew in Winnipeg who was willing to have conversations of longer than a minute with me. Those who knew that I could hear and wanted to know something from me would ask, read my response, thank me, and walk away. But Benjamin acted as if talking on paper were no different from talking in speech. We had long discussions, about the mountains in the United States where he was born, about the ocean and about books that we had both read. Sometimes we both wrote. He said it made him think more slowly. Then Rosalie would come in and they would go.

I was allowed to leave Papillon's house on one of his horses for three weeks every summer, so that I could go back home and keep up our house and the outbuildings on the farm. All the buildings were small and so their repairs were small. I made no additions or improvements; I kept things as they were.

Throughout the year, I imagined that I could live on the farm by myself and be happy and only lacked the nerve to do it. But by the second week, I would stay up long hours to finish painting the stable and clearing the spider webs from the eaves of our house so I could get back to Winnipeg sooner. The quiet which in my youth I had been terrified to leave was, in adulthood, almost as frightening to endure.

Rosalie never came with me. She talked about the farm endlessly, to me, to Benjamin, and to the other servants, but between our leaving, in 1881, and our return here, in the spring of 1895, she never saw this place. Maybe the painting of it in her mind became too perfect to risk violating by seeing it again.

I grew to abide the sound of many people speaking together. At dinner, the housekeepers, horsekeepers, groundskeepers and ladykeepers talked up a swarm of words and often I stayed in the dining room after dinner and picked out a person's voice from the crowd and listened to it for a while.

At the end of all the day's work, after we had put down our books and our journals, we would lay down to bed and Rosalie would tell me about the news or a passage from Aeschylus she'd been working on. We lived this way a long time.

Of course, Greek is a difficult language. What my sister tried to explain of its grammar seemed perfectly ridiculous. It was painful to listen to. When she read it out loud, I wrote on my pad of paper "it sounds like hoofs on slag to me." The characters, even, looked designed to be inscrutable. Even so, after twelve years of instruction, the last nine of which were free of the small tuition she had paid Benjamin, I suppose I should have suspected that my sister had that language more or less under her belt. The one time it occurred to me to wonder about this, I thought that maybe they had started in on Latin together, and put the thought away and forgot to ask her about it. I didn't suspect anything, I suppose, because it was unthinkable that my sister would ever deceive me. And she didn't deceive me, maybe she withheld some of her life from her brother—Lord, what I withheld from her—but she never lied. I'm certain that if I had asked, she would have told me the truth.

My blindness seems shocking, even reprehensible, to me now. That the darkest period of melancholy in her life—in which deep black rings grew up under her eyes; and her hitherto ceaseless talking thinned out to two or three mumbled "no thank you's" or "how do you do's" in a day; and I, in straightening our bed one morning, turned over her pillow and found it wet on the bottom—happened to coincide with Benjamin's engagement to the daughter of the boys' school's headmaster, that I who have never loved a person that way, should have been incapable of seeing that my sister did was perhaps the greatest failure of my brotherhood. For which I have been deservingly punished.

I began to fear that she would stop talking altogether. Each day her silences grew longer and my panic deepened. I found myself privately furious with her for keeping her voice from me though she knew how much I relied on it. How, I thought, could she be so treacherous, so cruel? Then for the first time I realized the extent of my own cruelty. For the first time I felt what Rosalie must have felt when she told me, "I am all alone." I had done, had continued doing for fourteen years, precisely the same thing to her. Rosalie's silence was only just.

I decided that something must be done, something drastic. I decided to speak to her. We were walking together along the edge of the field behind Papillon's house as the sun was setting red behind the trees and the wind bent the tops of rye. Then we stopped, and I turned to her, and tried to shape my mouth so that if I breathed properly, I would make the letter 'r'. Rosalie's mouth fell open. I tried to breathe out, but my throat seized. I tried to remember how to say the letter 'r'. Or to say any letter. The wind blew dust in our faces.

After five minutes, I saw that I could not do it and covered my mouth with my hand. Then she leaned over and kissed my cheek as the sun disappeared into the woods.

Two months after the engagement, Rosalie's lessons, which had stopped, began again, and although her depression seemed slowly to lift, and she began to speak and read to me at night again, she didn't talk as much or as loudly as she had before.

In the fall of 1891, while his son was at university in France, Papillon paid me a visit in the field. He was seventy-three then, but continued to ride his horse through the rye on his way out to speak to his "man" as he called me to his friends. "This is my man, Mr. Julius," he would introduce me. I would tip my hat. "Don't be offended, he's a mute, that's why he doesn't greet you. Ha ha!" he would say. On that day in 1891, he was trotting up to me where I was picking a burr from the mule's foot at the edge of the field and his mouth was open—maybe he had already started talking—and then his one eye started to twitch and his tongue came out of his mouth and he fell off the horse. I heard his head strike a rock. Of all the noises I have heard and hated in my life, that one was the ugliest, a skull on a rock. It was loud enough that I could hear it over the horse's legs rustling the rye, and I knew he must be dead. He wore very short riding boots, and when he fell from the horse, one of the boots remained on his foot but the other got caught in the stirrup. So as the horse bolted away, one boot went with it and bounced against the horse's ribs, looking as if there were a ghost, with its foot in the boot, kicking the horse clumsily along. When I reached his body, I took off one of my shoes for his naked foot and brought him to the house, slung over the mule's back.

Papillon's son returned from Europe and took control of his father's household, sold off all the asbestos mines, and invested his fortune in the securities market in New York. His wealth grew enormously. On one dinner, with three hundred guests, for which Rosalie had to hire twelve extra cooks, he spent £10,000. But he held many such dinners, and by 1893 nearly all the money was gone.

After his bankruptcy in 1894, the younger Papillon managed to hold on to his house for only another year. He sold everything of value in it, the chandeliers, the wine in the cellar. Eventually he even sold the land I had tilled since his own early youth. He let all the servants go, though he let us continue to live in his house. Then finally he sold the house too, or his creditors sold it. We all had to move out.

"Why shouldn't we go back?" Rosalie said. "Why've you been tending it all this time if we weren't going back eventually?"

"We have enough money to take a flat in town," I wrote.

"If you want to go, we should go," she said.

"It's not necessary."

"Julius, you never wanted to be here. I understand that. Let me pay you back."

"It will bore you."

"It will not. If you want to go, I will be happy to go. Besides, I am tired of this place. There are things I could stand to be rid of."

"Such as what?" I wrote.

"Oh, things. Things I'd rather be far from than near to."

"I don't understand."

"Don't fret yourself about it. I miss the prairie, I do."

"Promise me you'll say if you've changed your mind," I wrote.

"I won't change my mind," she said.

"Nevertheless."

"Anyway, I promise."

We left the next week. All the property we'd amassed in the fourteen years we lived in Winnipeg fit inside two trunks that lay under our feet on the train. At Brandon, we bought two horses and a wagon and rode north. After the first day's riding, we had reached Virden and spent the night in a stopping house there. We got home just before sunset the next day. That was two springs ago.

The prairie is a jealous place. My family and countless others laid claim to broad portions of it, or thought we did. In fact it was the prairie that claimed us. It permits you the delusion that you own it, while all the time it behaves with such perfect indifference to your wishes and so frigidly refuses to return to you any of the attention you give it that you begin to suspect, if it has a will or feeling, they do not concern themselves with you. After three months without rain, you ask that the grasses do not catch fire; maybe it rains peacefully and the prairie goes damp again, maybe lightning strikes and your fields turn to ash all around. You hope that the blizzard will hold off until the unaccounted-for heifer finds her way home; and she may or she may not. The prairie does not seem to hear you. However, if you leave the open prairie, if you move into town, as Rosalie and I did, you may find that, though it could never hear, it does speak, you may find that the prairie calls out to your thoughts, as if in longing, that though you may have no desire to return to it, you find yourself pulled back as by responsibility to leave whatever happiness you may have found elsewhere and return to the prairie, not for yourself, but out of loyalty to it. And if you return the jealous prairie will rob your mind of nearly all the tastes and sounds and smells of your other home. Like a wife burning the love letters her husband's mistress sent him. You may find, as I now do, watching the snowy bluff in the distance through this window, that you cannot recall the taste of an orange, the sound that a collection of tired people make as they settle in for supper, or the smell of a room you lived in for fifteen years even. Perhaps the prairie longed for you, perhaps it wanted only to dominate your imagination.

The trees were thicker now, Rosalie said, and there were more wild strawberries, and the trout in the Assiniboine seemed smaller than she remembered, but everything else looked the same. I grew barley, corn and wheat and kept the pigs and the cattle and fished a little more than I had in my youth. Rosalie did the canning and tended the vegetables and the chickens. She spent long hours watching the prairie. In the winter, from behind the window glass, and in the summer, from a chair on the porch. Even in the terrible mosquito season of June and July, she would watch calmly and smoke in Father's pipe some awful smelling plant she'd found in the woods which seemed to keep the insects away from her. She'd stare out at the bluff south of here, rapt, and looked fairly sad at these times.

Nine months ago, Rosalie and I rode into the town that had grown up about twenty miles southwest of here over the time we were away, and found that there was a letter for her at the post office. She didn't read it right then. She put it in her pocket, and tried to look calm but I saw that her hands were shaking. That night, she brought a lamp and walked to the bluff over the creek to read it. There was no moon and I could see the lamp on the bluff, even a mile away, from the window here. It was the only light anywhere. When she came back four hours later, she was still crying. I offered her a shot of the Scotch we'd bought in town, but she refused and handed me the letter.

I wrote, "This is to you. I shouldn't read it."

She pushed the letter into my chest.

The postmark said "PM January 24 1897 Baltimore MD"

I told her that I wanted her to go to him. What I meant was, since you are going, I will not keep you. Since a brother's love is not the same, since Benjamin postponed his other marriage repeatedly until he realized why, since he has asked you, and since you, I can see, said yes years ago, then I wish I wanted you to go to him, and though I want you to stay, I will say the opposite.

She has written four times since she left last May, imploring me, in each letter, to come live with them in Baltimore. Benjamin is now a professor at a college there and says that I am welcome and that he could find me work, but I do not feel capable of leaving the prairie again.

When Father came here, he forgot Kentucky. He said that he felt incapable of telling lies on the prairie, that this place asserted itself as the only possible reality—the sun set here and no place else; this particular rush of wind along the face of the grasses in spring was the only sound of wind in spring—and so you could not make fictions of other faces or other voices because the prairie did not permit you even to imagine them. Nor to imagine the true faces of your past. In time, he said, it stole Kentucky from his brain. It robs you piecemeal—one day you cannot remember the name of a face, the next you cannot picture the face either, the next you forget what it was you were trying to remember the day before, the next you forget that you were trying to remember something. Two months ago, I remembered the names of all of Papillon's horses; today I cannot remember how many of them there were. Today I remember why Rosalie did not take her Greek books with her when she left.

91

But since she is no longer here, I don't know that I will remember that in a week. Soon I will not remember her voice, as I do not remember mine. This place will have taken it. Eventually, it seems, the prairie will disburden my mind of all those strange memories and I will forget that I ever had a sister and will think only of what I am seeing and hearing on the plain.

Nominated by News from The Republic of Letters

NEW STAVES

essay by SEAMUS HEANEY

from THE THREEPENNY REVIEW

WHAT GOOD IS POETRY? Since Sir Philip Sidney's Apology for it and Shelley's Defence of it, there have been many other answers. One of the most cogent of these is W. H. Auden's poem "In Memory of W. B. Yeats," composed between Yeats's death in January 1939 and Germany's invasion of Poland later that year, which led to the outbreak of the Second World War. Its final lines are a kind of prayer to the shade of the dead poet, asking him to ensure the continuation of poetry itself and to sponsor its constant work of transformation: "In the deserts of the heart / Let the healing fountain start. / In the prison of his days / Teach the free man how to praise."

It would be hard not to read these lines as something more than an elegy. It isn't just hindsight that makes them ring like a gauntlet thrown down in the face of history: this is the voice of the spirit at bay and making a stand. Already, before the twentieth century had reached its halfway mark, there was plenty for poets and poetry to feel overwhelmed by, from trench warfare to the rise of the Nazis, and yet Auden's stanzas sound undaunted. There is a definite, unapologetic drive in the lines, emphatically rhymed and confidently metrical, which means that the poem comes across with indomitable force, as much a rallying cry as a lament.

It is a rallying cry that celebrates poetry for being on the side of life, and continuity of effort, and enlargement of the spirit. Indeed, the effect of Auden's conclusion is so powerful as to make it contradict something he says earlier in the poem, in a line which is perhaps the most often quoted and most frequently misrepresented line he ever wrote, the one which says: "For poetry makes nothing happen."

93

This, too, is a challenge of sorts, but it is one that is constantly misunderstood. The statement seems at first to be conceding that poetry is somehow falling short, failing in its function, but that can only be so if poetry's function is indeed to make something other than itself happen. But in fact Auden concedes neither of these things; his line occurs in a passage where there is no suggestion that poetry taken simply as itself is anything less than a necessity of life.

The paradoxical thing is, of course, that even as Auden was composing his famous line there were poets who were shaking the system in other totalitarian parts of the world, and they were doing so not by writing propaganda but by sticking to the self-entrancing, concentrated disciplines of lyric writing. It was, for example, Russian poets at work in what Auden called "the ranches of isolation and the busy griefs" who were among those causing the deepest political anxiety behind the walls of the Kremlin.

The 1930s were the decade of darkest Stalinist repression in the Soviet Union, the decade when poets and writers were silenced not just by the censor but by the executioner. In 1937, for example, Osip Mandelstam had not been published for years: he was living in banishment far from Moscow, living in fear for his life, but equally living in order that his poetry should survive and remain for ever what Auden called "a mouth." In the early 1930s he had returned to writing a kind of lyric poetry that was defiantly in tune with the laws of his own artistic nature—and this meant that it was fatally out of tune with the artistic law of the land in the Soviet Union.

Because he understood the rights and freedoms of lyric poetry to be the equivalent of the fundamental human rights and freedoms denied by the state, Mandelstam's vocation as a poet became the expression of a deeply committed and deeply oppositional humanism. It was as if he had taken an oath to be a kind of Antigone of the imagination, to obey the laws of his muse rather than the laws of his masters. For him, "the steadfastness of speech articulation" was of earthshaking importance. In one poem he even declares that a poet being struck by a line is like the earth being struck by a meteor, and from that image you could project the whole ground plan and elevation of his poetics and his philosophy.

In Mandelstam's thinking, there is no place for the doctrine of historical necessity, which in the end boiled down to the party line that Soviet poets were supposed to believe in and promote. As far as he is concerned, creative achievement in art and life involves the overleaping of necessity, the artful dodging of the next obvious move, the peremptory addition of the unpredictable. The thing arrives out of nowhere and yet cannot be judged out of place—this is what makes great poems both ungain-sayable and indispensable, makes them in fact happenings in and of themselves.

You could answer the question of what Mandelstam's poetry makes happen by saying that it opens a path towards the creation of other poems, and by poems I mean here not just works made up of words and then printed in books; I also mean the word in the much larger sense in which the poet Les Murray means it. For him, "poem" can signify a great system of belief or an ethic of behavior. And the twentieth century does indeed present us with a period during which the whole question of poetry's relationship to human values was worked out at extreme cost in the lives of the poets themselves, a period when the secular equivalent of sainthood was often attained by their devotion to vocation and when there has even been something like a martyrology of writers.

We have only to think of the names of Marina Tsvetayeva and Samuel Beckett and Paul Celan to be reminded of how rigorously and expensively and in what singular solitude they entered upon the way of art and followed it to the end. In its will—we might say, misquoting Dante—was their torment. Their path was along an ascetic way, not so much in a dark wood as a linguistic *via negativa*, and it was at the behest of artistic vocation that they changed their lives and spent them, for the sake of language, furthering language.

And yet the ascetic was not the only path taken by poetry in this century. The extraordinary fecundity and hypnotic force of poets such as Vladimir Mayakovsky and Federico García Lorca and Dylan Thomas must also be accounted a noble answer to the times. Their early deaths may have made them cultural heroes and glamorized them as Romantic stereotypes, but they still stand as a reminder of the daemonic strengths of the art, its covenant with the singing voice of Orpheus, the sheer spellbinding power of rhythmic speech. Dylan Thomas entered the ear of English speakers in the mid-century with apocalyptic confidence, but then, in the 1940s and 1950s, the light of trust in life itself began to dim.

After the Holocaust, there was a new darkness over the century. It entered consciousness like a second fall, one that was not part of some myth of creation and redemption but was actually a part of the historical record, the unimaginable at the back of any mirror in

95

which human beings might care to view themselves. It appears, for example, as a nightmarish backdrop in epoch-making poems by Sylvia Plath, such as "Daddy" and "Lady Lazarus," published in her 1965 collection *Ariel*. These poems and others by Plath went on to make something happen in a very political sense; the resurgence and defiance in her work, the combination of artistic achievement and personal liberation which it represented, all that very quickly began to drive the current of what was first of all called women's liberation and then feminism and then gender politics.

Plath's work, in other words, had definite kinetic effect. "Kinetic" is the word used by Joyce's Stephen Daedalus in order to describe art that has a carry-over effect in life. Art that can be coopted, say, for political purposes or as stimulation for erotic purposes. And such a carry-over effect of poetry into life is, of course, a common enough phenomenon.

If you ask to what extent the compassionate vision of a Neruda or a Brecht helped the poor and the repressed, or to what extent Hugh MacDiarmid helped a new national consciousness to evolve in Scotland, there is no exact answer but there is a certainty that something real and positive did occur. Likewise, there is no doubt that the work of the soldier poets of the First World War affected attitudes towards mass slaughter and loyalty to national mythologies; that Eastern European poets who refused to conform to the Communist ideologies kept alive the spirit of resistance which triumphed in 1989; that Allen Ginsberg and the Beats in general changed the weather of American culture, helped the anti-Vietnam War movement and accelerated the sexual revolution; that women poets in the wake of Plath's achievement gendered their agenda and affected the social and political climate; that poets of ethnic minorities have successfully made their poems part of a more extended work of solidarity and empowerment; and so on.

The work of all these poets did, in a most obvious sense, make something positive happen. I take it for granted, nevertheless, that no poetry worth its salt is unconcerned with the world it answers for and sometimes answers to. That answering function, as the American poet Robert Pinsky has pointed out, is precisely what makes poetry in the deepest sense responsible—able and willing to offer a response, but a response in its own terms. And it is those terms which often require poets to seclude themselves in Auden's "ranches of isolation and the busy griefs."

I began with an elegy for a poet because it is on the occasion of a poet's death that we experience the strongest sense of the poetry's necessity and the greatest gratitude to the poet for having made things, as Rilke said, "capable of eternity." When a poet dies, there is always a certain contradiction between our gratitude for what the art has gained and our feelings of personal loss, and this ambivalence is powerfully expressed in a couple of lines from the fifteenth-century Irish poet Tadg Dall O h-Uiginn, written in memory of his brother, who was also a poet. His mother's son was dead and so, in O h-Uiginn's words, "Poetry is daunted / A stave of the barrel is smashed / And the wall of learning broken."

There is intense grief here, but the images also give a magnificent sense of poetry's immemorial endurance, like the holding action of timber and stone. And that is why I quoted O h-Uiginn's lines in early November last year at the funeral service for Ted Hughes. With the death of this great English poet of the second half of our century, it became clear that he had re-minded England, as it were, put the country and the culture in mind again of much that its land and its language entail. He had, in a sense, rehooped the barrel and put in a new stave. This modern poet from Yorkshire who published in the 1960s a poem called "The Bull Moses" would have had no difficulty hitting it off with Caedmon, the first English poet, who began life as a farmhand in Northumbria, a fellow northerner with a harp under one arm and a bundle of fodder under the other.

At the end of a century which has seen the mushroom clouds over Japan and smoke from the gas ovens over Europe, seen the dustbowls and the melting icecaps, the acid rain and the eroding ozone layer, Hughes could acknowledge all the destructive truths and yet still sing like Caedmon about the glory of creation. In his elegy for his friend and father-in-law, the farmer Jack Orchard, Ted wrote lines which now express our own sense of loss:

> The trustful cattle, with frost on their backs,
> Waiting for hay, waiting for warmth,
> Stand in a new emptiness.
> From now on, the land
> Will have to manage without him.

Auden's phrase "the farming of a verse" comes to mind in this context; as does the old relationship, present in the word "cultivate," between farming and culture, a relationship deriving originally from the Latin verb *colere*. So I am reminded also of something that the Russian poet Joseph Brodsky once said in my hearing, something Auden-like in its simple clarity and conviction. Human beings, he said, are put on earth to create civilization.

And if we accept that definition of our human *raison d'être*, then we will admit that in a century when inhumanity was never far to seek, the poets have been true to that purpose, and have indeed proved central to it.

Nominated by David Wojahn

PU-239

fiction by KEN KALFUS

from PU-239 AND OTHER FANTASIES (Milkweed Editions)

SOMEONE COMMITTED a simple error that, according to the plant's blueprints, should have been impossible, and a valve was left open, a pipe ruptured, a technician was trapped in a crawlspace, and a small fire destroyed several workstations. At first the alarm was discounted: false alarms commonly rang and flashed through the plant like birds in a tropical rain forest. Once the seriousness of the accident was appreciated, the rescue crew discovered that a soft drink dispenser waiting to be sent out for repair blocked the room in which the radiation suits were kept. After moving it and entering the storage room, they learned that several of the oxygen tanks had been left uncharged. By the time they reached the lab the fire was nearly out, but smoke laced with elements from the actinide series filled the unit. Lying on his back above the ceiling, staring at the wormlike pattern of surface corrosion on the tin duct a few centimeters from his face, Timofey had inhaled the fumes for an hour and forty minutes. In that time he had tried to imagine that he was inhaling dollar bills and that once they lodged in his lungs and bone marrow they would bombard his body tissue with high-energy dimes, nickels, and quarters.

Timofey had worked in 16 nearly his entire adult life, entrusted with the bounteous, transfiguring secrets of the atom. For most of that life, he had been exhilarated by the reactor's song of nuclear fission, the hiss of particle capture and loss. Highly valued for his ingenuity, Timofey carried in his head not only a detailed knowledge of the plant's design, but also a precise recollection of its every repair and improvised alteration. He knew where the patches were and

101

how well they had been executed. He knew which stated tolerances could be exceeded and by how much, which gauges ran hot, which ran slow, and which could be completely ignored. The plant managers and scientists were often forced to defer to his judgment. On these occasions a glitter of derision showed in his voice, as he tapped a finger significantly against a sheet of engineering designs and explained why there was only a single correct answer to the question.

After Timofey's death, his colleagues recalled a dressing down he had received a few years earlier at the hands of a visiting scientist. No one remembered the details, except that she had proposed slightly altering the reaction process in order to produce a somewhat greater quantity of a certain isotope that she employed in her own research. Hovering in his stained and wrinkled white coat behind the half dozen plant officials whom she had been addressing, Timofey objected to the proposal. He said that greater quantities of the isotope would not be produced in the way she suggested and, in fact, could not be produced at all, according to well established principles of nuclear physics. Blood rushed to the woman's square, fleshy, bulldog face. "Idiot!" she spat. "I'm Nuclear Section Secretary of the Academy of Sciences. I fucking *own* the established principles of nuclear physics. You're a *technician*!" Those who were there recalled that Timofey tried to stand his ground, but as he began to explain the flaw in her reasoning his voice lost its resonance and he began to mumble, straying away from the main point. She cut him off, asking her audience, "Are there any other questions, any educated questions?" As it turned out, neither Timofey nor the scientist was ever proved right. The Defense Ministry rejected the proposal for reasons of economy.

Timofey's relations with his coworkers were more comfortable, if distant, and he usually joined the others in his unit at lunch in the plant's low-ceilinged, windowless buffet. The room rustled with murmured complaint. Timofey could hardly be counted among the most embittered of the technical workers—a point sagely observed later. All joked with stale irony about the lapses in safety and the precipitous decline in their salaries caused by inflation; these comments had become almost entirely humorless three months earlier, when management followed a flurry of assuring memos, beseeching directives, and unambiguous promises with a failure to pay them at all. No one had been paid since.

Every afternoon at four Timofey fled the compromises and incom-

102

petence of his workplace in an old Zhiguli that he had purchased precisely so that he could arrive home a half hour earlier than if he had taken the tram. Against the odds set by personality and circumstance, he had married, late in his fourth decade, an electrical engineer assigned to another unit. Now, with the attentiveness he had once offered the reactor, Timofey often sat across the kitchen table from his wife with his head cocked, listening to their spindly, asthmatic eight-year-old son, Tolya, in the next room give ruinous commands to his toy soldiers. A serious respiratory ailment similar to the boy's kept Marina from working; disability leave had brought a pretty bloom to her soft cheeks.

The family lived on the eighth floor of a weather-stained concrete apartment tower with crumbling front steps and unlit hallways. In this rotted box lay a jewel of a two-bedroom apartment that smelled of fresh bread and meat dumplings and overlooked a birch forest. Laced with ski tracks in the winter and fragranced by grilled shashlik in the summer, home to deer, rabbits, and even gray wolves, the forest stretched well beyond their sight, all the way to the city's double-fenced perimeter.

His colleagues thought of Marina and the boy as Timofey was pulled from the crawlspace. He was conscious, but dazed, his eyes unfocused and his face slack. Surrounded by phantoms in radiation suits, Timofey saw the unit as if for the first time: the cracked walls, the electrical cords snaking underfoot, the scratched and fogged glass over the gauges, the mold-spattered valves and pipes, the disabled equipment piled in an unused workstation, and the frayed tubing that bypassed sections of missing pipe and was kept in place by electrical tape. He staggered from the lab, took a shower, vomited twice, disposed of his clothes, and was briefly examined by a medic, who took his pulse and temperature. No one looked him in the eye. Timofey was sent home. His colleagues were surprised when he returned the next day, shrugging off the accident and saying that he had a few things to take care of before going on the "rest leave" he had been granted as a matter of course. But his smile was as wan as the moon on a midsummer night, and his hands trembled. In any case, his colleagues were too busy to chat. The clean-up was chaotically underway and the normal activities of the plant had been suspended.

Early one evening a week after the "event," as it was known in the plant and within the appropriate ministries (it was not known anywhere else), Timofey was sitting at a café table in the bar off the lobby of a towering Brezhnev-era hotel on one of the boulevards that radiated from Moscow's nucleus. A domestically made double-breasted sports jacket the color of milk chocolate hung from his frame like wash left to dry. He was only fifty years old but, lank and stooped, his face lined by a spiderwork of dilated veins, he looked at least fifteen years older, almost a veteran of the war. His skin was as gray as wet concrete, except for the radiation erythema inflaming the skin around his eyes and nose. Coarse white hair bristled from his skull. Set close beneath white caterpillar eyebrows, his blue eyes blazed.

He was not by nature impressed by attempts to suggest luxury and comfort, and the gypsies and touts milling outside the entrance had in any case already mitigated the hotel's grandeur. He recognized that the lounge area was meant to approximate the soaring glass and marble atria of the West, but the girders of the greenhouse roof impended two stories above his head, supported by walls of chipped concrete blocks. A line of shuttered windows ran the perimeter above the lounge, looking down upon it as if it were a factory floor. The single appealing amenity was the set of flourishing potted plants and ferns in the center of the room. As Timofey watched over a glass of unsipped vodka that had cost him a third of his remaining rubles, a fat security guard in a maroon suit flicked a cigarette butt into the plant beds and stalked away.

Timofey strained to detect the aspirates and dental fricatives of a foreign language, but the other patrons were all either Russian or "black"—that is, Caucasian. Overweight, unshaven men in lurid track suits and cheap leather jackets huddled over the stained plastic tables, blowing smoke into each other's faces. Occasionally they looked up from their drinks and eyed the people around them. Then they fell back into negotiation. At another table, a rectangular woman in a low-cut, short black dress and black leggings scowled at a newspaper.

Directly behind Timofey, sitting alone, a young man with dark, bony features decided that this hick would be incapable of getting a girl on his own. Not that there would be too many girls around this early. He wondered if Timofey had any money and whether he could make him part with it. Certainly the mark would have enough for one of the kids in ski parkas waving down cars on the boulevard. The young man, called Shiv by his Moscow acquaintances (he had no friends), got up from his table, leaving his drink.

"First time in Moscow, my friend?"

Timofey was not taken off guard. He slowly raised his head and studied the young man standing before him. Either the man's nose had once been broken, or his nose had never been touched and the rest of his face had been broken many times, leaving his cheeks and the arches beneath his eyes jutted askew. The youth wore a foreign blazer and a black shirt, and what looked like foreign shoes as well, a pair of black loafers. His dark, curly hair was cut long, lapping neatly against the top of his collar. Jewelry glinted from his fingers and wrists. It was impossible to imagine the existence of such a creature in 16.

Shiv didn't care for the fearlessness in Timofey's eyes; it suggested a profound ignorance of the world. But he pulled a chair underneath him, sat down heavily, and said in a low voice, "It's lonely here. Would you like to meet someone?"

The mark didn't reply, nor make any sign that he had even heard him. His jaw was clenched shut, his face blank. Shiv wondered whether he spoke Russian. He himself spoke no foreign languages and detested the capriciousness with which foreigners chose to speak their own. He added, "You've come to the right place. I'd be pleased to make an introduction."

Timofey continued to stare at Shiv in a way that he should have known, if he had any sense at all, was extremely dangerous. A crazy, Shiv thought, a waste of time. But then the mark abruptly rasped, in educated, unaccented Russian, "I have something to sell."

Shiv grinned, showing large white canines. He congratulated him, "You're a businessman. Well, you've come to the right place for that too. I'm also a businessman. What is it you want to sell?"

"I can't discuss it here."

"All right."

Shiv stood and Timofey tentatively followed him to a little alcove stuffed with video poker machines. They whined and yelped, devouring gambling tokens. Incandescent images of kings, queens, and knaves flickered across the young man's face.

"No, this isn't private enough."

"Sure it is," Shiv said. "More business is done here than on the Moscow Stock Exchange."

"No."

Shiv shrugged and headed back to his table, which the girl, in a rare display of zeal, had already cleared. His drink was gone. Shiv frowned, but knew he could make her apologize and give him another drink on the house, which would taste much better for it. He had that kind of respect, he thought.

"You're making the biggest mistake of your life," Timofey whispered behind him. "I'll make you rich."

What changed Shiv's mind was not the promise, which these days was laden in nearly every commercial advertisement, political manifesto, and murmur of love. Rather, he discerned two vigorously competing elements within the mark's voice. One of them was desperation, in itself an augury of profit. Yet as desperate as he was, Timofey had spoken just barely within range of Shiv's hearing. Shiv was impressed by the guy's self-control. Perhaps he was serious after all.

He turned back toward Timofey, who continued to stare at him in appraisal. With a barely perceptible flick of his head, Shiv motioned him toward a row of elevators bedecked with posters for travel agencies and masseuses. Timofey remained in the alcove for a long moment, trying to decide whether to follow. Shiv looked away and punched the call button. After a minute or so the elevator arrived. Timofey stepped in just as the doors were closing.

Shiv said, "If you're jerking me around . . ."

The usually reliable fourth-floor *dezhurnaya*, the suppurating wart who watched the floor's rooms, decided to be difficult. Shiv slipped her a five dollar bill, and she said, "More." She returned the second fiver because it had a crease down the middle, dispelling its notional value. Shiv had been trying to pass it off for weeks and now conceded that he would be stuck with it until the day he died. The crone accepted the next bill, scowling, and even then gazed a long time into her drawer of keys, as if undecided about giving him one.

As they entered the room, Shiv pulled out a pack of Marlboros and a gold-plated lighter and leaned against a beige chipboard dresser. The room's ponderous velvet curtains smelled of insecticide; unperturbed, a bloated fly did lazy eights around the naked bulb on the ceiling. Shiv didn't offer the mark a cigarette. "All right," he said, flame billowing from the lighter before he brought it to his face. "This better be worth my while."

Timofey reached into his jacket, almost too abruptly: he didn't notice Shiv tense and go for the dirk in his back pocket. The mark pulled out a green cardboard folder and proffered it. "Look at this."

Shiv returned the blade. He carried four knives of varying sizes, grades, and means of employment.

"Why?"

"Just look at it."

Shiv opened the folder. Inside was Timofey's internal passport, plus some other documents. Shiv was not accustomed to strangers shoving their papers in his face; indeed, he knew the family names of very few people in Moscow. This guy, then, had to be a nut case, and Shiv rued the ten bucks he had given the *dezhurnaya*. The mark stared up through the stamped black-and-white photograph as if from under water. "Timofey Fyodorovich, pleased to meet you. So what?"

"Look at where I live: Skotoprigonyevsk-16."

Shiv made no sign of being impressed, but for Timofey the words had the force of an incantation. The existence of the city, a scientific complex established by the military, had once been so secret that it was left undocumented on the Red Army's own field maps. Even its name, which was meant to indicate that it lay sixteen kilometers from the original Skotoprigonyevsk, was a deception: the two cities were nearly two hundred kilometers apart. Without permission from the KGB, it had been impossible to enter or leave 16. Until two years earlier, Timofey had never been outside, not once in twenty-three years. He now realized, as he would have realized if he hadn't been so distracted by the events of the past week, that it wasn't enough to find a criminal. He needed someone with brains, someone who had read a newspaper in the last five years.

"Now look at the other papers. See, this is my pass to the Strategic Production Facility."

"Comrade," Shiv said sarcastically, "if you think I'm buying some fancy documents—"

"Listen to me. My unit's principal task is the supply of the strategic weapons force. Our reactor produces Pu-239 as a fission by-product for manufacture into warheads. These operations have been curtailed, but the reactors must be kept functioning. Decommissioning them would be even more costly than maintaining them—and we can't even do that properly." Timofey's voice fell to an angry whisper. "There have been many lapses in the administration of safety procedure."

Timofey looked intently at Shiv, to see if he understood. But Shiv wasn't listening; he didn't like to be lectured and especially didn't like to be told to read things, even identity papers. The world was full of men who knew more than Shiv did, and he hated each one of them. A murderous black cloud rose from the stained orange carpeting at his feet and occulted his vision. The more Timofey talked, the more Shiv wanted to hurt him. But at the same time, starting from the moment he heard the name Skotoprigonyevsk-16, Shiv gradually became aware that he was onto something big, bigger than anything he had ever done before. He was nudged by an incipient awareness that perhaps it was even too big for him.

In flat, clipped sentences, Timofey spoke: "There was an accident. I was contaminated. I have a wife and child, and nothing to leave them. This is why I'm here."

"Don't tell me about your wife and child. You can fuck them both to hell. I'm a businessman."

For a moment, Timofey was shocked by the violence in the young man's voice. But then he reminded himself that, in coming to Moscow for the first time in twenty-five years, he had entered a country where violence was the most stable and valuable currency. Maybe this was the right guy for the deal after all. There was no room for sentimentality.

He braced himself. "All right then. Here's what you need to know. I have diverted a small quantity of fissile material. I'm here to sell it."

Shiv removed his handkerchief again and savagely wiped his nose. He had a cold, Timofey observed. Acute radiation exposure severely compromised the immune system, commonly leading to fatal bacterial infection. He wondered if the hoodlum's germs were the ones fated to kill him.

Timofey said, "Well, are you interested?"

To counteract any impression of weakness given by the handkerchief, Shiv tugged a mouthful of smoke from his cigarette.

"In what?"

"Are you listening to anything I'm saying? I have a little more than three hundred grams of weapons-grade plutonium. It can be used to make an atomic bomb. I want thirty thousand dollars for it."

As a matter of principle, Shiv laughed. He always laughed when a mark named a price. But a chill seeped through him as far down as his testicles.

"It will fetch many times that on the market. Iraq, Iran, Libya, North Korea all have nuclear weapons programs, but they don't have the technology to produce enriched fissile material. They're desperate for it; there's no price Saddam Hussein wouldn't pay for an atomic bomb."

"I don't know anything about selling this stuff . . ."

"Don't be a fool," Timofey rasped. "Neither do I. That's why I've come here. But you say you're a businessman. You must have contacts, people with money, people who can get it out of the country."

Shiv grunted. He was just playing for time now, to assemble his thoughts and devise a strategy. The word fool remained lodged in his gut like a spoiled piece of meat.

"Maybe I do, maybe I don't."

"Make up your mind."

"Where's the stuff?"

"With me."

A predatory light flicked on in the hoodlum's eyes. But Timofey had expected that. He slowly unbuttoned his jacket. It fell away to reveal an invention of several hours' work that, he realized only when he assembled it in the kitchen the day after the accident, he had been planning for years. At that moment of realization, his entire body had been flooded with a searing wonder at the dark soul that inhabited it. Now, under his arm, a steel canister no bigger than a coffee tin was attached to his left side by an impenetrably complex arrangement of belts, straps, hooks, and buckles.

"Do you see how I rigged the container?" he said. "There's a right way of taking it off my body and many wrong ways. Take it off one of the wrong ways and the container opens and the material spills out. Are you aware of the radiological properties of plutonium and their effect on living organisms?"

Shiv almost laughed. He once knew a girl who wore something like this.

"Let me see it."

"It's *plutonium*. It has to be examined under controlled laboratory conditions. If even a microscopic amount of it lodges within your body, ionizing radiation will irreversibly damage body tissue and your cells' nucleic material. A thousandth of a gram is fatal . . . I'll put it to you more simply. Anything it touches dies. It's like in a fairy tale."

Shiv did indeed have business contacts, but he'd been burned about six months earlier, helping to move some Uzbek heroin that must have been worth more than a half million dollars. He had actually held the bags in his hands and pinched the powder through the

109

plastic, marveling at the physics that transmuted such a trivial quantity of something into so much money. But once he made the arrangements and the businessmen had the stuff in *their* hands, they gave him only two thousand dollars for his trouble, little more than a tip. Across a table covered by a freshly stained tablecloth, the Don—his name was Voronenko, and he was from Tambov, but he insisted on being called the Don anyway, and being served spaghetti and meatballs for lunch—had grinned at the shattering disappointment on Shiv's face. Shiv had wanted to protest, but he was frightened. Afterwards he was so angry that he gambled and whored the two grand away in a single night.

He said, "So, there was an accident. How do I know the stuff's still good?"

"Do you know what a half-life is? The half-life of plutonium 239 is twenty-four thousand years."

"That's what you're telling me . . ."

"You can look it up."

"What am I, a fucking librarian? Listen, I know this game. It's mixed with something."

Timofey's whole body was burning; he could feel each of his vital organs being singed by alpha radiation. For a moment he wished he could lie on one of the narrow beds in the room and nap. When he woke, perhaps he would be home. But he dared not imagine that he would wake to find that the accident had never happened. He said, "Yes, of course. The sample contains significant amounts of uranium and other plutonium isotopes, plus trace quantities of americium and gallium. But the Pu-239 content is 94.7 percent."

"So you admit it's not the first-quality stuff."

"Anything greater than 93 percent is considered weapons-grade. Look, do you have somebody you can bring this to? Otherwise, we're wasting my time."

Shiv took out another cigarette from his jacket and tapped it against the back of his hand. Igniting the lighter, he kept his finger lingering on the gas feed. He passed the flame in front of his face so that it appeared to completely immolate the mark.

"Yeah, I do, but he's in Perkhuskovo. It's a forty-minute drive. I'll take you to him."

"I have a car. I'll follow you."

Shiv shook his head. "That won't work. His dacha's protected. You can't go through the gate alone."

110

"Forget it then. I'll take the material someplace else."

Shiv's shrug of indifference was nearly sincere. The guy was too weird, the stuff was too weird. His conscience told him he was better off pimping for schoolgirls. But he said, "If you like. But for a deal like this, you'll need to go to one godfather or another. On your own you're not going to find someone walking around with thirty thousand dollars in his pocket. This businessman knows me, his staff knows me. I'll go with you in your car. You can drive."

Timofey said, "No, we each drive separately."

The mark was unmovable. Shiv offered him a conciliatory smile.

"All right," he said. "Maybe. I'll call him from the lobby and try to set it up. I'm not even sure he can see us tonight."

"It has to be tonight or there's no deal."

"Don't be in such a hurry. You said the stuff lasts twenty-four thousand years, right?"

"Tell him I'm from Skotoprigonyevsk-16. Tell him it's weapons-grade. That's all he needs to know. Do you understand the very least bit of what I'm saying?"

The pale solar disc had dissolved in the horizonal haze long ago, but the autumn evening was still in its adolescent hours, alive to possibility. As the two cars lurched into the swirl of traffic on the Garden Ring road, Timofey could taste the unburned gasoline in the hoodlum's exhaust. He had never before driven in so much traffic or seen so many foreign cars, or guessed that they would ever be driven so recklessly. Their rear lights flitted and spun like fireflies. At his every hesitation or deceleration the cars behind him flashed their headlights. Their drivers navigated their vehicles as if from the edges of their seats, peering over their dashboards, white-knuckled and grim, and as if they all carried three hundred grams of weapons-grade plutonium strapped to their chests. Driving among Audis and Mercedeses would have thrilled Tolya, who cut pictures of them from magazines and cherished his small collection of mismatched models. The thought of his son, a sweet and cheerful boy with orthodontic braces, and utterly, utterly innocent, stabbed at him.

The road passed beneath what Timofey recognized as Mayakovsky Square from television broadcasts of holiday marches. He knew that the vengeful, lustrating revision of Moscow's street names in the last few years had renamed the square Triumfalnaya, though there was nothing triumphant about it, except for its big Philips billboard ad-

111

vertisement. Were all the advertisements on the Garden Ring posted in the Latin alphabet? Was Cyrillic no longer anything more than a folk custom? It was as if he had traveled to the capital of a country in which he had never lived.

Of course hardly any commercial advertising could be seen in 16. Since Gorbachev's fall a halfhearted attempt had been made to obscure most of the Soviet agitprop, but it was still a Soviet city untouched by foreign retailing and foreign advertising. The few foreign goods that found their way into the city's state-owned shops arrived dented and tattered, as if produced in Asian, European, and North American factories by demoralized Russian workers. Well, these days 16 was much less of a city. It was not uncommon to see chickens and other small livestock grazing in the gravel between the high-rises, where pensioners and unpaid workers had taken up subsistence farming. Resentment of Moscow burned in Timofey's chest, alongside the Pu-239.

Plutonium. There was no exit for the stuff. It was as permanent and universal as original sin. Since its first synthesis in 1941 (what did Seaborg do with that magical, primeval stone of his own creation? put it in his vault? was it still there?) more than a thousand metric tons of the element had been produced. It was still being manufactured, not only in Russia, but in France and Britain as well, and it remained stockpiled in America. Nearly all of it was locked in steel containers, buried in mines, or sealed in glass—safe, safe, safe. But the very minimal fraction that wasn't secured, the few flakes that had escaped in nuclear tests, reactor accidents, transport mishaps, thefts, and leakages, veiled the entire planet. Sometime within the next three months Timofey would die with plutonium in his body, joined in the same year by thousands of other victims in Russia and around the world. His body would be brought directly to the city crematorium, abstractly designed in jaggedly cut, pale yellow concrete so as to be vaguely "life-affirming," where the chemistry of his skin and lungs, heart and head, would be transformed by fire and wind. In the rendering oven, the Pu-239 would oxidize and engage in wanton couplings with other substances, but it would always stay faithful to its radioactive, elemental properties. Some of it would remain in the ash plowed back to the earth; the rest would be borne aloft into the vast white skies arching above the frozen plain. Dust to dust.

Yet it would remain intangible, completely invisible, hovering elusively before us like a floater in our eyes' vitreous humor. People get cancer all the time and almost never know why. A nucleic acid on a DNA site is knocked out of place, a chromosome sequence is deleted, an oncogene is activated. It would show up only in statistics, where it remained divorced from the lives and deaths of individuals. It was just as well, Timofey thought, that we couldn't take in the enormity of the threat; if we did, we would be paralyzed with fear— not for ourselves, but for our children. We couldn't wrap our minds around it; we could think of it only for a few moments and then have to turn away from it. But the accident had liberated Timofey. He could now contemplate plutonium without any difficulty at all.

And it was not only plutonium. Timofey was now exquisitely aware of the ethereal solution that washed over him every day like a warm bath: the insidiously subatomic, the swarmingly microscopic, and the multi-syllabically chemical. His body was soaked in pesticides, the liquefied remains of electrical batteries, leaded gasoline exhaust, dioxin, nitrates, toxic waste metals, dyes, and deadly viral organisms generated in untreated sewage—the entire carcinogenic and other-wise malevolent slough of the great Soviet industrial empire. Like Homo Sovieticus himself, Timofey was ending his life as a melange of damaged chromosomes, metal-laden tissue, crumbling bone, frag-mented membranes, and oxygen-deprived blood. Perhaps his na-tion's casual regard for the biological consequences of environmental degradation was the result of some quasi-Hegelian conviction that man lived in history, not nature. It was no wonder everyone smoked.

For a moment, as the hoodlum swung into the turning lane at the Novy Arbat, Timofey considered passing the turnoff and driving on through the night and the following day back to 16's familiar em-brace. But there was only one hundred and twenty dollars hidden in the bookcase in his apartment. It was the sum total of his family's sav-ings.

Now Shiv saw Timofey's shudder of indecision in his rearview mir-ror; he had suspected that the mark might turn tail. If he had, Shiv would have broken from the turning lane with a shriek of tire (he sa-vored the image) and chased him down.

In tandem the two cars crossed the bridge over the Moscow River, the brilliantly lit White House on their right nearly effervescing in the haze off the water. It was as white and polished as a tooth, having been capped recently by a squadron of Turkish workers after Yeltsin's troops had shelled and nearly gutted it. Shiv and Timofey passed the Pizza Hut and the arch commemorating the battle against Napoleon at Borodino. They were leaving the city. Now Timofey knew he was committed. The hoodlum wouldn't let him go. He knew this as surely as if he were sitting in the car beside him. If the world of the atom were controlled by random quantum events, then the macroscopic universe through which the two Zhigulis were piloted was purely deterministic. The canister was heavy and the straps that supported it were beginning to cut into Timofey's back.

He could have even more easily evaded Shiv at the exit off Kutuzovsky Prospekt; then on the next road there was another turnoff, then another and another. Timofey lost count of the turns. It was like driving down a rabbit hole: he'd never find his way back. Soon they were kicking up stones on a dark country road, the only traffic. Every once in a while the Moscow River or one of its tributaries showed itself through the naked, snowless birches. A pocked and torn slice of moon bobbed and weaved across his windshield. Shiv paused, looking for the way, and then abruptly pivoted his car into a lane hardly wider than the Zhiguli itself.

Timofey followed, taking care to stay on the path. He could hear himself breathing: the sound from his lungs was muffled and wet. Gravel crunched beneath his tires and bushes scraped their nails against the car's doors. The hood slowed even further, crossing a small bridge made of a few planks. They clattered like bones.

Timofey's rearview mirror incandesced. Annoyed, he pushed it from his line of sight. Shiv slowed to a stop, blinked a pair of white lights in reverse, and backed up just short of Timofey's front bumper. At the same time, Timofey felt a hard tap at his rear.

Shiv stepped from his car. Pinned against the night by the glare of headlights, the boy appeared vulnerable and very young, almost untouched by life. Timofey detected a measure of gentleness in his face, despite the lunar shadows cast across it. Shiv grimaced at the driver of the third automobile, signaling him to close his lights. He walked in front of his own car and squeezed alongside the brush to Timofey's passenger door.

"We have to talk," he said. "Open it."

Timofey hesitated for a moment, but the lengthy drive had softened his resolve and confused his plan. And there was a car pressed against his rear bumper. He reached over and unlocked the door.

Shiv slid into the seat and stretched his legs. Even for short people, the Zhigulis were too goddamned small.

"We're here?"

114

"Where else could we be?"

Timofey turned his head and peered into the dark, looking for the businessman's dacha. There was nothing to see at all.

"All right, now hand over the stuff."

"Look, let's do this right—" Timofey began, but then comprehension darkened his face. He didn't need to consider an escape: he understood the whole setup. Perhaps he had chosen the coward's way out. "I see. You're as foolish as a peasant in a fairy tale."

Shiv opened his coat and removed from a holster in his sport jacket an oiled straight blade nearly twenty centimeters long. He turned it so that the moonlight ran its length. He looked into the mark's face for fear. Instead he found ridicule.

Timofey said, "You're threatening me with a knife? I have enough plutonium in my lungs to power a small city for a year, and you're threatening me with a *knife*?"

Shiv placed the shaft against Timofey's side, hard enough to leave a mark even if it were removed. Timofey acted as if he didn't feel it. Again something dark passed before Shiv's eyes.

"Look, this is a high-carbon steel Premium Gessl manufactured by Imperial Gessl in Frankfurt, Germany. I paid eighty bucks for it. It passes through flesh like water. Just give me the goddamned stuff."

"No. I won't do that," Timofey said primly. "I want thirty thousand dollars. It's a fair price, I think, and I won't settle for anything less. I drove here in good faith."

Timofey was the first man Shiv had ever killed, though he had cut a dozen others, plus two women. He wondered if it got easier each time; that's what he had heard. In any case, this was easy enough. There wasn't even much blood, though he was glad the mark had driven his own car after all.

Now Shiv sat alone, aware of the hiss of his lungs, and also that his armpits were wet. Well, it wasn't every day you killed a man. But Timofey hadn't resisted, it hadn't been like killing a man. The knife had passed through him not as if he were water, but as if he were a ghost. Shiv sensed that he had been cheated again.

He opened and pushed away Timofey's brown sports jacket, which even in the soundless dark nearly screamed Era of Stagnation. The canister was there, still strapped to his chest. The configuration of straps, hooks, and buckles that kept it in place taunted Shiv with its intricacy. He couldn't follow where each strap went, or what was be-

115

ing buckled or snapped. To Shiv it was a labyrinth, a rat's nest, a knot. To Timofey it had been a topographical equation, clockworks, a flowchart. "Fuck it," Shiv said aloud. He took the Gessl and cut the thin strap above the cylinder with two quick strokes.

Already the mark's body was cool; perhaps time was passing more quickly than Shiv realized. Or maybe it was passing much more slowly: in a single dilated instant he discerned the two cut pieces of the strap hovering at each other's torn edge, longing to be one again. But then they flew away with a robust *snap*! and the entire assembly lost the tension that had kept it wrapped around Timofey's body. The effect was so dramatic he fancied that Timofey had come alive and that he would have the opportunity to kill him again. The canister popped open—he now apprehended which two hooks and which three straps had kept it closed—and fell against the gearshift.

Powder spilled out, but not much. Shiv grabbed the canister and shoveled back some of what was on the seat, at least a few thousand dollars' worth. He couldn't really see the stuff, but it was warm and gritty between his fingers. He scooped in as much as he could, screwed the cylinder shut, and then dusted off his hands against his trousers. He cut away the rest of the straps, leaving them draped on Timofey's body. He climbed from the car.

"Good work, lads."

The two brothers, Andrei and Yegor, each stood nearly two meters tall on either side of their car, which was still parked flush against Timofey's bumper. They were not twins, though it was often difficult to recall which was which, they were so empty of personality. Shiv, who had called them from the hotel lobby, thought of them as pure muscle. By most standards of measurement, they were of equally deficient intelligence. They spoke slowly, reasoned even more slowly, and became steadily more unreliable the further they traveled from their last glass of vodka. Nevertheless, they were useful, and they could do what they were told, or a satisfactory approximation of it.

"What do you got there?" said Yegor.

"You wouldn't understand, believe me."

It was then that he saw that Andrei was holding a gun at his hip, leveling it directly at him. It was some kind of pistol, and it looked ridiculously small in Andrei's hands. Still, it was a gun. In the old days, no one had a gun, everyone fought it out with knives and brass knuckles and solid, honest fists, and pieces of lead pipe. You couldn't get firearms. They never reached the market, and the mere possession of one made the cops dangerously angry. But this was democracy: now every moron had a gun.

"Put it away. What did you think, I was going to cut you out?"

Yegor stepped toward him, his arm outstretched. "Hand it over."

Shiv nodded his head, as if in agreement, but he kept the canister clutched to his stomach. "All right, you've got the drop on me. I admit it. I'll put it in writing if you like. They'll be talking about this for years. But you're not going to be able to move it on your own."

"Why not?" said Andrei. He raised the gun with both hands. The hands trembled. For a moment, Shiv thought he could see straight down the barrel. "You think we're stupid."

"If you want to show me how smart you are, you'll put down the fucking gun."

"I don't have to show you anything."

"Listen, this is plutonium. Do you know what it is?"

"Yeah, I know."

"Do you know what's it's used for?"

"I don't got to know. All I got to know is that people will buy it. That's the free market."

"Idiot! Who are you going to sell it to?"

"Private enterprise. They'll buy it from us just like they'd buy it from you. And did you call me an idiot?"

"Listen, I'm just trying to explain to you"—Shiv thought for a moment—"the material's radiological properties."

Shiv was too close to be surprised, it happened too quickly. In one moment he was trying to reason with Andrei, intimidate him, and was only beginning to appreciate the seriousness of the problem, and had just observed, in a casual way, that the entire time of his life up to the moment he had stepped out of Timofey's car seemed equal in length to the time since then, and in the next moment he was unconscious, bleeding from a large wound in his head.

"Well, fuck you," said Andrei, or, more literally, "go to a fucked mother." He had never shot a man before, and he was surprised and frightened by the blood, which had splattered all over Shiv's clothes, and even on himself. He had expected that the impact of the shot would have propelled Shiv off the bridge, but it hadn't. Shiv lay there at his feet, bleeding against the rear tire. The sound of the little gun was tremendous; it continued roaring through the woods long after Andrei had brought the weapon to his side.

Neither brother said anything for a while. In fact, they weren't

117

brothers, as everyone believed, but were stepbrothers, as well as in-laws, in some kind of complicated way that neither had ever figured out. From Yegor's silence, Andrei guessed that he was angry with him for shooting Shiv. They hadn't agreed to shoot him beforehand. But Yegor had allowed him to carry the gun, which meant Andrei had the right to make the decision. Yegor couldn't second-guess him, Andrei resolved, his nostrils flaring.

But Yegor broke the long silence with a gasped guffaw. In the bark of his surprise lay a tremor of anxiety. "Look at this mess," he said. "You fucking near tore off his head."

Andrei could tell his brother was proud of him, at least a bit. He felt a surge of love.

"Well, fuck," said Yegor, shaking his head in wonder. "It's really a mess. How are we going to clean it up? It's all over the car. Shit, it's on my pants."

"Let's just take the stuff and leave."

Yegor said, "Go through his pockets. He always carries a roll. I'll check the other guy."

"No, it's too much blood. I'll go through the other guy's pockets."

"Look, it's like I've been telling you, that's what's wrong with this country. People don't accept the consequences of their actions. Now, *you* put a hole in the guy's head, *you* go through his pockets."

Andrei scowled but quickly ran his hands through Shiv's trousers, jacket, and coat anyway. The body stirred and something like a groan bubbled from Shiv's blood-filled mouth. Some of the blood trickled onto Andrei's hand. It was disgustingly warm and viscid. He snatched his hand away and wiped it on Shiv's jacket. Taking more care now, he reached into the inside jacket pocket and pulled out a gold-colored money clip with some rubles, about ten twenty dollar bills, a few tens, and a creased five. He slipped the clip and four or five of the twenties into his pocket and, stacking the rest on the car's trunk, announced, "Not much, just some cash."

Yegor emerged from the car. "There's nothing at all on this guy, only rubles."

Andrei doubted that. He should have pocketed all of Shiv's money.

"I wonder what the stuff's like," said Yegor, taking the closed canister from Shiv's lap.

He placed it next to the money and pulled off the top, revealing inside a coarse, silvery gray powder. Yegor grimaced. It was nothing

118

like he had ever seen. He wet his finger, poked it into the container, and removed a fingerprint's worth. The stuff tasted chalky.

"What did he call it?" he asked.

"Plutonium. From Bolivia, he said."

Andrei reached in, took a pinch of the powder, and placed it on the back of his left hand. He then closed his right nostril with a finger and brought the stuff up to his face. He loved doing this. From the moment he had pulled the gun on Shiv he had felt as if he were in Chicago or Miami. He sniffed up the powder.

It burned, but not in the right way. It was as if someone—Yegor—had grabbed his nostril with a pair of hot pliers. The pain shot through his head like a nail, and he saw stars. Then he saw atoms, their nuclei surrounded by hairy penumbrae of indeterminately placed electrons. The nuclei themselves pulsed with indeterminacy, their masses slightly less than the sum of their parts. Bombarded by neutrons, the nuclei were drastically deformed. Some burst. The repulsion of two highly charged nuclear fragments released Promethean, adamantine energy, as well as excess neutrons that bounced among the other nuclei, a cascade of excitation and transformation.

"It's crap. It's complete crap. Crap, crap, *crap!*"

Enraged, Andrei hoisted the open container, brought it behind his head, and, with a grunt and a cry, hurled it far into the night sky. The canister sailed. For a moment, as it reached the top of its ascent beyond the bridge, it caught a piece of moonlight along its sides. It looked like a little crescent moon itself, in an eternal orbit above the earth, the stuff forever pluming behind it. And then it very swiftly vanished. Everything was quiet for a moment, and then there was a distant, voluptuous sound as the container plunged into the river. As the two brothers turned toward each other, one of them with a gun, everything was quiet again.

Nominated by Milkweed Editions

THE STREETCAR: AUGUST 6, 1945

by WILLIAM HEYEN

from THE OHIO REVIEW

For several hours just after the atomic bombing of Hiroshima,
a professional photographer,

Yoshito Matsushige, wandered the city, taking five pictures,
not taking many others,

as when he walked up to & looked inside a streetcar jammed
with dead passengers.

'They were all in normal positions,' Yoshito said, 'holding
onto straps, sitting

'or standing still, just as they were before the bomb went off.
Except that all

'leaned in the same direction—away from the blast. And all
were burned black,

'a reddish black, and they were stiff.' Yoshito put one foot
up on the streetcar,

raised & focussed his camera, fingered the shutter, but
did not take the picture. . . .

This streetcar with its stiff reddish-black & leaning passengers
   now travels our city,

stops & starts at crossings for our relentless traffic. Behind
   the dutiful driver,

no one is going shopping or visiting old parents or working figures
   on an abacus

or remembering a poem by an ancient master. We must not
   question or detain them, must not

stop this streetcar with our ideas in order to accept or understand,
   or to take their picture.

Nominated by The Ohio Review, Joyce Carol Oates, Elizabeth Spires, Michael Waters

GRAY

fiction by FANNY HOWE

from PLOUGHSHARES

SHE STOOD IN THE STREET, perplexed, as if she had just been dropped there. This was the late 1900's in a Western European city much like any other, when the streets at lunch hour teemed with office slaves, like herself, with their sandwiches slightly wet from sitting in ice all morning, and most of each month a cloud would cover the city, immovable and oppressive, wet all the way down to the pavement, wet in the fumes of buses and trucks slamming inches from the face.

She had gotten a temporary job working for an academic institution because of her nearly paranormal skills on a computer. Her hatred for the computer was part of her professional objectivity in dealing with their programs and systems. Sometimes the desire to kill a thing produces the profoundest understanding of it; it creates a powerful spell. Even now she was suffering from the inability to leave her computer work behind; to stop hating it and forget the case her boss had just dropped on her. She could not enjoy her lunch break.

What had happened was this. They were standing in the two-tiered office off a busy street that morning. The boss, a professor, and the office worker were both American, but he had a long-haired and sloppy look, along with a soft voice that somewhat masked his nationality. She wore the international student apparel that travels like mercury and her hair to her earlobes.

"While you are updating the system, I want you to keep your eye out for an error in there," the professor said. "It might be in the database. It might be human fallibility. The problem has existed for three years, so you have masses of material to plow through—three hundred files for each of those three years. And two different programs. But don't be daunted. The error is there somewhere."

"Why," she asked him, "is this so important? One error in three years is inevitable." She had never been asked to locate an error before; now it upset her.

"True, but our system is archaic. And the problem relates to a grade a woman received during the first year she was here and which is affecting her entire career. She will sue the institute—or bring us to court at least—if we can't prove that our grade was based on solid evidence."

"What kind of solid evidence?" she asked.

He explained—in the patient but remote tones of an academic— that the student, who had come over from America for one year, had received an A in a certain class. This excellent grade had given her the impetus to pursue a series of courses on her return to America that would lead to a career in some special kind of mathematics. However, somewhere along the line her A turned into a C, and this dropped her grade point average to a number that would put her out of the running for a top graduate school in her field.

"The written report she received with her A was apparently good, too," the professor said. "But at some point someone who worked in this office decided an error had been made, and her grade was dropped two points, turning up on her final evaluation as a C. By this time she had already left the country and spent another year and a half of her life operating on the assumption that she could pursue one career that now, of course, is closed to her. She can't go on to graduate school. The solid evidence would be hard copy—physical proof of this change in her grade."

"She must be really upset!" she cried, and her hand slapped at her cheek.

"Well, yes, to put it mildly. But we are unclear whether the new grade was based on new evidence that we received and stored somewhere—or whether the last girl working here screwed it up. And we have no way of tracing it humanly, by fax or phone, because the original grader and instructor has died and your predecessor has no recollection of this student. Usually girls like you are incredibly good at remembering these details."

The professor laughed and loosened his necktie awkwardly as if to acknowledge the completion of his first lecture in a long time.

"Let me tell you something," the office worker said. "With three hundred students a year—and the girl before me made a mess of the files—this is going to take me a long time. Couldn't we just—you know—tell the woman we made a mistake and give her the original A? I mean, this can't be worth the time."

The office worker looked up expectantly at his gray neck from where she was sitting at her desk.

"I mean, who's to know? I mean, I'll be working on the program anyway—and—if she is doing fine in her classes otherwise—why worry?" she asked.

"Well, this has occurred, of course, to me, but the case has gone so far, you see, she is obsessed with seeing the evidence, handing it to a lawyer and to the graduate institute that is now rejecting her. You understand. We can't fabricate the instructor's comments, and we also hope to learn from this error how not to repeat it. So you need to keep careful records of your research."

"If the instructor no longer exists, I'd give her a break," muttered the woman. "But then I'm not an academic."

She was soon left alone in the small, dark, thickly carpeted office. There were file cabinets stuffed with manila envelopes on her right. On her left a small window looked onto a little court and other office windows, lighted in the gray of noon. She had a large computer with a program in dazzling colors in front of her, and the name of the angry foreign student was scrawled on an envelope to the left of the computer, where her tea also sat.

She tugged at her hair as if, in response, a bell might ring in her brain. A musky smell hung around her, an air that was filtered through spotty light, violent light, a light that was sick-making but subtle—computer light. Snaky cords coiled from printer and computer down to the floor. She pressed her bare foot down on one and wondered if the Macintosh bitten apple sign referred to Eve. Forbidden bytes of knowledge. It struck her as ironic that she was seeking an original error inside the symbol of the first fruit bitten. These idle and ironic thoughts sidled through her consciousness while she worked, amounting to nothing. She was mesmerized by the light of the computer perhaps, or by the responsibility of her job, but nothing stronger than irony or mild empathy passed through her on a working day.

Outside that evening it was different. Her face was reflected everywhere later, walking around buildings. Her hair was like something illuminated underwater. The adolescent girls out on the street, as in Thomas Hardy's novels, and workers like herself, were always targets for male cunning and desire. No matter how intelligent and capable they were, there was a vulnerability to their bodies—supple, athletic, less pretty in face than in figure—that made the men rapacious, scheming, driven by a kind of homoerotic (because twisted by shame for someone not fully developed) desire. Androgynous in their long-waisted and sporty gestures, these female workers were destroyed not just by men but by time as a conspirator with the men—vacillation and the aging process—while they lived in dread and increasing sorrow at missing something. Always looking, always arriving and seeking. She knew that girls like herself felt that they might have taken the wrong step on the first day of their independence and could never retract that error.

Everyone in that decade was talking about God not existing in the usual sense anymore. God did not engage with creation or take sides or even care what happened on the last page of the story. Existence was now experienced as a calamitous state, an accident in space producing all the monkeys and bananas we have grown to love, and it was up to people alone to mend mistakes and abnormalities, to rebuild the machine from the inside.

The office worker began to wait with increasing irritation each day for her lunch break when she could escape the tedium of her quest—through manila envelopes stuffed with grade sheets, a pandemonium of instructors' comments, ever-changing lists of grade interpretations (what an A meant here was not what an A meant there), and her assignment to enter and organize all this information inside the Apple. She updated as she went along. The mysterious complaining student, Rosa Liu, had not yet emerged in all the papers, and weeks had passed. How could such a seemingly efficient institution allow such chaos to develop under a series of clever academics?

Lunch break meant fresh air, window-shopping, striding, staring, eating, and emptying herself of an unwanted and inexplicable desire for either love or praise. It was hard to tell the difference. She believed that office slaves are so named because they are a continuation of the economic model established in plantation America. They work for a set of individuals who are unknown to them and are managed by company men, like foremen, who are despised by both the owners and the slaves. In this case the foreman was a professor who had been given this "plum" (a couple of years abroad) for a number of good reasons to do with his academic record, his scholarship, and his interest in students. She guessed that professors, despised by the administrators of the institution, have the same kind of vanity that foremen did on the plantations, believing themselves to be indistinguishable from the power source for whom they work and respected enforcers of the highest social values. They abuse the institution verbally and complain constantly, but this is only a symptom of their comfort in it. People who gripe aloud are rarely those who change social structures.

Phenomenal architectures swelled like stone fruits around her: a city built to last for eons, rounded carvings, fountains, thick walls, and marble floors. Yet the domestic interiors were like extensions of gardens, seedy and earthy with long, long windows flung open on the coldest days. The people who had constructed such glorious buildings and efficient aircraft for their last war could not make a warm house, a bottle cap that would work, or a box of juice that would open quickly and neatly.

They were a strange people, even to a person as well-traveled and sophisticated as she was. Their culture was them. For them. Around them. They wanted no other but this that they had formally constructed. They married each other, even if it was a cousin, in order to ensure that the culture remained uncontaminated, fresh. They loved themselves, though they had weak bodies and chins, and made fun of themselves, wrote satirically about themselves, and succumbed to poisonous bouts of depression expressed in the gloomy weather of their land. They created the weather that they were famous for: that damp slop that hung over everything came out of their cells. It emanated, was generated.

She fluffed up her hair, checking as if some father Midas had turned it to gold, had stiffened her in space. To be unheld and unconsoled was awful. Her flat was tiny and green, on the ground floor of an exceptional building occupied by very rich foreigners who worked in finance and politics. She watched television there, read, called a few friends, woke up depressed, and prayed. Both of her parents had died, she had no one but an aunt and a cousin who didn't know her at all. She was a world-soul, well-traveled, passed from school to school and land to land, her father an unrecon-

126

structed communist, her mother a pianist, both of them suicides. By the time she was sixteen, she had no place prepared for her on earth.

A couple of boys had come across her, and she had loved being held, fondled, and whispered to. She had believed that she would be rescued, adored, made safe—but in neither case did this occur. Now there was this professor who had a fleshy tender face, unlike the American faces she could spot from afar—those faces exploding with ego. He seemed recessive and bored, pumping across the carpeting, shoes dragging. Often he stood behind her chair, facing her work on the computer, making comments, his hands resting near her hair, and she would feel herself seep downwards and ask him in a shaky voice about his family.

Finally one day she came on the missing file, and they were exuberant together and went to a restaurant to celebrate and study it. It was three pages of wrinkled and crushed paper, grade sheets, comments. At the time the student Rosa Liu was already a serious mathematics major. Here in these pages was the original A and the original comment from an instructor with an illegible signature saying, "Fine work—absolutely one of my best visiting students."

Over plates of Caesar salad the professor and his assistant became increasingly perplexed and agitated by the comment. The other pages were from other instructors in her field, all praising her, giving her top grades, and saying what a pleasure she was in class. How did this one grade get changed into a C?

"I think it was a human error, made before I got here," said the woman, "and we should just change it here and now and let her deal with it that way."

"You seem to be impatient—a bit," said the professor, wiping oil from his chin.

"Oh, no. I like mystery, the regular part of the job is routine."

"You like it here? I can, I'm sure, arrange to have you kept on."

"Don't worry, I'm fine," she said unaccountably.

"Where's home?" he asked.

"I have none, that's the problem . . .," she said, hoping he would call her indispensable and make her feel wanted.

He studied her face briefly, then paid their check, and she followed him out onto the wet gray street. She particularly liked the bones in his fingers, since they reminded her of her father, whose hands had been muscular from the labor they had endured. Yet her father had often said to her, "Everything is about power," as if his own life had been energetic and well-rewarded.

"I think you should keep looking for the error," the professor said to her over his shoulder, "but don't forget to update the system at the same time."

"That's what I was hired for . . . What should I be looking out for?"

"Probably it's a sheet of comments, like these ones, but sent later, maybe in an envelope still, and stuffed into the wrong file. You'll just have to rip everything apart. Do you mind? The last girl didn't have the patience."

They were at the bottom of the steps to the office.

"The salary is good," she replied. "Besides, I'm improving my own skills as I go along. By the time I'm done, believe me, there will be updated files and a new way of accessing them and a better way of entering the data."

"I hope so," he said grimly. "It will certainly be good on my record, if you get this sorted out. I'm always afraid this job was given to me as a form of gray-listing."

"Gray-listing? I've only heard of blacklisting."

"Age," he only remarked cryptically.

She answered the telephone, too, and sometimes talked to students who were worried or homesick. Usually, though, he did the counseling, and she would listen, suspended on her chair, to his voice in the next room; his kindness was palpable, he didn't judge. Other professors sometimes dropped in, and they would all go out for lunch or drinks, and she would hear their ironies, their bitter cracks about their work or their colleagues, and she would be astonished at his amendments to their snideness, the way he spoke no ill of others and expressed compassion for people described as idiots and jerks. Yet he never praised her.

She envied his wife and children. But she didn't covet him, she only desired to know that she was respected by him. Sometimes she thought it was physical love she desired, and she prayed that God would take away this hunger, and went to clubs with other office girls and pretended to be interested in anyone interested in her, but she wasn't. When he asked her, perfunctorily, to his house for dinner, she went obediently, but grieved throughout the occasion, watching the wife—as tall, flat, and serious as a door—and her clone daughter as they circled him with critical ease.

One day after Christmas—such a violent vacation—laden with

obligation and images of the Saint of Capitalism, fat and red-furred and white and full . . . she went to the office, it was closed, and almost miraculously put her hand into the file that contained the missing document. Of course it was in the wrong file, one belonging to another student from another year. It was in an envelope, stamped and mailed from the northern city where Rosa Liu's university was, and it contained a note from the late professor, correcting his original grade.

I would like to correct a grade I gave to one of your students, Rosa Liu, who took my class in Theorems in the Spring of 1993. It turned out that she plagiarized her written information. Then she wrote what amounted to psychotic accusations about me, which I am sure she has sent you. It is clearly too late to do anything but change her grade—she has already left the country—and I only hope that she didn't employ the same methods in order to receive the high grades she did in other classes here. Her grade should be reduced to a C, which in our country is no pass, but in yours is a low pass, I believe. She did after all attend all the classes.

Now the office worker, alone—it was Sunday, and she had left after church to come to the office as if it needed her—sat staring into the empty streets. She could destroy this letter, never find evidence of a change in the woman's grade, and continue to work in the office until she really was indispensable. This way she could continue to be close to something she wanted, whatever it was.

As a child she had been very sensitive to her parents' mood swings, their addictions to alcohol and pills, and had eyed them like a little rabbit in a big field because they often behaved like aliens. Their eyes reddened and grew wet and heavy, and they slogged across carpets and dropped suddenly asleep. But she had unformed memories—traces in her behavior—of good happy times with them, being rocked, held, kissed, read to, shown to, and the reason she prayed was because of those times, because she prayed really to them in the other world, and it might as well have been God who also liked to hide behind things.

Now she pocketed the letter and left the office and went for a long walk. A few fancy stores were open, she saw herself as light reflected in glass at several points, and wondered if there were any knowledge possible outside of experience. She took a bus and got out near the professor's flat, walking past it, back and forth, a few times. His car was gone. Her own activity disgusted and discouraged her, and that

129

night she went to a club and necked with a Lebanese man who was, like her father, a communist and spoke of Trotsky with mixed emotions. He said he was surprised that "a dumb blond would know about continuing revolution," and his finger snapped her panties.

Alone at home she considered suicide and following her parents to the place where they had gone. This was a common consideration.

She reread the note several times and wished she could talk to Rosa Liu about it, before deciding her next move. After all, what did she know about this plagiary, and if it really made any difference to the woman's abilities as a mathematician? Why did Rosa want so badly to find the evidence, if in fact it was incriminating, ruinous to her? She must have known what her crime was, and why her grade was changed. Why did the instructor, in his first letter, say that she was one of the best visiting students he had encountered if it weren't true? And what were Rosa Liu's so-called accusations?

The office worker wanted very much to destroy this letter. But some respect for facts made her hesitate. This respect was a kind of superstition. It was almost as if she imagined facts as bodies that could walk out of the chaos of time—even walk with a purpose—and that they could witness a false fact coming and steer surrounding events in a way that would release a kind of plague of lies. Indeed, out of revenge for her wickedness, the original fact would bend all first destinies into jammed-up paths.

Then she wondered if all this storing and collecting, which was embodied and embedded in the great leaden form of the computer, was perhaps driving her crazy. She felt a little uncoordinated mentally.

At work the next day she imagined herself showing the professor the letter and being pleased that he praised her for her diligence, for working on Sunday, and perhaps he would be worried that she might feel, now, compelled to quit the job, having discovered the root of the error. Don't quit, he might say, because now that you have updated the system, you are really indispensable, the only one who knows this thing in depth. You are all but an assistant registrar by now!

Pleased, she nonetheless didn't speak to him but went back into her office and turned on the computer, watching the colors pop up and wondering if colors like this would be reflected in a river. She gazed angrily into the screen, then returned to the files, hunched over them, determined to come to a decision about Rosa Liu. Her posture grew tense and threw sharp pains down her spine, and she began pulling out manila envelopes at random and spreading them around her on the floor, so that she could have greater ease sorting through them.

When the professor cast his shadow over her, from his position at the door, she looked at him with the same expression she had given the computer earlier. He removed himself, backwards, and she returned to her task. Days later, when she was still engaged in her pursuit through actual paper, on the floor, he insinuatingly wondered if she was still updating the computer system in the process of searching for this error. She told him that there was a basic flaw in the way the institute was processing grades, based on illegible notes from professors whose values and judgments bore no relationship to the home system.

"The only way," she said, "to make this work would be to acknowledge the radical difference between the systems and grade everyone who attended and did the work according to one universal standard—Task Completed Satisfactorily."

The professor laughed heartily, but the redness in his cheeks outlived the upturned shape to his lips. They argued for the first time. His voice grew loud, and he interrupted her, and said "Yeah yeah yeah" in impatient tones while she was explaining her point of view to him; he was in a hurry for her to stop talking, so he could talk better. She was on the floor, crouched, but her mind was outside, leaping up the steps of a store with spears of light shattering the time she was in.

Some people achieve a mystical perspective on the world by mental struggle, by unrelenting questioning of natural law, of time and imagination. Those lights that gathered around her protectively while she lived and walked were also part of her mind, extra parts. Now she crawled across the office floor past the professor's legs and told him she actually knew better than he about the failures in the grading system, because she was working with it daily. But he insisted on his perspective and on the need for maintaining equivalencies between universities in relation to a global vision. "We would be reverting to a kind of reverse snobbery if we let students get away without being graded according to the terms of the country they were in. The implications would be that we were just sending them over here to have fun."

"If the standards are different, how can the judgments be the same?" she muttered, then shut up. She grew depressed. But she kept up her hunt, daily, for some new piece of evidence. And then one night she found it, when she was alone, with the manila folders spilled on the floor under the colors of the computer and an overhead electric bulb. It was folded into long sections as if a child had been making a paper airplane from it. But the black e-mail print was immediately recognizable, in this case written like a poem in a narrow column.

> Dear profeser in the rest room
> you make me feel your big member
> you pull my hair call it part of
> the uncertanty world I was just there
> to clean toilets to pay my education
> but you stole my theorem
> but said I was unworthy of you.
> You stole my theorem for your use.
> You stole it for your carer. Big Phd man
> who done nothing for yers. No promotion!
> You think I don't know you fail?
> You don't care I died in industrial acident
> before I never maried my husband
> he was no profeser but only loved him briefly.
> Because of the one who came
> you call these the laws of imigration a finger bone
> to the one on the word procesor
> a stick for the fil clerk fethers for the cleanng women
> sex for this toilet washer who wrote a great theorem
> you stole and you know the persen
> who understans the problm is at the botom
> of the barell I used to think
> maths could solve anything profeser
> but maybe you could help me find a new solution
> or proof if you profer?
> See no mater what I was respected in my country.

> Rosa Liu

Now what could the office worker do with this information? She read and reread the e-mail several times. Her complexion silvered. She shut the door. It was drizzling on the dirty glass that looked out into an alley and across into other windows neon-lighted and filled with office workers like herself, facing full into the computer's screens.

What would influence her next move? Her parents' suicides? her belief in God? her Red upbringing? her loneliness? her need for the professor's love? her hatred of the computer? her hatred of the professor? the rain? the lights? the light? her temperament? her brain? I'll just think awhile, she decided. And she thought about calling the department at the university where Rosa Liu had been accused of plagiary. She wondered what story they would give her. But when she proposed doing this, the professor told her he had already called the department, and they had been close-mouthed, impenetrable. But she didn't quite believe him, because of the way his eyes were lowered and looking to the right.

For the next week she cleaned up the files from the floor and noted with some pleasure the effects of her work, her innate sense of sequence, so that the envelopes looked and now were in a form that no other office girl could fail to understand. And the computer system could now pop up the name of each former student including a grade point average and the classes they took and who taught them, in a matter of seconds. Yet with each grade she entered for this year's class, she made a little change, raising the grade a point or two. Why not? Sometimes it is almost intolerable that order, being so impersonal, is simultaneously so brutal.

That same evening she recalled the way God parted the waters, saying: "Let there be a dome in the midst of the waters, and let it separate the waters from the waters." And she felt a fellowship with this action. She hunched into her computer posture, face fixated on the glass as if she were seeing the arrival of warplanes over a swaying horizon, while in her lap she nervously attached Rosa Liu's e-mail to the professor's letter with a clip. She would reveal the results of her tireless search in the early winter darkness as they were each leaving to go home. The professor would be embarrassed because he would have guessed it was something like this. And so would she. And the embarrassment would bind them weirdly as they went up the stairs and together changed the grade to an A. The fact was, at her age, she would have a hard time finding a permanent new job.

Nominated by Joyce Carol Oates, Ploughshares

133

ALPHA IMAGES

by KARL ELDER

from BELOIT POETRY JOURNAL

A
In the beginning
God climbed Louis Zukofsky's
pocket stepladder.

B
We see from above
she faces east, her bosom
of the matriarch.

C
No great mystery,
he that rears on one hind leg.
Pegasus' hoof print.

D
Alfred Hitchcock as
pregnant with the devil as
with a certain air.

E
Where is the handle
and what hand stuck this pitchfork
into a snowbank?

F
Stand it on the moon
for a nation of ants, who
know not where they live.

G
Balancing a tray
with one hand, the other hand
poised to pluck the veil.

H
The minimalist's
gate to hell and heaven, these
corridors of light.

I
Blind to what's ahead,
behind, the ego takes this
pillar for a name.

J
Take pity on this
tattered parasol—too chic
for junk or joy stick.

K
What looks like a squawk
is to the ear a moth or
butterfly, clinging.

L
Lest we should deny
the ethereal we have
the hypothenuse.

M
Dragging its belly,
a mechanical spider,
its nose to the ground.

N

A scene from Up North
on a postcard, a timber
frozen as it's felled.

O

The rim of the moon.
Peephole into an igloo.
Shadow of zero.

P

How you choose to hold
it determines the weapon.
You may need tweezers.

Q

Might this be the light
at the end of the tunnel,
the visible path?

R

Head, shoulders, and chest—
who's the cameo inside
this dressmaker's bust?

S

Suppose our hero
tore the spent fuse from the stick.
Say the sound of it.

T

Though you can't see what
road you're on, the sign ahead
reads like calvary.

U

More mind than matter
is symmetry's mirror. You
should be that lucky.

V
V is for virgin.
Whether spread or locked, her legs
are the point of view.

W
Symbol of tungsten
and the filament itself,
its light is the white.

X
North—as if a place
as much as idea—four
needles pointing there.

Y
This flower has bloomed,
become so huge as to dwarf
both stem and petals.

Z
Swordplay with air—zip
zip zip—stitches which seem a
bout to disappear.

Nominated by Beloit Poetry Journal

THE SMALLEST MAN
IN THE WORLD

fiction by BONNIE JO CAMPBELL

from THE SOUTHERN REVIEW

Beauty is not a virtue. And beauty is not in the eye of the beholder. Beauty is a fact like height or symmetry or hair color. Understand that I am not bragging when I say I am the most beautiful woman in the bar.

Normally I can make this claim without hesitation, because this is my regular bar. But tonight the circus is in town, and there are strangers here, including four showgirls at a table between me and the jukebox drinking what look like vodka tonics—tall, clear drinks with maraschino cherries.

Whenever the circus comes to the Palace, I attend, as I did tonight with my sister, who now drums her fingers on the bar beside me.

"What did you like best?" she asks.

I shrug. My sister gets annoyed when I refuse to talk, but I do not like to answer questions I have not thought about.

"How about that rhinoceros?" she says. "It was sweating gallons out there. I'm surprised that woman didn't slide off."

"Yes."

"Why do you come here?" asks my sister, spinning around once on her stool. "There's nothing to do." She spins again. "You should tell them to get magnetic darts or something."

My sister always chatters this way. She is warm, communicative, and generous, and I am not—just ask any of my three ex-husbands.

138

If you want to know the other difficulties of being close to me, you will have to ask them or her, because I do not intend to enumerate my faults. My sister and I have similar eyes, mouths, and hair, and it is a puzzle why I am more beautiful than she. Perhaps it is because she has developed so many other interests. She is a social worker in a hospital, helping fifty families a day in whatever ways she can; she belongs to a softball league; she has a husband who is crazy about her. Within a year, she will probably have her first child. I work at a hotel, where part of my job is to look good.

"If you're not going to talk to me, I'm leaving," my sister says. "I've got stuff I can do at home." She downs her cranberry juice and heads for the door.

This is a typical end to our evenings together. I cannot explain to her that, though I love her company, I do not want to talk. As she exits, two big men in circus coveralls enter, accompanied by the smallest man in the world. The big men have identical builds, but one is white with blond hair and slightly crossed eyes, and the other is black and scruffy-headed. Both give the impression that the coveralls are the only clothes they own. When they reach the bar, these two bend in unison, and the small man straightens his arms and allows himself to be lifted onto a stool, where he stands and looks down on the bartender. To his credit, Martin the bartender does not ask for identification, but brings the small man his whiskey and soda in a professional way that does not suggest surprise that such a tiny man would want a drink, or indeed that a man would be so tiny.

As usual, I sit at the far end of the counter, on the brass-and-leather stool nearest the wall, so I can see everyone in the place. The wooden bar curves away from me and stretches thirty feet, halfway to the front door, and is stained a reddish color beneath layers of polyurethane. The wall opposite me is raw brick, lined with low-wattage fixtures designed to look like gas lanterns. After working all day in bright light, I find the dimness comforting.

The smallest man in the world looks at the patrons one by one, then settles his gaze on me and nods. His hair is thinning. With a closed mouth, I smile. He holds up his drink in my direction, in appreciation of my beauty, and I lift my drink in appreciation of his smallness.

I have compared beauty and height, but there is more in common between beauty and smallness: conciseness, the correct arrangement

139

of parts in a confined area. Space has not been wasted on the smallest man in the world. He is perfectly formed, with limbs, trunk, and ears all in proportion. Only at the most perfunctory glance does he look like a child, for he has a serious forehead and a square jaw. His face is slightly swollen, most likely from drinking, but his size obscures this fact. An art teacher once showed me the trick of making a black ink drawing and then shrinking it on a copy machine—in the reduction, the flaws are less perceptible.

As appears to be the case with the smallest man in the world, I sometimes drink too much. When I develop that swollen look, I disguise it by loosening my hair. Drinking is, of course, an ordinary addiction; it is not peculiar to persons who possess extreme qualities. Plenty of plain, normal-sized people drink too much. Take, for instance, the sweaty man who has been coming in for the last few months with his shirt buttons more and more strained—he has the look of a man embroiled in an unpleasant divorce. That woman at the other end of the bar must be seventy, maybe with grandchildren, and she drinks to excess nightly, done up in foundation and blusher. The edge of her glass is smeared halfway around with lipstick.

My sister appears in the doorway behind the made-up old woman and makes her way back to me, jangling her keys.

"I forgot that I drove you here. How are you getting home?"

"I can take a cab. Do not worry about me, little sister."

"OK, take care of yourself. I'll see you soon." She touches my shoulder to prove her concern. My sister is a caring person, no doubt, but I get the feeling she is worried less about me than about the people around me. "Wherever I came I brought calamity," Tennyson quotes Helen of Troy. My sister knows that when I get drunk I become friendly, and she knows that men who come into the bar with perfectly nice women or who have left at home women as pretty and caring as my sister will risk future happiness in order to spend the night with me. Some may consider my willingness to go home with such men reprehensible; you also may blame the Trojan War on Helen's misbehavior. Keep in mind, though, that Helen did not launch a single warship. And in the end she paid a great price for her affair with Paris: while you and I are able to toss off married names for fifty dollars and some paperwork, she remains Helen of Troy for all eternity. No matter that she settled happily with Menelaus in Athens and had a child.

140

My sister almost brushes against the circus men on the way out, and the white guy turns to watch her leave. She has a friendly, bouncy walk. She does not look back.

A pale-skinned couple enters and sits on stools halfway down. Perhaps they have been to a play. They move in unison, their once-independent bodies working as complementary parts of a whole. He helps her take off her coat, and she gets him something from her purse. The smallest man in the world jumps down and walks toward the jukebox, onto which his friends lift him. When a song skips, Martin the bartender looks over coolly, but to his credit does not yell, "Get off the jukebox." Though it has never occurred to me before, I consider this bartender a good friend.

Twenty years ago, when I was in high school, my mother and sister, hoping I could make friends, encouraged me to enter my first and only beauty contest. But even then I recognized most of those girls as shallow and hopeless bits of fluff, unaware of what freaks we were making of ourselves. And, of course, they hated me for winning. It should not surprise anyone that P. T. Barnum himself pioneered the modern beauty contest, recognizing that striking beauty was fundamentally no different from any other aberration. Such absurdly perfect integration of a woman's features and shape was not unlike a third arm growing from the center of another woman's back. Barnum was the first to realize that strangers would pay to see this sort of female oddity paraded before them.

The sweaty man with the strained buttons walks by on his way to the bathroom. When he glances at me, he trips over a carpet runner; he catches himself and regains his balance awkwardly, as though his body has recently become a stranger to him. I tend my body with such care that I cannot imagine losing touch with it—I am far more likely to lose my mind, something nobody notices. The man looks away as he straightens himself up, and a few minutes later he returns to his seat by a circuitous route.

In a thick accent, the smallest man in the world yells something to the table of showgirls, and at first they ignore him. "Brandy," he then shouts, several times, and I first think he is ordering a drink. "You looking pretty tonight." His voice is nasal and high-pitched, sadly comical.

The red-haired woman turns and shouts. "Why'd you follow us here? Find your own bar, shrimp."

"You are my loving, Miss Brandy." His voice is far more sad than

141

comic. The showgirl shakes her head and turns back to her friends, who laugh. She lights a cigarette.

At the jukebox the two men who accompany the smallest man in the world stand near him so they form an equilateral triangle, as if this can protect him. They are heartbroken at what transpires between their small man and the showgirls. After all, they must love him; they have become attached to his smallness the way men become attached to my beauty. When a man is with me, he cannot forget my beauty the way he forgets everything else. Intimate conversations and promises are forgettable, as are meals created with attention to every detail of taste and presentation. Even the loveliness of naked breasts can mean nothing when those remain covered for too long. But his size is a constant reminder, as is my face.

I do not like to see my own face, because, despite my makeup, I look sad—sometimes as sad as that rouged old woman slumped over the bar down the way. When I fix my face in the morning, it often occurs to me to make myself up as a clown by lipsticking a massive smile onto my cheeks. Or exaggerating the sadness by painting a frown and a few shiny tears. I have heard that each circus clown must register a face with the national clown organization, that they cannot co-opt the faces of others. Maybe women should have to do that, women who are famous for stealing the full lips and long, curving eyebrows of teenage runway models; perhaps women could be forced to be themselves, the way my sister is herself. This clown urge of mine becomes so overwhelming some days that I even fantasize about joining the circus, although anyone, including my sister and ex-husbands, will tell you that I am not funny.

The smallest man glances away from the showgirls and looks at me. He sways slightly, drunkenly, against the music. He whispers to the black man, sending him to the bar. The smallest man then jumps down, walks over to the showgirls, and disappears from my sight.

Martin brings another drink before I have finished the one in front of me. He nods over his shoulder and says, "The small guy sent this to you, says it's for 'the most beautiful woman.'" From him the compliment means something, and it means something to me that Martin conducted the message. "Have you been to the circus?" Martin asks.

"I went tonight with my sister. That was my sister with me." My arms, a bronze color that makes unclear precisely what my race is, stretch out brightly on the bar. Some people assume I come from an island where all the women are beautiful.

"She looks like you," Martin says. My hair is swept off my face, twisted softly at the back of my head so that my neck is bare. Martin's gaze washes over me; he never lets his eyes linger, perhaps out of respect or maybe because he doesn't trust me, having seen me leave with dozens of men. Martin is about to lift his foot and place it on a shelf under the bar, which means he will lean toward me and say something privately. But the look-alike couple interrupts our moment by motioning to him. They want a bag of nuts.

Shrieks erupt from the showgirl table, and I do not see the smallest man, but soon the red-haired woman screams, "You little pervert midget!" The smallest man emerges from under the table on all fours, brushes himself off, and returns to the jukebox. He holds a black platform pump and sniffs it until the redhead marches up in bare feet and grabs it from him. Her skirt is very short. The smallest man grins, but the two big men look anxious.

Though there is no table service on weeknights, Martin walks around the bar and brings the showgirls another round. The women must have been wearing wigs during the performance, because all of them have close-cropped hair. Their eyes are painted large. The redhead has long, muscular legs, the legs of an athlete, legs smooth and strong enough to turn a bartender into a waitress. Martin lets his gaze wander all over those legs, even after he returns to his post. These are probably the kind of women he prefers: energetic, acrobatic, clever.

One showgirl holds her fingers an inch apart toward the jukebox, and when the smallest man looks over, all the women burst out laughing. Their mouths seem large enough to swallow his whole head. When the red-haired showgirl notices me staring, she narrows her eyes. I turn back to the bar. I am accustomed to such looks. They think I have cheated in order to look this way. Have I had surgery? They wonder. They assume that, one way or another, I have sold my soul to the devil.

And I understand why the smallest man in the world can't leave them alone. For the same reason that I can't resist beautiful new men who come into this bar—because desiring them is uncomplicated. It is not the showgirls' fault that the smallest man humiliates himself—their cruelty is ordinary, and they could not possibly know what it means to be tiny.

The showgirls were best during the halftime show, when all the animals and performers came out in a Wild West spectacular; the showgirls wore fake-leather miniskirts with oversized pistols on their hips. I should have told my sister how much I liked the halftime show. My sister was right—the girl riding that sweaty rhinoceros practically had to do the splits as she bounced on its wide, slippery back.

There is no sideshow in the circus anymore. You have to go to county fairs for that kind of grotesquerie, or else watch television. This July I traveled thirty miles and paid two dollars each to see the world's smallest horse, the fattest pig, the longest alligator. You must take for granted that they really are the longest, the smallest, and the fattest. Who is to say that the posted weight, height, or length is even honest? Who is in charge of freak-show weights and measures?

Surely the man who bought me this drink is the smallest man in the world; the greatest show on earth would not lie so boldly. Before I finish my second, the smallest man has ordered his third. He seems drunk already, the way a regular-sized man would be had he taken three or four times as much.

On my way to the bathroom, I look straight ahead, avoiding the eyes of the red-haired showgirl, but on my way back, I walk slowly enough to study their heads and shoulders and to smell their perfume, which is flowery and applied too heavily, perhaps to disguise sweat. Though they portray beautiful women, they are not particularly beautiful. Real beauty would be too quiet on the arena floor, and it could not compete with the menagerie of elephants and horseback riders. Beauty cannot transmit over long distances, could not possibly stretch into the upper tiers of a stadium; costumes do a better job than the real thing. Helen's beauty was transmitted by hearsay; how many of those men who died at Troy ever saw her? The showgirls are not as young and foolish as they seem in costume. They are actors and magicians, good with the sleight of hand, the sleight of face.

Even the smallest man in the world used a few tricks. When he appeared in the center ring at halftime, sitting and then standing on the seat of a circus-painted stagecoach, he wore a suit jacket that had been cut long so his legs, which are actually in perfect proportion to

144

his body, looked short. The wagon was pulled by draft horses, beasts that would dwarf any human.

A crack like thunder sounds through the bar, but the showgirls do not look up. They are accustomed to elephants stampeding, vendors hawking, cannons blowing humans across arenas.

"Off the jukebox," says the bartender. He says it quickly, directly, without sharpness, and he is already turning away to avoid a confrontation. Martin is a genius. The smallest man in the world has not taken offense. He holds out his arms, signaling to his friends that he wants to be carried.

A man in a dark suit approaches this end of the bar and catches my eye. He has not been in here before. He is perhaps twenty-five and has on his face a look of mild astonishment. If my attention were not elsewhere, I might nod and invite him to sit beside me. He leaves one empty stool between us and motions to the bartender. His jacket hangs from broad, straight shoulders; the material is gray, tending toward blue in this light. Perhaps I will see him tomorrow at the hotel desk, or later tonight in a hotel bed.

At the hotel, I mostly work behind a glass wall, filling out forms, designing staff schedules, and making phone calls, unless there is a problem. In that case, I walk on three-inch heels from behind the glass, and I say in the most elegant voice you can imagine, "Is there a problem?" My mouth is perfectly darkened, and I do not open it again until the customer and the clerk have said all they want to say, and still I wait a little longer in silence. Only occasionally do I have to refund money.

Before I can speak to the man in the dark suit, the two men in coveralls carry the smallest man in the world to the bar. From here I cannot tell if the jukebox glass is cracked. Now they are playing a very old heartbreak by Hank Williams Sr.—the circus people have been playing all country-western.

I wonder if the smallest man in the world thinks about growing the way I think about growing less beautiful. Perhaps he and I could live together, drink less, entertain in our home. I know how difficult it would be to really know the smallest man in the world, to see beyond his height, and I would work for us not to be strangers. Along the stairway to our bedroom, beside the studio shots of our children, would hang photos of our old deformed selves. Thirty-five is not too late to start a family. My second husband, who already had two daughters, said I was too selfish to be a mother—but I could change.

145

My late-born children would have an easier time than his girls. When my girls looked at photos of me, they would say, "You were so beautiful, Mommy," and that past tense would be much easier on them at thirteen than "You *are* so beautiful." My husband would say, "I used to be the smallest man in the world until I met your mother."

You might suggest that if I genuinely looked forward to growing plain, I should skip the facials, the weekly manicures, and the constant touchups for my auburn highlights; I should let my hair hang in an easy style like my sister's, or cut it short and convenient as the showgirls have done. Well, you may as well suggest to a tall man that he slump; for me to neglect my beauty now would be a denial of the facts.

Though I try to ignore the stranger beside me, my body moves toward his the way a flower bends to the sun. I close my eyes in an attempt to resist, but when I open them he is looking into my face. He smells musky and a little smoky, and his eyes are cocktails with black olives. I would continue to slide closer, except that the smallest man in the world is making a fuss. He has jumped onto the bar and is standing with hands on hips, like the most outrageous, arrogant child in the world. Perhaps Martin has refused him a fourth drink.

"You're going to have to get down," says Martin.

The smallest man shouts in a language I have never heard in the hotel—Hungarian, perhaps. He is angry and hurt, but his two friends, black and white, continue to man the second and third corners of his triangle. They love him too much to encourage him to climb down. He is not a child, after all. He wears what look like a boy's sneakers, but his pants are tailored, and his safari-style jacket is cut to his figure. He stands tall, enraptured in hostility toward the bartender, and I hope I do not have to choose sides. The showgirls have finally noticed, and they are watching too—everybody loves a spectacle.

The smallest man in the world turns and looks across the room, not at them but at me. "Beautiful lady!" he shouts, in that accent. "Help me!" He hands his highball to his white man, and he starts down the bar toward me. The old woman with rouge clings to her drink at the other end. The smallest man leaps over most of the glasses between himself and me but knocks over both drinks of the pale look-alike couple. They lean back on their stools, a Siamese twin, both mouths limp in one expression of confusion. The man beside me jumps up and moves away. The smallest man in the world holds out his arms to me, and without hesitation I put down my drink and open my arms. With my beautiful but sad eyes I promise that if he reaches me, I will protect him. I will hold and shelter him like my own first child, embrace him as my blood brother, honor him as my true husband. I stand and step slightly back from the bar. If he is brave enough to jump, I will catch him.

Nominated by The Southern Review, Joyce Carol Oates

ELEGY FOR MY SISTER

by SHEROD SANTOS

from THE PARIS REVIEW

I

She was born *Sarah Gossett Ballenger*—
Sarah our mother's proper name, *Gossett* our mother's
family name, *Ballenger* the name of her father.
Following our mother's second marriage,
her name was changed to *Sarah Ballenger Santos*,
and when she herself got married, she became
Sarah Santos Knoeppel. After her divorce, she changed
her name to *Sarah Beth Ballenger*, though *Beth*
was selected simply because she "liked its sound,"
and because, for once, she'd felt entitled to name herself.

Following a stillbirth in the twelfth year
of her marriage, she instructed her daughters
to refer to her as *Mimi*—not *Mommy*, not *Mother*,
not *Mom*. At some point after she'd left home
(she was sixteen or seventeen at the time),
she changed the spelling of her familiar name
from *Sally* to *Salley*, and of her proper name
from *Sarah* to *Sara*, though here too the reasons
she gave were largely a matter of preference:
she just found those spellings more personal.

Thus all her life she felt her names referred to presences
outside of her, presences which sought to enclose

148

that self which separated *her* from who *they* were.
Thus all her life she was never quite sure who it was
people summoned whenever they called her by her name.
And, more specifically, she was never quite sure
they recognized *her* when, and if, she responded.
As she put it, at various periods in her life
she'd "lent" herself to particular names, only to reclaim
herself in time, only to suppose all over again.

II

                              . . . And so it is
I begin this now, a week after my sister's suicide,
because I can already feel her slipping beyond
the trace of words, and words, like bread crumbs
trailed behind her on the forest floor, are her way
back to us—or us to her—through the hemmed-in
reaches of the afterworld. But I begin this
for another reason as well. A more urgent
and perhaps more selfish reason, to answer
that question which day by day I fear
I'm growing less able to answer: *Who was she*
whose death now made her a stranger to me?
As though the problem were not that she had died,
and how was I to mourn her, but that some
stalled memory now kept her from existing.
And that she could only begin to exist,
to take her place in the future, when all of our
presuppositions about her, all of those things
that identified the woman we'd buried, were finally
swept aside. As if the time of her being
remained, as yet, a distant premonition within us.

III

Her hair was dark and irregularly parted,
and there was something undecided in the way
she chose to present herself to the world,
though her power over others (if not herself)
seemed to come from the confidence

149

of someone who felt she'd suffered more,
and so, perhaps rightly, assumed she possessed
the kind of spirit most favored by God.
But there was always something in the way
she dressed—an oversized brooch, a man's
sports watch, a garish hat or neckscarf—
which attempted to reverse that odd impression,
like those cowering dogs that so often appear
in seventeenth century religious paintings.
Those mongrel shapes that seem added to counter
some otherwise unabated spiritual yearning.

IV

As a rule, my sister didn't care for social gatherings,
though when she went she carried away
a palpable feeling of euphoria. This wasn't,
however, the euphoria of a "good time,"
but the accomplishment of someone who'd managed
to remain *incognito* under very exacting scrutiny.
When we were alone, this shyness proved self-
wounding, and I felt at times that many of the secrets
she confessed to me were things she actually
wished she regretted, more than things she suffered
for having done. In these and other respects,
she reminded me of those blue translucent birds
("so the hawks can't see them against the sky")
Marlon Brando describes in *The Fugitive Kind*.
Those legless birds that "don't belong no place
at all," and so stay on the wing until they die.

V

She was someone about whom people remarked:
She never seemed to find a life for herself. Or:
Her life was the story of a long collapse, its end
a dark, unlucky star she'd clung to hopefully,
for better or worse. Shortly after her death,
we discovered in her closet a large box containing

countless bottles of lotions, powders, lipsticks,
and oils. Many of them had never been opened,
still others had barely been used at all.
Sorting through the contents it occurred to me
the box contained some version of herself,
some representation of who she was—
a stronger? more serene? more independent self?—
that she'd never had the chance to become.
Sorting through the contents it occurred to me:
She once was becoming; she now ceased to become.

VI

Because of her "instability," doctors were reluctant
to write her prescriptions, though she was very adept
at describing those symptoms that called for the drugs
she wanted. She was also doggedly persistent.
One physician I telephoned defended his decision
by relating how, during one of her many unscheduled visits,
she'd remained in his office refusing to leave
until he'd written her a script for sleeping pills.
To be "cautious," he had written it out for only half
the normal number of pills. Which perhaps explains why,
on the floor beside her bed they found the empty vials
for four different drugs, each one ordered by
a different doctor—meprobamate, propoxyphene,
amitriptyline, and carisoprodol—a lethal combination
of anti-anxiety agents, painkillers, antidepressants,
and muscle relaxants. Clearly, killing herself
required the same cunning, and the same unspoken
complicity of others, that she'd needed to stay alive.

VII

Well, that what life's like. She'd say this
whenever she couldn't imagine what else
to say, or how her mind might disengage
that darkening shape-shift she could feel
was somehow, through her, handed down,

151

mother-to-daughter, daughter-to-child,
like the watercolors in her light-green eyes.
At the graveside, her two unkneeling daughters
closed in mute parenthesis around that space
(*Sarah Ballenger Santos Knoeppel*),
as if the soul encircled might recreate the ground
of being she'd unnamed; or lend new hope
to that vague impossibility: *Someone to love her*
for who she was . . . . A love I fear even she
finally felt incapable of when tears surprised
her stonewalled heart with what she'd done.

VIII

A dream I started having several weeks ago.
As in the newsreel of some dignitary-or-other
arriving in a foreign country, she's descending alone
the movable staircase from an airplane cabin,
and as she descends her face grows steadily younger
and more beautiful, like someone *coming into*
her own life. But instead of *the pathos of kindled hopes*,
I feel this moment as something that happens
to endanger her, something she is helpless to defend against,
as though the newsreel presaged an assassin's bomb.
This feeling brings with it a desperate urge
to "roll back the film," which succeeds only in slowing
it down to a pace that further accentuates the dread,
as though the newsreel'd slowed to capture the instant
the bomb goes off. Each step seems drawn out
endlessly, and falls so heavily on the heart
that I can feel—*in her*—the unearthly weight
a life takes on in the final moments it has to live.

IX

Is it inconceivable (I suspect this question haunts
us all) that all her life she was misunderstood?
That we'd shared a language which for whatever reasons
she herself had never learned? That all her attempts

to *draw us in* only further served to *hold us apart*?
That she'd had good reason to defend as *true*
what we'd perceived as *utterly false*? That what
she'd said in *love* or *affection* we'd heard as *confusion,*
anger, fear? Of course, these questions have no beginning
or end, and like posterity they fuel themselves
on a bottomless human vanity: the illusion that we can
know someone. Yet not to go on asking these questions
is to follow that line through time and space
that would lead us to experience her death (conclusively?
nostalgically? consolingly?) as "the final pages
of a novel." And how could she ever forgive us that?

X

My sister at thirty or thirty-one: stripping off table varnish
while her daughter naps on a folded towel beside her.

In the archangel section of the plaster cast gallery, she holds
her breath until the security guard stops looking her way.

On the table beside her bed: A bowl of dried wild roses
she would mist each morning with . . . was it rosewater?

Standing beside a photomat, staring at a strip of pictures, her look
of puzzlement slowly gives way to a look of recognition.

In the middle of the night—I was eight at the time—I wake
to find her patting my head, because *she* had just had a bad dream.

Her lifelong habit of momentarily closing her eyes, as if testing
the truthfulness of some emotion, then releasing a barely audible sigh.

Visiting hours over, her returning down the hall to her hospital room:
head down, shoulders stooped, her hands clasped behind her neck.

(That same morning, when she'd started to cry, she somehow managed
to distract herself by repeatedly crossing and uncrossing her legs.)

Overjoyed to be going home finally, then, mid-sentence, falling silent
at the thought of it, as though her mouth had been covered by a hand.

A warm spring night. A streetlamp beyond an open window.
Beneath the sill: a girl's hushed voice exhorting itself in whispers.

Nominated by David Baker, Jim Barnes, James Reiss, Grace Schulman, David Wojahn

COCK FIGHT

fiction by MARIANNA CHERRY

from CHELSEA

Y OU NEED UNDERSTAND. With us, was difficult business.

Like this with Kirsten: I am in *becak* like every day, straw hat sit on face. (At night growing chickens, at day paddling Javanese bicycle rickshaw. Is big stress!) Asleep under shiny sun which hot like a broken lorry engine. All us drivers was against one another street side, some sleep, or do a backgammon. Then suddenly, they shouting drivers, "O! O! O!" and stops game when dice throw because there is tourist woman have clothing scarce of clothing. (This street where museum and hotel have many tourist dress like this. As a further information, tourist women do not dress a lot. They say because heat, but so yes! Jawa hot!) Ibrahim wake up, remove hat, looks at a tourist in little skirt and shirt. With head down, walking, she. Embarass cheeks. Yo, man!! is funny! I laugh next my friend.

Courage, I walked off to her from becak. "Hey, where you want to go? *Mau kemana*?"

"Leave me alone," says she. Why? When she need ride and I offer. In her hand I see a paper with address.

"I take you," I say and reach out her hand, with polite. Skinny, tall woman, quiet. Face white, but not too so. I before like very white skin, but I think now it appearance such a person has died already. Long hair she, little orange, little brown. Eyes green like lime skin.

"Do you know this street? Jalan Batutenobang?" Her lips concentrate, as trying to speak the name bad like Ibrahim English.

"Of course," I read. "I know all Yogyakarta."

She tell she stay with her friend house, but do'nt know how to return. Tourist like children. They get lost.

155

"How much is a ride there?" she ask.

"Ten thousand rupiah," I say.

Of course it is that new tourists are very less smart, and they will not bargain one rupiah! Ten thousand for a one thousand ride! Silly *bule*!

"Four thousand," she tell.

"Come, come," I say, open the door.

"Four."

"Excuse me?" I say. "Where you want to go?"

"I know you understand me," she say.

"Eight and a half," I offer, thinking, relax, my honey.

"Look," she said. "I'm American, not Japanese. And in America I'm hardly rich."

I am told this, that Amerika is very expensive, yet all they have money for Garuda Airline.

"Give me your best price," I say.

"Fine—*zero*."

I laugh at the smart girl. Like my sister, whose smile trembles the day.

"Okay, Miss. I give you Jawa price. With Jawa price, is more cheap for taksi than walk for free—three thousand." She don't know. So much money by me, so little by her.

In jumping female in carriage with sunglass and packpack. Then peddling Ibrahim. Painful work is, wood coals for feet. With my muscles I earn such money as I push bicycle taksi.

"Are you married?" I asking. She not talk. "Are you married?" She turn round fast, mad. Wow!

"No," she say, strong.

I think, Relax, Max.

"Do you have boyfriend?"

She laugh, but not funny laugh. I push. Tourist is weirdo, man—I ask a little question, which they think I break their heart.

We go a way, and we past singing bird market and noodle carts. And we past Water Palace and she say "Oh, Stop!" for picture. And I okay. Hot Yogya, smelling city. Run to becak, smiling, "thank you!" And we past batik cart and she "Stop, please!" for buy scarf. She try green, she try blue. I stop with many becak driver, all many, who wait for tourist come back. Often I wait for bule-bule like this, and when they return and I approach, they say, "go way." I tell, "I am your driver," but they, "leave me a lone." I loose often money like this. Only they look my shirt and say, "oh yes, I remember you." But when she return at me, she thank me for waiting. She have take the blue scarf. I tell, "Is good color for you. You are pretty." Hereupon she looks me and reply, "I already have a boyfriend, okay?"

Sometime I think, less stress driving people of Jawa than tourist, but better money of tourist. Yet, it is really too bad that all people is a stress!

Riding off then, I ask, "What is your name?"

"Kirsten." That is all. But afterawhile, she turn round, say, "What's your name?"

"My name Ibrahim."

She smile hello.

She turn round, and put all the fingers to her hairs, which are windy, and touch her neck. "It's hot here," she tell soft, and I, yes, it is.

Kirsten pulling at little skirt cover one leg crossed an other when she see there are woman at the sidewalk have long Muslim dress, and turn, and point kodak, moving wrist side and side with concentrate before a push of the button. She looked at men cut chicken throat at sidewalk. And women at sidewalk sells fruit, cocoanuts, *jajan*. And later there is yellow petrol in bottles which Kirsten ask to stop for drink! She think is lemon drink, like in Amerika, says she. Along the street again, then basket shops and coffin shops, many of the row. All such yellow wood boxes. Is here she stop and make many potograp. There are many small coffins for a baby. She say she has never see coffins for a baby. And more we go: there is Utama Bank, and Kentucky Fried Chicken and Baskin-Robbin, which she point kodak, which I ask if she want to stop for *es krim*?

"It's sickening," she retort. She turn her head aside, so I can hear. The street noisy.

"I like es krim," I tell, "but sometime it get me sick at my stomach, too."

"These chains. I hear they're all over Vietnam."

"Chains?"

"Like that," she point to Kentucky Fried Chicken building. She make her fingers become O, and put together. "In America we call it a chain when one corporation—you know corporation?—has many businesses everywhere."

Building is all red and white, and many Indonesia flags a-circling it, all so red and white. Is funny—*merah putih!*

157

"Fast food is going to kill your culture. Do you know the word *culture*?"

"Yes, I know. And is not a problem, because Yogya have much culture."

"My country has a lot of culture, too. Modernization is fine, except the first thing we export is always heart disease."

"All is modernizing, yes, this Baskin-Robbin," I tell. "My sister have try for job at Dunkin Donut. Is good, what is new. Change."

"Just wait," all she say. She asks me if I know a word *oppression*.

"Yes, *penindasan*."

"Well, there you go." She removes from pocket small cloth to the nose to defend against salty auto exhaustion. She yell, "Think of it this way: you'll lose tourist money if Java looks just like Las Vegas." She speak me very slow.

"What is 'lasvegas'?" I ask, and all she say, "You're kidding," and then she think, laugh, tell, "Kind of like Borobodur with slot machines," smiling with merry eyeballs.

I don't know. I paddle, say, "What you do in Jawa?" I ask. "Bacation?"

"Visiting a friend. And traveling until school starts."

Only to practice English do I conversation with tourist. How old are you? and such and such. I learned English with school, some, and books, a little. For example, my dictionary is rubbing off. Kirsten says she is at university. She say that her friend's Matt father give him the job in Indonesia after finish school, maybe next year Singapura. There is many opportunity here. Before, was only tourists.

Where is Jalan Batutenobang, is less busy. Many big houses, some old, some modern. Nice stone carving walls. It have many many trees. In a little while, we arrive to Matt house. She stands out from becak, and with green eyes leaves to knock down the door. She puts one thousand rupiah to my hand, and says thank you very much.

Door is opened, and there Matt stand. Before she enter, she wave to me, and I wave all so. She will have tea, I think, and visit the day. The door is closed. I stand a moment, but then behind is old woman with basket—many bottle Fanta upon her head. She tell she need ride, and I must off again, away over the town.

Next day I see Kirsten walk alone with packpack on Jalan Malioboro, which have so many people, and all shops plastic, clothes and *peci* and *blangkon*, cassette, everything, then buses, car, taksi!

Everywhere smells leather and petrol. Mosque-singers sing to after-noon, and many man with *peci* find place to pray. There is shopping and many tourist here, so I find customer. Kirsten have worn a trousers today! Is better for Yogya.

"Hello!" I say. "Hey!" She see me, but not stop. "Where do you want to go?"

She displace the sunglasses to her face, and look me and look me. "Oh, it's you!"

"Where are you going today?"

"I don't know." She waggle her head. "Matt had to go to some city today for business. So I'm just . . ." She wave at the street. "You know."

"*Jalan-jalan*. Walkabout."

"Jalan whatever. Yes." She have tourist book, which she open, and says she wants to see batik-making and *gamelan* music.

"Come, Kirsten." I pet the becak and she enters.

Next, Kirsten like talk to Ibrahim. Help to study, and she laughed my English.

"Two years drive becak," I say. "And eleben years live in Yogya."

"Ele-VEN," says Kirsten, turning around can look me.

"V" and "b" in Jawa confuse. I know. Hard to tell and so always for-get. "Ele-BEN," I say, really try.

She was stops becak with polite. She speak to me, and point at lips and teeth. Kirsten makes "V" sound. Lips use Revlon, and eyes. Young red, if flower, and bird.

I point all so at the lip, say "Ele-VEN" with many hardship. Tourist and driver looking each other silly moment, fingers to lips.

"Good job," she say, and returns around in basket, not say nothing, and not me, and I push.

I think, I know there is better way of money today than driving, and I know there is a better sight-see than a batik factory. Where there is intersects, I go left, not right. Kirsten does nothing but watch the treetops—she don't know a difference.

We arrive to big building, where is very quiet, and around is houses, and a brown-gold river. She gets out the becak and thanks me. Silly tourist! There is no smell of wax.

"Kirsten," I tell. "This is not the factory. I take you to see cock fight."

"You're kidding." She look around, a nervous pigeon.

159

"Yes, I am kidding."

"I want to go." She hold her packpack very tight. "I want to go *now*."

"Everything okey-dokey," I tell.

"No, it isn't."

"Kirsten, you want Baskin-Robbin or Jawa culture? This Jawa culture."

She stand straight. To find my character, she look me and look me, head and hand and shoes. I am rummaged by her eyes.

She nod.

"Okay."

And then we enter together.

Fight is in a big building, like empty marketplace, have all dirt floor. Many men already, inspecting the chickens and decide how to make the bet. All men look me and Kirsten, because she is the first female present, but I know many here, is okay. There is big circle of dirt. Many teenager boy push in front, and men behind. Kirsten stay beside the door, and then approach amongst the shoulders to see inside. I am near to her. Inside circle, owners take cock out the bamboo cage and hold, and pat his feathers, and show all the men how strong is a bird. Many men—like the market with women pushing over food and argue a price, how now with those men, look and bet. One cock is red, small but fast. I think red chicken can win. We wait, wait, maybe twenty minute.

"Is interesting?" I ask her.

She ask, "Is this common?"

And I say, "Quite."

"May I take pictures?"

I say that it is just fine.

I hold up ten thousand rupiah, small money. I tell Kirsten, "I teach you bet," she say no, shake the head. "Is okay," I tell.

"I'll watch, but I won't bet," she say. "They kill each other."

"Certainly."

"Let's just say it's against my religion."

"What religion do you have, Kirsten?"

She makes film in the kodak. She say, "Live and let live."

I don't understand. She close up the camera.

I tell Kirsten, "If Kirsten bet or do *not* bet, does not change the fate of a chicken." I point the circle with my money. "In America, you can tell your friends."

She look the circle of men. She think. She take five thousand from the packpack.

I signal the man for bet.

Each chicken now under bell-shaped baskets. First man open basket of big, white-and-brown chicken. Green tail feathers shiny like big, old fly. Wings large and fat. It have one eye lost from a fight before—is a chicken that wins. Now both men smash each chicken face into the basket to make angry, and they are ready to fight—like squawking dog! Each their leg-nails are sharp—almost you can use for wood carving.

Both men release cock and then—zuk!—running atop each other! Chicken feathers fly off! They jump each other as starving dogs late the night, in quiet street. Red chicken, my chicken, jumps back, neck feathers protrude as India cobra snake. All men of circle, shout a bet and holding their money on top of their heads. It is as loud as people, when a bus did not stop—WAIT! Shouting, hands up. The cocks drive fast, jump high, feathers out, and bring the nail hard into the skin of the other. Red has one hit; blood drips from its wing. Is then, all men change bet, shouting again, bet on white chicken for easier money, or on my red chicken can return much money, if win, but probably not win. Chickens fall around and shake, until dust fly up, like rain from earth up the sky as chicken scratch out each other, really.

Kirsten, because she is female, is difficult to get inside circle for potograp because men who have give much money must see the fight. She try to stand tall.

"*Permisi,*" she say, to pass by, but difficult. She is besides the children, they touch her skin, she stand, try to picture the flying birds. Why can't she watch and remember? I look across everything, where Kirsten, she study this event. Her face follow the fight.

Soon is maybe fifteen minute of fight. The men watch the fate of money. Drops of red blood follow the animals, like a lorry leaking petrol to the road. The men of circle move around, like bees, because the fight rolls the dirt, hither and thither. She watch the pushing men. She laughs.

"It's like the New York Stock Exchange in here, you know?"

"No."

"It's fascinating," she say. "It's horrible! I mean, it's interesting, but I feel bad for the chickens."

161

"I think there is something else to worry, Kirsten."

Sometime chicken stop when tired and hold each another. But then other man put one basket-dome over both cocks, and there is a much wicked fluttering, like twenty men inside the gaol room. What I see underneath, is all color feathers, and chicken scream!

This man lift the basket, and chicken run apart. Stop. Turn. Circle circle. The head of my chicken held low, consideration—he is racking his brains out. Its wings of white cock stretches at both sides. Then they ran hard and there have wild splashing the feathers. The red chicken's leg falls upon the head of white, and much blood runs. White tries with much effort to walk, but one side off him limps to the ground, muscle breaking, while his another side try to proceed. I feel that this white bird will tear itself in half as trying to kill the other. He walks like drunk Australian.

Red cock watches the dying bird, which have won many fight. Almost does not care now, it waits for water to drink. Stupid bird. Other cock does not advance. The men of circle more quiet, because bet, because dying bird, have stopped. They watch.

"Is it over yet?" she ask quietly.

"No. A cock fight finish when one bird kill another."

"But the white one's on the ground. It can't fight anymore. What's the point?"

I tell, "It must finish, like decision cannot answer yes *and* no."

"It's mean."

"This normal. There is not money if chicken is not dead."

"Money," she repeated.

Now another man crowd both bird under one small basket. Then off basket—AND FIGHT! Neck feathers as cobra snakes. Jumping up, they, both, last time try to kill. Kirsten move away, behind me. She put her camera to the packpack and watches.

The nail of my cock cuts into the neck of white, and the bloods pour like slitting throat for market. The white chicken lies in window-sun with blood besides. My chicken walked a little uncertainly, then stop. It is a bird without thought.

I give Kirsten the thumb. We win! I collect money from a boy. I give her twelve thousand five hundred, say, "Now, when you go home, you can buy a new car."

She smile. "Or a sandwich." She looks the blue and red rupiah papers. "I don't feel right taking it. Here." She put the money to me.

162

It is easy to give small gifts, I think. I put it to her hand again. "You bet, you win," I tell.

She hold the money uncertainly. "I guess it's a more interesting souvenir than that scarf."

Behind is dead bird where is the men. Many money go around, hand in hand.

I invite Kirsten my house, after this.

She stepped into house Ibrahim. Is quiet, today, brothers at school, and sister working. Kirsten's head looks the ceiling. Looks one another corner, one another wall.

Herewith, I introduce her my mother and they are smiling and bowing and looking to Ibrahim for translation. My mother say that it is nice I can be home today. "Yes," I reply. I will give her the money I have won later tonight, and then she will not be angry with me anymore.

After enough, I carry Kirsten to outside where all my things for cock growing. The court: all is dirt where sun, outside house wall—here I with father or brother fight with chicken—and over thus, below house shade, a stuck of cages. I show best my chicken. But she ask—is funny—if she may pat this bird. First time she touch alive chicken, she tell. She is unbelievable that is warm! She tell, she think bird is more cold than people.

"Where I come from, chickens are usually frozen!" she laugh.

And I laugh for polite.

All of asuddenly, my mother carry tea. Ibu give tea and return away. Kirsten tell thank you, and drink without moment. Is this like in Amerika? I think, wow, so I drink too. Still, I believe Kirsten try for polite. And then Ibu bring two bowls of soap, but Kirsten say me that may not eat soap because with meat! Ibu tells, is interesting, she think Christian eat meat, and ask me translate a question what religion have Kirsten. Kirsten says is not Christian, and I ask if Yahudi, but she not understand. Many tourist that young, is Yahudi I think. Certainly she is, because people without religion are uneducated. I don't know. I think tourists understand religion uncertainly.

I eat soap, and Kirsten rice and egg. Afterawhile, Kirsten ask, and so I respond how I become becak driver for money, but need a better monies of sport chicken. Ibrahim tell, that still I seek job now, I was at university when I have studied electric engineer. This I have study when from villag to Yogya, but not yet find job. I am the most old son, so have responsibility my family. She look me like she is unbelievable. I say Kirsten, "I know you think whether becak driver can be engineer. Jawa not like Amerika. If you are rich, then university in California. Because I do not know high people for the job, even if I already have so much education, then I am forcing to drive becak. My friend of mine, Raharjo, he is best dancer at STSI, you know academy art and music? He study many year, he dance brilliant, and drive becak because who was won the position of teacher is brothers son (neese?) of direktor, whose less good dancer. Is like this in Jawa."

I from pocket matches and *kretek* cigarette.

"I'm sorry," she says. "I didn't understand."

"Yes, well," I say. "Is problem, Kirsten."

We speak each other of school, how she become science teacher at second school. I think she many study. Must diligent.

I smoke. She eat.

We have nice time together.

Then she looking the many cage, and looking me, along time till I am discomfortable.

"Yes?" says I.

"But I think it's wrong. Cock-fighting. I'm sorry. I think it's wrong."

"What you mean, wrong?"

"It's immoral to make one life kill another life."

"Immoral?"

"Wrong, bad." She think, say again.

"Wait minute," says me, and I take dictionary. (This how we talking each other!) I find "immoral." *Menyalahi kesusilaan.* I laughing, this! "Kirsten," I say, "is only a chicken! Chicken is not man."

"But it's a life."

"Is chicken life!"

"But they feel pain."

"Is chicken pain. Very different."

And she not say nothing awhile, but eat eat some rice and egg and vegetable, and she enter the kodak to bag, and hold bag.

"Today, Kirsten, you say the fight is interesting."

"Yes. But many things can be interesting precisely because they are wrong."

"For example?"

"For example American fast food restaurants in Asia—exporting a business that is destructive. You know 'destructive'?"

164

"Yes."

"But then you have Baskin-Robbins next door to a coffin shop. That's interesting. Or money in general—it's interesting because it creates problems."

"Like not having it," I tell, "is problem."

And she say, "*Or* having it."

Perhaps this is true.

Rice is finish. I say I take her see Ramayana ballet? She say no. She say Matt return very soon, may she go?

"Oh," I say, and "yes."

Is nice she have boyfriend.

"You know," she say. "Maybe Matt can help you. Not electrical engineering but, I don't know, something in the office."

"Is okay," I say.

"He works for USAsiaCorp. I'm sure there are lots of jobs for someone with a degree."

I smile because embarrass. Three days in Jawa I know she can help more than Ibrahim, who here twenty-four year.

After, we return at becak, all its metal dries in the sun. Chained by a fence, waiting. I look this piece machinery, and pray never drive again.

Is next day she find Ibrahim at museum, tell, come tonight by Matt house, and we go eat dinner. I am shy.

"Hi," Kirsten says from house when I arrive tonight, and Matt shake my hand, say, hello. He is tall. So young, have already been many places on earth.

"Ready to go?" he tell Kirsten.

As we walk from Matt house, Kirsten come to me, she touch my arm. She tell me quiet she have ask Matt about job. We use taksi. Matt tell driver where to go, he speak Indonesian. I tell him he speak very well.

I never eat a restaurant expensive like this night. Many tourist, and businessmen. Amerika, Indonesia, Australia, and Chinese many. I am discomfortable because I cannot pay. There is gamelan playing, twenty musician and singer, all such music for restaurant! But many tourist is good for musician, have many job.

Matt say the music is "trippy," a word he teach me.

"Actually, 'trippy' is an informal word," Kirsten say. "You would not say that about Mozart, for example. Have you ever heard of Mozart?"

"Yes, of course!"

165

"Fine," says Matt. "It's not trippy."

"You'd say it's beautiful," tell Kirsten. "The instruments are beautiful."

"They have carved in jackfruit wood," I tell. "I know a place where is made instrumen. I take you."

She turn to me above candleflame. She is curled of hair, and have green dress I think very nice.

"I would like that."

The food is arrived. It is Italy food. I ask the garçon for rice.

"I'm sorry," Matt say, "I thought you'd like something exotic."

"I am sorry too," I tell. "Only because rice is better for me. Thank you."

"I don't how you eat it every day. Where I'm from we change around: some days potatoes, bread, pasta. I'm up to here in rice." He laugh. Is nice guy.

"Well," say Kirsten, "you do live here. When in Rome."

"I've been here eight months, K. You try eight months of rice."

They look each other and then apart. I smile because I am discomfortable. Matt clink the glass to pour *anggur* wine. He speak to me in Indonesian.

"So, Kirsten tells me you raise chickens for cock fighting,"

"Yes."

He stop eating, consider. I know he is confusing. He make eyebrows. *"How does that business work, anyway?"*

"You try to sell them for as much money as you can." I tell him all the economie of cocks, how in Yogya, can get one, two hundred American dollars the chicken, and in Jakarta, maybe three—six hundred thousand rupiah. Is nice to speak with him. I wish Kirsten speak Indonesian all so.

"Three hundred dollars for a chicken?!"

"In Jakarta they'll gamble five times that."

Matt listen me tell my new business, his hands are folded and his chin on top of that. His shirtcuffs come away. It is beautiful watch he wears.

"Must be interesting work," Matt say.

I agree, but I have not yet no one can buy from me.

The waiter come, and Kirsten ask another beer.

"Kirsten also says you have a degree in civil engineering."

"Electric."

166

"And she said you're looking for work."

I look her, who kind to me, then to Matt. *"Yes, but—"* I stop. *"Yogya isn't easy for people who live in Yogya."*

"Yeah. But I think things are getting better. I really believe in what we do."

Kirsten touch her glass and touch flower atop the table. She eat little, little more from empty plate. Not understanding nothing, she can but watch the universe.

Matt tell me of big company.

"We consult with Southeast Asian companies develop infrastructure. Like Padang Corp.—road construction. Or SML—power supply. You can't have progress without infrastructure. I know there are problems with mining and logging and all that, but like it or not the business is here, so you've got to make it benefit the country, the people, as much as you can. And that means roads and reservoirs. Kirsten and I are very different that way. She wants things to be the way they should be, instead of how they are."

"Hey," Kirsten laugh and crack Matt with elbow. "I heard my name."

"It's nothing," Matt tell.

"I bet."

"Forgive me," I say.

We talk more. I tell about school, my qualifications. Which is I learn fast and have education. I grow chickens—is business—I drive becak—is work.

"And you know English."

"My English very bad."

Matt take another bit of meat, and remove something off his tongue, a seed maybe, or bone.

He nod at me, he pour my glass more red anggur wine, which I do not like, but drink for polite.

"I'm sure I can set you up," he say.

"You are very kind."

"I warn you, it won't be anything glamorous—you understand."
"Of course."

Kirsten have beer, and watch the gamelan. The man who play gong, he hit *kempul*, wait minute, then—*tak*—gong, which have deep water sound, like in the morning, awake, smoking. Kirsten close her eyes and mind this sound. I am glad it is she is happy, because

167

she have not understand anything. She is my fate to meet this Kirsten.

Life is too enough.

Is many day later, Monday. Matt have tell me, come my house Tuesday. He says is *"exciting time."* I am pushing, all day. After working, I bathe and return the house. I brang gift for Matt, small wood carving. There is a chair and table, where Kirsten sits with a book.

"Hello," I say.

She look up, no smile, does not stand up. She say hello. I think she does'nt read book because the sky grows over with evening.

"How long you wait?" I ask.

She wave her hand, shake her head. She is sad.

I laugh. She is with problem.

"Come on in."

She get up and I follow into the house. This house—Matt work for big company—have carving chairs, rug from India, and everything like a house on television.

"Isn't it beautiful?" she ask.

"Yes."

"See what you can do in a Third World country?"

She ask if I want whiskey. I sit the table and we have whiskey. I hold my gift for Matt.

After I drink, I tell, "Where is Matt?"

"Oh, Mr. Matt seems to have had another business trip. He called to say he was sorry, that he'll be back Wednesday."

I place the package atop the table. "He works very hard."

"Yes, he works very hard."

She pour another whiskey, but I say no. It hurt my stomach.

"I didn't expect this," she say. "I come out here, and he's changed. Matt. Now all he talks about is expansion and development and change."

"He have important job," I tell.

"It's become his religion."

I don't think she understand how important is economy.

"Ibrahim, do you understand? His company brings money here only because it destroys—electricity, freeways? All these 'good' things are really inconvenient, as it turns out."

She put her hand on mine, which I remove from her. She look to her empty cup which she have finished to drink.

168

"I'm sorry. I shouldn't say anything bad about Matt to you. He really liked you." She look up again. "Are you sure you don't want another drink?"

She pours. I wish Matt is here.

"Do you know what this job is? Making copies, filing—putting a piece of paper into one drawer, another piece of paper in another drawer. It's sitting in front of a computer all day." She point to her head. "It turns your brain into soup."

"I understand, Kirsten, what is work."

"I know. But you don't understand what carpal tunnel is. Or anxiety. The cultural legacy of the West."

"Ang— . . . excuse me?"

"Anxiety. Like stress. Do you know the word stress?"

"Yes, of course. Every day is a stress."

She takes more whiskey and look about the empty furniture. Is very big house for one person, what is bigger than a house for all my family. She put down the glass.

"I need a dip." She get up from the table and stand above me. "Do you want to go swimming?"

But I say no. "I do'nt swim."

"Never?"

"People in Jawa do'nt swim."

"It's hot. You live on an island. How can you not swim?"

"To me it is just fine."

"I need cold water. Excuse me."

She leave the room. I hear many footstep and doors, and when she return, she wear big T-shirt, and is all, I think. She stand by a glass door to outside, to garden. Many trees and flowers in the night. She nod her head toward outside. "Come on. You'll like it."

"I like to try new things, but not swimming."

She stand by the outdoors, tall and alone like an egret, and we behold one another. "Okay," she say, and go outside. Then I hear water, *cemplung*. On table is two glass, and whiskey, and Matt gift in pink paper.

Afterawhile, I approach the window. There is a square, and flowers and trees, stone statue, and a swimming pool, black, with moon. Kirsten drifts the water. This sounds gentle, deserted water, like carrying a buckets from water well. She said, "Hey, Ibrahim, come in. I'm sorry." She knows already a lot about Jawa—always she is sorry. I respond no. I go outside, and sit where there is a white chair. She say

169

how nice water is warm, how come in, and she observe up the moon. I smoke kretek. She exit pool, sit an edge and have one foot inside, and she look me. Kirsten comes to me, very wet, she have blue costume. She stand near.

"I know, Ibrahim, what I must look like to you." She wave the house, the things, the statue. "But could you trust me—believe—that I know more than you do? At least about traffic and pollution and office jobs."

"Perhaps."

This tourist, even if want to help, with such small understanding of things far from home. She does'nt like the Muslim dress, but does'nt like Baskin-Robbin. She want Jawa to stay same always in the future, but also want the chicken to live after the fight. What she like—rice and egg. I think it should bore my tongue.

She tell she need cloth from room, to dry. She puts her hand above the air to me. I touch her hand. I tell her, "You are cold."

Is Thursday when I go to Matt office. Is all gray inside, and clean, and many people are busy. There is a banana tree besides my chair, which made of wood, and a woman says, "excuse me" and talks on the *telpon*. I wait. After a moment, she say Mr. Matt may see me.

He open the door and "Hey there!" He have big smile, and he looks very relax. "I'll show you around."

We go to a room and another and another. All is computer and telpon. It is as my university and also *L.A. Law* on *televisi*. He show me where is the fax machine and copy. He show me where there is paper and ink.

"I said it wouldn't be glamorous right now," he say in Indonesian. *"But be patient."* He pet me on the shoulder. *"Like I said, it's an exciting time."*

It is Saturday I see Kirsten again. She waiting me where are many tourist. She have big bag, ask me help find hotel for her. I think she have many cry.

She make both her hand like a river go two direction. "He's too different." She remove hair off face. "You and me," she tell. "We're not corporate kind of people." All her hands and how she move like a butterfly. Lovely remember Kirsten. In between moments she appears me in a street, even beside dirty water.

I tell her I was at Matt office.

"That's great. I'm happy for you."

She has her bag. I dismount the becak. My brother will use it now.

"Hey, do you want to see Ramayana ballet?" she ask.

I am very busy because I start tomorrow, but Kirsten is sad.

"I cannot," I tell. "I am sorry, because I have responsibility today."

"Oh, okay. No problem." I am afraid she will cry. In her hand I see a paper with address. "Here you go," she give me. "Write me. Tell me how it's going." She put her sunglasses to her eyes, which I do not see. She touch my face. "Good-bye, Ibrahim."

I insert the paper to my pocket. Kirsten walk away on the street from Ibrahim. What I feel is pain and happy, and there is an uncertain bounty in my heart.

Nowadays it's a pain in the neck to remember her lovely picture. I never see her again.

I am going home. I pass the street where first I drive Kirsten, where is the coffin shop. I pass the Baskin-Robbin, then stop, return around. I think it is not "oppression," but es krim.

Inside is all white and white, young red, orange. It have air-condition, how like the chilly dawn. And then, "Hey!" I see my friend sister, Puspa. She is so beautiful—she was my girlfriend when I was very small. She was smart with singing, like her mother who sing for *wayang golek*. She have long straight hair under the white hat which spell "Rasa 31." She is happy to see me—"Ibrahim!" And her eyes are so big, wet flowers in the moonshine. When her brother and I are young, we play always! And we to university together. Her father is brilliant with herb for medicine. My mother and father ask for him in the villag when they become sick.

"Say hi to your brother," says me.

The sign have many es krim to choose from. I ask for jackfruit *coklat* Sunday. I eat where there is a small white table, and a window, where on the street there are the shoe-shiny boys and where walks a Catholic nuns that covered head and toe like bundling glass for the post. I smoke kretek and observe the window what passes away. Es krim make me only a little sick, I think. My friend of mine, he say if you eat more and more, afterawhile when you eat it, your stomach feels just fine.

Nominated by Chelsea

QUA QUA QUA

by HEATHER McHUGH

from MERIDIAN

Philosophical duck, it takes
some fine conjunctive paste to put
this nothing back together, gluing glue to glue—

a fine conjunction, and a weakness too
inside the nature of the noun. O duck, it doesn't
bother you. You live in a dive, you daub the lawn,

you dabble bodily aloft: more wakes
awake, where sheerness shares
its force. The hot air moves

you up, and then
the cool removes. There's no
such thing as things, and as for as:

it's just an alias, a form of time,
a self of other, something between thinking
and a thought (one minds his mom,

one brains his brother). You seem
so calm, o Cain of the corpus callosum,
fondler of pondlife's fallopian gore

knowing nowheres the way we don't
dare to, your web-message
subjectless (nothing a person could

pray or pry predicates from). From a log
to a logos and back, you go flinging
the thing that you are—and you sing

as you dare—on a current of
nerve. On a wing
and a wing.

Nominated by Susan Wheeler, Meridian

JASPER, TEXAS, 1998

by LUCILLE CLIFTON

from KESTREL and PLOUGHSHARES

i am a man's head hunched in the road.
i was chosen to speak by the members
of my body, the arm as it pulled away
pointed toward me, the hand opened once
and was gone.

why and why and why
should I call a white man brother?
who is the human in this place,
the thing that is dragged or the dragger?
what does my daughter say?

the sun is a blister overhead.
if i were alive i could not bear it.
the townsfolk sing we shall overcome
while hope drains slowly from my mouth
into the dirt which covers us all.
i am done with this dust, i am done.

Nominated by Cyrus Cassells, Toi Derricotte

THE CANALS OF MARS

memoir by GARY FINCKE

from SHENANDOAH

W<small>HEN</small> M<small>RS</small>. S<small>OWERS</small>, during the first week of sixth grade, showed us the canals of Mars, she traced the straight lines of them with the rubber tip of a wooden pointer. "Think of the Erie Canal," she said, holding the stick against the poster-sized map of Mars. "Better yet, think of the Panama and the Suez," she added, starting a list we were to memorize for one week's worth of geography.

"It's very likely," she said, "there were countries on Mars that fought over their technological marvels," and then she named, for our current events lesson, the nations threatening war for the Suez Canal, hissing out the names Nasser and the U.S.S.R., explaining the possible domino effect of the A-bomb.

The map, Mrs. Sowers went on to explain, had been drawn by Percival Lowell, a respected astronomer who had calculated the locations of Martian infrastructure. I believed her because up to that point I'd been relying for my information about Mars on a handful of science fiction movies I'd seen and a comic book Dave Tolley had brought to school the year before.

Through early September, before she brought us up to date on the Suez crisis, Mrs. Sowers ran a series of experiments for science. She demonstrated the water cycle; she wowed us with magnets and electric current that stood our hair on end.

Nature lessons were another matter. We fidgeted through two weeks on Pennsylvania plants. None of us liked the taste of the sassafras tea she brewed from a small tree on the hillside behind our school. It was like drinking the chewing gum our parents preferred to the sweet pleasures of Double Bubble and Bazooka.

What my friends and I wanted to know about were killer plants. Venus Fly Traps, for instance, or Pitcher Plants, or most of all, the whereabouts of those wonderfully gigantic man-eaters from the double features we watched on weekends at the Etna Theater.

All those enormous leaves. The suffocating, hair-trigger, relentless vines. Those plants were as dangerous as the giant squids created by atomic tests that left excess radiation in the ocean. If even one of their million fine-threaded leaves were brushed by careless explorers or women who wandered off from jungle camps against the advice of the guide, the horrible gulping would begin.

After one of those movies—a new Tarzan with Lex Barker— Charles Trout, the smallest boy in our class, was tossed into brambles behind the Etna Theater by boys we didn't know because our parents had saved enough money to make down payments on houses in the suburbs rather than stay in Etna, where the steel mills and railroad yards were showing signs of shutting down for good. "See?" my father would say, running his finger over his newly painted bakery wall. "See what Etna does to white?" And I nodded, thinking I could write my name and the names of all my friends with my finger through the soot.

Charles Trout laughed it off. None of us lived in Etna. We never saw those boys on the streets where we lived. And no matter, we couldn't get enough of those movies. We looked for plants in the neighborhood that might thrive on blood, dropped ants by the hundreds into any flower that grew wild, but never once did one close on the insects. It was as hard to find a carnivorous plant as it was to find quicksand. Apparently, we thought, you had to live in some steamy, forbidding place to watch anything being eaten by flowers.

Mrs. Sowers told us plants couldn't possibly get that large. She said we didn't study the Venus Fly-Trap because there weren't any in Pennsylvania. We were right, though, about one thing—they lived in bogs where other flowers seldom live. Worse, she insisted there weren't any within hundreds of miles of us.

That weekend Dave Tolley and I hiked to every marshy place we could find. It was late September, the weather, we thought, still warm enough for those traps to be working. Now that we had an important clue, we wanted to prove Mrs. Sowers wrong.

Meanwhile, we were glued to *You Asked For It*, where every Sunday on television we could see the impossible come true. Sooner or later, we thought, somebody would write in and ask to see a man-eating plant, but later that fall we settled for a man who could catch a bullet in his teeth.

While Dave Tolley and I watched, a bullet was marked by a witness from the audience so the rest of us would know it had really been fired. The camera, while the bullet was loaded, showed us the audience, all of the studio guests sitting up straight. They looked as if they were holding their breath. Every man was wearing a coat and tie, every woman a dress, and all of them were as old as our parents or older.

Even the man who could catch a bullet in his teeth was wearing a coat and tie as if he were going to church to pray for perfect timing. He furrowed his brow. He squinted. He concentrated. The marksman aimed carefully and fired. Across the studio stage the man was still standing. The camera panned in to show us it was the marked bullet he pulled from between his teeth, and we immediately set out to attempt a sort of beginners' lesson for bullet catching.

In Dave Tolley's refrigerator were bunches of green, seedless grapes. His parents played canasta on Sundays; they wouldn't be home for hours, and we threw those grapes across the living room at each other, never once catching even a lob toss between our teeth.

There were over a hundred grapes on the carpet. "Either he's a fake," Dave Tolley said, "or we're spastic." I shrugged. We had to pick all those grapes up and wash them, eating enough to make it look as if we were helping his parents rather than using their grapes as ammunition. Twenty grapes into the bowl, we decided to try one more time, and when Dave Tolley, a few minutes later, caught one of my tosses between his teeth, we shut up about impossible and decided that if somebody practiced longer than the ten minutes we'd just spent, maybe it could be done.

After all, Richard Turner, another boy in our class, could already juggle three balls. He'd learned to do it in one afternoon from his father. We thought of four balls, then five; we thought of swords and flaming sticks; we thought of increasing the speed of grapes until we could take on a bullet, how we could perform a feat so incredible that nobody would believe it.

Mrs. Sowers, of course, was no help. On Monday morning, when we told her, she said it was a silly thing to try. "Oh, that's just impossible," she said, even though we described the careful ways the program had made sure the whole thing was genuine. She shook her head and started current events, beginning with the Soviets invading

177

Hungary. "For a few days there, the Hungarians thought they were free. Nothing's the way it looks," she said, "when it comes to Communism."

She went on and on about misuse of power, how France and England had invaded Egypt. They equated power with authority, she explained, and everybody in our class wrote it down.

Dave Tolley and I had some authority. We were patrol boys. We directed traffic for a few minutes in the morning and the afternoon. I loved wearing that belt and the crossed white strap that sported the patrol badge. It showed Mrs. Sowers approved, that I was responsible and trustworthy, that even the low-readers from the Locust Grove trailer court had to wait for my signal to cross. The badges we wore were like magic that warded off danger. None of those thuggish boys had ever threatened us.

The Invasion of the Body Snatchers arrived at the Etna Theater. We'd been waiting so long, every boy in our sixth grade class but Jimmy Mason, who was thirteen and lived in the trailer court, watched it on Saturday afternoon. The Body Snatchers, it seemed, were plants. None of us could figure out how they'd changed the first human victims, but after that, people carried the big seed pods for them, placing the pods near the sleeping who woke up transformed into aliens. Sure enough, all the people in the movie who changed acted like plants. They didn't have emotions. They did anything they were told.

Just like in the Tarzan movies, it seemed scarier to be threatened by plants. You could recognize which animals were threatening. You stayed away from them. But plants? Except for poison ivy and the thorns on berry bushes and roses, there wasn't anything to be afraid of. Trees, bushes, flowers, weeds—if some of them could attack, we'd be out of luck because we were surrounded.

In the middle of November, Mrs. Sowers took Dave Tolley and me aside. "Listen, boys," she said, "I've come across a story you might enjoy. In England, a man came across a large meadow completely covered by sundews."

She looked at us for a moment. "Sundews are carnivorous plants," she said, and both of us started paying attention.

"There were a million plants," Mrs. Sowers said, and all of them, as far as the man could see, had just swallowed butterflies. An enormous flock of them had decided to settle on those flowers, and they had paid for their mistake, millions of them simultaneously eaten in minutes.

Dave Tolley and I nodded like carnival dolls. "Imagine," she said, "a whole field of insect-eating plants." We did, but like everything we wanted to see, the butterfly eaters seemed as far away as Mars.

"And as for *The Invasion of the Body Snatchers*," she said, "and all that big seed pod business, that's the Communists. Did either of you see *The Thing* a few years back? The alien in that movie was a vegetable that drank blood—it was a Communist, too. Korea and Red China—that's what all the to-do was about then. This thing in Egypt might be over for now, and all the Communists have to show for it is a canal nobody can use because it's full of sunken ships and broken bridges."

THE LAST DAY before Christmas vacation, beginning at lunch, was our party—the gift exchange, games with candy bars as prizes, mothers bringing cookies and potato chips and Coke—but first, Mrs. Sowers said, she had a surprise, flinging her arm toward a man in a dark suit who had materialized in the doorway.

"Who can remember their canals?" Mrs. Sowers said. The stranger smiled while we chorused Panama and Suez, and then pieced together the canals of Pennsylvania, pleasing Mrs. Sowers by conjuring Main Line, Schuylkill, Delaware, Lehigh and Morris.

The man in the suit, Mrs. Sowers said, had helped build the Pennsylvania Turnpike. That road had been completed, a wonderful success, nothing like that old dream we had studied in September, the Chesapeake and Ohio Canal, which was supposed to come right from the Chesapeake Bay to Pittsburgh and the beginning of the river seven miles from where we were sitting.

It turned out, after we had passed her retest, showing we remembered the long-closed canals of Pennsylvania and the still-open canals of the world, Mrs. Sowers was having that engineer show us a film on the first turnpike in America because part of that road ran through our county. And when Charles Trout, looking at the map of the turnpike, everything else in Pennsylvania blacked out, said it reminded him of the canals of Mars, the engineer told our class those lines on Mars weren't canals at all. Nobody said anything. Nobody looked at Mrs. Sowers. The engineer kept going, telling us those lines were just Martian forests that flourished on either side of the

179

canals, how irrigation would show itself to approaching spacecraft, how growth along our own lengthening turnpike system would tell the monsters coming our way we could think.

So that settled that, we thought. Mrs. Sowers wasn't wrong, but she wasn't infallible. If we knew who to ask, he'd lead us to carnivorous plants; if we talked to an expert, we'd learn to face a one-man firing squad and live to hear the applause. But when she told us, just before the gift exchange, that the troops were withdrawing in the Middle East, we all smiled because the inevitable atomic war had been postponed a while longer.

I gave her a gift-wrapped box my mother said contained a pair of stockings. "Thank you," Mrs. Sowers said, and I nodded, embarrassed, because I hadn't even seen the stockings before my mother wrapped them. Anything could have been in that box, as long as it lay flat, was light, and was less than ten inches long and six inches wide.

Because it was Friday, I got off the bus two miles from my house where a path between the Atlantic station and a car dealership made a shortcut to the Locust Grove trailer court. I walked, on Fridays, from the Atlantic station to my father's bakery in Etna. It was a mile, maybe, from that bus stop to the bakery, all of it along heavily-traveled Route 8, but there was a sidewalk most of the way, or parking lots to cut across, and I'd been walking that route once a week since fourth grade, during all that time talking to nobody who got off the bus there except Jimmy Mason after he flunked sixth grade and ended up in my class instead of the junior high school.

My mother worked until six o'clock on Fridays, but on that first official day of winter it was cold and gloomy and already nearly dark at four p.m. Instead of going up the path as he always did, Jimmy Mason fell in beside two older boys I'd never seen. All three of them caught up to me as soon as I crossed the Route 8 bridge where Pine Creek ran under the highway.

Jimmy Mason said the three of them had a job selling Christmas trees in Etna. He cut in front of me and walked backwards, slowing us down. If I had any money, he said, I should buy a tree from them, or better yet, just give the money to them and they wouldn't bother me any more.

"I don't have any money," I said, telling the truth.

"Not on you," Jimmy Mason said, but the other two boys bumped against me from either side.

"What's that badge for?" the biggest said. "You play cops and robbers at your school?"

"Safety patrol," I said. He turned and put his forearm against my chest, resting it across the badge. I noticed he had a mustache.

"You keep the babies safe?"

I didn't say anything. I already wished I hadn't said a word or had the stupidity to wear that patrol gear outside my winter coat. "Patrol boy," he said. "I want to cross here. Why don't you step out and stop those trucks?"

I cut to the inside, afraid he'd push me into the highway. I kept walking, down to the last section, a quarter mile of crushed cinder sidewalk, Pine Creek ten feet below us on one side, a hundred-foot cliff running down to the highway on the other.

All three lanes were patch-iced, the traffic one step from where he waved his arms. I could see the stoplight where businesses, including my father's, began. My mother would be wrapping bread and sandwich buns. In a few minutes she'd start looking out the window to see if I was coming.

He snapped the white straps crossed over my red jacket. "Safety patrol," he said. "Pussy." The badge blinked from the early sets of headlights. He pulled on a pair of black leather gloves. "Give me that badge," the boy said, "or I'll beat the shit out of you, patrol boy."

He shoved me toward the guardrail, and I looked down the hillside at the creek I could see moving beneath the thin ice. "Don't move," he said, sticking a blue pen in my face. "Patrol boy, you write this down: I died here, December 21," and then he shoved my arm toward the guardrail that made that pen skip along the metal's white and rust until I stopped where a string of *fuck yous* began.

"More darker," he said, and I went over and over the letters. "So the police," he said, "can read it when your body's found—now walk."

All four of us skidded down a path through the trees that lined the creek bank. Anybody driving a car along Route 8 couldn't see us anymore. On the other side of the creek an identical thick set of scrub trees covered a bank that sloped up and stopped where the leveled slag of the parking lot for National Valve began. Anybody in that factory, even if he was taking the time to stare out a window instead of shaping and cutting pipe, couldn't see us. Only someone overhead in a helicopter or a hot air balloon could have watched what was happening.

181

"You ever seen it hard, patrol boy?" he said. "You can fight back now or else you can kneel and suck it." I checked the bank on the other side of Pine Creek for an opening among the trees. For all I knew, nobody worked at National Valve after four o'clock. When he cocked his fist I stepped into water that ran over my shoes. "Cold?" he asked. "Wet?"

I watched his hands as I backpedaled to knee-high, the ice collapsing under me, and then I turned and slogged to the other side, eleven years old and dying at 4:15, December 21, in Pine Creek, all three of those boys screaming "Safety Patrol" across that ditch of factory run-off as I scrambled to the almost-empty lot where two cars were parked so near the edge, so close together, I thought, before I began to run toward the bakery, one driver was kneeling for another or both of them were waiting to kill me.

Nominated by Shenandoah, Lee Upton

BACKWARD POEM

by BOB HICOK

from HAYDEN'S FERRY REVIEW

This poem ends in death so I'll walk it

       backward home. The heart of an 87 year-old woman
starts on July 7th and immediately doctors
             syringe morphine from her veins

and her daughter puts a tissue

       together and steps from the room. There's
a general turning of days from dark to light
             and what she said to grandchildren

then she says to grandchildren now

       only the words face the other way and blood
removes itself from scraped knees and all
             her photographs resolve to black

as she lowers the camera from her eye

       and sleeps it back into the box. She waves
as if erasing the sky amid the turned-around
             hissing of the ocean and the elated

leaves retrieve their green and jump

into the trees and sex culminates with something
like warm proximity, a simple radiant fact.
                    Remembering her body old, she frets

the evaporation of liver spots

          and tightening of skin, interrogates the mirror
as gravity gives the curves back and begins
                    her first date with my grandfather

operating a quick stranger's stride.

          And soon I'll send the poem the other way and soon
she'll turn soft in bed as my mother shreds a blue
                    and powdery thing into finer dust

and just before the inevitable

          I'll write *a baby seeing the sky for the first time
floats without antecedent*, which naturally molts
                    to *the last wind to touch the body*

is all the body becomes. If time's

          no more than the flesh of space arching its back, what's
to stop the limber words from making geraniums
                    bloom in winter, what's to bind

my grandmother to an oath of death?

          I declare her young now and leaning on a sill with color
supplying the field, throats of the flowers open
                    to the pilgrimage of bees, the sun

dead above hoarding the shadows for itself.

Nominated by Hayden's Ferry Review, Roger Weingarten, Susan Wheeler, David Wojahn

IN THE BELLY
OF THE CAT

fiction by DANIEL S. LIBMAN

from THE PARIS REVIEW

THE SAME DAY that he canceled all his newspaper and magazine subscriptions, Mr. Christopher deveined a pound of jumbo shrimp by hand. He had never done this before, and used nearly a whole roll of paper towels wiping the snotty black entrails off his fingers one by one. He also grated a package of cheddar cheese with a previously unused grater that he uncovered in his silverware drawer, kneaded a loaf of oatmeal raisin bread, then called the escort service and arranged for a girl. "I want Carlotta; she's a Latina, right?"

He had called *The Tribune* earlier that morning. "Stop my subscription. The relationship is over; deliver it no longer. The advice columns just rehash the same situations—alcoholism, smoking, infidelity—although sometimes those columns are titillating, which I appreciate. The comic strips are contrived, and the punch lines aren't ever that good. That cranky columnist on page three ought to have his head examined; I think he's finally lost it, and your media critic is always biased towards the TV stations you own. But what I object to mostly, the reason I'm canceling, is because it comes too often: once a day, and anyway what good is it? I don't have that much time left and do you know how much I've wasted over the years slogging through, reading and cringing, hands and fingers covered in the ink, hauling paper-bloated garbage bags stuffed with Sports and Food sections, which I never even touch, down three flights of stairs every week?"

Mr. Christopher was hurt by the cavalier way the man at the *Trib* took care of the cancellation. After so much loyal readership he felt that they should have put up some sort of struggle, a little token of respect: "But Mr. Christopher, please think about it; you want to throw away sixty years just like that?" Not that it would have gotten them anywhere. His mind was made up.

He had been a widower now for a year and a half, retired, down to only two-thirds of what he weighed at forty, dentures, a toupee he no longer wore but kept hanging off his hall tree, an artificial hip; and a brother a couple of states to the east whom he didn't like with a mouthy know-it-all wife. This had come to him one evening earlier in the week, a cold-cut sandwich and a pickle on a plate in front of him, eyeing the pile of papers; he had enough of them.

Mr. Christopher canceled all the magazines too: *The East Coast Arbiter, Harbingers', The New Statesman,* even *The Convenience Store Merchandiser,* a holdover from work that they sent him for free.

He was bundling up the last week of *Tribs* he would ever receive, when his hands landed on a Food section. "Special Dishes to Commemorate Any Event," the headline said. I'll give you an event, he thought, How's finally ending sixty years of crap sound to you, Mr. Tribune.

Mr. Christopher decided to open up the Food section for the first time and cook those commemorative dishes. He mapped out what he needed to do in his head: buy fresh fruit, two pounds of shrimp; he'd need to take a bus to that specialty food store for some of it. . . . He even scanned the tips on what makes a good party: fancy utensils, music and special friends.

He was cubing the honeydew for the fruit slaw when she buzzed. He gave a start and walked to the intercom and thought how odd it sounded. No one had buzzed him for . . . weeks? months? decades? He leaned down to the grill, painted the same off-white as the rest of the apartment, and pressed.

Talk: Yes?

Listen: You call for me?

Talk: Who is it?

Listen: This is Monique. You call for me?

Talk: No. I called for Carlotta.

Listen: I'm Carlotta. Buzz me in.

Talk: Who are you?

Listen: Carlotta. You want me, baby?

He touched *door* and heard the faraway buzzing. She was in the building now; his heart raced. It would take a minute or two to climb the three flights, and then she would have to decide which direction to walk; that would take a few seconds. He was in 3A, towards the front of the building so she would have to look at 3B first, because it was right across from the stairs, and then make a choice, and she might choose right, which would take her to 3C—and in all this time he could back out, decide not to go ahead with this. He slid the security chain across the door.

But he had already gone to so much trouble. He had found the escort service in another part of *The Tribune* never before looked at, the match ads. At the very end were listings for adult services; these included descriptions of women, measurements and height and weight, and he wasn't born yesterday.

Mr. Christopher heard her footsteps and a knock. She had gotten to his door very quickly. Nervously, he touched his front pocket where he had put the money. It was a lot of cash to have at one time, the most he had carried in years. He looked down, considering himself, his paunch and his house slippers; he saw that the end of his belt was loose. He tucked it behind the proper loop in his corduroys, and she was knocking again, harder and faster.

"Yes, yes," he said quickly. "Hello."

"It's me," she answered, as if it might really be someone he knew. He was suddenly grateful that she hadn't said, "The whore you called for," or something equally provocative that might arouse suspicion, and he quickly undid the chain and opened the door.

She was about a foot taller, starchy white, with large fleshy legs that dropped out of a tiny skirt. Her midriff was showing, and her shoulders were bare, too. It was a lot of flesh for Mr. Christopher to mentally process, and he sputtered once before speaking.

"No," he said. "You are not a Carlotta. Not petite and not a coed."

"Carlotta sent me. I'm her friend, Monique."

She pushed past him. Mr. Christopher squinted against her redolent perfume as she breezed confidently into his living room. She had a small purse and tossed it onto his reading chair as if she had been in the apartment many times before.

His apartment building had once been a three-flat, but it had been sectioned off into nine uneasy units. His living room was long, but narrow; a wall had been added to make a bedroom where the other

187

half of the living room had been. Knowing that the other three units on the floor had once been part of his apartment made him curious to know what the other units looked like. On those rare occasions when a neighbor left the door open—like if they were getting ready to go out or trying to get a better breeze in the summer—and Mr. Christopher happened to be walking by, he would linger, just a little bit, craning his neck slightly to get a peek. He always wanted to know how the units fit together, and it vaguely irritated him that two-thirds of his apartment were being lived in by other people.

"Smells good," she said.

"You're smelling the onions and green peppers that I will be using to stuff the pork chops, our main course."

"Having a fancy party?" she asked, turning slowly and eyeing the elaborately set table for the first time. Although Mr. Christopher usually ate on his couch with his plate and a magazine on the ottoman, tonight he had set out the best plates he had, the good silverware, and had even put two candles right in the center.

"No no, it's just us," he said, taking a step to his cassette player.

"I already ate."

"No no. I told the man on the phone this was for dinner and . . . that it would be for dinner as well as the other stuff."

A tinny version of Benny Goodman's clarinet came out of the box.

"No one told me," she said. "I don't have that much time."

"I need you here for at least three hours. I told the man that; I told him. I can't get all the food prepared in an hour, let alone eat it. We're going to have salad and soup and appetizers and bread—the bread's not even completely baked yet."

"You have an hour from when I got out of the car, and that was a couple of minutes ago. If I don't get back to Mickey by then—"

"Who's Mickey?"

"Look out your window. Across the street."

The blinds were shut, but he shuffled between the table and the window and lowered a couple of slats with his hand.

In the no-parking zone, an enormous man sat on the hood of a town car, feet spread-eagle on the pavement, reading a newspaper. Even though it was a large and bulky car, it dipped under the weight of the man's bottom.

"What's he doing?" Mr. Christopher asked.

"Wasting time, now. But I'm telling you, if I don't get down in. . . fifty-three minutes, he'll come tearing up here. You've never seen

188

anything like it. You won't be able to reason with him, you won't be able to stop him. He'll come up those steps, bust down your door, and he'll clean your clock."

Mr. Christopher pulled his hands off the blinds and looked towards his kitchen. "Okay," he said. "We'll do it first, what you came here for, and that will give time for the bread to rise and also for the sugar—this is part of the dessert—to caramelize so that I can pour it, drizzle it, onto the flan. I need forty-five minutes for dinner. That gives me fifteen minutes for the rest of it. Can we do that in fifteen minutes, not even fifteen, but now it's already just twelve or eleven as you pointed out. Can it be done that fast?"

"Normally I have a routine I do, dancing and a rub down, and tickling on the genitalia to arouse you. If you want to skip all that, go right to it . . . Well, it's your money."

"I wasn't picturing dancing or a rub down, but now that I hear about it, it does sound like fun. This is my first time, Monique, so you'll have to guide me."

"Your first time, a guy of your age?"

"First time with a call girl. Okay, we're wasting time. I need to finish sautéing the onions. We better do this in the kitchen."

The kitchen had once been the hallway that connected Mr. Christopher's third of the apartment to the rest of the building. It was narrow and ended abruptly in a Sheetrock wall. The floor changed from hard wood to linoleum about a foot away from the wall, giving the impression that it might have led to a bathroom or a utility closet at one time. One side of the corridor was a narrow countertop, now covered in fruit peelings, shrimp shells and other food debris. Across the corridor was the sink, mini-refrigerator and a two-burner stove that was already covered with large pots. Another small countertop separated the two appliances.

He found the Food section and brushed some cheese shavings off the page and put his finger on the right passage. He took a sniff of her perfume and knew she was behind him. "Clear and soft . . . I'm going to add the green peppers and the cumin and then cook that . . . Then I have to slice the fat off the chops and carve little pockets—" He put a wooden spoon into his sautéing onions and turned his neck slightly so he could see her bare shoulder.

She reached around him unceremoniously and unbuckled his belt and lowered his pants. His legs were hairy with thick blue veins, but his underwear was shockingly white. When she pulled it down to his

189

knees she reached under and grabbed his limp penis. Her hand was so cold and dry that he jumped, but didn't scream. He reached over to the small counter without moving his feet and began to scoop the melon pieces into a large blue bowl.

"I can't get around you here," she told him from the floor. "Can I open one of these cabinets by your knees, so that I can move my head closer, and I'll be able to reach you while you're working?"

He said, "Hang on a second, I'll be able to turn around in a second. Do you think . . .," he took a pair of black food scissors and slowly began snipping away at the tips of a large artichoke. "Do you think you could take off some clothing too, maybe just your top. Otherwise I'd feel too self-conscious to enjoy it."

She pulled her tank top over her head, and when he turned around she was kneeling in front of him with her hands folded in her lap. Her shirt was lying next to her, and he allowed himself to stare at her breasts. They were the largest he had ever seen, which made him feel a flash of pride, as if he had gotten a surprisingly good return on a shaky investment. Her nipples were oval, straining to keep their shapes on top of such large breasts.

Monique looked right at him and took his balls in her hand. Uncomfortable at the strangely clinical turn this had taken, he cleared his throat once. "My, eh, testicles . . . They're much larger than they should be for the size of my . . ."

She waved the comment away, which did make him feel better. She surely had seen all sorts of genitalia; and she leaned down and put him in her mouth.

The tail on his kitty-cat clock swung back and forth with each second, matching the absurd ping-pong eyes in the cat's head. The clock, painted into the torso of the cat, showed that he had only six minutes left for this part of the night if he was going to have the minimum amount of time he needed to serve the meal. A burning spit of grease from the onions hit him on the back of the neck.

Concentration was difficult for Mr. Christopher and, without moving from his spot, he picked up the big wooden spoon and pushed his onions around in the oil. When he felt his legs getting wobbly, he put the spoon down and held the countertop.

He was losing time now, it was going by quicker than usual; the kitty-cat's eyes and tail had been sped up by some strange force. But he had to admit that it felt good, what she was doing. His legs shook and he was afraid he might fall. He dug in with the heels of his

190

house slippers and gripped tightly to the countertop. His hips involuntarily moved closer to the heat of her face. He wheezed from the back of his throat and felt her breasts against his legs, and he let himself go.

"Okay," he said. "You can spit that out in the sink."

She waved that comment away too, and put her shirt back on.

"Don't spoil your appetite," he said, as he did the top button on his pants and pulled his belt snug against his waist.

"I told you I ate already."

"Look," he told her. "I've got you for another thirty-three minutes. Go take a seat at the table."

She left, and he turned around and scooped the last melon pieces from the counter and used his hands to mix it all up in the bowl. He felt tired for a second, useless. He steadied himself against the counter and realized he just wanted to sleep—to pull the blanket up to his chest and open a magazine and relax. But the pot on the far burner began to bubble, and he remembered the magazines weren't coming anymore, although he couldn't remember why exactly. Mr. Christopher put the artichoke into the water and watched it simmer for a second before covering it.

She was already sitting when he walked back into the living room. He used a book of matches and lit the candles.

"You're going all out for this dinner, huh?" she asked.

Mr. Christopher wanted to smile, but he felt the pressure from the kitty-cat. The soup was done, and he went back into the kitchen, aware of the pathetic way his hip made him look when he was in a hurry. He ladled out two bowls, making sure each serving had the same number of shrimp and pineapple chunks.

"Lemongrass soup," he said, walking slowly out with the bowls. He placed them on the table and sat across from her.

"What is that smell?" she asked, cocking an eye at him.

"That's the lemongrass," he told her. "It's spicy, and I hope you like it."

"Should we say grace?"

Mr. Christopher had dipped his spoon in and was stirring his portion. "No time," he said, and slurped a loud mouthful. "Mmmm," he said, dabbing his lips with his napkin. "Okay, you keep eating, and I have to finish the fruit."

When he returned three minutes later, carrying four small bowls, he was breathing hard. Beads of sweat glistened on his forehead.

191

She looked up from her bowl and said excitedly, "You know, this is really good. Much better than it smells."

"I'm glad."

"You know what? The pineapple was even better than the shrimp. Pineapple in soup!" she said, and shook her head.

"This is fruit slaw, and this is a cheese and pea salad." He put both bowls in front of her and took her soup bowl. Her hand clenched momentarily, as if she might yank the soup bowl back and this pleased Mr. Christopher, but he didn't have time to think about it.

"Oh God, the wine," he said. He went towards the kitchen but turned around after a few steps and took the soup bowls with him. On the way, he limped to the cassette player and flipped the tape, which had stopped at some point.

The music was back on, and Mr. Christopher poured two glasses of wine. The song was one that he really liked—one of his favorites— Benny Goodman's "Belly of the Cat," and he suddenly felt self-conscious listening to it while pouring a woman wine. He quickly asked, "So, how do you like the salad?"

"It's okay," she said. "The soup was exotic, and this is sort of every-day type of food, so it's a strange menu."

"The food section said the salad is best served in a glass bowl. That way you can see the layers, the mayonnaise on the bottom, then the peas, then more mayonnaise, then the cheddar cheese, which I shredded myself. It's too bad I don't have a glass bowl."

"Why don't you sit down for a second?" she asked.

He twisted the blinds so he could see out the window. Mickey had put the newspaper away and was leaning against the car now, facing Mr. Christopher's doorway. He was dressed in a bow tie and a sporty tuxedo coat, like a bouncer at a banquet hall or a limo driver on prom night.

"I guess I'll sit down for a second," Mr. Christopher said, lowering himself uneasily into the chair. "And rest. I had planned on a nice conversation with you." He dabbed his forehead with the napkin, but he still felt sweaty. "So," he said, "how many people will you visit tonight?"

"I usually try to get five or six customers a night," she told him. "At least four, but six is a good night. Eight is the most I would do."

"When I worked retail, it was the same. Just like you, get to as many people as possible. So that's something we have in common, me and you," Mr. Christopher nodded once to himself. "But about you, eight times in one night? That's a lot. Good for business, I guess. Right?"

"That would be real good," she said. "Yes. It's not that tough. How many times do you do it a night?"

"Usually, none," he told her.

"But what's the most?"

He made a face.

"Come on, for a conversation. What's the most you've ever done it in a night?"

"If I've ever done it twice in a night, then two. But I can't remember. I usually get tired and there isn't enough time in a single night to rest up entirely. So we're different, that's why it's so nice to spend time with someone you don't know, to share different experiences. . . ." These sentences that he had prepared and even rehearsed a few times now sounded stilted and ridiculous in his mouth; although she was nodding in apparent agreement with him. Who was he trying to kid anyway? He looked at his watch to cover his embarrassment. "Okay," he said. "Time for the main course. Let's go, let's go."

He took her bowls away and returned a few minutes later with a platter. "We're going to eat dessert now, but save enough room for the pork chops. They're still a little pink and if we wait for them we might not have time for dessert. So we'll go out of turn."

She put her hand on her bare stomach. "That's fine with me anyway, because I'm not especially hungry. I told you that, that I had eaten already. I don't even know if I could eat another bite."

He brought four helpings of flan, each perfectly shaped like a large quivering eyeball. He had hoped she would want more than one helping, but he knew that wasn't going to happen, so he said, "I think it's time to make a toast."

She picked up her glass of wine, which was still full.

"To a lovely night," he said. "A lovely woman, a lovely meal and a lovely time."

He tipped his glass towards her slightly and she did the same in imitation, and they both drank.

"Okay," he said. "Now dessert."

He looked at his watch for a second and saw that he had nine minutes left. When he checked the window, he was surprised to see

Mickey was walking back and forth. His legs and arms and were thick, like sausages. Mickey checked his watch and looked up to the third floor of the building.

"It's time for the pork chops," he mumbled.

"Are you sure there's time? You don't want him—Mickey, coming up here. It's better that I should leave a few minutes early than he get mad—come up those stairs and start banging on your door."

"I have eight more minutes of your time," Mr. Christopher answered icily, and he walked into the kitchen.

When he returned a few minutes later, he was carrying a plate with two sickly pink and gray slabs of meat. Corn and onions had been stuffed into slits along the sides of the chops, but they oozed like puddles of sewage. Mr. Christopher skewered the largest one and tried to get it off the tray, but every time he lifted the fork, the chop slid off. Finally he pushed it with the prongs onto her plate and slid the other one onto his plate. He put the serving platter on the floor.

"Bon appetit, my sweet."

"Are you sure these are done?" she said, poking her chop with a knife. "You've really got to cook meat, pork especially; and I thought I saw these out on your counter, raw, when I was in the kitchen."

"That's right," he told her. He cut off a slice. It was dull pink on the inside and she looked away before he put it in his mouth. "But I turned the oven up as high as it would go and had them in since we began eating. Mmmm. Anyway, I don't have any more time." His lips were glistening and he sliced off another piece and waited for her to begin.

"It smells good," she stood up. "But I ate before I got here, and the custard and the soup, and that's it. I couldn't eat another bite. Thank you for the night. That'll be a hundred and forty bones, and that's not including a tip."

"Take a bite of the dinner. The bread isn't done yet and we'll forget about the liqueur; I haven't even begun to make the garlic butter sauce for the artichoke appetizer. So we'll forget all the rest, but I want you to at least try the pork chop. It's stuffed with corn and sautéed onions. You know, festively."

He wolfed down another bite, swallowing it as quickly as possible to show how good it was.

"My money," she said putting her palm out.

"My time," he said into his plate. "This is all I wanted, for you to

194

come here and have a nice meal and a nice time. It's my special day and this was all I wanted."

"Listen, old man. You didn't cook it long enough; I'm going to retch just from the smell and I'm already nauseous from the spicy soup and the bowl of mayonnaise."

He forced himself to take another piece of the pork chop. When it reached his tongue his stomach lurched, and the meat fell apart unnaturally. He put his napkin up to his mouth and spit it up. When he was done gagging and had wiped his lips hard onto the napkin, he said, "The money is in my front pants pocket. Seven twenty-dollar bills." He covered his head with his hands and rested his elbows on the table.

"Give it to me," she said.

"It's too late," he told her. "Check the window."

The door lurched in its frame and then popped open. Monique put her arm around Mr. Christopher's shoulders. "It's okay, Mickey," she yelled. "It's okay, I'm all right."

Mr. Christopher closed his eyes as a hand grabbed his shoulder and pulled him up off the chair. He opened them and saw Mickey's teeth, a row of little rat triangles.

"You see that door, buddy," Mickey snarled. "I suggest you hand over the money right this instant, or that's what's going to happen to your head."

"The money's in my pocket, sir," Mr. Christopher said, dropping back in the chair.

"The money's in my pocket," he repeated. He stood up and took a step back. "Here." He put the wad of folded bills onto the table.

"And hold on you two. Hold on a minute." He put up a finger towards Mickey and Monique and ambled into his kitchen. The pot with the artichoke was boiling over and Mr. Christopher turned off the burners and shut off the stove. A stack of old newspapers were piled under the counter, waiting to be taken to the trash.

"I know your time is valuable," Mr. Christopher called out. "And I know I've wasted some of it. I'm sorry about that . . ." Brightening up, he slipped on an oven-mitt and took the platter of pork chops from the oven. "And six customers is a lot, and I know you've got to be going . . . Believe me, I respect the need for speed. So maybe this will help, with dinner . . ." As he spoke, he wrapped in newspaper three of the juiciest chops he had. He pulled the artichoke out of the water with tongs and put it into a large zip-lock baggie. When that was done, he dumped the rest of the fruit slaw into another baggy, and the cheese and pea salad into a third. "I appreciate you coming over, Monique, and you too Mickey! I appreciate the time you spent with me . . ." Mr. Christopher pulled a brown shopping bag out of the garbage and put the moist newspaper packages and all the baggies into it.

The soup was hot, but he found a square tupperware in a cabinet and poured it in, burped the lid and put it in the brown bag with the rest of it. The flan was more delicate, but Mr. Christopher emptied an egg carton and filled the cups with the lumpy brown custard.

"I remember on Thanksgiving," Mr. Christopher called while skittering around his kitchen, "or any food holiday like that, Christmas and the Fourth of July—barbecues on the Fourth—and at the end the host always would ask what you wanted to . . . take home with you, leftovers . . ."

He had no plastic forks or spoons, but now wasn't the time to worry about his stuff. It would be a long time before he ever had guests over for such an occasion, if ever, so he put his nice silverware into the bag. Two of everything: two salad forks, two regular forks, two sets of each spoon—fruit, dessert, soup—two sets of steak knives and two butter knives. He pulled the bread loaf out of the oven, slapped the bottom of the pan with his mitted fist, and the oatmeal raisin mass fell solidly into the bag.

"That's when you know you've had a good time—didn't waste your time—when you walked out with an armload of food for the next couple of days . . ." He folded the top over twice, put his hand on his hip and walked into the living room.

The room was empty. Mr. Christopher held the warm shopping bag to his chest and looked at his door. It was only attached at the top hinge and looked like it might fall, and he could see past it, into the empty hallway, all the way to his neighbor's closed door.

Nominated by Jewel Mogan, George Plimpton

WEATHER UPDATE

by KARRI LYNN HARRISON

from MOUNT VOICES

A mechanical whirring runs inside machines nearby.
There's a hollow feeling in my teeth.
It's like I'm clean, my skin wet with bathwater still.
Instead the cotton knit of my spring sweater weighs slightly on my
    shoulders.
Around my wrists the sweater's loose.
Machines nearby cool themselves.
Tonight we wait for the Gulf front. We predict accumulation.
One of us warms her hands between her thighs.
I twist my silver rings as they seem to loosen on my fingers.
My hands are cold.
There's a hollow feeling in my teeth.
Tonight the redbuds are way down south spitting out the shades
    they keep down all winter.
We wait for accumulation.
The machinery nearby cools itself.
It's like I'm watching, my body dripping still, but instead I'm patient
    for the warm front to meet the cool.
A mechanical whirring is hollowing my skin; my teeth are clean.
The cotton knot of my spring sweater accumulates.
Way down south, the redbud warms her hands between her thighs.
Her skin is wet.
The silver rings loosen. Around the wrists I'm clean.
Over my shoulders, the front comes up from the Gulf, dripping still.
It's like I'm hollow.
It's like I'm silver.

One of us is watching, way down south all winter.
Inside, machines weigh — slightly.
I'm patient waiting, keeping the shades down.
On my fingers, they seem to loosen.

Nominated by Richard Jackson

THE POSSIBLE WORLD

fiction by ELIZABETH McKENZIE

from THE THREEPENNY REVIEW

IT WAS STRANGELY quiet outside, but maybe I had closed all the windows. This was the most well-built house I had ever lived in. The walls were creamy plaster, like those in an adobe mission. They were held together by strong oak beams which were exposed like whale ribs across the living room ceiling. Even the windows were made of a thicker, more interesting glass than normal windows. Tiny bubbles riddled the glass if you looked closely enough. I liked to walk around this house and examine its craftsmanship. Someone who appreciated a well-built house built this one.

I'm only a renter. I could dream of owning this house, but it would probably cost something like $575,000. Though well-built, it's small. And my husband, who is a software engineer over in San Jose, is afraid of owning big, cumbersome things. In them he sees nothing but trouble.

Anyway, it was suddenly quiet, and though I could see the trees whipping around in the wind, I couldn't hear a single groan or rustle. It was soothing but rather apocalyptic-feeling. I had the feeling I would not be staying in this house for long.

Yesterday Paul, who is my landlady's boyfriend, called me at exactly this time. It was 9:30 A.M. and I was in the kitchen watching a movie. He said, "I need some help on the Brocco-rabi project. As you know, I broke my leg dare-devil skiing and I need someone to drive me to Fresno to inspect the site of our first Brocco-rabi demonstration. Can you drive me? A hundred dollars?"

This isn't exactly what he said verbatim, but all of this was there. And even though it was an abrupt request, I was pleased. I didn't have anything to do yesterday except pick up my son after school. A drive to Fresno sounded out of the ordinary.

"Okay," I replied. "If I can find a way for Will to be picked up after school, I'll do it."

"Yeah, I've got that all figured out already," Paul said. "Virginia will be done with her meetings by then. She can pick him up."

Virginia is my landlady. I am aware of how much she likes my son. On Easter she dropped by a basket with Godiva eggs in it. Plus an expensive plush stuffed rabbit. It was almost embarrassing. Will couldn't care less about the price tag but it made me a little uncomfortable. Then on Halloween she made up a grab bag of candy and toys, very extravagant. Twice she'd asked me to bring him over and they'd baked cookies together.

Yesterday it was windy like today. I was to pick Paul up "asap," whatever that meant. I decided to take my time with my cup of coffee and my movie, seeing as he'd given me such short notice. But even so I could tell I was hurrying a little. This movie seemed like a strange choice for the morning. I could better imagine seeing this one on TV in the afternoon or evening, after the day had left its scratchy imprint on a person. A respectable businessman takes his daughter and son way into the outback of Australia, lights the car on fire and shoots himself in the head, leaving them to find their way on their own. Wandering in the desolate expanse they meet an aboriginal boy who shows them how to eat grubs and swim naked in a pool. How can anything be the same again?

Before Paul called, while watching the movie, I had made my daily list of things to do and among them were: go to library, go to bank, sort through Will's clothes and give away too-small things to Goodwill. Nothing that couldn't wait.

Sometimes you need to read between the lines of a list like that. I shouldn't short-change my plan for yesterday. Lots of other significant things could've happened. I might've heard something on the radio that would send me off on a really interesting mental tangent. Every time I'd hear a traffic report about an accident on Highway 17 I would wonder whether it was my husband or some other acquaintance, or I might receive a phone call that would get me going—from a friend with good news, say.

Two weeks ago, my sister, who calls me quite often, arranged for the largest radio station in her area to call and interview me. She loves to think of me back in the swing of things, and my involvement with Brocco-rabi was no exception. She called the radio station to see if they were interested, and they were. Can you believe it? I have tried to succeed in many different ways, and when I don't care, not invested at all, I'm in demand. Anyway, she told them I was the person to talk to when it came to Brocco-rabi. The radio station contacted me, and bingo, the next day I was scheduled to go on the air. It's a 50,000 watt radio station. It can be heard from Maine to South Carolina.

The thing is, I'm not really the person to talk to about Brocco-rabi. But my sister was so excited she'd put together this interview that I went along with it.

The host of this show was a man named Newt Barnaby. About five minutes before two, an assistant called. "Ready for Newt?" she asked. I said I was. I had practiced speaking with more authority the night before. I thought I should sound like the world's expert on Brocco-rabi.

Suddenly I could hear the actual radio show coming through the phone—a commercial for a car-wash. I sighed. Ultimately, nothing was resting on this. No one except my sister would hear it. If Virginia and Paul found out, they'd probably be irritated. Here I was, posing as the official spokesperson for Brocco-rabi. Just then the voice of Newt Barnaby began to talk over the end of the car-wash ad. My throat tightened up.

"And now we've got a very interesting feature for you today. Out in Salinas, California, a brand new vegetable is on the loose, and we've got Melissa Woods to tell us about it!"

"Hi, Newt," I said jauntily.

"Melissa! How's it going out in Salinas?"

"Actually, I'm not in Salinas. I live in Aptos." Why did I need to throw that in? Who cared? I concentrated harder.

"Where's Aptos?"

"Near Watsonville. This is a vast agricultural area, Newt. The Pajaro and Salinas valleys are among the richest growing areas on earth."

"Lucky you! We easterners know the good veggies always seem to come from California. So, tell us—what exactly is Brocco-rabi?"

I was doing better now. My voice was coming on strong and clear.

"Well, Newt, Brocco-rabi was genetically engineered. As you can

201

probably guess, it's half broccoli and half kohlrabi. It's a hearty grower and has five times the vitamins of both combined. It's quite large and kind of looks like a big green cow udder."

"Yeow! The Frankenstein of vegetables!" Newt Barnaby emitted a resounding, fully committed laugh. And I smiled. I was staring out the thick, bubbly window into my backyard. From the inside of my house, the outside had never looked more interesting.

"Yes, and it's the first new vegetable to be created since 1937, when scientists masterminded the Brussels Sprout."

"Really! Melissa, this is absolutely fascinating."

Did he really think so? I was afraid I had my dates wrong, and surely some know-it-all would call the station to correct me. Better get back on firm ground.

"Furthermore, we're about to introduce Chucky Brocco-rabi, a larger-than-life super hero. He wears a cape and a little bikini like most of the other superheroes do—"

"Ho ho. Tell us, does Brocco-rabi taste good?"

"Sure. Everybody loves it."

"Where can I find Brocco-rabi? Can I drive over to Price Chopper and buy some right now?"

"I certainly hope so. We believe it's now in every state, and it's catching on in Europe, too."

"What's the bottom line on Brocco-rabi, Melissa? Why should America open its heart to a new vegetable?"

"Newt, what with the government's five-a-day plan, we need all the options we can get at the lunch and dinner table. Kids are really going to love Brocco-rabi too. The weirdness of it."

"Weird! Weird! I love it! Thanks, Melissa Woods from Aptos, California!"

Newt disappeared and all the sound collapsed into a vacuum in the phone. I thought my eardrum was going to get sucked into it, too. That was it? No goodbyes? I was suddenly alone again in my kitchen, looking at the soaking skillet from the wild-rice dish I'd prepared the night before. I slowly hung up the phone. Then, a minute later, my sister called. She said I sounded like a natural. She said she was sure Brocco-rabi sales would skyrocket.

Later, I thought it was kind of foolish for me to have gotten so worked up about this radio interview, broadcast over states where nobody I knew would be listening.

Anyway, yesterday I vacuumed the car before I drove to pick up

Paul. I sprayed some room freshener around and packed up a tin of cookies. Then I went and filled the tank with gas and squeegeed the windows. For some reason I wanted to do a really good job of driving Paul to Fresno. I admit I was disproportionately excited about this trip.

Remember, it was windy yesterday. But I like weather. It's one of the few things that can make everything seem different when you're in exactly the same place.

My husband thinks Paul is something of a blowhard but he likes him. One day, shortly after we moved into this house, it was a beautiful day and my husband had the day off. He planned on doing a little lawn mowing, making himself a martini, then lying out on a chaise in the freshly threshed grass. He doesn't get to enjoy our yard often, and wasn't even aware until that day that I had planted an extensive summer garden that had provided us with most of our salad materials recently. At any rate, he had only just turned off the roaring two-horsepower engine on the mower when Paul showed up with a box of wires and switches. "Hey, buddy," he said to my husband, "I need to put lights down in the crawl space and even though I'm an aeronautical engineer I know a hell of a lot about electronics and you can come down there and shoot the shit with me."

This wasn't exactly what he said but if you read between the lines it was clear this was his meaning. And even though my husband never does anything he doesn't want to do, he put aside his martini and chaise lounge and disappeared into the basement crawl space with Paul for the rest of the afternoon. Then that night he was amazed at himself.

"Why did I spend my afternoon off crawling on my belly in the dirt?" he asked me.

"I was wondering. What did you talk about all that time?"

"He insisted on installing five different switches and bulb outlets. Two would have been more than enough. That Paul is pretty proud of himself. Was some kind of boy genius. Did some engineering contracts for the military and spent a year in a tunnel under Japan. Said they had golf courses down there."

"Golf courses? How deep were the tunnels?"

"He did mention. I think he said two miles."

"Two miles deep. Amazing! Golf courses!"

"I don't know. Maybe I wasn't listening."

"Not listening? It really sounds much more interesting than I expected."

In fact, as the afternoon wore on, I had crawled over to the heavy, scrolled wrought iron heater vent and pressed my ear to it. I stayed there for a long time trying to hear the sound of their voices. The smell of moist soil came up through the vent in gentle waves. It made my mouth water. Sometimes I heard a roar like the ocean and for awhile I heard scratching like a squirrel making a nest. But that's it. I guess it's such a well-built house, sound doesn't travel. I determined I wasn't missing much.

"Well, maybe he feels at home down there," I said, wondering why I wanted to prolong this discussion.

"Who?"

"Paul."

"Where?"

"Under the house. Maybe it reminds him of Japan."

"Oh, right. Let's hope he doesn't decide to put a golf course down there," my husband joked.

It pleased me to see my husband interacting with someone, that's what it was. He had few friends and worked forty-five miles from our house. Only once had I come to his office, and that was to bring him his briefcase, which he had forgotten. When I found him there he seemed glad to see me and the briefcase, but asked me to talk quietly, and I remember how we ended up speaking in whispers. I had already decided my husband didn't like the sound of the voice. He had been raised an only child by old, quiet parents, and couldn't help it, but this was the truth about him. Say I started speaking in the yard to a neighbor over the fence. My husband would come out on the porch and stare. If I was on the phone laughing, he would walk into the room with a funny look on his face. That's the way he was. To talk to someone all afternoon in the moist soil under the house meant my husband liked them. I wanted him to like someone.

So yesterday Paul descended from Virginia's other house in his full-leg cast. I leapt from my car and offered to help him in. "I've got it, Melissa," he said. "Thanks." Like an excellent chauffeur, I opened the passenger door for him. "So thanks for hopping to on such short notice," he said. "You're a trooper, and besides, I know you didn't have anything else to do today."

Of course, he really said something else, but I knew what he was thinking. Paul and Virginia ran a small ad firm. After we moved into their house and they found out that I had done some publicity work before, they offered me jobs from time to time. I never asked for them and I often wondered how they knew I was willing to do these jobs. I guess because I lived in Virginia's house I imagined they could see me rattling around inside it. So I spent one week coming up with names for a new organic shampoo that would be sold pyramid-style, by couples working their own neighborhoods like hungry coyotes. Then a couple months ago Paul and Virginia wangled the Brocco-rabi account, a fairly sizable one, I gathered, and I started taking on assignments regularly. There were press releases and so forth. And then this grand opening for Chucky came up. I'd been on the phone to all kinds of official people in Fresno for the past month. The actual event was now only a few weeks away. And yet even though I'd tagged along with Paul and Virginia on meetings with N & B, and attended all the planning for the commercial that would be made during the event with the video people, I couldn't help worrying that this might not be the best way to market Brocco-rabi. Get the kids excited by Brocco-rabi and they'll bug their mothers into buying it, that was the cornerstone of their strategy. They had created 3-D cartoon activity books all about Chucky with glasses to boot. They planned on bringing Chucky himself into the schools. But I already knew there was nothing lovable about Chucky Brocco-rabi. He wasn't funny. He had no personality. He couldn't even talk, that was the bottom line. A costume designer was preparing about a dozen of the mute green getups at this very moment. Paul and Virginia were spending a lot of N & B's money on this. Paul and Virginia had their own ad agency, but they didn't have any kids. How could they know?

As the two of us drove along the two-lane highway to Fresno, I thought of the movie I'd been watching that morning. Would one of us self-immolate on this trip? The hills were golden and so was the sky, filled as it was with crop dustings and smog and embers from a fire put out near Paso Robles only the day before. The wind had whipped that fire, then moved up here. It was whipping my car. "I hope Virginia doesn't wimp out on me," Paul said. "I mean, she's the most intelligent woman I know and yet she's utterly insecure. I need to help her get over it. Same problem destroyed my first marriage. I was off overseas all the time on high-security missions and so finally to make her feel competent I bought her a store."

"A store?" I said. "That was nice of you."

"Yeah, well, it didn't work. After a while she didn't think she could handle it."

"What kind of store was it?"

"Needlecraft, stuff like that. She was an expert at needlecraft."

"Just because she was a needlecraft expert doesn't mean she could run a needlecraft store," I offered.

"She lost her confidence. Tried to kill herself with knitting needles."

"Is that a joke?" I asked.

"If you think that's a joke you've got a strange sense of humor," Paul said.

There was something about Paul that bothered me, I decided.

"It's a tragedy when someone underestimates their talents. By the way, are you aware of how smart your son is?"

"Of course I am," I said. Will was smart, no doubt about it. He started reading when he was three, almost like spontaneous combustion. Pow! Suddenly he knew how. It definitely amazed me, and not only that, he could identify all the states by shape when he was only two. He had memorized them all on his own. I had been incredulous and grateful.

"I just hope you realize how smart he is. It would be terrible if you didn't." This irritated me for some reason so I didn't reply. I didn't need to. After all, I was driving and had to be vigilant because cars kept passing us. Not that I was going the bare speed limit; however, I found passing to be too fleeting a form of triumph to be useful to me. So I just kept on guard against other passers. Paul kept blabbing about the uncertain future of Will's intellect while I guarded our lives. The two and a half hours passed after a while.

The supermarket we had chosen for this event was on the outskirts of town, in a new suburban area full of cul-de-sacs and shopping centers that had only been in existence for fifteen to twenty years. The suburb still touched on original almond orchards, full of flowers in the springtime, as grey as ghosts by Thanksgiving.

We entered the store and inspected the produce department to make sure it was suitable as a backdrop for both the commercial and the event itself. And it was. It was actually an extraordinary produce section. Vegetables of every color and shape, fresh and waxy, filled enormous rough-hewn bins which were spotlighted from above. Automatic sprayers jetted over never-dehydrating greens in tiers along the mirrored walls. Paul and I nodded at each other with approval.

A quick talk with the produce manager assured us of his cooperation on the day of the event. "He's going to be a phenomenon," Paul bragged to the produce manager, showing him a blueprint of Chucky. "As big as the California Raisins, as big as Joe Camel. We've got a million-dollar budget just to play with. So if you display our product prominently, we can do all kinds of great things for you."

I started to feel sucked in. Paul's droning voice began to compel me to think I was on an important mission. I could tell I was beaming as the produce manager listened and was impressed. At last, completely satisfied, we took off for destination two, the suburban junior high.

"Good work," Paul said.

"Thanks. You too," I added.

At the junior high we met with the leader of the drill team. Two hundred girls were quickly promised to be at our disposal for the event. We would have them do a few routines, substituting Chucky's name for the name of their junior high. This drill team was the top-placing team in the state. We would make a generous contribution to their travel budget. Paul and the drill team leader fawned over each other as they closed the mutually beneficial deal. Then, as the drill team leader went on a little long about the special routines her special core squad could do, and the baton-twirling that could add to Chucky's luster, I could see the gulf of Paul's insincerity widening. I could tell he didn't like her. For some reason, this was something of a relief, after having to hear about how great Virginia was all morning.

We finished off in Fresno by visiting the Chamber of Commerce. There we picked up more endorsements for Chucky and the event. Promises of publicity and even the possibility of a cameo by the Mayor. The truth is, I love being included on other people's missions. This trip was lightening my spirits. As we walked out to my car we gave each other "five." Paul was bubbling.

"I'll actually spend a few dollars on you to thank you," Paul said. "Let's go over to the restaurant at the Hilton. Okay?"

"Great," I said. I looked at my watch. All that accomplished, and it was still only 3:00.

"Virginia's probably got Will by now," Paul mused.

"True," I said.

"That's nice. For Virginia. She really wants kids."

I parked in the underground garage under the Fresno Hilton. I helped Paul get out of the car and he limped beside me into the lobby. The restaurant was closed between lunch and dinner so we sat in the bar. Paul ordered an Irish Coffee, which sounded exactly right to me, so I ordered one too.

"This is good," I said, when it came.

"Want anything off the bar menu?"

"Umm, well, crab cakes sound good."

"Virginia will be incredibly psyched about all of this," Paul said. "It's all working out. Now all I need to do is contact that reporter from the *Bee* and then the radio station. You want to take care of that?"

"Sure," I said.

"And then I'll show Virginia the results and she'll think I did all the work, and she won't resent having to support me" seemed to be what he was thinking. "Miss, can we have a kettle of clam chowder, and an order of crab cakes?"

"You know," I said, "I think this is going to be a lot of fun. I think a lot of people are going to come. That was a great idea you had, about raffling the roller blades."

Paul nodded in complete agreement. "The main thing to remember, though, is that the commercial is the most important aspect of the event. So as long as the video people get all the shots they need, it doesn't matter if things don't go perfectly smooth. Doesn't that take a load off your mind?"

"You mean, since I'm the coordinator?"

"Right. Can I ask you a question, Melissa?"

"Okay."

"Do you think Virginia is attractive?"

I had thought he was going to ask me if I was a happy, fulfilled person—something that would put me on the spot but make me feel like I had an interesting secret. "Sure," I said sullenly.

"I mean, is she what another woman would call a beautiful woman?"

"Yes, I guess so," I said. I pictured Virginia. She was short and round and had hair like Liza Minelli's. I suppose you can say anyone is beautiful, really.

"Do you mind if I tell her you said that?"

"But it's not as if I said, 'Virginia's beautiful,' out of the blue."

"But you think so."

Who wanted to argue over something like that? "Yeah, sure, whatever."

Paul smiled at me. It was the first time I could remember him attempting to look pleasant for my benefit. Foolishly, I had looked forward to some new company today in the form of Paul. But try as I might, I didn't have a sense of us connecting.

The crab cakes came and at least they were good. Paul dipped into his clam kettle. "Chow down," he said.

"Yeah," I said.

"Did you know Virginia wanted to write a postcard to Letterman about Will?" Paul slurped. "Get him on the show."

"What?"

"That state thing. The way he bites Fig Newtons into the shapes of states? That's incredible."

I laughed. "He did that for you guys?"

"Virginia was in shock. I tell you, she's a little bit in love with your son. Who wouldn't be, he's a great kid. But the truth is, we've actually talked about taking care of him if anything ever happened to you and your husband. I mean, we'd go the whole way. We'd adopt him."

I looked at Paul quizzically. "You mean, if both of us died?"

"We're not going to adopt him if you're still alive, obviously."

"You mean you imagined us being dead?"

"All I'm saying is that we would like to volunteer to be the ones who would take care of Will if anything ever happened. That's all."

I slumped in my seat. What was bothering me? Then I had it. Never before had anyone discussed the possibility of my own death with me. It felt intimate and indifferent at the same time. As if the wind had stripped me of my clothes but not stopped to look. A real insult.

"Let me see. You and Virginia were sitting around one day, maybe talking about how nice it would be to have children, and then one of you said something like, 'That Will boy over at our rental is pretty nice,' and then the other one said, 'Maybe our tenants will die suddenly and we can have him'?"

"Of course not," Paul said. "Virginia and I put a lot of thought into this."

"And anyway, even if we did die, what makes you think we'd want you two? We have family and friends!"

"Forget I said anything."

"No, no, I'm glad you told me," I said. "Because, you know, the idea makes my blood curdle."

"Oh come on," Paul said. "You're overreacting!"

209

"Yes. It makes me feel really sick, like the crab cakes are trying to crawl out of my stomach."

"You're funny," Paul said, smiling the way he did at the drill team leader. "Virginia and I really appreciate that in your work."

I excused myself. I was in a huff. I wanted my husband to go pick up Will at Virginia's house right away. But at the office they told me he was already gone. When I called home, my husband answered and was really worked up. "What happened?" he shouted. "The school called me at work. At work! No one ever came to pick up Will. He was just sitting there in the school office a couple of hours!"

"Virginia didn't come get him? She forgot about him?"

"If I had been out of the office today, what would have happened? It took me an hour and a half to get there because of traffic, which I always avoid by leaving later."

I said, "You know what? It's just as well he wasn't there, and I'm not going to be working for Paul and Virginia anymore!"

"Why on earth would it be just as well?"

"I'm not going to be working for Paul and Virginia anymore," I said again. "Don't you want to hear why?"

"Someone better explain something," my husband said. "How would you like to be left at school? My mother never did that to me."

As we headed back to Aptos, the wind wrestled the car and the passers passed and the sun was going down right before our squinting eyes. Sometimes the road vanished into a dwarfed sunburst on the windshield, and Paul gasped and dug into the floor with his bad leg. I hoped his hair would turn white. For some reason, this driving was the easiest thing I'd done in a long time. Far be it from me to judge, but it was really starting to seem like you couldn't do anything with some people. Take, for example, people who thought you could sell a stenchful green vegetable by dressing it in a costume, and people who made love to their wives with their shoes on. I was surrounded by unthinking types. Last night I crawled out of bed as my husband slept, stretched out flat on the living room floor and closed my eyes. I imagined traveling to another place where I started over with nothing. I don't know why that scenario appealed to me so much, but it was the only thing I could think of that carried me through the night.

Nominated by Ron Tanner

RECORDED MESSAGE

by PHILIP DACEY

from THE DEATHBED PLAYBOY (Eastern Washington University Press)

"Your call is important to us.
Thank you for holding."
—Norwest Banks

Your call is important to us.
That is why, although we are not now answering,
we will, as soon as possible, answer,
provided you keep holding.
If you do not keep holding,
we assure you
we will not answer.

Your call is important to us
because you are holding,
because you are the kind of person who,
when asked to hold, keeps holding,
at least so far.
As difficult as it might be for you to believe,
not everyone holds.
Some stop holding even before we have finished
asking them to hold. Some, we are coming to suspect,
take special pleasure
in not holding.

Lest you begin to doubt us, remember
that if we did not intend to answer,
we would not let you hold,
as you will note we continue to do.
We thank you for holding.
We are thanking you now
so that later, should you have held
long enough for us to answer,
we needn't spend time
thanking you then
for having held.
We know your time is important to you,
as our time is important to us.
Unfortunately, we have none of our own right now
to answer you.

Finally, let us emphasize that
the importance to us of your call
is demonstrated by our
not answering
in this particular way.
In fact, this particular way of not answering—
when considered from the angle
from which we would like you
to consider it—
can be construed
as our way of answering.
We hope our answer, such as it is,
is as important to you
as your call is to us,
so important
that you are now ready
to hear it again.

Nominated by Collette Inez, Timothy Geiger

REGENERATION

fiction by PAULS TOUTONGHI

from BOSTON REVIEW

I‍F THE DEVIL WORE COLOGNE, the workers muttered, hacking into a stubborn flank, a thighbone.

Each of the seven dead elephants weighed close to five tons. This number, Hulbert understood, was an approximation. Whether it was slightly more or slightly less, though, he reflected as he dug at the dirt on either side of a dirty yellow tusk, didn't matter all that much. By now—gracelessly splayed at the back of its pen in the Berlin Zoo, its tusks sunk in the dirt, half of its carcass stripped of skin and sectioned into ten-pound packages of bone—the elephant did not care much about its self-image. *Too fat? Too thin? Too concave, too convex? And my trunk—too serpentine and scaly?* The elephant could rest; the elephant could cease from worrying.

—Maria, no. No. I'm too tired.
—You're all dust, Hully. I'm all dust. We need a bath.
—Maria, I—
—What? We'll lick each other clean.
—Maria—
—My name? An epiphany. My name. Lights, an angel, a repetition.

The asparagus can dig? this morning's supervisor had asked, his forehead drawn into a jumble of creases and folds. Then he'd sighed and extended a shovel. Among the prisoners of war—the large men with bony forearms and shaved heads—Hulbert was immensely foreign. But he did work for a single ration coupon. For flour, for bread, for soap. He was economical.

—Do they hurt?
—A little. Only when I touch them.

If the devil wore cologne, the workers muttered, hacking into a stubborn flank, a thighbone.

Hulbert Hecht leaned against the bone, the exposed ivory that was stained with rivulets of blood and the truculent, yellowish mud. Tiredness gathered in his muscles, in the arms that had been digging for hours, in the burning backs of his heels and his knees. Last night, lying on the tattered mattress that he shared with Maria, he had looked down at his legs in wonder. His knees were swollen as cabbages, almost luminous in the damp light of the cellar.

—Boy!
Hulbert flinched mid-motion. This meant him.

And she had kissed his mouth and his hairless, thin-ribbed chest. And now, standing in the swirling dust of the cold November day, wearing his only sweater—the sweater he wore every day to ramble around Berlin, to search for work among the clean-up crews—he had found a job repairing the wreckage of the zoo. And it stank, even though most of the bodies of the dead animals had been removed. Only the elephants remained—seven of them—and they had to be ponderously dissected, cut into manageable chunks, and carted off to the landfill.

—*Spargel!* Asparagus! Are you listening to me?
—Yes, sir.
—How is the tusk coming, Asparagus?
—Almost free of the ground, sir.
—Well, hurry up, hurry up. When you dig it clear I want you to saw it off. And then, I have a delivery for you to make. You think you can lift this tusk?
Hulbert looked at the thing, still solid in the jawbone of the beast. The prisoner closest to him laughed, briefly, a sound that skittered

into nothing as soon as it began, a muffled exclamation. The *Unteroffizier* spun around.

The elephant could rest. The asparagus can dig. Maria delivered notes to the wives of the executed men. The war widows. Soldiers, politicians, bureaucrats. Sometimes she whistled as she walked down the street; once she tripped over a dictionary. It was stained and torn, coverless, in the gutter. Had someone tried to burn it? What an odd book, she thought, lifting the heavy, wet paper. Mud on the first few pages. She picked a word at random. *Kompott*, she said aloud. Stewed fruit.

At the doorway to the first woman's house she paused. Didn't she remember this place from some other time?

—What? Are you laughing? Are you, *taube*?
Pigeon.
—No, sir. I . . . I . . . cough.
—Coughing?
He kicked the man hard, in the abdomen. Already weak from hunger, the prisoner curled over onto his side, his lips opening and closing, trying desperately to tongue the air into his chest.

Ruth Wagner gave him bread and lemon jam, dirty yellow, the color of dried moss. *Your beautiful mother*, Ruth said, *gave me lemon jam when I was sick. In my tea.* The light was almost texture, marbled in the panels of the dust. Hulbert coughed into the towel that Ruth held to his face, just short of his lips, a dishtowel. Crane-light, light like the neck of a crane, and she touched his light brown hair with two hesitant fingertips.

—They'll pick each other clean. Like animals. Like vultures.
She thought for a moment, brushing the bruises on his chest.
—No, Hully. We did the right thing. We were beautiful today.

Even this section of it was heavy. He felt it burrow into the plane of his shoulder. What address did he need? The dust was abrasive against his skin, his eyes. Unter den Linden. First left. South on Wilhelmstrasse. And then, a wound in the ground, great as some reptilian mouth, and there, in the half-dim, a pair of boots with the legs

215

still in them. No body, just legs. *But these are such good boots*, he thought, and sighed, continued walking. *What a shame to waste such good boots.* And the city was a sewer. It stank of shit and decay and corrupted flesh. He continued walking. Water pipes cut from a rubbled span of gravel, a citrine column of water cut through the grimy noon fog. If the devil wore the air, Hulbert thought, his body would be such sweet cologne.

Yesterday, Hulbert had seen the *Unteroffizier* execute a man in the wildebeest pen, shoot him in the head for eating raw meat off a carcass. Afterwards, Hulbert had heard the commander talking to the other officers; the man had to be shot, he'd said, because he had become sub-human. *Just imagine*—and here the Unteroffizier had raised his hands in the air and paused, looked quickly to the left and to the right, a conductor initiating the orchestra's responsive swell— *just imagine kneeling over the dead body, and chewing at the bloody, fatty flesh.* Zoofleisch. *Just imagine. It was, quite clearly, the sickness of his race, coming through under adversity. But still. . . . And we work so hard to educate them. Barbaric Slavs.*
Maria had kissed his mouth and his hairless, thin-ribbed chest. She remembered this even as she handed over the first of her letters, the first of the swastika-embossed envelopes. A small and brittle laughter at the memory, even as she released her hold on the paper, gave this woman—fat as a pickle, wrapped in a body-length lilac scarf—notification of her husband's death. The poor, obese, oblong woman—she'd smiled at the girl's hopeful face—and Maria felt guilty about this later, lying in bed, her knees swollen as cabbages.

—Wagner? No. It can't be. Ruth Wagner?
—That's what it says.
—Open it.
—To Ruth Wagner, registered post, hand-delivered, certified agent. That's me.
—They use the guillotine, you know.
—Bill for execution . . . the usual . . . Alfons Wagner, husband of Ruth.

Hulbert put his hand to his face, rubbed his forehead with the tips of his fingers. This was a gesture he had learned without noticing, somehow, and now—he dreamed it, the weariness on him like an overcoat, a fully inhabited second skin.

For flour, for bread, for soap. Soap was the best, but the rarest. No one had permission to take a bath, anyway, except the rumors of a few officers, once a week. The rumors were always the cleanest. Maria and Hulbert, of course, had no bathtub, no plumbing at all in this cellar where they'd squatted, where no one else had come in five weeks. The *Mietskasernen*, the rental barracks, had become a great emptiness, bare as the war itself. The spiders were their sole inhabitants.

Look, Maria said of one in particular, a wolf spider that was poised in the half-dark, a meter from their pillow. *It's listening. It wants to talk, Hulbert. Say something to it. It wants a conversation.*

—Cough now. You can cough now. Go on. I don't mind.

He turned to Hulbert. The prisoner he'd kicked was still writhing on the ground. The *Unteroffizier* unbuttoned his pistol's leather holster.

—But I need this quickly, *Spargel*, so hurry. You're the only one who can leave, as you can see. . . .

At the war's beginning, still only a child, he had crumpled into panic whenever he saw the black uniforms, the seamed wool trousers that tucked so neatly into the oversized boots. Now, he'd learned to negotiate their space, to say yes quickly, to leave as soon as he could. For some reason, these soldiers seemed to love children.

Ruth Wagner marked another day off on her calendar. It had been five months, now. She stood at her fourth-floor window, looked out over Berlin. What had been an awful view—the back of an appliance warehouse, red brick and a shadow of a fire escape—was now a panorama of rubble.

One chimney jutted from the wet ruin, solitary as a lamppost.

Ruth's building was the last on her block.

In the center of the street, a crater dug a five-meter pit in the concrete; in the crater's center was an overturned sofa—green and yellow, a noxious plaid.

Ruth stood at the window and rolled the pen between her palms.

She sighed and leaned forward against the glass, thinking of her husband.

—How old are we, Maria?
—Twelve, yesterday. Twelve, still, today.
The asparagus can dig?
—Who said that?

—Do they hurt?
The *Unteroffizier* had raised his hands in the air and paused, looked quickly to the left and to the right, a conductor initiating the orchestra of slaves.
—Do they feel it, you mean?
—Yes, sir.
—Of course, lieutenant, but not like us. Take that boy over there.
He pointed with his pistol, the barrel still warm.
—If I shot him, he would feel his life, his consciousness, slipping away. Even if for only an instant, he'd feel it. This corpse, he didn't feel a thing. Not like we would, not like that boy would.
And he'd seen Maria at the alley's end, walking, of all things, towards him. Seeing her face, her beautiful, luminous face, he began to run, to sprint, towards her. The heaviness on his shoulders—the section of tusk, thick and pearled and another knot, a new part of his chordate spine—dissipated, clattered against him easily, weightless as canvas or heat.

—How is the tusk coming, *Spargel*?
—Almost free of the ground, sir.

He sat on an older man's shoulder. A prisoner. Bony hands on his thighs, the hold of a skeletal structure. Hulbert sawed back and forth, curls of the ivory rising from the tusk's seam. It was a cold November day, and his own hands? They hurt as they wrapped around the blade of the saw. They were pink and moist, and they were sweating, making the handle damp.

Did the devil eat cabbages? He must eat cabbages, she thought, and stirred her broth—it was all bacon fat and celery. Ruth looked at her hands; they were sagging into wrinkles, the skin was beginning to hang off of her wrists, towards the tips of her fingers. The skin, once

218

clean and colored like a lump of putty, was now spotted and creased and stained. She stared at the steam from the boiling water and then she heard the knock at her door.

—What are you doing?
—No, what are *you* doing?

They kissed, a sudden collision. Maria wasn't sure if this was what they were supposed to do—this kiss upon seeing each other unexpectedly—but she felt the now-familiar press of Hulbert's lips and could think of nothing else. She touched his chin with her mouth, ran the flat of her tongue over the faint hairs that had only begun to accumulate there, beneath his lip. She held his shoulders in her hands and licked his eyes—they had closed now—tasted the salt of his skin, its sharpness.

—It can't be.
—It is. Look. Read it.
—Board per day: 1.50. Transport to Brandenburg Prison: 12.90. Execution of sentence: 158.18. Fee for death sentence: 300.00. There must be over five hundred marks here—
—474.84. Exactly. It's almost always the same.
—But we can't give this to her.
—It's a bill. She has to pay it—
—For her own husband's execution?
—Hully, it's my work. I'm lucky. Like this, at least we can eat.

The *Unteroffizier* had just shot another man. This one had been trying to escape. In the pucker of November cold, he licked the barrel of his pistol, felt its sear against his tongue. He always did this when he fired the Luger.

How beautiful, how the bodies steam, he thought, *after they die. This is truly a beautiful, and, of course, such a necessary, art.* He turned to his subordinate officer.

—Is that boy back yet? Has he delivered my tusk to Celeste?

Ruth walked to the door. She hated the door, wished it didn't exist. People were always leaving through doors—that's all they were good for—and Ruth hated people leaving. Once you lost someone you loved, who you truly loved, she realized, you never wanted to see another door again. Because there was always a last time, a last departure, a last aperture to traverse. She undid the latch with her spotted hands. Opening it slightly, she saw the space of nothing at eye level and then, at her ankles, leaning against the drawn-in frame. . . . What was it? Was it petrified wood? Was it a rock, a jagged rock, placed here as a joke? She leaned down to look.

—I have an idea, Hully.
He was sitting on the curb, drawing his hands back and forth through the dirty water of the gutter.
—What is it?
—Let's take your tusk. I know what we can do with it. I know where it should go.

Ruth put the tusk—unwieldly, heavy, caked with blood—in her fireplace. *Of all the things*, she thought, *of all the things to find on your doorstep.* She smiled. *And I didn't even know they shed.* Ruth brushed its texture with her hand. It was the first surface she'd touched in such a long time, she realized, that seemed like it actually was there.

If the devil wore cologne, the workers muttered.

The S-Bahn was bombed out again, so they had to walk. The dust from the city was horrific; it choked you, coated your clothes and face as soon as you left a building. Hulbert and Maria worked outside all day—by night, their lungs were sore and their faces webbed with dust. Near the *Meitkasernen*, in the park with a few last, swollen linden, Hulbert stepped on a nail. It went cleanly through his shoe and his skin, went deep into the flesh of his foot. He folded downward, crooked, off-balance.
—Maria.
They'd been walking for almost an hour. They were close to home. Everything around them looked like a photograph of itself, all granulate and shadow. He was crooked, off-balance; he began to topple.
—Maria.
And she was there, of course, her swollen knees and her tired, stiff body. And then she had his shoe in her hands and she was putting pressure on the dirty, bleeding skin. His foot was stitched with scabs

and raw abrasions and now, this solid puncture. The blood was oddly pale, colored like a mouth.

—Maria, it's not stopping.

His voice was thin. He was so tired.

—It's not stopping.

—Quiet, Hully, hush. It will stop.

She kissed his sweat-thickened hair. Behind her, the city was burning. The smoke was burgeoning upward, humming softly and rising, a kindling of marrow and of bone.

Nominated by Boston Review

MY DEAD DAD

by DAVID KIRBY

from THE SOUTHERN REVIEW

Our rue Albert apartment has this pre-Napoleonic water heater
      that lurches to life with a horripilating bang
when, for example, Barbara is taking a bath, as she is now,
      and every time she turns the handle for
more hot water, the heater hesitates a second, then ka-pow!

as though there's a little service technician sitting inside
      working a crossword, his elbows on his knees,
and suddenly he gets the more-hot-water signal and jumps up
      off his little dollhouse chair and runs down
the walkway and throws a shovelful of coal in the furnace

and then walks back, wiping his brow, only to have Barbara
      crank that faucet again, and thwack! he's off
and running while I'm sitting in our French living room
      reading *Journey to the End of Night* by Céline,
whose prose is sweaty and overheated in the first place,

and boom! there he goes once more, sprinting toward
      the furnace, and in the other room
Barbara is giving these little cries of either pleasure
      or surprise or both, as she often does
when bathing, and ba-boom! there he goes again.

I imagine him in neatly pressed khakis and a hat
          with a patent-leather brim,
like the gas-station attendants of my youth,
          and I wonder if he is not a relative of the equally little man
in the refrigerator whose job it was, according to my dad,

to turn the light on whenever anyone opened the
          door and off when they closed it
and who, in my child's mind, bore a striking resemblance
          to my dad not only in appearance
but also patience and love of word games and other nonsense.

And if there is such a little man in my French refrigerator
          and water heater and one
in my refrigerator and water heater back home,
          and if there are five billion of
us big people in the world, there must be twenty billion of them!

I think, like us, they'd have entertainments, such as
          circuses, barbecues, and *thés dansants*,
but also wars and horrible acts of cruelty!
          Though when peace returned, entire towns of
little people would finish the evening meal and then go on

the *passeggiata* the way the Italians do, the young flirting,
          the old sighing as they admire and envy the young,
the children and dogs getting mixed up in everybody's legs
          as they stroll and chat and ready themselves for
sleep as the clock in the little clock tower strikes eleven,

twelve, one, and the moon comes up—the moon! Which also
          has its little men, according to my dad,
though these are green and, to our eyes, largely invisible,
          since they live on the dark half,
though every once in a while they, too, become curious,

and a few will sneak over into the glary, sunlit side,
          so that when the moon is full, he said,
we should stare at it with every optical instrument at our

disposal, because if we do, we just might see
one of those little fellows nibbling the piece of cheese

he holds in one hand as he shields his eyes with the other
       and squints down at us. And I haven't even got
to the good little people who live inside each bad one
       of us, according to pop psychologists,
though I don't think my dead dad would have bought that one;

yet since the few people left who knew us both often say
       how much I remind them of him, then I think
if my dead dad lives anywhere at all, he lives inside me.
       Well, and my brother, too, if not
our mother, though there's nothing unusual about that,

because the older I get, the more widows I know, and
       none of them ever says anything about
her dead husband, suggesting perhaps these champions
       weren't so fabulous after all, at least
to them. Sad thought, isn't it, that these men should live

only in the minds of their children. Or maybe my dead dad's
       on the moon, since the alternate point
of view to my smug phenomenological one is that people
       go to heaven when they die,
and heaven's in the sky, and so's the moon,

so who's to say that's not my dead dad up there, his mouth
       full of Limburger or provolone,
shielding his eyes as he tries to find the house
       where we used to live, but he can't,
because it's been torn down, though he'd have no way

of knowing that, so he looks for my mother, and she's there,
       but she lives in a retirement community now,
and he can't believe how old she is, and he's shocked
       that she's as beautiful as he always knew
her to be, only she can't walk now, can't hear, can't see.

And he looks for my brother in Ohio, and he's there,
	and me in Florida, where he left me,
but I'm not in Florida anymore. Hey, Dad! Over here! It's France!
	No, France! Great country! Great cheese.
I wish I could take you in my pocket with me everywhere I go.

Nominated by The Southern Review, Philip Levine, Tony Hoagland,
David Baker, Edward Falco

OTHER PEOPLE'S SECRETS

memoir by PATRICIA HAMPL

from GRAYWOLF FORUM THREE: THE BUSINESS OF MEMORY (Graywolf Press)

THE RIVER IS STILL NOW. Nighttime, and I have come here to sit alone in the dark in the wooden boat under its canvas roof, to tally up, finally, those I have betrayed. Let me count the ways. Earlier, white herds of cloud, way up there and harmless, buffaloed across the sky. A beautiful day, and everyone, it seemed, was on the water.

But now the pleasure craft that tooled back and forth all day, plying the marina's no-wake zone, are gone. Only a flotilla of linked barges rides high and empty, headed downriver to Lock Number Two at Hastings, intent on the river's serious business. The massive lozenges look strangely sinister as they part the dark water. By day these barges seem benign—riverine trucks, floating grain or ore or gravel between Saint Paul and the great Elsewhere. But now they pass by spectrally, huge and soundless.

Spotlights from the county jail send wavering columns of moon-colored light across the water from that side of the river to the marina on this side. I once saw a woman, standing on the Wabasha Bridge, lean as far over the guardrail as she could, and blow kisses toward the jail while traffic rushed around her. I followed her gaze and saw a raised arm clad in a blue shirt, indistinct and ghostly, motioning back from a darkened window. The loyal body, reaching even beyond bars to keep its pledge.

The boat groans in its slip, the lines that hold it fast strain as they absorb the wake from the barges. Boat, dock, ropes rub companion-

226

ably against each other, sending out contented squeaks and low, re-assuring moans that sound as if they're saying exactly what they mean—*tethered, tethered.*

This is the location in-between, not solid land, not high seas. Just a boat bobbing under a covered slip, the old city of my life laid out before me—the cathedral where my parents were married, the great oxidized bulb of its dome looking like a Jules Verne spaceship landed on the highest hill of the Saint Paul bluffs; on the near shore of Raspberry Island, an elderly Hmong immigrant casting late into the night for carp poisoned by PCBs; and downtown, in the middle distance, the bronze statue of the homeboy, F. Scott Fitzgerald, a topcoat flung over his arm even in summer, all alone at this hour in Rice Park, across from the sane neoclassical gray of the public library where it all began for me. "You'll like this place," my mother said, holding my hand as we entered—impossible luck!—a building full of books.

Let's start with mother, then, first betrayal.

It was all right to be a writer. In fact, it was much too grand, a dizzy height far above the likes of us. "Have you thought about being a librarian instead, darling?" At least I should get my teaching certificate, "to fall back on," she said, as if teaching were a kind of fainting couch that would catch me when I swooned from writing. But I knew I mustn't take an education course of any kind. Some canny instinct told me it is dangerous to be too practical in this life. I read nineteenth-century novels and Romantic poetry for four years, and left the university unscathed by any skill, ready to begin what, already, I called "my work."

I knocked around a jumble of jobs for ten years, working on the copy desk of the Saint Paul newspaper, recording oral histories in nursing homes around town—Jewish, Catholic, Presbyterian. I edited a magazine for the local public radio station. I lived in a rural commune on nothing at all, eating spaghetti and parsley with others as poetry-besotted as I, squealing like the city girl I was when a field mouse scurried across the farmhouse floor. I went to graduate school for two years—two more years of reading poetry. A decade of this and that.

Then, when I was thirty-two, my first book was accepted for publication, a collection of poems. My mother was ecstatic. She wrote in her calendar for that June day—practically crowing—"First Book Accepted!!" as if she were signing a contract of her own, one which committed her to overseeing an imaginary multiple-book deal she had negotiated with the future on my behalf. She asked to see the manuscript out of sheer delight and pride. My first reader.

And here began my career of betrayal. The opening poem in the manuscript, called "Mother/Daughter Dance" was agreeably imagistic, the predictable struggle of the suffocated daughter and the protean mother padded with nicely opaque figurative language. No problem. Only at the end, rising to a crescendo of impacted meaning, had the poem, seemingly of its own volition, reached out of its complacent obscurity to filch a plain and serviceable fact—my mother's epilepsy. There it was, the grand mal seizure as the finishing touch, a personal fact that morphed into a symbol, opening the poem, I knew, wide, wide, wide.

"You cannot publish that poem," she said on the telephone, not, for once, my stage mother egging me on. The voice of the betrayed, I heard for the first time, is not sad. It is coldly outraged.

"Why not?" I said with brazen innocence.

Just who did I think I was?

A writer, of course. We get to do this—tell secrets and get away with it. It's called, in book reviews and graduate seminars, courage. *She displays remarkable courage in exploring the family's. . . . the book is sustained by his exemplary courage in revealing. . . .*

I am trying now to remember if I cared about her feelings at all. I know I did not approve of the secrecy in which for years she had wrapped the dark jewel of her condition. I did not feel she *deserved* to be so upset about something that should be seen in purely practical terms. I hated—feared, really—the freight she loaded on the idea of epilepsy, her belief that she would lose her job if anyone "found out," her baleful stories of people having to cross the border into Iowa to get married because "not so long ago" Minnesota refused to issue marriage licenses to epileptics. The idea of Iowa being "across the border" was itself absurd.

She had always said she was a feminist before there was feminism, but where was that buoyant *Our Bodies, Ourselves* spirit? Vanished. When it came to epilepsy, something darkly medieval had bewitched her, making it impossible to appeal to her usually wry common sense. I rebelled against her shivery horror of seizures, although her own had been successfully controlled by medication for years. It was all, as I told her, no big deal. Couldn't she see that?

Stony silence.

She was outraged by my betrayal. I was furious at her theatrical se-

228

crecy. Would you feel this way, I asked sensibly, if you had diabetes?

"This isn't diabetes," she said darkly, the rich unction of her shame refusing my hygienic approach.

Even as we faced off, I felt obscurely how thin my reasonableness was. The gravitas of her disgrace infuriated me partly because it had such natural force. I was a reed easily snapped in the fierce gale of her shame. I sensed obliquely that her loyalty to her secret bespoke a firmer grasp of the world than my poems could imagine. But poetry was everything! That I knew. Her ferocious secrecy made me feel foolish, a lightweight, but for no reason I could articulate. Perhaps I had, as yet, no secret of my own to guard, no humiliation against which I measured myself and the cruelly dispassionate world with its casual, intrusive gaze.

I tried, of course, to make *her* feel foolish. It was ridiculous, I said, to think anyone would fire her for a medical condition—especially her employer, a progressive liberal-arts college where she worked in the library. "You don't know people," she said, her dignified mistrust subtly trumping my credulous open-air policy.

This was tougher than I had expected. I changed tactics. Nobody even reads poetry, I assured her shamelessly. You have nothing to worry about.

She dismissed this pandering. "You have no right," she said simply.

It is pointless to claim your First Amendment rights with your mother. My arguments proved to be no argument at all, and she was impervious to any blandishment.

Then, when things looked lost, I was visited by a strange inspiration.

I simply reversed field. I told her that if she wanted, I would cut the poem from the book. I paused, let this magnanimous gesture sink in. "You think it over," I said. "I'll do whatever you want. But Mother . . ."

"What?" she asked, wary, full of misgivings as well she might have been.

"One thing," I said, the soul of an aluminum-siding salesman rising within me, "I just want you to know—before you make your decision—it really is the best poem in the book." Click.

This was not, after all, an inspiration. It was a gamble. And although it was largely unconscious, still, there was calculation to it. She loved to play the horses. And I was my mother's daughter; instinctively I put my money on a winner. The next morning she called

229

and told me I could publish the poem. "It's a good poem," she said, echoing my own self-promoting point. Her voice was rinsed of outrage, a little weary but without resentment.

Describe it as I saw it then: she had read the poem, and like God in His heaven, she saw that it was good. I didn't pause to think she was doing me a favor, that she might be making a terrible sacrifice. This was good for her, I told myself with the satisfied righteousness of a nurse entering a terrified patient's room armed with long needles and body restraints. The wicked witch of secrecy had been vanquished. I hadn't simply won (although that was delicious). I had liberated my mother, unlocked her from the prison of the dank secret where she had been cruelly chained for so long.

I felt heroic in a low-grade literary sort of way. I understood that poetry—my poem!—had performed this liberating deed. My mother had been unable to speak. I had spoken for her. It had been hard for both of us. But this was the whole point of literature, its deepest good, this voicing of the unspoken, the forbidden. And look at the prize we won with our struggle—for doesn't the truth, as John, the beloved apostle promised, set you free?

· · ·

Memory is such a cheat and privacy such a dodging chimera that between the two of them—literature's goalposts—the match is bound to turn into a brawl. Kafka's famous solution to the conundrum of personal and public rights—burn the papers!—lies, as his work does, at the conflicted heart of twentieth-century writing, drenched as it is in the testimony of personal memory and political mayhem.

Max Brod, the friend entrusted to do the burning, was the first to make the point in his own defense, which has been taken up by others ever since: Aside from the unconscionable loss to the world if he had destroyed the letters and the journals with their stories and unfinished novels, Brod, as his good friend Kafka well knew, was a man incapable of burning a single syllable. Kafka asked someone to destroy his work whom he could be sure would never do so. No one seriously accuses Brod of betraying a dying friend. Or rather, no one wishes to think about the choice in ethical terms because who would wish he had lit the match?

But one person did obey. Dora Diamant, Kafka's final and certainly truest love, was also asked to destroy his papers. She burned

230

what she could, without hesitation. She took Kafka at his word—and he was alive to see her fulfill his command. She was never wife or widow, and did not retain any rights over the matter after Kafka's death, but even Brod, Kafka's literary executor, felt it necessary to treat her diplomatically, as late as 1930, and to present his case to her when he set about publishing the work.

As she wrote to Brod during this period when they tried to come to an understanding about publication of Kafka's work:

> The world at large does not have to know about Franz. He is nobody else's business because, well, because nobody could possibly understand him. I regarded it—and I think I still do so now—as wholly out of the question for anyone ever to understand Franz, or to get even an inkling of what he was about unless one knew him personally. All efforts to understand him were hopeless unless he himself made them possible by the look in his eyes or the touch of his hand. . . .

Hers is the austere, even haughty claim of privacy, a jealous right, perhaps. She knew it: "I am only now beginning to understand . . . the fear of having to share him with others." This, she freely admits to Brod, is "very petty." She does not claim that her willingness to destroy the work was a wholly noble act. She is surprisingly without moral posturing.

Still, she could not bear to give the world those works she had not destroyed. As Ernst Pawel says in *Nightmare of Reason: A Life of Franz Kafka*, she denied that she had them until after her marriage to a prominent German Communist when their house was raided by the Gestapo in 1933 and every piece of paper, including all the Kafka material, was confiscated, never to be located to this day. She was, finally, distraught, and as Pawel says, "confessed her folly" to Brod.

Pawel, an acute and sensitive reader of Kafka and his relationships, puzzles over this willful act of secrecy. "The sentiment or sentimentality that moved this otherwise recklessly truthful woman to persist in her lie," he writes, clearly perplexed, ". . . may somehow be touching, but it led to a tragic loss."

Yes—but. The lie Dora Diamont persisted in was a simple one—her refusal to admit to Kafka's editors or friends that she still possessed any of his papers. But her letter to Brod (written three years

231

before the Gestapo raid) is not the document of a woman who is simply "sentimental." She is adamantly antiliterary. The papers she refused to hand over—and which, terrible irony, were swept away by the Gestapo into that other kind of silence, the wretched midcentury abyss—were, no doubt quite literally to her, private documents. After all, most of Kafka's works were written in—or as—journals. There is no more private kind of writing. The journal teeters on the edge of literature. It plays the game of having its cake and eating it too: writing which is not meant to be read.

The objects Kafka asked Dora Diamant to destroy and those she later refused to hand over to editors did not have the clear identity of "professional writing" or of "literature." They were works from a master of prose writing, but they were still journals and letters. They must have seemed, to the woman who had lived with them, intensely personal documents. If it is understood even between lovers that a journal is "private," off limits, not to be read, it doesn't seem quite so outrageous that Dora Diamant, who loved the man, would choose to honor his privacy as she did. In fact, it is not a mystery at all, but quite in keeping with her character as a "recklessly truthful woman."

Privacy and expression are two embattled religions. And while the god of privacy reigns in the vast air of silence, expression worships a divinity who is sovereign in the tabernacle of literature. Privacy, by definition, keeps its reasons to itself and can hardly be expected to borrow the weapons of expression—language and literature—to defend itself. To understand the impulse of privacy that persists against every assault, as Dora Diamant's did, her position must not call forth the condescension of seeing her adamant refusal as being merely "touching."

In her 1930 letter to Brod, Dora Diamant is trying to express what she maintains—against the institutional weight and historical force of literature—is a greater truth than the truth that exists in Kafka's papers. She is determined to remain loyal to his appalling absence and to the ineffable wonder of his being, "the look in his eyes", "the touch of his hand."

This is not sentimentality. She speaks from a harsh passion for accuracy—nothing but his very being is good enough to stand as his truth. Literature at best is a delusion. It is the intruder, the falsifier. She makes an even more radical claim—it is unnecessary: "The world at large does not have to know about Franz." Why? Because their "knowing" (possible only through the work now that he is dead) is doomed to be incomplete and therefore inaccurate. A lie, in other words. In her terms, it is a bigger lie, no doubt, than her refusal to admit to those eager editors that she did indeed have the goods stashed away in her apartment.

No writer could possibly agree with her. Except Kafka, of course. But maybe Kafka wasn't "a writer." It may be necessary to call him a prophet. In any case, Dora Diamant wasn't a writer. She belonged to the other religion, not the one of words, but the human one of intimacy, of hands that touch and eyes that look. The one that knows we die, and bears silently the grief of this extinction, refusing the vainglorious comfort of literature's claim of immortality, declining Shakespeare's offer:

> So long as men can breathe or eyes can see,
> So long lives this, and this gives life to thee.

The ancient religions all have injunctions against speaking the name of God. Truth, they know, rests in silence. As Dora Diamant, unarmed against the august priests of literature who surrounded her, also knew in her loneliness: what happens in the dark of human intimacy is holy, and belongs to silence. It is not, as we writers say, material.

• • •

There is no betrayal, as there is no love, like the first one. But then, I hadn't betrayed my mother—I had saved her. I freed her from silence, from secrecy, from the benighted attitudes that had caused her such anguish, and from the historical suppression of women's voices—and so on and so forth. If Dora Diamant was someone who didn't believe in literature, I was one who believed in nothing else.

This defining moment: I must have been about twelve, not older. A spring day, certainly in May because the windows, and even the heavy doors at Saint Luke's School are open. Fresh air is gusting through the building like a nimble thief, roller shades slapping against windows from the draft, classroom doors banging shut. The classrooms are festooned with flowers, mostly drooping masses of lilac stuck in coffee cans and mason jars, placed at the bare feet of

233

the plaster Virgin who has a niche in every classroom: *Ave, ave, Ma-ree-ee-ah*, our Queen of the May.

For some reason we, our whole class, are standing in the corridor. We are waiting—to go into the auditorium, to go out on the playground, some everyday thing like that. We are formed in two lines and we are supposed to be silent. We are talking, of course, but in low murmurs, and Sister doesn't mind. She is smiling. Nothing is happening, nothing at all. We are just waiting for the next ordinary moment to blossom forth.

Out of this vacancy, I am struck by a blow: *I must commemorate all this.* I know it is just my mind, but it doesn't feel like a thought. It is a command. It feels odd, and it feels good, buoyant. Sister is there in her heavy black drapery, also the spring breeze rocketing down the dark corridor, and the classroom doorway we are standing by, where, inside, lilacs are shriveling at the bare feet of Mary. Or maybe it is a voice that strikes me, Tommy Howe hissing to—I forget to whom, "OK, OK, lemme go."

These things matter—Tommy's voice, Sister smiling in her black, the ricochet of the wind, the lilacs collapsing—because I am here to take them in.

That was all. It was everything.

I have asked myself many times about that oddly adult word—*commemorate*—which rainbows over the whole gauzy instant. I'm sure that was the word, that in fact this word was the whole galvanizing point of the experience because I remember thinking even at the time that it was a weird word for a child—me—to use. It was an elderly word, not mine. But I grabbed it and held on. Perhaps only a Catholic child of the 1950s would be at home with such a conception. We "commemorated" just about everything. The year was crosshatched with significance—saints' feast days, holy days, Lent with its Friday fasts and Stations of the Cross. We prayed for the dead, we prayed *to* the dead.

How alive it all was. Commemoration was the badge of living we pinned on all that happened. Our great pulsing religion didn't just hold us fast in its claws. It sent us coursing through the day, the week, the month and season, companioned by meaning. To honor the moment, living or dead, was what "to commemorate" meant. This, I sensed for the first time, was what writers did. Of course, being a Catholic girl, I was already sniffing for my vocation. Sister was

234

smiling, her garments billowing with the spring wind, and here was "the call," secular perhaps, but surely a voice out of the whirlwind.

• • •

The sense of the fundamental goodness of the commemorative act made it difficult to believe "commemoration" could be harmful. Beyond this essential goodness I perceived in the act of writing, I felt what I was up to was a kind of radiance, a dazzling shining-forth of experience. I never liked the notion that writers "celebrated" life— that was a notion too close to boosterism and the covering-over of life I thought writers were expressly commissioned to examine. But who could be hurt by being honored—or simply noticed? Who could object to that?

A lot of people, it turned out. My mother was only the first. "You can use me," a friend once said, "just don't abuse me." But who, exactly, makes that distinction?

"You're not going to *use* this, are you?" someone else asked after confiding in me. She regarded me suddenly with horror, as if she had strayed into a remake of *Invasion of the Body Snatchers* where she played a real human who has just discovered I'm one of *them*.

Later, I strayed into a scary movie myself. I'd become friendly one year with a visiting writer from one of the small, indistinct countries "behind the Iron Curtain," as we used to say. It was a year of romantic upheaval for me—for her too. God knows what I told her. We met for coffee now and again, and regaled each other with wry stories from our absurdist lives. Then she went back where she had come from.

A year later I received in the mail a book in a language completely unknown to me. When I saw her name on the cover I realized this was the book she had been writing in Minnesota. "Just wanted you to have my little American book!" the cheery note said. An American publisher was interested in releasing an English translation, she added. I flipped through the incomprehensible pages. Suddenly, two hideous words cleared the alphabet soup with terrible eloquence: *Patricia Hampl.* Then I saw, with increasing alarm, that my name— me!—popped up like a ghoulish gargoyle throughout the text, doing, saying, I knew not what.

"I don't think you'll be too upset," someone who could read the incomprehensible language told me, but declined to translate. "It's a little sticky," she said vaguely. Sticky?

Later still, at a workshop with a Famous Novelist, I raised my hand and posed the question. "You've said in interviews that your fiction is autobiographical," I began, notebook ready to take down his good counsel. "I'm wondering what advice you might have on writing about family or close friends?"

"Fuck 'em," he said. And I shivered the body-snatcher shiver. So you *do* have to become one of them?

Over the years, as other books followed my first, I told the story of how I had spoken for my mother who could not speak for herself. I had all my ducks lined up in a row—my belief in the radiance of the commemorative act, my honorable willingness to let my mother decide the fate of the poem, her plucky decision to let me publish the poem, which at first she had seen as a cruel invasion but which—the real miracle—she came to recognize was nothing less than a liberation for her. She and I, together, had broken an evil silence. See what literature can do?

Then one day I got a call from a poet who was writing a piece about "personal writing." She had been in an audience where I had told my mother-daughter story. There had been many; by this time I had my patter down. It was a wonderful story, she said. Could she use it in her essay as an example of . . . ?

The words "wonderful story" hung above me like an accusation. The blah-blah-blah of it all came back and stood before me, too contemptuous even to slap me in the face. I felt abashed. I told her I wanted to check the story first with my mother.

She answered the phone on the first ring. She was still working, still at her library job. *Remember that poem in my first book,* I said, *the one that has the seizure in it and you and me?*

Oh yes.

Remember how I told you I wouldn't publish it if you didn't want me to, and you said I could go ahead?

Yes.

Well, I was just wondering. Is that something you're glad about? I mean, do you feel the poem sort of got things out in the open and sort of relieved your mind, or—I sounded like a nervous teenager, not the Visiting Writer who had edified dozens of writing workshops with this exemplary tale—*or . . .*

What *was* the or? What was the alternative?
Or did you just do it because you loved me?
Without pausing a beat: *Because I love you.*
Then the pause: *I always hated it.*

• • •

Bobbing again on the water in the old boat, still in-between. A nightly ritual, but now, as if on cue for the climax, lightning has begun to knife the sky, and thunder has started its drumrolls. Hot summer night, waiting to break open the heat, and spill.

No wonder I like to come down here, to this floating place. I was attracted too to the in-between position of the writer. More exactly, I was after the suspended state that comes with the act of writing: not happy, not sad; uncertain of the next turn, yet not lost; here, but really *there*, the there of an unmapped geography which, nonetheless, was truly home—and paradisal.

The elusive pleasure to be found in writing (and only *in* it, not the *before* of anticipation, not the *after* of accomplishment) is in following the drift, inkling your way toward meaning. My old hero, Whitman, that rogue flaneur, knew all about it: "I am afoot with my vision!" he exulted. It was an *ars poetica* I too could sign up for, basking in the sublime congruence of consciousness "afoot" in the floating world.

There are, it is true, memoirists who are not magnetized by memory. They simply "have a story to tell." They have the goods on someone—mother, father, even themselves in an earlier life, or on history itself. "Something" has happened to them. These stories—of incest or abuse, of extraordinary accomplishment or exceptional hardship, the testimonies of those who have witnessed the hellfire of history or the anguish of unusually trying childhoods—are what are sometimes thought of as the real or best occasions of autobiography.

Memory, in this view, is a minion of experience. It has a tale to tell. Its job is to witness the real or to reveal the hidden. Sometimes the impulse to write these accounts is transparently self-serving or self-dramatizing. But at least as often, and certainly more valiantly, this is the necessary literature of witness. Historic truth rests on such testimony. The authority of these personal documents is so profound, so incriminating, that whole arsenals of hatred have been arrayed in mad argument for half a century in a vain attempt to deny the truth of a little girl's diary. These kinds of memoir count for a lot. Sometimes they are the only history we can ever hope to get.

Still, memory is not, fundamentally, a repository. If it were, no question would arise about its accuracy, no argument would be fought over its notorious imprecision. The privacy of individual experience is not a right as Dora Diamant tried to argue with Max Brod, or as my mother begged me to see. Not a right, but something greater—it is an inevitability that returns no matter what invasion seems to overtake it. This privacy is bred of memory's intimacy with the idiosyncrasy of the imagination. What memory "sees," it must regard through the image-making faculty of mind. The parallel lines of memory and imagination cross finally, and collide in narrative. The casualty is the dead body of privacy lying smashed on the track.

Strangely enough, contemporary memoir, all the rage today as it practically shoves the novel off the book-review pages, has its roots not in fiction, which it appears to mimic and tease, but in poetry. The chaotic lyric impulse, not the smooth drive of plot, is the engine of memory. Flashes of half-forgotten moments flare up from their recesses: the ember red tip of a Marlboro at night on a dock, summer of 1954, the lake still as soup, or a patch of a remembered song unhinged from its narrative moorings—*Glow little glow worm, glimmer, glimmer*, and don't forget the skinned knuckle—Dad's!—turning a dead ignition on a twenty-below winter day. Shards glinting in the dust.

These are the materials of memoir, details that refuse to stay buried, that demand habitation. Their spark of meaning spreads into a wildfire of narrative. They may be domesticated into a story, but the passion that begat them as images belongs to the wild night of poetry. It is the humble detail, as that arch memorialist Nabokov understood, which commands memory to speak: "Caress the detail," he advised, "the divine detail." And in so doing, he implicitly suggested, the world—the one lost forever—comes streaming back. Alive, ghostly real.

Kafka called himself "a memory come alive." His fellow townsman, Rilke, also believed that memory, not "experience," claims the sovereign position in the imagination. How strange that Kafka and Rilke, these two giants who preside as the hieratic figures, respectively, of The Writer and The Poet for the modern age, were both

238

Prague boys, born barely eight years apart, timid sons of rigid fathers, believers in the word, prophets of the catastrophe that was to swallow their world whole, and change literature forever. Canaries sent down into the mine of history, singing till the end.

In *Letters to a Young Poet*, the little book it is probably safe to say every young poet reads at some point, Rilke wrote to a boy who was a student at the very military academy where he himself had been so notoriously miserable. He wrote, no doubt, to his younger self as well as to this otherwise unknown student poet Franz Zaver Kappus. Although the boy was only nineteen, Rilke sent him not forward into experience, but deeply inward to memory as the greatest "treasure" available to a writer.

"Even if you found yourself in some prison," Rilke says in the first letter, "whose walls let in none of the world's sounds—wouldn't you still have your childhood, that jewel beyond all price, that treasure house of memories?"

This is not an invitation to nostalgia—Rilke had been painfully unhappy as a boy, stifled and frightened. He was not a sentimentalist of childhood. He is directing the young poet, rather, to the old religion of commemoration in whose rituals the glory of consciousness presides. He believes, as I cannot help believing as well, in the communion of perception where experience does not fade to a deathly pale, but lives evergreen, the imagination taking on the lost life, even a whole world, bringing it to the only place it can live again, reviving it in the pools and freshets of language.

• • •

I have gone to visit my mother. She is in the hospital, has been there now many weeks. "It's hell to get old," she says, barely-voiced words escaping from the trach tube from which she breathes. Almost blind, but still eager to get back to her e-mail at home. She smiles from her great charm, a beatific smile, when I say "e-mail," when I say "home." There is a feeding tube in her stomach. There was a stroke, then her old nemesis, a seizure, a heart attack, respiratory this, pulmonary that—all the things that can go wrong, all the things that have their high-tech solutions. She is surrounded by beeps and gurgles, hums and hisses. She'll get home. She's a fighter. At the moment, fighting her way out of the thick ether of weeks of sedative medicines.

239

She is glad I have come. She has been, she tells me, in a coffin at Willwersheid's Mortuary. Terrible experience, very confining.

I tell her she has not been in a coffin, I assure her she has not been at a funeral parlor. I tell her the name of the hospital where she is.

She looks at me as at a fool, not bothering to conceal her contempt. Then the astonishing firmness that kept me in line for years: *I have been in a coffin. Don't tell me I have not been in a coffin*.

Well, I say, you're not in a coffin now, are you?

No, she says, agreeing with vast relief, *thank God for that*.

The trip, she says animatedly, trying to express the marvel of it all, has been simply *amazing*. Shipboard life is wonderful. Skirting Cuba—that was beautiful. But the best part? The most beautiful, wonderful black woman—a real lady—came to her cabin with fresh linens. The ironing smelled so good! That was what made Port au Prince especially nice. People everywhere, she says, have been so lovely.

Why not? It's better than the coffin at Willwersheid's. Then, the air, saturated by weeks of medication, suddenly clears, and we're talking sensibly about people we know, about politics—she knows who's running for governor, and she wouldn't vote for Norm Coleman if he were the last man on earth. We see eye-to-eye. She asks about my father, she asks about my work—our usual subjects.

"Actually," I say, "I'm writing about you. Sort of."

She's in a wheelchair, the portable oxygen strapped to the back. We have wheeled down to the visitors' lounge and are looking out the big picture window that has a view of the capitol building and the cathedral, and even a slender curve of the Mississippi in the distance where I will go when I leave here, to sit again to brood in the little boat under the canvas slip. She can make out the capitol and the cathedral. Storms grizzle the sky with lightning, and her good eye widens with interest.

I say I am trying to tell the story again of the poem about the seizure. "I'm trying to explain it from your point of view," I say.

She nods, takes this in. "Yes," she says slowly, thoughtfully. "That's good you're doing that finally. It's very important to . . . to my career." Her smile, the great rainbow that the nurses have remarked on, beams in my direction, the wild sky behind us, flashing.

Her career. Yes. Her own passage through this life, the shape she too has made of things, her visions, the things she alone knows. The terrible narrowness of a coffin and the marvels of Port au Prince, the astonishing kindness of people, the pleasure of sweet-smelling linen. I can see now that she was standing up for the truth of her experience, the literal fact of it, how it jerked and twisted not only her body but her life, how it truly *seized* her. My poem and I—we merely fingered the thing, casually displaying it for the idle passerby. What she knows and how she knows it must not be taken from her.

I never understood the fury my desire to commemorate brought down upon me. The sense of betrayal—when I thought I was just saying what I saw, drawn into utterance, I truly believed, by the buoyancy of loving life, all its strange particles. I didn't have a dark story of abuse to purvey or even a horde of delicious gossip. I was just taking pictures, I thought. But then, doesn't the "primitive" instinct know that the camera steals the soul? My own name skittering down the pages of a foreign book, sending alarms down my spine. The truth is: to be written about feels creepy. The constraining suit of words rarely fits. Writers—and readers—believe in the fiction of telling a true story. But the living subject knows it as the work of a culprit.

Years ago, when I was living in the poetry commune, eating spaghetti and parsley, I had a dream I knew would stay with me. A keeper, as my father says of fish. I was behind the wheel of a Buick, a big improbable Dad car I couldn't imagine driving in real life. I was steering with my eyes shut, traveling the streets of my girlhood— Linwood, Lexington, Oxford, even Snelling with its whizzing truck traffic. It was terrifying. I understood I must not open my eyes. And I must not turn the wheel over to the man sitting beside me in the passenger seat although he had his eyes wide open. If I wanted to reach my destination (murky, undefined), I must keep driving blind. My companion kept screaming, "You'll kill us all!"

I've lost quite a few people along the way. And not to death. I lose them to writing. The one who accused me of appropriating her life, the one who said he was appalled, the poet miffed by my description of his shoes, the dear elderly priest who said he thought I understood the meaning of a private conversation, this one, that one. Gone, gone. Their fading faces haven't faded at all, just receded, turned abruptly away from me, as is their right.

I have the letters somewhere, stuffed in a file drawer I never open. The long letters, trying to give me a chance to explain myself, the terse ones, cutting me off for good. The range of tone it is possible for the betrayed to employ—the outrage, the disgust, the wounded astonishment, the quiet dismay, the cold dismissal. Some of them close friends, some barely known, only encountered. All of them "used," one way or another, except for the baffling case of the one who wrote to complain because I had *not* included her.

Mother and I are safe inside, staring out the big hospital window as our city gets lost in sheets of gray. "Is it raining?" she asks. The storm is a wild one, bending old trees on Summit Avenue, snapping them easily, taking up clots of sod as they go down. At the river the boat must be banging against the dock.

My mind scrolls up again the furious swirl of repeating phrases in those letters from people who no longer speak to me. And me, surprised every time. *I cannot believe that you would think . . . Maybe it seemed that way to you, but I . . .*

But I'm getting too close again, hovering at their sides where they don't want me, trying to take down the dialogue. Better not. Leave the letters in their proud silence. No quotes, no names. Or else, someone, in a dream or elsewhere, is likely to rise up in fury, charging with the oracular voice of the righteous dead that I've killed again.

Nominated by Joyce Carol Oates, Michael Collier

THE IMPOSSIBILITY OF LANGUAGE

by BETH ANN FENNELLY

from TRIQUARTERLY

1.

"Blackberries," says one, rolling it in the barrel
of the mouth. "Yes," says the other, "oak."
"Well aged, aroma of truffles," adds the third.
They nod. Roll it and roll it, the way God
must have packed the earth in his palms.
Discuss the legs of it running down the glass.
They bring the valley into it. And color: "The light
staining the glass at Sainte Chapelle." Back to taste:
"Earthy. A finish of clove." They leave nodding—
such faith in the opaque bottles of their words.

2. How I Became a Nature Lover

Suppose I said, "Honeysuckle,"
meaning stickysweet stamen,
the hidden core you taught me,
a city girl, to find. How I crave
the moment I coax it from calyx,
tongue under the bulbed tip
of glistening stalk, like an altar boy
raising the salver under blessed bread

243

the long Sundays of my girlhood,
suppose my tongue caught that mystery
the   single   swollen   drop
                    O
               honey-
               suckle

The irony of metaphor:
you are closest to something
when naming what it's not.

3.

1934: Imagine Mandelstam, who loved
words too much, with his poet friends,
how they passed the bottle of slivovic.
"Osip," they pleaded, "chitáy, chitáy."
And so he did read about Stalin,
"the Kremlin mountaineer," with "laughing
cockroaches on his top lip," who rolled
"executions on his tongue like berries."
How could Mandelstam have known
one man fisting the table in laughter
would quote the poem to the mountaineer?

Think of Mandelstam in winter: the water
freezes in the water jug. In summer:
the prison mattress shimmies lice.
But Nadezhda visits him. They do not speak
of hope or love or death. He recites his poems
in a whisper that she memorizes. Even in his cell,
"this shoe-size in earth with bars around it,"
as long as he has lips, he has a weapon.

Imagine how much each word weighs
on Nadezhda's tongue. She bears
them home like eggs in that time of no eggs.
She nests them deep inside the secret book.
He dies, committed to her memory.

4.

"I ask you to cinema, coffee, wine,
        you say me, 'no.' You gave my heart
the fire, and now you give me the heart
        burn. Why, when eyes of you
are sympathetic like some fox?"
        We speak barest when we barely
speak—love letters from the foreigner
        before the invention of cliché.

Teaching immigrants English,
        I gave them crayons to draw families,
taught them words for each brown,
        orange, tan face. Guillermo's page
was blank. "I am alonesome," he wrote.

5.

Meaning? Language can so not.

The government releases
films of nuclear testing
from the fifties.
A plane bellies over
an atoll in the Pacific.
It drops a bomb.
The camera,
at a "safe distance"
some dozen islands away,
flips over. The sky
falls. The narrator surmises,
"at this juncture
of maturation,
premature impactaction
necessitates further study."
The mushroom cloud
is a balloon caption
for which earth can't
find words.

6.

Is the ear bereft if an alphabet dies
that it has never heard?

> *The latest extinction of language*
> *occurred last month with the death*
> *of the lone speaker of Northern Pomo,*
> *a woman in her eighties.*

Are we weaker without the word
in Northern Pomo for begonia?
Does the inner hammer numbly
strike its drum? Does it grow dumb
mourning sounds that it will never hear?

7. Unfinished Poems

rise
from trashcans
sewers & pulp mills
& bind themselves under
elaborate covers
for the endless library
of the unborn
who climb mahogany
ladders to finger
thick volumes
& with vague lips
sound out what's there
& what's not

8.

Synonyms are lies. Answer the question
with *stones* or *rocks*:

Q. When Virginia Woolf, on the banks
of the Ouse, walked into the water,

swallowing her words, with what objects
had she loaded the pockets of her dress?

A. *Stones. Rocks* is wrong, as in
"She took her life for granite."

9. The Myth of Translation

Try a simple sentence: "I am hungover."
For Japanese, "I suffer the two-day dizzies."
In Czech, "The monkeys swing inside my head."
Italians say, "Today, I'm out of tune."
Languages aren't codes that correspond—
in Arabic, there's no word for "hungover."

Does the Innuit woman, kept on ice all winter,
sucking fat from ducks for her hunter's leggings,
not divine the boredom her language doesn't name?
Or would the word's birth crack the ice for miles,
drowning the hunter who crouches with a spear
beside the ice hole for the bearded seal? She sucks
the fat slowly, careful not to quill her throat
with feathers. She grows heavy. It is, as it was
from the beginning, a question of knowledge.
If she bites into the word, she'll be alonesome.

Nominated by TriQuarterly

WOMEN'S PANTOMIME

fiction by BEN MARCUS

from BOMB

THE FIRST OBSTACLE to excellence in women's pantomime is the surplus of small bones in the face, feet, hands, and body. True mime is best done from a near boneless approach, when the flesh can "rubberdog" various facial and postural styles. The kind of mime most often produced by men with a full set of bones (a "stack"), is stiff and lumbering, hardly believable as an imitation of real behavior. There are simply too many non-pliable bones in the body to allow for the covert shapes and postures that lead to useful emotion purges. A woman who tries to mime away her excess emotions while operating with a full stack of bones will find little success. Only a "short stack" mime style can effectively contribute to the quiet heart.

The chief way to determine the gratuitous bone content in the female head (shabble) is to tap its surface with a facial mallet over an extended period of a month or more, using a mallet style more like *worrying* than actual smashing. Worrying the same area of the head with the mallet will eventually break down the excess bone matter, much of which is at the back or crown of the head, and it will pass naturally from the body, through the tears or saliva or sweat. Any bones that can be shed this way are not important to the life of the body, but are a disposable shell that simply needs to be cracked free and passed.

A small-boned woman who can add at least seven pounds of pure facial weight, without increasing mass to the rest of her body, would not need to remove any bones from her head. The added flesh would be sufficient for even the most elastic of mimes, including the "pancake" and the "puddle" styles. The best way to fatten the face through spot gaining is probably to drink cream at the rate of a gallon a day. Another option is a fat transfer, from a richer area of the body like the thighs or hips. With the fat transfer, the fat is brusquely massaged up the torso, into the head, then tied off with a tourniquet about the neck until the fat "catches" and takes root in the cheeks and around the eyes.

Barring these difficult methods, which only work with the small women, every woman can safely achieve a short stack of bone content by sacrificing several pounds of small bones in the hands and feet, two rib bones, some gratuitous material on and near the spine (flak), the knee caps, and parts of both shoulder blades. The bones, once broken, dislodged, and pulverized, can most safely leave the body from a bone exit zone introduced near the sternum.

Other bone removals are riskier, but the rewards of mime adaptability are all the greater. Removing a portion of the jawbone allows a woman to perform the "hammerhead" mime, good for quieting nearly all of the emotions, but envy in particular. Boneless hands can be pulled into excellent shadow shapes and silhouettes, enabling the "chicken" and the "waterfall." The armless mimes of Geraldine include the "weather vane" and the "elephant," not to mention the "sleeveless John Henry." Since all teeth but the front two are disposable, their removal allows for inner mouth and foreign language mimes that are widely effective with conditions of empathy and awe.

Given this rather dire recommendation for such an excess of self-surgery, it should be cheering to hear that the disposable bones, once broken and dislodged, don't always have to be removed from the body; they can be migrated under the skin to the belly area, or pushed around into the excess flesh of the buttocks, where they will keep for months, provided the buttocks are regularly massaged and soaked in water. Restoring the bones to their original locations is easy; they can be shuttled through the skin until they arrive at the home area, then a body vice, a so-called Restorer, might be layered underneath a denim body suit for a week or so, until the bones have rooted down again and returned to their former function.

What Do I Do with the Bones after I Remove Them?
If enough hardened bone remains after removal, a behavior whistle, or body flute, should be carved. Music played through an instrument derived from a woman's own body will tend to calm her feelings,

pacify the various rages of the day, and offer a sense of collapsed time, which aids in decreasing attachments and affection for persons or things. The songs from the body flute may also be effective in halting the motion of others, or causing them to sleep or cry or harm themselves, depending on the tune that's played.

Animal Mimes

It is only natural that miming an animal (slumming) would produce an internal animal state of reduced feelings. Most persons, including women, regularly slum an animal without knowing they are doing so. A basic zoological catalog of actions, such as the *Behavior Bible*, can be followed by the miming woman (the quiet Gladys) looking to cool down the intensity of her feelings, and these animal actions can more or less be subtly integrated into daily life, appended to the so-called human behavior a woman exhibits, so that basic tasks like walking, swimming, reading, and speaking can be augmented with various animal behaviors; stamping the feet, mewling, scratching, bucking, kicking, lumbering, hissing, skulking in the grass. It will be for each woman to determine which animals offer the behavior models she most needs to eliminate or conceal. There are so many animals in the world now, and the history of behavior has become so vast, that a woman should have no trouble finding a creature that corresponds to her emotion surplus (fiend quotient), but the search for an appropriate animal should very likely begin on the American farm.

My animal mime practice centered on a creature known as the horse. The horse postures, stances, and attitudes I pursued—the trot, gallop, canter, feeding from a bag, shaking my "mane," rearing up with my "hoofs" when I was introduced to people—including an intricate program of neighing, whinnying and snorting, which I deployed orally at every opportunity, until I had successfully and legibly integrated bursts of these noises into my everyday speech so that I appeared merely to be loudly clearing my throat—these horse intrusions required so much attention from me that the result, at the end of the day, was inevitably to leech me of every active feeling I was aware of and thus clean my rioting heart down to the simplest, pumping thing. Indeed perhaps the chief effect of miming an animal is a kind of deep exhaustion not possible otherwise. Just looking at an animal is tiring. Pretending to be one can be fatal.

My earliest memories of my father involve his dog mimes, then later a "wolf" act that became indistinguishable from his real behavior, a kind of addition to his fatherhood that kept him out of doors, knocking about in the yard, hard to please. During his dog phase, in the mornings at our Ohio home, he prowled outside my bedroom door and growled and scratched and barked, sending up moans and howls and threatening sounds, sometimes gnashing his mouth as though he were tearing at a piece of meat. Indeed he often pretended he was eating me. If I went to the door, still cautious and confused from sleep, to determine what was the ruckus, I'd only hear him scamper away and discover in his place nothing but scratch marks and slobber and a strange odor, along with a hard, dark nugget of waste. Upon my return to bed, he'd be back at it, barking his hard, father's bark and pawing at my door, throwing himself into it, whining.

My mother's animal of choice appeared to be a creature I could only fathom to be another woman, very much older, probably her own mother, who was stooped and sad and sometimes aimless. It was a quiet mime with only the subtlest style, the most refined behavioral imitation I've ever observed, entailing long days of stillness by the window, elegant use of her hands to hide her face, and a deep expulsion of sighs that bordered on language but lacked, always, the requisite shape of the mouth to carve the air into words.

Is There Anything I Should Not Pretend to Do?
Miming an emotion is the most dangerous gestural pretense, for obvious reasons. If an emotional condition is unintentionally mimed, such as weeping, laughing, wincing in fright, doubting, even when done as a joke, as though to suggest: "wouldn't it be funny if I actually felt something?" the only real antidote can be an extended performance of the "Nothing Mime," a stationary pose held outdoors for a full day, which requires a woman to do exactly nothing until the mimed emotions begin to subside. The danger of a mimed emotion is that there is very little difference, if any, between pretending to feel something and actually feeling it; in some cases the pretense is even stronger, the imitation cuts deeper and lasts longer. Thus the Nothing Mime, conducted in any weather and deployed with the use of a full-body mood-mitten, which registers a woman's emotional activity on its surface, is prescribed.

The Thrust Mime
The gestures of intercourse (stitching), when undertaken without another body or prop, are useful in purging feelings of confusion and

doubt. If I do not believe I can accomplish a task, performing the thrust mime, an extended stitch and volley, tends to erase my doubt and send me back into my life with renewed commitment.

My common stitch occurs with a wide-stance against a waist-high table, one arm crossed behind my back for balance, the other leaning on the table (military push-up style). On the count of three, I begin to thrust, a slow pace at first, smooth and solid, with a striding tilt to my hips, as though I were probing a stiff pudding. I drive deep with arched back and clenched buttocks. At the full thrust position, I "flurry" with short, fast strokes, then pull back and "go long," slowing the thrust almost to a stop and drawing all the way back (the seesaw); intermittently, I withdraw and hold a long pause, then "nozzle" at the threshold, which involves rising up and down on my toes (also called Peeking in the Window), before returning to the basic thrust and flurry rhythm, the parry, the dodge, the throw. This style also works over a staircase, though both arms are used for support (the civilian). When practiced against a wall, a shoulder can be relied on for pivoting, with both arms clasped behind the back (the gentleman). People will naturally have to discover an authentic thrust mime for themselves, based upon the primary gesture that brings about release. They may also employ a Bump coach, if their budget permits it. If the act of thrusting is not the chief sexual gesture, then the mime should be changed accordingly. Knitting and pecking are other useful intercourse paradigms. I have seen women perform the elegant "fade-away jumper" mime, the elaborate "sauté," the arched mime of "hula hoop," and the "rise and shine," a somberly grave sexual style that always saddens me, and I suspect these actions were based on sexual experiences, given the gentle facial tremors I observed and the strained gestures of concentration. There are probably thousands of different ways to mime human intercourse—to stitch the air with one's hips—not to mention the many animal styles that also have their uses, yet a woman should not be discouraged if her intercourse mode is different or unusual to witness, if it requires a complicated and new physical presentation that might frighten other people who could mistake her stitch for a seizure or rough sleeping. A deceitful, conservative stitch is helpful to no one, nor will anyone be fooled. More and more women, during moments of doubt and confusion, will be pausing in their daily affairs to briefly mime a personalized moment of intercourse, however strenuous and interruptive it might first seem, and thus recover their courage to move about in the world.

The Good-bye Mime

The good-bye mime is probably the most therapeutic behavioral imitation available, yet the very notion of therapy involves a promise of relief, which itself is one of the more stubborn American feelings, and not to be succumbed to, so this form of fake behavior should be treated carefully. If too much "comfort" is derived from performing the good-bye mime, it should be discontinued. In short, the good-bye mime involves constructing non-flesh "enemies" who can be "killed" through mime weaponry, strangling, drowning, and other means decided by the woman "waving" good-bye. The kill function, as a general behavior in this world, is not available to very many women without legal consequence, yet a certain *love reduction* can probably only be accomplished through the mimed slaughter of persons orbiting the woman's life, especially those doing so to an excessive degree, the fathers, the brothers, the so-called lovers, the strangers. A non-flesh duplicate of these enemies, or mannequin equivalents, can be aggressively mistreated by a woman at will—stabbed, shot, punched, and pummeled—and the result is an outrush of attachment sensations (friendliness), which can be the most resistant to emotion flushing. The good-bye mime should be executed at a private "kill site," where vocalizations may be freely released and a wide cache of weaponry is available. A woman should kill her fathers, brothers, friends, and relevant strangers in this way whenever the *trap of devotion* begins to feel too real.

In turn, the suicide mime (carpenter), done when a woman's personal shame volume (PSV) has become overly loud in her body and threatens to produce undesirable acts of contrition and apology, is a useful self-killing mime that, if performed frequently enough and with great gusto, can accelerate the zero heart attempt. In my experience the suicide mime must be "arpeggiated" to work well. I must rapidly fake many suicides, through gunshot, hanging, and knife wounds, miming the actual death moment each time. Women might prefer to "shakespeare" the death moment and draw it out over a full day, while others may find that "cartooning" it is more effective for shame reduction.

253

Equipment

The very notion of women's pantomime is to conduct a life without things, so equipment itself becomes a paradox, and with one or two exceptions should be refused in favor of a pure mime life that could occur anywhere in the world without alteration. Although some women prefer to wear the full-body mood mitten and the empathic storm sock throughout all of their daily activities, I view this choice of attire as an arrogant display of reduced emotions, somewhat too preening and boastful, insulting to those persons who still are addicted to expression and emoting.

Yet one important device is indispensable to the frontier of women's mime, and that is the body-correction full-length glass, the "Translator," which serves as a window in front of the miming woman and distorts her actions in various ways: it "janes" her to make her seem more friendly, it "males" her or ages her, it delays her gestures and plays them back later, for behavior festivals, and it creates a mirror template of refined women's actions, for her to model her body after when she is practicing her behaviors.

Would it hurt if You Mimed your Father?

Miming a member of one's own family (ambush) can create an interesting behavior-minus that can nearly last forever, particularly if the family can work as a team to mime each other's behavior (a figure eight), doing so in real time throughout their daily lives, swapping roles during those hard hours between sleep sessions. A camouflage mime occurs when several family members suddenly mime a single person (bullseye), as when parents mime their son, for instance, and do not relent or admit that they are doing so; this is also called over-miming, or "love," and can cause a very durable behavior-minus in the boy whose behavior is being imitated, particularly if he goes by the name "Ben Marcus." The over-mime absolves the boy from being himself, given that his behavior is so well covered in the actions of others. He can watch his parents acting as he would, imitating him, until his head and heart become so quiet and small that quite possibly no one in the world can see him, and he can make his exit from all visible life without report.

Nominated by Bomb, Diane Williams

SSSHH

by SHARON OLDS

from THE AMERICAN POETRY REVIEW

There was someone asleep in the next room,
so my lips were pressed closed, what was happening seemed
to be happening through me, almost not to me,
though in me, but to our species, or through it
to some other, as if I were a message conveyor,
a flesh Morse, which did not even
seem to be sending love, but, within the
certainty of love, to be sending the pure
specifications of the womb, blue
and vase-shaped, or the duration and strength
of its pulses, as if that swallowing throat
could appear, now, were appearing, now,
in some other world. I lay along him,
home, as if I lay face-down on an
uncrushable garden, sweet odor
and whisker of earth. Where does it come from
when it rises again, using you to the
perimeters, the air around the scalp, making
you testify, agony-mouthed—you hold
hard to the beloved as if that will save you,
it saves you, you come to, on the solid
sea of that body, it lifts you up
and down, you ride its long swell.
And then the pure joy comes,
the sheerest bliss—as if the first had been
conception; the second, birth; now

you are a living being made of this.
And now, it may be, the open eyes,
and the sight of the corner of that eye, that shape
of loving gaze, brings it on,
and now the hour of the bestial masks
seen. I feel his seeing of them drive
its tremors through his hardness, now hands and body
and face dance. You may be smiling while the gnarlings
cross your smile with their diagonal distorts,
then kissing, while the waves pass through
and crinkle head and mouth. The last
minutes—I almost want to draw
a curtain around them, as if they are
invisible, or seeing would warp
the ripple of the kissings and crossings
so it could not be said. Perhaps the end
is unspeakable,
but here where we have come, past doubt,
through into love in the face of death,
I did not cry out as it approached, I looked
and looked at him, as if calm, a direct
fearless look, straight from the cunt,
a look that is the cunt looking
through the eye, the soul looking through the cunt through the
eye in love as coming travels
stately wrenching through, like a message
sent by matter, through us, to spirit,
but who is there to hear it, only
the lovers, and now, in the paper whisper,
ssshh, ssshh.

Nominated by Len Roberts, Diane Williams, Robert Phillips

I DRIVE YOU
FROM MY HEART

by JANA HARRIS

from ONTARIO REVIEW

Frances Stanton, Snake River Crossing, Cottonwood, Idaho 1889

With thorn bushes,
with a flailing razor strop,
I drive you from my heart,
throw rocks at you,
throw gravel shards
at your two burnt matchstick
eyelid slits. The black
coachwhip snake
of your smile I hatchet
with a dull carving knife;
with the sharpest pick
pummel your bloodless cyanide
peach pit heart. With knitting
needles, nails, I drive you
from every cell of memory.
I stab slivers through
the bridge of your nose,
your brow's overhang,
then hammer down
your high-peaked cheek bones.
From my body I purge

you like the crabs
of cancer, like a heavy
affliction of the lungs, like
misery in my joints.
I drive you, drive you
from my heart.

Scarecrow, scarecrow,
I infect the straws of you
with scorpions. Armies
of stinging ants march you
from my thoughts. Your silent
secretive glacial soul I drive
away from me. Your once seraph
face turns to cabbage,
a common worm-eaten
scalped head-of-a-cabbage.
I bruise your ears
with gunpowder screams.
I drive you, drive you out.

I see you sleeping under houses,
see your scarred dog face snarling up.
I put the feral dog you are
in a river skiff come unmoored
in an ice floe when flood waters
hide the rocks, watch you trudge
to shore, legs bleeding as you
labor through hip-deep snow,
face shining with hoarfrost.
I hold furnace slag
to the frayed seams
of the clothes I made for you,
to the rags that are your hair.
The pitiful fire you become
empties my heart of you.
I throw your bones into the rain-
soaked street, make you
no different than mud, throw
your ashes to the Nor'easters so

no part of you will have another
for companionship. My hands,
arms, my clothes covered
with grit, the soot of you
thick on me.

When I am bathed
and empty of you, I sweep
you into the corner
of an unheated room,
bury tintypes of you
in a trunk under the bed where
your onyx eyes pale
from mold never again
to glare at me as if to spit.
With your face
driven into history, I finally,
finally free the river
of the mire of you,

and cross over.

Nominated by Joyce Carol Oates, Ontario Review

BERNA'S PLACE

fiction by JANE McCAFFERTY

from WITNESS

Mᴀ HUSBAND AND I worked together so that the house would be presentable for our only son and his new girlfriend. "It's serious, this time," our son had told me. "I think I've found my life." Life, he said, not wife. But really, he'd found the whole package.

Jude, my husband, was a newly retired art professor, and an artist—working in oil and acrylic—and over the years our entire house had turned into a studio. We had paint thinner on the back of our toilet, smocks on the railing, art magazines piled into the corners of the dining room. I told myself this was inevitable: how could a man like Jude be contained in one room? Even the front porch had been conquered by his old cans, the dried brushes piled in a heap below the swing, the scrappy canvases he never seemed to move out to the curb for the trash collectors leaning against the wall by the door. (I'd given up.) In his art he was somewhat successful; the best galleries in Philadelphia had shown his work, and Jude was gratified by a number of fellow artists who seemed to think he was some kind of genius. Articles in the 1970s about his early neo-Expressionism said as much. Though he'd never admit it, and often made the joke that he was a has-been that never was, I knew Jude *needed* to think he was a genius. In his heart he still wrestled with that tiresome affliction that most men trade in for a kind of reluctant humility by the time they turn fifty. Jude, at sixty-four, was still going strong, sometimes painting all night long in the attic, Billie Holiday or Bach for company, a view of the skyline out the window.

He was also very kind. He knew when I was tired from a day at work, where I sat behind a counter in a crowded hospital trying to help exasperated, sometimes furious people figure out their health care insurance. When I was mopping the floor to prepare the house for our son and his girlfriend, Jude climbed out of the cave of his work and told me to go take a nap. He'd clean, he said, his eyes still glazed with his art. And I knew he'd apply the same fierce, concentrated energy to housework as he did to his painting. The place would shine.

My son rang the doorbell that evening at dusk; I was struck by that since usually he burst through the door with no warning. I was used to him raiding the refrigerator as if he were still in high school. This night was different, though. This was the night we were to meet his girlfriend.

I was the one to answer. There they stood in the dusk, my handsome son in his maroon sweater and ponytail, a twenty-five-year-old young man who liked his dog, reading, Buddhist meditation, and hiking, and beside him, holding his hand, stood his girlfriend, as he'd been calling her, despite the fact that she was, at least compared to him, old. Sixty, I'd soon learn. Sixty. Nine years my senior. She wore a beige raincoat, and moccasins. She was very tall, with high cheekbones and lank, dark hair parted on the side, and my first thought was that she looked like my pediatrician from childhood, a woman who'd visited my home when I'd had German measles. The resemblance was so uncanny that for a moment I thought it was her, Doctor Vera Martin! I was almost ready to embrace her, for she had impressed me deeply as a child, with a sense of authority that seemed rooted both in her eloquent silences and the sudden warmth that transformed her serious face when she finally smiled. My son's friend smiled and the resemblance only deepened.

"Hi!" I said, and stared at this woman who I knew could not be my childhood doctor, who was, in fact, long dead. So who was she? Not his girlfriend. Not really.

"Invite us in, Ma," said my son, and I could see he was enjoying my shock. "This is Berna, Ma. Berna, this is Marian, my ma."

Berna reached out to shake my hand. Her eyes were dark and warm. As she opened her coat I saw her sweatshirt was covered with decals of cats.

"I wasn't able to dress appropriately," she said. "I'm coming from work. You'll pardon me, I hope?"

"Work?"

"She's a vet," my son jumped in, beaming at her. He was more animated than I'd seen him in years. "She makes house-calls. A traveling vet. I went with her today. She's excellent. Harry (that was his dog) loved her. That's how we met. She's the only traveling vet in town." He took a deep breath, he seemed filled with a kind of desperate, nervous excitement—so different from his usual taut calm.

"A traveling vet," I said. "Well well. That's something. Please come in, sit down."

The two of them followed me into the living room. I felt I was dreaming. Berna sat down. She made no noise as she sat. No little groan of pleasure. No sigh. She sat with her long back as straight as the poised tails of the cats on her sweatshirt, her eyes and the eyes of the cats too alert so that I felt like a small crowd was quietly assessing me. Griffin sat beside her, and held her hand, and suddenly I asked him if I could speak to him in the kitchen. I felt toyed with, and wanted him to know.

"Why didn't you mention she was old enough to be your grandmother?" I hadn't meant to hiss at him. In the kitchen light his brown eyes widened.

"What's your problem?" he said. "Did you turn into Dad or something?"

"Griffin, this is ridiculous! Don't act like you're not enjoying the shock value of this! She looks like my childhood pediatrician, who was old then, and dead now!"

He scrunched up his face in a sort of disgusted confusion. All the composure I'd seen for the past two years, composure that had struck me as false, had left him. I knew his palms were sweating. I felt for him, but it struck me as comical, his expecting me to take this in stride.

"I want to marry this woman," he said. "I want to marry her. This has nothing to do with your childhood doctor, or shock value." I saw he was deadly serious. So, I thought, this is how his strangeness has found itself a home. Let's hope it's temporary, a pit stop.

Berna appeared in the doorway, a tall, long-limbed sixty in a cheap, baggy cat sweatshirt that somehow was dignified enough on her.

"Look," she said. "Let's be up front here, shall we? Let's get it all out on the table. Go ahead and tell me what's pressing in on you: I'm old enough to be his mother."

"Grandmother," I said.

"Grandmother then," Berna said, with a kind of pride that lifted her chin. "Though I'd have to have given birth at an awfully young age to make that a true statement." Her voice was soft and steady with confidence.

"I've finally brought Berna here because she's the first woman I've really loved. That needs to be known and digested."

"That's what you're telling her?" I said to him, remembering a string of girls named Cindy, and the three Jens, two of whom I'd become quite friendly with.

"I told her because it's true, Ma. OK? Now it's all out in the open. You want a beer, Bern?"

"Sure," said Bern.

And I heard my husband coming down the steps. Here we go, I thought.

My husband and son never got along. I used to blame Jude—he'd been so absent during Griffin's childhood, so self-absorbed, and my son had been born, it seemed, awestruck by his father. Terrible combination. In those early years we lived out in the country and Jude painted in a large shed; Griffin was like a dog, waiting too patiently for the master to finally notice him and play. The more absorbed his father was, the keener Griffin's need became; Jude claimed there was something manipulative in this, but my heart broke for my child, and I think I rightly feared his very soul was being shaped by the intensity of his longing. Maybe that can be said of all children.

I'd beg Jude to give the boy a little attention, and he did, but it was the wrong kind. He'd take Griffin to the art museum. He'd try to make him memorize paintings, learn perspective, listen to facts about the artists. Griffin tried his best, and told Jude he wanted to walk into Pierre Bonnard's paintings and live there, but you shouldn't do this with a seven-year-old unless the kid is oddly brilliant, a prodigy, which Griffin never was, and I know this disappointed his father, and I know, also, that his father blamed my genes. I come from a long line of Midwestern farmers. If I said any big words in my mother's presence, she cocked her eyebrow, which meant for me to get down off my damn high horse. Intelligence was a force to be tamed into utility.

After years of rejection, Griffin finally gave up. He was twelve, then. He got a dog for his birthday that year. It seemed to me that all his love for his father got transferred onto the dog, a mutt from the

263

shelter Griff named Roberto, for the great ballplayer Roberto Clemente. Roberto was a bit mangy and looked heartsick, but loved Griffin the way dogs love boys. A simple solution, I thought. Roberto went everywhere with Griffin—they even let that dog into the grocery store. Things were easier for Griffin after that. He became a teenager who said very little to either of us. In high school he found an enormous friend named Jack J. Pree, who wore thick glasses, and who managed to attract certain girls despite his obesity. Jack lived with his aunt and uncle, drove a monstrous, ancient gold Buick, called himself *the fatso existentialist* and called Griff *Brother Soul*. It was the sort of mythology Griff needed. Brother Soul and The Fatso Existentialist spent days just driving around with aging Roberto hanging out the window, the three of them listening to old blues and new punk. Nights they read philosophy books aloud, or had water balloon fights in Jack J. Pree's tiny hedged backyard, which was five doors down from us. Through a hole in the bushes, I spied on them. I loved my son, and I'd become a spy in his life.

Jude walked into the kitchen that evening, and I saw, for a moment, how handsome he was, which still happened when I was aware that someone else would be looking at him for the first time. Griffin, Berna and I had taken seats at the oak table by the glass wall that looked out onto a little patio. Berna had first stood at the window and admired that space. "Lovely," she'd said.

"Hey Griffin," Jude said, and looked at Berna. "Where's your girlfriend?"

Berna got up from the table.

"Hello," she said. "I'm Berna Kateson." She walked over and shook his hand. She was nearly as tall as Jude.

Griffin watched them with utmost seriousness, waiting for his father to do something wrong.

"Griffin and I have been together for quite a while now, so we thought it was time to meet you," Berna said, again with her distinct, almost imperceptible chin-raising pride.

"Uh huh," said my husband. "I see." He shot a look at Griffin, then his eyes settled on my own, and I looked down, away from him, so that he was stranded in his shock. Berna sat back down.

"I realize this isn't a typical scenario," she said. "I realize one might feel a little baffled when faced with the possibility of their son marrying an older woman, even a very successful one."

Jude opened the refrigerator and pulled out a bottle of wine, poured himself a glass, and sat down with us at the table.

"So," he said to Berna, and looked at her with coldly urgent eyes. "Why don't you tell us about yourself. About your success."

"That seems a kind of power-play question," Berna said. "So maybe I should ask it to you. Why don't you tell me about yourself? Your success?" She smiled back at him, without malice.

I could feel Griffin loving this. Her simple composure must have seemed like real bravery to him.

"Well," said my husband, "I'm sure Griffin here has told you all about me. I'm sure it's been a stellar father-son relationship report. It was all little league and fishing trips with Griff and me."

Berna laughed, generously, I thought. Jude squinted his eyes at her, then looked at me as if to say, are we dreaming?

"We're both wiped out, actually," said Griffin. "We had a day that was hard on the heart, didn't we, Bern? I mean, we should tell the story of our day and put things in perspective, right? Rather than spend more time on this petty American bullshit?"

Whenever Griffin didn't like something he called it American. This had been his habit for years.

"We had to put two cats down, and tell a dog owner that his dog had one week of life left," Berna said. "Nobody took this well. We became on-the-spot grief counselors, which isn't unusual." She massaged her temples. She stuck her limp dark hair behind her ears.

"We?" said my husband. "Did my son go to veterinary school since I last saw him? Or is he simply Granny's sidekick now?"

"He's studying to be an assistant," Berna said. "I'm sorry you're obsessed with age, but I'd have been foolish not to expect it."

Berna sipped her beer. Then a great burst of laughter escaped from her mouth. Very, very odd. A shocking contrast to her whole bearing, which was elegant reserve.

"Excuse me," she said, as if she'd burped. Her eyes flashed, widening; her lips suppressed a smile.

"Can we go into the other room where it's more comfortable?" I said, as if we would all turn into different people if our chairs were softer.

"So anyhow," Berna said, almost as soon as we sat down, "Griffin is gifted, utterly gifted with animals. By that I mean he's not only got the brains to be a vet, he's got the heart. He's already on his way to being a certified assistant, but I think that's just the beginning."

Jude sat with his arms crossed in a high-backed green chair, his eyes peering over his glasses. I sat on the couch on one side of Berna, and Griffin sat very close to her on the other side. I was really hoping they didn't do anything like kiss. Griffin had been known to kiss his other girlfriends quite blatantly, with a kind of hostile showmanship in our presence.

"It's easy to find a brain," Berna continued. "And it's easy to find a heart. I've had a whole string of assistants that were all heart. Near disasters, I have to say. The last gal, Peggy, who I thought might be good since she looked exactly like a horse—so often the ones who most resemble animals are good—I know, that's odd—but anyhow, every time we had to go to someone's house and put their pet down, she'd gallop out of the room and sob. The person losing the animal they'd loved for twenty years would be quietly welling up with tears, and then they'd stop, too concerned with Peggy's sobbing to even feel their own sorrow."

"So what happened to Peggy?" I said. I imagined her grazing in a field, chewing on hay. "Did she find another profession?"

"Peggy's all right," Berna said. "Peggy has a job in a bank now. She needs numbers. Numbers don't die."

Jude sighed. It was the sigh that said he wasn't getting enough attention.

"Before Peggy it was Michael Bent. Michael Bent turned out to be a bit of a Nazi. I suppose that's irresponsible of me, using that term when he really did nothing at all. But his eyes had me constantly on the alert. I'd never seen such icy eyes. The eyes of an imprisoned soul. The only time I saw pleasure in those eyes was when he was giving shots. Before Michael Bent it was Darren Sedgewick, a very short, witty man in his fifties who quit a big corporate job to be my assistant, and then after three weeks died of a heart attack one evening in my car. I'm sorry to go on like this. May I go get myself another beer?"

Griffin ran to get her one; now he was back.

"Tell them about Emily Donnerbaum," said Griffin, enraptured, a child hearing stories he already knows.

"Yes, do tell us about Emily Donnerbaum," said Jude, "and then, why don't we start planning your wedding?"

266

A silence fell.

"How many children will you be having, Griff?" Jude said, smiling, his arms still crossed.

Griffin moved even closer to Berna. He rolled his eyes and gave his father a look of exasperation.

"You think I'd even consider bringing children into *this* world? You think I'd want them sucking down the energy of global terrorism? And as I mentioned to you a few years back, the fact that we have enough children on the globe *already* makes a *difference* to me. I'm not so big on *propagating* my own genes to gratify my own ego, which I know you think is too big, and you may be right, in fact I *know* you're right, but at least I'm trying to *subdue* it. Not to mention stray animals without homes. Why does everyone I meet have this 1950s American thing about having kids?"

Griffin spoke with such passion that Jude looked at him for a moment with love. We hadn't seen any passion from Griffin for a few years. We'd seen composure. We'd heard descriptions of what he called his "practice." His practice was sitting on a pillow and counting each one of his breaths for one hour a day, before going to work as a telemarketer for Greenpeace. (He'd quit his very lucrative computer job.) His practice purified his thoughts, he said. It helped him deal with "afflictive emotion." It allowed, I suppose, for un-American transcendence.

"And we'll have a house full of animals, that's for certain," Berna said, in a voice that was soothing no matter what she was saying. "I have four cats now, and two dogs, and I've managed this restraint only because it's difficult for one person to have more than this. More than six and you start cheating them out of a superb life. But with a man around the house, especially a good man like Griff, there's no telling how many we'll be able to take in."

"Our grandchildren," I mumbled, and barked out a laugh in spite of myself.

"Actually," Berna suddenly said, looking at Griffin, "it's not in my nature to lie this way. Nor is it in yours. What were we thinking, Griff? We'd let them down easy?"

Lying?

She looked at us. "Look," she said, holding up her hand to show us the ring. "We're already married. I'm your daughter-in-law now, all right? There will be no big wedding." She smiled over at Griffin.

267

"OK," said Griffin, "now you know. Bern, tell them about Emily Donnerbaum now! You gotta hear this!"

That night, after they left, I lay in bed in our dark room and started to laugh. Jude sighed, exasperated with me; this wasn't funny. In fact, each time he closed his eyes he said he pictured them in bed, naked together, and it made his skin crawl. At this I laughed harder, then settled down to scold him.

"Jude! That's rather unkind," I said. "She may be getting on in years, but she's not disgusting. Her face is beautiful. Those cheekbones I'd like to have."

"Naked," Jude said. "I keep seeing her naked, and it is disgusting. It's like a fairy-tale image I can't shake. I guess this marks me as pathetic and shallow. I always said you'd eventually discover this."

"No, not pathetic, Jude, but a little harsh. And in ten years I'll be her age. Will I be a fairy-tale image?"

"You'll be you."

"I think old bodies are beautiful," I said, and smiled to myself, my eyes on the twisted black branches of the tree that scraped our window. I had never really thought this before. In fact, I'd always found old bodies disturbing, male or female, but especially female. As a young woman I'd been one to sit on the beach and cringe at the old ladies walking by, I'd been one to promise myself that I'd always stay covered up when I got up in years. But in the darkness that night, remembering Berna's vivid vet stories and my son next to her, holding her hand and waiting to be alone with her, a clenched fist inside of me opened up. I lay there remembering my son's waiting—the feel of his waiting—everything was boring to him near the end of our night because he wanted her, he wanted her alone, and in bed. How long had it been since Jude had experienced that sort of waiting? Waiting to have *me*? Ten years? Twenty?

"Jude?" I said.

"Mmmm?"

"I think we need to put aside our bias and learn to love Berna. She's highly intelligent, and graceful, and actually quite funny. And she brings out the *life* in Griff. Whether we like it or not, she's going to be part of us."

"You're losing your mind," he grumbled. "A young man doesn't marry a woman thirty-five years older than himself. Thirty-five fucking years! If he does, the parents should step in and interpret it as mental illness, and begin looking for appropriate institutions."

"Jude! He's always been different, but he's never been mentally ill."

"I'd rather he had brought home a little bald Buddhist girl," Jude said. "If I were him right now, some part of me would be hoping my parents would step in."

"Jude, he's an adult, and he's married. We have no power anymore."

"He's a good-looking kid missing out on beautiful young women! He's missing out on the best life has to offer! He's trading all that in—the best years of his life—for an eccentric brain whose dogs probably sit in chairs at the dinner table."

Jude sat up and flicked on the light.

He looked around the room as if he'd never seen it before.

"Why would he do this?" he said, to the wall. "I bet she buys the dogs plaid raincoats like that woman we knew in Sea Isle."

"No, Jude. Berna is not the dog-raincoat type. You know that." I was exhilarated. I was, moment by moment, growing more proud of my son, and less interested in my husband, whom I knew I could taunt right now—I knew I could talk to him about all the men he knew who'd left their wives and married women half their age. (We had two very good friends in fact, who'd done this, and we'd gone to their pretty, hushed, little weddings, and despite my initial cynicism I'd felt moved and happy for everyone.) And I knew I could bring up Anita Defranz, a talented twenty-year-old painter he'd had an affair with eight years ago, a girl he brought to dinner after confessing the affair to me, wanting it all to be in the open, wanting me to like the girl, and I did, I did like her quite a bit even as I wanted her to vanish, even as my face grew hot at the thought of her. But I never told Jude that something ended for me during that dinner, nothing dramatic—but some part of my story with Jude *ended* as Anita Defranz told me how delicious the casserole was. "May I please have the recipe, please?" she'd said.

Jude had so trusted me to understand him, to understand his longing for Anita Defranz, who indeed was beautiful, with perfect skin and long, shiny dark hair, that I felt oddly touched by that trust, almost as if Jude were a child whose neediness made him a little dense. And now, in bed, feeling Jude's protest fill the room, feeling his confusion thicken the air in the room, I again saw him as a child, a child who could not see beyond its own sense of things. I felt sorry for him, really, and hated that pity, because it was pity that catapulted him from the realm of anyone I could unequivocally desire. Maybe I'd pitied him ever since Anita Defranz in her red silk shirt had sat so primly at our table.

"I'm going out for a walk," Jude said, pulling on his jeans. "I need some fresh air to help me figure this out."

I remember how after he left, and I was alone in the room without his protest, suddenly I was protesting myself. My one boy! This would be his life? This? How sad! Fundamentally sad, and it all must mean something sadder. And what kind of woman would do this? Such presumption! She was crazy, no doubt. My sentimental visions of going to stay with his young wife after the birth of their first child, a girl, of course, the girl I'd never had myself, pressed in on me.

I wept stupid tears knowing I'd stop all this just as soon as Jude came back with the energy of his rant.

I'm a reactor, Griffin once told me, not an actor.

Jude had vaguely obsessive tendencies; it showed up in his painting (one year he painted nothing but unremarkable gray rooms with brown floors), it showed up the year he drove two miles every morning at five a.m. to get a cream donut and black coffee from Winnie's Diner, in the way he had worn only black canvas shoes by day, and construction boots in the evening. He was a man who went on kicks—and I could look back over our life and organize my memories around them. *The tofu jogging year. The gambling year. The year he understood Republicans. The year of Ancient Greece books.*

And now he could not stop visiting my son and his new wife.

"Come on," he'd say. "Let's go on out and see what they're doing tonight."

"We should call ahead of time."

"No," he'd say. "I want to see what they do when they're not prepared."

"That's not polite," I argued, but somehow we'd be on our way by then, in Jude's little Chevy, his head almost touching the ceiling, the radio tuned into a sports show—the one kick he never abandoned, and me looking out the window at the starless city night.

We'd drive nine miles into the country dark, into the wild array of brilliant stars, then up along their bumpy dirt driveway, and we'd see

270

the one lit window in their house—a kitchen window—and invari-
ably we would find the two of them on the Murphy bed—you know,
those beds that fold down out of the wall—they had one in their
kitchen—someone who'd owned the house long ago had nursed an
invalid. So we'd look in through the window and knock and they'd
call, "Come in," having no idea who we were. They were fearless; I
suppose their love had rendered the whole world benign. Or maybe
Berna had always been that way.

We'd step into the dimly lit kitchen. They had a Franklin stove
filled with fire for heat. The air felt good. Charged, somehow, with
good, unspeakable things. With spirits and spices. Both loved cook-
ing. Griffin, I'd always thought, should have gone to chef school.
He'd always seemed most happy at the stove.

"Hi," we'd say, "just thought we'd drop in and say hello." I'd look
at Jude regarding them. His face looked so troubled, all mixed up
with criticism and deep interest and profound bafflement.

The two of them would be on the Murphy bed in old flannel paja-
mas and surrounded by three or four cats. They were always so
bright-eyed, and tucked under quilts made by Berna's mother, a
woman who we'd learn had joined the Peace Corps when she was
seventy-four, after teaching mentally retarded adults for thirty-eight
years. (My heart lurched forward, hearing this.) They'd quickly slip
out of bed, smile at us and tell us to sit down at the table. In the soft
light of that kitchen, with the old, creaking wooden floor and the
white lace curtains and the enormous spice rack and the big cheap
painting of the wild ocean, Berna looked beautiful, I noticed. Not
just beautiful for an older person, but *beautiful*. Griff, who always
looked perfect to me, was more so. Under the table, a black dog usu-
ally slept, snoring quietly. In the room just beyond the kitchen, a
chameleon lived in a plant that touched the ceiling. To feed the
chameleon Berna kept crickets in egg cartons on the solar porch in
the back; she fed them powdered milk and fruits. You could always
hear their song. When you closed your eyes it was as though the
memory of a peaceful August night from the heart of childhood had
been brought to life.

"Can I get you some tea?" Berna asked us, moving toward the cab-
inets.

"Tea would be good," I said. She had long, bare feet, and her nails
were painted, which surprised me, since she wore no makeup.

"You haven't had tea until you've had Berna's," my son said.

271

She served us ginger tea in small blue flowered teacups, with lemon and bamboo honey. It was true, the tea was better than any we'd had. She put the teapot on the table, and sat down. Again, I noticed how she never sighed, or groaned as she moved about, as she sat or got up from chairs. (I'd begun groaning in my late thirties.)

"So," Jude wanted to know one fall night, "where are you from, originally?"

"Nova Scotia," she said, her teacup in her hand. She had wrapped herself in an orange and yellow afghan.

"Nova Scotia!" he said. "Such a beautiful place."

"Indeed. I miss it every day, even as I'm utterly rooted here."

"I was there once, in my twenties," Jude said. "We hiked, and slept near the coast, and swam in the lakes. It was stunningly *gentle* land. That's my memory of it. Damn, I'd like to go back. And that wild water. Nova Scotia! I'll be damned."

"You never told me about that," I said. "I thought I knew everything."

Jude smiled at me, from a Nova Scotian distance.

Was it my imagination, or did discovering that she was from Nova Scotia change everything for Jude? He was mysterious that way—unpredictable just when you started to feel his predictability too keenly.

I remember the red leaves flying beyond the window that night, my son trying not to glare at his father, while Jude leaned in toward Berna, to hear more about her homeland, his eyes warm. She told us of her father, an old fisherman who wrote poetry and was living now in a hut by a lake. A man who coaxed the sweetest carrots out of bad soil. Berna tried to talk to all of us, but really she was speaking to Jude, responding to his own sudden interest. When Jude's interested, it's like he gets a lasso out and ropes the person in.

"We usually hit the hay about now," Griffin finally said that night, because his father and Berna were still talking about Nova Scotia, and some great, irrational fear in him was taking over all his better impulses. He was imagining the object of his desire running off with his father, of course. He was imagining they looked good together. I remembered being in that kind of love, where everyone's a threat. I was far enough away from such pain to envy its intensity.

"Griffin," I whispered in his ear as we were leaving, "relax, she loves you. Nobody is going to take her away. Most certainly not *him*."

His body stiffened at this intrusive intimacy. He had to pretend he was fearless with me. And yet, as we were pulling out of the driveway, he came out onto the stoop and waved, and I felt the wave as an offering of his thanks.

In those early months we had many evenings like this, with Berna, in her silken, dusky, calming voice, telling us stories of her family, or stories involving her work, and my son listening, marveling at this articulate, strange wonder of a wife, and watching us closely, usually. After a while he'd relax, forget to be vigilant, and we'd see his own charm as he told his own story. We saw his youth, his thoughtful eyes, his wild energy for life, his mind, unhinged from worrying about the opinions of others (except maybe ours) and we understood how Berna had fallen for him.

How do I say this? Six months after I met Berna, I became involved with a thirty-year-old groundskeeper named Abraham. Perhaps it's predictable that a mother whose son is married to someone so old would feel she's been granted a kind of license. Many would say it's Freudian, but that's too easy. I only know that after we began to accept the marriage as real, after we had seen them countless times in their Murphy bed in their eccentric pajamas, bizarre but beautiful really, with their animals and radiant regard for each other, after we had spent several Sunday afternoons walking in the woods behind Berna's house, and nights under stars she, like Jude, could name, after all that I felt a kind of penetrating amusement, a profound sort of humor infecting the whole world, and a newfound belief in surprises. I was waiting to be surprised. I was open. I wasn't walking around looking for a younger man—that sort of literal answer wouldn't have appealed to me at all. And yet, the day I visited my friend Noreen in her old home near the graveyard, I knew that when she pointed out the window at a certain groundskeeper named Abraham and said, "Isn't he adorable?" that this certain Abraham was meaningful to me, somehow. He wasn't, for me, adorable, but rather a man, and I liked his name and how he looked in the gray light, with his black eyes and his faded red hooded sweatshirt, and while it's true that I wouldn't have moved beyond a whimsical admiration of the young man had I not known Berna, I stood at the window beside Noreen and felt absolutely fired with lust for a moment. I may have blushed when she told me I shouldn't stare at children that way.

"Speaking of that," Noreen said, "how's Griffin doing with the old lady? Bernadette?"

"Berna," I said. "She's really not that old. She's younger than we

273

are, Noreen, in a way. I mean, her spirit is roughly Griffin's age. And she's got hardly a line in her face. (This part wasn't true and I was embarrassed to find myself lying.) And she moves so gracefully. I understand now, I think."

"God!" Noreen said. "I hate how everyone ends up understanding everything! It's weird, completely weird, and now you think it's normal."

I could have said, "Noreen, look at you, in this lovely old house that you keep so nice, you who fears the water and chooses to get seasick every other weekend so your husband can have his boat and eat it too, you who spends a fortune getting your hair bleached twice a month because you're terrified of looking old, look at all that and then we can talk about normal."

But I said nothing. I was not an aggressive person. I hated to hurt anyone, so avoided challenging conversation. And I was, perhaps, already planning how to talk to Abraham. I'd known Noreen for twenty-six years. We'd pushed children in strollers together. Nothing I could say would make her able to understand what I was feeling about life. She was a dear friend, but all the limits I had to respect with her made me lonely.

Abraham sat in his truck listening to music and eating a piece of bread. I walked up to the truck and said, "How long had you been a landscaper?" I was nervous, and said *had*, rather than *have*, and felt the tips of my ears grow hot.

"A landscaper?" Abraham said. "Is that what I am?"

He looked bored, at first.

"If not that, then what? What do you call yourself?"

"Abraham Horell. And you? What do you call yourself?" The boredom in his face had given way to a kind of bemused smile. It was a windy spring day, with gray light and silence surrounding us. I was aware that I'd relive this moment in memory.

"I haven't come up with a word for myself yet. Don't know *what* to call myself."

"Oh," he said, flatly, and I worried I'd been too odd.

"My name is Patricia," I said. "Some call me Trisha."

"Trisha," he said. "Nice name."

He got out of his truck. He was tall, in loose khakis. He left the music on. Miles Davis. He asked me why I was standing there at the edge of Noreen's yard. Did I know her?

274

"She's an old friend."

"Do you know the old man?"

"Not as well as I know Noreen."

"The old man takes her for granted. That's my opinion. And I've only been around him three times. My father would've called him a horse's ass."

That was all I needed. It was fuel. If he could see that much, he could see a lot of things.

I looked toward the massive garden he had planted, the rich soil dark as his hair.

"You do good work," I said. And I stepped closer to him. I looked at his face. My heart was pounding because I knew that even this subtle gesture might look as wildly transparent as it felt.

"Thank you," he said, and I saw he wore a tiny star of an earring on one ear. "If you come back later, you can see the whole garden, the whole thing, finished."

"I think I will," I said. And I tried to imagine that the final look we exchanged demolished any innocence between us.

It didn't. I did come back later, and he walked me around the garden, like a proud boy with a curious parent. My heart sunk as I told him how lovely it all was. I came back twice that week, and it wasn't until I brought him coffee the following week that he understood. I could tell by the way he took the coffee, brushed hair out of my eyes, lowered his chin to his chest, and held my gaze.

Later that same day Abraham and I went to a place called The Deluxe Luncheonette. And I got to hear all about the sweet young man who had dropped out of med school five years ago, who was divorced, who had a child named Zoe Clare, whose ex-wife was "remarried to a rich dude" but still demanding child support, whose father, whom he'd adored, had recently died.

Abraham spoke with ease, fueled by the bad, strong coffee of the luncheonette. His legs moved back and forth under the table, knocking against each other. I didn't particularly like his style of conversation—it had that windblown quality, where you feel the person could be talking to anyone, but I didn't admit this to myself at the time.

As it turned out, we were there because Abraham lived upstairs, in a room.

After coffee, and rice pudding, and saltines, and water, up we went. My head felt full of blood. My eyes watered. I bit down on the lipstick I'd applied hours before, then wiped it off on a tissue.

275

You could stand at the window of his book-lined room and look down on the little main street, the unspeakably mundane work-a-day world, and the view gave me more reason to be there. He came up behind me, placed a kiss on my neck, which felt too cold, too wet, but I was relieved not to have to talk anymore, and relieved that the room was dusky, so that both my body and the pictures of his child framed on the dresser, a girl in a red hat jumping rope, were slightly muted.

"Are you on the pill?" he whispered, and I told him I was, but he should use a condom anyway—diseases, I whispered. I hadn't been on the pill for years, and the truth was, it had been two years since I needed to worry about any of it. The change, as they called it, was something I'd walked through as if it were a simple doorway. What change? I'd wanted to ask someone.

I did not like his kissing—too pointed, almost mock-aggressive. I kept turning my face. But soon after, when he entered me, speaking to me gently, saying "it's OK, it's OK," and I whispered back, "I know it's OK," I did not expect to be weeping with the odd shock of joy that was simply intense sexual pleasure. I clung to him with misplaced emotion, as if he were someone I'd fallen in love with. And since no real love was anywhere in that room, save for in the face of that jump-roping little girl on the dresser, the pleasure ended in embarrassment for me.

For Abraham, I'm not sure. He may have been used to these things. He ran down to the luncheonette and brought me up a Coke and a plate of fries. We ate them together in silence, and I kept my eyes wide on the window, and listened to the sound of my own chewing as if it could protect me from thinking things like *here I am, a middle-aged slut!*

As I sat there dipping fries into ketchup, Jude's face, Jude's voice, broke through like a light. I was gratified to feel I missed him. Missed my husband, whoever he was.

I had four more late afternoons just like this one, and put an end to them because I understood how quickly they would put an end to themselves. Abraham's last words to me were so ironic they provoke my laughter even now. "You're wild," he'd said. How unknown I felt, but not as foolish as you might imagine.

I saw Abraham only one other time—two months later, driving through a blue day in his truck, with a dog, and a young woman,

276

whose yellow hair streamed out the window. I honked my horn and waved, in spite of myself, and then he was gone.

"Jude," I said one night in the dark. It was raining, and we'd just watched a bad movie on television, both of us enduring insomnia. "I had an affair, you know."

"No, I didn't know."

"He was very young. He worked on Noreen's yard. It ended up meaning very little to me, but I thought I'd tell you. You've always been open with me."

"Have I?"

"As I recall, a girl you loved ate dinner with us. She loved my cooking."

"True. True enough."

"Jude, where are you? I can't feel your reaction."

"I can't either."

"Excuse me?"

"Maybe I'm relieved."

"Relieved?"

"That you're outside the shell of this marriage when I've been outside it for years."

He sat up and put his head in his hands. I felt that he wanted to weep, but had no tears.

"Jude?" My face was red; why had I told him?

"Just don't say you're sorry."

"I won't."

"Because I've been terribly unfaithful. More than once, you know. More than twice. You probably know this. Do you know this?" I didn't say a word, but felt alone now, when I had imagined I'd already been alone. Does loneliness have floors like an endless skyscraper, and you keep descending?

"Four times. Four affairs. The last one ended last year. I've been dying to tell you."

"Really? Why don't we go downstairs and have us a drink, Jude. And you can tell me the story of our lives. You know, the one you forgot to tell me for the past twenty years or so. I'm such a good listener but you'll need to give me some details." I was on this new cold floor in the same old skyscraper and it seemed I had a new voice to go with it, a lower, more detached sort of voice, which was the very opposite of what I felt in the dead center of my heart. It was terror I felt. Because he'd stolen my sense of our past, and I had nothing to replace it with yet.

I got all their names. Besides Anita there was Lisa, the same Lisa again a year later, Savannah, and Lily. I sat and wrote the names down on a yellow tablet. I wrote them in a list, while Jude sat and rubbed his eyes. "Oh," he said, "Patty, I forgot Patty. She was manic-depressive."

"No, Jude, not yet, I don't want the stories yet. Just the names."

"If you count one-nighters there was also Rhonda Jean."

"Rhonda Jean," I murmured, writing it down. "Rhonda Jean! Was she a country-and-western singer, Jude? Was that the year you were always listening to Tanya Tucker?" I held the list up so he could see. "Does that look like all of them?"

He nodded. "You're stooping pretty low with this."

"Just meeting you on your own ground, Jude."

"Certainly. But it's ground well beneath you. You'll probably leave me, too, and that's understandable."

"Is that your hope? That I'll leave you?"

"No, no, of course not." He yawned, and I thought tears filled his eyes. He looked down at his own hands.

I was not ready to baby him. I took it girl by girl. I made columns for the following categories: duration of affair, age, hair color, height, weight, breast size, intelligence, family background, hobbies. This *was* beneath me, embarrassing even at the time. I was driven by an old fury finally coming to life.

The affairs had happened *before* Anita Defranz, most of them when Jude was in his thirties. Only Lily had been recent.

"So we can start there," I said. "We can start with Lily. You tell me the story, and I'll listen up."

I spoke with calm authority. I spoke in unconscious imitation of Berna.

"Lily is nobody you'd ever want to meet," he said.

"But I need the story, Jude."

"It will mortify me to tell you."

"So be it."

"She was in her twenties, she called herself a poet, I met her at Reed Carone's house, he was her professor at the time, she wore a beaded top, she was nice enough, in the summer she worked with deaf children, she was a *girl*, can we stop now?"

"Jude, it's interesting to me."

"It was physical attraction, that's all. The most elemental kind. I'm sorry. We'd go to her crummy apartment. She was a slob, and I had to endure the presence of her roommate who called me the pig. Finally the roommate said the pig could no longer enter the sty, so it was Howard Johnson's hotel. We went there weekly for seven weeks. Then she fell for a young buck from Cuba, introduced him to me so I'd get the picture of how far up in the world she was moving. I was relieved. And after that I've been faithful, and will be until I die."

"Faithful."

"I certainly love you. Nobody else."

"Nice words, Jude, but who are we? I want to hate you. But then, that would be like hating my life. I don't want to do that. Do I."

My eyes stung with tears. *My life* echoed in my brain, and I saw myself as a little girl running down a road in Indiana, the first time I'd ever felt that sense of *my life*! I'd been stung by a bee. I remembered my father in the doorway of the kitchen, scooping me up. I cried, not from the bee sting but because I knew I had a life, and was alone living it.

"So what did Lily look like?" I said. "Like Anita Defranz?"

"More or less."

"I'd like to hate you, Jude. For all those nights you fell asleep beside me, so exhausted, so spent. You wouldn't even talk to me! I'd like to kick you, and slap you. But I'm a dignified person who is now going out for a walk."

I felt him watch me rise from my chair, and I was gratified that he was speechless.

We lived in silence for nearly a week—avoiding each other when we could, and then 120 roses were delivered to my door, the card simply saying "From Jude Harrison," which made me laugh until tears streamed down my face.

"Jude!" I hollered that day—he was upstairs painting. "Jude Harrison, this lunacy solves absolutely nothing! Where will we put them?"

He came downstairs—I stopped laughing as soon as I saw him, my heart recoiling—and together we quietly found vases and jars for each rose, and the whole house filled up with his apology. For a while, I was touched, and then not so touched. Now we had a friendly silence, sometimes broken with, "Want some scrambled eggs?" or "I need to paint in the kitchen today, if it's all right? I need that light" or "How 'bout we go see Berna and Griff tonight?"

In the car that night Jude and I rode in silence. I felt so eager to get to Griffin's house, as if it were a holiday and I were a child in love with ritual. I knew we'd be served tea, I knew they'd be in pajamas, I knew I'd hear stories, I knew the house would have that inexplicable atmosphere. *Electrified by something*, I thought, *by mystery*, I decided, though even that word did not capture what I felt there.

They had company. It was only the third time we'd come to find them not alone. The first two times it had been old Jack J. Pree, no longer a fatso or an existentialist, but married and the father of twin girls. He was still Jack J. Pree, though, full of loud laughter, and no dull judgments, and when he left he lifted Bern off the ground for a hug. His wife was more like a stunned, wide-eyed owl. You could feel her observations were grist for the mill for the tale she'd tell her friend on the phone the next day.

Tonight the company was a stranger, an old man, very old, who we saw first through the window. I wondered if it was Berna's father.

We stepped inside; the kitchen felt like deep water. Berna's eyes were sad. Griffin was nowhere.

"What happened?"

"This is Charlie Demato," Berna said. "He's staying with Griff and me for a while."

Charlie Demato, the old man, sat at the kitchen table with a bowl of oatmeal in front of him. He had sharp elbows perched on the table's edge, and he smiled up at us. "A pleasure to meet you," he said. "You'll excuse my spirits," he added.

"We had to put down Mr. Demato's dog today. He lost his wife three weeks ago."

Jude and I expressed our sympathy. I felt we should leave. Surely Mr. Demato didn't need strangers like us. I said as much.

The old man looked up at me. "Please," he said. "Please stay. Don't go."

It was as if he were demanding that there be no more departures in life—nobody, ever again, would be leaving.

"Just sit down," he ordered.

Griffin appeared, smiled at us from the doorway.

"Berna," the old man said, "tell these people about Belle. Tell them so they know she wasn't just some dog."

Berna said that he should tell the story. That it would help him.

"Excuse me while I get my album of photographs," said Mr. Demato, and walked into the other room.

"He's staying with us," Griffin said.

"We know."

"It's part of how Bern runs the business. If some old person loses a pet and they live alone and they can't bear it, she invites them out here."

"Doesn't have to be an old person," Berna said. "Loneliness comes in all ages. A girl of twenty lived with me for six months one time. Turned out she had a lot to teach me. She stayed too long, she got herself pregnant, she ate too much, and made it impossible for me to meditate. But she was a teacher for me, I knew that all along."

Mr. Demato was coming back to us, his enormous album in his arms.

"Ain't I a sight for sore eyes?" he mumbled, and laughed. "This goddamn album weighs more than I do."

He sat down in the chair and opened to the first page.

"My wife, six years old!" he said, and clapped. "Deprived child. Never had a dog. Her mother claimed to be allergic. Her mother was a big liar. She hated me. My wife took after her father. Her father fell off a rooftop and died when he was thirty-two. Broke my wife's heart. Just a little girl. Never the same again."

He flipped through a few pages. His breathing quickened.

"I am unprepared," he said. "I am very unprepared. And I did many things to prepare myself. I rejoined the Catholic church."

We were all looking at him, trying to express something with our faces. Berna was up taking bread out of the oven. I saw that Mr. Demato's hand had started to tremble. "I went into the confession booth. 'Bless me father for I have sinned,' I said. 'But God who made death is the real sinner,' I said. The priest said, 'It is normal to be angry at death, and it's good to express your anger.' "

He looked up at us. He had urgent blue eyes. "You're all too young to understand," he said. "You live with a woman for forty-eight years. Her biggest fault is too much garlic on her food, and maybe she had to get the last word in. Bitchy once a month, even after menopause. We got the dog twenty years ago. A mutt. A pup. She took care of it just like it was a baby. She talked to it that way. We'd had a baby together. A smart girl. The girl grew up and moved to San Diego. The girl got breast cancer when she was forty. Survived. We lived through that together. Luck was on our side. How lucky we were. And look here, she played piano!"

He closed the book of pictures before we could see. He rested one of his hands on top of it, the other hand coming up to cover his eyes. He stood up. "I'm sorry, I am not prepared. I wasn't prepared. For the weight of it. I am sorry to go on. Berna, may I go to my room? I thank you. The dog died a peaceful death in my arms. A lovely way to go. They should do it for human beings. You have a fine son. Good night, now. The dog was named Belle."

As he walked away Jude's hand took my own under the table.

"He's a nice old man," Jude said. "I wish I'd known one good thing to say."

"Yes." I said. "Me too."

Jude squeezed my hand.

Then, we heard the old man singing. Not softly. He was belting it out in there, a song I'd never heard. *All the lilies, all the lilies, lighting up her face!* He had a terrible voice, a comic voice, and who would have thought he could be so loud?

We sat and wondered if we should go to him. If this was a sign of unraveling. But nobody moved.

"The man needs to sing," Berna said. She smiled.

We ate her warm, fresh bread. *The lilies, the lilies, the lilies in the snow!*

We laughed a little. The song did not soften, if anything he got louder and more off key. It went on and on. We almost got used to it.

We learned Griffin had been accepted to veterinary school in Philadelphia. We drank to that—brandy. I kissed him.

When the old man fell silent, we all rose from the table. *He's sung himself to death*, I thought, as we all seemed to tiptoe toward his room.

But the old man met us halfway there. He was bundled up in a parka. He said he was going out for a walk. He was going to sing in the great outdoors he said. He was not prepared, he said. We saw he was weeping.

I wanted to embrace this man. But he was nobody you could embrace. He was a force for whom you simply had to get out of the way. You had to move aside and let the old man go into the great outdoors, unprepared.

We saw him, later, Jude and I. We were in our car, beginning our ride back home. The old man was headed back to Bern and Griffin's house where he would find fire in the stove, and some companionship, and something else I'd never name. We didn't stop and ask the old man if he needed a ride up the hill.

"If I lost you," Jude said, "I'd be walking like that. I'd be out walking alone for the rest of my life."

His words had the near ring of sincerity, and touched me for a moment, even as I didn't believe them.

"I couldn't stand it," he said. "You're my whole life."

"Well I hope if you sing you sound better than he did," I said, and Jude said nothing, wounded, perhaps, that I wasn't engaging his fears.

For the first time in years, I rested my head on Jude's shoulder as he drove. This was more awkwardness than it was comfort. But it was something. We rode through the dark like that, in a new kind of silence, a silence made of fading echoes, the echo of an old man's song, the echo of pain and resentment and lies that break hearts, the echo of all we'd ever meant to be for one another.

We were hungry. We stopped and had a meal in an all-night diner, Jude and I. The booth was aqua and small. We ate in silence. We could hardly take our eyes off each other. *We are what we are*, we seemed to be saying in that quiet. *We are what we are.*

We were filling up so we could go home to continue our broken, indelicate story.

Nominated by Carolyn Bly, Kent Nelson, Gibbons Ruark, Witness

HAMMERING STONES

by WILLIAM WENTHE

from THE SOUTHERN REVIEW

On the gospel channel, bodybuilders:
one rolls up a frying pan, one uncurls
a horseshoe's steel Omega; one lays hands
on a pair of Georgia license plates, rips
them in half. Leather weight-belts, talc,
sweat, glutted veins in bicep, neck;
gnashing teeth, grunts bowel-deep, pecs
that surge and stress the words
on T-shirts: GOD MADE YOU TO WIN.

It's more than just a ten-foot log
one of them cleans and jerks above his head;
nor do they believe the single-mindedness
of the man hammering stones with his forehead
is enough. That something other moves
in the knuckles of the man clobbering nails
into hickory with his fists is concrete
proof: here is grace made tangible.

In a motel room, the thumb of a man
clicks along the remote, looking
for something to distract him from one
moment to the next. Above the neon lot,
a few stars visible, spiked into the dark;
bats lift *themselves* in jagged wreaths

around the streetlamps. All day, with one foot
and one hand, he moved two thousand pounds of Chevy
across four states. If he can lift tomorrow
his eight-pound head from the damp pillow
it will be enough. The sun could do no more.

Nominated by Jeffrey Harrison

I REMEMBER TOSCANINI

by MICHAEL BLUMENTHAL

from DUSTY ANGEL (BOA Editions)

I was too young to know the voice of Enrico Caruso,
But my father was a lover of Mario Lanza
And I still remember the white hair of Toscanini,
Well before there was a hall named Avery Fisher
Or I had heard the deep, cantorial tones of Richard Tucker
And the soft, more earthly chords of Perry Como.

I had never even heard of clear Lake Como
High in the country of our beloved Caruso,
Or bowed to "Kol Nidre" sung by Richard Tucker,
But just hummed "The Student Prince" along with Mario Lanza
In the years young Liz Taylor was with Eddie Fisher
And we stood at the Old Met watching Toscanini.

There was a legend to the mere name: Toscanini,
So far from the mundane ditties of Perry Como
As to seem like the sea nymph in Goethe's "Fischer."
Or that island-stricken, shipwrecked Crusoe,
As if he "walked with God" (as we sang along with Lanza),
Or wore a prayer shawl and yarmulke, just like Richard Tucker.

I wanted, someday, to sing stirringly like Richard Tucker,
Or conduct with the grace and power of a Toscanini,
And be a hero to my father (and to women) as was Lanza,
But never chime to Christmas bells with Perry Como.

I wanted to endure by singing, just like wild Caruso,
Not just croon "O My Papa" with charming Eddie Fisher.

Now I no longer dwell on almost-silent Eddie Fisher,
Though I still listen, yearly, to my Richard Tucker
Singing his "Kol Nidre" like a young Caruso
With a Jewish lilt and accent, led by Toscanini,
Whom I saw last night on TV, at Lake Como,
Driving a black car far more regal than a Lanza.

Yet I know they are mostly gone, even Mario Lanza,
And soon, no doubt, dear boyish Eddie Fisher,
Though I saw just the other day that Perry Como
(His new wig flattened to resemble Richard Tucker)
Would have a TV special of his own, just like Toscanini,
As if he had survived to be our new Caruso,

Proving all things equal in the end: Comos and Fishers,
The Richard Tuckers and the young Carusos, though in my heart
I still hear Lanza, and will sway, until I die, to dear old Toscanini.

Nominated by Grace Schulman, BOA Editions

TUSK

fiction by A.A. SRINIVASAN

from TRIQUARTERLY

Hᴵɴᴅɪ, ᴛᴀᴍɪʟ, ʙᴇɴɢᴀʟɪ, Gujarati, Malayalam, Marathi, Punjabi. I brought all of them to the cyberworld of local advertising and graphics. Of course, without the help of scholars who felt themselves quite intimate with each of the languages, I could not have accomplished this task. I have earned my fortune in the world of technology, and I assure the squeamish entrepreneur there remain princely amounts of money to be made in the realm of electronic reality, after my own small contribution.

I began my career in a more mundane field, developing electronic mail transferring programs. My software development served as a better way to send memorandums, documents, haiku and love letters through fiber optic lines quick, bang. Within the next two years, my program would have become obsolete due to my lack of enthusiasm for the business, but for a stroke of genius; I sold the project to Permasoftware for a hefty sum. At thirty-two I am more than ready to retire, emotionally as well as financially. I will work again one day. When? I don't know.

To say I do not work is not entirely true. Some might term me a type of physician of the future; for many people, I am more important than their own GPs. I carry a pager, and when a new computer enters the home, I feel a gentle vibration on my hip. An anxious voice on the line pleads for my help.

Nitin Aggarwal was my first house call after I sold my company. "Vinay," he boomed, "we've bought a new computer. Bigger than my own son! But, you know, this thing, I can't get the damned monitor to show a bloody . . . uh, you know . . . this thing. When are you available? Are you going to Ganapati Chathurthi on Sunday? We are. Priya wants the priest to bless the computer, but there is no way in hell I am going to drag it all the way down there. Almost three-thousand dollars we spent on this thing. I bought a lot of software stuffs to go with it. You will have to come over and teach me how to use it."

This same man never did have This Thing blessed by a priest, but three years later, it seems to work fine. He gave it to his son (who is now bigger than the CPU) and bought himself another component which refuses to fit under his desk. Now he possesses the perfect excuse to purchase new office furniture.

I make regular house calls to Nitin. Today he expounds on the same subject I hear about every time I pay a visit. "You know, Vinay, you are like family to me, like my own son. Why is there a giraffe walking across my screen? Damn thing. Parag must have loaded one of those . . . screen-savers on there. Wait until my clients catch a glimpse of this. Don't you want to have children, Vinay? Don't you miss having a home cooked meal?"

He doesn't realize I am served a home cooked meal every time I make a house call to set up, repair, or remove a computer from a residence. "Vinay," they say, "you must be hungry. My husband can wait to set up his computer. Come, sit down. Have some dosai. Have some puris. Have some naan. Have some rice, yogurts, alu, dal, bharta, raita, sambar, bhindi, vada, papadums picklejalebisgulabja-muns."

I smile at my old friend sitting across from me, who tinkers with his computer, running the giraffes, monkeys, and toucans off the screen with the click of a key. I rub the heftiness around my middle and laugh to myself. As far as meals are concerned, I am well taken care of.

My mother also tries to please and appease everyone with food. It is her way of getting my father to shut up for a few minutes. And my mother *does* spend most of her time attempting to pacify my father, just as I had tried years ago. My parents are champions of domestic strife, and when they are not engaged in verbal combat, they immerse themselves in silence. No one knows why my father is so angry. He never discusses anything with us. My mother always says: "He's a businessman, Vinay. Rich people didn't get rich by being nice."

As a child, it was imperative for me to gauge my father's moods be-

289

fore I said anything and especially before I made a request. The first time I asked him for a computer, he nearly knocked my head off, for he had lost big time in the stock market that day. I learned to decipher the Dow Jones at an early age. I spent most of my days watching television while my parents were at work, until they did finally buy a computer for me. Television became only a memory. My father bought me a new computer every two years, a bribe, I think, a way of preventing me from pestering him. I loved my first computer the same way a child loves a pet, a sibling, a parent, even. My mother would come in with my dinner in hand, and she would play with the keyboard and the mouse while I ate. This was her way of getting me away from my personal terminal for a few minutes; she knew I would always move for her.

Nitin's wife reminds me of my mother. She is one of the best cooks around, and after eating one of her meals, I feel as if the whole universe (or perhaps just a decent-sized computer) will fit into my stomach. For his wife, I developed a Hindi script on the computer, enabling her to write a well-designed cookbook for the Venkateswar Temple fund-raiser. All the women ooh-aahed at her designs and typesetting skills, then immediately placed an order for her cookbook, as well as for a copy of the homemade program, which created the visual feast. The husbands phoned me, one by one, shouting, "Vinay, you're a bloody genius! Why didn't you think of this sooner? Why didn't I think of it sooner? Do you want to work for my company? We're thinking of getting into import/export, you know? I have a friend who wants to publish a SoCal Gujarat newsletter *in* Gujarati, but I said, 'No way, *bhai*, no way. You'll have to publish it in English, or nothing.' But, when Seema showed me that cookbook of yours, I rang him *immeedjiatly* and shared the news, my genius friend." When I reminded him the font was in Hindi, not Gujarati, he replied, "Yes, but you know Gujarati, no?" No. I don't even know Hindi. A consultant and friend wrote out the alphabet for me since English is my one and only language, I'm afraid.

I hired a Gujarati doctor to write the alphabet to aid me and delivered the program to Mr. Shah the following month. Before I finished with the Gujarati text, Sri Subramanian phoned, asking for the development of a Tamil alphabet and a collection of clip art depicting Rama, Sita, Arjuna, Krishna, Ganesha. I hesitated for a moment, wondering how long it would take me to develop a South Indian language. Too long, I thought, and too many headaches. Already, I dreamt of demonic dancing alphabets all night, but Subramanian begged, "*Enna?* What's wrong? South Indian languages are beneath you?" I replied, "Not beneath me, perhaps beyond me." He chuckled and phoned me three more times before I agreed.

For him, I developed all of the items he requested: an unrefined version of the Tamilian alphabet as well as a screen-saver of Krishna and Arjuna rolling across the battleground with Hanuman dancing around behind them, setting the field alight with his tail. I seemed to have gotten a bit carried away and muddled my myths, but Subramanian cared little and overlooked any flaws. We both viewed it as an experiment anyway, a highly successful one.

A designer helped me develop a Ganesha screen-saver as a gift for my mother. The elephant-headed god rides along on his mouse and falls off of his vehicle, His stomach bursting open from the collision with the ground. The animation is fantastic, as balls of rice pudding and other sweets come tumbling out of Him, brightly-colored desserts fly across the screen. He scoops up His food and places it all back inside of Him as the Moon watches and laughs. Ha ha ha! The Moon rotates round and round, gleefully, while the mouse scampers back and forth! An indignant frown settles across the face of the god. He breaks off one of His tusks and hurls it at the laughing lunatic, but the Moon catches the sacred ivory in his mouth and refuses to return it. Then, the scene begins again, with a jolly Ganapati strolling across the monitor on his mouse-steed. The program has become very popular with children.

In came orders of all sorts, forcing me to produce more and more alphabets. A poet friend insisted I develop his native language on the computer, for his earnest labors were presently dedicated to a collection of Bengali haiku. Also, a married Punjabi woman was having an affair with another Punjabi, but her husband, a man originating from the state of Karnataka, could not read the love letters they sent back and forth via the electronic mail's attached documents.

And every time I delivered a new alphabet to a family, they sat me down at the dinner table, asking if I wanted any pakoras, bhajees, bharta, khatrika, rasgollah, basmati pillau, thair sadham, dum-alu . . . food flying at me from all directions.

Nitin now reminds me of my age and of the enormous house I bought last year, all empty and sad. "It is *sooo* sad and lonely, I can't even bear to visit you there. Why do you own such a big place, *bhai?* A palace isn't a palace without a woman and couple-of-three kiddies running round." I shake my head and smile, thinking it might not be such a bad idea if I begin a family, have someone to help me spend my money, but still, I don't know if it's wise to take advice from an accountant who believes couple-of-three is a legitimate numerical description. I tell Nitin how to turn off his Jungle Life screen-saver and head home.

I share my house with a boarder named Subash, who, when he is not at work, sits in front of the television waiting for the next cricket match. "Vinay, you are my godsend," he told me when he moved in. "In New York, I had to ride down to Greves Cinema in the middle of the night and catch the matches there, but that satellite dish you've got makes for the happiest home in the whole world." I am unsure of my reasons for buying the dish in the first place. I hate watching television, and I usually pick up *India West* if I want to know cricket scores, but Subash's passion for the sport refuses to be appeased by a few lines in a weekly dispatch. He threatens to kill himself if India fails to win the World's Cup this year. "Its been too long, Vinay, too long for us."

When I arrive home, Subash sits at the dining table grinning like a jolly Buddha. "Good chances! We're in the running. Australia and Sri Lanka are the big opponents this year. West Indies, not so good. South Africa, Pakistan, no way." He rocks back and forth, rubbing his palms together like an anxious fan waiting for the bowler to let go of the ball. "You are good luck. Did you know that? Ever since I met you, good things have been happening. There is some fish curry in the fridge. Have some. Have all you like. You need to eat. You'll bring me good luck, won't you?" He smiles at me, enjoying his own little joke.

I envy Subash sometimes. The look in his eyes during a cricket match, the tightened fist on his lap, the roaring of his voice, make the house come alive, as if there are a hundred people pumped up, living under one roof, this roof.

His passions extend beyond cricket. Subash threatened to kill himself once before, said he intended to jump off my balcony (which probably would *not* have killed him) if he missed the chance to put his hands on the brand new Microsoft Windows software the very day of its release. At 2:00 A.M., he danced in the street, waving his box back and forth in the air after standing in line at the computer store for two hours. I should have been embarrassed to be with him.

"We're having a cricket party on Tuesday, and you're coming. You need to bring the dessert."

"I can't come."

"Why not?"

I can't think of any reason.

"Of course, you're coming. You never go anywhere. You sit in front of your computer all day, researching God-knows-what, and you need to start getting out more, dating, doing something. I'm not going to be here forever, satellite dish or not. I have plans for my future: parties to attend, food to eat, countries to visit, weight to gain, women to charm. You are wasting your life making house calls and sitting in front of a computer. I can barely remember what your voice sounds like. Say something."

I laugh.

"Say something."

"Hello. My name is Vinay."

"Something interesting."

"I don't care much for cricket."

"Say something that isn't blasphemous."

My stomach growls, and I wander to the refrigerator for some fish curry.

"Ganesha has a fat stomach and big ears. That's why my mother named me Vinay."

Subash laughs, staring down at his stomach. "Then, most of us should be named after dearest Ganapati."

I once dated a girl who said, "Vinay, you don't talk much and this bothers me. It makes one think you might, perhaps, be a murdering psychopath. A silent man is a bad sign, means he might combust at any given moment. Please say something. Don't just nod like that. You look like an imbecile. Do you sing? You aren't an imbecile, but you need to speak up. Speak up, speak up. I need to know what you're thinking, and for gods' sake, don't whistle. That is another sure sign of a lunatic." I loved her, although I never discovered where she derived her knowledge of psychopaths. She married her singing teacher, and the two later opened a sari shop. Her name was Leela. The store has been named after her.

She asked me to set up a computer inventory system for *Leela's Palace* before they opened to the public, and I agreed. While I unhappily loaded the software onto their computer register, Leela took

293

a rest from decorating the mannequins in the front window. "You are the only one I trust to do this, to not rip us off," she said, sipping on a Coke. She held the can out to me and I ignored the gesture. "Some might say I've taken advantage of you because I knew you couldn't say 'no.' In fact, you can't say a damn thing. How did a man without a tongue become so successful? I always thought you would amount to something if you could just burst out of that feeble life you lead." I said nothing. The computer system was ready for operation. Leela picked up a bag of samosas sitting next to her chair and dropped them in front of me, then turned on her heel and resumed her dance with the half-naked mannequin.

Subash points a finger at me. "You haven't dated anyone since Leela. What you saw in her, I don't know. There is a woman I want you to meet at this party, so you must come."

I put up a struggle but not a terribly convincing one. Something in my voice or the way I concentrate a little too hard on reheating the fish displays a glimmer of excitement. When Leela left me, she asked, "So, what will you do now?" I shrugged, replying, "Work. I have a lot of work to do, projects. I'll have more time for them now." She laughed, no, she guffawed at my response. It took me two years to understand the meaning behind that roar of laughter.

"Does she like computers?" I ask casually, poking at the fish in the microwave.

Subash bangs his palm flat on the table and laughs the way Leela laughed when she left. "My god, you must be kidding, chap! You think I would set you up with someone who liked computers? No way! Vimmi hates most things with a plug attachment. For a while we all thought she was the Unabomber. She said she'll be carried into the information age weeping."

I laugh, agreeing with him that an egghead in my life might not be the best woman suited for me.

"Although," Subash says, scratching his chin, "If you're curious, you can find a picture of her on the Web. Her brother created his own page."

"What is her brother's name? Maybe I know him," I say.

"Vimal Narayan."

Bingo. The only clue I need. "Never heard of him." I sit down at the table, next to Subash, with my dinner in hand.

"Will Vimal be at the party, too?" I ask, still attempting an air of nonchalance.

"I think he'll be in Detroit until next week, but *you* must be there! She knows all about you now. I told her she needs to save you from your sorry life, my friend. And I am doing this for my own selfish reasons, too. The happier you are, my dear Ganapati, the more luck you will bring to me! Pakistan, get ready to give up your title!"

"We haven't even met each other yet," I say. "I wouldn't place any bets on account of me. What if she hates me, makes my life miserable? What if I hate her in return? What if we never even speak to each other?"

"Look, Vimmi is a hundred times nicer than Leela, and she doesn't have a mouth like a turbine. She's a little shy sometimes, but not *too* shy, always smiling. She's a painter."

"Really?" I ask, too quickly. "Have you seen any of her paintings?"

"No," he says, picking out the onions from the fish curry, one by one, and dropping them into his mouth. "She's a big cricket fan, so she's all right with me."

"Then why don't you ask her out, yourself? All this makes me very suspicious."

"She isn't Bengali, and that *is* a must. She has got to speak my language, chap."

"The only language *you* know, *chap*, is cricket. Your vocabulary is limited to batsman, bowler, wicket, Azharuddin, and Tendulkar."

He laughs. "True, very true, but Mums wouldn't like her very much then, would she?"

After polishing off all the onions, not bothering to leave me any, Subash washes his hands and heads out the door to collect betting money from his friends for the Cup finals. An hour later, he arrives home with two fistfuls of cash accompanied by a check or two. He drops everything on the table, in front of me, covering the newspaper I read half-heartedly. I want to wait until Subash has gone to sleep before looking up the picture of the woman who doesn't possess a mouth like a turbine.

"Okay, Vinayaka, here it is. All on Mother Bharat. Six-hundred whopper-oonies." He snaps a hundred-dollar bill in front of my face. "Tomorrow it all begins. Do your thing."

"Stop it," I say laughing, pushing the money out of view. "You're incorrigible."

"Alas, chap, only one of my many virtues."

"Then I don't think I want to know what your other virtues are."

"Oh, but dedication is my finest one!" He leans over the table and scoops up all the money to his chest. "Who else would sacrifice a week's vacation to monitor their team's performance?"

"I can only think of nine-hundred-million other people." He waves my comment away with one free hand.

True. Subash did in fact use up his vacation time, a whole week, to watch the last of the Wills Cup matches. Beyond the subcontinent, a person such as this might prove difficult to find.

He yawns and says, "I'm going to bed. Get plenty of sleep tomorrow. The match is live, live! 1:30 A.M." He fondles the green lump of bills close to him as if it were his teddy-bear.

I wait for the light to turn off in his bedroom before I head upstairs to my office. Subash has a tendency to barge in, late at night, yelling, "God help me, Vinay, I'm going to smash that thing to smithereens if you can't fix my damn computer. Everything lost! Who asked Microsoft to make my life easier anyway?" After I would fix the problem, he would simply slap his hands together in an overly dramatic *namasté* and sigh, "I worship you, *bhai*, I really do."

I sit down at my desk and log in. My sister often laughs at me, at the fact I have a password to get into my personal computer at home. "Who the hell will break into your files here, brother dearest?" She's right. I disable the program, allowing me to enter my files without logging on the next time I use it. I have been using my computer less and less and will eventually forget my complex password anyway.

I enter the realm of the World Wide Web and perform a search for Vimal Narayan. After arriving at the correct address, the colorful page explains that the creator is an attorney, originally from Kentucky. His favorite sports are badminton, squash, and tennis, none of which I am remotely good at. In college, he was the head of a speech and debate team, which I now interpret as a euphemism for an argumentative and confrontational person. (Dearest Leela was also the head of her speech and debate team.) Vimal is handsome, with his evenly proportioned features and muscular physique. The photo shows him holding both a tennis racket and a gavel. His ambition is to serve on the United States Supreme Court. Click HERE, it says, to meet my MOTHER, FATHER, SISTER, SAINT BERNARD. I click where it says, SISTER. The image loads while my fingers drum against the mouse.

A photo of a woman comes up, crisp, clear. She casually holds a sculpture under her arm of a rat or hamster with wings. Her hair falls to her shoulders, one side tucked behind her ear. Her round eyes question why a camera sits in her face, a face which resembles a cherub in its perfect circularity. Her incisors nervously gnaw on the edge of her bottom lip. She wears an AUDUBON shirt which shows a hedgehog or beaver sitting under the logo. The screen reads: My sister Vimala is an artist/sculptor. She lives in Los Angeles with a dog, a parrot, a mouse, and a ferret. She has just finished a Ph.D. in bio-chemical engineering at the University of Illinois, and plans to do absolutely nothing with it! But I love her anyway. Her favorite sports are diving for clams and bungee jumping, and she loves to cook and paint. She doesn't have an e-mail address. Click here to meet my MOTHER, FATHER, SAINT BERNARD, ME. I click on all of them, one at a time, to see if there are any more pictures of Vimmi. There are none.

I turn off the computer, bored with everything else it has to offer. Attempting to sleep tonight seems futile now. Too bad India isn't playing a match today. Then I would have a reason for pacing the hallways during all hours of the night, although I really could care less about the outcome. Subash would know something else haunts me; he is spastic but far from stupid or unobservant. Perhaps I should wake him, ask him what he has told her about me. Does she *really* want to meet me? No, it will excite him too much. Then I'll feel foolish and embarrassed when I meet her. What am I saying? I can't date a woman whose favorite sport is bungee jumping. I'm terrified of heights. Clam diving? What is that? It doesn't sound like much of a sport to me. And what does one do after picking up the clams? She can't possibly eat them. Can she? How disgusting. All right, I *have* tried squid. I can live with clams—I suppose. And why a ferret? Where can I get one? What is it? Are they rodents? Marsupials? Felines? I'm allergic to cats. Will I also suffer an allergic reaction to ferrets? Women always choose animals over me, complete beasts. How do the mouse and the ferret interact? What about the parrot? I've met one before, and it never shut its yap, sort of like Subash, but I like *him*. Perhaps Vimmi's parrot doesn't speak, or enunciate properly. Do all of these various creatures get along? It is obvious that she's already too complicated for me. There is no way I can go through with this, no way. Subash will call me a coward, no doubt. I've done this to him several times before, but then, he didn't understand I was afraid of another Leela, and I was afraid of *not* having another Leela. Perhaps I should rid myself of my computer, throw it to the dogs . . . and the mice and the ferrets and the parrots and throw myself at Vimmi. God, why didn't I take speech and debate? I think I'm hungry again.

❊

In the early morning hours, I dress and hurry to my office in the same way Subash has been running around for a month like a mouse in a plastic ball. I print out the photo of Vimmi and hide it in my shirt pocket after folding it neatly into a square. A few pens prevent the photo from falling out. I remove it two or three times when time passes too slowly, then fold it up straight-away every time the house creaks. I train my mind to erase any thoughts of computers. Should I ask her about her animals? How would I know of her interests? I can't betray myself, divulge my late night research. Subash flies through the door just as I tuck the paper to my chest.

"Hey chap!" I feel a heavy slap on my back. "What are you doing? You *really* need to get out more. I am going to throw that computer out the window if you don't stop sitting in front of it all day, all night, all day. You make me want to scream. How can you fiddle with things like that when, in only seventeen hours, the match of the century will begin?" Subash waves an arm in the air as if he is rounding up cattle, then scampers out of my office. I hear him shouting, "Ganapati, ho!" as he runs down the hall, toward the kitchen. The countdown has begun.

❊

The shouting, booing, hissing, cheering begins at 1:30 A.M. Five cricket fanatics, a sleeping wife, and me, sitting around a fifty-two-inch television watching the first semifinals televised from Calcutta's Eden Gardens. Not a word was mentioned about Vimmi. I sit at the table in back of the sofa, where I pick at the gulab jamun I bought from the Indian grocery shop. The five men help themselves at different intervals to the snacks, the dinner, and the dessert. One of the men has lost his voice from his inability to contain his emotions over the last month; however, he does manage to croak, "Hi, Vinay." Subash stands up and stretches after shouting, "Dammit! Let's beat those Ravanas!" During a lull in the match, he says, "I forgot about dessert. Hand me some of those, my 'Good Luck Ganapati.' " (This is how he has introduced me to his friends.) He holds out a plate to me, and I ration out three fried dough balls. He rolls his eyes to the heavens

298

and yells, "Brilliant!" After finishing the second gulab jamun, he turns to his mates and says, "Hey, where is Vimmi?" The men ignore him. One man shrugs. "I don't think she lives too far away," Subash mumbles, his eyes now glued back on the television screen. "Maybe she only wants to catch the end of the match." He wanders back to the sofa.

The Bengalis are now rioting. (In Calcutta, not the living room.)

I've eaten half of the gulab jamuns. I should save some in case Vimmi comes.

Shouldn't she have arrived by now? Perhaps I'll meet her another time. We always tend to run into one another, we Indians, somehow, somewhere, sometime, in Los Angeles. I know what she looks like. I wonder if she would be impressed by my artistic creations, my alphabets. Maybe I could bring her slowly into my own world, show her a few things on the computer. I feel one side of my chest. Yes, the printout is still there. Would Vimmi and I cook together? Would she create a cookbook of her own? She would probably handwrite the damn thing herself. Or maybe I could entice her into using the computer. Would she eventually develop a fondness for it, the way I once developed an insatiable appetite for gulab jamun? Would I, one day, find love letters from her to someone I didn't know, written in a language foreign to me?

I see Subash eyeing the last gulab jamun, but I snatch it up first, placing the sweet ball near me.

I wander out onto the back porch and seat myself near the pool. What if Vimmi and I hit it off like long lost friends? I wonder if she wants to have children. Wouldn't this surprise my dear friend Nitin? Would I entertain him in my home and compare my couple-of-three kiddies to the size of computers? Probably not in Vimmi's presence. Or would she and I have pets only?

Subash beckons me inside before I can make myself comfortable. "They've lost! We've lost. Forfeited. Damn riots started again!" He turns away, his despair expressed by silence. The guests leave one by one. Subash manages to open his mouth to say something, though he looks like someone dying of malnutrition. "Hey, Vinay." He called me Vinay, not Vinayaka, Ganapati, Ganesha. I would even settle for chap. "Vimmi phoned while you were outside. She said she didn't set her alarm correctly. She sounded half asleep."

"Who?" I ask. "Oh, yes. Vimmi." I shrug and laugh. "Well, she didn't miss much then, did she?"

He nods weakly, turning his eyes toward the blank face of the television.

I drive home, carrying the last gulab jamun in a plastic baggie. Subash stays at Shankar's house for the night, the best thing for him right now. He needs the company of someone with whom he can share his grief.

The night is clear and cool. I look at the moon, its half-smile. Sometimes I wait for something to happen when I stare at it for too long, wait for it to give something back to me, and at other times I think it is simply laughing.

Nominated by TriQuarterly

INSIDE GERTRUDE STEIN

by LYNN EMANUEL

from THEN, SUDDENLY (University of Pittsburgh Press)

RIGHT NOW as I am talking to you and as you are being talked to, without letup, it is becoming clear that gertrude stein has hijacked me and that this feeling that you are having now as you read this, that this is what it feels like to be inside gertrude stein. This is what it feels like to be a huge typewriter in a dress. Yes, I feel we have gotten inside gertrude stein, and of course it is dark inside the enormous gertrude, it is like being locked up in a refrigerator lit only by a smiling rind of cheese. Being inside gertrude is like being inside a monument made of a cloud which is always moving across the sky which is also always moving. Gertrude is a huge galleon of cloud anchored to the ground by one small tether, yes, I see it down there, do you see that tiny snail glued to the tackboard of the landscape? That is alice. So, I am inside gertrude; we belong to each other, she and I, and it is so wonderful because I have always been a thin woman inside of whom a big woman is screaming to get out, and she's out now and if a river could type this is how it would sound, pure and complicated and enormous. Now we are lilting across the countryside, and we are talking, and if the wind could type it would sound like this, ongoing and repetitious, abstracting and stylizing everything, like our famous haircut painted by Picasso. Because when you are inside our haircut you understand that all the flotsam and jetsam of hairdo have been cleared away (like the forests from the New World) so that the skull can show through grinning and feasting on the alarm it has created. I am now, alarmingly, inside gertrude's head and I am thinking that I may only be a thought she has had when she imagined that she and alice were dead and gone and someone had to carry on the work of

301

being gertrude stein, and so I am receiving, from beyond the grave, radioactive isotopes of her genius saying, take up my work, become gertrude stein.

Because someone must be gertrude stein, someone must save us from the literalists and realists, and narratives of the beginning and end, someone must be a river that can type. And why not I? Gertrude is insisting on the fact that while I am a subgenius, weighing one hundred-five pounds, and living in a small town with an enormous furry male husband who is always in his Cadillac Eldorado driving off to sell something to people who do not deserve the bad luck of this merchandise in their lives—that these facts would not be a problem for gertrude stein. Gertrude and I feel that, for instance, in *Patriarchal Poetry* when (like an avalanche that can type) she is burying the patriarchy, still there persists a sense of condescending affection. So, while I'm a thin, heterosexual subgenius, nevertheless gertrude has chosen me as her tool, just as she chose the patriarchy as a tool for ending the patriarchy. And because I have become her tool, now, in a sense, gertrude is inside me. It's tough. Having gertrude inside me is like having swallowed an ocean liner that can type, and, while I feel like a very small coat closet with a bear in it, gertrude and I feel that I must tell you that gertrude does not care. She is using me to get her message across, to say, I am lost, I am beset by literalists and narratives of the beginning and middle and end, help me. And so, yes, I say, yes, I am here, gertrude, because we feel, gertrude and I, that there is real urgency in our voice (like a sob that can type) and that things are very bad for her because she is lost, beset by the literalists and realists, her own enormousness crushing her, and we must find her and take her into ourselves, even though I am the least likely of saviors and have been chosen perhaps as a last resort, yes, definitely, gertrude is saying to me, you are the least likely of saviors, you are my last choice and my last resort.

Nominated by Gary Fincke, Andrew Hudgins, Alicia Ostriker, Ed Ochester, William Olsen, The University of Pittsburgh Press

HOMESICKNESS

memoir by VIRGINIA HOLMAN

from DOUBLETAKE

EVERY FEW YEARS I go on a pilgrimage to a place I once called home: the small town of Poquoson, a formerly remote community on the northern tip of the Virginia peninsula. My mother's family there dates back to pre-Revolutionary War times, and traces of Old Poquoson's Elizabethan lilt remain in my speech, cropping up at odd times and making me feel childish or, rather, like the child I was when we lived there. I still have family in Poquoson—a widowed great-aunt, an aunt and uncle and cousins at various removes—whose names gleam from battered black mailboxes at the end of long oyster-shell-paved drives, drives and property that I used to cut across as a child but don't dare to now, as an outsider and as an adult. I've become what old Poquosoners matter-of-factly call a "foreigner," though a few visits to the marina and B. C. Smith's general store would quickly reestablish my blood privileges. I have an aunt who has lived in Poquoson for thirty years, but she's from Pennsylvania and has never been completely welcomed because of her foreigner status.

Friends find it odd that every time I go home to Poquoson it is not to see people, but to see our house, which remains on our property nestled between the property of my great-aunt and that of my uncle, in a piney, bayberry-filled patch of woods near the water. I rarely visit Poquoson, though it's a mere half-day's drive from my current home, but when I do, it is always on impulse. I am consoled by the fact that I can drive back to the place where I grew up and walk in and touch my past—the refrigerator, our upright piano, a sofa, paintings—walk the rooms I walked as a child. It's not exactly the same, though, not because someone is living in our old house, but because no one has

303

lived there since we left, twenty years ago. Our house is abandoned. One aunt occasionally mows down the field by the long drive, but other than that, it is respectfully and, for the most part, benignly ignored by my Poquoson relatives.

A house never belongs to anyone as fully as it does to a child. As children we claim spaces inside a house that are ours alone. The dusty undersides of beds and tables, slim kitchen cabinets we can tuck ourselves into, closet shelves, attic rooms, and cool sandy crawl spaces filled with prehistoric crickets and pale running weeds.

Our house in Poquoson is tiny—a seven-hundred-square-foot summer cottage constructed by my grandfather with shipyard scrap—and built by design for short-term summer inhabitancy. Its foundation is two inches of poured cement that also serves as the floor. The metal shower stall was purchased at a battleship auction. The front-door handle is an elbowed pine branch—to lock the house requires a chain and combination lock. A curious fact: the house has no ceilings. The top of the walls end where regular walls end, but above them is space and unpainted rafters. As a girl, I would hitch my foot onto the door handle of my room, pull myself up and balance myself astride the wall—one leg in my parents' bedroom, the other in the living room. From this perch I'd observe my family—my baby sister playing on the floor of our room, my mother in the kitchen pacing and talking to herself, my father adjusting the television antenna—like the disinterested, ever-present spy I imagined was God.

There are fewer and fewer abandoned houses these days it seems, even in Poquoson. A NASA facility is nearby. There is money to be made. There is property value. When I was a child, an abandoned house was a thrilling sight—I had no sense of life's foreshadowing— and I'd risk dogs and the threat of bird shot to get inside. A half-mile up Pasture Road was my favorite empty house, abandoned for at least twenty years by everyone's account, and loaded down with things: furniture and boxes and fold-up, roll-away metal beds, and books of family members who had passed on since this house was abandoned that were left here in storage for someone, someday to claim. I spent long winter afternoons wandering around that house, opening brittle mildewed handbags and once found a lovely silver and mother-of-pearl compact, which I thought to steal, but didn't,

304

and in another, discovered the elegantly printed personalized tithing envelopes for the local Methodist church, which I immediately pocketed. I spent hours arranging snug little bird's nests and translucent snake sheds along one sunny windowsill, like offerings at an altar.

I've lately been feeling pulled back to Poquoson, to visit the house. Acutely so, since the house two doors up from my present home was deliberately burned one night last month and its tenant, a new neighbor, murdered elsewhere.

My son is fascinated and horrified by the burned house, as am I. On two sides, the blackened, skeletal frame is all that remains. My three-year-old son comments on how now we can not only see inside the house but look clean through it, how now the rain gets in, how now the house is broken. We watch the men come to tear down the house, which they do slowly, as if they are peeling it away. When all that is left is the foundation and an enormous Dumpster full of the broken house, I tell my son that soon a new one will be built on the same spot, and he is disturbed by this news. Where the broken house was? he wants to know. I think he senses that there is something inappropriate afoot, that if a new house is built where the burned house was, then there will be no tangible evidence of what was, of what happened here. Later that same day he brings me a long, scorched, pungent scrap of cloth that has blown into our yard from the burned house. Part of my murdered neighbor's red batik dress.

When our loved ones are gone, we remember them, and the person we were with them, by visiting those places we shared. Who hasn't wanted to knock on a stranger's door and say, I used to live in this house? And who hasn't resisted that urge, knowing if the current occupants welcome you inside, you must cross the threshold from your memories into their home?

Though we lived in Virginia Beach, the house in Poquoson was the place my mother always fled to in times of crisis. It was safe and familiar and hers; the one place she could truly call home. So it was natural that when she first became aware of her madness, she abruptly set up residence in the cottage. She refused to live elsewhere, and due to this simple fact we all moved into the cottage together. Its temporary structure was forced to endure us year-round, through sudden floods that littered silver minnows across our floors and four winters, one so bitter it froze the inlets and raised pier pilings until the planks of every dock in town curled back toward shore.

Ultimately, my mother's illness estranged us from our relatives who live there. She's alive. Schizophrenic. Institutionalized. Never improving, slowly declining. One day she will die. Always, there is the house. And there is some form of comfort there. Even though it is the place where my mother was claimed despite her resistance, despite my family's best efforts to save her.

Before we came to live at the house in Poquoson, my mother would take my baby sister and me on day trips to the house. Her trips, like mine, I now realize, were impulsive and urgent. One snowy morning we drove to cut flowers from her mother's camellia tree to place on her grave. Today, as I write this, it is snowing, and I have just cut camellias from the tree in our backyard and placed them in my grandmother Virginia's battered silver pitcher. I see my mother in her trench coat, her black hair tied back with one red ribbon, her calmness in this task of cutting the flowers from the tree, her coral red lips, the dry snow filling up the deep green leaves. In memory she looks graceful; just like the pictures I have seen of my mother as a young girl, dancing everywhere in this landscape. In one photo she stands in the forked trunk of a black cherry tree on pointe, her hands raised above her head so the entire afternoon's sun shines in them.

Those pictures are different from the flat-faced young woman I see in pictures taken one snowy winter morning at my grandmother's funeral. My grandmother's death was sudden, and my mother did not love her mother at the time she died. What I understand only now is my mother's rage, frozen and suspended like the whole sun caught in her young hands.

After my neighbor's house burned, I saw her family for several days, parked in front of my house, while arson dogs and police crews worked in the charred house to bring out its secrets. They didn't talk to the officials, nor did the officials speak to the family. Their daughter, their sister, was gone, yet her house remained, and that was where they went to understand. Even now, I see the family drive by the house, which is mere foundation now, heavily dusted with lime, to slow and look at the ruins.

Once, driving through the countryside with a friend, I was astounded as she mused on the trashy nature of the owners of one falling-down house left standing in front of a trailer. The ugliness of the site offended her. Especially, she conjectured, since the land the house and the trailer occupied was valuable and could be sold to elevate the family. They'd buy a new house elsewhere, someone would raze "the mess" that they'd made, and no one would need to know how bad things had been. I found I couldn't speak. These were my people she wanted to eliminate from her sight. Did she really think that the answer to their plight was so simple—level and bury their history, walk away from it as quickly as possible, revise as they see fit? At that moment, I had no alternative to supply that seemed acceptable. But what I knew was that those people were hanging on to all they had left. They were still hoping.

I am preparing to return to my abandoned house. This time I am resisting the desire to rush back. This time I am making lists. This time I may take my son. I need this visit to be deliberate, made with my mind, not the impulsiveness of my body furiously running home. Close and curious friends volunteer to go back with me, and I momentarily consider their offers. But this house is a place I have taken only one dear friend from childhood, and that was before it was completely abandoned. Since then, I've returned alone, or with my sister and husband.

The last time I visited, I rememorized the three stops on the ancient combination lock to enter. When I arrived I didn't bother with the lock, I merely entered through the hole that had been kicked in the rotting front door. Once inside, I saw that someone had used our home as temporary shelter, more temporary than the four years we spent here. But beneath the beer cans and bread wrappers and a neatly folded army blanket on the sofa were the remains of our other life. The piano up on blocks to save it from the inevitable flooding, a can of corn on the shelf, a bottle of Bacardi on top of the fridge. A painting done by my uncle's first girlfriend hung in shreds from its frame. There were grimy oil lanterns and a row of seashells on the mantel. A polyester brown suit of my father's still hung in the closet. A gust of wind blew and the chimney scraped to life—raccoons or birds. An old teakettle that had rusted into the top of the space heater clattered as the stovepipe wheezed. In one corner was a bright red chiming apple toy that belonged to my sister when she was a baby. Everything seemed sad and neglected. Even though we'd had fires in the fireplace; even though there'd been happy days.

In the bathroom the cabinets were still full of old medicines—

Creomulsion, Goody powders, big blue diuretic pills, empty syringes (who did those belong to?). The hinges of an old Band-Aid box were clotted with rust, and I suddenly remembered the fresh gin-and-tonic smell of Bactine. A bar of soap sat small and cracked and moldy in the dish. I looked in the sink and noticed hair in the drain. Was it ours? Was it my mother's? Mine as a child? I stared at it and wondered perversely if I should pluck it out and keep it for some girlish spell to save my family, retroactively, from all the sadness I knew was to come. I ran my fingers tentatively along the bowl of the sink and I was surprised to find it gritty and wet. I raised my fingers to my nose and smelled pure man. At first I was still in the dream of the past and thought weirdly that my father had been here, maybe that morning, shaving. Then I realized that couldn't be—I'd been at my father's house only hours before, listening to him shave as I lay in bed. Whoever had been here was here recently—that morning, or only a day or two before. I ran my thumb over the razor slot in the cabinet and thought of all the rusting metal in that wall that had stroked the faces of my grandfather, my uncle, my father. When I raised my eyes to look in the mirror, I jumped on cue, expecting to see a strange face behind me, watching. But what I saw was my own back, reflected from the full-length mirror mounted on the door.

When it was well past time to leave, I sat on the sofa and bit my nails. Why couldn't I go? I realized then I'd been waiting, even hoping, for the other person to return. Did I really believe the transient who'd occupied our house could tell me something of my mother from simply having lived in her house? Did I think he could tell me why she'd gotten sick? Why we had to suffer here? Why she always ran to the cottage? And, now, why I run here? I looked up at the rafters. Now the stranger felt unwelcome. Now I felt unwelcome. I crawled out through the broken door, covered it with a folded tarpaulin from the shed, and left.

Later, I stopped to walk on old paths through the woods to a place I knew as a child. A place where two smooth rocks are etched with "1780" and initials. Further up from these stones is an odd, sundappled patch in the shady woods where irises and daffodils bloom. I sat on the ground and tried to picture the homestead that was once here; the way the light must've fallen through the windows. I scraped through the pine needles and into the black soil looking for another clue to the people who lived here. My people.

My father talks of selling the land and with it, naturally, the house. Perhaps that time will come. Right now, I still need to need the house. Someday, facts and memory will be enough. But that house is mine and my sister's, passed down from our grandmother to my mother to us. It is the place we've all returned to, that my mother ran to, because the people we love, the people we need to talk to, our mothers, are gone. This need of mine and my sister's is also my mother's need and was her mother's need—an atavistic urge—and our grief is expressed fully only in the context of that house, abandoned and decaying.

Some day our house will be claimed as completely as that old homestead. I'll go back before then. But what is it I will want to know on that day I do return? What will I tell my son as we approach the abandoned house for the first time in years? I wonder: will my son's family return? Will they notice the crape myrtles arranged amid the tangle of trees on this land? Will they care that once, we were here?

Nominated by Nancy Richard

THE SPELL

by JONATHAN DAVID JACKSON

from PLOUGHSHARES

Everything rots but flowers leave memories.
I was the boy who loved flowers, dried, fresh,
not just their fragrance but their bee-stung
bodies prayerfully folded into dusty skin.
I was the boy who walked limp-limbed, scent-drunk,
with the smell of spit on my hands, swearing:
Relinquish me of my desire
to be sunlit, beautiful.

They sat in vinegar water, blooming
past their time, their mouths open, white roaring
tigers perched high on the mantle top
in the robe room, down in the church cellar—
I moved swiftly on my tiptoes, stealing
a petal and a stem, wiping dust
from their long, knotty tongues onto my lips.
What was I to do with such big wet lilies?

I was a fire-eater, a witch. I opened
my eyes during the humming benediction
and tipped down to the cellar, stopping time,
dropping the prayer book, its pages fluttering,
and I laid my body in the moist dark
of the robe room, closing the door tight,
eyes not used to the dark, eyes wet, alive

breathing quietly, taking stems in reed-like
halves to wet my lips . . .

When the deacons found me, their arms reaching,
their faces molded into black masks,
I was honey-eyed, softly burping.
They called out my name in the darkness
of the robe room, and probed my mouth until
the flaking bits and evidence was found
and they whispered in my ear:
Girls have names like flowers . . .

Boys have names you can yell . . .
What is your name? Do you know your name?
But all my secrets were silent and heat
flowed through me like fire in glass.

Nominated by Cleopatra Mathis, Elizabeth Spires

THE SHARPSHOOTER

fiction by JOYCE CAROL OATES

from CONJUNCTIONS

> *The secret meaning of the evolution of civilization is no longer obscure to us who*
> *have pledged our lives to the struggle between Good and Evil, between the in-*
> *stinct of Life and the instinct of Death as it works itself out in the human species.*
> *So we vow!*
>
> —Preface, *The Book of the Patriot in America*

It was my Daddy's pioneer wisdom. *There is always something*
deserving of being shot by the right man.

When I was eleven my Daddy first took me out onto the range to
shoot *butcher birds.* I date my lifelong respect for firearms & my
prowess as a Sharpshooter from that time.

Butcher bird was Daddy's name for hawks, falcons, California con-
dors (now almost extinct) & golden eagles (ditto) we would shoot out
of the sky. Also, though scavengers & not predators actively threaten-
ing our barnyard fowl & spring lambs, Daddy despised turkey vul-
tures as unclean & disgusting creatures there could be no excuse for
existing & these ungainly birds too we would shoot out of trees & off
fence railings where they perched like old umbrellas. Daddy was not
a well man suffering the loss of his left eye & "fifty yards" (as he said)
of ulcerated colon as a result of War injuries & so he was filled with a
terrible fury for these predator-creatures striking our livestock like
flying devils out of the air.

Also crows. Thousands of crows cawing & shrieking in migration
darkening the sun.

There are not enough bullets for all the targets deserving, was another of Daddy's firm beliefs. These I have inherited, & Daddy's patriot pride.

Those years, we were living on what remained of our sheep ranch. Fifty acres mostly scrubland in the San Joaquin Valley midway between Salinas to the west & Bakersfield to the south. My Daddy & his older brother who'd been crippled in the War, though not Daddy's war, & me.

Others had deserted us. Never did we speak of them.

In our Ford pickup we'd drive out for hours. Sometimes rode horse-back. Daddy made a gift to me of his .22-caliber Remington rifle & taught me to load & fire in safety & never in haste. For a long time as a boy I fired at stationary targets. A living & moving target is another thing Daddy warned. Aim carefully before you pull any trigger, remember someday there's a target that, if you miss, will fire back at you & without mercy.

This wisdom of Daddy's, I cherish in my heart.

I am over-cautious as à Sharpshooter, some believe. Yet my belief is, where a target is concerned you may not get a second chance.

Our barnyard fowl, chickens & guineas, & in the fields spring lambs were the *butcher birds'* special prey. Other predators were coyotes & feral dogs & less frequently mountain lions but the *butcher birds* were the worst predators because of their numbers & the swiftness of their attacks. Yet they were beautiful birds, you had to concede. Red-tailed hawks, goshawks & golden eagles. Soaring & gliding & dipping & suddenly dropping like a shot to seize small creatures in their talons & bear them aloft alive & shrieking & struggling.

Others were struck & mutilated where they grazed or slept. The ewes bleating. I'd seen the carcasses in the grass. Eyes picked out & entrails dragged along the ground like shiny slippery ribbons. A cloud of flies was the signal.

Shoot! Shoot the fuckers! Daddy would give the command & at the exact moment, we both shot.

They praised me for my age all who knew me. Sharpshooter they called me. & sometimes Little Soldier.

The golden eagle & the California condor are rarities now but in my boyhood we shot many of these & strung up their carcasses in warning! *Now you know. Now you are but meat & feathers, now you are nothing.* Yet there was beauty in contemplating such powerful creatures of the air, I would have to concede. To bring down a golden eagle as Daddy would say is a task for a man & to see its golden neck feathers close up. (To this day I carry with me, in memory of my boyhood, a six-inch golden feather close to my heart.) The condor was an even larger bird, with black-feathered wings (we'd measured once at ten feet) & vivid white underwing feathers like a second pair of wings. The cries of these great birds! Gliding in wide circles & tilting from side to side & what was strange in such creatures was how, feeding, they might be joined by others swiftly flying from far beyond the range of a man's vision.

Of the *butcher birds* it was goshawks I shot the most of, as a boy. For there were so many. & when their numbers were depleted in our vicinity I would go in search of them; farther & farther from home, in ever-widening circles. Choosing to travel cross-country, I would ride a horse. Later, when I was old enough to have a driver's license, & the price of gasoline not yet too high, I would drive. A goshawk is gray & blue & their feathers like vapor so that drifting against a filmy sky they would vanish & reappear & again vanish & reappear & I would become excited knowing I must fire to strike a target not only speeding but not-visible & yet this I would do, by instinct, sometimes missing (I concede) but often my bullet struck its target to yank the soaring creature from the sky as if I held an invisible string attached to it & had such power over it, unknown by the goshawk, & unguessed, I might yank it down to earth in an instant.

On the ground, their beautiful feathers bloody, & eyes staring open, they lay still as if they'd never been alive.

Butcher bird now you know—I would speak to these calmly.

Butcher bird now you know who has dominion over you, who cannot fly as you fly—never would I gloat, almost there was a sadness in my speech.

For what is the melancholy of the Sharpshooter, after his beautiful prey lies crumpled at his feet? Of this, no poet has yet spoken; & I fear, none ever will.

Those years. I lived in that place yet spent long days roaming, & often slept in the pickup, following I know not what thread of unnameable desire drawing me sometimes as far south as the San Bernardino Mountains & into the vast desert spaces of Nevada. I was a soldier seeking my army. I was a Sharpshooter seeking my calling. In the rearview mirror of the pickup a fine pale-powdery ascension of dust & in the distance before me watery mirages that beckoned &

314

teased. *Your destiny! Where is your destiny!* Driving with my rifle beside me on the passenger's seat, sometimes two rifles, & a double-barreled shotgun, loaded & primed to be fired. Sometimes in the emptiness of the desert I would drive with boyish bravado, my rifle slanted at an angle on the steering wheel as if I might fire through the windshield if required. (Of course, I would never do such a self-destructive thing!) Often I would be gone for days & weeks & by this time Daddy was dead & my uncle elderly & ailing & there was no one to observe me. Not *butcher birds* exclusively but other birds too became my targets, primarily crows, for there are too many crows in existence, & such game birds as pheasants & California quail & geese, for which I would use my shotgun, though I did not trouble to search out their carcasses where they fell stricken from the air.

Rabbits & deer & other creatures I might shoot, yet not as a hunter. A Sharpshooter is not a hunter. With binoculars scanning the range & the desert seeking life, & movement. Once I saw on a mountainside in the Big Maria Mountains (near the Arizona border) what appeared to be a face; a female face; & unnatural blond hair, & unnatural red mouth pursed in a teasing kiss; & though trying not to stare at this apparition I was helpless before it, & my pulses pounded, & my temples, & I reasoned it was but a billboard & not an actual face & yet it teased & taunted so, at last I could not resist aiming my rifle at it as I drove slowly past, & fired a number of times until the terrible pressure was relieved & I'd driven past; & no one to witness. *Now you know. Now you know. Now you know.*

Soon after that my excitation was such, I was drawn to target-shoot sheep & cattle, even a grazing horse provided the countryside was empty of all witnesses. For *how easy to pull the trigger* as they would tell me one day in the Agency. There is a sacred wisdom here, I believe it is a pioneer wisdom. *Where the bullet flies, the target dies.* Subtle as poetry is *What is the target is not the question, only where.* Sometimes I would sight a vehicle far away on the highway scarcely more than a speck rapidly approaching & if there were no witnesses (in the Nevada desert, rarely were there witnesses) at the crucial instant as our vehicles neared each other I would lift my rifle & aim out my rolled-down window & taking into account the probable combined velocities of both vehicles rushing together I would squeeze the trigger at the strategic moment; with the supreme control of the Sharpshooter I would not flinch, though the other driver might pass close enough by me to see the expression on his (or her) face; I would proceed onward without slackening my speed, nor increasing it, observing calmly in my rearview mirror the target vehicle swerving from the highway to crash by the roadside. If there were witnesses what were they but *butcher birds* gazing down at such a spectacle from their high-soaring heights; & *butcher birds* despite the keenness of their eyes cannot bear witness. These were in no way personal vengeful acts, only the instinct of the Sharpshooter.

Shoot! Shoot the fuckers! Daddy would command. & what could a son do but obey.

It was in 1946 I would be hired by the Agency. Too young to have served my country in Wartime, I pledged to serve my country in these interludes of false peace. For Evil has come home to America. It is not of Europe now nor even of the Soviets exclusively but has come to our continent to subvert & destroy our American heritage. For the Communist Enemy is both foreign & yet close to us as any neighbor. This Enemy can be indeed the neighbor. *Evil is the word for the target* as it is said in the Agency. *Evil is what we mean by our target.*

Nominated by Conjunctions, Richard Burgin

V. (PSALM 37 AT AUSCHWITZ)

by JACQUELINE OSHEROW

from THE ANTIOCH REVIEW

Nourish yourself with faith (Psalm 37:3)

Just a little longer and there will be no wicked one; you'll contemplate his place and he'll be gone (Psalm 37:10)

I was young; I've also grown old and I've never seen a righteous man forsaken or his children begging bread (Psalm 37:25 and Birkat Hamazon—*Grace after Meals*)

All those boys who'd started *heder* at three,
After licking a page of letters smeared with honey,
Who, legend has it, by the age of ten,
Could track the route of an imaginary pin

Stuck through the *Gemarah,* word for word—
Surely it was nothing to the likes of them,
Who clung to every holy thing they heard,
To learn by heart the words of every psalm,

And surely, even given the odds, one,
Despite his scholar's pallor and his puniness,
Made it, by some miracle, to the workers' line
And didn't go directly to the gas.

What I want to know is: could he have tried,
Before his slow death from starvation,
To bring himself a little consolation
By reciting all those psalms inside his head?

Just a little longer and there will be no wicked one,
He'd murmur to a shovel full of ash,
You'll contemplate his place and he'll be gone.
Unless he was too busy saying *kaddish*

For his father—lost a few days before
Along with his own reservoir of psalms,
Still stunned by the crudeness of the cattle car,
A man known to go hungry giving alms,

Who'd walk to *shul* the long way, on a muddy road
So as not to crush a blade of grass on *shabbos*—
Was he to say his father wasn't righteous
That his only son should go in search of bread?

Though the psalm does say *begging* bread:
And begging was of little use at Auschwitz:
There, you had to have something to trade—
A sock, a shoe, a blanket, cigarettes—

For what someone who did favors for a dishwasher
Had managed to scrape off dirty SS plates.
Our scholar wouldn't eat—it wasn't kosher—
Though the rules didn't really apply at Auschwitz;

The Torah, after all, says, *to live by them;*
You can even eat vermin in the face of death
But our young man kept singing that one psalm
Over and over: *nourish yourself with faith.*

(Is that why David says he's never seen
The children of the righteous begging bread?
They're meant to be sustained by faith alone?)
And was our scholar, singing that line, comforted?

And his fellow prisoners? Could they have heard?
Did he sing the other psalms or just that one?
Maybe all the psalms had left his head.
He'd contemplate their place and they'd be gone.

I could try asking my father-in-law
If, in all his years at Auschwitz-Birkenau,
He ever once overheard a psalm.
But I know the answer just imagining him

Giving me the slightly baffled stare
He keeps in reserve for these conversations
That says: where do you find these foolish questions?
And then: how could you know? you weren't there;

If I hadn't been, I wouldn't believe it either. . . .
Aloud, he'd tell me: *Psalms, I didn't hear,*
You were lucky to put two words together
Without some SS screaming in your ear

But this was nothing. This was nothing.
Most of his descriptions end like this.
He almost never says what *something* was.
Whatever it may have been, he'll always sing

That bit about the children begging bread
When it's quoted in the *Birkat Hamazon.*
I refused to sing it as a kid—
Though, unless you're counting television

I could honestly have said I'd never seen
Or known I'd seen, a single person starving—
My poor rabbi found me so unnerving
When I'd balk at his effort to explain

That the line wasn't meant to be historical
But something to hold onto as a dream.
I love to sing it now. Only a fool
Would try to be literal about a psalm

But then I'd argue: but it says *seen*.
The past tense. A single person's life-span.
Read it. *I've been young and I've grown old.*
Even now, singing it, I'm still compelled

To wonder what the line's supposed to mean.
Maybe the key word really is *seen*
And David's trying to make us a confession:
That, for all his affect of compassion,

He never, even once, bothered to look.
Or maybe it was just that he couldn't see.
A man who, with a slingshot and a rock,
Could conquer a nation's greatest enemy. . . .

A slingshot at Auschwitz? Can you imagine?
Though once, in a film, I heard a Vilna partisan
Describe his girlfriend crippling a Nazi train
Loaded with guns and bombs and ammunition

With a single handmade ball of yarn and nails. . . .
But that was only one Nazi train.
She did, for a week or so, tie up those rails,
But, before she knew it, trains were running again,

Taking whoever hadn't died of gunshots
In graves they'd dug themselves in nearby woods
To slower, but less messy, deaths at Auschwitz—
Some, with entire books inside their heads—

And what I'm saying is, there were so many of them—
Let's forget about my scholar with the shovel—
I'd admit it; he had no thought of a psalm—
But think of the others, many religious people,

Standing there, waiting in the other line,
First, for the barber, to have their hair cut,
Then, for whoever did the tooth extraction,
All these things took time; they had to wait.

I know it sounds crazy, but couldn't one of them—
Not that it matters, they all died anyway—
But still, so many people, and enough time
For reciting what the dying are supposed to say

(*Hear O Israel*, etc.) and a psalm.
Or not even a whole psalm. Just one line.
All those people waiting. Couldn't one of them
Have mumbled to a brother, a father, a son

(The women, of course, were on another line
And this was not a psalm they would have known)
Just a little longer and there will be no wicked one;
Just a little longer . . . he'll be gone.

Nominated by Agha Shahid Ali, Edward Hirsch

COMMENDABLE

fiction by JOAN SILBER

from PLOUGHSHARES

MARCIA'S PARENTS, who still lived in New Jersey, were truly happy when she came to live in the East again. Her father said, "Hey! That's more like it," when she first told them she was moving to New York. "About time!" her mother said. Nobody mentioned the years when they had been so bitterly against her. Her parents were old now, and the fights were over long since. And what had they fought about? Sex, Marcia would say. Sex in various forms. And who had asked them to be so nosy? Marcia had lived with some men who were not great people, she had danced in a topless club, she had been in one dirty movie that very few people saw. But it had never been her idea to share this news or to try to make it intelligible to them. Her poor parents, how raging and mean they had been. And the whole thing had been one spell of time for Marcia, among many, and not the most regrettable. For years now she'd been a regular person who worked at a job, and her parents said, "Sweetheart, you are so gorgeous," when they saw her, and, "Don't be a stranger," when she left.

Now that Marcia was living nearby, she could see that her parents had changed quite a lot. They had once been sociable people, bridge players and party givers, but now they hardly went out. Her father was convinced that the teenage boy next door was casing the house when he walked around in his own backyard, and her mother believed that someone was stealing gravel from their driveway. They gave their dire reports with foxy satisfaction; oh, they knew what was going on, they were well-aware. "It's a different world," they said, correctly, although its difference made them read it wrong, Marcia thought.

They were still in the same house where Marcia had grown up, a roomy Colonial that got good sun. And the town seemed remarkably the same, Marcia decided, when she came for a weekend and was sent out to shop. Mitchell's Hardware was still there, only with a new sign, and Garfield's Fine Footwear was in the same spot on Franklin Avenue. Even the shoes in the window looked eternal—patent Mary Janes for little girls, brown oxfords for men, pointy pumps for women.

On the other hand, where the Sweet Shoppe had been was a store that sold exercise equipment, and next door was a Caffe delle Quattro Stagioni, which smelled deliciously of espresso. The Caffe was all chrome and tile, sleekly authentic, but the woman coming out of the door, as Marcia went by, could have been one of the mothers from her youth. She had a look of breezy competence that Marcia had almost forgotten about, a modest but sturdy expression; she wore a blouse and Bermuda shorts, and she had her hair in a short, tidy cut (like a little cap, Marcia's mother would have said). "Hello, hello," the woman said. "What are you doing here?" She was definitely speaking to Marcia.

"Visiting the old homestead," Marcia said. "How are you?" She had no idea, not a clue.

The woman chuckled, a little spitefully, and said, "You don't know me, do you?" but from that dark chuckle Marcia did know. It was Kaye Brightley, older sister of Ivy, who had been Marcia's best friend in junior high.

And what was Kaye doing here? She lived here, had always lived here; she had a job at the pharmaceutical company on the highway, and she had her own house out by where Heiling's Ice Cream used to be. "How's Ivy?" Marcia said.

"In London still. She likes it. You know she's divorced? Her kids are fine, they're old now. She's good, she's living with someone. How are *you* doing?"

Marcia said she was just now on her way to buy tomato plants for her mother.

"I wouldn't get them at Mitchell's, if I were you," Kaye said. "The really good place is the nursery in East Brook. That's where Jimmy gets his, and he has an amazing garden."

"Jimmy McPhaill?" Marcia said.

Was nothing changed here at all? Jimmy had been Kaye's constant companion all through high school. For a while they'd had a romance (of some kind, Ivy and Marcia had done a lot of wild guessing about what kind), but this had fallen apart soon, and after a brief cooling-off period they'd gone back to being buddies. Marcia thought later that Jimmy was probably gay. An opera lover, a sports hater, an impassioned fan of Emily Dickinson. Although now when she thought of him, he seemed corny and avuncular and hearty, someone whose jokes would be all wrong in most gay circles.

She and Ivy, the young pests, had hung around Jimmy as much as he would let them, pale and unhandsome though he was. He had been quite nice to them. He lent them books and made them listen to Gilbert and Sullivan. He took them out for sundaes, with Kaye, and acted tickled by their greed for chocolate, their crushes on the counter guy. Marcia and Ivy were goofy, feverish creatures then; by the time they were more composed, he was gone. Kaye was always shooing them away—"Hey, kidlets, go take a short walk off a long pier"—but she put up with them better than most older sisters would have.

"He's a stupendous gardener," Kaye said. "Every square inch of his yard, back and front, has something sprouting out of it. Every year there's more."

"Say what you will," Marcia groaned, "New York does not have real vegetation. They chain down the saplings."

Marcia went on so long about New York's pathetic, scraggly ginko trees that before she knew it, she was agreeing to go see Jimmy's place. "He can tell you everything you need to know about tomatoes," Kaye said. "He's the one who knows. And then you can get a quick view of the garden, which you really have to see."

Marcia followed Kaye's car out of the town's old center, onto a road with a little mall of newer stores, into the hillier, wealthier, more countrified expanses where Jimmy's parents had always lived. The parents were both dead by now, Marcia had just been told, and he was in their house alone.

Even from a distance you could see that these grounds were like nothing else around them. Marcia's first impression was of an illustration from a Victorian children's book, with roses on trellises and sweet peas clinging by their tendrils to a fence. Everything seemed lush and innocent. And that was only the side of the house. When

324

they parked in the back, they walked out into something more formal and rhythmic—beds of red and pink and blue, trailing arches of lavender and white, and even a sculpted bramble in the shape of a spire. Marcia, who did not know the names of many flowers, was dazzled by the cunning, intricate shapes, the bell-shaped cups, and the open, flat blooms, big as cymbals, and the cascades of frothy white bushes. Sitting on a bench was a large person in a striped shirt and khakis who was Jimmy.

"I didn't know you were coming!" he said to Kaye. He got up to greet her. He was better-looking as a grownup, more evenly proportioned. He'd become a broad-faced man with a beard, quite substantial. Still a little soft around the edges, maybe. When Marcia was explained to him, he said, "Well, well, well."

He thought she didn't like him. He thought she still found him clumsy and unimpressive. Once, when he was home from college, he had taken her out for ice cream, and she had acted quite superior with him. Marcia had forgotten all about this part of it.

Kaye made Jimmy give a tour of every petal and leaf in the garden, which Marcia was genuinely thrilled by. "What do you think?" Kaye said. "Unbelievable, right?"

"You're amazing," Marcia told Jimmy. "I'm amazed. This is too much, this place."

"Right," he said.

"This is a whole kingdom here. You must work your fingers to the bone, just to get the tea roses like that."

Marcia was gushing, but he was hard to talk to, and it was often her instinct to flatter men. She supposed she wanted to stop this; maybe not.

"I've never seen a private garden as incredible as this."

"Shucks," he said.

"No, really."

"I could show you the potting shed," he said. "That's what makes it easier, that I had that built here. The hideaway."

"She doesn't want to see that ratty piece of architecture," Kaye said. "Let her sit down."

Uh-oh. Marcia sat down, just in case Kaye thought she was after Jimmy.

"Do you like root beer?" Kaye said. Jimmy was sent inside to bring them some.

"This place *is* incredible," Marcia said, one more time.

"Every night when I come over, he's playing in the dirt," Kaye said. "He wouldn't do vegetables for a long time, but I talked him into it."

Jimmy was back with the root beer in glass mugs. "The Kaye does not believe in ice cubes for this beverage."

If they weren't a couple, they managed to sound like one. And they matched: the primly casual clothes, the streaks of gray in their hair. But perhaps they were both thinking that Marcia looked foolishly juvenile with her bleached ponytail and her short sundress. They wanted to hear about whatever she'd been up to. A long story; Marcia stuck to the here and now. She had a little, little apartment in New York—the size of a gym locker—and she was a program counselor at Planned Parenthood.

"I see a lot of teenage girls," she said. "You would not believe some of the outfits. They're a cute group. And quite hip. We didn't know about getting our own birth control at that age."

"Speak for yourself," Kaye said.

"Why, Kaye," Marcia said.

"I mean boys knew to buy condoms. Another idea that's come around again."

"Car fins are next," Jimmy said.

"We didn't have the risks," Kaye said, "that they have now."

Had Kaye had sex in high school? Marcia had never imagined her doing any such thing—Kaye with her boxy body, her flat voice. When things got wild in America, Kaye was already out of school. Marcia, who was only five years younger, thought of herself as from another generation, on the boat Kaye had just missed. But who knew what Kaye had been up to? Perhaps she and Jimmy had ventured into those waters, and then turned back.

"Condoms aren't the only things we send people out with," Marcia said. "It depends."

"Better than having them on welfare, right, Jimmy?" Kaye said.

"I'm not against freedom for anybody," Jimmy said. "I just wish they had husbands so the taxpayers wouldn't have to marry them."

"Those stubborn girls," Marcia said, "turning away those eager husbands."

They probably thought she sounded bitter, which she was not, or not about those things; heartless desertions hadn't been her problem. She liked men still, she still cooed and trilled around them, and when would this end? She hoped before it became ridiculous.

Jimmy said, "Okay, blame the boys. Go ahead." On that last trip

326

out for a sundae with Jimmy, she remembered now, he had turned caustic when she'd said she was going to be very, very busy the next few days. "Thank you for your time this afternoon," he had said. And she had not told Kaye, although she had tried earlier to brag about things like that to Kaye.

"Jimmy gets stuck on one idea," Kaye said. "Who could believe that husbands are the answer?"

"I couldn't, personally," Marcia said. "I've had three. One of them isn't quite done yet. You ever have one?"

"Not me," Kaye said.

"Me, neither," Jimmy said.

"I got to see things, at least, because of them," Marcia said. "I lived in Mexico, and before that I was in Senegal for a while."

"I've only been to England," Kaye said. "To see Ivy."

"Where I'd like to go someday is Japan," Jimmy said. "I'd be interested to see the gardens."

"Me, too," Kaye said. Jimmy had money. What was stopping them?

"Asia," Jimmy said, "is great for games." He went and got his mahjongg set to show Marcia; the tiles were antique ivory. Marcia said the set was beautiful, but she begged off on joining their tournament, which had been running for years, according to the score sheets. Actually in Mexico, where she'd had a lot of leisure, Marcia had been quite a passable mah-jongg player.

By the time Marcia got advice about the tomato plants, she decided it was too late to drive over to buy them in East Brook. When she called home to explain where she was, her mother didn't seem to mind. "I've been hanging out with Kaye Brightley and her boyfriend," Marcia said. "Remember Ivy? Kaye's the sister."

"I know who she is, she's been around here for years. Boyfriend who?" Marcia's mother said. "I thought she liked girls."

It was Marcia's first summer in the East in many years, and she had underestimated how hot New York could get. The wiring in her building was too old for air conditioners. She took dips in the municipal pool on Carmine Street, remnant of a nobler civic vision and safe even now, but so crowded it was like swimming on the subway. As a child, she had swum in Russell Pond in Russell Park, a few blocks from her house. The pond's bottom was as muddy as ever, she found out one weekend; the water was warm and smelled like tadpoles. Local children were surprised to see her there; adults almost never went in, and most of the morning you had to be a kid taking a class to use it. Several times Marcia swam there in the late afternoon, when the light was bright and dappled.

Neither Kaye nor Jimmy would go with her. Too public, and Kaye had once seen a leech in the water. (So had Marcia, but not lately.) But whenever she could, Marcia stopped in at Jimmy's garden before she went home, and had gin and tonics with the two of them; the root beer, it turned out, was only for before three. "Greetings, thirsty voyager," Jimmy would say. Marcia was still stumped on the question of whether they were a couple or not. They seemed to spend together every minute that Kaye wasn't working. (Jimmy lived off what he referred to as family holdings and seemed to have quite an open schedule.) They went out for movies and dinners and drives to the country, and their conversation was as full of old stories and minor bickering as any couple's. Marcia had never seen them embrace, but they were Episcopalians, as Marcia's mother liked to point out, and not young. But then why did they live separately, why wouldn't they marry each other? Kaye's house—small and ugly, in a new development—was bare and provisional inside, as if she were waiting to see about it, although she had lived there for years.

On weekends Kaye did go off without Jimmy for a few hours, to play basketball with a group of women, and it was this—and her square-torsoed, no-nonsense sturdiness—that had given Marcia's mother her ideas about Kaye's sexual preference. "And her manner," Marcia's mother said. She found Kaye gruff and unaccommodating. "A person who is not trying to be pleasant."

"Mother," Marcia said. "Nobody goes through the day being girly and sugary anymore. Kaye has a responsible job. She wears a suit and bosses people around."

"I heard. She makes a nice living," Marcia's mother said.

"They all have to now," Marcia's father said. "Am I right?"

Marcia could not imagine Kaye having sex with another woman (something she had watched in person, in fact, more than once), but she knew that watching was unnatural, and so anyone was almost impossible to picture swept away in the mechanics. Marcia herself had never much liked mirrors; she liked to close her eyes. So perhaps Kaye had known unspeakable splendors. And Jimmy was a whole other set of secrets.

Neither of them seemed at all miserable. Kaye liked her job, as far as Marcia could see. She talked about it with a possessive irritation, a

328

pride in its vexations, always, Marcia thought, a sign of love. She complained about how she always had to check every little thing her "people" did without making them feel like nincompoops; she was probably good at all this.

One night Kaye telephoned Marcia at home for advice about what to wear to a company awards banquet. "A swank affair," she said. She must have been to this kind of thing before, but she probably knew that her type—the dowdy woman of great integrity—wasn't what was wanted for corporate display; she was a respected throwback. "Dark red silk would be good with your coloring," Marcia said. "Spend money." But they both knew Kaye would look like Kaye, anyway.

Otherwise they never spoke to each other outside Marcia's visits; neither Kaye nor Jimmy showed the slightest interest in setting foot on the island of Manhattan. Marcia could go for a few weeks without thinking about either of them; her job was busy and packed with other people's crises, and at night she had long, ill-advised phone conversations with Alejandro, the man she had left her husband, Mike, for, and also with Mike, who was now living with a twenty-five-year-old but was balking about the divorce.

Marcia was glad for her solitude, with its peace and freedom, but she was sorry she was never going to sleep with either Mike or Alejandro again. And perhaps with no one else, either; she knew lots of people—men and women both, her age and other ages—who did without. She could see the advantages, but she had lived a good part of her life trying to be faithful to the currents of desire, sworn to that, if to nothing else. At nineteen, in the topless bar, prancing around on that little catwalk stage, she'd thought she was dancing out the most urgent truth, repeating what everyone knew, only more prettily, with her smudged eyes and her rouged breasts; what a vain girl she had been and how caught up in one single idea. And even later, when she couldn't stand to be anywhere near the Carnival Club, nothing had seemed clearer to her than the primacy of sexual feeling. But maybe her own fate was that she had passed now into another stage, another state. She could imagine it, or almost. But she would have to move to another line of work, where she wasn't all the time explaining to teenagers where their cervixes were.

In a general way, she was fine now, with her tiny apartment, her ambling routines, her touristy pleasure in the noise and sociability of the New York streets. She had a few old friends here from other places, and a few cronies at work whom she liked. In autumn the weather was clear and pleasant; Manhattan (she told Alejandro) was a handsome city, garbage and all.

In the brightest part of October, Kaye called to ask if Marcia wanted to come spend a weekend with them in the country, in a house Jimmy's father had owned, near the Delaware Water Gap. Another relative used it in the summer, but Jimmy wouldn't leave his garden then, and Kaye said they liked it in the fall. "Come be a leaf peeper," Kaye said. "We don't do anything more strenuous than that, I promise."

"You always missed the autumns in the East," Mike said, when she told him she was going.

On Saturday morning she took the train to New Jersey, where Kaye and Jimmy met her at the station, and they rode over highways whose bordering trees were suddenly blazing with color. All that miraculous color, the backlit leaves glowing against the sky, made Marcia fiercely homesick for Alejandro and for Mike, for things over and done with.

The house, which had been quite isolated when he was a kid, Jimmy said, was now on a road dotted with new chalets and A-frames. In the afternoon, joggers of all ages went past and waved to the three of them on the porch; they sat sipping bourbon and sodas, Kaye's drink of choice for the season. The hillside behind them was dazzling.

At dusk they went inside, and Kaye brought out a Scrabble set. "Don't let Jimmy try his fake words. He's ruthless," she said. They were clever players, both of them, good at placing their letters on the high-scoring squares and reusing *q*'s and *x*'s; Marcia was beaten badly. "The Kaye is unstoppable tonight," Jimmy said.

In the kitchen, Kaye stood at the stove, with a bib apron over her wool slacks, and made them what she called a lazy dinner, chicken baked in some sort of salad dressing, not bad. "Children," she said, "you may pick up your drumsticks. We're in the country."

Would Kaye have made a good mother? You could say she had the life of a suburban matron, without the family to go with it. Had she been cheated of her best fate, or would she have been one of those sour, hotly resigned mothers of Marcia's childhood? If Kaye mourned the road not taken, it didn't show. And she did have Jimmy, who at the moment was gnawing away intently at his bone. "You can't get a better bird than this," he said. "Not if you shot it yourself." They were three middle-aged adults without children, although Marcia had at least done things you wouldn't want kids along for. Not that anyone was handing out medals for that.

"In Senegal the chicken, when you got any, was as tough as shoe leather," Marcia said. "At dinners, conversations would hit these long pauses while people were chewing." She noticed she wanted to brag about herself, where she had been and with whom.

"I'd like to go to Africa," Jimmy said.

"He doesn't even have a passport," Kaye said.

"Actually, mine is expired, too," Marcia said.

"Really?" Kaye said. "This shocks me, about you."

"Oh, boy," Marcia said. "My current life would really shock you, then. I don't do a thing."

"What qualifies as a thing?" Jimmy said.

"Don't ask," Marcia said. He looked sly and laughed his old laugh, a hawing guffaw. Marcia felt very racy, not happily. It might be harder than she'd thought, spending a whole weekend with the two of them.

But then Kaye brought out the dessert—do-it-yourself sundaes, with fudge sauce and Reddi-wip and shredded coconut and a jar of walnuts in syrup. "You don't do this all the time, do you?" Marcia said.

"Sure we do," Kaye said.

"Sundae comes once a week," Jimmy said. "Isn't that the idea?"

"I'm in heaven," Marcia said.

Where were Jimmy and Kaye each planning to sleep? That was the question. Marcia's own suitcase had been taken to a dark corner room with sloped eaves, charming in a gloomy way, across the hall from the master bedroom, whose open door showed that somebody's method of unpacking was to dump all the stuff on the floor. When they all went upstairs to bed, Jimmy went into this room, and Kaye stood in the hall saying, "Sweet dreams," and then she went into another bedroom, next door to Marcia's. That's it, then, Marcia thought, I should have known.

Marcia was probably glad, more or less. Lying in the single bed, under a weighty mound of wool blankets, she liked to think of all three of them tucked up in their separate realms, cozy enough. Like children, or like commendable old people in a British novel. To each his own, she thought.

331

But in the middle of the night Marcia was awakened by a single, soft cry. From Jimmy's room she could hear gasping and short, quick breaths. Ah, well, she thought, let them, but she felt like a man in the audience at the Carnival Club, trapped in his own rapt attention, dumb and hooked and mocked. (*Who doesn't want to watch?* the owner had said. *What else is interesting?*) Then Marcia heard Kaye calling, "Jimmy, Jimmy," but the voice came from next door, from Kaye's own room. The door opened, and Kaye ran out into the hall.

It was not sex—what was wrong with Marcia, that that was all she knew about?—it was a medical crisis or a bad dream. Marcia was probably not wanted in the second case, and she lay still for a minute—Jimmy's voice, a low monotone, seemed to be reassuring Kaye—and then she got up, anyway. How could she pretend not to have heard? Wasn't she here in the house with them? Kaye turned on the light just as Marcia stood in the doorway, and there was Jimmy sitting up in bed, red-faced and sweating; he looked as if he'd been boiled. His hair and his beard were as wet as a swimmer's.

"Are you all right?" Marcia said.

"I woke you up," Jimmy said. "We should've put you downstairs."

"He has medicine he takes," Kaye said. "Don't worry about it. Go back to bed."

"Sorry," Marcia said, and got out of there.

Oh, Jimmy, she thought back in her room, you could have just told me. How long had he had night sweats? Kaye's face had been heavy with a tight, mournful anger. But they might've kept her away from the house overnight, if they really had wanted to keep all of this private and hidden.

Perhaps Marcia was not supposed to say anything about it to them. As if she didn't hand out pamphlets every day urging people to get tested in four languages. She wondered if Jimmy had a wild and separate nocturnal life with other men, or a longtime lover he just didn't tell people like her about. Jimmy acted as if he didn't know what year it was, Marcia thought, and yet he must know.

At breakfast Kaye was still angry, or plenty miffed, at any rate. "I tell him to just do the *basics* to take care of himself," she said. "It's the least he could do, don't you think? Does he get monitored by the doctor when he's supposed to? No. Does he exercise at all ever? No. Not him."

332

"He has to be careful. It can make a big difference," Marcia said.

Jimmy, who was sitting right across from them spooning up his cereal, said, "He has to put up with everybody's free advice."

"What are they giving him?" Marcia said to Kaye.

"That's another thing," Kaye said. "Nitroglycerine pills dissolved on the tongue—that can't be the best they can do for angina. Really. Does that sound like a nineteenth-century treatment or what?"

"The heart," Jimmy said, "is a nineteenth-century organ. I have a quaint, outdated malady."

Marcia saw Jimmy's heart, a sequestered valentine, pulsing in its wine-velvet casing. Apparently she was never going to guess right about it.

"Your *father* took those little nitro pills," Kaye said. "How state-of-the-art can they be?"

Jimmy carried his bowl to the sink and walked out of the kitchen.

"None of my beeswax," Kaye said. "That's his little way of letting me know."

"Is he all right?" Marcia said.

"He's not all right," Kaye said. "He knows he's not."

"You can't make him take care of himself if he won't."

"Who, then?" Kaye said. "Who else?"

Marcia was about to say, *He has to do it himself*, but that was just some California jive; perhaps it was her own jive.

"He just goes on in his merry, pigheaded way," Kaye said. "He leaves it to me to worry. I'm the one. It's my job." Kaye was washing the breakfast dishes as she spoke. Steam was rising from the sink like a staging of her ire.

She went at the counter with a sponge, scouring hard. "He just goes off. And you see how he leaves the kitchen. Look at this crud."

"You could ignore the crud," Marcia said. "That's kind of my philosophy."

"Yes," Kaye said. She went on rub-a-dub-dubbing.

"Do you do this whenever you come out here?" Marcia said. "Clean the house?"

"Well, I have to," Kaye said.

"Mike, my husband, was a great housekeeper," Marcia said. "I think I got neater because of him."

"Jimmy hasn't gotten neater," Kaye said. She was taking a broom out of a closet. Marcia followed her into the hallway, where she began sweeping.

333

"I'll do something," Marcia said. "Do you want me to do something?"

"You're the guest," Kaye said.

Kaye was raising a lot of dust, attacking the floor with great lunges of the broom. She seemed invigorated by her proprietary housework and her wifely griping. Marcia sat down to watch her and felt left out.

Music came suddenly from the living room. A jolly tenor was telling them that he was the captain of the *Pinafore* and a right good captain, too. "Ah," Kaye said. "He's put that on for me. He's sick of it, but I still like it."

Jimmy came out of the living room then, doing a little two-step to the chorus that was giving three cheers and one cheer more. If it was his way of ending their quarrel, it worked. Kaye knew the words to all the verses. Jimmy held the dustpan for her, and they bobbed around in time. "What movie are we in?" Marcia said.

After this Jimmy went out to get the Sunday paper, and when he came back they all sat in the now dustless parlor and read through every part of the paper. Jimmy and Kaye muttered at the articles and read bits of news aloud every so often, and they did the crossword puzzle together, seated next to each other with rival pencils. What if sex were just taken out of the world? Marcia thought. Kaye and Jimmy were like an illustration from a book explaining how this could be done.

What would you do if you were blind? What if you couldn't walk? People always imagined how their senses got sharpened, their appreciations grew within a smaller focus; less stood in the way of their attentions; they became keen and sharp. Marcia was remembering all this.

"This puzzle was designed by a sadist rogue computer," Jimmy said.

"Anybody want to go for a walk?" Marcia said. "A little pre-lunch constitutional?"

"Jimmy sort of has to take it easy today," Kaye said. "Normally I encourage him to move his butt, but now, no."

This meant that Kaye was not going, either, and when Marcia took off for a quick stroll, the two of them waved to her from the porch. It was not Jimmy's fault he had to rest, but they were both so generally quiet in their habits, not to say pokey. Marcia always felt young and coltish next to them, but she wasn't so young, was she?

334

The weather was not as bright today—a white sky, a dampness in the air—and the foliage looked less fiery, but still panoramically terrific. Marcia went around gathering up the best leaves, the deepest reds and flashiest combos; she did this for something to do, but also with the idea of sending a few in the mail to Alejandro, who had never seen the leaves change.

When she got back to the house, Jimmy was napping on the porch, and Kaye was inside reading a mystery and looking drowsy; neither of them could have slept much the night before. Marcia showed Kaye her leaf assortment—"to send to a friend in California."

"Press them first," Kaye said.

Kaye didn't ask anything about the friend, which disappointed Marcia; she seemed to want to speak about him. "My friend Alejandro," she said. "Who's never been north of Marin County."

A little flush of affection for Alejandro had crept over her on the leaf hunt. "My pen pal," she said, although really they were phone pals.

"I see," Kaye said. She did her knowing chuckle.

"He's a total Californian," Marcia said. "He's never been to New York."

"I've never been to the West Coast."

"It'll be his first visit. He's coming probably in the winter," Marcia said. "I like the idea of showing him the snow." Why was she saying this? She was making it up.

"Better tell him to bring a lot of layers to wear," Kaye said.

"I told him to wait till spring, but he wants to come after Christmas." Marcia knew it was childish to lie like this, but she couldn't stop. She didn't even *want* Alejandro to come, she was fairly sure. She watched Kaye's expression, which was mildly amused and a little put out that Marcia had been keeping secrets.

"It's so small in that apartment," Marcia said, "but we'll manage." She couldn't help it, she felt better. "The man snores," she said, "and hogs all the room in the bed."

Over lunch, which was BLT sandwiches, Marcia said, "I used to cook more, but I stopped."

"Better produce in California," Jimmy said.

"Alejandro likes to cook. It spoiled me. On camping trips, even, we ate well," Marcia said. "You wouldn't believe I would go camping, would you?"

"There are trails around here," Kaye said. "Somewhere."

335

"We had good equipment. One of those dome tents, one of those amazing lightweight sleeping bags. It was Alejandro's stuff, actually." Kaye looked amused again.

By late afternoon, it was time to drive back; Kaye and Jimmy didn't like to drive at night. On the highway Marcia was afraid they were going to want to play one of those family car games—count all the signs with S in them, that sort of thing—but instead they listened to a tape of *The Mikado*. If you want to know who we are, we are gentlemen of Japan. Kaye insisted on driving, although Jimmy looked much better than he had in the morning.

"Alejandro drives like a nut," Marcia said. "He's good, but he's too fast. It's hold-on-to-your-hat time when he's behind the wheel."

"That's California, isn't it?" Kaye said.

"Are you freezing?" Jimmy said to Kaye. "You look like you're freezing." He took off his cardigan and put it around her shoulders. It was one of those old man's sweaters, droopy and gray, and even from the back seat it made Kaye look like Margaret Rutherford. "Better? Okay?" Jimmy said. What scared Marcia was that she was starting to envy them.

"It's the way Alejandro takes the turns," Marcia said. "Too much."

She was making Alejandro sound pretty dashing. He was actually a fairly quiet person, aside from his driving habits. She didn't think it was Alejandro she wanted to see, but he was the phantom object of desire now, the readiest emblem of plain and definite lust. Even now, Marcia thought she didn't really understand what life was without this, and she hoped she never knew, but in time it was likely she would. How little she had imagined before now, how slender her horizons had been.

"Campers," Kaye said, "I see a Dairy Queen ahead. What do you think?"

"Let our lovely guest decide," Jimmy said.

"Stop we must," Marcia said.

Listen to this, will you? she thought. Incredible. They had her talking like them.

The girl behind the counter at the Dairy Queen wore puce lipstick heavily outlined in brown, and she made Jimmy repeat his order three times. Marcia talked to girls like her all day (you could win them over by just admiring their earrings) and had once been that girl, but Jimmy was rattled. Marcia put her arms around Jimmy and

Kaye while they waited. "Hello, three musketeers," the girl said when she came back with their orders.

They took the ice cream—two double chocolates and one vanilla-chocolate swirl—and they each tucked into their cones with a happy concentration that Marcia decided (with some effort, and it wasn't easy) not to see as any sort of erotic pantomime. It seemed to be her job to take on innocence now, a trait she had never admired or had any use for before. And she was doing fine at it. Oh, who would have thought?

"The intrepid travelers find refreshment," Jimmy said.

Nominated by Debra Spark, Pat Strachan, Maxine Kumin,
Barbara Selfridge, Eugene Stein, Robert Boswell

PENUMBRA

by BETTY ADCOCK

from SHENANDOAH

The child in the cracked photograph sits still
in the rope swing hung from a live oak.
Her velvet dress brims with a lace frill.

Her pet bantam is quiet in her lap.
It is the autumn day of a funeral
and someone has thought to take a snap-

shot of the child who won't be allowed
to go to the burying—the coffin in the house
for days, strange people going in and out.

She's dressed as if she'd go, in the blue church-
dress from last Christmas, almost too short.
The rooster loves her. She guards his perch

on her lap, his colors feathering the mild air.
She concentrates on this, now that her father
is unknowable, crying in the rocking chair.

Her mouth knife-thin, her small hands knotted hard
on the ropes she grips as if to be rescued,
she is growing a will that won't be shed.

And something as cold as winter's breath
tightens in her, as later the asthma's vise
will tighten—hands on the throat, the truth.

Black and white, she is hiding
in every one of my bright beginnings.
Gold and deep blue and dark-shining

red the cockerel's feathers, gold the sun
in that skyblue southern fall, blue
over the four-o'clocks and the drone

of weeping draining like a shadow from the house
where someone is gone, is gone, is gone—
where the child will stay to darken like a bruise.

I am six years old, buried
in the colorless album.
My mother is dead.
I forgive no one.

Nominated by Shenandoah

HALF-ANSWERED PRAYERS

memoir by ANDREW HUDGINS

from THE AMERICAN SCHOLAR

W HEN I WAS A CHILD, I longed to hear the voice of God. I prayed and prayed, begging to be heard, begging to be answered. I prayed not to die. I prayed that I wouldn't be whipped for kicking my brother. And I prayed to get things I wanted. A dog. A Cub Scout uniform. A baseball glove. A radio.

In bed at night, I spent uncountable hours in an almost mindless orgy of greed, pleading and whining for a transistor radio. Every night for months, I troubled "deaf heaven with my bootless cries," as Shakespeare phrases it. I wanted the radio so I could huddle beneath the covers after I was sent to bed, and listen to baseball games and country music. Even then, years before I could envision terminal cancer patients praying frantically for a miracle cure and years before I read of Jews in Nazi death camps beseeching God for justice, I knew that asking for a radio, a thing, was ignoble—a vulgar abuse of my Protestant right to address the godhead directly. But I wanted the radio so much I persisted in my supplication.

Though I've never doubted that the impulse behind the two was pretty much the same, my childhood avarice, over time, changed into spiritual longing. In either case, I've wanted something I didn't have—whether it was a radio when I was ten, world peace when I was twenty, homes for the homeless when I was thirty, a job that offered personal fulfillment when I was forty, or spiritual serenity as I near fifty. I now scorn my youthful avarice and materialism, but at least, after months of bootless crying, I got the radio.

That answered prayer may have owed more to my earthly father's growing tired of my badgering than to my heavenly father's finally extending his grace. Or perhaps, as I was taught to think at church, my father was God's agent on earth. However I came by the radio, I was not allowed to take it to bed with me. My mother said, "Your bed is for sleeping in and nothing else, young man. You have no need for a radio there." And neither was I allowed to listen to country music. Songs about drinking, loving, and cheating were too adult for a young boy like me, my parents gravely informed me, putting their fingers precisely on the reason I was fascinated by them.

This was how prayers seemed to go. When I did get what I wanted, I got it in a way that was almost exactly like not getting it. Every child learns these lessons about the gap between expectation and reality, but in a Baptist family they are so tied to God, the giver of all blessings, that I came to understand him as an especially cunning lawyer who parsed every prayer, looking for loopholes, looking for perverse ways of answering the letter of my request while frustrating the spirit of it. Into the familiar Christian dialectic of the Old Testament God of wrath and the New Testament God of mercy, I insinuated a malicious, mocking figure—a Loki, a Coyote, a Pan, a Reynard the Fox. But I prayed to him anyway. I was expected to pray to him, and besides, who else had the power to give me the things I desired?

Except for trying to wheedle things out of God, I prayed hesitantly because, as a matter of principle, I'd never been taught how to pray. For Baptists, prayer was simply opening your soul to God, and how can that be taught? the preachers asked scornfully. Just talk to God, they said. From the grace we said before meals, I knew to offer thanks for food, and because it was the one thing always mentioned by the laymen who self-consciously and haltingly offered the public prayers during the Sunday services, I knew to be thankful for my health. My parents, grandparents, and the preachers also emphasized the importance of health. If you've got your health, they intoned, you've got everything. But even as I thanked God, I thought: But I've always had good health. Aren't you *supposed* to have good health? Isn't it something you should take for granted, and when you age and you no longer have it, isn't it like God is taking it away? I

341

took these questions as evidence that I didn't have much aptitude for the more spiritual side of prayer. And the response I was getting from God—none—reinforced that sense. But I kept praying anyway.

Like 90 percent of Americans, I pray regularly. But unlike 96 percent of my fellow citizens, I'm not sure that I believe in God. It's an awkward, if not entirely untenable, position. The God I pray to is an external God, one who exists, if he exists, outside of me. I resist the idea of an internal God simply because it seems to me a slightly camouflaged way of worshiping myself, solipsism magnified to its most repulsive level. But of course, as I pray to the external God that I'm not sure is there, I'm also talking to myself, clarifying my own thoughts, trying to place myself in the spiritual tradition that I have inherited, trying to understand things that resist understanding. My prayers are then, despite my discomfort with an interior God, both centripetal and centrifugal, directed both inward and outward. And even if the external God does not exist, I benefit from the exercise of trying to put what is beyond words into words. In "East Coker," T. S. Eliot writes about words, speech, writing, but he might just as well be talking about prayer when he says that

> each venture
> Is a new beginning, a raid on the inarticulate
> With shabby equipment always deteriorating
> In the general mess of imprecision of feeling,
> Undisciplined squads of emotion. And what there is to conquer
> By strength and submission, has already been discovered
> Once or twice, or several times, by men whom one cannot hope
> To emulate—but there is no competition—
> There is only the fight to recover what has been lost
> And found and lost again and again: and now, under conditions
> That seem unpropitious. But perhaps neither gain nor loss.
> For us, there is only the trying. The rest is not our business.

I pray to reach outside myself, to position and understand myself against, beside, parallel to, and perhaps even at one with a God who very well may not exist, and in doing that I push, against my will sometimes, into self-understanding.

Though I've learned to pray mostly for my own moral and spiritual betterment, not for things, the hunger for God-knowledge has per-

342

sisted and grown. The prayer I've prayed since I could see my way clear to formulate it when I was ten, eleven, twelve is "Let me hear a word from you. Let me know you are there." By the time I was fifteen I didn't even mind much if God said no to my petitions; I just wanted to hear the no. I'd have settled, I told myself, for the harsh response Job provoked from God. After God strips him of everything—health, fortune, family—Job finally cries out for justice, for an explanation: "Let the Almighty answer me!" The audacity of the demand thrills me as much now as it did when I was a teenager.

The King James Version tells us contemptuously that Job is "righteous in his own eyes," and God answers Job's perfectly reasonable questions with more questions, and trumps his bafflement with scorn:

> Then the Lord answered Job out of the whirlwind, and said,
> Who is this that darkeneth counsel by words without knowledge?
> Gird up now thy loins like a man; for I will demand of thee, and answer thou me.
> Where wast thou when I laid the foundations of the earth? declare if thou hast understanding.
> Who hath laid the measures thereof, if thou knowest? or who hath stretched the line upon it?

Three chapters later God is still berating poor Job:

> Canst thou draw out leviathan with an hook? or his tongue with a cord which thou lettest down?
> Canst thou put an hook into his nose? or bore his jaw through with a thorn?
> Will he make many supplications unto thee? will he speak soft words unto thee? . . .
> None is so fierce that dare stir him up: who then is able to stand before me?
> Who hath prevented me, that I should repay him? whatsoever is under the whole heaven is mine.

Job's response to such hectoring is to "repent in dust and ashes":

> I know that thou canst do every thing, and that no thought can be withholden from thee.

Who is he that hideth counsel without knowledge? therefore
have
I uttered that I understood not; things too wonderful for me,
which I knew not.

I understood as a boy that God was pulling rank on Job. He was
overwhelming Job with his magnificence, his realms of divine knowl-
edge that left puny human understanding so far behind as to render
it meaningless. Putting myself in Job's place, I resented God's tone of
voice. I felt the way I did when my parents dismissed my questions
by telling me that I wasn't supposed to understand, say, the lyrics of
a country song about drinking and slipping around. Those were adult
concerns and I would understand them when I was an adult. End of
discussion.

Nonetheless, I was as thrilled by God's answer as I was by Job's
question, just because it was an answer. Job was persuaded, as I was
not, by the thunderously poetic non sequitur of God's reply, but at
least Job knew for certain that he was struggling with a God who ex-
isted, and I envied him his certainty.

Certain or not, I've continued to pray, and as I've aged, I've taken
more and more comfort in the idea of prayer as a way to help those who
are beyond my help. One of my students is waiting to hear the results of
her spinal tap. Does she have multiple sclerosis? She'll find out next
week. Please, Lord, do not let this young woman have MS. Does it
help? Or is praying merely a primitive denial of my own helplessness? I
don't know. I hope for the former and fear the latter. But at the very
least, I can say to her the next time I see her, "I'm praying for you," and
that speaks to her, I hope, of a deeper level of human concern and con-
nectedness than "Hey, Patty, I'm keeping my fingers crossed!"

Twenty years ago, while I was taking classes to prepare me for con-
firmation in the Episcopal Church (a process I decided not to go
through with), I was taught a simple form of prayer: Adoration, Con-
trition, Thanksgiving, Supplication. The rector teaching the class
helpfully pointed out that we could remember this because the first
letters spelled out "Acts—as in the Acts of the Apostles." Though I
cringed in embarrassment and then cringed again at my aesthetic re-
sponse to the mnemonic device, I've used it virtually every night of
my life since then.

The last three parts of the prayer give me no trouble. Contrition is
useful. It's humbling to spend a few minutes every night reviewing

and evaluating my day, trying to understand how I have failed to do right by others and by my own sense of myself. But I also try to look from what I take to be God's perspective at how I've lived my last twenty-four hours. And for a pessimist like me, a person too apt to get caught up in the pleasures of self-excoriation, remembering to move on and enumerate my blessings with gratitude is just as useful as contrition. Supplication, though I still occasionally lunge at it with my old transistor-radio greed, is starting to lose some of its grip on me. I am always slightly pleased when I wake up in the morning and realize that I've fallen asleep before I get to my list of desires.

But adoration flummoxes me. What possible gratification does an omnipotent being derive from my telling him how great he is? Flattering God with a list of his attributes seems like a primitive, even anachronistic, exercise. The few times I've tried it I've felt like an especially obsequious minor official from Bactria who, with his mouth hanging open, has entered Babylon through the gold and ivory of the Ishtar Gate. Ushered into the presence of Xerxes, the Great King, he mumbles his way through a memorized list of superlatives in a language he barely understands, and the Great King, who hears his own titles recited to him a hundred times a week, still listens closely, making sure the satraps pay him due reverence.

In trying to praise God, I also feel most strongly the troubling historical connections of Christianity to the worship of Baal and Mithras, and all the cults of the sacrificed god. Though I know the real purpose of praise is not to flatter God but to help me understand my proper relation to him, I balk at praising the presence who, if he exists, has presided in this century alone over two world wars, the Holocaust, the murder of the kulaks, the rape of Nanking, the bombing of Hiroshima and Nagasaki, the Chinese cultural revolution, the killing fields of Cambodia, and the influenza pandemic of 1918. The problem of theodicy—why does God allow evil in the world?—leads all too quickly to asking how, given all the evil in the world, there can be a God. I confess to, thank, and ask for help from a God whose existence I doubt, but to praise him without confidence in his existence and his goodness twists my tongue into baffled silence. Not knowing what else to do, I repeat by rote the opening words of the Lord's Prayer, trying to find some way to inhabit them.

My desire for the mystic took some non-Christian turns when, in high school, I began to read about occult practices. I'd lie on my bed

345

for hours, trying to project my soul out of my body, up through the roof. I imagined my soul—me!—wafting through the Sheetrock and roof joists, through the pink fiberglass insulation, through the plywood sheathing, through the asphalt shingles, and up into the night sky. Still rising, I'd look down on my house and my neighborhood dwindling beneath me. It was always the night sky I rose into, even if I was attempting my astral projection as the Alabama sun pounded through the window. The sky was always full of stars, and I always floated with my arms held out from my sides, my hands and fingers feeling the wind that I knew I wouldn't feel if I were really pure soul.

And there I lost my grip on the vision that I was trying to make real. I couldn't truly imagine what it would be like to be a soul free in the air. Where would I go? What would I want to see? I could, I supposed, float into the houses of my friends and spy on them—or waft into the Statehouse and spy on government officials. I could even watch people make love, a subject about which I had much interest and no knowledge. But these seemed base uses of the gift I hoped to acquire, and in truth, I wasn't really interested in being a mystical Peeping Tom. Plus, I could never quite conceive of my soul as a free agent in the sky. Even in my best imaginings, my incorporeal soul was still subject to the vagaries of the wind, like a balloon or a kite. And like a kite, my imagined soul seemed anchored to the ground, to my body, to the house in which I lay on the bed, imagining—solid, earthbound, leaden. This was not astral projection. Even as a teenager, I suspected that my loving attention to Sheetrock and fiberglass kept me from slipping effortlessly through them. A real mystic, I thought, would know that all was maya, illusion. He wouldn't even think "roof" as he rose though an undifferentiated mass of material to swoop and gambol in midair, at play in the fields of the sky, freed of the limitations of flesh.

I realized that the only religion I was ever going to begin to understand as a faith, even if I didn't confidently share that faith, was the incarnational one I was born into. Christianity's deep divisions reflect my own. The incarnation of God in the body of Jesus, fully God and fully human at the same time, presents a Möbius strip of logic. It boggles my understanding, yet perfectly represents the way I experience my life, as my body and soul strain to go their separate ways while at the same time struggling for the unity that Christ represents. Pauline Christianity, with its all but horror of the corrupted body and its love of the pure soul, balances against the God who became the

346

son of a rural carpenter. Christ, the Christian ideal, takes these opposing essences—body and soul—and fuses them into one essence, an act of philosophical synthesis that defies my understanding while it defines my yearning. And that yearning is so strong it holds my natural skepticism in yet another uneasy balance.

When I was a boy, thirteen or fourteen, I prayed my truest prayers in bed, after the family prayers had been said and the light snapped out. This was my real praying, pouring out to God what I hoped was my soul. After the "Amen," I'd masturbate, and then, wretched with guilt, I'd pray again, pleading for forgiveness. But why should God forgive me? We both knew I was going to commit the same sin again, perhaps within the next fifteen minutes. My prayers and my sins wound around each other in an orgy of urgency, release, guilt, and terror of hellfire that repeated itself nightly and often several times a night. This lascivious cycle of despair prepared me to read the *Inferno* with the eyes of one of Dante's sinners, or *Pilgrim's Progress* with the eyes of one of the many pilgrims who founder in the Slough of Despond and never come near the Celestial City. To me, those books felt absolutely contemporary, a vital reflection of life as I and many of the people around me understood it.

Now, though, I see those frantic bouts of prayer and release as complementary. The hoped-for ecstatic union of the body in sex directly parallels the hoped-for ecstatic union of the soul with God in prayer: bodily and spiritual intercourse. Under the sweat-damp sheets of my bed, I was discovering a metaphor that the mystics have known since at least the Song of Songs. Whitman sang it in "Song of Myself," and even the medieval church tacitly acknowledged it in one of the legends collected in *The Little Flowers of Saint Francis*. While Francis is in Babylonia (where, by the way, he secretly converts the sultan to Catholicism), he is approached by a lustful woman. He works out a deal with her. If she will do what he wants, then he will do what she wants.

She accepts, and suggests that they immediately prepare a bed for their lovemaking. But Francis says, "Come with me, and I will show you a very beautiful bed," and he leads her to the large fire burning in the central hearth of the house:

> And in fervor of spirit he stripped himself naked and threw himself down in the fireplace as on a bed. And he called to her, saying: "Undress and come quickly and enjoy

this splendid, flowery, and wonderful bed, because you must be here if you wish to obey me!" And he remained there for a long time with joyful face, resting on the fireplace as though on flowers, but the fire did not burn or singe him.

The legend tells us only that the woman was so terrified and remorseful at seeing the miracle that she converted on the spot and "became so holy in grace that she won many souls for the Lord in that region." What is left for us to understand is that when the woman saw Francis lounging luxuriously in the fire, she saw the purified vision of the longing for passion, union, ecstasy, and fulfillment that had driven her to prostitute herself.

Even now I envy this fictional character the unambiguous certainty of her sudden faith. In those intense, troubled nights, I too was reaching out desperately for the God I already doubted, asking for a word, for some assurance that the body was not all I had, that the material world was not the only world. I heard nothing.

Through my late teens and into my middle twenties, I declared myself an agnostic, even an atheist. Still, I never quite stopped praying. It was too natural a part of my life for me to stop.

But three times—long after I quit consciously listening—I have heard God's voice speak directly to me. I wonder what the average number is for a man my age.

The first time I have forgotten almost entirely. My first wife and I were separated and I was on the edge, I suspect, of a nervous breakdown. One morning in the bathroom, shaving, I heard a voice clearly not my own say something to me. Whatever the voice said, it was something so trivial and inscrutable that I laughed out loud. Still, I was thrilled to have heard the voice, and for a day or two I felt a sense of serenity and otherworldly detachment that I had never felt before. I'm sorry, but those clichés, which are almost invariably used to describe experiences like this, are all I have to offer. As I knew it would, the sense of peace dwindled over the next three days. But in that short period of grace, I laughed at and accepted my own immediate questioning of what had happened: "This could just be stress. People often hear voices when they are stressed." "If it was really God, why didn't he tell you something useful?" "If it was really God, why do you find it so hard to remember what he said?" Whatever I

348

heard, it was already abandoning me, sliding out of my mind, and I didn't want to write it down because I knew it would look silly in print.

I never mentioned to anyone that I'd heard the voice. I was too embarrassed to talk about it. And I distrusted it. I thought I might be nuts. I have talked to myself all my life, and my mother, who was both amused and slightly disturbed by this habit, used to say, "It's okay to talk to yourself, but when you start hearing answers, you know you're in trouble." I also remembered a strange psychology class I had taken at Huntingdon College, a small Methodist school in my hometown of Montgomery, Alabama. Dr. Statum, the hard-nosed psychologist who taught the class, told us that one of the questions frequently asked on psychological tests was "Do you hear God talking to you?" Since he was a born-again Christian, he always answered yes. He paused to let that sink in. Someone in the class tittered nervously. But we should remember, he went on, that answering yes to one of the "trick" questions wasn't enough to get you declared insane. You had to answer yes to several of them before you were deemed truly, clinically over the line. His point was that psychological exams didn't really know how to deal with religious people, so they simply built in some slack.

For a long time, I pondered Dr. Statum's comfortable acceptance of the idea that many religious people had at least one of the primary earmarks of insanity, unsure what to make of it or of him. And I wondered what it meant about my father and all the people I sat next to in church every Sunday. Now, though, I returned to that moment in Dr. Statum's class for reassurance. Sure, I'd heard a voice speak to me out of thin air, and my impulse at the time—and my impulse now—was to think it was the voice of God. If it was, I wasn't crazy. And if it wasn't—well, Dr. Statum (I reminded myself) had said that you had to have more than one symptom before you were officially nuts.

In truth, I didn't worry too much about my sanity. The experience was clearly a positive one, and through a difficult time in my life, I was buoyed by the idea that God had spoken to me and reassured me—while I also held in mind the understanding that I might have had a momentary schizophrenic delusion. Though I did not know it at the time, the voice I heard meets the third of St. Ignatius's "Rules for the Discernment of Spirits": "I call consolation any increase of faith, hope, and charity and any interior joy that calls and attracts to

349

heavenly things." In *St. Ignatius of Loyola: The Psychology of a Saint*, W. W. Meissner, who is both a Jesuit and a psychiatrist, considers Ignatius's own mystical visions. "Was Ignatius psychotic?" he asks.

Meissner admits that some psychiatrists "have not hesitated to call mystical phenomena psychotic." Both psychotics and mystics see visions (or, more rarely, hear voices), fall passive during the experience, develop a sense of mission, lose a sense of time and space, and undergo rapid mood shifts. And both are ashamed of the experience; it belongs to a realm that cannot be shared with others. But Meissner seems to be more persuaded by scholars who point out that mystics, unlike psychotics, maintain a steady grasp on reality, are humble rather than self-aggrandizing, and possess a "serene optimism." Meissner quotes the psychiatrist Silvano Arieti as saying, "Religious and mystical experiences seem instead to result in a strengthening and enriching of the personality." Meissner answers his question about Ignatius's sanity by saying that a modern psychiatrist, diagnosing the future saint's condition in the turmoil surrounding his conversion, might well have concluded he was psychotic. But psychosis would have been the last word that would have sprung to mind if he or she had examined the extraordinarily self-possessed and forceful Ignatius who governed the Society of Jesus and conducted its "world-wide operations and complex and difficult relations with royalty and the papal court."

While the voice I heard is small spiritual potatoes next to Ignatius's visionary feast, the saint, like me, was sometimes absentminded about what had been served at the banquet. In his autobiography, which is told in the third person, Ignatius records that God unveiled to him how the world was created, but he has forgotten the details: "One time the manner in which God had created the world was revealed to his understanding with great spiritual joy. He seemed to see something white, from which some rays were coming, and God made light from this. But he did not know how to explain these things, nor did he remember very well the spiritual enlightenment that God was pressing on his soul at that time."

I remember more clearly the second time I heard God's voice. I was visiting my father in north Alabama while the woman I am now married to was in California. She and I weren't seeing each other at the time. She had some personal problems to sort out without the distraction of a man in her life. Wondering if I was being strung along or manipulated by a woman I didn't yet know very well, and wondering if I should forget her and move on, I was agitated and unhappy. All this was in my head as I got up one morning and made the bed. The bedspread was in midair, ballooned above the mattress, when I heard a voice say, as clear as God calling Samuel's name in the night, "Isn't she doing everything she can?"

Immediately I felt a sense of calmness. Yes, I said to myself. Yes, she is doing everything she can.

Pondering what had happened, I walked into the dining room and had breakfast with my dad. I sipped my coffee, ate my Raisin Bran, and read the *Birmingham News* in silence, trying to hold onto the moment for a little longer before it began to fade into the noise of everyday life. I did not tell my father what had happened. What could I say—"Hey, Dad, I just heard God talk to me in your guest bedroom, and he was offering advice for the lovelorn"? Of course, as I munched my Raisin Bran, I was already wondering why God, if that is who it was, talked to me only when women abandoned me. And why did God ask a question? Why didn't he just *tell* me that she was doing everything she could? But the question the voice asked was clearly rhetorical. It presupposed its answer. And the slightly comic nature of the whole scene reassured me. My love life, though important to me, hardly seemed of divine importance. Perhaps that's the point—that the first two times I heard God speak to me, he was concerned with my personal life. That's not what I expected.

When I had prayed as a boy for God to speak to me, I had both longed for and dreaded the words that he might say. From all the stories I'd heard preachers tell, from all the devotional books I'd read, and from the Bible itself, I thought God almost invariably called the unbeliever to believe and the believer to preach. I was afraid that God would order me to be a missionary or a street-corner preacher. I was truly terrified that God would tell me to spend my life serving the poor. In church, as the preachers exalted evangelists like Billy Sunday and Billy Graham and missionaries like Lottie Moon, I identified both with these religious models and with Jonah sailing in the opposite direction from Nineveh, where God had commanded him to go. I even identified fully with Jonah's rage at God for showing mercy and sparing Nineveh. After Jonah had walked through that great city crying that God would destroy it in forty days, the people fasted, covered themselves and their beasts with sack-

351

cloth and ashes, and repented. But what gratification is there in actually being listened to when you had relished the image of God striking dead all the unbelievers who had scorned and mocked you?

From my childhood fear of being called by God, I well understood Jonah's petulance and rage. When my father and the other deacons in his church went witnessing door to door, I shrank from them, afraid they'd ask me to accompany them and testify to strangers. Sharing their greatest happiness and their faith in eternal life was meant as an act of generosity, but confronting complete strangers with one's beliefs has always seemed to me like a very intimate violation of other people's selfhood. I spent many childhood hours imagining how I would do it, and how I would respond when people brushed me off, as I would brush them off if our positions were reversed.

Though I have known plenty of born-again preachers, I have known only one person who underwent a dramatic conversion, like the one I feared, and became a street-corner evangelist. When I was teaching part-time at a small university in Montgomery, I'd sometimes go out for drinks after class with the older students. One of the regulars was a rowdy chop-haired blonde in her mid-twenties. Part hippie, part redneck, Liz drank as heavily as men who outweighed her by eighty pounds and smoked unfiltered Camels as if smoke were sustenance. She left her illegitimate child with her mother, and though she talked about him a lot, she never seemed in a hurry to get home. She wore cheap tube tops and tight jeans artfully frayed to single threads across her thighs, and she laughed with a rough heehaw that I loved.

Several months after the class ended, Liz called and told me that she'd been born again. She'd moved back in with her mother. She'd noticed me driving by her mother's house on my way to visit my girlfriend, and she wondered if I'd like to stop by for a cup of coffee.

At her mother's kitchen table, she told me about her ministry, and whenever her eyes grew faraway as she got lost in the telling, I studied her face. She looked relaxed, almost peaceful, telling of the rebuffs she'd suffered as she, along with her new preacher Brother James, witnessed for two days every week on street corners in downtown Montgomery. They worked twelve-hour days, exhorting crowds, stopping passersby, and simply preaching to the empty street when there were no people to preach to. Her clothes were clean and modest. She didn't smoke, she didn't swear, she didn't drink, and she

352

was plowing ahead at school, determined to get her degree and go on to a small seminary I hadn't heard of. But as she told stories about the rude remarks and threats that people made while she was witnessing, she occasionally let out one of those vulgar, braying laughs that I admired.

When her son—he looked to be about ten—wandered into the kitchen and demanded orange juice, she politely told him that she was talking and she'd get him some juice when she was done.

"I want it now. Now! Now! Now!" he chanted in an ascending pitch, his face turning purple.

Liz grabbed him by the upper arm and swung him around till he was face to face with her. "Mommy said she'd get you some juice in a minute. But you are not allowed to interrupt me when I'm talking to company."

The boy sucked a long breath, preparing to scream. Liz held up the index finger of her right hand and said, "Johnny, don't act like a baby. If I have to spank you, I will."

He snuffled for a moment or two, and then leaned forward, resting his head on her arm for a few moments. She gave him a quick hug. "You go play and I'll bring you your juice in a few minutes."

While he was still in the room she gave me a quick, apologetic smile, and said to me, but speaking so he could hear, "It's hard for him. I let him run wild for ten years and it's hard for him to learn that he now has a mother here to take care of him."

As I left, she said—she said it casually when I paused at the door to say good-bye—"You know I pray for you."

That simple sentence ran me through a whole array of emotions as I stood in her mother's doorway, looking at as changed a human being as I have ever seen in my life, and changed for the better.

"Thank you," I said. "Thank you." I was supposed to say, "I'm praying for you too," but I couldn't get the words out of my mouth.

When I was younger, between about twelve and twenty-five, I hated it when people told me they were praying for me. And I hated it even more when they didn't say it but I could tell from the look on their faces that they were mentally adding me to their prayer lists. I hated it with the passion of a self-conscious boy and young man who wanted to think he was invisible, unnoticed by adults. Also, I perceived other people's prayers as their desire to coerce me mystically—prayer as the voodoo of the middle class. I thought that, under the guise of caring for me, they were using God as an invisible robot

353

arm to make me do things that they couldn't make me do themselves: join the church, be a better student, stay out of trouble. I felt as if I were a billiard ball that might not be making its true run across the table because they were using God as a sort of mystical body English to affect my movements, even to tilt the table.

But now that I have a stronger, steadily stronger, sense of mortality and of the limitations of human effort, I find myself longing for their prayers. I want the table tilted. I want to be remembered by them, and I have a superstitious faith in the faith of believers like my wife, my father, my cousin Julie, my friend Randall. And of course if I want them to pray for me, I have to pray for them. It is unthinkable that I would withhold my prayers from those who pray for me, just because I am skeptical that my words to God do any good.

The only other time, the most recent time, I heard God speak, his voice was coming out of my mouth. One morning several years ago, as I woke from a deep sleep, I was chanting "God loves me" over and over again—a slow, intense, two-beat repetition that was part of my own breathing. "God," I said, as I inhaled. "Loves me," I said, as I exhaled. I lay in bed awake for fifteen or twenty minutes, repeating "God loves me" as if possessed. At any time during those fifteen minutes, I could have stopped myself with a simple act of will. But why would I want to? The feeling was wholly pleasurable, and deeply reassuring on any number of levels—personal, spiritual, and even intellectual. I'm well acquainted with Carlyle's "The Everlasting No." This was my strongest brush with "the EVERLASTING YEA, wherein all contradiction is solved: wherein whoso walks and works, it is well with him." I think of this voice as God's because it said something that until then I would never have said myself, and it is in fact something that I don't say even now, except sometimes late at night when I am having trouble sleeping. Then, I will try to work my way back into the strange, serene rhythm of that morning: "God" on the inbreath, "loves me" on the out-breath.

So of the three times I have heard God's voice, I remember two sentences: an embarrassingly personal rhetorical question and Christianity's most mind-numbingly obvious cliché. But I hear the Sunday school simplicity of the phrase "God loves me" as a reminder that spiritually I am a beginner, a child, a tyro—and that before I can go any further I must absorb this basic lesson. Sometimes the most basic lesson is the most profound. Toward the end of his life, Karl

Barth, in a story that has become a favorite of contemporary pulpits, was asked if he could sum up his lifework in systematic theology. He replied with the words of the children's song, "Jesus loves me, this I know, for the Bible tells me so."

I feel especially grateful for the last voice. I feel God put those words in my mouth because I would never say them myself; I would never even begin to feel the feeling without his forcing the issue. In my mouthing of the cliché there is the odd mixture of divine subtlety and ham-handedness that the mystics speak of. And despite my doubts and misgivings, I believe, with a tentative and anxious faith, that my prayers for a sense of the presence of the godhead are being answered. The next step is harder; it's even more daunting than trying to believe that God loves me. In Carlyle's *Sartor Resartus*, the phrase immediately before "This is the EVERLASTING YEA" is "Love God." But for me that is like looking at the last chapter of the trigonometry text on the first day of class. I can't imagine ever getting there.

Sometimes I ransack various translations of the Bible, trying to get a grip on a verse that eludes me. For a long time I was puzzled by a sentence from John 5:17. "My Father worketh hitherto, and I work" is how the King James Version renders it. "Hitherto what?" I wondered, until, after some years, curiosity overtook lethargy and I checked other translations. "My Father is working still, and I am working," says the Revised Standard Version. The New Jerusalem Bible is even clearer: "My Father goes on working, and so do I."

On the in-breath: "God." If he exists. On the out-breath: "Loves me."

Nominated by The American Scholar, John Drury

FOLDING THE FOX

by ROBERT GIBB

from ARTS & LETTERS

My son, discovering numbers
   And the laws of structure
      In the crystal's walls, the gray
Comb woven in the wasp's nest,

Comes to me this evening bearing
   A sheaf of paper and the book
      In which the ancient art lies
Charted, the animals are creased

Into being. Together we practice
   Intricacies of wing fold
      And crimp fold, water bomb base,
Learning to master the basic

Emergence of their shapes.
   My son turns out cups like lilies
      And those severe white birds,
Almost Egyptian in their beauty,

While I finally muster up
   A squash fold from the wrinkles
      And misguided pleats, recalling
The simpler veer of paper airplanes

Into flight, the kites I boxed
  Together like cartons of light.
    When I was nine, my Uncle Arch
Taught me how to knot a tie,

Standing behind me in the mirror,
  Kind hands on mine as they
    Fashioned the loops of fabric
And drew them tight. Now, tonight,

I try to guide hands which ache
  To vanish among the crisp
    Divisions of paper, as together
We follow the fox through petal

And bird base, five-sided square,
  To where the flame-shaped tail
    Plumes before us
Across newly emblazoned air.

Nominated by Michael Waters

IN CUBA I WAS
A GERMAN SHEPHERD

fiction by ANA MENENDEZ

from ZOETROPE: ALL STORY

THE PARK where the four men gathered was small. Before the city put it on the tourist maps, it was just a fenced rectangle of space that people missed on the way to their office jobs. The men came each morning to sit under the shifting shade of a banyan tree, and sometimes the way the wind moved through the leaves reminded them of home.

One man carried a box of plastic dominoes. His name was Máximo, and because he was a small man, his grandiose name had inspired much amusement all his life. He liked to say that over the years he'd learned a thing or two about the "physics of laughter," and his friends took that to mean good humor could make a big man out of anyone. Now, Máximo waited for the others to sit before turning the dominoes out on the table. Judging the men to be in good spirits, he cleared his throat and began to tell the joke he had prepared for the day.

"So Bill Clinton dies in office and they freeze his body."

Antonio leaned back in his chair and let out a sigh. "Here we go."

Máximo caught a roll of the eyes and almost grew annoyed. But he smiled. "It gets better."

He scraped the dominoes in two wide circles across the table, then continued.

"Okay, so they freeze his body and when we get the technology to unfreeze him, he wakes up in the year 2105."

"Two thousand one hundred and five eh?"

"Very good," Máximo said. "Anyway he's curious about what's happened to the world all this time, so he goes up to a Jewish fellow and he asks. 'So, how are things in the Middle East?' The guy replies, 'Oh wonderful, wonderful, everything is like heaven. Everybody gets along now.' This makes Clinton smile, right?"

The men stopped their shuffling and dragged their pieces across the table and waited for Máximo to finish.

"Next he goes up to an Irishman and he asks, 'So how are things over there in Northern Ireland now?' The guy says, 'Northern? It's one Ireland now and we all live in peace.' Clinton is extremely pleased at this point, right? So he does that biting thing with his lip."

Máximo stopped to demonstrate, and Raúl and Carlos slapped their hands on the domino table and laughed. Máximo paused. Even Antonio had to smile. Máximo loved this moment when the men were warming to the joke and he still kept the punch line close to himself like a secret.

"So, okay," Máximo continued, "Clinton goes up to a Cuban fellow and says, 'Compadre, how are things in Cuba these days?' The guy looks at Clinton and he says to the president, 'Let me tell you, my friend, I can feel it in my bones, any day now Castro's gonna fall.' "

Máximo tucked his head into his neck and smiled. Carlos slapped him on the back and laughed.

"That's a good one, sure is," he said. "I like that one."

"Funny," Antonio said, nodding as he set up his pieces.

"Yes, funny," Raúl said. After chuckling for another moment, he added, "But old."

"What do you mean old?" Antonio said, then he turned to Carlos. "What are you looking at?"

Carlos stopped laughing.

"It's not old," Máximo said. "I just made it up."

"I'm telling you, professor, it's an old one," Raúl said. "I heard it when Reagan was president."

Máximo looked at Raúl, but didn't say anything. He pulled the double nine from his row and laid it in the middle of the table, but the thud he intended was lost in the horns and curses of morning traffic on Eighth Street.

Raúl and Máximo had lived on the same El Vedado street in Havana for fifteen years before the revolution. Raúl had been a govern-

359

ment accountant and Máximo a professor at the university, two blocks from his home on L Street. They weren't close friends, but friendly still, in that way of people who come from the same place and think they already know the important things about one another.

Máximo was one of the first to leave L Street, boarding a plane for Miami on the eve of January 1, 1960, exactly one year after Batista had done the same. For reasons he told himself he could no longer remember, he said goodbye to no one. He was forty-two years old then, already balding, with a wife and two young daughters whose names he tended to confuse. He left behind the row house of long shiny windows, the piano, the mahogany furniture, and the pension he thought he'd return to in two years time. Three, if things were as serious as they said.

In Miami, Máximo tried driving a taxi, but the streets were still a web of foreign names and winding curves that could one day lead to glitter and another to the hollow end of a pistol. His Spanish and his Havana University credentials meant nothing here. And he was too old to cut sugarcane with the younger men who began arriving in the spring of 1961. But the men gave Máximo an idea, and after teary nights of promises, he convinced his wife—she of stately homes and multiple cooks—to make lunch to sell to those sugar men who waited, squatting on their heels in the dark, for the bus to Belle Glade every morning. They worked side by side, Máximo and Rosa. And at the end of every day, their hands stained orange from the lard and the cheap meat, their knuckles red and tender where the hot water and the knife blade had worked their business, Máximo and Rosa would sit down to whatever remained of the day's cooking, and they would chew slowly, the day unraveling, their hunger ebbing with the light.

They worked together for seven years like that, and when the Cubans began disappearing from the bus line, Máximo and Rosa moved their lunch packets indoors and opened their little restaurant right on Eighth Street. There, a generation of former professors served black beans and rice to the nostalgic. When Raúl showed up in Miami in the summer of 1971 looking for work, Máximo added one more waiter's spot for his old acquaintance from L Street. Each night, after the customers had gone, Máximo and Rosa and Raúl and Havana's old lawyers and bankers and dreamers would sit around the biggest table and eat and talk, and sometimes, late in the night after several glasses of wine, someone would start the stories that began with "In Cuba I remember . . ." They were stories of old lovers,

360

beautiful and round-hipped. Of skies that stretched on clear and blue to the Cuban hills. Of green landscapes that clung to the red clay of Güines, roots dug in like fingernails in a good-bye. In Cuba, the stories always began, life was good and pure. But something always happened to them in the end, something withering, malignant. Máximo never understood it. The stories that opened in the sun, always narrowed into a dark place. And after those nights, his head throbbing, Máximo would turn and turn in his sleep and awake unable to remember his dreams.

Even now, ten years after selling the place, Máximo couldn't walk by it in the early morning when it was still clean and empty. He'd tried it once. He'd stood and stared into the restaurant and had become lost and dizzy in his own reflection in the glass, the neat row of chairs, the tombstone lunch board behind them.

"Okay. A bunch of rafters are on the beach getting ready to sail off to Miami."

"Where are they?"

"Who cares? Wherever. Cuba's got a thousand miles of coastline. Use your imagination."

"Let the professor tell his thing, for god's sake."

"Thank you." Máximo cleared his throat and shuffled the dominoes. "So anyway, a bunch of rafters are gathered there on the sand. And they're all crying and hugging their wives and all the rafts are bobbing on the water and suddenly someone in the group yells, 'Hey! Look who goes there!' And it's Fidel in swimming trunks, carrying a raft on his back."

Carlos interrupted to let out a yelping laugh. "I like that, I like it, sure do."

"You like it, eh?" said Antonio. "Why don't you let the Cuban finish it."

Máximo slid the pieces to himself in twos and continued. "So one of the guys on the sand says to Fidel, 'Compatriota, what are you doing here? What's with the raft?' And Fidel sits on his raft and pushes off the shore and says, 'I'm sick of this place, too. I'm going to Miami.' So the other guys look at each other and say, 'Coño, compadre, if you're leaving, then there's no reason for us to go. Here, take my raft too, get the fuck out of here.' "

Raúl let a shaking laugh rise from his belly and saluted Máximo with a domino piece.

361

"A good one, my friend."

Carlos laughed long and loud. Antonio laughed, too, but he was careful to not laugh too hard, and he gave his friend a sharp look over the racket he was causing. He and Carlos were Dominican, not Cuban, and they ate their same foods and played their same games, but Antonio knew they still didn't understand all the layers of hurt in the Cubans' jokes.

It had been Raúl's idea to go down to Domino Park that first time. Máximo protested. He had seen the rows of tourists pressed up against the fence, gawking at the colorful old guys playing dominoes.

"I'm not going to be the sad spectacle in someone's vacation slide show," he'd said.

But Raúl was already dressed up in a pale blue guayabera, saying how it was a beautiful day and to smell the air.

"Let them take pictures," Raúl said. "What the hell. Make us immortal."

"Immortal," Máximo said with a sneer. And then to himself, *The gods' punishment.*

It was that year after Rosa died, and Máximo didn't want to tell how he'd begun to see her at the kitchen table as she'd been at twenty-five. Watched one thick strand of her dark hair stuck to her morning face. He saw her at thirty, bending down to wipe the chocolate off the cheeks of their two small daughters. And his eyes moved from Rosa to his small daughters. He had something he needed to tell them. He saw them grown up, at the funeral, crying together. He watched Rosa rise and do the sign of the cross. He knew he was caught inside a nightmare, but he couldn't stop. He would emerge slowly, creaking out of the shower and there she'd be, Rosa, like before, her breasts round and pink from the hot water, calling back through the years. Some mornings he would awake and smell peanuts roasting and hear the faint call of the *manicero* pleading for someone to relieve his burden of white paper cones. Or it would be thundering, the long hard thunder of Miami that was so much like the thunder of home that each rumble shattered the morning of his other life. He would awake, caught fast in the damp sheets, and feel himself falling backwards.

He took the number eight bus to Eighth Street and Fifteenth Avenue. At Domino Park, he sat with Raúl and they played alone that first day, Máximo noticing his own speckled hands, the spots of light

362

through the banyan leaves, a round red beetle that crawled slowly across the table, then hopped the next breeze and floated away.

Antonio and Carlos were not Cuban, but they knew when to dump their heavy pieces and when to hold back the eights for the final shocking stroke. Waiting for a table, Raúl and Máximo would linger beside them and watch them lay their traps, a succession of threes that broke their opponents, an incredible run of fives. Even the unthinkable: passing when they had the piece to play.

Other twosomes began to refuse to play with the Dominicans, said that Carlos guy gave them the creeps with his giggling and monosyllables. Besides, any team that won so often must be cheating, went the charge, especially a team one-half imbecile. But really it was that no one plays to lose. You begin to lose again and again and it reminds you of other things in your life, the despair of it all begins to bleed through and that is not what games are for. Who wants to live their whole life alongside the lucky? But Máximo and Raúl liked these blessed Dominicans, appreciated the well-oiled moves of two old pros. And if the two Dominicans, afraid to be alone again, let them win now and then, who would know, who could ever admit to such a thing?

For many months they didn't know much about each other, these four men. Even the smallest boy knew not to talk when the pieces were in play. But soon came Máximo's jokes during the shuffling, something new and bright coming into his eyes like daydreams as he spoke. Carlos's full loud laughter, like that of children. And the four men learned to linger long enough between sets to color an old memory while the white pieces scraped along the table.

One day as they sat at their table, the one closest to the sidewalk, a pretty girl walked by. She swung her long brown hair around and looked in at the men with her green eyes.

"What the hell is she looking at," said Antonio, who always sat with his back to the wall, looking out at the street. But the others saw how he stared back, too.

Carlos let out a giggle and immediately put a hand to his mouth.

"In Santo Domingo, a man once looked at—" but Carlos didn't get to finish.

"Shut up you old idiot," said Antonio, putting his hands on the table like he was about to get up and leave.

"Please," Máximo said.

The girl stared another moment, then turned and left.

Raúl rose slowly, flattening down his oiled hair with his right hand. "Ay, mi niña."

"Sit down, hombre," Antonio said. "You're an old fool, just like this one."

"You're the fool," Raúl called back. "A woman like that . . ."

He watched the girl cross the street. When she was out of sight, he grabbed the back of the chair behind him and eased his body down, his eyes still on the street. The other three men looked at one another.

"I knew a woman like that once," Raúl said, after a long moment.

"That's right, he did," Antonio said, "in his moist boy dreams— what was it? A century ago?"

"No me jodas," Raúl said. "You are a vulgar man. I had a life all three of you would have paid millions for. Women."

Máximo watched him, then lowered his face, shuffled the dominoes.

"I had women," Raúl said.

"We all had women," Carlos said, and he looked like he was about to laugh again, but instead just sat there, smiling like he was remembering one of Máximo's jokes.

"There was one I remember. More beautiful than the rising moon," Raúl said.

"Oh Jesus," Antonio said. "You people."

Máximo looked up, watching Raúl.

"Ay, a woman like that," Raúl said and shook his head. "The women of Cuba were radiant, magnificent, wouldn't you say, professor?"

Máximo looked away.

"I don't know," Antonio said. "I think that Americana there looked better than anything you remember."

And that brought a long laugh from Carlos.

Máximo sat all night at the pine table in his new efficiency, thinking about the green-eyed girl and wondering why he was thinking about her. The table and a narrow bed had come with the apartment, which he'd moved into after selling the house in Shenandoah. The table had come with two chairs, sturdy and polished—not in the least institutional—but he had put one of the chairs by the bed. The landlady, a woman in her forties, had helped Máximo haul up three potted palms. Later, he bought a green pot of marigolds that he saw in the supermarket and brought its butter leaves back to life under the window's eastern light. Máximo often sat at the table through the night, sometimes reading Martí, sometimes listening to the rain on the tin hull of the air conditioner.

When you are older, he'd read somewhere, you don't need as much sleep. And wasn't that funny, because his days felt more like sleep than ever. Dinner kept him occupied for hours, remembering the story of each dish. Sometimes, at the table, he greeted old friends and awakened with a start when they reached out to touch him. When dawn rose and slunk into the room sideways through the blinds, Máximo walked as in a dream across the thin patterns of light on the terrazzo.

The chair, why did he keep the other chair? Even the marigolds reminded him. An image returned again and again. Was it the green-eyed girl?

And then he remembered that Rosa wore carnations in her hair and hated her name. And that it saddened him because he liked to roll it off his tongue like a slow train to the country.

"Rosa," he said, taking her hand the night they met at the La Concha while an old *danzón* played.

"Clavel," she said, tossing her head back in a crackling laugh. "Call me Clavel." She pulled her hand away and laughed again. "Don't you notice the flower in a girl's hair?"

He led her around the dance floor lined with chaperones, and when they turned he whispered that he wanted to follow her laughter to the moon.

She laughed again, the notes round and heavy as summer raindrops, and Máximo felt his fingers go cold where they touched hers. The *danzón* played, and they turned and turned, and the faces of the chaperones and the moist warm air—and Máximo with his cold fingers worried that she had laughed at him. He was twenty-four and could not imagine a more sorrowful thing in all the world.

Sometimes, years later, he would catch a premonition of Rosa in the face of his eldest daughter. She would turn toward a window or do something with her eyes. And then she would smile and tilt her head back, and her laughter connected him again to that night, made him believe for a moment that life was a string you could gather up in your hands all at once.

He sat at the table and tried to remember the last time he saw Marisa. In California now. An important lawyer. A year? Two? An-

365

abel, gone to New York. Two years? They called more often than most children, Máximo knew. They called often and he was lucky that way.

"Fidel decides he needs to get in touch with young people."

"Ay ay ay."

"So his handlers arrange for him to go to a school in Havana. He gets all dressed up in his olive uniform, you know, puts conditioner on his beard and brushes it one hundred times, all that."

Raúl breathed out, letting each breath come out like a puff of laughter. "Where do you get these things?"

"No interrupting the artist anymore, okay?" Máximo continued. "So after he's beautiful enough, he goes to the school. He sits in on a few classes, walks around the halls. Finally, it's time for Fidel to leave and he realizes he hasn't talked to anyone. He rushes over to the assembly that is seeing him off with shouts of 'Comandante!' and he pulls a little boy out of a row. 'Tell me,' Fidel says, 'what is your name?' 'Pepito,' the little boy answers. 'Pepito, what a nice name,' Fidel says. 'And tell me, Pepito, what do you think of the Revolution?' 'Comandante,' Pepito says, 'the Revolution is the reason we are all here.' 'Ah, very good Pepito. And tell me, what is your favorite subject?' Pepito answers, 'Comandante, my favorite subject is mathematics.' Fidel pats the little boy on the head. 'And tell me, Pepito, what would you like to be when you grow up?' Pepito smiles and says, 'Comandante, I would like to be a tourist.' "

Máximo looked around the table, a shadow of a smile on his thin white lips as he waited for the laughter.

"Ay," Raúl said. "That's so funny it breaks my heart."

Máximo grew to like dominoes, the way each piece became part of the next. After the last piece was laid down and they were tallying up the score, Máximo liked to look over the table like an art critic. He liked the way the row of black dots snaked around the table with such free-flowing abandon it was almost as if, thrilled to be let out of the box, the pieces choreographed a fresh dance of gratitude every day. He liked the straightforward contrast of black on white. The clean, fresh scrape of the pieces across the table before each new round. The audacity of the double nines. The plain smooth face of the blank, like a newborn unetched by the world to come.

"Professor," Raúl began, "let's speed up the shuffling a bit, sí?"

"I was thinking," Máximo said.

"Well, that shouldn't take long," Antonio said.

"Who invented dominoes, anyway?" Máximo said.

"I'd say it was probably the Chinese," Antonio said.

"No jodas," Raúl said. "Who else could have invented this game of skill and intelligence but a Cuban."

"Coño," said Antonio without a smile. "Here we go again."

"Ah, bueno," Raúl said with a smile, stuck between joking and condescending. "You don't have to believe it if it hurts."

Carlos let out a long laugh.

"You people are unbelievable," said Antonio. But there was something hard and tired behind the way he smiled.

It was the first day of December, but summer still hung about in the brightest patches of sunlight. The four men sat under the shade of the banyan tree. It wasn't cold, not even in the shade, but three of the men wore cardigans. If asked, they would say they were expecting a chilly north wind and doesn't anybody listen to the weather forecasts anymore. Only Antonio, his round body enough to keep him warm, clung to the short sleeves of summer.

Kids from the local Catholic high school had volunteered to decorate the park for Christmas, and they dashed about with tinsel in their hair, bumping one another and laughing loudly. Lucinda, the woman who issued the dominoes and kept back the gambling, asked them to quiet down, pointing at the men. A wind stirred the top branches of the banyan tree and moved on without touching the ground. One leaf fell to the table.

Antonio waited for Máximo to fetch Lucinda's box of plastic pieces. Antonio held his brown paper bag to his chest and looked at the Cubans, his customary sourness replaced for a moment by what in a man like him could pass for levity. Máximo sat down and began to dump the plastic pieces on the table as he'd always done. But this time, Antonio held out his hand.

"One moment," he said, and shook his brown paper bag.

"Qué pasa, chico?" Máximo said.

Antonio reached into the paper bag as the men watched. He let the paper fall away. In his hand he held an oblong black leather box.

"Coñooo," Raúl said.

He set the box on the table, like a magician drawing out his trick. He looked around to the men and finally opened the box with a flourish to reveal a neat row of big heavy pieces, gone yellow and smooth like old teeth. They bent in closer to look. Antonio tilted the box gently and the pieces fell out in one long line, their black dots facing up now like tight dark pupils in the sunlight.

"Ivory," Antonio said, "and ebony. They're antique. You're not allowed to make them anymore."

"Beautiful," Carlos said, and clasped his hands.

"My daughter found them for me in New Orleans," Antonio continued, ignoring Carlos.

He looked around the table and lingered on Máximo, who had lowered the box of plastic dominoes to the ground.

"She said she's been searching for them for two years. Couldn't wait two more weeks to give them to me," he said.

"Coñooo," Raúl said.

A moment passed.

"Well," Antonio said, "what do you think, Máximo?"

Máximo looked at him. Then he bent across the table to touch one of the pieces.

He gave a jerk with his head and listened for the traffic. "Very nice," he said.

"Very nice?" Antonio said. "Very nice?" He laughed in his thin way. "My daughter walked all over New Orleans to find these and the Cuban thinks they're 'very nice?' " He paused, watching Máximo. "Did you know my daughter is coming to visit me for Christmas? She's coming for Christmas, Máximo, maybe you can tell her that her gift was very nice, but not as nice as some you remember, eh?"

Máximo looked up, his eyes settled on Carlos, who looked at Antonio and then looked away.

"Calm down, hombre," Carlos said, opening his arms wide, a nervous giggle beginning in his throat. "What's gotten into you?"

Antonio waved his hand.

A diesel truck rattled down Eighth Street, headed for downtown.

"My daughter is a district attorney in Los Angeles," Máximo said, after the noise of the truck died. "December is one of the busiest months."

He felt a heat behind his eyes he had not felt in many years.

"Hold one in your hand," Antonio said. "Feel how heavy that is."

When the children were small, Máximo and Rosa used to spend Nochebuena with his cousins in Cárdenas. It was a five-hour drive from Havana in the cars of those days. They would rise early on the twenty-third and arrive by mid-afternoon so Máximo could help the men kill the pig for the feast the following night. Máximo and the other men held the squealing, squirming animal down, its wiry brown coat cutting into their gloveless hands. But god, they were intelligent creatures. No sooner did it spot the knife, than the animal would bolt out of their arms, screaming like Armageddon. It had become the subtext to the Nochebuena tradition, this chasing of the terrified pig through the yard, dodging orange trees and the rotting fruit underneath. The children were never allowed to watch, Rosa made sure. They sat indoors with the women and stirred the black beans. With loud laughter, they shut out the shouts of the men and the hysterical pleadings of the animal as it was dragged back to its slaughter.

"Juanito the little dog gets off the boat from Cuba and decides to take a stroll down Brickell Avenue."

"Let me make sure I understand the joke. Juanito is a dog. Bow-wow."

"That's pretty good."

"Yes, Juanito is a dog, goddamnit."

Raúl looked up, startled.

Máximo shuffled the pieces hard and swallowed. He swung his arms across the table in wide, violent arcs. One of the pieces flew off the table.

"Hey, hey, watch it with that, what's wrong with you?"

Máximo stopped. He felt his heart beating.

"I'm sorry," he said. He bent over the edge of the table to see where the piece had landed. "Wait a minute."

He held the table with one hand and tried to stretch to pick up the piece.

"What are you doing?"

"Just wait a minute." When he couldn't reach, he stood up, pulled the piece toward him with his foot, sat back down and reached for it again, this time grasping it between his fingers and his palm. He put it face down on the table with the others and shuffled, slowly, his mind barely registering the traffic.

"Where was I—Juanito the little dog, right, bowwow." Máximo took a deep breath. "He's just off the boat from Cuba and is strolling down Brickell Avenue. He's looking up at all the tall and shiny build-

369

ings. 'Coñooo,' he says, dazzled by all the mirrors. 'There's nothing like this in Cuba.' "

"Hey, hey, professor. We had tall buildings."

"Jesus Christ!" Máximo said. He pressed his thumb and forefinger into the corners of his eyes. "This is after Castro, then. Let me just get it out for Christ's sake."

He stopped shuffling. Raúl looked away.

"Ready now? Juanito the little dog is looking up at all the tall buildings and he's so happy to finally be in America because all his cousins have been telling him what a great country it is, right? You know, they were sending back photos of their new cars and girlfriends."

"A joke about dogs who drive cars, I've heard it all."

"Hey, they're Cuban superdogs."

"All right, they're sending back photos of their new owners or the biggest bones any dog has ever seen. Anything you like. Use your imaginations." Máximo stopped shuffling. "Where was I?"

"You were at the part where Juanito buys a Rolls Royce."

The men laughed.

"Okay, Antonio, why don't you three fools continue the joke." Máximo got up from the table. "You've made me forget the rest of it."

"Aw, come on, chico, sit down, don't be so sensitive."

"Come on, professor, you were at the part where Juanito is so glad to be in America."

"Forget it. I can't remember the rest now." Máximo rubbed his temple, grabbed the back of the chair and sat down slowly, facing the street. "Just leave me alone, I can't remember it." He pulled at the pieces two by two. "I'm sorry. Look, let's just play."

The men set up their double rows of dominoes, like miniature barricades before them.

"These pieces are a work of art," Antonio said, and lay down a double eight.

The banyan tree was strung with white lights that were lit all day. Colored lights twined around the metal poles of the fence, which was topped with a long looping piece of gold tinsel garland.

The Christmas tourists began arriving just before lunch as Máximo and Raúl stepped off the number eight bus. Carlos and Antonio were already at the table, watched by two groups of families. Mom and

370

Dad with kids. They were big, even the kids were big and pink. The mother whispered to the kids and they smiled and waved. Raúl waved back at the mother.

"Nice legs, yes?" he whispered to Máximo.

Before Máximo looked away, he saw the mother take out one of those little black pocket cameras. He saw the flash out of the corner of his eye. He sat down and looked around the table; the other men stared at their pieces.

The game started badly. It happened sometimes, the distribution of the pieces went all wrong and out of desperation one of the men made mistakes, and soon it was all they could do to knock all the pieces over and start fresh. Raúl set down a double three and signaled to Máximo it was all he had. Carlos passed. Máximo surveyed his last five pieces. His thoughts scattered to the family outside. He looked up to find the tallest boy with his face pressed between the iron slats, staring at him.

"You pass?" Antonio said.

Máximo looked at him, then at the table. He put down a three and a five. He looked again, the boy was gone. The family had moved on.

The tour groups arrived later that afternoon. First the white buses with the happy blue letters WELCOME TO LITTLE HAVANA. Next, the fat women in white shorts, their knees lost in an abstraction of flesh. Máximo tried to concentrate on the game. The worst part was how the other men acted out for them. Dominoes is supposed to be a quiet game. And now there they were shouting at each other and gesturing. A few of the men had even brought cigars, and they dangled now, unlit, from their mouths.

"You see, Raúl," Máximo said. "You see how we're a spectacle?" He felt like an animal and wanted to growl and cast about behind the metal fence.

Raúl shrugged. "Doesn't bother me."

"A goddamn spectacle. A collection of old bones," Máximo said.

The other men looked up at Máximo.

"Hey speak for yourself, cabrón," Antonio said.

Raúl shrugged again.

Máximo rubbed his left elbow and began to shuffle. It was hot, and the sun was setting in his eyes, backlighting the car exhaust like a veil before him. He rubbed his temple, feeling the skin move over the bone. He pressed the inside corners of his eyes, then drew his hand back to his left elbow.

371

"Hey, you okay there?" Antonio said.

An open trolley pulled up and parked at the curb. A young man, perhaps in his thirties, stood in the front, holding a microphone. He wore a guayabera. Máximo looked away.

"This here is Domino Park," came the amplified voice in English, then in Spanish. "No one under fifty-five allowed, folks. But we can sure watch them play."

Máximo heard shutters click, then convinced himself he couldn't have heard, not from where he was.

"Most of these men are Cuban and they're keeping alive the tradition of their homeland," the amplified voice continued, echoing against the back wall of the park. "You see, in Cuba it was very common to retire to a game of dominoes after a good meal. It was a way to bond and build community. You folks here are seeing a slice of the past. A simpler time of good friendships and unhurried days."

Maybe it was the sun. The men later noted that he seemed odd. The ties. Rubbing his bones.

First Máximo muttered to himself. He rubbed his temple again. When the feedback on the microphone pierced through Domino Park, he could no longer sit where he was, accept things as they were. It was a moment that had long been missing from his life.

He stood and made a fist at the trolley.

"Mierda!" he shouted. "Mierda! That's the biggest bullshit I've ever heard."

He made a lunge at the fence. Carlos jumped up and held him back. Raúl led him back to his seat.

The man of the amplified voice cleared his throat. The people on the trolley looked at him and back at Máximo, perhaps they thought this was part of the show.

"Well," the man chuckled. "There you have it, folks."

Lucinda ran over, but the other men waved her off. She began to protest about rules and propriety. The park had a reputation to uphold.

It was Antonio who spoke. "Leave the man alone," he said.

Máximo looked at him. His head was pounding. Antonio met his gaze briefly then looked to Lucinda.

"Some men don't like to be stared at is all," he said. "It won't happen again."

She shifted her weight, but remained where she was, watching.

"What are you waiting for?" Antonio said, turning now to Máximo, who had lowered his head onto the white backs of the dominoes. "Shuffle."

That night Máximo was too tired to sit at the pine table. He didn't even prepare dinner. He slept, and in his dreams he was a blue-and-yellow fish swimming in warm waters, gliding through the coral, the only fish in the sea and he was happy. But the light changed and the sea darkened suddenly and he was rising through it, afraid of breaking the surface, afraid of the pinhole sun on the other side, afraid of drowning in the blue vault of sky.

"Let me finish the story of Juanito the little dog."
No one said anything.
"Is that okay? I'm okay. I just remembered it. Can I finish it?"
The men nodded, but still did not speak.
"He is just off the boat from Cuba. He is walking down Brickell Avenue. And he is trying to steady himself, see, because he still has his sea legs and all the buildings are so tall they are making him dizzy. He doesn't know what to expect. He's maybe a little afraid. And he's thinking about a pretty little dog he once knew and he's wondering where she is now and he wishes he were back home."
He paused to take a breath. Raúl cleared his throat. The men looked at one another, then at Máximo. But his eyes were on the blur of dominoes before him. He felt a stillness around him, a shadow move past the fence, but he didn't look up.
"He's not a depressed kind of dog, though. Don't get me wrong. He's very feisty. And when he sees an elegant white poodle striding toward him, he forgets all his worries and exclaims, 'O Madre de Dios, si cocinas como caminas . . .' "
The men let out a small laugh. Máximo continued.
" 'Si cocinas como caminas . . .' Juanito says, but the white poodle interrupts and says, 'I beg your pardon? This is America, speak English.' So Juanito pauses for a moment to consider and says in his broken English, 'Mamita, you are one hot doggie, yes? I would like to take you to movies and fancy dinners.' "
"One hot doggie, yes?" Carlos repeated, then laughed. "You're killing me."
The other men smiled, warming to the story again.
"So Juanito says, 'I would like to marry you, my love, and have gorgeous puppies with you and live in a castle.' Well, all this time the

373

white poodle has her snout in the air. She looks at Juanito and says, 'Do you have any idea who you're talking to? I am a refined breed of considerable class and you are nothing but a short, insignificant mutt.' Juanito is stunned for a moment, but he rallies for the final shot. He's a proud dog, you see, and he's afraid of his pain. 'Pardon me, your highness,' Juanito the mangy dog says, 'Here in America, I may be a short, insignificant mutt, but in Cuba I was a German shepherd.'"

Máximo turned so the men would not see his tears. The afternoon traffic crawled westward. One horn blasted, then another. He remembered holding his daughters days after their birth, thinking how fragile and vulnerable lay his bond to the future. For weeks, he carried them on pillows, like jeweled china. Then, the blank spaces in his life lay before him. Now he stood with the gulf at his back, their ribbony youth aflutter in the past. And what had he salvaged from the years? Already, he was forgetting Rosa's face, the precise shade of her eyes.

Carlos cleared his throat and moved his hand as if to touch him, then held back. He cleared his throat again.

"He was a good dog," Carlos said, pursing his lips.

Antonio began to laugh, then fell silent with the rest. Máximo started shuffling, then stopped. The shadow of the banyan tree worked a kaleidoscope over the dominoes. When the wind eased, Máximo tilted his head to listen. He heard something stir behind him, someone leaning heavily on the fence. He could almost feel their breath. His heart quickened.

"Tell them to go away," Máximo said. "Tell them, no pictures."

Nominated by Tom Paine, Chris Spain, Zoetrope: All Story

DEATH'S MIDWIFE HAS THE SMALLEST HANDS!

by CLAIRE BATEMAN

from HARVARD REVIEW

That's what they exclaim every time—
not "My God, I'm dead!" but
"What adorable little hands!" or
"Quelle petite matins!"—meaning *mains*,
of course, not *matins* or *mornings*, but surely,
under the circumstances, some difficulty
matching words with concepts might be expected—
& actually, those hands *could* be mistaken
for mornings; little twin dawns, they move
with a genuinely lapidary speed
("Wie Können solche kleine Hände
so rasch sich bewegen?").
Yes, though she has the bulky body of a
fullback raised solely on raw beef,
her hands are not only doll-tiny, but
tidy as well, with glossed nails gleaming
a subtle shade *between* peach & coral.
O hands of ferocity & tenderness!
Some of their other areas of expertise include
coaxing show tunes from her miniature piano,
penning microscopic calligraphy
on their own little maple desk,
carving elaborate soap bar flotillas, &

375

playing poker solitaire—you can scarcely
see them, they flow so fluently
laying out the tableau! Also,
they're so deliciously pale, nearly
translucent, sometimes she imagines they're
made of spun sugar or wax. It's true that
occasionally, during an extra-busy night with
more than the usual number of
transitions to attend to, they do
seem to fade out, even to the brink of
invisibility. This, however, troubles her
not in the least. She just lights their tips
like wicks, & keeps on working.

Nominated by Thomas E. Kennedy, Arthur Smith

AGAINST A CERTAIN KIND OF ARDENCY

by CHARLES MARTIN

from THE HUDSON REVIEW

1

I know someone so ardent of the past
He finds it hard to let bygones be gone,
And says that since the present will not last,
Yesterday only can be counted on

To offer him the one true paradigm
For keeping bad enough from turning worse.
It isn't that he minds the present time,
If he could just approach it in reverse—

Yet he'd be happy to go on repeating
What has been done (as though such repetition
Were anything but wholly self-defeating),

And seems to be unbothered in the least
That he might lose the present through attrition
By yielding so much ground to the deceased.

2

If I believed that I'd be listened to,
And not accused of soiling his white banner,

I'd offer him a very different view,
Propounded in my best post-modern manner:

I'd argue that the past would be no more
Unless *we* made it—made, by our making,
What *it* could never be mistaken for:
We bring it into being by forsaking

Its ready consolations and rewards,
And thereby setting it against the new.
And so the *arrières*-and-*avants-gardes*

(So like in every way except direction)
Are both mistaken about what's to do—
Though neither would have need of my correction.

3

A long-dead Roman poet said it better
("Better" will have to do: if I say "best"
I'll lose my argument) in a verse letter
He may have meant for us, though it's addressed

To Augustus Caesar: "Who would not lament
The way we shun the new? If innovation
Had been abhorred by the Greeks to the same extent
That it is by the citizens of *our* nation,

There'd be no ancients for us now to read;
Where, in what trackless wasteland, would we be?"
No ancients without moderns, they agreed.

With Horace, I would argue to the last
Against a certain kind of ardency;
For what, if not the present, makes the past?

Nominated by Jay Meek

LOVE SONGS OF FRUIT FLIES

fiction by E.S. BUMAS

from THE GETTYSBURG REVIEW

STEPHANIE, I ASK HER, if only to test my hypothesis. Don't you find me terribly boring? Not asking for an essay but an assay, just a yes/no, a true/false, negative or positive, reactive or nonreactive, pink or blue. I avoid her big, round, coffee-colored eyes and instead look at the large, round eye of the surface of my coffee. I have heard it argued that one of our evolutionary adaptations is that when we see creatures with big, round eyes (as children have big, round eyes), we are driven to protect them. With Stephanie, who is no child, I might have a homologous reaction and need to protect her from being bored: I'm so boring it must be painful. And so impossible, I've already wandered in my mind from asking her if she finds me boring to wondering whether other species such as insects have analogous reactions to eye size, and how I would prove it, and whether certain animals find members of their own species boring.

Not yet, she says, grimacing from her ginger tea (no bourgeois coffee, not like the boring brew I'm drinking), I don't find you boring yet, but I'll be sure to let you know.

Fair enough. But when?

When I think I get confused. I think my internal clock must have three hands that move at different speeds to indicate geological time, evolutionary biological time, not to mention everybody else's time. Which is to consider the rise and fall of the Roman empire with a fifteen-second commercial for a miniseries based on *The Rise and*

Fall of the Roman Empire. Only more so. The time of humanity: well, take all my weight, bulging daily from spending too much time in the lab, and say that I am the time of the earth, little old me sipping boring coffee on my mattress by an open window. Oh, no, pollen spores. I sneeze. The weight removed from my body would cover all the time that humans have been alive. Humans and perhaps two or three of our ancestors: *Australopithecus*, Lucy. I am approximating. Biologists have little patience for geology, or for anything other than biology. Then there's the time of fruit flies, the official species of evolutionary biology, our mascots, that live, on average, two to three weeks and in that time make the mating call hardwired in their genes and hear the mating call of other insects and reproduce and disappear forever except in the palimpsest of genes of future flies. A one-week generation, and for all we know an instant generation gap (we do not know). Love at first sight a must. Mating, more accurately.

When I tell Stephanie this, she doesn't quite get my point, or rather she wonders aloud if the sneeze, the head descending quickly, was in some way an inspiration for some of the African dance she has studied with a certain Mr. Cromwell, if the sneeze could represent some ancient idea of insemination from the days of matriarchy, before men realized their small but indispensable role in reproduction and messed up, in Stephanie's approximation, virtually everything.

I have to take off my shoes.

I hold her ginger tea. She bangs on the floor, ball heel ball ball (I worry about the neighbors), snaps her head up (*ah*, she says), thrusts her head down (*choo*); she takes four steps backward (maybe the neighbors will know it is her and not me), then drops her shoulders and slowly lifts her head (I've forgotten about the neighbors), ball heel ball ball.

You might have something there, she says, but it wasn't really my idea. History, she believes, is preserved in movement. I stay very still.

I ask myself, *What is the probability of this thing working out, and what is the probability of my becoming a character in one of her performances?* I have learned what she will say to calm me down when I get panicky, why not both? Why not both, and have some valerian tea that stinks like sweaty sweat socks; it will calm me down. I go to the lab, which calms me too.

She came late to pick me up for lunch. I introduced her to Nellie down the hall, who is the only woman professor in the department and who works on the communication system of Jamaican fruit bats. There are more women in biology than in other sciences, but I have noticed a large attrition rate: 50 percent graduates, 30 percent post-docs, and only one professor in our department. There are very few black biologists. We are not a representative sample of the population. Nellie took Stephanie to the bat cages, where there were some Missourian insectivores that she keeps for trips to high schools, and let her pet their soft fur and fragile wings.

Are they happy here? Stephanie asked.

With eyes rolled in the cave of her brow, Nellie took back the bat, and Stephanie and I went out. I had a gel running and so was in no particular hurry.

When I returned, Nellie called me into her lab, scrunched her face as though trying to look like a flying fox, the famous tropical dog-faced bat, and said, You could do a lot better. She means, I take it, another biologist.

Stick to what you're an expert in, I told her. Fruit bats.

Other fields—as the Javanese say—other grasshoppers.

I am checkers to Stephanie's chess, though, as she reminds me, she does not even know how to play chess, and I do, not too shabbily in fact. She is if anything above my station, and wouldn't she prefer someone who knows more about what she does, who could do it himself, or maybe herself, someone she could collaborate with, someone skinnier?

We sort of do collaborate, she insists. Her new piece is called *If Fruits Were Meant to Fly They'd Have Wings.* She has glued plastic angel wings onto grapefruits, oranges, mangoes, and a melon, suspended them from bouncing bungee cords, and accompanies them with a metallic dirge played on her loud electric harp. A clock behind her runs very fast, and when it has made two full twelve-hour rotations, she stops playing and cuts a string so the mobile falls to the floor. Do I find my fruit flies boring?

She always starts off interested in my work, but then changes the subject until it is more interesting to her. I don't necessarily mind, but I wonder if she finds what I do with grasshoppers sick, some sort of insect rights stance. What prebiotic pond did I ooze from, anyway? In my own defense, it's not as though I am using their fur.

Did you ever hear of this one experiment, I ask her, when some researchers isolated the fruit fly gene for producing eyes? Now we can stimulate the development of eyes in non-eye tissue and grow eyes anywhere on a drosophila, on the legs, on the wings.

When I was a kid, she says, I used to trace my hand with a crayon and put a big blue eye where the lines of the palm ought to be. If it was pencil, I'd just make the eye lighter. I stopped when I thought it was silly, then years later I saw some cave paintings with the same idea, but it was too late.

To Stephanie, any science seems as practical as changing light bulbs. I often wonder what the relation of my work is to the rest of the world, whereas all my colleagues seem convinced that they are involved in the most important project on the planet, and that their funding problems only indicate the rest of the world's inability to fathom what is truly important. Evolution is not, as my harder colleagues from biochemistry point out, a hard science. Instead, it is a self-proclaimed squishy science, dealing with the probable instead of the predictive, which is all right by me. Some evolutionary biologists do have this totalizing problem that we only rid ourselves of over time, this attitude that we can explain the existence of anything off the tops of our heads. Any characteristic of a species, we tend to figure, must have taken so long to develop that it had to have helped the species survive. From there our logic works backward over millennia. To survive, it is as though a species must grow its own adapter kit to fit the ill-shaped world. Just-so stories, as senior ecologists call our explanations. Many of them believe that populations change at random, because of sampling errors. I believe everything, having an almost instinctual understanding of freak errors, but I still consider adaptation and selection important enough to justify some just-so stories.

Stephanie's latest project, *Sleeping on the Street*, involves her living in the display window of a local gallery. She comes in when the gallery closes, wearing my pajamas, and watches TV in bed. Then she brushes her teeth and goes to sleep. I am a little jealous because really, I think though I do not say it, only I am supposed to see what she looks like in my pajamas (much better than I do) and when she sleeps (like a gentler harp player). People turned out for the opening, but soon there is only me and the occasional stragglers who stumble by drunk and do double takes, but no one who will literally be sleeping on the street. With my can opener that I had been looking for, Stephanie opens a can of peas and offers me a forkful. The fork bangs into the window, and the peas spill. She shrugs and picks up the peas.

At first I was skeptical. Some of these performance artist types—I believe the word is *whooboy*—rubbing themselves with paint while spewing excerpts from their diaries, sticking pins through themselves as though they were the insect and the entomologist. And what did they even know about sterilizing instruments? Less than any self-disrespecting Saint Louis junkie. Mind boggling. I would rather not think about it. The kind of artists that laminate their dogs and then complain if labs use a white mouse to test a medicine. Not that I am opposed either to the rights of animals I will never study or to art I will never see. Other fields, other grasshoppers. I don't, I have to admit, understand the urge to get on stage. Teaching lab techniques is enough to give me leather tongue. Lecturing makes me hyperventilate. I think of the stage on my microscope and try unsuccessfully to imagine that the grasshoppers' DNA is performing for me there, that the stains are abstract painting, but they are saying something specific usually, if I know how to phrase the question. Grasshoppers I have a chance of understanding in ways they could not just as easily tell me.

Though every day I think I understand more of the genetics of grasshopper behavior, I don't know anything about any one grasshopper. I can't learn the name of any of them. Not the grasshopper with the most beautiful song. Not the grasshopper that mates like ten. Not the grasshopper that all other grasshoppers shun. What if I found that they had names for each other, not necessarily given names, but genetically destined names written out in the alphabet of nucleotides: adenine, cytosine, thymine, guanine, or as we label them, A, C, T, and G. When Stephanie calls me Eric, I am Eric, for what it's worth. But the word *Stephanie* feels so good to speak, to have in my mouth, starting out stiff and getting funny, I might call all the grasshoppers Stephanie. At least the females.

I'm learning Stephanie.

We met at Idem's, the bookstore-café at the corner, where the books smell like coffee and cigarette smoke, where she serves mediocre cakes and exotic teas and specialty coffees also available with syrups that no one orders, ever. Actually, we met at the dictionary that sits on its own stand next to the counter. I had just been hoping for coffee and a muffin and a book in the evening after a (failed) experiment. There was this young man talking into a microphone, performing, that is, who said he was salacious, and he and his friends knew what that meant because they were English graduate students. An English graduate student, I was suddenly happy to say, I was not. I went to the big unabridged because I hate that people might consider me stupid. I especially hate thinking myself that I am stupid. I hate it so much that I forget to resent the people who wanted me to feel stupid in the first place.

He thinks it means he's horny, she said, leaning over the counter and closing the big fat book on my hand. It also means he's a jerk.

The salacious English graduate student said, This is what I think of the canon, and he dramatically brought up phlegm that sat on the floor and looked like a gob of DNA thrown clear of a centrifuge. Then he apologized to the canon and fell to his knees and begged its forgiveness.

Stephanie put her elbows on the counter and held her face until it was over.

When no one wanted coffee or tea or cake, she came over and sat at my table and explained to me that she was not bourgeois, while I glanced over her shoulder to make sure no one wanted coffee or tea or cake. We talked about dictionaries. She was opposed to them on principle, some stuffy old book telling her what a word meant. To me, like all big books—the Bible, *Gray's Anatomy*, the encyclopedia—it is a thing to be in awe of and deserves to lie open on its own stand because it is always in use. She smelled of salted corn chips. I like salted corn chips.

She assured me that she was much more interesting than the salacious English grad student and that I should come see her perform.

Perform? Oh, perform, so you're a—I pointed toward the microphone—a performer.

And you don't perform. . . . Oh, you do perform.

I perform, well, I perform experiments.

Oh, experimental.

In a lab.

Oh, that's interesting, she said, without making an effort to decide what kind of experiments or what kind of a lab.

I stayed until closing and helped her clean up. She had to scrub the floor where the salacious English graduate student performer had spat.

I was in no hurry to go home and watch talk shows, and neither was she. Her roommate was seeing the English graduate student who was indeed salacious and who had practically moved in, and their apartment was getting a bit small. Stephanie was looking for a new place.

Where do you live? she said, and I told her the address. Oh, she said, maybe I'll move in there.

I said nothing. I walked her to her place, shook her hand, and then when I finally went home, I noticed a For Rent sign on the front lawn. I was relieved. I had thought Stephanie had wanted to move not into my building but into my apartment. I had a corn chip and slept.

Three hours later I was up for work and in the lab by the coffee machine, waiting for it to drip and feeling as I imagined a zombie would.

Late night? said Mike, the professor I work under.

Don't let it interfere with your project, said Nellie. Your work is important. She means well, I realized. She would like to instill in me the massive egotism required for success in the field.

Thanks, Nellie.

Stephanie came in my pickup truck, which her roommate had helped her load. I helped her unload. There were boxes and boxes of books and paints and fabrics and cassettes, and my truck never seemed to empty. She had framed posters that looked like schematics of a computer with a technology I couldn't quite grasp and that turned out to be a notation form for certain dance steps: meringue, twist, pony. She cradled what looked like a zither without a soundboard.

It's a mini-harp, she said as would a mini-angel.

But she doesn't play it like a normal harp. She hooks it up to several distortion boxes and to pedals and to an amplifier. This music is all but random. Aeolian, she says, bouncing a ball off the strings, which make a sound like raucous dolphins. I don't think she could repeat a song if she wanted to. Aeolian feedback and aeolian reverb. The wa-wa she has to pedal. Doesn't sound like a harp, more like some laboratory with a future technology. She took a comb and combed the strings, then she brushed them with a toothbrush and flossed them with dental floss. It sounded like words, and then it sounded like it was screaming in pain (those times it hurt to hear), and then it sounded as though it were laughing.

Hearing the strange random noises, some soothing but mostly grating, and following the changing keys and tempos and timbres was a bit of a revelation because I had never suspected that anything might be as crazy and all over the place as my own brain, that anyone else's brain might produce such noisy thoughts.

She screeched to a halt. What do you think? she asked.

You know exactly what I think.

Too loud? The neighbors? Do they hate me already?

That's not what I mean. I mean I think exactly what your harp said.

It's true that my brain can get a little confused. That's part of the trouble with having three distinct senses of time. That's the security of the measured order of the lab—everything is graduated, everything is gradual, all hypotheses can be proven or at least proven wrong. Outside of the lab everything is unquantifiable, everything overflows, like Stephanie. It's a good thing really that I am so boring. Otherwise my brain might spontaneously combust. The gradual feeling of lab work is very calming. And then when your hypothesis is proven, there is the feeling that in some way your brain has connected you to the world, in some way you are right. That's also how I felt when Stephanie first played her harp.

She gave me a housewarming present: a vial of sand from the Sahara. Last summer, before I knew her, she went out riding a jeep through the desert, where guerilla fighters let her fire a machine gun, a huge machine gun, into the apparent emptiness. In a tobacco tin, she rattles spent cartridges she plans to use one day, though she doesn't say what for: How did she get them through customs? I would love to go to the Sahara. The number of variations in the insects would be fantastic. Many of the species haven't even been named. Maybe I could shoot off a machine gun if I were absolutely sure no one was coming and no animals or plants might be injured. My last field trip I had hunted down a herd of grasshoppers on the Arkansas-Missouri border. I brought back samples, as I suppose Stephanie did. I knew enough not to remind her that she, and not I, was the one with the new place, because if I had, she would have taken back the sand.

We celebrated her move by making sandwiches, opening cans of food, and going to a movie that was French and about a romantic triangle, as she assured me all French movies were. They are all shown at the artsy movie theater that was about to be condemned—not for showing artsy French movies about romantic triangles, but for structural flaws—and we signed a petition for clemency handed to us atop a clipboard by a skinny bald man in spectacles.

Oh, you're at the same address? Then you're, he said, continuing by pointing at her then at me so that, inadvertently I suppose, he made a gesture of disapproval.

Same mail slot. I get journals and magazines, she gets invitations to openings and calendars of events. Different apartments, usually. She comes in when she wakes up to ask, referring to my degree, What's up doc? and for just a sip of my coffee that she smells more than drinks, as though caffeine works by inhaling. Why is she here? I ask myself, and try to find an answer that is scientific, that is predicated on testable hypotheses. She marches right in without having to knock because: this is Saint Louis and we have no need to lock the doors to our apartments (a type two error, acceptance of fallacy, adopted civic pride reminds me that this year we had the nation's highest homicide rate); or at least that is a habit I have left over from growing up in Arkansas (type one error, rejection of truth). Actually, I like that she comes right in while I am drinking coffee on my mattress on the floor (a more reasonable hypothesis, and perhaps she likes to come in without having to knock). She walks right onto my mattress in her kimono and stiletto heels and sits down. I wouldn't like it any less if I had a water bed. I'll brush off the mattress later.

Eric, she asks inquisitively, massaging moisturizer into her palms, aren't we going to sleep together?

Yeah? I guess correctly.

She says I ring her bell. When she says that, I think of her as one of those strong-man tests at a fair—I've seen these only in cartoons, never at state fairs—where I pound on her feet and a visible impulse rises up her body to her head where her bell is. But I am not a strong man. Instead, I hold her feet a lot, not that they are so beautiful; in fact, they are rather torn apart by twenty years of dancing, and before that she was hammertoed, so her littlest toe bends underneath her foot. Her feet look like the result of the kind of foot binding the Chinese communists illegalized. And for good reason. Yet her fingers are long and elegant; I can hardly believe that the hands and feet belong to the same person. I stroke her feet a lot because I think she's very beautiful except her feet, and that makes me love her feet more. These are the feet of someone who would be with me.

Her fingers are full of lines, and when I look closely at them, she pulls back her hand. Then she realizes she should not try to hide her aging and lets me look. About aging, she says that, yes, she hears her biological clock going tick-tock-tick but has rolled over and hit the

387

snooze button. The lengths of her fingers are striped with shallow furrows, wavelike patterns, a lake of time. The tops of her fingers spiral like jetties or reaction to magnets, and her knuckles and the web between her thumb and forefinger are in a grid pattern like a slide used for counting cells. I point out that clocks that go tick-tock-tick do not come with snooze buttons. She rubs in moisturizer like Lady Macbeth.

I watch her practice the zombie step barefooted. I wouldn't have to learn that one. Comes natural to me. I've been working on walking like the living. Up until recently I have not spent that much less time in the lab than the flies and bats and grasshoppers do. She pounds the floor and I worry about neighbors—so bourgeois am I. The dance she is learning, she explains, is a ritual that reenacts the creation of the world. That is, in this tribe's explanation of it. When perhaps they thought sneezing had something to do with insemination.

Instead of killing time in the lab waiting for a culture to grow, I stop by her dance class in a hot and sweaty high school gym. The teacher is Mr. Cromwell, an impossibly tall and muscled man, what's left of his hair kept very short, a striking beauty in need of some restoration, sweatpants pulled a little higher than maybe they used to have to be because Mr. Cromwell has a bit of a stomach, paunch by no means, not paunch as I have paunch, but on this body anything imperfect is obvious. He tells the bongo drummers to begin with a samba rhythm. When he counts time, one-two-three—bare foot pounding on the floor, shaking the right side of the muscles all the way up to his bald head—four-five-six-seven, his stationary body seems an elaborate choreography in which each muscle is a separate dancer. Stephanie is good, that's for sure, though she never believes it for more than a minute, but when Mr. Cromwell shows the students their parts, he is a beautiful woman then again a beautiful man, changing gender as do some species of frog.

Move that jelly butt, he tells Stephanie. To another who is too stiff, don't save it, don't be afraid to give it away, there's an unlimited supply, child. And he splendidly demonstrates hips I hardly noticed before. Then he is a strict disciplinarian. Drummers—they slow to a halt—Drummers, I said samba. Is that samba? And then they begin again, and now it is apparently samba. The class began just a few weeks ago, and the students do the movements I know from my apartment—the zombie, the ape walk—only they are completely asynchronous, and it is rather painful to look at them, keeping their hips as though they were in a limited supply. The other two dozen women (and two fit men) are bigger than Stephanie is, more muscular, but they are not her, so I iris in on her. Stephanie's crooked feet clasp the wooden floor, heel ball heel, her arms not quite in the circle Mr. Cromwell has asked for, then she is lost between a centrifugal explosion of braids and the more generous swing of another woman's pelvis.

The dancers provide encouraging applause to each other.

Nuh-uh, I think you'll have to save it. Back in line, says Mr. Cromwell.

And back in line they go.

After class they go all sweaty to the local bar to smoke and drink, which I would not have thought so many dancers do, but we must hurry home because we have to get up early the next day for one of Stephanie's projects. Mr. Cromwell is disappointed, and Stephanie and I each defer to the other. If you really want to. If *you* really want to. And Mr. Cromwell buys us each a beer.

Is he okay? Mr. Cromwell asks Stephanie, and she asks me if something is the matter.

It is just that the dance was about creation myths and has got me thinking about what we know from science about our creation, that our existence as a species is predicated on the sheer luck that sixty million years ago our ancestors, unlike so many mammals, did not go extinct in the cold meteorite shade.

Mr. Cromwell and Stephanie look worried, as though I am going to, if not just bore them, perhaps even embarrass them.

Let us bring the scale down to our fruit fly size. Had I seen the microphone and embarrassedly stepped out of Idem's, then I would never have met Stephanie. I suppose I would be sadder, or perhaps some other life might have opened up like a major motion picture. Had our species died out, I don't know how much sadder the world would have been. I am thinking of the ozone and the rain forest. Me for sure. I don't know, our species' existence is so unlikely as to seem implausible.

Think of all the stories, Stephanie says, that just miss happening, the movements no one choreographs.

What's so nice about you two, Mr. Cromwell says from his great height, a hand on Stephanie's shoulder and his beer on mine, is that each one can't believe the other would even look at you—which I don't find funny, but he laughs his drag queen laugh until the muscular professional surfaces, finds himself funny, and then he laughs deep.

I ask rhetorically if that means we are good together and by accident mention mating and then realize that I mean being a couple, but I use the word *coupling*, and the right word, I try to correct myself, is *marriage*.

Mr. Cromwell actually looks shocked, as though he could accept that heterosexuals have the right to lead their own lives, even to mate and to couple, but that the institution of marriage is too sacred for them.

Stephanie doesn't answer for me.

I have exposed myself as bourgeois.

My brain is overflowing, and I would like to have peeked in on the lab.

We drive silently except for the motor's hum, until she asks me, What is it? and I say, Nothing, and she says, But what is it? and I ask her if she finds me as boring as I find the question I always ask her. Not an essay, just an assay.

Yum yum, she says. These are the oppositions I love to deconstruct for breakfast. Can we stop for a muffin and tea? You think I'll get it on my dress?

Of course she will get it on her dress. She leaves no beverage unspilled. She deconstructs my heart: left ventricle on the right and right ventricle on the left; atria orbiting like satellites. Then she reconstructs it in a heart shape and strings the veins and arteries tight as harp strings. I should mention that Stephanie is wearing a wedding dress, which does not add to my comfort.

Can't I like the way you bore me? she says.

I know I shouldn't keep talking, but my paradigm of the way the world should be and is is taking on some very serious anomalies. How could she love me when I've not received any genes implanted from someone better looking and with some talent?

A multiple choice. Take out a sharp number two pencil. If you don't know leave it blank, or at least guess C.

C.

Oh, C, I say. What is C?

Just when you ask these boring, boring questions.

So right now you find me boring.

Eric, stop.

I pull over. I can't see, and I can't breathe.

That's not what I meant, she says, then realizes she can get a muffin where I have stopped.

When she gets back in, she rubs my knees, and I can see and breathe and drive. Seventy-five-mile-per-hour wind rushes into my lungs and works like inhaled coffee. Just getting out of the city and driving this far southwest makes me feel more peaceful because of all the trees, just like in the four-hectare patch of pine that my parents had until they sold it to pay for my college. She asks what it was like growing up. Childhood was a modest affair. I can barely remember when I learned to ride a bike or hunt, but, at fourteen, when my dad said I had become a man and taught me integral calculus, I knew I was onto something.

We have no reservations and end up in the Transcendence Encampment, which looks less like a nature-buff preserve than like some refugee camp, wall-to-wall tents from the highway to the river, company store selling plastic cases and beef jerky and cold canned beer at outrageous prices. The plastic cases are to keep cigarettes and sandwiches dry on the river. A man with a wheelbarrow brings a load of wooden blocks that he and some other men pile into a tall pyramid for a bonfire. There are a few cabins, really one cabin divided into rooms with beds and stoves, of which we take one, feeling bourgeois, especially as we are only two people, whereas there seem to be families in the neighborhood of dozens crammed into the others. Stephanie is a dart board for mosquitoes, slapping her arms, tucking her hands into the sleeves of her wedding dress and, as we walk to our part of the cabin, using the hands gloved in cuffs to lift the dress above the mud. Around her I am safe from bites. Skinny blond children sit out on the porch as though they have never done anything other than sit on porches. When we go inside, they peek through the windows to get a glance at our honeymoon.

Here the sport of choice is floating. Those who splurge rent a canoe and are driven upriver. The aluminum canoe is dropped in the water and the passengers given oars, not to row (where's the hurry?), but to steer away from fallen trees, though still some canoes thwack hard against the trunks, waking and sending turtles diving off branches. The better deal is getting a huge inner tube from some ancient truck and sitting with one's jelly butt in the middle through the whole trip. I wear a large bathing suit, and she the wedding dress hitched up around her thighs; and because there are pointy rocks in the riverbed, I wear plastic shoes, and Stephanie old sneakers she should have thrown out long ago but had hoped to use for some installation. I have on sunblock and she, despite my protest, nothing. It's cold at first, but you get used to it, and cold is always better during ninety-odd-degree Missouri summers that are only pleasant if you happen to be a mosquito.

Floating is not, I dare say, a sport for the bourgeois. We did it on vacations in Arkansas when I was a kid, even had our own tubes, but Stephanie's family went sailing in Illinois, as they have today, without inviting me. Sailing with Stephanie's family, she has explained to me, would be too much work to leave energy for real work. Here we float with other hillbillies, the best prepared of whom have, tied to their own, an extra tube, a spare tire, in which a cooler of beer has been wedged, and tied around their necks, water-resistant plastic cigarette holders, like the bright orange one in which Stephanie is keeping her poems dry.

The river winds through pines. The water is clear and cold, and we get used to the cold and drag our hands and wrists, and folks paddling by in the convex mirrors of canoes look at us enviously and do not even congratulate us. The heat has evaporated much of the Transcendence River, though, and sometimes we can see the rocks that will grate against Stephanie's bottom. She takes out her poems and, with the pages veiling her face from the sun, reads her ever wetter words.

> Were I to praise you properly
> I would have to sing the beauty
> of all your cells
> (doing whatever cells do),
> and in their nuclei
> read out every strand of DNA
> each as long as this float trip
> and sing the genius of every gene
> (whatever they happen to do right).
> The poets, they're okay, but
> the scientists have some idea
> of what's going on.

Her project is called *Transcendance*. I think she intended to weird folks out, but only I am a bit embarrassed, and it is much too hot between banks of baking mud to care too much. I doubt they lynch performance artists. In these parts, evolutionary biologists are more scandalous. Here we are cosmopolites from Saint Louis, city slickers with our slick jelly butts in the water. And besides, the people floating around us seem to like the entertainment, or at least they humor us. It's her or the trees.

This is better than a TV in a tube, says one woman, continuing portentously, I had a swimming suit just like yours, honey, but I almost drowned.

Love your poem, says a man floating backward in a floppy fishing hat and wet T-shirt. He is firmly planted in a tire that says *Barney's*. Have a dry cigarette.

Thank you, Barney.

Take one of these cold ones, says his friend to me, and let's drink a toast to your wonderful genes.

My job is to snap photos with a disposable camera in a plastic bag. The floaters ham it up, while the canoeists are aloof and expose just their dignified profiles. Stephanie runs out of poems quickly, but the trip takes us several hours.

My poetry is short, she apologizes, and the river is long.

We stop at several embankments to seek out shade because Stephanie is turning pink, and at deep patches of water to swim in and to jump into from rocks. I take pictures of a bride jumping off a cliff screaming, I do.

The next day we return to Saint Louis early because I have to get back to the lab—the grasshoppers do not know of weekends—and Stephanie has practice with Mr. Cromwell, who is dancing a solo piece accompanied by several drummers and Stephanie on harp.

The gym is full, and everyone seems to know each other. Mr. Cromwell wears long, loose priestly robes. The drummers begin, and Stephanie shakes bubbles of sound from her harp. Mr. Cromwell does what he has been trying to tell his students to do. Over your toes, he said last time, and now he is way out over his toes, moving like evolution in reverse, his knuckles grazing the floor. The drums get louder. And jump, he told them, and he jumps so high, his arms straight up, a leap really, so high that I remember we are in a basketball court, and Mr. Cromwell could easily slam like a pro. And side, he said, and he jumps again and drops his arm to touch his bare foot and lands with the bang of his impact muffled by the factory screech of the harp. And side, and he jumps and this time touches his left foot, and for a moment, he is suspended in midair, frozen like a bow about to release its arrow. All this with Stephanie's music, so it seems as though this dance is a clarity somewhere within my rattled brain, too distracted to understand evolution. I know these steps, but I don't know the power, and I'm seeing the movements Stephanie practices only now in some improved form, some abstracted version where they are virtually perfected. On the level of form, there is Mr. Cromwell defying gravity. Then he falls loudly to earth. On earth, there is Stephanie.

At the bar to celebrate, Mr. Cromwell is in a mood so wonderful one fears its end. What did you think? he asks. I tell him, and he asks, So then what is the matter, Baby? More about your job, isn't it?

My brain sounded like Stephanie's harp. More biology.

You've seen what I do. What do you do? Miss Stephanie, you know what he does all day, presumably.

I don't want to bore anybody, and Stephanie, stalled halfway through her beer, seems already exhausted from performing and from sunburn.

He's a molecular biologist, with training in population genetics.

I see.

He works with grasshopper DNA, she says, but I guessed she did not know either what I do, and that she was realizing that she did not know exactly what I do. She asked me to say what I was trying to accomplish anyway, and, as I was not trying to accomplish anything, what I was trying to prove. Okay, somewhere between prove and accomplish.

There was a very famous experiment done with *Drosophila*, this was years ago, that isolated the gene involved in mating song production. The gene was then transposed to a drosophila of another species. Do you follow still? The drosophila of the second species now had the first species' mating-song gene. Well, a drosophila from the first species heard the song and went to and tried to mate with the drosophila from the wrong species.

I don't think this story has a happy ending, says Mr. Cromwell.

Well, they tried, but no go.

Looking for love in all the wrong places, he concludes, tsk-tsking.

What I'm doing is the same thing, isolating song genes in one species of grasshopper and implanting them in another to see if they'll try to mate. If the experiment works, it means that there are other species that sing their own songs and not just *Drosophila*.

Our love songs, Stephanie says, pointing to her chest, are in our genes?

Very unscientific of me, but sometimes I think I know what goes on in the mind of an insect, although I know they don't even have brains. I can't believe I'm admitting this. Even my fantasies are boring.

Poor poor *Drosophilum*, Stephanie says, and I shrug my shoulder. Singing love songs and nobody can hear them right. Singing the wrong song. And the other one flies right by and doesn't even know he's being serenaded.

She really was exhausted. She starts to cry, and Mr. Cromwell says, There there, not turning away from the soft stalactite that extends from her nostril until she retracts it.

You guys, she says, you like my songs, don't you?

We love your noisy songs, Baby.

Another evolutionary adaptation of our species, I have heard it argued, has been that, when we see other members of our species crying, we want to comfort them, to make them stop crying. Probably this keeps us, when it works, from hurting children, as with the large-eye theory. Though this sounds like just another just-so story, perhaps some hormone could be isolated and eventually the gene that signals its production. I try to calm Stephanie, but I guess I'm not evolved enough to cheer her up. I guess I'm not well adapted. But I want to hold her and stop her crying and, if possible, get my shoulder loose so I can rub away the tear that is welling up in my left eye for the poor flies and my poor grasshoppers and for poor us who are lucky to have heard each other's songs and almost did not.

I can't say what one drosophila sees in another drosophila except rightness, appropriateness, you'll-do-ness. *Drosophila* sing their own songs, and we sing ours with varying degrees of musicality. And even when Stephanie's song is played by a harp that feeds back or drums in the wrong rhythm, it is the song that I want, I want her, I want to get into her genes. I know that it is impossible to see human things in other species, but there is no other way for me to see than, at best, humanly. I know it is impossible to apply what other species do to what we do, but I know that Chinese martial artists have had some success imagining themselves cranes and grasshoppers and mantises and dragons. Everything is impossible, and yet we go on. Human life seems so improbable that we sing it to each other if only to reassure

395

each other that our lives could exist at all. When that does not work, we resort to just-so stories.

I get loose and blow my nose.

All mankind, Stephanie says, puff.

Can't you just say bless you?

Mr. Cromwell wraps his long arms around both of us and tells us, There there.

Someone must have done something with our genes because we may not be the same creatures. But for some reason, her songs go right to my very genetic blueprint, especially when she sings them throatily in my ear. We are together like a café attached to a bookstore, not the same, but not a bad idea, like our two names in the same sentence: Eric loves Stephanie.

I am willing to consider love an evolutionary adaptation.

Nominated by The Gettysburg Review

TESTAMENT

by GLENNA HOLLOWAY

from MICHIGAN QUARTERLY REVIEW

Saint James described it as a raging fire.
That little muscle anchored in our throats
Is flexed by pride, cupidity, desire.
It curves and curls, incessantly misquotes,
Embroiders, burns, inveigles with a twist,
Spews bile and guile then batters like a fist,
Misleads the innocent, derides the weak.
Sometimes it poses quasi-truth oblique
Against a noble theme, a vital rung,
Or revels in the taste of its own cheek.
Ah, James, how well you knew the human tongue.

How keen a marriage tool, a smoking pyre
For any wife or husband who promotes
A fine-tuned knack for probing to acquire
Superiority: each one devotes
Delicious care to making up a list
Of most effective subjects used for grist.
As ancient mills begin to grind and squeak,
The mighty organ primes its pipes to speak,
And from its depths supported by a lung,
Sound bites arise to start the day's critique.
Ah James, how well you knew the human tongue.

A bit can curb a horse, control his ire.
The softest member in his mouth denotes

Where his own power ends, serves to rewire
Intentions as it channels all his oats
In service to the reins he won't resist
Once understood. He minds, unprejudiced,
Just so he's fed and watered at the creek,
De-cockleburred and brushed until he's sleek,
And stabled where they've shoveled out the dung.
It only takes a bit to make him meek.
Ah, James, how well you knew the human tongue:

For ours cannot be tamed. Always for hire,
It plies its ancient trade by modern rotes,
Aflap in wayward winds or stuck in mire.
The people it infects, the self it bloats
As every snaky syllable is hissed,
Sometimes don't know they're bitten till they've missed
A beat, a byte, as they attempt to sneak
In idioms of kindness, strange as Greek.
Then only laughter licks the newly stung
Who quickly emulate the top technique.
Ah, James, how well you knew the human tongue.

Toxicity and acrid ash conspire;
The residue of curses, lies, and gloats
Impedes all good. The status quo is dire
With little research into antidotes.
Hell's blaze, said James, backlights our words; the gist
Of what is said defines the casuist.
Prognoses for reform are worse than bleak,
This implement, aligned with Satan's clique,
Might change if every owner started young
To rid it of corruption's tainted streak.
Ah, James, how well you knew the human tongue.

Despite the odds, a few die-hards still seek
To douse the damning flames and maybe wreak
A miracle to purge the body hung

With this bizarre appendage, this antique.
Oh, James, may God forgive the human tongue.

Nominated by Michigan Quarterly Review

OFF THE ROAD
OR THE PERFECT
CURVE UNFOUND

memoir by GLEN CHAMBERLAIN BARRETT

from NORTHERN LIGHTS

It WAS THE GEESE that took me to that world without words. And that is how I came, for a summer, to be off the road.

It was May, and I was just leaving Three Forks, Montana, heading east on the Interstate, wondering if it was those words the man had said that wrecked us. *I love you*, he'd told me, and I sensed when he said that a devotion to language rather than to me, which meant an approaching break up, a faithlessness. He was a writer, you see, and he spoke of how language should be like engineer's curves—perfect tools by which to measure accurately. I liked his metaphor, and the fact that he ignored his goal of exactness when it came to loving me, that he used such a generic phrase to establish his affection, suggested that he was lying.

And so I left him. I left Seattle, the world of our watery love, to go home to another watery world—my home in Michigan. There I would live on a perfect curve of beach, placing my footprints in the sand next to no other footprints in the sand, a solitary figure needing nobody—no body.

In the late afternoon on the day I left for Michigan, I pulled into Three Forks to buy gas. When I paid, I picked up a pamphlet to read about the history of this confluence of rivers. It said that the Indians considered it one of the centers of the world, and as I drove off, I wondered if this was one of the centers, then where were the others? And how wise was it to have more than one middle to something? I knew enough about Einstein's theory of relativity to suppose it was possible, but then with his theory everything was possible. Then I wondered if the Indians knew about the theory of relativity without ever having to talk about it, name it, get words into it, unlike my poet lover.

Given relativity, given springtime in the Rockies, and given that Three Forks is the place where the beating currents of three rivers come together to make the headwaters of the Missouri, I was willing to consider the proposition. And so I pulled off the road to a state park to see what it felt like to be in one of the centers of the world.

That's when the geese came. Out of the deteriorating sky, luminescent as candles in a vee, lit by the dying glow of day and the spark of inheritance which drove them north, they were flying homeward. I, too, was going home. But they were flying. I was fleeing. And they were going together, while I was alone. Once again alone, once again making the decision to leave before being left.

Because of them, I didn't go back to that perfect curve of Michigan beach. I drove for an hour or more thinking about those birds, and then, past Livingston, with an easy turn of the wheel, I exited the Interstate at a green sign that simply said, *Crazy Mountains*. With that turn, I forsook the one constant companion I'd always had—water— and headed north, north toward the mountains and the geese. I drove along a two-lane tar road for quite a while, crossed its center line onto a dirt lane, and finally travelled onto two tracks. By then it was pitch black, so I crawled into the back of my car to sleep that kind of darkness away.

In the morning, I awoke to snow. The world was as cold as my soul, I figured, and it made me feel good about where I'd gotten off, for I'd never spent time in a landscape that fit my personal geography; I'd always lived in lush, verdant places. Getting out of the car, I stretched while I looked around, and, seeing no one, squatted and watched my own warm waters, gathered during the night, dissolve the snowy crystals on the ground. And there in the dissolution, mixed amidst the pebbles between my shoes, were snails—lake or sea snails—empty and dry. I stood up and scuffed at the snow and dirt around me, where I discovered more and more of them, and then I went to look at a rock outcropping. Embedded in it were the same tiny shells, and imprinted in it were the fans of clams. I spun slowly around looking at this white breast of a dim sea. It was a dead ocean, and it promised a silence I felt I wanted. Why, I didn't know, other than that it had something to do with love and its absence.

I got back in my car and drove on down the two tracks toward the emptiness, until I came to a faded two-story frame ranch house that sat beneath a cliff. When I knocked on the door, an old man answered. He was pulling a canister of oxygen and had a mask over his face. He didn't talk—he couldn't because it would take too much of his air, I figured—so he just motioned me in with his long, skinny, blue, index finger. Then he dragged his oxygen can like a golfer would his bag back to the LazyBoy in the corner; he sat down and watched me with eyes that because of the mask looked unnaturally big.

I watched back.

A long time passed before a woman came in. She was strong and handsome, a palomino-colored woman with big, strong, square teeth and a ponytail. Her name was Eleanor, Eleanor Tate, and she was the owner of this operation, she told me, and the man in the chair with the oxygen tank was Franklin, Franklin Coil, her father.

What did she mean by operation, I asked.

Horsebreeding.

Did she need help, I asked, even though I didn't know anything about horses.

Yup, she said.

That summer, I came to know horses—more particularly, Arabian horses. The distinguishing feature of this pedigree is not the spooned out head; those are typical of the Egyptian—the third-world branch—of the family, which leaves the other side—the Anglos—looking normal rather than dinko-cephalic. Nor should Arabs be thought of as black, as kids' storytellers would have us believe. While many start out as jet as shoe polish, just as many within two years have turned a scuffed gray. No, the distinguishing features of full-blooded Arabian horses are their unpronounceable names (the whole stable sounded like a professional basketball team) and their short backs. Most horses have six lumbar vertebrae; Arabs have just five. That short-coupled back is what gives them their smooth gait.

The other owner of this operation was Bill. Bill Tate. I didn't know he existed until he opened the door one night—about a week after I'd arrived—and walked in, stomping the slush and mud off his shoes, for it had continued to snow. Bill was Eleanor's second husband, and over the course of the summer I pieced their story together. She was from New York state and had always loved horses. At some point early on, she had mixed up her passion for horses with her love of men and married one, a chemist who taught at the university in Bozeman. She said he cheated on her first, but I came to believe otherwise. Oh, she didn't have affairs; she just had a heart filled with 35 Arabs. I suspected that whenever her chemist tried to come close, he got trampled. Finally he had enough and found a young co-ed with an empty heart.

After that, Eleanor took up with Bill, who had once been a dairy farmer in Maine, until his wife fell off a horse and died. Bereft, he sold the farm and came west in search of a new life. He found Eleanor who really didn't want a lover but needed a hired man. If she married him, she calculated, he would work for free. He was a victim, if ever there was one. That first night I met him I could tell because his eyes were set far apart, almost on the outsides of his high cheekbones, like the eyes of deer and elk and antelope—the eyes of those destined to be prey. He was silent like prey animals, too, aware that if he made too much noise, Eleanor would find him and put him to some chore.

Of the three of them, I liked Franklin the best. Most often, he was in the LazyBoy, except when he dragged himself over to the moss rock fireplace, which Bill had built two years before; it was made from his very own harvest of rocks from one of his own fields, and as I came to know Bill it became clear that this was one of his more successful attempts at agriculture. Once the rock hearth was in place, Franklin had taken it upon himself to keep the moss alive by watering it. He would stand there with his oxygen hissing and a little spray can in one upraised arm, pissing out at the moss that never grew. I admired his desire to have a purpose.

I liked him for another reason, too. He liked my piano playing. The piano was in the basement room Eleanor let me use. It had gotten stuck down there when the house was built. Its first owners, who had come west right after World War I on the last and least homestead act, were so enthusiastic about free land that they decided to work from below the ground up, making the basement of a house to which they would add stories as they prospered. They put everything they owned, including the piano, in the hole in the ground and then built above it. When it came time to move their belongings up in the world, they discovered that they'd made the doors too skinny. And so the old piano sat forlornly below ground, ultimately as forgotten as the new dreams it once made melody for.

I liked to play it. I had never been very good, but I'd become used to my lack of talent and enjoyed picking at the keys. I don't think I ever enjoyed playing a piano more than that one in the Crazy Mountains because it was so out of tune it made Mozart sound Oriental. In the concussion of East meeting West, I couldn't hear my mistakes, and it sounded so good. When I finished, I would come around the corner and up out of the tunnel of stairs, and at the top would be Franklin and his oxygen tank, listening and hissing. He reminded me of a fish out of water, standing on its tail, gills panting in and out, desperate for water, and there isn't any, and it is dying. Sometimes I thought a sweet clunk to Franklin's head with a stick would be good, except that he derived pleasure from moss rocks and Chinese music, and pleasure, I have come to know, in whatever paltry form, is what makes life valuable.

It was not long before my thoughts of mercy killing were ended. One June Sunday, a misty moisty morning, I came back to the ranch from my day off. When I walked in the door and looked towards the LazyBoy to wave to Franklin (for I was becoming as mute as he), it was empty. Only the grease smudge where his head had rested and his air can with the mask hanging forlornly over its silver top valve verified that he had ever been there.

Bill was sitting in his chair reading one of his favorite Zane Grey books.

"Where's Franklin?" I asked, hanging up my dripping coat.

"Dead." He did not look up. He offered no explanation.

"That's it?" I asked. "Dead?"

"Yup."

"Where's Eleanor?"

He turned a page. "Ridin' Sad."

Sad was Sahid, Eleanor's honest-to-God black stallion, the one that didn't turn gray, 22-years-old, her true love and her main livelihood. It was his color that brought mares from all over the country for a costly game of genetic roulette. If heritage spun out right, a new foal would be born black and stay black, and his name would be something like Sahid-al-Jasmine-al-Fed, and he would be worth $25,000

404

for his color alone. Eleanor hardly ever rode Sahid except in a couple of parades each year. She worried about him getting hurt. I had never seen her ride him, or seen her ride, so busy was she managing the herd. Curious, I put my coat back on and went out.

In the drizzle I walked around the house to the back, where the cliff was. It was a fault, really. The Crazies are full of them. A fault is a crack in the earth where two landforms are exposed when the world crashes against itself, crumpling, bending, pushing, and ultimately cracking. A cliff can be one of the results of this crazy self-destruction. The land leading up to this particular crack I was living under was shale, made of the old ocean bed, and the cliff was made of rich, soft, volcanic soil. It was up there, too, where Eleanor had her arena, the location selected because the ground was softer on the horses' feet. It didn't matter that it was windier and ripped the noses and ears off anyone riding her horses. The riders, after all, were just people.

At first I didn't see anything but an ink blot moving in the gray fog, kind of an animated Rorscach test. I moved closer and squatted along the fault line, watching Eleanor materialize straight-backed, riding that horse around in a prance, his front legs coming up in a high bend before snapping down elegantly. She rode by me, and I could see her back. In all that precision of movement there were big blotches of mud upon her coat from Sahid's hooves. The horse was now crossing the arena diagonally, his front outside leg stepping over his inside one while his strong hind end muscled him forward. He was beautiful. When he got to one corner, Eleanor rode him to the other corner and then crossed him back over the other direction, making a big X in the earth. After that, she posted a trot and made voltés, little circles all curlicued around the perimeter, and then she disappeared out of the arena and into the fog. I could see the precise script of the horse's feet, a perfect, geometric language signifying nothing. I had an inkling then of what it was like to live without words. I think I had come out to say I was sorry about Franklin. But Eleanor didn't need to hear that from me, any more than she needed any words from Bill or her first husband.

When I got back to the house, Bill asked, "Sad okay?"

"Yup," I said, and went to the basement to make imprecise noise on the piano.

The weather worsened that day, and by night there was a terrible wind coming out of the east—a bad sign. When I got up the next morning, two inches of snow had been blown in, turning the green world into a blank page.

Bill and I climbed into his old blue truck to go check his cattle— 28 head of Hereford cows who were calving. Way out on a high meadow, we came upon a heifer who stood beside a still form in the slush. "Aw, Gaw," Bill whined, showing more emotion than he had for poor old Franklin, I thought. He jumped out of the cab, scooped the calf up and put it on my lap, then punched out of the field as he headed for the house.

"Elnor, Elnor," he screamed, "it's a calf!" and Eleanor came running with towels as Bill carried the baby into the bathroom. He swaddled it, rubbing it dry, until the calf began to shiver. "There," he said, "it'll be awright. Leave it stay here an' warm up."

After breakfast, the calf still lay on the cracked linoleum, making no effort to move. As I cleaned my teeth, I was disconcerted by its big baby blue eyes, circled white with terror, staring at me. It breathed hard, and mucous sprayed out its nose; it was as if its whole body was filled with liquid that shouldn't be there, and little squeaks, like birds caught in a chimney, came from its lungs. That calf reminded me of Franklin, the way it looked and never spoke and the way it couldn't breathe. I looked away from it into the mirror, where I caught the reflection of Bill, who was filling a big dripper with whiskey. "Get down here and rub its legs," he told me as he knelt and squirted the amber liquid into the calf's mouth.

I clenched my jaw, and we worked silently together. As I sat there on a peeling bathroom floor massaging a cow while it drank Ten High whiskey from a crazy man and it snowed outside in June, I figured I had no idea what to say about my life. I was coming to understand the ease of silence.

After the whiskey, the calf's breathing bubbled more. "Don't wanna git the little feller drunk," Bill said. "Come on." He headed to his chair and picked up Zane Grey. I looked at Franklin's empty chair and the air tank and grabbed his squeeze-it bottle to water the fireplace. The world was quiet but for the sigh of mist and the hiss of wet wood burning. It seemed so foolish of me, so foolish of Franklin, to try to keep up with the drying elements of the fire which had overcome any water in the logs and now crackled happily, the only happy noise in the house. The only happy noise. The only noise. The only. The . . . The words in my head were evaporating as quickly and easily as water when I heard a clickety clack of hooves in the bathroom. Bill and I ran in, and the calf was still on its side, its legs galloping in a convulsion.

"It cain't breathe!" Bill shouted, and he loped out of the room, leaving me with the thrashing baby whose big wad of tongue, turning blue, was stuck to the floor. In a flash Bill was back, dragging Franklin's oxygen tank. He turned the lever, making the can hiss, and grabbed the mask, slipping it over the bovine muzzle.

The opaque plastic cup, which used to cover all of Franklin's face, just fit over the big pink nose of the calf. Its thin lower lip jutted from underneath, and the pastel ridge of its ungulate gums gave a faint promise of teeth, just like a little human baby's. Pretty soon, the steady hiss had a regular rhythm, and the cow took its tongue back into its mouth. Bill removed the mask and gave it another shot of Ten High. "A coupla weeks of this, and the Nips'll want him," he said.

"What's that mean?"

"Kobi."

"What's that mean?"

"Beef."

"What's that mean?" I followed him out of the bathroom, but he didn't answer. I stood, not knowing what to do. Through the living room windows I could see that the weather was lifting, the sun filtering through the clouds, melting the slush, and the new grass outside was the color of cartoon green. I felt an intimation of hope. But just then there came a long, plaintive cry from the bathroom, so I turned back to see what the calf was up to. Its skin lay caved in around its soft ribs, the oxygen all gone from it, air and life expelled.

We loaded the corpse into the back of the pickup and drove it down and away from the cliff far out and onto the ancient seabed. There we lowered it down like sailors would a body into the green ocean of land for the scavengers to eat. On the way back through the shimmering little grass I thought about how that calf had died on bad whiskey and pure air. And that was all right. That was all I could think.

The rest of Bill's calf crop slipped with ease into summer, and then Eleanor's baby horses started coming, and the small ranch in the Crazy Mountains was like a miniature Genesis. It was all do and no talk for the most part, and it made me think of the Bible, how I never believed that in the beginning was the Word. I believed that in the beginning was the Deed, which wasn't invented; it was just done.

407

The week the world started must have been a busy one, with light coming on and going off and water fountaining and land scaping and grass and herbs and trees and fruit popping and man and animals self-generating. There wasn't any time to sit down and put words to it all. In fact, it wasn't until years later, when Adam and Eve had to name the results of their deeds, and Abel and Cain theirs, and all those generations of begats theirs, that humans decided to write Genesis, and they lied, saying, *In the beginning was the Word.* I felt myself becoming more and more like Eleanor and Bill, accepting that words were inaccurate and unnecessary. My longings for the poet lover became as dry and dead as the ocean which now grew fragile grass.

The summertime came and went, flashing a dusty green and humming a busy song as it passed. And when it was gone, the place was quiet. There were few chores for me to do, so I began to take walks, and I would look at the high autumn clouds like dapples in the sky, grass that curled and spiraled into thin air, aspen leaves that sparkled like meteors as they fell in the sun, and pine that wove itself into the shade of mountainsides. The world that early fall was like a giant lens, smoke-hazed from range fires and casting a filtered but intense light on everything. I waited and waited silently, for what I didn't know—the horizon to the north to burst into flame, maybe, and the firefighters to scurry on it like the freezing flies were doing on the spotted and indifferent rumps of Eleanor's mares.

The first cold snap came then, and the quiet pools of the stream glassed over, entrapping a late hatch in the ice. The little black bugs looked like print emerging on its own out of the middle of some old parchment, indecipherable. I didn't care that I couldn't read it, though, for I had given up reading along with speech. Total silence came when the ravens left, their barks no longer rising on the thermal currents. I was passive with the weather and the landscape, just taking in the particulars of that Crazy world, beautiful and finely etched as foreign script.

Though they hadn't said anything, I sensed that Bill and Eleanor wanted me to leave. There was, after all, nothing for me to do anymore. But their silence continued, for I had come to let them treat me as they treated each other—not overtly unkind, but indifferent. Since they did not articulate their desire for me to leave, I did not need to articulate my reaction. What I would—wanted—to do remained unknown because it was unspoken.

Then one morning I woke with a start of fear. Maybe they would never ask me to go. Maybe I would stay on forever as the crazy hand who sprayed the moss rocks in the fireplace and played Chinese music in the dark. With a momentary energy fueled by panic, I came out of my dark basement dreams, out of the dark basement, up the stairs, out the door, and into the dark dawn. As the black ink slowly washed out of the sky, I skirted around the cliff behind the house and up to the arena where Eleanor had ridden Sad, then down again and into the seabed field.

My breath was shaky because I'd been running and I was scared, so scared all of a sudden, about becoming dumb. I felt unmoored, and I yawed around that land as the light changed from blue to yellow. There had been no blue to purple to red to orange to yellow, it seemed to me, and I sat down, winded, and wondered how the sky could go from one primary color to another. Given our invention of the color wheel, it seemed impossible. Then I remembered that I was living in a world which had not been overtaken by human invention. It just was. And that was what I thought I wanted.

I sat there frustrated and shivering, staring at the cured grass between my legs, and when I brought my head up, not twenty feet in front of me was a small blue rib bone. I stared at its blueness and its perfect curve which made a parallel arc with the horizon. Crawling toward the rib, I saw the blue fly away, and the bone turned white. It's a vision, I thought, but it wasn't. It was butterflies, tiny blue butterflies, and at least five hundred flitter-fluttered off the rib into the yellow air. I knelt on the ground like a dog staring at a bone, and then I saw the other ones scattered about. These belonged to the calf, the one that drank whiskey and used up the last of Franklin's air. I looked around for my bearing, to make sure it was the right spot. Right spot, hell; it was one of the centers of the universe, a hole in that September morning air where different spaces and times came together and for a crack were measurable with a curve of landscape.

I remembered that once, before I'd given up on love and words, I'd read the Romantics. I learned from them that you can't have continuous epiphany, a kind of spiritual orgasm. If you try, your life becomes mechanical, a kind of platonic sex manual where you put inappropriate tabs in improper slots. Samuel Coleridge tried to stay in an epiphanous state: it was an illusory place he called Xanadu, and he thought he could remain within its clear borders if he smoked opium. It didn't work, and he went crazy. Or crazier.

Maybe that was what had happened to Eleanor and Bill. Maybe that Crazy Mountain ranch had been a place where they thought they could just experience things, like Eleanor's horses did, without talking, without trying to figure out, for instance, what the word love meant, or how to use it in the dialects of body and soul. Since they couldn't speak it, maybe they couldn't feel it—or anything else, and so they went crazy. Or crazier.

On that autumn morning, I knew I was crazy for having sought a place where words didn't exist. But I decided I didn't want to be crazier, so I went to the house and packed, and then I told them I would be leaving and tried to explain why. My voice was hoarse from lack of use, and my sentences were faltering. They didn't say anything. My words or Eleanor or Bill.

I haven't been much off the road since. In fact, I live in Bozeman where I teach language arts at the university. The world here is not as pretty as that one in the Crazies. Nor is it so immediate, and at five o'clock on a weekday, its borders are fogged with sulfur dioxide, carbon monoxide, and ethylene—substances more dangerous than color wheels and language. I try to tell the man I love and the children we have borne about that pure and silent summer long ago, but the words fail me.

Nominated by Northern Lights

PARADISE COVE

by STEPHEN YENSER

from THE YALE REVIEW

My daughter in the coastal sunset asks for Plato. "Plato,"
She begs, *"blue* Plato, please, *Plato*" . . . Finally, I understand

And rummage from the picnic basket the Playdough, the blue can,
And the pink as well—which I henceforth call "Aristotle."

"Ariso'l, Ariso'l," she repeats—then, swallowing the glottal,
"Aerosol," and there we are, playing with both ideas that there are.

For one, the mixogamous world is all one thing, and for the other,
This increasing unicity is two (or more, which is the same,

Since to rub two things together in a ruttish realm is to get others,
And those yet others, viz. our daughters and our sons).

The temporizing third idea—that these two are somehow one—
Returns us to the first. So Marcus Aurelius thought. Maybe Lao Tzu.

In any event, Nietzsche teaches that each thinker's goal
Is to become as serious as a child at play, even as the sun sinks,

Even when again the sun is setting—or rather, here in Los Angeles,
City of Angels, City of Angles, the set is sunning,

Stunning, even, in the ever acuter, gentler rays that with the smaze
Turn the horizon Technicolor blues and lavenders and pinks.

Nominated by Susan Wheeler, Agha Shahid Ali

MATES

fiction by EDITH PEARLMAN

from PLEIADES

KEITH AND MITSUKO MAGUIRE drifted into town like hoboes, though the rails they rode were only the trolley tracks from Boston, and they paid their fares like everyone else. But they seemed as easy as vagabonds, without even a suitcase between them, and only one hat, a canvas cap. They took turns putting it on. Each wore a hiker's back frame fitted with a sleeping bag and a knapsack. Two lime green sneakers hung from Mitsuko's pack.

That afternoon they were seen sharing a loaf and a couple of beers on a bench in Logowitz Park. Afterwards they relaxed under a beech tree with their paperbacks. They looked as if they meant to camp there. But sleeping outside was as illegal twenty-five years ago as it is today; and these newcomers, it turned out, honored the law. In fact they spent their first night in the Godolphin Inn, like ordinary travelers. They spent their second night in the apartment they had just rented at the top of a three-decker on Lewis Street, around the corner from the house I have lived in since I was a girl.

And there they stayed for a quarter of a century, maintaining cordial relations with the downstairs landlord and with the succession of families who occupied the middle flat. Every fall they planted tulips in front. In the spring Keith mowed the side lawn. Summers they raised vegetables in the back; all three apartments shared the bounty.

Anyone else in their position would have bought a single-family house or a condo, maybe after the first child, certainly after the second. Keith, a welder, made good money; and Mitsuko, working part-time as a computer programmer, supplemented their income. But the Maguires kept on paying rent as if there were no such thing as equity. They owned no television; and their blender had only three speeds. But although the net curtains at their windows seemed a thing of the moment, like a bridal veil, their plain oak furniture had a responsible thickness. On hooks in the back hall hung the kids' raingear, and Keith's hard hat, and Mitsuko's sneakers. The sneakers' green color darkened with wear; eventually she bought a pair of pink ones.

I taught all three of the boys. By the time the oldest entered sixth grade he was a passionate soccer player. The second, the bookish one, wore glasses. The third, a cut-up, was undersized. In each son the mother's Eastern eyes looked out of the father's Celtic face; a simple, comely, repeated visage; a glyph meaning "child."

Mitsuko herself was not much bigger than a child. When the youngest began high school even he had out-stripped his mother. Her little face contained a soft beige mouth, a nose of no conse- quence, and those mild eyes. Her short hair was clipped every month by Keith. (In return Mitsuko trimmed Keith's receding curls and rusty beard.) She wore tees and jeans and sneakers except for public occasions; then she wore a plum-colored skirt and a white silk blouse. I think it was always the same skirt and blouse. The school doctor once referred to her as generic; but when I asked him to iden- tify the genus he sighed his fat sigh. "Female parent? All I mean is that she's stripped down." I agreed. It was as if nature had given her only the essentials: flat little ears; binocular vision; teeth strong enough for buffalo steak, though they were required to deal with nothing more fibrous than apples and raw celery (Mitsuko's cuisine was vegetarian). Her breasts swelled to the size of teacups when she was nursing, then receded. The school doctor's breasts, sometimes visible under a summer shirt, were slightly bigger than Mitsuko's.

The Maguires attended no church. They registered Independent. They belonged to no club. But every year they helped organize the spring block party and the fall park clean-up. Mitsuko made filligree cookies for school bake sales and Keith served on the search com- mittee when the principal retired. When their eldest was in my class, each gave a What-I-Do talk to the sixth grade. At my request they re- peated it annually. Wearing a belt stuffed with tools, his mask in his hands, Keith spoke of welding's origins in the forge. He mentioned weapons, tools, automobiles. He told us of the smartness of the wind, the sway of the scaffolding, the friendly heft of the torch. "An arc flames and then burns blue," he said. "Steel bar fuses to steel bar." Mitsuko in her appearances before the class also began with history. She described Babbage's first calculating machine, whose innards nervously clacked. She recapitulated the invention of the Hollerith code (the punched card she showed the kids seemed as venerable as papyrus); the cathode tube; the microchip. Then she too turned personal. "My task is to achieve intimacy with the computer," she said. "To follow the twists of its thought; to help it become all it can." When leaving she turned at the doorway and gave us the hint of a bow.

Many townspeople knew the Maguires. How could they not, with the boys going to school and making friends and playing sports? Their household had the usual needs—shots and checkups, medications, vegetables, hardware. The kids bought magazines and notebooks at Dunton's Tobacco. Every November Keith and his sons walked smiling into Roberta's Linens and bought a new Belgian handkerchief for Mitsuko's birthday. During the following year's special occasions, its lace would foam from the pocket of the white silk blouse.

But none of us knew them well. They didn't become anyone's intimates. And when they vanished, they vanished in a wink. One day we heard that the youngest was leaving to become a doctor; the next day, or so it seemed, the parents had decamped.

I had seen Mitsuko the previous week. She was buying avocados at the greengrocer. She told me that she mixed them with cold milk and chocolate in the blender. "The drink is pale green, like a dragonfly," she said. "Very refreshing."

Yes, the youngest was off to Medical School. The middle son was teaching carpentry in Oregon. The oldest, a journalist in Minnesota, was married and the father of twin girls.

So she had grand-daughters. She was close to fifty, but she still could have passed for a teen-ager. You had to peer closely, under the pretext of examining pineapples together, to see a faint cross-hatching under the eyes. But there was no gray in the cropped hair, and the body in jeans and tee was that of a stripling.

She chose a final avocado. "I am glad to have run into you," she said with her usual courtesy. Even later I could not call this remark valedictory. The Maguires were always glad to run into any of us. They were probably glad to see our backs, too.

"You are a maiden lady," the school doctor reminded me some

months later. We have grown old together; he says what he pleases. "Marriage is a private mystery. I'm told that parents feel vacant when their children have flown."

"Most couples just stay here and crumble together."

"Who knows?" he shrugged. "I'm a maiden lady myself."

The few people who saw Keith and Mitsuko waiting for the trolley that September morning assumed they were going off on a camping trip. Certainly they were properly outfitted, each wearing a hiker's back frame fitted with a sleeping bag and a knapsack.

The most popular theory is that they have settled in some other part of the country. There they work—Keith with steel and flame, Mitsuko with the electronic will-o-the-wisp; there they drink avocado shakes and read paperbacks.

Some fanciful townspeople whisper a different opinion: that when the Maguires shook our dust from their hiking boots they shed their years, too. They have indeed started again elsewhere; but rejuvenated, restored. Mitsuko's little breasts are already swelling in preparation for the expected baby.

I reject both theories. Maiden lady that I am, I believe solitude to be not only the unavoidable human condition but also the sensible human preference. Keith and Mitsuko took the trolley together, yes. But I think that downtown they enacted an affectionate though rather formal parting in some public place—the bus depot, probably. Keith then strode off. Mitsuko waited for her bus. When it came she boarded it deftly despite the aluminum and canvas equipment on her back. The sneakers—bright red, this time, as if they had ripened—swung like cherries from the frame.

Nominated by Pleiades

HER LITERAL ONE

by ALBERT GOLDBARTH

from THE GEORGIA REVIEW

As for the light—it was a city light
as I was a city ten-year-old, a flower that was actually
half weed, a scraggly Jewbloom on the north side of Chicago,
call it Scaredy-Blossom, Bookhead, Clinging Wondereyes;
whatever, the light and I sufficed, although the dingy bloat
they call a sky there wasn't anybody's standard idea
of island-paradise blue, and I was nobody's notion
of first-prize hothouse exotica. The seasons turned,
a wheel at a carnival booth: some sucker-you-win
and a lot more sucker-you-lose. In a family
photograph album: nodding, waxily pallid heads
of Indian Pipe, like lackeys in obsequious salaams;
but also the Buddhaly bulbous bodies
of Skunk Cabbage, confident, radiating a *thereness*.
This was Chicago, remember; tailpipes in winter
offered great gray blossoms showier than anything
in a horticultural text. I like particularly the ones
with double lives, so that March Marigold
is also Cowslip; Bouncing Bet is Soapwort;
Spotted Joe-Pye Weed is Gravelroot; Fire Pink
is Catchfly. As for sex—the nectary woo
of the *Habenaria* Orchid is engineered
so that the pixilated bee, on exiting
that clever sanctum, manages to pull the entire pollen sac
along with it, so fertilizes the next free Orchid it enters.
The fur of an animal is sex for them, a cotton sock,

the wind. Sex is an engine that powers us even
in repression: think of the passion elevated
out of a nun, think of the one emphatic annual flower
worn like a boutonniere by the Desert Cactus.
I grew, I was dew and sap. The seasons turned,
a tire on a drum to check for a puncture: what
was this one, maybe my mother's grave, my father's,
my divorce. And as for love—I wouldn't say "evergreen"
was the word, although love reappeared on a semiregular basis
in a sticky burst of the pistil and the stamen that we
long ago embodied, in the way we did
the sea. In a family photograph album: the one in a snood;
the one elucidating a point; the lank vamp
and her sumo beau; the famished epicurean . . .
they're all here, in their hoed rows
or their potting soil—sometimes you can see a mass of leaves
snap up at the sun like a school
of piranha crazy on blood. So many—Thoreau says
the Virginia Meadow Beauty looks like
"a little cream pitcher." I've always thought that
Yellow Lady's-Slipper looked less like footwear
and more like a saddle canteen that might be sized
to one of the plastic horses from my Fort Apache set
when I was six. The yellow stamens
of the Fragrant Water Lily look like blasts from the hell
of the fundamentalists, shot through vents in the planet's surface.
The quiet white star that we've named Wood Anemone
reminds me of the fading of a bass chord,
given a visible body. Arrowhead is also
Duck Potato. Touch-Me-Not is also Jewelweed,
and its bilateral petals droop like golden testicles.
Forget-Me-Not is Mouse-Ear. Yet we *do* forget:
the seasons turn unchanged, but for their passengers
the stars bear down like an emery wheel,
grinding away. And as for death—if even
Shakespeare and Dante acquiesced, who are *we* to say no?
As for death—traditionally, Jews visiting graves
set stones there as memoria, instead of flowers;
after all, why pretend? A gravel quarry
at the edge of a Jewish cemetery serves us for a florist,

and I like the hard idea of a dozen little stones
for a bouquet. I hope I haven't overlooked the pink idea
of the vulvas that a man knows in his lifetime
as a privilege, as a kind of lush botanical display.
As for the spirit—I hope I haven't neglected the gospel
lifting invisibly from the Calla Lily's throat. Yes,
as for the spirit—I remember an afternoon
when sun had touched, had brought alive, a church's
stained-glass Eden scene, and fifty members of the choir,
their white robes suffused deep green by this, all
turned to face that shining as if they
were phototropic. I *swear* a petal of Canadian Dwarf Cinquefoil
is, assuming my astronomy book is accurate, the visual twin
of the radiation emitted by a white dwarf star
4,000 light-years from Earth. As for remarriage,
Skyler is kneeling outside right now in her floppy
shade hat, with her hand rake and her spade.
As for my students—this is metaphor at work,
applied with a bricklayer's trowel, and then happily
pile-drivered into place. Do you see
how mimetic it is, of the frail *us* that wakes with us,
inside us, every day to meet whatever random
nurturing or savaging the light is going to do?
As for my wife—this is my garden, this is the best
I can tend, while she's all sweat and song and bent
to the difficult needs of her literal one.

Nominated by The Georgia Review, Michael Waters, Marilyn Krysl,
Stephen Dunn, Lucia Perillo

BAD JUDGMENT

by CATHLEEN CALBERT

from BAD JUDGMENT (Sarabande Books)

It's on the line,
    the sun's in your eyes,
        the time you thought it would be all right
            to go for a drive alone at night,
                he didn't mean it,
            he'll never do it again,
        you can trust him,
    I think she's really a friend,
I bet the child will be all right where he is,
    it doesn't get dark until late,
        I'll take the red-eye,
            have the cheese steak,
                you keep track of the receipts,
            we'll only meet for coffee,
        I'll weigh less in a couple weeks,
    I'll take the job,
I'll marry him,
    I'll see my mother in the spring,
        no hurry,
            I'm not even sleepy,
                I can drive all night, don't worry,
            shall we get some cigarettes?
    How about chocolate martinis?
Is the water supposed to be green?
It's all right, I'm not ovulating,
    it's all right, I'm clean,

it's all right, I haven't been with anyone else lately,
having a baby will bring us closer together,
I can stand another cup of coffee,
let's get the puppy,
let's get the aquarium,
let's get another puppy,
I think that's as big as a dog like that gets,
he's just lonely,
why don't we not plan anything?
If the book's good, they'll publish it eventually,
why don't we paint the whole thing?
We could knock down a wall,
we could dig up these trees,
I think I'll wait to have a baby,
I bet these sores don't mean anything,
my doctor knows what's best for me,
my dentist knows what's best for me,
my therapist knows I'm trying,
I feel I'll never lose you, we'll keep writing,
you're sensitive, that's why you do these things,
I'll just watch a little TV,
I'll talk to him, but I won't say anything,
we'll talk, but we won't do anything,
if I tell him how I feel,
if he tells me how he feels,
I want him to be honest with me,
I only want to know the truth,
not knowing hurts worse,
henna just makes your hair shiny,
it's too overcast to burn,
he's staying for the children,
she doesn't understand him,
they're not even sleeping together,
everybody parks here,
they never ticket,
they almost never tow,
there's an undertow
but you hardly feel it,
this will pinch a little,
this might smart,

you'll only feel a tug,
    are you crazy, they love company!
        I don't think she meant anything,
    why don't you go talk to her?
    I bet the two of you can straighten it out,
if I were you, I'd leave him,
I'd perm my hair,
    I'd get that outfit,
      I only want what's best for you,
    I know you do,
      I love you too.

Nominated by Rosellen Brown, J. Allyn Rosser, Sarabande Books

THE MAN WITH
THE PAPER EYES

fiction by BAY ANAPOL

from STORY

IRENE WAS HANDCUFFED when we met. The corrections officer told me her name was John. Nothing surprised me then. In those days I was a social worker for the Catholic Diocese at Twin Streams, a dismal men's medical correctional facility on the far and rainy end of the California coast. Twin Streams was the arm of the state prison system where cons were sent for evaluation. It was where any mental or physical problems could be isolated, medicated, warehoused, and—with any luck—forgotten.

I specialized in the motley collection of preoperative transsexuals (mostly drug busts and soliciting, a couple of timid armed robberies) housed in C block. The pre-ops were transferred to Twin Streams because it was illegal to remove them from hormone dosage while they were incarcerated and this was the only place to dole out the medication. It was hard to imagine them in the mainline population of another prison anyway, what with their long hair, resilient breasts (implants or 'mones), and brittle, amateur manicures.

The morning before Irene came to my weekly therapy group, I drank cold coffee out of a plastic cup I'd clipped from the front CO's station and listened to Mrs. Hernandez, an inmate's mother. I watched the cigarette swoop in and out of her peach-colored mouth. I'd quit smoking weeks before. Coffee, I'd read, was a cigarette cue. I tried to focus on the gold bracelet sliding up and down Mrs. Hernandez's wrist, the first bright object I'd seen all day. The weather was gray and misty and my office smelled of unwashed bodies and old tobacco.

"Raymond is doing a GED class." Mrs. Hernandez pronounced the three letters carefully: gee-eee-dee. "That's good, right? Right?" She ended all her sentences there. She wore dangling seagull earrings and white sunglasses and around her crepey neck hung two clinking strands of rosaries, one wood, one ivory. If my attention strayed a moment, she plucked up a strand and hummed Hail Marys until it returned.

"Education is important to the parole board." I knew Raymond as Angel, a pre-op transsexual with a bored, languid air and Mrs. Hernandez's pillowy breasts. Angel's boyfriend was important in the Mexican Mafia. This gave her status. She had a husky soprano voice, and whenever anyone asked her anything she moaned: don' make me *tired*.

"My lawyer he says maybe Raymond could be transferred to a work camp, the minimum place. He didn't do anything *vi-o-lent*. Oh, just drugs, right? Right?" Mrs. Hernandez's thin black eyebrows moved up and down like worms. Angel still had a nickel to serve and each time her mother entered my office and pulled out her cigarettes I felt I was doing hard time with her.

"He can't be transferred and stay on 'mones."

"So Raymond will stop taking hormones, right? Right?"

"—but you see he *reads* as a woman and he *feels* he's a woman—"

"Mother of Jesus." Mrs. Hernandez removed her sunglasses. I could tell from her deep brown eyes she'd once been pretty. "Tell me, Miss Mary Claire. You believe in abortion?"

I swallowed more coffee. "Would you like to discuss abortion?"

"I'll tell *you*." She wrapped two fingers around her wooden rosary and looked about as if Father Allen was hiding under my desk. "Between the wall, right? Right? I didn't want Raymond. He was my fifth. But the nuns said I'd burn. You think I'd have burned?"

"Some people do believe that but—"

Her eyes narrowed slightly. "What do you believe?"

"I'm not sure what I believe, Mrs. Hernandez." It was the first truly unguarded response I had ever given her, and we both sighed at the rarity.

"Maybe I should burn." She clutched at her rosary. "I'm a bad person for thinking like that."

"Of course you're not a bad person." But how did I know? There was a certain kind of woman who settled in and never worried. I'd seen their bland faces in the supermarket, wheeling babies past counters laden with Pampers and Cheerios, hands sparkling pin-sized diamonds. Their homes were neat and smelled of potpourri. I was not one of them. I was an escape artist, the kind who broke iron-clad leases and left startled men in my wake. When I drove away from the prison gates each day, I saw the outside world beckon like a string of lights from a far-off city. And like Mrs. Hernandez, I buckled my seat belt and hoped for the best.

"You're not bad," I said again. But Mrs. Hernandez was praying and she didn't hear me.

It was my idea to hold a therapy group at noon. This meant scurrying from Mrs. Hernandez to eat the inedible but quick cafeteria food: beans cold from an industrial-size can, hard bread, fishy-smelling apple pie, and an extra serving of raisins. The inmates on canes or crutches bolted lunch and tapped along the corridors toward their work assignments or by the infirmary for their meds and joked *sell my body to science* before swallowing. Some looked forward only to the time when breakfast was served again on a metal tray with a blunt fork and a bent spoon, heavy oatmeal, a tiny carton of milk with a waxy straw, like grade school. Most of my group was like this, their rage beaten out of them from years of institutionalization. When I pushed open the door to the chapel, they nodded expectantly, a hodge-podge of child molesters, pre-ops, a couple of disables like Tiny on his crutch and Waggy in his wheelchair. I closed the doors and pulled a chair into the circle.

Angel spoke first. "My mother says she don't like having a daughter. She says she got plenny of daughters. Man, she make me *tired*." Angel and Marcelline always sat together, giggling like stoned high school girls. I thought of them—and all the other pre-ops—as "shes." The two gave the illusion of being made-up, although their faces were bare. They had a remembered beauty, like refugees.

"You just tired," Marcelline said. She giggled and slapped her thigh. "You just one tired girl." She looked so happy and alive, I knew she was using. Tiny, who had Aryan Brotherhood ties and thick muscle from the waist up, watched Marcelline giggle and looked pleased. He supplied crystal as a romantic gesture, like carnations before a prom date.

"It can be difficult for a parent to accept change," I said. "We've talked about this. Making peace with our parents."

Marcelline nudged Tiny, in for stabbing his stepfather, a biker who had stranded him on a drug deal.

"Would you like to say more about your mother, Angel?"

"She think if I can get my GED I'd be a boy again." Angel's eyes zipped around the room. "Damn, she dumb," she said tenderly.

Then it was Waggy's turn. He talked about the way his mother cried at his trial, then slapped his face and walked away. He had not seen or heard from her in ten years. Waggy was one of my favorites. He was tall and lean in his wheelchair, with the sad dignity of the young Leslie Howard in *Gone with the Wind*. His paralysis had been caused by a guard's bullet during an escape attempt. He'd continued to crawl through the fence opening even after he'd been shot.

"I forgive my mother," Waggy said. "I guess it's good she never saw me like this, but I'd give anything to know if she knows. Maybe she just don't care."

"So OK then," Tiny said. "Write her a letter."

"Call," Marcelline said. "Say, momma it's your fault I'm a *cripple*."

"Only she might not accept charges," a quiet little child molester put in.

Waggy stared down at his useless legs, covered by a thin brown blanket. "I don't have no address or number or nothing," he said softly.

"You can still write your thoughts in a letter," I said.

"Can't send it," Waggy said:

"It would be just for you."

The room shrugged collectively, as if to say *damn, she dumb*.

At that moment the heavy chapel doors swung open and there was Irene, the fat corrections officer leading her like a captured princess in the hands of savages. She had the air of someone volunteering to participate in an interesting but primitive tribal rite.

"This is a new one, Mary Claire," the fat officer said. "John Adams. He's in PC, but Dr. Dryer thought maybe he should come to your group?" Protective custody was another way to say "trouble" but Irene looked too quiet for that. She stared into the distance as the CO released her wrists. Marcelline patted the empty chair next to her. "Rest your sweet ass," she said. "While you still got the *chance*."

The new inmate waited until it was her own idea, then she sat gracefully, unfolding her long legs like a complicated origami construction.

"Well, John," I said. "Welcome to the group—"

"I'd like to be called Irene," she said.

I thought it was a strange name. Usually they took something frilly: Dandelion, Angel, Wildflower.

"Will you call me that?" Irene had a Southern voice, hoarse and melodic, dipping at some words and elongating others, the kind of voice made for lulling. No implants. You would have to look closely to see the faint rise and fall of her breasts.

"Of course, Irene. Please feel free to share when you're comfortable—"

"Just butt right in, no ifs or buts." Marcelline slapped herself on the backside. Irene did not move an inch in response. I was accustomed to the jittery, malleable girlishness of Angel and Marcelline. Irene did not seem male or female; she was a curious hybrid, like a child who resembled both parents but looked singular. I remembered a famous drawing I'd been shown in school: looked at from one side, a young man. A shift of focus and the shape of the man became an old woman. Irene smiled. Her front teeth were slightly crooked. Everyone in the joint had crooked teeth. I'd never known any of them to come from a family with money for braces. She narrowed her strange and nearly black eyes at me and I saw all at once the charismatic man she had been and I thought I could spend the rest of my days waiting to see that crooked smile again.

"We're dealing today with issues of forgiveness," I said.

"Jesus—he forgives everyone," Angel said.

"But it's more 'bout how we should forgive ourselves," Marcelline told her. She waved her long nails. "For, you know—whatever."

I passed out some paper and blunt pencils. "I want all of you to try writing a letter to someone you want to ask forgiveness of. Or a person you want to forgive. It could be anyone. It could be yourself. Write something you weren't able to tell them before. What they mean to you."

Tiny stared at his piece of paper and scratched one word then two. Waggy took a drink like a shot of whiskey from the plastic cup in the holder taped to the side of his wheelchair. Marcelline did not pretend to write. She picked at her nails.

"Tiny," I said, "would you like to share with the group?"

427

Tiny shifted his crutch and cleared his throat. " 'Bits. I forgive you for sleeping around like you maybe did. You were just lonely is what I guess and didn't know what was good for you. Anyway, it's OK. Tiny.' " He looked up. "She has my kid."

Marcelline made a bitter, jealous sound in her throat.

"Thank you, Tiny," I said. "Angel?"

Angel shrugged. " 'Mama. If you don't wanna give me cigarette money or nothing I forgive you and for liking Juan more than me even though I'm youngest and you should like me better and give me more money and pay for my op and all. You just old and set in your ways.' " Angel put down the paper and thought a minute. "Maybe I wouldn't end about her being old and all that."

"What would you say, Angel?"

" 'Bout how I love her and shit."

I nodded encouragement.

"See, that way she send what I need, you hear what I'm saying?"

This time the group nodded.

"What," I said, "would you write if you didn't ask for anything?"

Angel looked perplexed. "It don't make sense to spend time writing a letter if you ain't gonna ask for money or something. Letters make me *tired*."

"Here she go," Marcelline said, "someone wind her up again."

I smiled at Angel. "OK. Well, it's a good thing to think over this week."

The others read letters to their wives, their girlfriends, their daughters, their sons, their fathers. *When I'm on the out baby I'm gonna be good to you thought about so much here ain't never coming back here no way.* They forgave unreliability, stolen money, stolen drugs, infidelities large and small, missed visits, sexless evenings, unreceived Father's Day cards. While they read, Irene sat silently. Her wrists were red from where the handcuffs chafed. I could always tell a transsexual from a biological woman, even the good ones. I'd learned to look at the wrists, the bony lines. They can whittle down the Adam's apple, and the genitals can be switched like chess pieces, but some things just can't be changed—not yet anyway.

"Would you like to read, Irene? If you don't feel comfortable, you don't have to share with us yet."

Irene considered. Then she stood like a student forced to recite. "Does this letter have to be addressed to anyone?"

"Well. It's helpful to understand the—"

She cleared her throat and fixed me with her stare. " 'When I took your mouth on mine it was like lighting a candle—' "

There was a slight rustle as the group leaned forward.

" 'Like the love candles we bought at Madame DeFarge in the Quarter, the one we scratched in our names before we burned it. I think about that candle. I think about the way you sucked on the candle and passed it to me before you lit the flame.' "

I could not look away. I knew my face was warm.

" 'You know,' " Irene continued, " 'that nothing is forgivable. Mistakes we've made are imprinted on our skins. We read them from bus windows, across highways. What we believe is always a half step away from what we need to believe which is this: nothing is stronger than will and magic. I want to take that love candle from your mouth and light it once again. I want to drip hot wax on our—' "

"Irene," I whispered.

" 'Souls,' " Irene said. She sat.

The group was silent.

"You go, girl," Marcelline said finally. "You go."

I could feel Irene's dark eyes on me. I could feel them reach right into my skin.

When I asked that afternoon where Irene was housed, the C block officer just shrugged the direction. She was busy shuffling a group back in, a bored pied piper followed by a long trail of denimed cons. C block was a little quieter than the others because it housed the hated child molesters on meds, as well as transgenders, and the baby-rapers were only too grateful to be out of the way of the other cons to mix it up much. Even in all that silence, Irene's cell was a tiny oasis. Like all the protective custody cells, it was a three-sided observation cage in the middle of the tier. She sat with a notebook on her lap and did not look up when I approached.

"I knew you'd come," she said. She put the notebook down slowly, as if I'd awakened her. "This is like that place. Where all the souls kind of circulate before they're sorted."

"Purgatory?"

"That's it. I like that word. Sounds like an organ warming up at church." Her eyes were stranger than I remembered.

"We have a nice mass here. Father Allen comes in Sundays at ten—"

"I don't do church. Went with Louise just once. She found out they used grape juice for the sacraments." Irene grinned. She rubbed her wrists, still slightly reddened from the cuffs. "Louise liked her religion a little stronger."

"Louise. Is she a—friend?" I felt a tiny stab of jealousy.

"No," Irene said. She opened her hands and closed them.

"What are you writing?" I asked when the silence grew too long.

She didn't answer. I thought maybe she was writing a screenplay, a thriller for money. A lot of inmates dreamed of selling their story, making it big.

"You don't have to tell me."

Big Eddy shouted across the block about someone being a punk and nothing but a punk.

"You're always welcome to come to group. It's a good place for sharing your feelings. Writing your thoughts down. Have you ever tried a support group before?"

"You mean some new 'girls' talking about how hard it is to buy a matching bra and panty set in their size?" Irene lit a cigarette and slipped the pack back into her pocket. "No thank you maaaam."

"They aren't all that way."

"When I was *evaluated*"—she smoked like a man, the cigarette caught between her thumb and forefinger—"I asked if I could keep the fern I was carrying when I was clipped. Inmates, they said, cannot maintain plant life. But we *are* plant life, I said. They didn't think that was funny. I was in the hole for a week. The way they looked when I said that, it was worth every day of stale bread." She inhaled like a man, too, holding the smoke deep in her lungs, as if she was reluctant to allow it to escape. How old was she? Her hair had no trace of gray. Female hormones had probably kept her looking a decade younger than her age. She rubbed out her cigarette. I wanted to reach in, relight it, take a hit.

"I'm curious how long it's been since you called yourself John."

"Oh, I don't know. I used to change the names of my toys when I was little, depending on the day of the week. The place."

"Why stay with the name Irene then?"

Another pause. "It's after someone. I took her name. The first Irene was someone I knew."

"Someone you cared about? Someone you miss?"

"She was *someone*."

The way Irene looked in that half-light made me understand that John had been the kind of man who could walk into a room and tame

430

women like snakes. "But I knew I'd be an Irene way before that. You want to hear about the fortune-teller? I met her when I was twelve. It was nearly Mardi Gras."

"Mardi Gras," I said. "You're from New Orleans. That's a city I've always wanted to visit—"

"I spent my boyhood in New Orleans," she said. "Isn't that funny? Not many women have a boyhood to remember."

"No."

"My first cigarette was that summer, under the Irish Bayou Bridge. They wanted to fix my teeth too but I wouldn't let them."

"Who wanted to fix your teeth?"

Irene waved her hand. "You know. The ones who tidy everything up."

"I see."

"Don't let nobody tell you any romantic tales of the Bayou, cause it's all a damned lie. Just hot hot hot. It was almost Mardi Gras and it was a heat wave and everyone was drunk. Doesn't have to be Mardi Gras for everyone to be drunk though, that city is always just a flood of beer and hurricanes. We were new people but I wanted to sail a float that year and ride up top. We didn't have money but I got it in my head that I could build one. Why not? I'd build us a float like the others, I knew a little carpentry, and I had a fist of dollars to get a costume for Fat Tuesday—"

"Where'd you get a fist of dollars?"

"Never mind. I got it. But it wasn't enough. So I ran from the costume shop to the wharf where they built the floats. Just to see. The weather turned that day, it rained. I watched the rain and the baby mosquitos buzzing around me and I thought I could sit there for years and when I got up nothing would have changed. You ever feel that way?"

"I think so."

"When I did get up everything had changed."

From male to female, I thought. But I knew it wasn't that simple.

"It was Southern rain. You know, that's kind of heated. It doesn't cool the air, just hits the surface like steam. I got to three little kids fishing off the pier, they were used to everything, little poor children like that, even the rain beating on their backs and puddling their sneakers. It rainin' hard, the little girl said to me. She had a real serious look. She was a beautiful little girl. Yes, I said, it sure is, and it was. I didn't care. I was thinking of the float and what I would have

431

worn throwing beads to the people in the crowd unlucky enough not to have their own float, like the little children next to me. I would be a god to them that day but they didn't know it. They didn't know any of it. We got to the big building on the pier and I threw open the doors and there was a real float and she was sitting on it, like she was waiting for me." Irene stopped.

"The fortune-teller," I said.

"The float was just like I imagined, gold tiers and fake doorways, places where you could wave at the crowd and yards and yards and yards of beads. A gypsy sat, playing her cards at a special spangled table. She wore jet beads and wide gold earrings and she had the blackest hair I'd ever seen, darker than mine. When she smiled a tooth shone in her mouth like a star. She dealt all four of us a hand and told our future."

Irene dealt me an invisible hand describing this. She was a wonderful, gifted mimic. I'd known jailhouse magicians and card-tricksters and ventriloquists and one silent wife abuser who could make whole gardens of paper flowers from a few sheets pulled from a notebook. But when Irene snapped imaginary cards to me they were so real I could almost turn them over.

"Was that the first Irene?" I asked. "The one whose name you took?"

"*No.* It was a gypsy. You ever hear of a gypsy named Irene?"

"I guess not. What did the gypsy tell you?"

"She told the little girl first. She said she would marry a man with eyes the color of paper, and that she would never know whether he loved her, and this would be great pain. The gypsy knew if he would love her, but she wouldn't say, because it was important for the little girl to suffer and learn. And her children would also have paper eyes, and she would never be able to read them either. She said she would live in a house with people she loved but they would be strangers. This was her fate, to get everything she wished for, then to wonder why she wished for it."

"That is everybody's fate," I said. Irene spread her hands against the bars of the cage in agreement. Our fingers almost touched.

"She told the boy who had caught the most fish that he would spend much of his life on water. He would have a sailing house, but he would never find a woman to share this place. He would watch sunsets alone, with only a three-legged cat for company. He would love the little girl who married the man with the paper eyes, but he would never have her. The little boy blushed. Then she told the last little boy, the one with silky blonde hair, that he would never lose his hair, but that was the only riches he'd ever have. Golden hair. That all? the boy whined and she was angry. She said the future was wasted on him. She wrapped her cards in a square of silk and got up from the chair." Irene smiled. "Then she turned around and asked if I wanted to hear mine."

"And what was yours?"

"This," she said. "All this." She motioned to include the whole cell block. "She told me I'd be Irene and I laughed. Of course later I thought here I had known the future, all its wrinkles and blessings, but I couldn't *change* anything. People think if you know the future you can change it. But you can't."

"Did you see the gypsy again?"

Irene shook her head. "No. But I taught myself to read the cards after that. She said I had a gift. When I have my cards again, I'll read yours and you'll see."

"No," I said, chilled. "I don't want to know my future."

"I guess not." She stared at me with her strange eyes, sizing me up. "What's your name? Your Christian name, I mean?"

I told her.

"It's a funny thing about names though." She drew out all the syllables in her slow, Southern way. "Nothing is really alive until it's *named*." We looked at each other. Rather we shared a look, which is an important distinction. And then she stood closer and stretched and I could see through the bars and wire the power of her body, how well she lived within those strong limbs and I thought how wonderful the boy John must have been, running through the hot streets of his city.

"Mary Claire," she said, as if she could read my thoughts, "John's still here." Then she pointed to the place where nothing stronger than bone concealed the steady and complicated beat of her heart.

Nominated by Daniel Orozco

SIX APOLOGIES, LORD

by OLENA KALYTIAK DAVIS

from THE ANTIOCH REVIEW

I Have Loved My Horrible Self, Lord.
I Rose, Lord, And I Rose, Lord, And I,
Dropt. Your Requirements, Lord. 'Spite Your Requirements, Lord,
I Have Loved The Low Voltage Of The Moon, Lord,
Until There Was No Moon Intensity Left, Lord, No Moon Intensity
    Left
For You, Lord. I Have Loved The Frivolous, The Fleeting, The
    Frightful
Clouds. Lord, I Have Loved Clouds! Do Not Forgive Me, Do Not
Forgive Me LordandLover, HarborandMaster, GuardianandBread,
    Do Not.
Hold Me, Lord, O, Hold Me

Accountable, Lord. I Am
Accountable. Lord.

Lord It Over Me,
Lord It Over Me, Lord. Feed Me

Hope, Lord. Feed Me
Hope, Lord, Or Break My Teeth.

Break My Teeth, Sir,

In This My Mouth.

Nominated by The Antioch Review, Eugene Stein

THE DOLL

fiction by EUDORA WELTY

from THE GEORGIA REVIEW

SHE DID NOT drive away immediately. She thought dreamily, if Charles looks down from his office window he will certainly recognize my leghorn hat with the red cloth apple on it; and more obscurely, my hat will stand for me and for the words I said last night. Wondering if indeed he might not look down, she took off her glove and let the diamond flash in the sun, momentarily faint at the sudden accusing charge of light into her eyes: this was love. Quickly she hid her hand again. Charles had given her the ring the night before. She used her hand gently, as though it had been hurt, to touch the rag doll in the white dress which she had just bought at the church bazaar. She thought of Charles sitting leanly at his desk above, answering one at a time the questions of other people, his long hand to his head, thinking about problems of law: a chained myth when he was not with her.

It had been very warm inside the shop, very dark. Large groups of ladies talked at the tops of their voices. Her happiness, as though it were a scented flower, had in that crowded place become almost suffocating, and it seemed now to have put out queer shoots, like a disturbing tropical plant. Resentment, a queer sort of envy turned inside out, returned to her as she thought, lifting her chin, what do ladies shopping know of my love that has me bound so close to it that I am prostrate with its nearness. She was safer in feeling defensive; then she was not frightened.

°Editor's Note: first appeared in the little magazine *The Tanager* (June, 1936). Never before reprinted.

When she had lifted a cloth to examine it, she had felt that she moved with secrecy, that her flesh was packed snugly to her bones, that the very apple on her hat was shrinking into an enigma. By being a secret from other people, she might be more known to Charles . . . but she shut her eyes tightly, in a sort of modest numbness toward this other side of the secrecy. She considered helplessly going to his office now. She was tempting the fear, that new tendril on the tropical plant, to clutch at her again. The sensation of faintness and nausea was becoming rhythmically gratifying. She would show him the doll. She laid her finger on its red crayon mouth; it had a strange, crooked smile, one undoubtedly drawn by a sewing lady, an amateur. Charles might tell her what it meant.

She looked up hurriedly and gazed at the stream of shoppers in the sun.

Slowly she realized that her eyes had found someone in the crowded street and were threading with him in and out among the other people. It was Charles.

He was alone. He was across the street, walking slowly north in her direction. She was half-smiling at once, forming her lips to say his name. Yesterday she would have called him. But how could it be Charles, who was sitting at the desk above her head, coming to the window to look down and recognize her leghorn hat? Was it Charles?

He did not wear his hat, if it were. His face looked darker, with the dark hair blowing over it in the late summer breeze that floated dreamily up the street.

She looked down at the doll, as if to adjust the image in her eyes, and then looked back. This could not be Charles. She reassured herself. This man was fatter. His stomach above his white summer trousers looked almost plump. If it were he, it looked like him in another time, in another place, which was not to be borne.

But it was Charles; impossibly, it was.

It was the way he was holding himself, the way he was walking, that made the mystery. In the hot afternoon sun he seemed utterly relaxed, even a little tired. He moved up the street in long, slow steps, carrying his coat slung over his shoulder in a way she had never seen in him, placing his legs out before him in an unhurried easy manner that was somehow proud and inscrutable. He walked more slowly than anyone else in the street. She noticed suddenly how graceful he was.

But she had never thought of Charles as being graceful! When she

437

was walking with him she thought of his nearness; she held with her hand the sinews of his arm running under the cloth of his coat. She was certain that together they walked much faster than Charles was now walking alone; compared with Charles now, they appeared in retrospect almost to have run; and she knew that Charles did not bend his head down attentively and yet with superiority, as he did now, and look into every shop window that he passed. Filled with panic, she saw that he was then observing a window full of automobile tires which were round and staring, undulating his head to them as he passed. She looked at the window too, but as at something she could not comprehend.

He was almost across the street from her. She knew that he could not see her; he was nearsighted; and he never saw me from his office window, she thought falteringly, and yet gladly and ashamedly. She smoothed the doll's dress. He was so calm. He spoke to no one. He was there, he was bared to her eyes, he was displayed, he had taken off his coat and lost his hat; she stared at him, but it was impossible not to know that he was wrapped in a cloak of himself which he thought unobserved, and from which the touch of her hand would roll like a drop of rain, if, indeed, she should dare to touch him. Tears coming into her eyes suddenly angered her, that she should be crying on Main Street.

With an imperious gesture, one of her habits before she had become engaged, she laid her hand on the automobile horn. She would sound it, and call him to her. The ring sparkled in the bare sunlight. Fear stopped her. Where was he going? What was he doing, so slowly, unhurriedly and alone? She saw him stop and look attentively into a window displaying flashlights, his shoulders broadened and relaxed into a downcurved line. She could see that across his shoulders his shirt was wet; the line of his underwear showed through. The back of his head, dark and angular, familiar, always touched her deeply. She clutched the doll, wanting to jump from the car, run across the street to him and touch his arm. "I saw you," she would say. But she could not.

He stood there only a moment. At last she leaned back in the car. Who was the more hidden, the more hiding, she thought, pressed against the cushion. Again he walked in his slow, obscure way up the street: she was watching him in the driving mirror. He crossed at an intersection and moved on, other people walked near him and around him, meeting him and passing him, and she lost sight of him.

Charles had been there. She looked at the little stores, their false fronts waving under the dense sky, and at the people. Charles? He was another person. He was not herself, and yet neither was he any of the others in the street. The slowness of his step remained with her. It seemed to tramp softly and heavily within her blood. She was sickened with some perception of mystery.

Dumbly she laid the doll in the seat beside her, where it lay with its arms outstretched, and drove away.

That night she took particular pains with her hair. She wore as many of the things he had given her as she could, the gold chain, the little pin from London. She was careful to lock the other things in the case. Fastening the pin, feeling its slender point at her trembling fingertips, she remembered her terror on the night of their first dance together, when she had just met him, when she had just come back from her boarding school in the north.

She heard his car door, his step on the walk, quick and eager.

Even while she was greeting him, she was leading him to the dark porch. She felt his footstep beating in the veins at her temples, the way it had been in the afternoon, in counterpoint against his faster step on the tile beside her. She was confused and shy, and drew back into the swing. He talked. Finally she leaned in a rush against his coat and shut her eyes, putting her fright against the smell of starched linen and the lotion he used on his face.

"What have you been doing today?" he asked her after a while.

"Oh, I did a little shopping. Nothing much."

She turned her head and looked into the magnolia tree. She heard him tearing open a cigarette package and striking a match. She could not ask him what he had been doing. In dread she looked up at his face. She saw his mouth, in the oblique matchlight, made of curves and bulges and its dark canyons, its size uncertain. Strange, often-kissed mouth. She remembered wonderingly, he has even been in the War, and a scratchy black and white landscape in a moving picture she had seen stood still in her head.

"You haven't given me a kiss," he said, turning his face down to hers.

She swept herself instantly free from his look and flung her shoulders against a pillow in the corner of the swing. She began to sob convulsively.

"Marie!"

439

It was her name in his voice, but she heard herself answering childishly, "That's my name!"

He stood over her pulling gently at her arms.

She did not know whether she said it or not. "I can't kiss you."

He turned her by the shoulders so that she was looking up at him. His face was in the dark, part of the still leaves. His body in white was like a shaft being sunk into her stupid brain. She stopped crying finally. Stretching her arms up to his head she pulled herself up and caught her lips to his in a kiss the end of which she dreaded more than she could bear.

"Now!" he said gently. He seemed a little shocked by her behavior. He sat down beside her. She raised her head and looked up at him but he said nothing else. She jumped up.

"Look, dear, what I bought today."

She led him in tumult into the lighted room. Her eyes throbbed with pain. The doll lay on its face on a table. She picked it up. Under the lamp the ring blazed into her eyes.

"What is it? What's it for?" he asked.

"It's just a doll. Just a funny doll. I bought it while you were busy today. I was going to surprise you."

"I thought you would be at home all afternoon sleeping," he said.

They stood apart, at a loss. She touched her engagement ring, with a gesture strangely like wringing her hands. Then quickly holding the doll by its un-elbowed arms, she made it glide in its long dress over the tabletop. He began to smile, but did not offer to take the doll and look at it.

"It was just something I decided I wanted."

"You're so strange tonight," he said. "My darling."

"What's she smiling for?" continued Marie. She pouted like a little girl, and listened askance for his reply.

Suddenly, as if signalling from the uncurious outside world to their dilemma, came the sound of the fire-siren, and the close-coming, penetrating roar of firetrucks. They laughed suddenly, suddenly snatched from their aloneness and projected into the world.

"Let's go to the fire!" they cried together.

In the car they saw where the sky was red and went in that direction.

It was a house on the other side of town. They left the car and walked closer. Leaves of the trees they stood under framed the red spectacle, which crowds of people stood silently watching; they were the new-comers.

Black, round clouds of smoke rose rhythmically from the yellow box the fire made, and floated away to the south. The burning made a vibration, a trembling, invisible curtain in the air, and now and then leaves from the trees over their heads would suddenly ignite and quickly perish in dying triangles of blaze.

They stood side by side watching. Separately, and then slowly together as if hypnotized they saw the long, red scarves of flame part and disclose a little square window, and there, standing with stick arms raised like a doll, a woman waiting to be rescued; then, lowering their gazes, which were twisted together into one strand, they saw the ladder and the fireman in his helmet ascending. It was like the crude action of opera, they felt, and then, their arms tightly touching, believed gradually, as the man climbed, that indeed they were the ennoblers as well as the helpless projectors of this fiery danger, this cheap rescue pantomime: they were the music of the opera, the reason for this compulsion and crudity; and in tumultuous peace and self-worship at last they threw themselves with haste into each other's arms, hiding their eyes from the glare of the burning house in the shadows of each other.

In their throbbing pride they walked to the car and drove for a while over the little square blocks of the city, feeling like precious jewels, not like people who might be afraid again. They were in horror of speaking.

Finally Marie lay in sudden exhaustion against Charles, her whole body relaxing and feeling dead and tender toward him.

He was saying something softly. "I wonder how we can be so sweet to each other—what makes us be so sweet to each other—and sometimes we seem a thousand miles apart—until—do you know—?"

"No." Her whole flesh began to rally about her surfeited heart, and she was glad at last to hear him, to desert her fear for his own. "No," she said, comfort and contrition deepening her voice until it was round in her throat like fruit. "Don't wonder. Just—*now*—"

Nominated by Cleopatra Mathis, Robert Phillips, The Georgia Review

A PRIMER FOR THE SMALL WEIRD LOVES

by RICHARD SIKEN

from INDIANA REVIEW

1

The blond boy in the red trunks is holding your head underwater
because he is trying to kill you,
     and you deserve it, you do, and you know this,
          and you are ready to die in this swimming pool
    because you wanted to touch his hands and lips and this means
              your life is over anyway.
     You're in the eighth grade. You know these things.
    You know how to ride a dirt bike, and you know how to do
      long division,
and you know that a boy who likes boys is a dead boy, unless
         he keeps his mouth shut, which is what you
              didn't do,
because you are weak and hollow and it doesn't matter anymore.

2

    A dark-haired man in a rented bungalow is licking the whiskey
from the back of your wrist and dreaming with your mouth.
     He feels nothing,
         he could slit your throat,

keeps a knife in his pocket,
                    peels an apple right in front of you
        while you tramp around a mustard colored room
in your underwear
                    drinking Dutch beer from a green bottle.
        After everything that was going to happen has happened
you ask only for the cab fare home
            and realize you should have asked for more
                    because he couldn't care less, either way.

3

        The man on top of you is teaching you how to hate, sees you
as a piece of real estate, just another Kansas,
                    just another fallow field lying underneath him
                            like a sacrifice.
He's turning your back into a table so he doesn't have to
            eat off the floor, so he can get comfortable,
pressing against you until he fits, until he's made a place for himself
                            inside you
that turns like a wheel, that eats away at you like acid or an animal.
        The clock ticks from five to six.
                    Kissing degenerates into biting.
So you get a kidney punch, a little blood in your urine.
                    It isn't over yet, it's just begun.

4

        Says to himself *The boy's no good. The boy is just no good.*
            but he takes you in his arms and
pushes your flesh around to see if you could ever be ugly to him.
                    You, the now familiar whipping boy, but you're
        beautiful, he can feel
                    the dogs licking his heart.
Who gets the whip and who gets the hoops of flame? He hits you
                            and he hits you
        and he hits you, desire driving his hands right into your body.
            Hush, my Sweet. These tornadoes are for you.
You wanted to think of yourself as someone

443

who did these kinds of things.
You wanted to be in love and he happened to get in the way.

5

The green-eyed boy in the powder blue shirt standing next to
you in the supermarket recoils as if hit, repeatedly,
by a lot of men, as if he has a history of it.
This is not your problem.
You have your own body to deal with.
The lamp by the bed is broken.
You are feeling things he's no longer in touch with.
And everyone in the donut shop is speaking softly,
so as not to wake each other.
The wind knocks the heads of the flowers together.
Steam rises from every cup at every table at once.
Things happen all the time,
things happen every minute that have nothing to do with us.

6

So you say you want a deathbed scene, the knowledge that comes
before knowledge,
and you want it dirty.
And no one can ever figure out what you want,
and you won't tell them,
and you realize the one person in the world who loves you
isn't the one you thought it would be,
and you don't trust him to love you in a way
you would enjoy.
And the boy who loves you the wrong way is filthy.
And the boy who loves you the wrong way keeps weakening.
You thought if you handed over your body
he'd do something interesting.

7

Maybe it was the snow, or something in the snow
that was confusing.

444

Maybe if you didn't limit your hungers
                    to the things that never hold you
                              you'd find something satisfying.
The ice in the punchbowl makes the sound
                    of chandeliers being dragged up from the lake.
    The man wants you to sign something.
            Being friendly but no longer trusting it,
                                    not even the existence of it,
            while the man slumps in a chair, smokes your cigarettes,
and looks at your mouth as if to say
                    It's Spring. You smell good. Lie to me.

                              8

    Sometimes you have to take the road that's longer, you know this,
but you want to say
            Oh no, I'm not swallowing this again.
                          And then you find yourself in the dark,
        come home to where he's trying to destroy the building.
Falls asleep with his hands at your throat,
                leaves his story on your parchment skin
                              with the language of his hands.
    We rub each other until we're smooth and blurred
            or we peel back the skin to see what we're lined with:
                        the buttercreme dreams, the walnut heart.
We do this, we do, we take the things we love and tear them apart
        or we pin them down with our bodies and pretend they're ours.

                              9

    The stranger says there are no more couches and he will have to
sleep in your bed. You try to warn him, you tell him
                    you will want to get inside him, and ruin him,
            but he doesn't listen.
By lunchtime he's mowing your lawn with a weed whacker.
            You can tell he needs a glass of water, but you aren't going
                    to give him one, you aren't going to
                                    give him anything.
    But then you kiss him, and he doesn't move, he doesn't pull away,

it sounds like his eyes are rolling around in his head, but you keep
    kissing him.
And he hasn't moved, he's frozen, and you've kissed him,
    and he'll never forgive you, and maybe now he'll leave you alone.

Nominated by David Jauss, Stacey Richter, Indiana Review

TWILIGHT OF THE APPLE GROWERS

essay by JANE BROX

from THE GEORGIA REVIEW

THE EARLY New England farms all had their apple trees that grew along a fence line or in a small block; stalwart, long-lived, their bearing limbs pruned to a craggy, turned grace. Apples—old work-horse crop—crushed for cider, dried beside the fire, or simmered into sauce. Touched with frost, the late-ripening storage varieties—Baldwins, say—were packed away into March, and as the days lengthened their skins toughened then wrinkled, their flesh softened, and the dank, stone-sealed air of the apple cellar deepened to a winy depth.

In 1920, over a quarter million bearing apple trees ranged across the drumlins and eskers of Middlesex County—far-spread, full-sized trees producing more than a million bushels of fruit. We are so far from an agricultural economy now, I can't help but think at first that a million bushels of apples must have meant the early century was a propitious time for farming here, yet by then agriculture in New England had been in decline for years. Even by the mid-nineteenth century Henry Thoreau, walking his own corner of Middlesex County, could see the falling off: *none of the farmer's sons are willing to be farmers, and the apple trees are decayed, and the cellar holes are more numerous than the houses, and the rails are covered with lichens, and the old maids wish to sell out and move into the village, and have waited twenty years in vain for this purpose. . . . lands which the Indian long since was dispossessed of and now the farms*

447

are run out, and what were forests are now grain-fields, what were
grainfields, pastures. . . .

By the time my father planted his last orchard in the 1980's, apple growing in Middlesex County had diminished to little more than a thousand acres of orchards spread across seventy-four farms. In 1992, 819 acres remained on fifty-three farms. And they, tucked in among spreading suburbs and industrial complexes, are without context in the county or in the eastern part of Massachusetts. In tough weather—a droughty mid-summer, say—when growers wonder how the apples will ever size up, they listen for news of rain in the beach and boating forecast, the rush-hour weather, and the weekend weather.

Our own farm claims little more than three hundred of the county's remaining apple trees. The main orchard, sloping behind the barns and houses and bordered on its far side by a stand of hundred-foot white pines, is hardly noticeable, except in blossom time, to a passerby. Most of the year our farm is dominated by the row crops—fields of corn and trellised tomatoes and vines of cucumbers and squashes, yet even so, when I think of the possibility that all of it may pass away, it's the apple trees I can't imagine going—maybe because through all the changes here, there's always been an orchard.

In 1901, along with the house, the gradey herd of milking cows, the barn and its contents—pails, hammers, plows, scythes—my grandparents gained ownership of the Baldwins, Gravensteins, Red Astrakhans, and Ben Davis. A few of those trees hang on—thickset now, and crusted with lichen—in the far corners of the farm, but by midcentury most had been replaced by my father's plantings of McIntosh, Red Delicious, Cortland, and Northern Spy. By then he had sold the herd and had begun to concentrate on growing fruits and vegetables for the nearby city dwellers, hauling his produce to the corner markets in Lowell and Lawrence until the cities emptied of their prospects, the family stores failed, and the world around us turned suburban.

As new ranches and split-levels were set down on old fields and in old woods, the local traffic became constant and we sold on our roadside stand nearly all the produce we grew. By then the varieties of apples we offered included Macoun, Jonah Reds, Paula Reds, and a redder strain of Cortlands—red had become important in marketing—as the last orchard my father planted started to bear. Those trees cover only a few acres, but their wood is grafted to semidwarf rootstock, which means easier-to-pick smaller trees that produce higher yields per acre. Not so long-lived, they'll be replaced after a quarter-century or so, and will never look as tough and wind-staunch as the old Baldwin trees.

When most of the row crops have been plowed under and the fields are deep in rye, apples—like winter squash and pumpkins— bring in money after the killing frosts. Though they may extend the season, my father never counted apples among his most productive or lucrative crops. He always said corn was the draw. Even now, come July my mother will return from Sunday Mass saying, "All anybody wanted to know was when the corn would be ready." The stand opens with corn, and with the first sparse pickings everyone crowds the table and watches anxiously as a young boy tosses bushel after bushel on the table and packs the pile down into dozens and half dozens; they watch the dozens disappear and the bushels empty, afraid all will be gone before they get their turn. The stand—last stop on a Friday afternoon before the road to the beach, to the White Mountains, to the lake country in Maine—runs with corn all through the summer, and the demand hardly lets up until summer itself lets go.

Never such a story for apples, which appear after corn and then tomatoes and peaches have contented everyone—and even the first astringent smells of the early Gravs and Paula Reds and Jerseymacs are lost when set beside the sweeter smells of peaches and cornsilk. Apples gain their true place in the cooler, drier air after Labor Day— the world back on its axis—when those who stop do so on the way home from work, or during a weekend morning in the middle of errands. *I love the smell of fall*, some will say, as they breathe in the cold, sharp scent of apples. The first red leaves are falling one by one. The days are already growing brief.

If the scent of apples closes one year, pruning the orchard opens the next, bringing a kind of relief on the other side of winter restlessness: work to shake off the quiet contemplative months in a time not crowded by countless other chores and a shortness of time. Come late February or early March my father would take out his snips and saw and begin to work down the rows of the orchard. I like to remember him alone under the wide winter sky, studying the shape of each tree before making his cuts. He always liked to be doing some-

449

thing, even after the arthritis in his knees made it difficult to walk without the help of a cane. In his last years he'd drive his truck nearly from tree to tree. I can still see him as he'd pause after turning out of the seat to brace himself for the sure pain that would come when he put his weight on his knees. Down to bone on bone the doctor had said. Even so, he stayed with it—that was always his advice to me: *stay with it*—until he was eighty-five, his last spring, when he hired the man to prune the orchard for him.

After my father's death—the fields buried in snow—it was the dormant trees with their gray, turned branches that loomed large to me and made the farm feel like too much to care for. In the weeks afterwards, as I tried to square his affairs, I didn't give a thought to the summer row crops. I just wanted—beyond reason really—to see the orchard pruned as it had always been. I looked through all the cards and the several list-finders on his desk in an effort to find the name of that pruner he'd hired the spring before, and once I found the listing, heart in my throat, I called.

"I'd be glad to do it," he answered. "You've got a nice setup—an old romantic orchard. They don't make them that way anymore." He was glad to do it, and though his price was higher than my father ever would have settled on, I didn't know what else in the world to do but agree. In those months I'd probably have paid anything just for things to be the same. It was worth it to see the man show up, snips and loppers in hand—strange with his radio, sunglasses, and wide-brimmed hat—on the first open day in late February. Even with all the corn snow still on the ground—we'd had over ten feet of it that winter—he worked deftly up and down the rows, and the shapes of the trees clarified in his wake.

Here is another spring. It's a late Wednesday afternoon, and our farm manager David and I are traveling west through the broad length of Middlesex and into more rural Worcester County on our way to the first Twilight Meeting of the year for apple growers. The interstate belies any sense of distance or towns-traveled-through as it cuts across the rolling, wooded hills of our region. The grasses are just starting to turn green, and the light feels a little milder as the sun slants toward the western hills, though the cold comes in quickly still.

We've both been pruning the orchard this year—Dave has taken a chain saw to the tops of the older trees, while I've been working from the ground, pruning the lower limbs the best I know how, looking

450

into the tangle of the crowns, trying to clear out what's growing down, or in, or crossing another branch. The water sprouts, the winter damage, the deer-bitten branch tips. You could hear me mumbling to myself: *That won't do any good—that should go—this one, maybe this.*

We still have a ways to go with the pruning even though the buds have been swelling for a while. As we left today for the Twilight Meeting—named so because it's held at the end of a work day—the buds, having already passed dormancy, silver tip, and green tip, were at the stage called half-inch green where you can see the leafy folds just starting to break out. In the weeks to come there will be tight cluster, pink, full bloom, petal fall, fruit set, then the June drop. Through all the variants of the April days—the warming trends, the cloudy, cold, gray setbacks, and the freak snows—the buds push forward toward their blossoming, softening the harsh winter forms of the trees. All the long months I've looked out on the severe turns of the long-pruned branches, and now at dusk, especially, the orchard feels full of peace, with the haze of incipient silver-white and green floating around the crowns of even the oldest, craggiest trees. For the moment they seem to be made only half of substance, and hardly bearers of fortunes and tradition.

The trees are clearly on our mind as we head into the Nashoba Hills. "I can't imagine the orchard paying for itself," I say casually.

"I know," Dave answers.

"Who will you get to pick all the apples?"

"I have no idea."

At the meeting there'll be apple growers from the northeastern region of Massachusetts, which includes Essex, Middlesex, and Worcester counties. Each meeting is held at a different host farm every month of the spring and early summer. The owner or manager leads a tour of his orchards, packing houses, and storage areas, and afterwards the extension agents from the University of Massachusetts Tree Fruit Program report on recent field trials and the insect migrations and hatches. They give out certification points for those with pesticide applicator's licenses.

The host farm this month is in the Nashoba Hills, which has always been the prime apple growing region in the area and where the largest orchards remain. The Soil Survey of 1924 praises the Charlton loam of these hills, *derived from glacial-till deposits which are*

451

commonly from 10 to 40 feet thick over the bedrock. This soil occurs on low, smooth, rounded, oblong or drumloid hills, and in many places caps the tops of ridges and hills having more or less stony hillsides. . . . Drainage is thoroughly established, but the soil has an excellent moisture-holding capacity, and crops rarely suffer even in dry seasons. . . . Apples do exceptionally well. The trees make a healthy growth, and the fruit is of good quality. . . .

As we turn off the interstate and approach the farm, the road is nearly swallowed by high round hills on either side. Slender dwarf trees cross them in soldierly rows, trees light and airy after their spring pruning. Though it's higher and colder here than at home, the green on these buds is breaking out, too. We pull into the parking lot of a broad, beamy, closed-for-the-winter farmstand. The windows are dark and bare, a fading See You In The Spring sign covers one of the doorpanes. The parking lot is filled with pickups. Some, high-riding shiny new four-wheel drives with elaborate detailing; others, with rusting fenders and slatted wooden sides on the beds to give them some depth. On the doors, the names: *Wheatley Orchards, Barstow Farms, Flat Hill Orchards . . .*

We meet up with the others behind the farmstand in the apple storage area. There may not be many left, but the apple growers range in prosperity and experience from a bewildered couple who've just bought into an old neglected orchard to third or fourth generation farmers who manage state-of-the-art operations. Most are men in their fifties and sixties, some in their seventies. April is the time to finish up what pruning is left, and—just from work—they're dressed in workpants, jackets, peaked caps, and boots. They've already been working outside for many weeks, so their cheeks are rough and red from the spring winds. There are a few women, and a scattering of younger men. We, with our five or six acres of orchard, half of which are aging, standard trees, belong with the smaller enterprises. Much of the meeting—discussion of the breakdown of senescent fruit, comprehensive spray programs, and the shipping market—is banked towards larger growers and will be beyond our immediate concerns. Still, it feels like something we can't afford to miss.

Maybe there are forty or fifty of us gathered in a long hall that runs alongside the refrigeration areas. As I sit, I suddenly get a scent—round and deep—of long-stored apples, and with the chill in the air I forget the spring, and feel for a moment as if winter is still to come. I remember the way the smell of apples filled our car when I

452

was a child. On longer trips my father always traveled with a bag of them on the floor behind the driver's seat. Northern Spies. When he pulled in for gas, if he had started in talking to the owner or attendant, he'd reach back and offer him an apple as he paid up.

I come around again to realize it's the scent of last fall's crop I now smell. The host pulls out a couple of stored samples to show how they've held up all these months. Beautiful, large, streaked with red. I remember the pruner telling me *Massachusetts apples are renowned outside Massachusetts—they're exported all over the world—McIntosh sell for a dollar apiece in England.* This time of year you'd find few in the nearby supermarkets, which are full of New Zealand Bracburns, Australian Granny Smiths, and Washington state Red Delicious. Oversized, a waxed shine, $1.19 a pound. Even if the Massachusetts crop failed completely, the supermarkets would still have their apples. Except for a few brief fall weeks, imports always take up most of the allotted display space in the produce sections, even when the early regional varieties—Paula Reds, Jerseymacs—appear in late August. No matter the flavor, people buy with their eyes, and everyone here would tell you those Washington state Red Delicious are meant for eyes alone.

Most of the men are large, and the tables feel a little crowded. Many haven't seen each other all winter, and there's a rumble of catch-up talk: *Retire, no, Christ, that's when they plant ya . . . I was going to put out some oil next week, if it warms up a bit. Going to be a cold spring . . .* Many are talking about the cider situation. In recent years, several E. coli outbreaks have sent a scare through health officials and the public, and now the rumors are all about requiring pasteurization for cider. No drops in the mix either, nothing that's touched the ground: *We might try running it through the milk pasteurizer. I tell you, regulations are what will kill us. It's ridiculous.*

The voices all feel familiar to me—this is the kind of talk I've overheard for much of my life. Still, I feel shy. I recognize a few old acquaintances of my dad. One or two step over to see me for a moment—"How's it going over there? How's your mother holding up? If I can be of some help . . ." We talk politely for a few minutes until the conversation trails off, and they amble away to join another group.

The orchard tour is first, and the large lot of us pile into the backs of some of the pickups and jostle along the cart path to higher ground to look at some Galas that had been planted half a dozen years ago. The top of the hill is crowned with a nineteenth-century white clapboard homestead, which is shaded by a few ancient specimen apple trees long past production now. I guess they're what's left of an old orchard meant to span years and years. They—with their rough gray bark, more bullish trunk than crown, the new growth of long slim branches weeping towards the ground—make us almost believe such trees always were, and that it's we who are the first to change. But the idea of beauty that they suggest and that we hold (*old romantic orchards*), of trees planted in rows across open land, began only when apple growing became a deliberate occupation, going back no more than a few lifetimes. The earliest New England farmers tucked in wild apple trees where they could, and the result was nothing like the blocks and rows we've all come to know and love. Theirs was a disorder Thoreau loved, and saw passing in his time:

I fear that he who walks over these hills a century hence will not know the pleasure of knocking off wild apples. Ah, poor man! there are many pleasures which he will be debarred from! Notwithstanding the prevalence of the Baldwin and the Porter, I doubt if as extensive orchards are set out to-day in this town as there were a century ago when these vast straggling cider-orchards were planted. Men stuck in a tree then by every wallside and let it take its chance. I see nobody planting trees today in such out of the way places, along almost every road and lane and wallside, and at the bottom of dells in the wood. Now that they have grafted trees and pay a price for them, they collect them into a plot by their houses and fence them in.

So we also are aftercomers of a kind, and cannot guess the beauty been.

"It's good to be up high," someone says, and it is, as I look west towards the Connecticut River Valley and the long blue of the greater hills. The sky is already deepening in the east. The cold sun, low in the west. Frail branches of the small trees cast long shadows. The farm manager talks about his Galas, his successes and failures, and as we stand among the trees some of us hang on his words, others look at the pruning job or the way the buds are breaking. Then we trundle back down the hill to the storage house to drink coffee, eat hotdogs, and listen to the extension agent from the Department of Plant and Soil Sciences give a rundown on rootstock trials and foliar calcium sprays for apples. Another takes his turn and discusses the oil spray schedule. Specific, scientific—where does such knowledge go beyond this room and these few people? An undertow of small talk begins to break out. It's been a long day, and attention is drifting away.

The agent brings us round by raising his voice a bit: "OK, listen up. One last thing. The Pesticide Disclosure Act is in front of the Ag Committee in the House. I thought we had the chair's support, but it doesn't look that way. Give a call. If this goes through it will require you to notify every abutter a week before every application. We'll have a hard time doing our job." His sense of urgency quiets the group down. Some pull out paper and scribble a note down. He gives them some numbers to call. One thing you can count on to make this crowd feel like a group again—themselves alone—is the threat of new regulations and legislation.

There isn't anyone here, I imagine, even among the successful ones, who isn't staring off into the unknown. Farms have always been lost, many more lost than ever revived. Middlesex County has been going certainly away from this way of life for a century and a half. The farmland here, with its cleared, well-drained soils, has been sought out for development for a long time, and when it passes from one generation to the next, unless it qualifies for special valuation, unless the children commit themselves to ten years of farming, the land is assessed for highest and best use, which prices it far beyond any agricultural future.

However uncertain the future, it's also true that those who remain must love the work—from the countless hours of pruning in the lengthening days of late winter to the final harvest in the brief days of autumn—even if it doesn't seem they've had a choice except to carry on from the ones who've gone before them. And some, maybe many, who love it still have not survived for a thousand reasons—family, finances, and hard luck among them. But in a world of choices, whoever doesn't love the work has no chance at all. Next meeting, next month, in a longer twilight, in warmer air, the apples will be in pink, and it will be a busier time for work, though most who are here will attend that meeting also.

After the last talk dies down, everyone drifts off to the parking lot. I stand at our truck waiting for David, who's stayed behind to talk to one of the extension agents. I look back at the storage house where we all met, and the building suddenly seems overlit in the growing dark. I can hear bits of conversation in the distance. *They're saying frost in the lower valleys. Can you still take care of my cider apples this year? Let's talk about it before next meeting.* Yes, if and when the farms go, all the particular talk will go, too. The words and their fullest meanings: *petal fall, fruit set, June drop, stay with it.* The last truck doors slam shut.

The evening commute has passed, so the road is quiet; the birds are already silent, the silver-green tips of the apple trees are glinting. Lights go out in the storage house. One by one the engines turn over and the trucks drive off. Silence. A lingering sting of gasoline in the air, then the smell of the spring buds returns.

Nominated by Stephen Corey

BIBLICAL ALSO-RANS

by CHARLES HARPER WEBB

from LIVER (University of Wisconsin Press)

Hanoch, Pallu, Hezron, Carmi,
Jemuel, Ohad, Zohar, Shuni:
one Genesis mention's all you got.

Ziphion, Muppim, Arodi: lost
in a list even the most devout skip over
like small towns on the road to L.A.

How tall were you, Shillim?
What was your favorite color, Ard?
Did you love your wife, Iob?

Not even her name survives.
Adam, Eve, Abel, Cain—
these are the stars crowds surge to see.

Each hour thousands of Josephs,
Jacobs, Benjamins are born.
How many Oholibamahs? How many

Mizzahs draw first breath today?
Gatam, Kenaz, Reuel? Sidemen
in the band. Waiters who bring

the Pèrignon and disappear.
Yet they loved dawn's garnet light
as much as Moses did. They drank

wine with as much delight.
I thought my life would line me up
with Samuel, Isaac, Joshua.

Instead I stand with Basemath, Hoglah,
Ammihud. Theirs are the names
I honor; theirs, the deaths I feel,

their children's tears loud as any
on the corpse of Abraham, their smiles
as missed, the earth as desolate

without them: Pebbles on a hill.
Crumbs carried off by ants.
Jeush. Dishan. Nahath. Shammah.

Nominated by Kirk Nesset, Edward Hirsch

WHEN IT'S YOU

fiction by FRED LEEBRON

from THE THREEPENNY REVIEW

IT STARTS with a slight but unusual feeling of fullness after each meal. Or it starts with pain in the center of your back, along the spine, that gradually inches to the ribs. Or one day you lift your arm because you feel like there's an extra pocket of air under there. And it's a lump. Or perhaps you have a persistent cough, a weird insistent shortness of breath, strange numbness sheathing one side of your chest. You see blood in the urine, or blood or mucus in the stool. Or you cough blood or sneeze blood out your nose. Or your fingernails inexplicably grow yellow. Or your breath smells unexpectedly foul, as if you've been chewing on sweat.

We say, it's nothing. We say, Wait, maybe it'll go away. We say, Give it time. We say, How long have you had this? When was the last time you saw a doctor? Maybe you should see a doctor. You could see a doctor. I think it's time you saw a doctor. Let's see a doctor. I'll go with you. I'm calling the doctor. Now. I'll make the appointment. I'm calling the doctor. You'll call? When? Okay. If you haven't called by then, I'm calling. I'm calling the doctor.

They say, So how are you feeling? You're not feeling that great today? When did it start? Where does it trouble you? Could you climb up on the table? Take your shirt off? Take your pants off? Breathe deeply. Let me look in those ears. Open your mouth. Breathe really deeply. Lie down. Put pressure on it. Again. More pressure. Pressure till I say you can stop. You feeling something there? There? Here? Put pressure on it. Breathe deeply. Cough. Maybe we should run some tests. I think we ought to run some tests. We're going to have to do some tests. You need some tests. We need to schedule some tests. How about a few tests? Nothing invasive. Nothing too invasive. Nothing that will cause you any substantial discomfort. Nothing to be afraid of. Well, it's a little invasive. It's pretty invasive, but we really need to have a look. Actually, there's a small percentage of risk, but we need to do this. I think we need to do this. We have to do this. Now, we don't want to speculate. We'll just wait and see. We'll just let the results speak for themselves.

We sit in the kitchen, by the pot of coffee. Decaf. Maybe we're standing at the counter. The room is as cheerful as it's going to get. The lamps are lit, the faux marble buffed. All the other rooms feel too large and deserted for us, as if we've just moved in. Maybe it's nothing, we say. He didn't say it had to be something. I don't think it's nothing, you say. I want it to be nothing. You push the coffee away. I want a glass of water. We get you water. Everyone says drink eight glasses of water a day. It's good for the lymph nodes. It replaces you. You want to be replaced. You want everything new, right now. What are you thinking? I'm not thinking about anything. We could go buy some books about it. We don't even know what it is yet. Maybe it's nothing. God this kitchen is depressing. Do you think we should call anyone? Who should we call? I was asking you. You want to call your mother? Not yet. Sister, brother, daughter, son? Father? Lover? You laugh.

The tests. You have to call in sick to work. Maybe you are sick. You haven't had solids for six hours, or twelve hours. Or you haven't had anything but water for twelve hours. Or you haven't even had water. They numb you locally. Or they put you under to the max. You like that. You wake up thinking, Hey, that wasn't so bad. The room is cheerful. There are flowers. People wearing smiles. Then you feel it. That *was* something. That test. I should have studied, you joke. The doctor laughs and pats your arm. The other arm is hooked to an IV at the hand. We'll know in a few days, the doctor says. Thank you, you say. Because it is important to be gracious.

Again, we go home. We sit in the kitchen. Outside it is as gray as an overcoat. You're almost giddy. It is wonderful, you think—we think—to have these days of not knowing. It's so freeing. We can't do anything. We don't know. Your face is drawn. You look pale. You've lost a bit of weight. Stress. Stress isn't healthy, but it can sure take the weight off. We sit around the rest of the day. For dinner we eat soup. We don't even drink. We watch the Duraflame. We slump on the couch, legs intertwined. The phone doesn't ring. Nobody knows. We don't know either.

The next morning I leave for work. Sorry. You don't feel like going in but you may have the rest of your life to call in sick, so in the office you spend the time filing and secretly packing for your imagined successor. Or you've figured you'll call in sick until you know. You're still sore. They've taken something from you, those guys in the smocks and scrubs and lab coats. You sit around all day in the smallest room you can find. Maybe you're on the floor of the front hall coat closet. Or maybe you're in our bathroom, although there's something so antiseptic—so medicinal—about plumbing that suddenly it terrifies you. You can't talk to anyone. You dig in the home medical manual. Of course you know what it could be. Something unspeakable. You don't speak it. You drink twelve glasses of water, just to be sure. The home manual says that coming to terms with your mortality can be a process of great personal growth and discovery. You feel around inside yourself for the weird feeling that sent you on this expedition in the first place. It's still there. Right there. Goddamn.

I come home. You've got the will out. That's thinking ahead, I say.

The next day, ten A.M. sharp, we have our appointment. You don't know quite what to wear for the occasion. I'm dressed for work, thinking I'll go in after. You dress in denim and flannel and hiking boots—a kind of survival gear. Or you dress in the corporate manner befitting the appropriate buttoned-down approach to the crisis proportions of your situation. The doctor's in his office by himself. Of course he's by himself. So far it has always been just him. Who else could it be? He stands up and shakes our hands. We sit down. He coughs. Perhaps he smiles inappropriately. He looks at you. Unblinkingly. It's terminal, he says. Or, it's time to get your affairs in order. Or, I'm sorry, there's not much we can do. Or, I'm afraid there's nothing we can do. He can't say, We've done the best we could. Because there's nothing anyone has done yet, which is a relief or an opportunity or in your case just not applicable. He spells it out. He explains it, exhausts it, as if to a class of freshmen premed students interested in the onset and etiology of disease. He is frank, we'll call him afterwards endlessly—frank—so endlessly that we just call him that, Frank. That's his name. Frank. Frank.

You're dying. We're on the hunt for a second opinion. It takes three weeks or four weeks or two weeks to arrange and the insurance won't cover all of it or won't cover any of it. No matter, when you're dying you just want enough opinions to be sure. You want to know. Actually, we both sometimes think but never utter, it may be better

461

not to know. Another time, another life, perhaps we'll give that strategy a try. I still go to work. You have been put, indefinitely, on sick leave. Only your immediate supervisor knows. She's discreet. You have to begin to tell people. Your parents, your siblings, kids if you have them. Maybe that lover if you have one and I still don't know about it. What a mess, the telling, the endless retelling. Then you think, Email. You create an alias. You keep them all posted when you feel like typing. They know to stop calling. You're saving your energy. For recovery.

The second opinion guy is so fancy that his underlings have underlings, and those underlings have underlings, and you don't actually speak to him directly until you've run the underling gauntlet, been interrogated by them and examined by them and coughed up a couple thousand dollars in the name of the big cajuna, the grand poobah. The guy himself is as tall and broad and convincing as you'd like him to be. He sits down, just the one lieutenant at his side, and looks at you, looks at us, looks at you again. "Your doctor did an excellent job working you up," he says. "I confirm the diagnosis." Or, "I've reviewed all the tests and read all the charts and your doctor did a good job. I agree with the diagnosis." Or, "I've run some tests on your tests and I've spoken with your doctor and I feel that there is a 100% chance that his diagnosis is correct." He leans back in his chair. He looks at you, he hasn't stopped looking at you, he is seeing what you look like and to him you don't look much different from everyone else who has pushed through his door. "So what can you do?" he says. His long fingers begin to count. "Well, you can try hormones. You can try drugs. You can try a combination of hormones and drugs. Or you can do nothing."

Do nothing? We bandy that around in the back of our heads while going over all the options that aren't really options so much as stalling tactics or running-out-the-clock tactics or tactics that just defy comparison, what the big cajuna calls palliative rather than curative. There is nothing curative. Not for you. At the end of the tiresome Q and A he stands up, shakes my hand, shakes your hand, says, "Good luck." Twenty-three hundred dollars for good luck. Wow.

We buy books. We visit therapists. You take nutritional supplements. We click our way through the Internet. We apply to alternative treatment centers, centers which some whisper are in it just for the money, and they decline us and they don't even give us a reason why. Or they accept you and it's a minimum $172,000 in uninsurable care and they want to open up a vein at your collarbone and teach you how to pump yourself with biological agents to wage war against the biological enemies in your system. Or they put you on a wait list that is five years long when you only have one and tell you that they're sorry, that's the roll of the dice, the spin of the wheel, and they wish it could be otherwise. They cannot explain it any better than that because it's you and you are dying and this fact hits either of us at any odd time of day all day all the time, actually all the time. We pay bills, we make dinners, we answer the phone—sometimes. We're no longer terribly interested in television. We hate the phrase, Next year, next season, next week.

People begin dropping by. Old high school friends whom you haven't heard from in decades, former college roommates, your first boss, your parents' friends shabby in their wrinkledness because we're all wondering why not them instead of you, old colleagues, colleagues from the office from which you've just retired with a meaty far too generous package that leaves us thinking it's because they don't expect you to last too long, they've called around, they know. We're always cleaning the house before these people come and after they leave, and while they visit we try to sit patiently on the couch, projecting relaxation, projecting grace, and sip our decaffeinated tea and nibble at carrot sticks and wait, oh wait, for them to go.

During the week I go to work, where I immerse myself in numbing numbers and letters and you stay at home and attend to the business of dying. It really is a full-time occupation and each day you get a little closer to its long-term objective. No matter how much water you drink or how many relaxation tapes you listen to or how often you take those postmodern orange translucent tablets of yours, your wrists grow as thin as my thumb. You discover a list in a corner of your brain of all the people you had hoped to outlive and now it's becoming increasingly clear you won't. You try to make amends with your mother, your father, whose last wish on earth—so help them god—was to outlive you and in whose grave faces you can read your own doom. You watch comedy after comedy on the VCR and subscribe to comedy servers on the Internet. You're the first to read the latest jokes on politics and entertainment and sex. You want to have sex. We try. It is one emotional field intersecting with another emotional field, the combination of which is like drowning in mud.

We plan a Caribbean trip and cancel it. We plan a weekend bed-and-breakfast and cancel it. We plan dinner out and cancel it. The best we can do are lunches out, here and there, nothing too special but that doesn't matter, you can barely taste anything anyway. If haughty waiters make us wait, we call them over and say, Excuse us but could you please get your ass out of your mouth and deliver to us in a prompt and courteous manner that which we require? Any delay from anyone and we stomp on their faces. We *don't* have time. We have humor, we have dignity, we have restraint. But time is not what we have.

One morning, one bleak, meek morning, you say, I can't get up. You say it like you say, It's time.

Is this, I wonder, at all what it would have been like if we'd ever had the opportunity, the chance, to say, I'm in labor?

I call Frank. I call the hospital. I call Frank's assistant. I call the insurance company. I call the hospital supply store. You lie there in short breaths, then long breaths, then short breaths. In pill form we have percoset, morphine, codeine, percodan. Frank says they have run their course, done their job, lost their efficacy.

I only want to breathe, you say.

The hospital bed comes. A day nurse comes. Oxygen, IV, bedpans, a commode, vacuum-packed catheterization kit, boxes of latex gloves.

How long can we afford this, you say.

Don't ask me that, I say.

However long it takes, you answer slyly.

I wish you'd quit thinking this way. I wish we'd both quit thinking, that the roof would open and the sky would be there, that the world would stop turning on its stupid tender resilient axis, that the sun would implode, that your mother would stop calling, that I didn't have to work—not ever again, thank you—that the nurse didn't have to stay, that you didn't just keep on lying there, that the clock in the hall didn't tick so loudly and relentlessly, that the hospital bed would stop looking so much like a hospital bed because it is in our house goddamn it and what is the point if it can't stop looking like a hospital bed, that we hadn't married, that we'd never met.

What was that, you say.

Are you sure you want to do this, you say.

Want to do this? *Want* to watch you die, pay the bills, eat microwaved dinners, see everyone else in the whole goddamn world so unchanged by what is changing us—the president on the television, the newsstand guy in the subway, the asskisser at my office? The

464

nurse presses her lips together and her eyes clang with the message, Pull yourself together. In the kitchen she has left the radio on to a Buddhist talk show. I was honored to be at his passing, a woman says. It was a beautiful passing, probably the most beautiful passing I have ever witnessed. There was blue in the room and the sky. It was quite a blue and decided aura. A truly beautiful passing. There is faint applause. Faint applause on a talk show? Or maybe it's a tape on the tape deck and the nurse has brought Live At The Monastery for our comfort. Or the nurse smiles at my struggle, a struggle so familiar to her in her blue cardigan and tennis shoes, stethoscope dumped in one of the blue pockets like some kind of loose wire.

I tell you I'm fine and that no I don't want to do this but this is the only way to do this if it has to be done.

The nurse nods and shuts her eyes. Then she lines up the IV stand to begin titrating your new painkiller.

Will it dull me, you ask. I don't want to be dull.

Don't worry, she says. I'll adjust it.

She's good. She taps that line for pain without any pain and now you are attached, each step another air-sucking sock to my stomach.

I sit. You fade in and out of sleep. I argue with the nurse about the painkiller and she says it's not that, it's part of The Process. Your not-in-the-hospital hospital smell begins to fill our house and I think I can't go on like this and you're not going to go on. You're going to go. You're waiting to go. This is where I'm supposed to say it's okay. I'm going to be okay. It's okay to go. I release you. Go ahead now, go. I'm supposed to say I love you but I understand and you can go now and you know I just love you because I can't say I'll see you or I'll be with you because I don't believe that I can't just change my beliefs for this I can't lie in the face of it. I can't even say it's okay. It's not right, it doesn't fit, it's not right, you're too young, it's not fair. There is nothing good about it. I can't say any of that. Where is the comfort in that? Just take the painkiller, I think, just up that painkiller, just numb it, just numb it, just numb it and be done with it. And then what? Then what? I can't say it, I can't say any of it. I couldn't say, we couldn't say, that's what I came to say, that I couldn't say, that I couldn't do, that I couldn't be. That it isn't beautiful. That it isn't growth. When it's you.

Nominated by Pinckney Benedict, Jane Hirshfield, Threepenny Review

THE DOVE'S NECK

by GERALD STERN

from THE AMERICAN POETRY REVIEW

The dove's neck is so thin
and his head so small he almost
disappears like a turtle when
he turns round to stare
but he goes up to sleep
and he comes down to eat
and he can see my lavender
from where he does it though he has
no fear of the bees, I think,
who curl around the flowers
and fly from one to the other
only to eat, not sleep,
and carry the food on their backs;
but I would lie in lavender
if I had the chance, I have
already lain in alfalfa
once in tupelo and in
western Pennsylvania in Clarion county
I lay in a field of clover and daisies almost
free for once of envy
as if my neck were also
thin and my head like a turtle's,
though he should envy me, that
sex-idiot, I who lay there
for almost an hour, practically
sleeping, a short drive east

of Ohio, near the abandoned
coal-mines, half a century
after the grass had hidden
the disgusting earth including,
fair or not fair, the anger,
for all I knew, underneath that
field which seemed to tilt
in such a way that stretching
my arms and legs the flowers were
always there and the wind
was always blowing, one of
my bitter personal heavens.

Nominated by American Poetry Review, Philip Levine,
Susan Hahn, Chard de Niord, Len Roberts

THE END OF
THE TUNNEL

memoir by NANCY McCABE

from PRAIRIE SCHOONER

W HAT I REMEMBER is waking to light like the light that begins
and ends our lives. Still under the inarticulate influence of dreams, I
might just have been born into that first bright light or I might be
traveling down a tunnel toward that last brilliant one. Then I feel the
weight of my hands against the blankets, the weight of something
wrong. Bewildered terror drags a sound from my throat, a hoarse,
ragged yell.

Every night, a cat scratches its way up my bedroom screen, then
leaps to the ground and claws its way up again. Sometimes it yowls,
in heat; sometimes I wake to the long silhouette of its body against
the window. More often I sleep through its climbing; I sleep right
through the snarl and scramble and hiss and tumble of it and another
cat beneath the window. Usually I just absorb the cat into my
dreams. I've been dreaming about the cat tonight. It hooks its claws
into the mesh and scales the screen, stretching higher and higher. I
wait for the usual closure, the cat thumping to the pavement. In-
stead, silence stirs me awake.

I open my eyes to a blinding beam of light. For a few seconds, I
have no idea who or where I am, am only aware of some primal in-
stinct that shouts danger.

The light wavers and steadies.

That's when I return to my body, impaled on that beam. That's

468

when I sit up and scream, or mean to, but my voice fails me. Where is the piercing scream I practiced throughout childhood, long and high enough to outscream anyone? I produce only the barest croak.

A voice drones. For a long time, all I'll let myself recall is the cheerful, soothing tone, a little apologetic as if to a third person on my behalf. The tone makes me feel instantly calm and a little embarrassed, unnecessarily hysterical. We'll just come back later, says the voice. For now we'll leave her alone. Scrambling, and then my blind slaps against the wall. Spots of light jump in front of my eyes as my bedroom comes into focus, the hulking shapes of my chest of drawers and bookshelves. It's 3:30 A.M., a time my body will never forget.

I have lived in Springfield, Missouri, for only six months. Here, I've maintained an illusion left over from my Kansas childhood that harm can never come to me. This Midwestern way of thinking results from a humility so extreme it edges toward arrogance. We are landlocked, far from the coasts—far from the action, we think. The vast plains, the vast sky, remind us of our insignificance. We belong to the fly-over, the treeless flatlands where cars break down on their way to Colorado vacations. Alphabetically we never come first or last, the positions of most emphasis; in the Miss America pageant and listings of national temperature highs, we remain buried halfway through.

And so I wander into my kitchen at 3:30 A.M. and wash my dishes, because I am not used to believing that bad things can happen to me or recognizing them if they do. After a while it occurs to me that maybe I should call the police.

A patrol car coasts silently into my driveway. Light flashes blood red against the pavement and the dark house.

An officer trails a light along my bedroom window frame. "He cut out your screen," the officer says.

While I slept only an arm-length away, someone sliced a knife through my screen. I back into the house.

The officer tries to take fingerprints, but my intruder was wearing gloves.

"He won't return. They never do," the officer says after questioning me briefly, mostly questions I am too stunned to remember the answers to. He gives me a slip of paper with my case number on it in the event that I remember anything else. There are two lines. One says, "Crimes against persons." The other says, "Crimes against property." That's the one that has been checked.

I want to protest. Instead I fold the paper into a tiny square and put it in my pocket.

The patrol car coasts silently away.

Obsessively checking my doors and windows, I am disturbed by the pitch black of the porch. The light switch stands at attention, in the on position. I flick it off: no change. Peering out I find an empty fixture: no bulb, no globe-shaped cover.

In the kitchen, the sliding glass door stands open half an inch, enough to admit insects. The lock has been jimmied, but a security bar in the track caused the door to stick.

It is so calculated, this effort to pass unnoticed into my house while I slept.

In my bedroom, the screen has been cut meticulously—no frayed ends, no incomplete grids, only frame and cool night air.

Then the phone rings.

"I'm calling about your ad," says a cheerful male voice, a tad apologetic. I struggle to hold onto the sound: timbre, pitch, tone. "The one for free underwear," he says.

I wrote a story, not long before, involving a series of help-wanted ads and a lingerie party at which the protagonist wins free underwear. Suddenly, it feels like someone has invaded not just my house, but my thoughts; a stranger has swept a searchlight across my most secret self. But that's silly, I tell myself; I've read that story twice to audiences. Still the rooms of my apartment and the rooms of my mind no longer belong to me.

Jan and Doris come to get me. We drink tea in their kitchen as dawn lightens the windows. We go over and over what happened but can't make any sense of it. My hands want to push away the memory of the light that forces me to its center, that penetrates the crevices of my brain. I imagine flailing my arms, swimming and clawing my way out of that pool of light.

I often practiced screaming as a child; for the neighborhood girls, screaming was a form of entertainment, a way to assert our presence and keep the landscape from swallowing us up. We liked to scream in the network of drainage tunnels under the highways and roads, some of those tunnels so small I felt crammed into a tin can. I often panicked in those dark, tight spaces where rolls of snake skins shimmered and crumbled beneath my knees, where my face broke through sticky spiderwebs and the shadows of my descending hands sent lizards and beetles darting into cracks. I went on crawling through these passages because I didn't want to be a coward, but I much preferred the larger tunnels under the Kansas Turnpike. Though dark and dank, at least they were big enough for a child to stand. We usually ran through them, screaming as always, our pounding footsteps and piercing screams enlarged by tunnel acoustics until two or three of us sounded like a mob. We ran through the cacophony of our own echoes that preceded and followed us like ghosts of ourselves. The sensation of being chased through that shadowy underworld gave me goose bumps on the hottest day. As we drowned out the muffled sound of cars rumbling above, I focused on the widening promise of sunlight ahead.

All that practice screaming, I tell Jan, and where was that skill when I really needed it?

A newscaster comes on with an item about some guy in Minnesota called the Underwear Outlaw. He steals women's panties and mails them back. We laugh uneasily. Doris snaps off the TV.

Once I am safely in bed, Jan cuts off the spare room light. Instantly, colors burst in front of my eyes as if someone has just taken my picture without permission, freezing me in a position I wouldn't recognize. Finally I drift into dreams about locks picked with credit cards, glass doors pried with crowbars, chains broken by shoulders hurtling against wood. At 3 A.M., I wake completely to a storm. I feel myself flinch at every flash of lightning, jolt with every roll of thunder, but I can't find my voice.

Closing my eyes, I watch a stranger unscrew a globe-shaped light cover and bulb, then move in complete darkness down the side of my house to break the lock on my sliding glass door. He tugs it half an inch until it sticks.

Creeping on down the side of the house to my open bedroom window, he can see me, through the downturned blind slats, sleeping soundly. I watch him watch me. I watch him cut away my screen.

At 3:29, I watch myself struggle from sleep, fixed like a small animal in the glare of headlights.

At 3:30, at the flicker of lightning and whip-crack of thunder, I hear myself scream. Once I start, I can't stop. I scream and scream as I wish I'd screamed the night before.

In another gray dawn, Jan and I wait for tea to steep. My screams

471

echo in my ears; my throat feels raw. Beyond that shrill memory of my own voice, the faintness of the pats of rain on the roof come as a surprise.

I was eleven the summer afternoon that a strange man chased my friend Tanya and me. We'd been lazily dangling our feet in the jigsaw cracks of the dried creekbed, nearly asleep in the hot sun when a snatch of rock music on the gravel road drove us upright, alert. A car pulled over abruptly, raising a cloud of dust, and a dirty, bearded man with long hair slid down the embankment, yelling something unintelligible. We recognized him as one of those hippies we'd been warned might force us to take drugs. We leapt to our feet and darted into the tunnels under the Kansas Turnpike like rabbits into holes, I like to think. The man's footsteps stopped at the tunnel entrance. I imagine him ducking down to peer in at us, making our escape, running hard and fast toward the light on the other side, toward safety.

That night we vowed never to tell our parents what had happened, partly to protect them and partly to avoid the inevitable limits on our freedom. We huddled in my backyard and Tanya told me what her mother had said about rape: "When a woman is raped, she usually dies, but if she doesn't, she wishes she had."

I wasn't quite sure what rape meant and I was too embarrassed to ask. I only knew that it had to do with women, so I pictured a woman shivering behind a curtain. My friend Shelley says she pictured a woman with long scratches across her face. We didn't know what rape meant, so we pictured the closest things we knew: women who were draped, women who were raked.

I resolve to drive away all fear by force of will. After all, except for instant eyestrain around candles or bright lights, except for muscles that will not give up their tension, except for unaccountable terror when I enter my apartment, I am unhurt. But no matter how firmly I vow to get over it, the power of my subconscious amazes me. For months, without fail, I will wake each morning at precisely 3:30 A.M. It is as if I house another person, a secret mind that keeps time while I sleep and wakes me at the moment of danger. Eventually I name that other person The Sleepwalker because of the way I wake to find her wandering all the rooms, patrolling window latches, checking the blinds. Or sometimes, in the morning, I discover heaped beside me keys, mace, shoes, bug spray, window rods: provisions for escape, items to be used as weapons. The Sleepwalker lets me sleep, but she is ever vigilant.

During that first week, alarmed by my perfect record of waking every 3:30 A.M., Jan calls a friend who works for the Rape Crisis Center and then reports back to me. The guy with the flashlight has been around for years. He blinds women, then orders them to undress and touch themselves while he masturbates. He's known, among Rape Crisis workers, as the Flashlight Molester, although he tends to run if women fight back.

My attempt to scream, no matter how meager the results, was not worthless after all, Jan tells me. Inadequate as it seemed, that yell had declared me a fighter.

I muster every remaining bit of energy I have to dial the police and ask questions. Reluctantly, a detective fills me in on the man the Springfield police refer to as the Flashlight Burglar, who has attacked twenty or thirty women in the last couple of years.

"Why didn't anyone tell me that?" I ask.

The detective tries to reassure me. "Hey, it could have been worse. It could have been the Ether Bandit."

This is what I learn: that the Ether Bandit used to break into houses and knock his victims out with ether-soaked rags. When they came to, they had no idea what he'd done to them. "At least this guy, the Flashlight Burglar, he doesn't usually enter people's houses, and he doesn't come back," the detective says.

I protest: He did try to enter my house, and he did promise to return.

"Hey, the Ether Bandit really did come back. He knocked one woman out three times."

I abandon my protest.

"Yeah," the officer says, taking my silence for awe. "Someone finally shot him. We followed the trail of blood to the hospital and arrested him."

I vaguely remember reading about this, back when I thought I was immune.

"We'd like to get this jerk, too," the detective says. "But he makes it tough. We have a suspect but no proof. He doesn't leave fingerprints."

I ask about the phone call I reported later that morning, but my report has not made it into the file. The detective explains that the call, obscenely early in the morning not long after the departure of the Flashlight Man, my only crank phone call in six months at that number, is probably a coincidence.

"This guy doesn't do things like that," the detective says. "He's just your basic Peeping Tom. He sees something he wants to look at and he looks."

I complain to the local paper for ignoring the Flashlight Man's apparently copious activity. Between the spring of 1990 and the summer of 1992, when I leave Springfield for good, I read story after story about a man with a flashlight who continues to enter women's bedrooms by force. He tells them that he'll be watching them, that he'll return if they call the police. In at least one case, he pays a return visit. In another, he physically assaults a woman.

In 1991, during the most brutal rape in Springfield's history, the attacker refers to himself as "we," and talks about his victim in third person while he stuffs carpet fibers and tape inside her and breaks her shoulders, wrists, pelvis, and ankle.

"We'll just leave her alone," I remember the voice saying, the voice on the same continuum that has led to such brutality. "We'll come back later," says the voice in my memory.

Before the Flashlight Man, I imagine, my life was a straight line, mostly, with its little peaks and valleys, a heartbeat on a monitor. Now the line has been twisted into question marks, disconnected curves and dots without continuity or routine, punctuated by sudden starts and sharp prickles of adrenaline, and it's dawning on me that there may never be any answers. It's not just the larger questions that drive me crazy: Who is the Flashlight Man? What if he's someone I know and trust? Or if not, why me? What made him choose me? I can't shake off the smaller questions, either: the Flashlight Man must have been carrying a crowbar, a knife, and a flashlight; when he left he took my bulb, my light cover, and my screen. Why? Where did he put these things? Does he have a special toolkit for breaking and entering that he lugs with him despite the possibility that he may have to run? I picture him with a knapsack slung over one shoulder, making a run for it down dark streets, the light cover knocking against his spine. Does he display my screen, my light bulb, that heavy globe-shaped cover on a shelf or in a case, like trophies? How does he explain this bizarre collection to the landlord or the exterminator?

I become obsessed. If the police really have a suspect, why don't they search his home for the things missing from mine? Clearly, the police don't think his activity is significant; clearly they aren't trying very hard to catch him. Clearly, it is up to me.

My friends become alarmed by this new vigilante phase. I spy on people, eavesdrop on voices. From the computer lab down the hall from my office, I hear a voice that gives me pause. Its owner emerges from the lab. He is a short blond guy with a mustache, and with an electric jolt I realize that he is enrolled in a class where I gave a reading of my story. He glances toward me and I think, he knows I know. I scurry down the hall to my office and lock the door.

I've stayed late to grade papers because Jan has a night class. Now I can't concentrate on the papers. My heart is so loud in my ears it might be footsteps. But no: the halls are empty and silent. Then I hear a shuffling, and I stare paralyzed through the vent in the door at the tips of two black shoes. Any second a hand will test the doorknob. The lock is a flimsy one; how long does it take to pick a lock? I wonder.

Then, outside my door, a familiar voice calls to a passerby. I fling open the door to confront the journalism professor and newspaper columnist whose office adjoins mine.

Mike feels so bad about scaring me, he asks me to talk anonymously about what happened and he prints the interview in his weekly column. Letters trickle in, including one from a woman who writes that the column raised terrible memories for her. The guy who broke into her house still calls periodically and reads to her from her daughter's diary—a diary that remains intact in her daughter's bedroom.

Another Flashlight Man encounter, I think. Another writing link.

Mike offers to set up a meeting between the woman and me. Mania grips me, a wild certainty that I am on the verge of catching the Flashlight Man.

When Deanne passes me a glass of Coke, an ice cube pops. We both jump. Then we laugh.

I expected a smaller, frailer woman. In her late forties or early fifties, Deanne is, instead, tall and solid, with a mole on her chin, an armor of metal bracelets clanking along her forearm, and crepesoled shoes.

"So you think we might have run into the same man." Deanne crosses her legs and takes a grim sip of Coke. "I'm all for getting him. Tell me what happened to you."

475

She shakes her head and clicks her tongue while I talk. Suddenly, the door rattles as if someone is frantic to break it down. I feel myself go rigid.

Deanne leaps up to let in the cat. "Stop that, Lamby, you're scaring our guest," she says.

She pats her lap until the cat settles in it. "So you never got a look at him? Well, I got a good look at mine. He was about 35, 5'8", with blondish hair and a mustache."

I have to steady my glass. "That sounds just like a student I was wondering about. Would you recognize him? You have to come by and see this guy."

"So we're going to catch him, huh?" Deanne laughs, a big throaty laugh that trembles her whole body. "Let me tell you what happened to me."

About three years ago, she was dozing in a chair when she felt a tap on her shoulder. She thought it was the cat.

Cats. The cat on my window screen, in heat, the cat howling as it climbed and dropped, climbed and dropped. Cat claws, scratching, like a knife against a screen. I lean forward, feverish.

Deanne had opened her eyes to the dark shape of a man, hovering over her.

"Back then, I had a job working with psychotics," Deanne says. "I was used to keeping my wits about me in unusual situations." She closes her eyes and continues her story.

"Are you an angel from heaven?" Talking in a slow, bright voice, Deanne rose and tiptoed to the chain hanging from the ceiling bulb. The man tiptoed behind her. As she reached up, he imitated her posture and mimicked her gesture, pulling an imaginary chain above his head.

The light didn't come on.

She yanked the chain again. Still, nothing. He continued the weird game of Follow-the-Leader, reaching up to grab at his invisible chain.

"Let's go upstairs," she said. When he didn't object, she led the way, brushing her fingers against light switches. The rooms remained shadowy. Behind her, his fingers repeated her flicking motions.

"Let's talk." She edged toward the front door. "Tell me your name."

"I'm Ken." He spoke so softly she almost didn't hear him.

476

"Did you remove my fuses?" She hardened her tone.

He hung his head and nodded.

"All right, Ken," she said. "I want you to leave my house. I want you to go into my garage and replace the fuses, and then I want you off my property."

He obeyed, exiting through the garage. She locked the doors, then watched from the front window until he finally emerged into the driveway. Hitting the porch switch, she caught him in full light, wearing her gardening gloves.

"Later I realized I shouldn't have done that," Deanne tells me. "I was afraid he'd come back to get me so that I wouldn't be able to identify him."

But Deanne didn't recognize him in any police photos. The next week, a man who said his name was Ken called and read passages from her daughter's diary, which had never left her bedroom.

"He must have copied pages while he was here was all I could figure," Deanne concludes. Tipping her glass into her mouth, she peers over the rim at me. "So we're going to catch him, huh?"

At first, listening to her story, my brain has raced, filtering out events, clinging to isolated details: cats, surprise, light, fear. But as Deanne continued, I felt oddly shamed by her competence and frightened at the crazed fervor she reflected back to me. Mine drains slowly away, crowded out by disappointment and then just plain exhaustion. It is as if the last couple of days someone else has astrally projected herself into my body, turning me ridiculous. Now as that other person abruptly departs, I want only to go to Jan and Doris's and sleep. I feel a letdown so final, it is indistinguishable from relief.

Jan and Doris laugh hysterically at Deanne's story, and Doris renames Ken The Mime Intruder. That cracks us all up, not because it's that funny, but because we haven't laughed in days. It feels like loosening my belt a notch, giving up some tension. The Flashlight Burglar, the Ether Bandit, the Underwear Outlaw, the Mime Intruder: do we diminish or merely downplay their impact with these cartoonish names?

We drink tea late, our nightly ritual, and I recall bouts with bronchitis, how only what is hot enough to blister my tongue succeeds in soothing my throat. Now, anything hot enough to burn reminds me that I'm still alive. Sometimes I reheat the tea to boiling, concocting little tests, little reassurances: the possibility of a burn forces me to

477

stay alert, and avoiding the burn reminds me that I have some power to protect myself. I sip tea with Jan and Doris and struggle for reasons to laugh and try to accept what I will never know, every scalding passage a journey toward calm.

Later, in bed, I will picture the deft cloth-covered hands of a faceless man. The hands twist loose my porch light. I watch a dark shape move on to my sliding glass door; I watch hands quickly pry the lock and jerk at the door; I hear muttered cursing. As a knife slashes its way around the screen, I slip out of bed, creep to the window, and slam the frame on the imaginary fingers of the Flashlight Man. And then I open the front door and stare down his apparition, taking a cue from Deanne. "I want you off this property," I tell him in a full, confident voice. "I want you out of my life." And slowly, gradually, he fades away.

Years ago, the city of Wichita widened Highway 54, making the system of drainage tunnels inadequate, creating a flood plain. With every rain, the creek bursts its restraints and turns the bottom level of the house where I grew up into a sloggy swimming pool. In our early twenties, Tanya and I confessed to our mothers about the man who chased us into the tunnels. Tanya's mother had her own confession: one day she'd glanced out the window to see us trotting across yards from the David's store. Three feet behind us, a man followed, matching his pace to ours. He stopped when we stopped, picked up speed when we did. Tanya's mother shot out the door, shouting our names, and the man bolted.

Tanya and her mother, my mother and I, all stared at each other, caught in an almost reverent silence. Our mothers looked queasy; they looked as if they could barely fathom the miracle of our survival. But we savored these memories they would have willingly erased, our lives suddenly more exciting and more charmed than we'd ever imagined. I knew nothing bad could really happen to me; I was too unimportant to be attacked or murdered.

And then, a few years later, I woke. The light I woke to failed to draw my soul like a magnet or to suggest comfort and warmth like those lights at the ends of Near Death Tunnels. No life flashed before my eyes. For those brief moments, past and future no more existed than when the cold water tap gushes hot and the hand jerks back, the whole present focused on sudden surprise, sudden pain. Only later did I understand that I, we all, are always in greater danger than we imagine; the past follows, ghost-like, into the present, the knowledge of our deaths weaving underneath like tunnels underground, like blue veins under skin.

I woke, this subterranean knowledge rising abruptly to the surface, bursting its restraints, so that six weeks later, the ordinary experiences I have temporarily left behind have the capacity to amaze me. I am mesmerized by the fruit and vegetable aisles at the grocery store, at pyramids of lettuce, oranges, apples, cucumbers, bananas, carrots, kiwi, at a range of possibilities I have forgotten, reds and greens and yellows, leaves and stalks and globes, beaded with the rain of the overhead sprinkler system, doubled in the mirrors above. That night, in the clubhouse of my new apartment complex, we prepare for aerobics class, opening doors and windows, pulling back curtains so that for a second I remember the cowering draped woman in my childhood image. Our reflections dance in the glass of the patio door, and I don't care that from outside, anyone can see in. The shadows of our circling arms sweep the wall, and my heart pounds, blood races with all the choices I forgot during weeks of tension and fear: grapevine, jazz square, mambo step, kick ball change; Jonathan apples, Red Rome, Granny Smith, Golden Delicious; anger, sorrow, wonder, joy. In the glass, there's another me, as if on the other side of light, a shadow self, my Sleepwalker, also dancing.

Nominated by Prairie Schooner, Gerald Shapiro

FROM THE VEGAS CANTOS

by GREG RAPPLEYE

from MISSISSIPPI REVIEW

> *"Hey, I like to swing as much as anybody, but this ain't a plan, it's a pipe load of the crazy stuff."*
> Dean Martin, *from the original shooting script for* Ocean's Eleven.

January 1960. Klieg lights, Sinatra
at the Sands, filming underway
for the Rat Pack movie, the Strip
blazing neon. The plot, such as it is:
Eleven ex-soldiers, led by Frank,
rob five casinos on New Year's Eve,
after Sammy knocks out the power lines.
Every day, the production shoots into dusk.
Cesar Romero as Duke Santos,
trying to intimidate the boys,
Sammy driving the truck full of money
through the Sheriff's blockade,
Angie Dickinson telling Ilka Chase
just how it is between Angie and Frank,
how it's always going to be, five different bands
playing *Auld Lang Syne,* over and over,
dancing into The New Frontier.
It's hard work and at night they unwind

with vodka martinis, a bottle
of Jack Daniel's, a splash of soda,
unfiltered Chesterfields. *Smoking is all
in the wrist,* Lawford says.

* * *

At 1 a.m.,
Frank backs away from the piano
in the Copa Room, says, *The action here
is getting old,* to Sammy, Sammy nods at Dean,
the Pack rises, pushes toward the exit.
In the parking lot, three El Dorado
convertibles: One pearlescent blue,
one lemon chiffon, one green mist,
all courtesy of Jack Warner.
They load the cars, tops down.
It's January in the desert, but a warm front
has burgeoned up from the Sea of Cortez,
and Dean says, *It's ragtop weather, baby,*
nudging the strapless breasts
of a showgirl's sequined gown.
Frank and Dean in front, Angie, Ilka,
then Sammy driving the chiffon El Dorado,
Lawford sipping a traveller, more girls,
Joey Bishop, the only sober one,
driving the third car and *worried,* Romero,
drunk and laughing, Shirley MacLaine
and another chick in back. *Does Frank know
where he's going?* Joey wants to know.
It's your job to be the mother! Romero says.
And too often, Joey thinks, *Right,* I'm the one
left paying for broken windows
and slipping fifty to the maitre d'
while the others scoot through the kitchen,
playing pat-ass on the way. Behind
the third Cadillac, the parking attendant,
Paco, drives his '53 Chevy pickup—
Richard Conte, already swan-songed
in the movie (*Your guy buys the big casino,*
Frank had explained), flat-drunk

481

in the bed of the truck, Henry Silva,
Norman Fell, and a couple of broads
holding stakes that rise from the sides,
everyone singing *Come Fly With Me,*
Frank's number-one hit.

* * *

On they go,
ten, twenty miles into the desert,
until Romero begins to wonder if this is
such a good idea, until the singing stops
and the girls have started to shiver.
Dean lights another cigarette, looks
sideways at Frank, who has said almost nothing.
Just as Dean is about to ask, *What's up, amigo?*
Frank goes, *This is the place,* jerks the car
onto a two-track, bottoms through the alkali flats
and drives on. Sammy, his good eye almost hypnotized
by the dashing lines of U.S. 95,
comes to, chases the pearlescent blue
El Dorado off the road,
the green Cadillac and flat-gray pickup
follow suit. Frank finally stops, hops
out, his car in park, headlights
still on. *Circle up!* he yells, looping a finger
in the air. Frank backs the drivers off,
making sure they leave enough space
in the middle. Everyone piles out.
Paco! Frank snaps. *You and Normie
grab some branches off that pile of mesquite!
Dean, Sammy, get the booze and blankets
outta the trunk. You girls, there's a cooler
and snacks in the yellow El Dorado.
And while you're up,* Dean,
*tune all the radios to that Mexican station
we've been listening to!*
Sammy squirts the mesquite
with lighter fluid, tosses a match,
the oily flames rise into the sky,

the radios begin three hours of Basie,
Ellington, and Dorsey, between songs
the announcer hawking headache powders,
Geritola and *laxantes*.

✿ ✿ ✿

A chill in the air. Stars swirl overhead,
miles from the neon clutter of the Strip.
Some pair off under blankets.
Sammy has a few drinks, smokes,
takes a chick he's been eyeing
into the lemon El Dorado. Her head
disappears, Sammy lies back
against the creamy leather.
You are the craziest, he says, over and over.
Dean chases Shirley around the fire.
She lets him catch up, paw her, stick his tongue
down her throat, bending her
in the crook of his left arm, martini balanced
in one hand, cigarette in the other.
Baby, he says, *let's rehearse our scene.*
She laughs, pushes him away, the pursuit begins
again.

✿ ✿ ✿

Night goes by. Constellations rise.
Paco tends the fire, Romero falls asleep,
Norman Fell nods off, Silva wanders away,
Sammy snores in the El Dorado,
the sweet head of a showgirl in his lap.
How Are Things in Glocca Morra?
Take the "A" Train,
Ac-cent-tchu-ate the Positive,
50,000 watts of Ensenada clear-channel
play on. Only Frank, Angie,
and Joey stay awake, Frank listening
to music, pacing, singing a scrap lyric,
cupping a cigarette to his face,
pushing a black Panama snap-brim

483

back on his head, occasionally lighting
a Chesterfield for Angie. A sweet smell is
in the air, a redolence Frank knows
from the early forties—
the bad boys in the saxophone section.
Frank looks toward the pickup.
He sees the glow: Paco, Dean, and Lawford
passing a pipe of Mary Jane,
wacky tabacky, the crazy stuff.
Frank frowns. They're in the desert, okay,
no one around and if you stay clear
of the Mormons, anything goes,
but he doesn't need any hopheads
hanging around, capisce?
He looks at Angie, nods toward
the pickup, she shakes her head
in disapproval. *Take care of it,* Frank snaps
at Joey, then turns and walks
to the other side of the fire.

* * *

Stars turn. The fire burns down.
Frank looks at his watch. Almost 6 a.m.
He tells Joey, *Radios off. And roust Dean*
outta the truck, he's got to see this.
Frank steps fifty yards into the desert.
A few minutes later, Joey and Angie follow.
Dean, his head pounding, stumbles toward them.
Suddenly, the horizon ignites—soundless,
a half-moon of orange, yellow, and white fire
swells in the distance. Frank's face flashes
in the ignited air, he squints, heads jerk
back in alarm, a reaction to light,
Oh my God, Angie mouths, and Joey and Dean
just stand there. The blankets stir.
Sammy's head wobbles,
his good eye opens, a sleepy head
rises from his lap. Paco moans to consciousness,
begins to cross himself,

and before he gets to *Espiritu Santo,*
a windstorm sweeps through—
dust glows red below
the expanding mushroom cloud,
a concussion washes their bodies,
the earth begins to roll.
Everyone is awake now—even Conte's head rises
behind the pickup cab.
To the east, the air is on fire, electric
with the bomb's ignition.
That's what I brought you to see,
Frank says, *the Big Kahplowie!*
Raising a glass of bourbon
toward the towering firestorm,
Salud to Armageddon! he yells into the dust, turns
and tells everyone, *Pack it in*
before the fallout hits! He throws the keys
of the blue El Dorado at Dean.
You're sober. Drive. Joey,
take the yellow one. Lawford, the green.
Paco drives his own. Angie, you ride with me.
The caravan sets out. Conte stirs again,
Silva wipes atomic dust from his eyes.

✳ ✳ ✳

      In the back of the blue El Dorado,
Sinatra curls into the fetal position, his head
nested in Angie's lap. She smooths his cheek,
his face softens in the courtesy lights.
The radio is off, Dean in front, smoking
and driving, the horizon beginning to glow
with the orange and streaky pink
of a bombed-out desert sunrise. Ahead,
the other-glow of the Strip. Dean
finishes a cigarette, looks at it for a second
then flicks it over the side. In the mirror,
he watches it bounce and spray sparks
across the road, until it disappears
in the headlight-wash of the lemon El Dorado.

He begins to sing his new song
from the movie, scatting it, arriving
at the chorus, tapping his fingers on the wheel.
Ain't that a kick in the head?
he sings, *Ain't that a kick in the head?*

Nominated by Mississippi Review

THE ORDINARY SON

fiction by RON CARLSON

from THE OXFORD AMERICAN

The story of my famous family is a story of genius and its conse-
quences, I suppose, and I am uniquely and particularly suited to tell
the story, since genius avoided me—and I, it. I remain an ordinary
man, if there is such a thing, calm in all weathers, aware of event but
uninterested and generally incapable of deciphering implication. As
my genius brother, Garrett, used to say, "Reed, you're not screwed
too tight like the rest of us, but you're still screwed." Now there's a
definition of the common man you can trust, and further, you can
trust me. There's no irony in that or deep inner meaning or Freudian
slips—any kind of slips, really—simply what it says. My mother told
me many times I have a good heart, and of course she was a genius,
and that heart should help with this story. But a heart, as she said so
often, good as it may be, is always trouble.

Part of the reason this story hasn't come together, the story of my
famous family, is that no one remembers they were related. They all
had their own names. My father was Duncan Landers, the noted
NASA physicist, the man responsible for every facet of the photogra-
phy of the first moon landing. There is still camera gear on the moon
inscribed with this name. That is, Landers. He was born Duncan Lrs-
dyksz, which was changed when NASA began their public relations
campaigns in the mid-'60s. The space agency suggested that physi-
cists who worked for NASA should have more vowels in their names.
They didn't want their press releases to seem full of typographical er-
rors or foreigners. Congress was reading this stuff. So Lrsdyksz be-
came Landers. (My father's close associate Igor Oeuroi didn't just get

487

vowels; his name became LeRoy Rodgers. After *le cowboy star*, my mother quipped.)

My mother was Gloria Rainstrap, the poet who spent twenty years fighting for workers' rights from Texas to Alaska. In one string, she gave four thousand lectures, not missing a night as she drove from village to village throughout the country. It still stands as some kind of record. Wherever she went, she stirred up the best kind of trouble, reading her work and then spending hours in whatever guest house or spare bedroom she was given, reading the poems and essays of the people who had come to see her. She was tireless, driven by her overwhelming sense of fairness, and she was certainly the primary idealist to come out of twentieth-century Texas. When she started leaving home for months, and then years, at a time, I was just a lad, but I remember her telling my father, Duncan, one night, "Texas is too small for what I have to do."

This was not around the dinner table. We were a family of geniuses and did not have a dinner table. In fact, the only table we did have was my father's drafting table, which was in the entry so that you had to squeeze sideways to even get into our house. "It sets the tone," Duncan used to say. "I want anyone coming into our home to see my work. That work is the reason we have a roof anyway." He said this one day after my friend Jeff Shreckenbah and I inched past him on the way to my room. "And who are these people coming in the door?"

"It is your son and his friend," I told him.

"Good," he said, his benediction, but he said it deeply into his drawing, which is where he spent his time at home. He wouldn't have known if the Houston Oilers had arrived, because he was about to invent the gravity-free vacuum hinge that is still used today.

Most of my father's, Duncan Landers's, work was classified, top-secret, eyes-only, but it didn't matter. No one except Jeff Shreckenbah came to our house. Other people didn't "come over." We were geniuses. We had no television, and we had no telephone. "What should I do?" my father would say from where he sat in the entry, drawing. "Answer some little buzzing device? Say hello to it?" NASA tried to install phones for us. Duncan took them out. It was a genius household and not to be diminished by primitive electronic foo-fahs.

My older sister was named Christina by my father and given the last name Rossetti by my mother. When she finally fled from MIT at nineteen, she gave herself a new surname: Isotope. There had been some trouble, she told me, personal trouble, and she needed the new name to remind herself she wouldn't last long—and then she asked me how I liked my half-life. I was eleven then, and she laughed and said, "I'm kidding, Reed. You're not a genius; you're going to live forever." I was talking to her on the "hot line," the secret phone our housekeeper, Clovis Armandy, kept in a kitchen cupboard.

"Where are you going?" I asked her.

"West with Mother," she said. Evidently, Gloria Rainstrap had driven up to Boston to rescue Christina from some sort of meltdown.

"A juncture of some kind," my father told me. "Not to worry."

Christina said, "I'm through with theoretical chemistry, but chemistry isn't through with me. Take care of Dad. See you later."

We three children were eight years apart; that's how geniuses plan their families. Christina had been gone for years, it seemed, from our genius household; she barely knew our baby brother, Garrett.

Garrett and I took everything in stride. We accepted that ours was a family of geniuses and that we had no telephone or refrigerator or proper beds. We thought it was natural to eat crackers and sardines for months on end. We thought the front yard was supposed to be a jungle of overgrown grass, weeds, and whatever reptiles would volunteer to live there. Twice a year the City of Houston street crew came by and mowed it all down, and daylight would pour in for a month or two. We had no cars. My father was always climbing into white Chevrolet station wagons, unmarked, and going off to the Space Center south of town. My mother was always stepping up into orange VW buses driven by other people and driving off to tour. My sister had been the youngest student at MIT. My brother and I did our own laundry for years and walked to school, where, about seventh grade, we began to see the differences between the way ordinary people lived and the way geniuses lived. Other people's lives, we learned, centered fundamentally on two things: television and soft foods rich with all versions of sugar.

By the time I entered junior high school, my mother's travels had kicked into high gear, so she hired a woman we came to know well, Clovis Armandy, to live with us and to assist in our corporeal care. Gloria Rainstrap's parental theory and practice could be summed up by the verse I heard her recite a thousand times before I reached the age of six: "Feed the soul, the body finds a way." And she fed our souls with a groaning banquet of iron ethics at every opportunity. She wasn't interested in sandwiches or casseroles. She was the kind of person who had a moral motive for her every move. We had no refrigerator because it was simply the wrong way to prolong the value of food, which had little value in the first place. We had no real furniture because furniture became the numbing insulation of drones who worked for the economy, an evil in itself. If religion was the opiate of the masses, then home furnishings were the Novocain of the middle class. Any small surfeit of comfort undermined our moral fabric. We live for the work we can do, not for things, she told us. I've met and heard lots of folks who share Gloria's posture toward life on this earth, but I've never found anyone who could put it so well, present her ideas so convincingly, so beautifully, or so insistently. Her words seduced you into wanting to go without. I won't put any of her poems in this story, but they were transcendent. The *Times* called her "Buddha's angry daughter." My mother's response to people who were somewhat shocked at our empty house and its unkempt quality was, "We're ego-distant. These little things," she'd say, waving her hand over the litter of the laundry, discarded draft paper, piles of top-secret documents in the hallway, various toys, the odd empty tin of sardines, "don't bother us in the least. We aren't even here for them." I loved that last part and still use it when a nuisance arises: I'm not even here for it. "Ego-distant," my friend Jeff Schreckenbah used to say, standing in our empty house, "which means your ma doesn't sweat the small stuff."

My mother's quirk, one she fostered, was writing on the bottom of things. She started it because she was always gone, for months at a time, and she wanted us to get her messages throughout her absence and thereby be reminded of making correct decisions and ethical choices. It was not unusual to find ballpoint-pen lettering on the bottoms of our shoes and little marker messages on the bottoms of plates where she'd written in a tiny script. Anything that you could lift up and look under, she would have left her mark on it. These notes primarily confused me. There I'd be in math class and would cross my legs see something on the edge of my sneaker and read, "Your troubles, if you stay alert, will pass very quickly away."

I'm not complaining. I never, except once or twice, felt deprived. I like sardines, still. It was a bit of a pinch when I got to high school and noted with new poignancy that I didn't quite have the wardrobe it took to keep up. Genuises dress plain and clean but not always as

490

clean as their ordinary counterparts, who have nothing better to do with their lives than buy and sort and wash clothes.

Things were fine. I turned seventeen. I was hanging out sitting around my bare room, reading books—the history of this, the history of that, dry stuff—waiting for my genius to kick in. This is what had happened to Christina. One day when she was ten, she was having a tea party with her dolls, which were two rolled pink towels. The next day she'd catalogued and diagrammed the amino acids, laying the groundwork for two artificial sweeteners and a mood elevator. By the time my mother, Gloria Rainstrap, returned from the Northwest, and my father looked up from his table, the State Department "mentors" had been by, and my sister, Christina, was on her way to the inner sanctums of the Massachusetts Institute of Technology. I remember my mother standing against my father's drafting table, her hands along the top. Her jaw was set, and she said, "This is meaningful work for Christina, her special doorway."

My father dragged his eyes up from his drawings and said, "Where's Christina now?"

So the day I went into Garrett's room and found him writing equations down a huge scroll of butcher paper on which, until that day, he had drawn battle re-creations of the French and Indian Wars, was a big day for me. I stood there in the gloom, watching him crawl along the paper, reeling out figures of which very few were numbers I recognized, most of the symbols being x's and y's and the little twisted members of the Greek alphabet, and I knew that it had skipped me. Genius had cast its powerful, clear eye on me and said, "No, thanks." At least I was that smart. I realized that I was not going to get to be a genius.

The message took my body a piece at a time, loosening each joint and muscle on the way up and then filling my face with a strange warmth, which I knew immediately was relief.

I was free.

I quickly took a job doing landscaping and general cleanup and maintenance at the San Jacinto Resort Motel on the old Hempstead Highway. My friend, Jeff Schreckenbah, worked next door at Alfredo's American Cafe, and he had told me that the last guy doing handiwork at the motel had been fired for making a holy mess of the parking lot with a paintbrush. When I applied, Mr. Rakkerts, the short little guy who owned the place, took me on.

For me, these were the days of the big changes. I bought a car, an act that at one time would have been as alien to me as intergalactic travel or applying to barber college. I bought a car. It was a four-door lime-green Plymouth Fury III, low miles. I bought a pair of chinos. These things gave me exquisite pleasure. I was seventeen, and I had not known the tangible pleasure of having things. I bought three new shirts and a wristwatch with a leather strap, and I went driving in the evenings, alone, south from our subdivision of Spring Woods with my arm on the green sill of my lime-green Plymouth Fury III through the vast spaghetti bowl of freeways and into the mysterious network of towers that was downtown Houston. It was my dawning.

Late at night, my blood rich with wonder at the possibilities of such a vast material planet, I would return to our tumbledown genius ranchhouse, my sister off putting new legs on the periodic table, my mother away in Shreveport, showing the workers there the way to political and personal power, my brother in his room, edging closer to new theories of rocket reaction and thrust, my father sitting by the entry, rapt in his schematics. As I'd come in and sidle by his table and the one real light in the whole front part of the house, his pencilings on the space station hinge looking as beautiful and inscrutable to me as a sheet of music, he'd say my name as a simple greeting. "Reed."

"Duncan," I'd say in return.

"How goes the metropolis?" he'd add, not looking up. His breath was faintly reminiscent of sardines; in fact, I still associate that smell, which is not as unpleasant as it might seem, with brilliance. I know he said "metropolis" because he didn't know for a moment which city we were in.

"It teems with industrious citizenry well into the night," I'd answer.

Then he'd say it, "Good," his benediction, as he'd carefully trace his leadholder and its steel-like wafer of 5H pencil-lead along a precise new line deep into the vast white space. "That's good."

The San Jacinto Resort Motel along the Hempstead Highway was exactly what you might expect a twenty-unit motel to be in the year 1966. The many bright new interstates had come racing to Houston and collided downtown in a maze, and the old Hempstead Highway had been supplanted as a major artery into town. There was still a good deal of traffic on the four-lane, and the motel was always about half full—never the same half, as you would expect. There were three permanent occupants, one of them a withered old man named Newcombe Shinetower who was a hundred years old that summer and had no car, just a room full of magazines with red and yellow covers, stacks of these things with titles like *Too Young for Comfort* and *Treasure Chest.* There were other titles. I was in Mr. Shinetower's room on only two occasions. He wore the same flannel shirt every day of his life and was heavily gone to seed. Once or twice a day I would see him shuffling out toward Alfredo's American Cafe where, Jeff told me, he always ate the catfish.

"You want to live to be a hundred," Jeff said, "eat the catfish." I told him I didn't know about a hundred and that I generally preferred smaller fish. I was never sure if Mr. Shinetower saw me or not as I moved through his line of sight. He might have nodded; it was hard to tell. What I felt was that he might exist on another plane, the way rocks are said to; they're in there, but at a rhythm too slow for humans to perceive.

It was in Mr. Shinetower's room, rife with the flaking detritus of the ages, that Jeff tried to help me reckon with the new world.

"You're interested in sex, right?" he asked me one day as I took my break at the counter of Alfredo's. I told him I was, but that wasn't exactly the truth. I was indifferent. I understood how it was being packaged and sold to the American people, but it did not stir me, nor did any of the girls we went to school with, many of whom were outright beauties and not bashful about it. This was Texas in the '60s. Some of these buxom girls would grow up and try to assassinate their daughter's rivals on the cheerleading squad. If sex is the game, some seemed to say, deal me in. And I guess I felt it was a game, too, one I could sit out. I had begun to look a little closer at the ways I was different from my peers, worrying about anything that might be a genius tendency. And I took great comfort in the unmistakable affection I felt for my Plymouth Fury III.

"Good," he said. "If you're interested, then you're safe—you're not a genius. Geniuses," here he leaned toward me and squinted his eyes to let me know this was a groundbreaking postulate, "have a little trouble in the sex department."

I liked Jeff; he was my first "buddy." I sat on the round red Naugahyde stool at Alfredo's long Formica counter and listened to his speech, including "sex department," and I don't know, it kind of made sense to me. There must have been something on my face, which is a way of saying there must have been nothing on my face, absolutely nothing, a blank blank, because Jeff pulled his apron over his head and said, "Meet me out back in two minutes." He looked down the counter to where old Mr. Shinetower sucked on his soup. "We got to get you some useful information."

Out back, of course, Jeff led me directly around to the motel and Mr. Shinetower's room, which was not unlocked, but opened when Jeff gave the doorknob a healthy rattle. Inside, in the sour dark, Jeff lit the lamp and picked up one of the old man's periodicals.

Jeff held the magazine and thumbed it like a deck of cards, stopping finally at a full-page photograph, which he presented to me with an odd kind of certainty.

"There," he said. "This is what everybody is trying for. This is the goal." It was a glossy color photograph, and I knew what it was right away, even in the poor light: a shiny shaved pubis, seven or eight times larger than life size. "This makes the world go round."

I was going along with Jeff all the way on this, but that comment begged for a rebuttal, which I restrained. I could feel my father in me responding about the forces that actually caused and maintained the angular momentum of the earth. Instead, I looked at the picture, which had its own lurid beauty. Of course, what it looked like was a landscape, a barren but promising promontory on not this, but another world, the seam too perfect a fold for anything but ceremony. I imagined landing a small aircraft on the tawny slopes and approaching the entry, stepping lightly with a small party of explorers, alert for the meaning of such a place. The air would be devoid of the usual climatic markers (no clouds or air pressure), and in the stillness we would be silent and reverential. The light in the photograph captivated me in that it seemed to come from everywhere, a flat, even twilight that would indicate a world with one or maybe two distant polar suns. There was an alluring blue shadow that ran along the cleft the way a footprint in snow holds its own blue glow, and that aberration affected and intrigued me.

Jeff had left my side and was at the window, on guard, pleased that I was involved in my studies.

"So," he said. "It's really something, isn't it?" He came to me, grabbed the magazine, and took one long look at the page the way a thirsty man drinks from a jug, then set it back on the stack of Old Man Shinetower's magazines.

"Yes," I said. "It certainly is." Now that it was gone, I realized I had memorized the photograph, that place.

"Come on. Let's get out of here before he gets back." Jeff cracked the door and looked out, both ways. "Whoa," he said, setting the door closed again. "He's coming back. He's on the walk down about three rooms." Then Jeff did an amazing thing: he dropped like a rock to all fours, then onto his stomach, and slid under the bed. I'd never seen anyone do that; I've never seen it since. I heard him hiss, "Do something. Hide."

Again I saw myself arriving in the photograph. Now I was alone. I landed carefully, and the entire venture was full of care, as if I didn't want to wake something. I had a case of instruments, and I wanted to know about that light, that shadow, I could feel my legs burn as I climbed toward it step by step.

What I did in the room was take two steps back into the corner and stand behind the lamp. I put my hands at my side and my chin up. I stood still. At that moment we heard a key in the lock, and daylight spilled across the ratty shag carpet. Mr. Shinetower came in. He was wearing the red and black plaid shirt that he wore everyday. It was like a living thing. Someday it would go to lunch at Alfredo's without him.

He walked by me and stopped for a moment in front of the television to drop a handful of change from his pocket into a mason jar on top and messed with the television until it lit and focused. Then he continued into the little green bathroom, and I saw the door swing halfway closed behind him.

Jeff slid out from the bed, stood hastily, his eyes whirling, and opened the door and went out. He was closing it behind him when I caught the edge and followed him into the spinning daylight. When I pulled the door, he gasped, so I shut it. We heard it register closed, and then we slipped quickly through the arbor to the alley behind the units and ran along the overgrown trail back to the bayou and sat on the weedy slope. Jeff was covered with clots of dust and hairy, white goo-gah. It was thick in his hair, and I moved away from him while he swatted at it for a while. Here we could smell the sewer working at the bayou, a rich industrial silage, and the sky was gray, but too bright to look at. I went back to the other world for a moment, the cool, perfect place I'd been touring in Mr. Shinetower's magazine, quiet and still, and offering that light. Jeff was spitting and pulling feathers of dust from his collar and sleeves. I wanted so much to be stirred by what I had seen. I had stared at it and wanted it to stir me, and it had done something. I felt something. I wanted to see

495

that terrain, chart it, understand where the blue glow arose and how it lay along the juncture, and how that light, I was certain, interfered with the ordinary passage of time. Time? I had a faint headache.

"That was close," Jeff said finally. He was still cloaked with flotsam from under Mr. Shinetower's bed. "But it was worth it. Did you get a good look? See what I'm talking about?"

"It was a remarkable photograph," I said.

"Now you know. You've seen it, you know. I've got to get back to work; let's go fishing this weekend." He rose and, still whacking soot and ashes and wicked whatevers from his person, ran off toward Alfredo's.

"I've seen it," I said, and I sat there as the sadness bled through me. Duncan would have appreciated the moment and corrected Jeff the way he corrected me all those years.

"Seeing isn't knowing," he would say. "To see something is only to establish the first terms of your misunderstanding." That I remembered him at such a time, above the effulgent bayou, moments after my flight over the naked photograph, made me sad. I was not a genius, but I would be advised by one forevermore.

Happily, my work at the motel was straightforward, and I enjoyed it very much. I could do most of it with my shirt off, cutting away the tenacious vines from behind each of the rooms so that the air conditioning units would not get strangled, and I sweated profusely in the sweet, humid air. I painted the pool fence and enameled the three metal tables a kind of turquoise blue, a '50s turquoise that has become tony again just this year, a color that calls to the passerby: Holiday! We're on holiday!

Once a week I poured a pernicious quantity of lime into the two manholes above the storm sewer, and it fell like snow on the teeming backs of thousands of albino waterbugs and roaches that lived there. This did not daunt them in the least. I am no expert on any of the insect tribes, nor do I fully understand their customs, but my association with those subterranean multitudes suggested to me that they looked forward to this weekly toxic snowfall.

Twice a week I pressed the enormous push broom from one end of the driveway to the other until I had a wheelbarrow full of gravel and the million crushed tickets of litter people threw from their moving vehicles along the Hempstead Highway. It was wonderful work. The broom alone weighed twenty pounds. The sweeping, the painting, and the trimming braced me—work that required simply my back and both my arms and legs, but neither side of my brain.

Mr. Leeland Rakkerts, my boss, lived in a small apartment behind the office and could be summoned by a bell during the night hours. He was sixty that June. His wife had passed away years before, and he'd become a reclusive little gun nut. He had a growing gallery of hardware on a pegboard in his apartment, featuring long-barrelled automatic weaponry and at least two dozen huge handguns. But he was fine to me, and he paid me cash every Friday afternoon. When he opened the cash drawer, he always made sure, be you friend or foe, that you saw the .45 pistol that rested there, too. My mother would have abhorred me working for him, a man she would have considered the enemy, and she would have said as much, but I wasn't taking the high road or the low road, just a road. That summer the upkeep of the motel was my job, and I did it as well as I could. I'd taken a summer job and was making money. I didn't weigh things on my scale of ethics every ten minutes, because I wasn't entirely sure I had such a scale. I certainly didn't have one as fully evolved as my mother's.

It was a bit like being in the army; when in doubt, paint something. I remeasured and overpainted the parking lot. The last guy had drunkenly painted a wacky series of parentheses where people were supposed to park, and I did a good job with a big brush and five gallons of high mustard yellow. When I finished, I took the feeling of satisfaction in my chest to be simply that: satisfaction. Even if I was working for the devil, the people who put their cars in his parking lot would be squared away.

Getting into my Plymouth Fury III those days, with a sweaty back and a pocketful of cash, I knew I was no genius, but I felt—is this close?—like a great guy, a person of some command.

That fall my brother, Garrett Lrsdyksz (he'd changed his name back with a legal kit that Baxter, our Secret Service guy, had gotten him through the mail), became the youngest student ever to matriculate at Rice University. He was almost eleven. And he didn't enter as a freshman; he entered as a junior. In physics, of course. There was a little article about it on the wire services, noting that he had, without any assistance, set forward the complete set of equations explaining the relationship between the rotation of the earth and "special atmospheric aberrations most hospitable to exit trajectories of ground-fired propulsion devices." You can look it up, and all you'll find is the title, because the rest, like all the work he did in his cataclysmic year at Rice, is classified, top secret, eyes-only. Later, he explained his research this way to me: "There are storms, and then there are storms, Reed. A high pressure area is only a high pressure area down here on earth; it has a different pressure on the other side."

I looked at my little brother, a person forever in need of a haircut, and I thought: he's mastered the other side, and I can just barely cope with this one.

That wasn't exactly true, of course, because my Plymouth Fury III and my weekly wages from the San Jacinto Resort Motel allowed me to start having a little life, earthbound as it may have been. I started hanging out a little at Jeff Shreckenbah's place, a rambling hacienda out of town with two outbuildings where his dad worked on stock cars. Jeff's mother called me "Ladykiller," which I liked, but which I couldn't hear without imagining my mother's response; my mother, who told me a million times, "Morality commences in the words we use to speak of our next act."

"Hey, Ladykiller," Mrs. Shreckenbah would say to me as we pried open the fridge, looking for whatever we could find. Mr. Shreckenbah made me call him Jake, saying we'd save the last names for the use of the law-enforcement officials and members of the Supreme Court. They'd let us have Lone Star longnecks, if we were staying, or Coca-Cola, if we were hitting the road. Some nights we'd go out with Jake and hand him wrenches while he worked on his cars. He was always asking me, "What's the plan?"—an opening my mother would have approved of.

"We're going fishing," I told him, because that's what Jeff and I had started doing. I'd greet his parents, pick him up, and then Jeff and I would cruise hard down Interstate 45, fifty miles to Galveston and the coast of the warm Gulf of Mexico, where we'd drink Lone Star and surf cast all night long, hauling in all sorts of mysteries of the deep. I loved it.

Jeff would bring along a pack of Dutch Masters cigars, and I'd stand waist-deep in the warm water, puffing on the cheap cigar, throwing a live shrimp on a hook as far as I could toward the equator, the only light being the stars above us, the gapped two-story sky-line of Galveston behind us, and our bonfire on the beach tearing a bright hole in the sky.

When fish struck, they struck hard, waking me from vivid daydreams of Mr. Leeland Rakkerts giving me a bonus for sweeping the driveway so thoroughly, a twenty so crisp it hurt to fold it into my pocket. My dreams were full of crisp twenties. I could see Jeff over there, fifty yards away, the little orange tip of his cigar glowing, starlight on the flash of his line as he cast. I liked having my feet firmly on the bottom of the ocean, standing in the night. My brother and sister and my mother and father could shine their lights into the elemental mysteries of the world; I could stand in the dark and fish. I could feel the muscles in my arm as I cast again; I was stronger than I'd been two months ago. And then I felt the fish strike and begin to run south.

Having relinquished the cerebral (not that I ever had it in my grasp), I was immersing myself in the real world the same way I was stepping deeper and deeper into the Gulf, following the frenzied fish as he tried to take my line. I worked him back, gave him some, worked him back. Though I had no idea what I would do with it, I had decided to make a lot of money, and as the fish drew me up to my armpits and the bottom grew irregular, I thought about the ways it might be achieved. Being no genius, I had few ideas.

I spit out my cigar after the first wavelet broke over my face, and I called to Jeff, "I got one."

He was behind me now, backing toward the fire, and he called, "Bring him up here and let's see."

The top half of my head, including my two hands and the fishing pole, were all that was above sea level when the fish relented, and I began to haul him back. He broke the surface several times as I backed out of the ocean, reeling as I went. Knee-deep, I stopped and lifted the line until a dark form lifted into the air. I ran him up to Jeff by the fire and showed him there, a two-pound catfish. When I held him, I felt the sudden shock of his gaffs going into my finger and palm.

"Ow!" Jeff said. "Who's got whom?" He took the fish from me on a gill stick.

I shook my stinging hand.

"It's all right," he assured me, throwing another elbow of driftwood onto the fire and handing me an icy Lone Star. "Let's fry this guy up and eat him right now. I'm serious. This is going to be worth it. We're going to live to be one hundred years, guaranteed."

We'd sit, eat, fish some more, talk, and late late we'd drive back, the dawn light gray across the huge tidal plain, smoking Dutch

Masters until I was queasy and quiet, dreaming about my money, however I would make it.

Usually this dream was interrupted by my actual boss, Mr. Leeland Rakkerts, shaking my shoulder as I stood sleeping on my broom in the parking lot of the hot and bothered San Jacinto Resort Motel, saying, "Boy! Hey! Boy! You can take your zombie fits home or get on the stick here." I'd give him the wide-eyed nod and continue sweeping, pushing a thousand pounds of scraggly gravel into a conical pile and hauling it in my wheelbarrow way out back into the thick tropical weeds at the edge of the bayou and dumping it there like a body. It wasn't a crisp twenty-dollar bill he'd given me, but it was a valuable bit of advice for a seventeen-year-old, and I tried to take it as such.

Those Saturdays, after we'd been to the Gulf, beat in my skull like a drum, the Texas sun a thick pressure on my bare back as I moved through the heavy, humid air, skimming and vacuuming the pool and rearranging the pool furniture, though it was never ever moved because no one ever used the pool. People didn't come to the San Jacinto Resort Motel to swim. Then, standing in the slim shade behind the office, trembling under a sheen of sweat, I would suck on a tall bottle of Coca-Cola as if on the very nectar of life, and by midafternoon as I trimmed the hedges along the walks and raked and swept, the day would come back to me, a pure pleasure, my limegreen Plymouth Fury III parked in the shady side of Alfredo's American Cafe, standing like a promise of every sweet thing life could offer.

These were the days when my brother, Garrett, was coming home on weekends, dropped at our curb by the maroon Rice University van after a week in the research dorms, where young geniuses from all over the world lived in bare little cubicles, the kind of thing somebody with an IQ of 250 apparently loves. I had been to Garrett's room on campus, and it was perfect for him. There was a kind of pad in one corner surrounded by a little bank of his clothing, and the strip of butcher paper—covered with numbers and letters and tracked thoroughly with the faint gray intersecting grid of sneaker prints—ran the length of the floor. His window looked out onto the pretty, green, grassy quad.

It was the quietest building I have ever been in, and I was almost convinced that Garrett might be the only inmate, but when we left to

500

go down to the cafeteria for a sandwich, I saw the other geniuses in their rooms, lying on their stomachs like kids drawing with crayons on a rainy day. Then I realized that they were kids, and it was a rainy day, and they *were* working with crayons; the only difference was that they were drawing formulas.

Downstairs there was a whole slew of little people in the dining hall, sitting around in the plastic chairs, swinging their feet back and forth six inches off the floor, ignoring their trays of tuna-fish sandwiches and tomato soup, staring this way and that as the idea storms in their brains swept through. You could almost see they were thinking by how their hair stood in fierce clusters.

There was one adult present, a guy in a blue sweater-vest who went from table to table urging the children to eat: "Finish that sandwich, drink your milk; go ahead, use your spoon; try the soup, it's good for you." I noticed he was careful to register and gather any of the random jottings the children committed while they sat around doodling in spilled milk. I guess he was a member of the faculty. It would be a shame for some nine-year-old to write the key to universal field theory in peanut butter and jelly and then eat it.

"So, Garrett," I said as we sat down, "How's it going?"

Garrett looked at me, his trance interrupted, and as it melted away and he saw me and the platters of cafetería food before us, he smiled. There he was, my little brother, a sleepy-looking kid with a spray of freckles up and over his nose like the Crab Nebula and two enthusiastic front teeth that would be keeping his mouth open for decades.

"Reed," he said. " *'How's it going?'* I love that. I've always liked your acute sense of narrative. So linear and right for you." His smile, which took a moment and some force to assemble, was ancient, beneficent, as if he both envied and pitied me for something, and he shook his head softly. "But things here aren't going, kid." He poked a finger into the white bread of his tuna sandwich and studied the indentation like a man finding a footprint on the moon. "Things here are. . . . This is it: things. . . ." He started again, "Things aren't bad, really. It's kind of a floating circle. That's close. Things aren't going; they float in the circle. Right?"

We were both staring at the sandwich; I think I might have been waiting for it to float, but only for a second. I understood what he was saying. Things existed. I'm not that dumb. Things, whatever they might be—and that was a topic I didn't even want to open—had essence, not process. That's simple, that doesn't take a genius to decipher.

"Great," I said. And then I said what you say to your little brother when he sits there pale and distracted and four years ahead of you in school, "Why don't you eat some of that, and I'll take you out and show you my car."

It wasn't as bad a visit as I'm making it sound. We were brothers; we loved each other. We didn't have to say it. The dining room got to me a little until I realized I needed to stop worrying about these children and whether or not they were happy. Happiness wasn't an issue. The place was clean; the food was fresh. Happiness, in that cafeteria, was simply beside the point.

On the way out, Garrett introduced me to his friend, Donna Li, a ten-year-old from New Orleans, who he said was into programming. She was a tall girl with shiny hair and a ready smile, eating alone by the window. This was 1966, and I was certain she was involved somehow in television. You didn't hear the word "computer" every other sentence back then. When she stood to shake my hand, I had no idea what to say to her, and it came out, "I hope your programming is floating in the circle."

"It is," she said.

"She's written her own language," Garrett assured me, "and now she's on the applications."

It was my turn to speak again, and already I couldn't touch bottom, so I said, "We're going out to see my car. Do you want to see my car?"

Imagine me in the parking lot then with these two little kids. On the way out I'd told Garrett about my job at the motel and that Jeff Shreckenbah and I had been hanging out and fishing on the weekends and that Jeff's dad raced stock cars, and for the first time all day Garrett's face filled with a kind of wonder, as if this were news from another world, which I guess it was. There was a misty rain with a faint petrochemical smell in it, and we approached my car as if it were a sleeping brontosaurus. They were both entranced and moved toward it carefully, finally putting their little hands on the wet fender in unison. "This is your car," Garrett said, and I wasn't sure if it was the *your* or the *car* that had him in awe.

I couldn't figure out what floated in the circle or even where the circle was, but I could rattle my keys and start that Plymouth

Fury III and listen to the steady sound of the engine, which I did for them now. They both backed away appreciatively.

"It's a large car," Donna Li said.

"Reed," Garrett said to me. "This is really something. And what's that smell?"

I cocked my head, smelling it, too, a big smell, budging the petro-carbons away, a live, salty smell, and then I remembered: I'd left half a bucket of bait shrimp in the trunk, where they'd been ripening for three days since my last trip to Galveston.

"That's rain in the bayou, Garrett."

"Something organic," Donna Li said, moving toward the rear of the vehicle.

"Here, guys," I said, handing Garrett the bag of candy, sardine tins, and peanut-butter-and-cheese packs I'd brought him. I consid-ered for half a second showing him the pile of rotting crustaceans; it would have been cool, and he was my brother. But I didn't want to give the little geniuses the wrong first impression of the Plymouth.

"Good luck with your programming," I told Donna Li, shaking her hand. "And Garrett, be kind to your rocketry."

Garrett smiled again at that and said to Donna, "He's my brother."

She added, "And he owns the largest car in Texas."

I felt bad driving my stinking car away from the two young people, but it was that or fess up. I could see them standing in my rearview mirror for a long time. First, they watched me, and then they looked up, both of them, for a long time. They were geniuses looking into the rain. I counted on their being able to find a way out of it.

Nominated by Melissa Pritchard

THE WORKFORCE

by JAMES TATE

from HARVARD REVIEW

Do you have adequate oxen for the job?
No, my oxen are inadequate.
Well, how many oxen would it take to do an adequate job?
I would need ten more oxen to do the job adequately.
I'll see if I can get them for you.
I'd be obliged if you could do that for me.
Certainly. And do you have sufficient fishcakes for the men?
We have fifty fishcakes, which is less than sufficient.
Would fifty more fishcakes be sufficient?
Fifty more fishcakes would be precisely sufficient.
I'll have them delivered on the morrow.
Do you need maps of the mountains and the underworld?
We have maps of the mountains but we lack maps of the underworld.
Of course you lack maps of the underworld,
there are no maps of the underworld.
And, besides, you don't want to go there, it's stuffy.
I had no intention of going there, or anywhere for that matter.
It's just that you asked me if I needed maps. . . .
Yes, yes, it's my fault, I got carried away.
What do you need then, you tell me?
We need seeds, we need plows, we need scythes, chickens,
pigs, cows, buckets and women.
Women?
We have no women.
You're a sorry lot then.
We are a sorry lot, sir.

Well I can't get you women.
I assumed as much, sir.
What are you going to do without women, then?
We will suffer, sir. And then we'll die out one by one.
Can any of you sing?
Yes, sir, we have many fine singers among us.
Order them to begin singing immediately.
Either women will find you this way or you will die
comforted. Meanwhile busy yourselves
with the meaningful tasks you have set for yourselves.
Sir, we will not rest until the babes arrive.

Nominated by Richard Jackson

TWO PRAYERS

fiction by PAUL MALISZEWSKI

from MCSWEENEY'S

PRAYER AGAINST THE TYRANNY OF ANOTHER'S SHOES

> *Beckett even wore pointed-toe patent leather pumps that were too small because he wanted to wear the same shoe in the same size as Joyce, who was very proud of his small, neatly shod feet. Joyce had been vain about his feet since his youth, when poverty forced him to go about Dublin in a pair of white tennis shoes, the only footwear he owned.*
>
> —Deirdre Bair, *Samuel Beckett: A Biography*

DOWN ONSTAGE there is a play going on. My neighbor, whom I don't know from Adam, leans way over toward me and speaks into my ear. "Hey," he says, "why don't you put yourself in my shoes?"

I look down at the floor. His shoes are unlaced. His feet are resting on top of them. He's flexing his toes in his socks. One with a hole.

I look back at the stage. This play's been going on for some time. I think, sure, why not. So I move to drag his shoes toward me.

"Wait," he says. "Put yourself in my seat before you put yourself in my shoes."

"You want to trade seats, too?" I ask.

My neighbor nods, and then he's talking to the person to his immediate right. Finally he looks back at me.

"Who's that lady beside you?" he asks.

I look to my left. I turn back to my neighbor. "I don't know," I say.

My neighbor says, "You got to talk to her."

"Why?" I ask.

He looks at me blankly. "We're all moving to the right. She's going to have to put herself in your shoes. Now, go," he says. "Make arrangements."

And so I do.

By the fourth act I'm sliding around in my neighbor's wingtips. My neighbor is wedged into a pair of sequined pumps. His skin, his sock, the fat of his foot, droop over the top of the pump like a muffin. Everywhere I look: incongruity. The woman in the off-the-shoulder gown, in cowboy boots; the man in the tweed jacket, in espadrilles; the boy in his father's shoes; the husband in his wife's; his wife now in two-tone tasseled loafers.

After the play there's a dance for all of us and our new shoes. I find the woman who relinquished her zip-up half-boots for my black dress shoes (bought for a funeral—distant relative) and ask her to dance. I take her by the hand to right out in front of the band. This is not a learning experience, I can't ignore that. We all want to like each other's shoes and we all want to fit in and play along and go with the flow, but none of us can ignore the discomfort. I started out thinking, What a great idea! How simply whimsical! When the play ended, however, and I still didn't have my shoes back I thought, What a story this will make. Now the dancing has reached its tenth hour. There are rumors circulating that we'll be trading again before the night's out, to try yet one more person's shoes. It's hard not to be disgusted.

I am uncomfortable. I can't keep my mind off that.

Where does this discomfort go? Up toward the ceiling, with the music? Into our drinks? When we excuse ourselves to the restroom, are we hoping to lose it in the plumbing or rinse it from our mouths? Me, I solemnly try to dance this discomfort away. I am not alone in my endeavor; many of us take to the floor. We ignore the person who has our shoes or whose shoes we wear and dance, dance, dance. We dance in the modern style, we look down at the floor, at our feet, and watch ourselves move.

PRAYER FOR THE STRENGTH OF THREAD

I was told to give up looking for my grandmother. I was told she was lost. Gone for good. After two and one half weeks of trying to follow the red thread looped three times around her waist, I heard from

507

friends, neighbors, and officials all separately positing that her red thread was now irretrievably tangled with the other threads out there, ones looped three times and tied around other grandmothers and grandfathers, themselves also gone for good. I was told these things also by my family, who wanted me at home, they said, to lead the nightly grace for instance and attend to some other unspecified things, and told too by my wife, who wanted me at home because she heard it said by other people that to search for so long was not advisable.

I pray for faith, in both my grandmother, who could be irascible in her own way, and the red thread, which seemed sturdy enough. I looped it around her three times one night while she slept. Lacking a real icon or even a photograph of her, I direct my prayers toward the seat where she sat. Beside the chair, a stocky reading table overburdened with cooking magazines, community newsletters, a crossword puzzle dictionary. On the other side, a great spool of red thread. It unwinds through the living room, out the entry hall and under the door. The spool buzzes slightly, barely as it turns. It has not stopped unwinding since she left. In some circles this is interpreted, however cautiously, as a good sign.

I am not alone in my searching. There are many of us out here tracking threads, hunting grandmamas and grandpapas. We are professionals, some of us, and first-timers others; we have one thing on our minds: find our elderly, find them before we are elderly too and tied fast with thread. We search out of love, yes, but also fear. Fear of being gone for good like them.

Would you believe that I met a woman out here? She was also following a line of red thread, if you can believe that. Down the same street as me. Coincidence was our first attraction, as is usually the case. When the excitement of coincidence flagged, we discovered something else to take its place: we both love coffee!

Now we are sitting at a sidewalk cafe. It is little! It is delightful! This cafe is the sort of place made expressly for the adjectives "little" and "delightful." We've been here for days, though we swear to each other it's seemed like weeks, for we know each other so well. We are ordering all the desserts, one at a time, from the little and delightful menu. The waiter promises every item is delightful. He loves them all, he says. We ask him for two forks and we share.

This is how it looks at our delightful cafe: we are leaning over the little table. Underneath our knees rub. We each hold one hand out and let the threads slip through our fingers. If you didn't know better you'd think we were merely relaxing, that's how casual we appear. This searching cannot be rushed. Though we occasionally touch each other (on the arm, on the face) and even have a bit of a kissy thing going, we never let loose the threads. We are careful that way, cautious even. We tell each other we want love, and we mean it, in a way.

The threads run on, unwinding, and the desserts just keep coming. My God, this torte! It's great. This carrot cake and the crème brûlée. Waiter! Oh, waiter!

Nominated by Michael Martone

SYNOPSIS: THE SONGS OF THE JOLLY FLATBOATMEN

by PAUL VIOLI

from FRACAS (Hanging Loose Press)

Row your boat gently.
You're headed downstream anyway.

Save your strength for the mudflats.

Never discourage merriment.

If anyone concludes that life
is but a dream and thinks
that's worth singing about
exuberantly, exultantly,
over and over again,
toss him overboard
into the maw of rock and ice,

and row on,
                gently, gently.

It will amaze you,
what you can get away with

and yet remain a jolly
decent, generally compassionate,
semi-competent flatboatman.

Nominated by Lee Upton

MEDALLION

by MICHAEL HEFFERNAN

from THE GETTYSBURG REVIEW

I'm going to go out and walk around a little,
because it's a nice day, in the seventies,
after a night where the temperature dropped
just below freezing. There isn't much here
in the anteroom of the self, I don't think,
so why should I go on investigating
what last night's dream meant, or the subtleties
of the numerology of the soul as evidenced
in cryptanalytical encodings in the poems
of Bertran de Montsegur? I'm out of here,
and off on a little walk in the neighborhood,
but first I'd like to tell you I appreciate
your letting me share. It meant a lot to me.
Quite candidly, I'm not sure what to do
on days like this, or any day, really.
It all runs together, into a place
the good seem to have occupied as their own
and spruced up so nicely others of us who aren't
so good, but not the worst of citizens,
can't help but feel a little out of pocket,
as the saying goes, and I for one would like
to reach into my pocket and pull out
the ruby medallion my mother gave to me,
which fell out of my coat into the grate
by the front tire of the bus I'd waited for
across the street from the Schubert Theatre

in Detroit in 1959. I'd say,
to anyone around inclined to listen,
here is a little something you can have.
I hope you like it. Why don't you just keep it
and give it to another good person some day.
Tell them it used to be Bertran's, who came here once
on a horse all spangled with rubies and golden bells.

Nominated by Gibbons Ruark, Philip Levine, Rebecca McClanahan, Alan Michael Parker

NOGALES AND THE BOMB

fiction by ALBERTO RÍOS

from GLIMMER TRAIN

I WAS FIVE YEARS OLD, which isn't so important all by itself, but it was 1929, or maybe 1930. This was a big time in the world. I was living in Nogales, Sonora, with my parents. I don't remember if it was a weekday or a weekend, or even if it was winter or summer, but I do remember the hour when everything happened.

In those days my mother would get us all up at seven o'clock, and we would eat cereal, eggs, or sweet bread, and invariably milk. It wasn't so different from now. We always wanted coffee, but coffee, my mother said, would make us sick. Our drink was milk. Or something like milk, anyway. Sometimes to make milk my mother would put Eagle condensed milk in water. It might not have been Eagle brand, but it had an eagle on it. This had vitamins, she said. But the truth is, it was cheaper than milk, and some days this made a difference.

But it was the coffee we wanted. My mother used to make the coffee herself. It was called *caracolillo*, and she learned how to make it on the *rancho* she grew up on. *Caracolillo* was made of pea beans, not coffee beans, but it still had a good taste, and it was still called coffee. A lot of people drank the already-made Café Combate, but not us. My mother would roast the beans, which were small, and then she would grind them.

First, she would light a match and turn on the stove. Then she would put a big pan on the stove. She would put the *caracolillo* beans

514

in dry, and then stir them around so that they wouldn't burn. As she was stirring she would put sugar on the beans, and it would stick to them, making a kind of skin. When the heat changed them from green to black, my mother would pick up a bean with her fingers and snap it in half. That's how she would know if it was done, although I couldn't tell one way or the other. I was still too young.

Then quickly she would pick up the pan and dump out all the beans onto a clean tablecloth. She'd leave the beans there to cool and to dry. When they were ready, she would put them in a large jam jar and seal them tight. Whenever she wanted to make coffee, she had a small grinder, which you had to hold between your knees. I had to do it, and I hated it because it was real work and it hurt my legs. But I would grind the beans, and the powder would fall into a small box at its base.

The fire and the beans and the sugar and the grinding—it all had a loud and happy smell that could not be ignored. Even as kids we understood something of that magic. It was as if the coffee had hands, which it would put around our faces and try to draw us to its chest. They were strong hands, and would not give up. Even after the coffee was made, the hands came up out of it as steam, and they still tried to wave us over.

But no, my mother said, no coffee for us, and that was that. She would send us outside, then, to play in the garden with our small cups and saucers that we had made ourselves out of white clay. We liked playing best under the peach trees, but sometimes we ventured under the apricots and the mulberries.

There were some hills made of clay, and we used their funny dirt to make things. Usually it was red. Sometimes there was some white. We would mix it up with some water and make a *masa*, like for tortillas, and then we would roll it out and form things. We would let whatever we made bake in the sun, and this is how we made our toys, except for dolls. My mother, when she made our dolls instead of buying them, used old pieces of cloth or worn-out pillowcases, which she would fill with smaller rags and tie off at the most important points—a head, some arms. She would get the soot off the stove and paint a face on the dolls. They had big eyes, sometimes. You took your chances. She would make hair out of yarn and whatever else was around. And she made them in all sizes, although I'm not sure this was on purpose.

I always wanted a doll with a china face, but they were too expen-

515

sive. These years were a hard time in the world. The dolls my mother bought me, the only ones she could afford, were always made out of cardboard, but they could eat pretend food just as well as china dolls. I played a game we called *comadritas*, or little mothers, with my sisters, and sometimes a neighbor. We'd dress up with rags on our heads and we'd tie ourselves up with material or old drapes so that it looked like we were wearing long dresses. People wore long dresses and head coverings then, and not just in church.

We'd decide where each of us lived in the garden, and each one of us had our own tea set and table with chairs. We'd invite each other over, very grown-up. Then we would wait for someone to visit and it was always a surprise. Someone would knock, and we'd say, "Who is it? Oh, *comadrita*, it's you. Come right in."

"Oh, thank you, *comadrita*."

"Not at all, *comadrita*. Would you care for some coffee?"

"Oh, *comadrita*, I really can't, my husband will be home any moment."

"Oh, just a cup, *comadrita*."

"Well, okay, *comadrita*, just a cup."

All our games had rules like that, and they all had songs to help us remember, but all the words and ways to act were from the grown-up world. We were making fun of them, but practicing to be grown-ups as well. There were so many, but I remember them all.

Have you ever heard of the *pobrecita huerfanita,* the poor orphan? *Sin su padre, sin su madre, le echaremos a la calle, a llorar su desventura . . .* The orphan was one of us, who would have to get in the middle of our circle. We would sing to her, "Without your father, without your mother, we send you into the street, to cry out your misfortune."

Yo no tengo padre, ni madre, pero las tengo a ustedes. "I don't have a father, or a mother," the one of us who was playing the orphan would sing, to answer us. "But I have all of you."

Whereupon we would all jump forward to hug her and kiss her. Then the next one in the circle became the orphan, and we did it all over until we each had a turn. And there were so many more. *Bebeleche*, which is hopscotch. The *pajara pinta.*

In the *pajara pinta*, someone would be in the middle of the circle, again, with eyes covered. We would sing a song like in the other game, but the person in the middle would then touch someone in the circle without knowing who it was. She would kneel and ask if this were her true love.

"Would you give me your left hand, would you give me your right hand, would you give me a kiss?"

That's what we would do on regular days, but today was different. On regular days my mother would do her chores and my father would go to work. He worked as much on the American side of the border as the Mexican side, which is where we lived. He was a carpenter, though sometimes he sold houses. One could do that in those days. His most regular employer was Mr. Contreras's funeral home. It was on his days off that my father sold houses.

We didn't live on a regular street. We lived at the top of one of the many hills, and there were only trails leading up to the houses. Our address was Calle del Cerro No. 10, which was really the name of the trail that went through the little canyon between hills. That kind of place is called a *callejón*. The house was pink, and made of adobe and brick, with two large rooms and a kitchen, all covered by a roof made of tin with laminate. The house was very warm in the winter, and we didn't use a heater. When it was hot, the house was fresh and cool. It was built right up against the side of the hill, right into it, with the hill being almost its fourth wall, and this helped. We weren't on top of the hill—we were part of the top of the hill.

It meant we could see everything, which was going to help us on this day. And not only could we see everything, we could smell everything as well. This wasn't as bad as it sounds. Every day at midafternoon, about three, my mother would make the coffee. She would send us to the bakery for fresh sweet bread, usually to the Norteña—there were two we could choose from in the neighborhood. There were bakeries all over in those days. The bread they baked was ready every day at three o'clock exactly, and we would wait for the smell, which was like a clock. The smell told us when it was time for the afternoon coffee.

If my mother had a guest, even a neighbor, they would go inside and drink the coffee, or sometimes Chinese tea. But they would never stand outside in those days. I had heard the grown-ups talking, that there was a revolution coming, a change of government. They talked in secret, which just meant that they were always talking in low tones.

The neighbors would gather, and talk inside their houses all the time. This was all before it happened, what I'm going to tell you, and I didn't understand much of what they were saying. There were rumors, though, and as a child I was always curious. I always wanted to listen, even though what they said was mysterious and in big words. Maybe I wanted to listen just because it was mysterious. That's how I was. The talk was like a magnet to me.

Well, on this day, in the morning, my mother didn't let us play under the peach trees. We had been hearing airplanes flying all around, and coming close to houses. At least we thought they were airplanes. That's what people were saying, but they made all the kids stay inside and so I never got to see any. But even from inside the house we could hear the people standing outside and saying things like, "Here come the Obregonistas," and, "We better do something."

They were all shouting as the morning went on, and then crying. We went out of the house, too, finally, when my mother couldn't stop us, and I saw my father running toward us up the hill. It was almost noon, but too early for him to be coming home for lunch. Because we were so high up, we could see people crossing the line to the American side. They had opened up the *garitas*, the guard stations, and seemed to be letting people go right through.

My father arrived scared. He said to my mother the hour is here, and that they're going to kill everyone. My mother made us all go inside and get on top of the bed. I don't know why, but at least that way she would know where we were.

"Let's go, let's go to the other side," my father said.

But my mother was very calm. Quietly, she said, "No. We're not going. If we're going to die, we're going to die together, and right here." I don't know what else they said to each other because, by this time, we were all hiding under the sheets and pillows.

The noises of the airplanes got louder, and we began to hear explosions. There was noise everywhere. One of the neighbors yelled to everyone that they were bombs, but I didn't know what that meant. But I could hear the people in the *callejón*, which echoed everything up to us. I could hear as the whole street cried and moaned.

Between the stove and the wall, in the kitchen of our house, there was a little space, and that's where my mother put us. It was a very small space, and there were five of us. My parents put their arms

518

against us, and held us tight against the wall. I don't know how long the bombs and the noise lasted. It wasn't a day. It might just have been an hour or two hours when the noises finally started to go away. But that hour or two is bigger than almost any other day I can think of. It's bigger than some months.

My mother said, finally, "They're gone."

My father said, "I'm going to look out the door." Everything was quiet, which was as loud now as the noise had been. "Yes, they're gone, there's nothing out there. *Se repintieron*," he said. They must have felt bad for what they had done, he figured, and given up. Who wouldn't? But he didn't really know.

We went outside and we could see the neighbors coming out, and the people farther down in town. The neighbors were all checking with each other—did anything happen to you? Were you afraid? I was. I hid. We didn't know what else to do.

There was some laughter, but it wasn't like other times. People seemed to shiver and shake this feeling off like a dog throws off water. They didn't mean to do it, but I could see the way they suddenly moved.

After this, we heard that they actually were bombs that had fallen. One had fallen close to the house. The hole is still there in the *callejón* to this day. They left it on purpose. An airplane also fell. The authorities did not have airplanes of their own, but they managed to shoot one down on Canal Street.

The pilot was alive, we heard, but we never knew what happened to him. And nobody else died, either. Afterward, it was kind of funny, in that it all went off so badly. They had just been dropping bombs out of the airplanes, but they had to steer them as well, so they never could aim very well at anything. Things would be different today, I know, but that's how it was.

We don't know why they bombed the town. To this day, we don't know. That's how the Revolution was. That was the year President Obregón was assassinated, and the bombs may have had something to do with that, but we didn't know. Everyone just shook their heads a lot when they talked about it.

The funny thing is, the bombs did not end there. During World War II, the Japanese had a secret weapon. They had the idea of putting bombs on hot-air balloons and letting them float across the

Pacific to the United States. They were supposed to kill people when they blew up, and start fires, forest fires, and destroy buildings. Whatever a bomb could do.

People didn't really know very much about the wind yet. The Japanese had just discovered that the winds came in this direction, that they blew for over five thousand miles all the way from Japan to the United States. They had to make the balloons light enough to fly but strong enough to last. They used some kind of a paper that came from mulberry trees, just like the ones we used to have around the house. Remember the peach and apricot trees, too?

Well, the plan didn't work very well, but they did do it, and the bombs did reach several places. But it was like the bombs they dropped from the airplanes when I was young—they couldn't aim these very well, either, not over five thousand miles. And the thing is, one of them reached Nogales. It was on the American side, but, you know, it's still Nogales. But it was like the other bombs—nobody got hurt, and nothing much happened. They just found the balloon-paper and some bomb things.

Nobody ever really believed they came all the way from Japan, but it turns out they did. The people who knew how to figure these things out figured it out, but nobody was supposed to talk about any of this, no matter which side of the border you were on. Nobody was supposed to let the Japanese think that their plan had worked. Of course, we heard all this a long time after the war was over. Even so, we still weren't supposed to say anything. I still feel funny talking about it.

So there we were, being bombed again. And it was just as silly, and accidental. I say it was an accident because we never did anything to be bombed for. Not that anyone ever does, but we really didn't. It just seemed like a good idea to someone somewhere else. I don't know what it is about this place.

The second bomb didn't amount to much. But I was five years old when I heard those first bombs, and they were loud enough to last up to now, to the end of the century. If they meant to scare five-year-olds, then it worked, and very well. But I remember the coffee from that time, too, and that must mean something.

Nominated by Melissa Pritchard, Barbara Selfridge

SEVEN ROSES

by FRANK X. GASPAR

from THE GEORGIA REVIEW

Three red, one white, one purple, one yellow, one pink.
Seven roses in a jar on the kitchen table, the morning
paper, Kona coffee, a plate of sliced melon and banana.
I'm in a fogbank. I was out wandering the keeps
of some mind or another far too late. Now all I can do
is stare at the roses, which smell wonderful, as does
the fruit, as does the coffee. The truth about life is
that it is good, but it comes with a lot of strings attached.
The rose bushes were here when we bought
this house, though we have added to them, subtracted
from them. Frankly, I don't like them much. They
demand so much of you. They want to be fertilized
and pruned and mulched. Then they get sick, they
get rusty and moldy, and things live in them and you
must resort to despicable substances, you have to
wear yellow gloves. All that time out in the heat
when you could be bodysurfing or reading a book.
If I were Rumi I could make a parable about the roses,
I could dance into a fainting spell and someone on my staff
would write down the poem I uttered, or if I were Francis Ponge
I could study the roses in a way that a cubist might,
just before painting them all up and down a stretched canvas.
I've looked at the hard truth: that my heart might be just
too dark for roses. Or my soul too weary. Or my mind
too confused. Yet they are beautiful here in their cut
ripeness, their delicate bowing to earth. See how the air

beads into water all along the jar. And the white rose,
its delicate, almost invisible kiss of red at the edges of
its inner petals. It is all so strange in the morning when
I cannot think, and when my body at rest wishes to remain
at rest, which is the law, after all. I know it's the way
of the world that the roses and I have so much to do
with one another. It's one hand washing the other hand.
It's morning and I take to the day slowly, grow
into my senses slowly. And maybe the roses puzzle after me
in their fashion, the seven lovely roses sitting on my table,
scenting the sunlit room. Maybe they know that I know
how they hate the way they are softly, softly dying for me.

Nominated by Elizabeth Spires, Ellen Wilbur, Dorianne Laux, Cleopatra Mathis,
Bruce Beasley, Richard Garcia, Pamela Stewart, Stephen Corey

WE TAKE OUR CHILDREN TO IRELAND

by LYNNE McMAHON

from THE SOUTHERN REVIEW

What will they remember best? The barbed wire
still looped around the Belfast airport,
the building-high Ulster murals—
but those were fleeting, car-window sights;
more likely the turf fires lit each night,
the cups of tea their father brought
and the buttered soda farls, the seawall
where they leaped shrieking into the Irish Sea
and emerged, purpling, to applause;
perhaps the green castle at Carrickfergus,
but more likely the candy store
with its alien crisps—Vinegar? they ask,
Prawn cocktail? Worcestershire leek?
More certainly still the sleekly syllabled
odd new words, *gleet* and *shite*.
and grand responses to everyday events:
How was your breakfast? Brilliant.
How's your crust? Gorgeous.
Everything after that was gorgeous,
brilliant. How's your gleeted shite?
And the polite indictment from parents
everywhere, the nicely dressed matrons
pushing prams, brushing away their older kids

with a Fuck off, will ye? which stopped
our children cold. Is the water cold,
they asked Damian, before they dared it.
No, he said, it's not cold, it's
fooking cold, ye idjits.
And the mundane hyperbole of rebuke—
You little puke, I'll tear your arm off
and beat you with it, I'll row you out to sea
and drop you, I'll bury you in sand
and top you off with rocks—
to which the toddler would contentedly nod
and continue to drill his shovel
into the sill. All this will play on
long past the fisherman's cottage and farmer's
slurry, the tall hedgerows lining the narrow
drive up the coast, the most beautiful
of Irish landscapes indelibly fixed
in the smeared face of two-year-old Jack—
Would you look at that, his father said
to Ben and Zach, shite everywhere, brilliant.
Gorgeous, they replied. And meant it.

Nominated by Jim Barnes, Grace Schulman, David Baker, James Reiss

YOUR NAME HERE

by JOHN ASHBERY

from CONJUNCTIONS

But how can I be in this bar and also be a recluse?
The colony of ants was marching toward me, stretching
far into the distance, where they were as small as ants.
Their leader held up a twig as big as poplar.
It was obviously supposed to be for me.
But he couldn't say it, with a poplar in his mandibles.
Well, let's forget that scene and turn to one in Paris.
Ants are walking down the Champs-Elysées
in the snow, in twos and threes, conversing,
revealing a sociability one never supposed them as having.
The larger ones have almost reached the allegorical statues
of French cities (is it?) on the Place de la Concorde.
"You see, I told you he was going to bolt.
Now he just sits in his attic
ordering copious *plats* from a nearby restaurant
as though God had meant him to be quiet."
"While you are like a portrait of Mme. de Staël by Overbeck,
that is to say a little serious and washed out.
Remember you can come to me anytime
with what is bothering you, just don't ask for money.
Day and night my home, my hearth are open to you,
you great big adorable one, you."

The bar was unexpectedly comfortable.
I thought about staying. There was an alarm clock on it.
Patrons were invited to guess the time (the clock was always wrong).

More cheerful citizenry crowded in, singing the Marseillaise,
congratulating each other for the wrong reasons, like the color
of their socks, and taking swigs from a communal jug.
"I just love it when he gets this way,
which happens in the middle of August, when summer is on its way
out, and autumn is still just a glint in its eye,
a chronicle of hoar-frost foretold."
"Yes and he was going to buy all the candy bars in the machine
but something happened, the walls caved in (who knew
the river had risen rapidly?) and one by one people were swept
    away
calling endearing things to each other, using pet names.
Achilles, meet Angus." Then it all happened so quickly I
guess I never knew where we were going, where the pavement
was taking us.

Things got real quiet in the oubliette.
I was still reading *Jean-Christophe*. I'll never finish the darn thing.
Now is the time for you to go out into the light
and congratulate whoever is left in our city. People who survived
the eclipse. But I was totally taken with you, always have been.
Light a candle in my wreath, I'll be yours forever and will kiss you.

Nominated by Conjunctions

WHEN SHE IS OLD AND I AM FAMOUS

fiction by JULIE ORRINGER

from THE PARIS REVIEW

THERE ARE GRAPE LEAVES, like a crown, on her head. Grapes hang in her hair, and in her hands she holds the green vines. She dances with both arms in the air. On her smallest toe she wears a ring of pink shell.

Can someone tell her, please, to go home? This is my Italy and my story. We are in a vineyard near Florence. I have just turned twenty. She is a girl, a gangly teen, and she is a model. She is famous for almost getting killed. Last year, when she was fifteen, a photographer asked her to dance on the rail of a bridge and she fell. A metal rod beneath the water pierced her chest. Water came into the wound, close to her heart, and for three weeks she was in the hospital with an infection so furious it made her chant nonsense. All the while she got thinner and more pale, until, when she emerged, they thought she might be the best model there ever was. Her hair is wavy and long and buckeye-brown, and her blue eyes have a stunned, sad look to them. She is five feet eleven inches tall and weighs one hundred and thirteen pounds. She has told me so.

This week she is visiting from Paris, where she lives with her father, my Uncle Claude. When Claude was a young man he left college to become the darling of a great couturier, who introduced him to the sequin-and-powder world of Paris drag. Monsieur M. paraded my uncle around in black-and-white evening gowns, high-heeled pumps and sprayed-up diva hairdos. I have seen pictures in his attic

527

back in Fernald, Indiana, my uncle leaning over some balustrade in a cloud of pink chiffon, silk roses at his waist. One time he appeared in *Vogue*, in a couture photo spread. All this went on for years, until I was six, when a postcard came asking us to pick him up at the Chicago airport. He came off the plane holding a squirming baby. Neither my mother nor I knew anything about his having a child, or even a female lover. Yet there she was, my infant cousin, and here she is now, in the vineyard doing her grape-leaf dance for my friends and me.

Aïda. That is her terrible name. *Ai-ee-duh*: two cries of pain and one of stupidity. The vines tighten around her body as she spins, and Joseph snaps photographs. She knows he will like it, the way the leaves cling, and the way the grapes stain her white dress. We are trespassing here in a vintner's vines, spilling the juice of his expensive grapes, and if he sees us here he will surely shoot us. What an end to my tall little cousin. Between the purple stains on her chest, a darker stain spreads. Have I mentioned yet that I am fat?

Isn't it funny, how I've learned to say it? I am fat. I am not skin or muscle or gristle or bone. What I am, the part of my body that I most am, is fat. Continuous, white, lighter than water, a source of energy. No one can hold all of me at once. Does this constitute a crime? I know how to carry myself. Sometimes I feel almost graceful. But all around I hear the thin people's bombast: *Get Rid of Flabby Thighs Now! Avoid Holiday Weight-Gain Nightmares! Lose Those Last Five Pounds!* What is left of a woman once her last five pounds are gone?

I met Drew and Joseph in my drawing class in Florence. Joseph is a blond sculptor from Manhattan, and Drew is a thirty-seven-year-old painter from Wisconsin. In drawing class we had neighboring easels, and Drew and I traded roll-eyed glances over Joe's loud Walkman. We both found ourselves drawing in techno-rhythm. When we finally complained to him, he told us he started wearing it because Drew and I talked too much. I wish that were true. I hardly talk to anyone, even after three months in Florence.

One evening as the three of us walked home from class we passed a billboard showing Cousin Aïda in a gray silk gown, and when I told them she was my cousin they both laughed as if I had made some sort of feminist comment. I insisted that I was telling the truth. That was a mistake. They sat me down at a café and made me talk about her for half an hour. Joseph wondered whether she planned to complete her schooling or follow her career, and Drew had to know whether she suffered from eating disorders and skewed self-esteem. It would have been easier if they'd just stood in front of the billboard and drooled. At least I would have been able to anticipate their mute stupor when they actually met her.

Aïda rolls her shoulders and lets her hair fall forward, hiding her face in shadow. They can't take their eyes off her. Uncle Claude would scold her for removing her sun hat. I have picked it up and am wearing it now. It is gold straw and it fits perfectly. What else of hers could I put on? Not even her gloves.

"Now stand perfectly still," Joseph says, extending his thumb and index finger as if to frame her. He snaps a few pictures then lets the camera drop. He looks as if he would like to throw a net over her. He will show these pictures of Aïda to his friends back home, telling them how he slept with her between the grapevines. This will be a lie, I hope. "Dance again," he says, "this time slower."

She rotates her hips like a Balinese dancer. "Like this?"

"That's it," he says. "Nice and slow." Surreptitiously he adjusts his shorts.

When Drew looks at my cousin I imagine him taking notes for future paintings. In Wisconsin he works as a professional muralist, and here he is the best drawing student in our class, good even at representing the foot when it faces forward. I am hopeless at drawing the foot at any angle. My models all look like they are sliding off the page. I've seen photographs of Drew's murals, twenty-foot-high paintings on the sides of elementary schools and parking structures, and his figures look as though they could step out of the wall and crush your car. He does paintings of just the feet. I can tell he's studying Aïda's pink toes right now. Later he will draw her, at night in his room, while his upstairs neighbor practices the violin until the crack of dawn. "If she didn't live there, I'd have to hire her to live there," he tells me. She may keep him up all night, but at least she makes him paint well.

There are certain things I can never abide: lack of food, lack of sleep and Aïda. But she is here in Italy on my free week because our parents thought it would be fun for us. "Aïda doesn't get much rest," my mother told me. "She needs time away from that business in France."

I told my mother that Aïda made me nervous. "Her name has an umlaut, for crying out loud."

529

"She's your cousin," my mother said.

"She's been on the covers of twelve magazines."

"Well, Mira"—and here her voice became sweet, almost reverent—"you are a future Michelangelo."

There's no question about my mother's faith in me. She has always believed I will succeed, never once taking into account my failure to represent the human figure. She says I have a "style." That may be true, but it does not make me the next anybody. Sometimes I freeze in front of the canvas, full of the knowledge that if I keep painting, sooner or later I will fail her.

My cousin always knew how important she was, even when she was little. Over at her house in Indiana I had to watch her eat ice-cream bars while I picked at my Sunmaid raisins. I tried to be nice because my mother had said, "Be nice." I told her she had a pretty name, that I knew she was named after a character from a Verdi opera, which my mom and I had listened to all the way from Chicago to Indiana. Aïda licked the chocolate from around her lips, then folded the silver wrapper. "I'm not named after the *character*," she said. "I'm named after the *entire opera*."

The little bitch is a prodigy, a skinny Venus, a genius. She knows how to shake it. She will never be at a loss for work or money. She is a human dollar sign. Prada has made millions on her. And still her eyes remain clear and she gets enough sleep at night.

Joseph has run out of film. "You have beautiful teeth," he says hopelessly.

She grins for him.

Drew looks at me and shakes his head, and I am thankful.

When she's tired of the dance, Aïda untwines the vines from her body and lets them fall to the ground. She squashes a plump grape between her toes, looking into the distance. Then, as though compelled by some sign in the sky, she climbs to the top of a ridge and looks down into the valley. Joseph and Drew follow to see what she sees, and I have no choice but to follow as well. Where the vines end, the land slopes down into a bowl of dry grass. Near its center, surrounded by overgrown hedges and flower beds, the vintner's house rises, a sprawling two-story villa with a crumbling tile roof. Aïda inhales and turns toward the three of us, her eyes steady. "That's where my mother lives," she announces.

It is such an astounding lie, I cannot even bring myself to respond. Aïda's mother was the caterer at a party Uncle Claude attended during his "wild years;" my own mother related the story to me years ago as a cautionary tale. When Aïda was eight weeks old her mother left her with Claude, and that was that. But Aïda's tone is earnest and forthright, and both Joseph and Drew look up, confused.

"I thought you lived with your dad in Paris," Joseph says. He shoots a hard glance at me as if I've been concealing her whereabouts all this time.

"She does," I say.

Aïda shrugs. "My mother's family owns this whole place."

"This is news." Joseph looks at me, and I shake my head.

"My mom and I aren't very close," Aïda says and sits down. She ties a piece of grass into a knot, then tosses it down the hill. "Actually, the last time I saw her I was three." She draws her legs up and hugs her knees, and her shoulders rise and fall as she sighs. "It's not the kind of thing you do in Italy, tote around your bastard kid. It would have been a *vergogna* to the *famiglia*, as they say." Aïda looks down at the stone house in the valley.

Joseph and Drew exchange a glance, seeming to decide how to handle this moment. I find myself wordless. It's true that Aïda's mother didn't want to raise her. I don't doubt that it would have been a disgrace to her Catholic family. What baffles me is how Aïda can make up this story when she knows that *I* know it's bullshit. What does she expect will happen? Does she think I'll pretend to believe her? Joseph's eyebrows draw together with concern. I can't tell what he's thinking.

Aïda stands and dusts her hands against her dress, then begins to make her way down the slope. Joe gives us a look, shakes his head as if ashamed of himself, and then follows her.

"Where the hell do you think you're going?" I call to Aïda.

She turns, and the wind lifts her hair like a pennant. Her chin is set hard. "I'm going to get something from her," she says. "I'm not going back to France without a memento."

"Let's stop this now, Aïda," I say. "You're not related to anyone who lives in that house." In fact, it didn't look as if anyone lived there at all. The garden was a snarl of overgrown bushes, and the windows looked blank like sightless eyes.

"Go home," she says. "Joe will come with me. And don't pretend you're worried. If I didn't come back, you'd be glad."

She turns away and I watch her descend toward the villa, my tongue dry in my mouth.

These past days Aïda has been camping on my bedroom floor. Asleep she looks like a collapsed easel, something hard and angular lying where it shouldn't. Yesterday morning I opened one eye to see her fingering the contents of a blue tin box, my private cache of condoms. When I sat up and pushed the mosquito netting aside, she shoved the box back under the bed.

"What are you doing?" I asked.

The color rose in her cheeks.

"It's none of my business," I said. "But if you meet a guy."

She gave an abbreviated "ha" like the air had been punched out of her. Then she got up and began to look for something in her suitcase. Very quietly she said, "Of course, you're the expert."

"What's that supposed to mean?" I said.

She turned around and smiled with just her lips. "Nothing."

"Listen, shitweed, I may not be the next *Vogue* cover girl, but that doesn't mean I sleep alone every night."

"Whatever you say." She shook out a teeny dress and held it against herself.

"For God's sake," I said. "Do you have to be primo bitch of the whole universe?"

She tilted her head, coy and intimate. "You know what I think, Mira?" she said. "I think you're a vibrator cowgirl. I think you're riding the mechanical bull."

I had nothing to say. But something flew at her and I knew I had thrown it. She ducked. A glass candlestick broke against the wall.

"Fucking psycho!" she shouted. "Are you trying to kill me?"

"Get a hotel room," I said. "You're not staying here."

"Fine with me. I'll sleep in a ditch and you can sleep alone."

Her tone was plain and hard, eggshell white, but for a split second her lower lip quivered. It occurred to me for the first time that she might feel shunted off, that she might see me as a kind of baby-sitter she had to abide while her father had a break from her. Quickly I tried to replay in my mind all the names she had called me, that day and throughout our kid years, so I could shut out any thoughts that would make me feel sorry for her. "Get out of my room," I said. She picked her way across the glass and went into the bathroom. Door-click, faucet-knob squeak and then her scream, because in my apartment there is no hot water to be had, ever, by anyone.

Drew and I shuffle sideways down a rock hill toward the dried-up garden. Fifty yards below, my cousin sidles along the wall of the house. I cannot imagine how she plans to enter this fortress or what she will say if someone sees her. There's a rustle in a bank of hedges, and we see Joseph creeping along, his camera bag banging against his leg. He disappoints me. Back in New York he works in a fashion photographer's darkroom, and he speaks of commercial photography as if it were the worst imaginable use for good chemicals and photo paper. For three months he's photographed nothing in Florence but water and cobblestones. Today he follows Aïda as if she were leading him on a leash.

Aïda freezes, flattening herself against the house wall. It seems she's heard something, although there's still no one in the garden. After a moment she moves toward a bank of curtained French doors and tries a handle. The door opens, and she disappears inside. Joseph freezes. He waits until she beckons with her hand, then he slides in and closes the door behind him. They're gone. I am not about to go any farther. The sun is furious and the vines too low to provide any shelter. A bag containing lunch for four people hangs heavy on my back. I am the only one who has not brought any drawing tools. It was somehow understood that I would carry the food.

"We might as well wait here," Drew says. "Hopefully they'll be out soon."

"I hope." The bag slides off my shoulders and falls into the dust.

Drew reaches for the lunch. "I would have carried this for you," he says. His eyes rest for a moment on mine, but I know he is only trying to be polite.

There was a time when I was the one who got the attention, when my body was the one everyone admired. In junior high, where puberty was a kind of contest, you wanted to be the one with the tits out to here. I had my bra when I was nine, the first in our grade, which made me famous among my classmates. My mother, a busty lady herself, told me she was proud to see me growing up. I believed my breasts were a gift from God, and even let a few kids have an accidental rub at them. It wasn't until high school, when the novelty wore off and they grew to a D-cup, that I started to see things as they really were. Bathing suits did not fit right. I spilled out of the tops of sundresses. I looked ridiculous when running or jumping. Forget cheerleading. I began smashing those breasts down with sports bras, day and night.

It doesn't matter what the Baroque masters thought. The big breasts, the lush bodies, those are museum pieces now, and who cares if they stand for fertility and plenty, wealth and gluttony, or the fullest bloom of youth? Ruben's nudes made of cumulus clouds, Titian's milky, half-dressed beauties overflowing their garments, Lorenzo Lotto's big intelligent-eyed Madonnas—they have their place, and it is on a wall. No one remembers that a tiny breast meant desolation and deserts and famine.

Take Aïda on the billboard in Florence, wearing a gray Escada gown held up by two thin strands of rhinestones. Where the dress dips low at the side, there is a shadow like a closed and painted eyelid, just the edge of Aïda's tiny breast, selling this $6,000 dress. That is what you can do today with almost nothing.

The fact is, Aïda guessed right when she said I was a virgin. There were other girls at my high school, fat girls, who would go out by the train tracks at night and take off all their clothes. There were some who would give hand jobs. There were others who had sex for the first time when they were eleven. Few of these girls had dates for homecoming, and none of them held hands at school with the boys they met by the tracks at night. At the time, I would rather have died than be one of them.

But sometimes I think about how it might have been for those girls, who got to touch and be touched and to live with exciting varieties of shame. When I look at my drawings of men and women, there's a stiffness there, a glassiness I'm afraid comes from too little risk. It makes me dislike myself and perhaps it makes me a bad artist. Can these things be changed now that I am, in most ways, grown up? Is there a remedy for how I conducted my life all those years? Where do I begin?

Drew lies back on his elbows and whistles "Moon River." I wish I could relax. Somewhere below, my cousin stalks an artifact of her non-mother. I picture the tall, cool rooms with their crumbling ceilings and threadbare tapestries woven in dark colors. Maybe she will burn the place down. In another few months, I imagine, she will need to do something to get herself on the evening news. Being on a billboard can't be enough for her.

I put on Aïda's sun hat and tie its white ribbons beneath my chin.

534

Just as I'm wondering if either of us will speak to the other all afternoon, Drew asks if I've decided to submit any works for display in the Del Reggio Gallery in Rome.

"*What* works?" I say. "You've seen my sliding people. Maybe I could do a little installation with a basket underneath each painting to catch the poor figure when she falls off the page."

"You have a talent, Mira. People criticize *my* work for being too realistic."

"But I don't plan to draw them expressionistically. They just come out that way. It's artistic stupidity, Drew, not talent."

"Well, then, I guess you'd better quit now," he says, shrugging. He picks up some fallen grapes, waxy and black, and throws them into the hammock of my skirt. "How about another profession? Sheepherding? Radio announcing? Hat design?"

"There's a fine idea." The words come out clipped and without humor. A dry silence settles between us, and I'm angry at myself for being nervous and at him for bringing up the exhibition. He knows his work will go into the show.

At times I think it would be terrible to have him touch me. I can imagine the disappointment he would show when I removed my dress. One hopes to find a painter who likes the old masters, like in the personal columns I've read in *The Chicago Tribune*: Lusty DWM w/taste for old wine and Rubens seeks SWF with full-bodied flavor. Would I ever dare to call?

"So what do you think of my little cousin?" I ask.

"Why?" he says. "What do you think of her?"

"She's had a hard past," I say, in an attempt at magnanimity. Because if I answered the question with honesty, I would blast Aïda to Turkmenistan. All our lives she has understood her advantage over me, and has exercised it at every turn. When I pass her billboard in town I can feel her gleeful disdain. No matter how well you paint, she seems to say, you will remain invisible next to me.

Perhaps because Drew is older I thought of him as enlightened in certain ways; but I saw how he looked at my cousin today with plain sexual appetite. I hand him a plum from our lunch bag and turn my face away from the sun because I am hot and tired and want to be far away from here.

As we eat, we hear the foreign-sounding *ee-oo* of an Italian police siren in the distance. Dread kindles in my chest. I imagine Aïda be-

535

ing wrested into handcuffs by a brown-shirted Italian policeman, and the shamefaced look she'll give Joseph as her lie comes crashing down. Will I be too sorry later to say I told her so? I can almost hear my mother's phone diatribe: *You let her break into a house with some boy? And just watched the police haul her off to an Italian jail?* Drew and I get to our feet. The house below is quiet and still. A boxy police car sweeps into the lane, dragging a billow of dust behind it. It roars down the hill and screeches to a stop somewhere in front of the house, where we can no longer see it. After a moment someone pounds on the front door.

Drew says, "We'd better go down."

"They'll see us."

"Suit yourself." He flicks the pit of his plum into the grapevines and starts down the hill.

I follow him toward the front of the house until we see the paved area where the car is parked. He is about to step onto the piazza. Panicked, I take his arm and pull him behind a stand of junipers at the side of the driveway. There are just enough bushes to hide both of us. The shadows are deep but there are places to look through the branches, and we can see the police officer who had been pounding on the front door. The other officer sits quietly in the car, engrossed in a map.

"This is ridiculous," Drew says. "We have to go in."

"No way," I whisper. "There's enough trouble already. What's the minimum penalty for breaking and entering in this country?"

Drew shakes his head. "Tell me I came to Florence to stand in a bush."

The front door opens slightly, and the policeman goes inside. After a few minutes the officer with the map gets out and goes to the door, then into the house. Everything is still. A bird I can't name alights near Drew's hand and bobs on a thin branch. We stand together in the dust. The heat coming off his body has an earthy smell like the beeswax soap nuns sell in the marketplace. If I extended my hand just a centimeter, I could touch his arm.

"Uh-oh," he says softly.

There are Aïda and Joseph being led from the house by the policemen. Aïda's hair is mussed as if there has been a struggle, and her dress hangs crooked at the shoulder. Joseph walks without looking at her. A woman in a black dress—a housekeeper from the looks of her—curses at them from the doorway. They're not in handcuffs, but the police aren't about to let them go, either. Just as the first police-man opens the car door, a chocolate-colored Mercedes appears at the top of the drive. The steel-haired housekeeper stiffens and points. "*La padrona di casa*," she says.

They hold Aïda and Joseph beside the police car, waiting for the Mercedes to descend into the piazza. When the car arrives and the dust clears, the lady of the house climbs out. She squares herself to-ward the scene in front of her villa. She is tall and lean. Her hair is caught in the kind of knot the Italian women wear, heavy and sweep-ing and low on the neck. Beneath her ivory jacket her shoulders are businesslike. She looks as if she would be more at home in New York or Rome than out here on this grape farm. She lowers her black sun-glasses. With a flick of her hand toward Aïda and Joseph, she asks who the two criminals might be.

Aïda raises her chin and looks squarely at the woman. "*La vostra dottore*," she says. Your doctor.

The policemen roar with laughter.

The maid tells her padrona that Aïda was apprehended in the boudoir, trying on shoes. She had tried on nearly ten pairs before she was caught.

"You like my shoes?" the woman asks in English. She tilts her head, scrutinizing Aïda. "You look familiar to me."

"She's a model," Joseph says.

"Ah!" the woman says. "And you? You are a model too?" Her mouth is thin and agile.

"A photographer," Joe says.

"And you were trying on shoes also in my house?"

There is a silence. Joseph looks at Aïda for some clue as to what she wants him to say or do. Aïda looks around, and I almost feel as if she is looking for me, as if she thinks I might come out and save her now. Her eyes begin to dart between the padrona and the policemen, and her mouth opens. She lets her eyes flutter closed, then collapses against a policeman in an extremely realistic faint.

"Poor girl," the woman says. "Bring her into the house."

The police look disapproving, but they comply. One of them grabs her under the shoulders and the other takes her feet. Like an imper-ial procession they all enter the house, and the housekeeper closes the door behind them.

"She must be sick," Drew whispers. "Does she eat?"

"In a manner of speaking."

537

He climbs out of our hiding place and starts down toward the house. I have to follow him. I picture being home in bed, lying on my side and looking at the blank wall, a desert of comfort, no demands or disappointment. As I navigate the large stones at the edge of the piazza, my foot catches in a crevice and I lose my balance. There's a snap, and pain shoots through my left ankle. I come down hard onto my hip.

Drew turns around. "You okay?"

I nod, sideways, from the ground. He comes back to offer me his hand. It's torture getting up. My body feels as if it weighs a thousand pounds. When I test the hurt ankle, the pain makes my eyes water. I let go of Drew's hand and limp toward the door.

"Are you going to make it?" Drew asks.

"Sure," I say, but the truth is there's something awfully wrong. The pain tightens in a band around my lower leg. Drew rings the doorbell, and in a few moments the housekeeper opens the door. Her eyes are small and stern. She draws her gray brows together and looks at Drew. In his perfect Italian, he tells her that our friends are inside and that we would like to ask forgiveness of the lady of the house. She throws her hands heavenward and wonders aloud what will happen next. But she holds the door open and beckons us inside.

The entry hall is cool and dark like a wine cavern itself. There is a smell of fennel and coffee and dogs, and the characteristic dampness of Florentine architecture. Supporting myself against the stone wall, I creep along behind Drew, past tall canvases portraying the vintner's family, long-faced men and women arrayed in brocade and velvet and gold. The style is almost more Dutch than Italian, with angular light and deep reds and blues. In one portrait a seventeenth-century version of our padrona holds a lute dripping with flower garlands. She looks serene and pastoral, certainly capable of mercy. I take this for a good sign. We move past these paintings toward a large sunny room facing the back garden, whose French doors I recognize as the ones Aïda slipped through not long ago. My cousin is stretched out on a yellow chaise longue with Joseph at her side. The policemen are nowhere to be seen. I imagine them drinking espresso in the kitchen with the inevitable cook. La Padrona sits next to Aïda with a glossy magazine open on her lap, exclaiming at what she sees. "Ah, yes, here you are again," she says. "God, what a gown." It's as though royalty has come for a visit. She seems reluctant to look away from the photographs when the maid enters and announces us as friends of the signorina.

538

"More friends?"

"Actually, Mira's my cousin," Aïda explains. "And that's Drew. He's another student."

Drew gives our padrona a polite nod. Then he goes to Aïda and crouches beside her chaise longue. "We saw you faint," he says. "Do you need some water?"

"She'll be fine," Joseph says, and gives him a narrow-eyed look.

Drew stands, raising his hands in front of him. "I asked her a simple question."

The padrona clears her throat. "Please make yourself comfortable," she says. "Maria will bring you a refreshment." She introduces herself as Pietà Cellini, the wife of the vintner. She says this proudly, although from the state of their house it seems the family wines haven't been doing so well in recent years. As she speaks she holds Aïda's hand in her own. "Isn't she remarkable, your cousin?" she asks. "So young."

"I'm awfully sorry about all this," I say. "We should be getting home."

"She's darling," says Signora Cellini. "My own daughter went to study in Rome two years ago. She's just a little older than Aïda. Mischievous, too."

"Is that so?" I say. The pain in my ankle has become almost funny. My head feels weightless and poorly attached.

"Aïda was just showing me her lovely pictures in *Elle*," our host says. "The poor girl had a shock just now, all those police. I'm afraid our housemaid was quite rude."

"I'm sure she was just protecting your house," I say.

Aïda sips water from a porcelain cup. Joseph takes it from her when she's finished and sets it down on a tiny gilt table. "Is that better?" he asks.

"You're so nice." Aïda pats his arm. "I'm sure it was just the heat."

Black flashes crowd the edges of my vision. The ankle has begun to throb. I look past them all, through the panes of the French doors and out into the garden, where an old man digs at a bed of spent roses. Dry-looking cuttings lie on the ground, and bees dive and hover around the man. He is singing a song whose words I cannot hear through the glass. I rest my forehead against my hand, wondering how I can stand to be here a moment longer. Aïda laughs, and Joseph's voice joins hers. It seems she has done this intentionally, in reparation for the thrown candlestick or the words I said to her, or even because all my life I have had a mother and she has had none. What a brilliant success I would be if I could paint the scene in this sunny room, glorious Aïda in careful disarray, the two men repelled by one another and drawn to her, the elegant woman leaning over her with a porcelain cup. Sell it. Retire to Aruba. I can already feel the paint between my fingers, under my nails, sliding beneath my fingertips on the canvas. And then I hear the padrona's voice coming from what seems a great distance, calling not Aïda's name but my own. "Mira," she says, "Good God. What happened to your ankle?"

In defiance of all my better instincts, I look down. At first it seems I am looking at a foreign object, some huge red-and-purple swelling where my ankle used to be. It strains against the straps of my sandal as if threatening to burst. "I got hurt," I say, blinking against a contracting darkness, and then there is silent nothing.

It is nighttime. I do not recall getting back to the apartment, nor do I remember undressing or getting into bed. The room is quiet. There is a bag of crushed ice on my ankle, and an angel bending over it as if it had already died. Translucent wings rise from the angel's back, and its face is inclined over my foot. Its hair shines blue in the moonlight. It murmurs an incomprehensible prayer.

The mosquito netting fills with wind and then hangs limp again, brushing Aïda's shoulders. Her face is full of concentration. She touches the swollen arch of my foot. I can hardly feel it. You could help me if you wanted to, she might say now. You have lived longer than I have and could let me know how it is, but you don't. You let me dance and giggle and look like an idiot. You like it. You wish it. Is she saying this?

"How did we get home?" I ask her. My voice sounds full of sleep.

"You're awake," she says. "You sure messed up your ankle."

"It feels like there are bricks on my chest."

"Signora Cellini gave you Tylenol with codeine. It knocked you out."

Sweet drug. My wisdom-tooth friend. One should have it around. "Where are the guys?"

"Home. We made quite a spectacle."

"You did."

"That's what I do, Cousin Mira."

"*I* don't."

"Was I the only one to faint today?" She raises her eyebrows at me.

"Well, I didn't do it on purpose."

"You'll have to go to a doctor tomorrow."

"So be it. This is your fault, you know," I tell her. I mean for it to be severe, but the last part comes out *falyuno*. I am almost asleep again and grateful for that. With my eyelids half-closed I can see the wings rising from her shoulders again, and her feet might be fused into one, and who knows, she might after all be sexless and uninvolved with the commerce of this world, and I might be the Virgin Mary, receiving the impossible news.

The next morning Aïda calls a cab and we go down to the university infirmary, where an American nurse named Betsy feels my ankle and shakes her head. "X-ray," she says, her blond ponytail swinging back and forth. "This looks ugly." My ankle, if I were to reproduce it on a canvas, would require plenty of aquamarine and ocher and Russian red. The doctor handles me gently. He tells the technician to take plenty of pictures. In another room the doctor puts my films up on a lighted board. He shows me a hairline fracture, which looks to me like a tiny mountain range etched into my bone. He does not understand why I smile when he gives me the bad news. How can I explain to him how apt it is? Drew would recommend a self-portrait.

When I return to the waiting room wearing a fiberglass cast from toes to mid-calf, I find Aïda holding a croissant on a napkin. I feel as if I will faint from hunger.

"Hi, gimp," she says. There's a smirk. I'd like to whack her with my new weapons. Instead we head for the door and walk down Via Rinaldi toward a trattoria where I can find some breakfast. The sun is out, and the *zanzare*. Big, fat ones. Unlike American mosquitoes, these actually hurt when they bite. It's the huge proboscis. At least my ankle is safe from that for a while.

The doctor has prescribed normal activity, with caution until I learn to use the crutches better. It's my first time on them—I always wanted them when I was a kid, but somehow managed to escape injury—and I think I will stay home as long as possible. Time to paint. No more vineyards. Aïda can do what she likes for the last two days of her visit.

At the trattoria we have a marble-topped table on the sidewalk, and a kind waiter looks at me with pity. He brings things we do not order, a little plate of biscotti and tiny ramekins of flavored butter for our *pane*. Aïda twirls her hair and looks at her feet. She is quiet today and has neglected to put on the customary makeup: something to

541

make her lips shine, a thin dark line around the eyes, a pink stain on the cheeks. She looks almost plain, like anyone else's cousin. She actually eats the free biscotti.

Our waiter sets espresso cups on the table. Aïda's growth will be stunted forever by the staggering amount of caffeine she has consumed in Florence. Of course, her father doesn't allow it back home. "Does it hurt?" she asks, pointing to the ankle.

"Not so much anymore," I say. "All that good pain medicine."

"Too bad about the cast. I really mean it. They itch something awful."

Great.

"Now, can I ask you one question, Aïda?" I say.

"One." She lifts her cup and grins at her sneakers.

"What was all that malarkey about your mother? I mean, for God's sake."

There's a long silence. Her lips move slightly as if she's about to answer, but no words come. She sets the cup down and begins to twist her hands, thin bags of bones, against each other. The knuckles crack. "*I* don't know," she says finally. "It was just something to say."

"A little ridiculous, don't you think? Making Joseph break into the house with you?"

"I didn't make anyone do anything." She frowns. "He could have stayed behind with you."

"You sorcered him, Aïda. You knew you were doing it."

Aïda picks up her tiny spoon and stirs the espresso, her eyes becoming serious and downcast. "I did look up my actual mother once," she says.

The admission startles me. I sit up in the iron chair. "When?"

"Last year. After the accident. I imagined dying without ever knowing her, and that was too scary. I didn't tell my dad about it, because you know, he wants me to see him as *both* parents."

"But how did you find her?"

"There was a government agency. France has tons of them, they're so socialized. A man helped me locate a file, and there she was, I mean her name and information about her. Her parents' address in Rouen. My grandparents, can you believe it?"

I imagine a white-haired lady somewhere on an apple farm, wondering to whom the high, clear voice on the phone could belong. It sounds like the voice of a ghost, a child she had who died when she was twelve. She answers the girl's questions with fear in her chest. Does a phone call from a spirit mean that one is close to death?

"They gave me her phone number and address. She was living in Aix-en-Provence. I took a bus there and stood outside her apartment building for hours, and when it rained I stood in someone's vestibule. I didn't even know which window was hers. It's just as well, I guess. She wouldn't have wanted to see me anyhow."

I don't want to believe this story. It seems designed to make me pity her. Yet there's an embarrassment in her face that suddenly makes her look very young, like a child who has admitted to a misdeed. "Are you going to try again?" I ask.

"Maybe sometime," she says. "Maybe after my career."

"That might be a long time," I say.

"Probably not," she says, her eyes set on something in the distance. "I'll have a few good years, and I'd better make enough money to retire on. I don't know what other job I could do."

I consider this. "So what will you do with yourself afterward?"

"I don't know. Go to Morocco with my father. Have kids. Whatever people do."

I think of those pictures of my uncle in couture evening gowns, his skin milky, his waist slender as a girl's. His graceful fingers hold roses or railings or *billets-doux*. His hair hangs long and thick, a shiny mass down his back. He now wears turtlenecks and horn-rimmed glasses; there are veins on the backs of his hands, and his beautiful hair is gone. I wonder how this can happen to Aïda. She seems eternal, the exception to a rule. Can she really be mortal? Even when she fell off the bridge and chanted fever-songs, I knew she would survive to see international fame. In the glossy pages of Signora Cellini's magazines and those of women all over the world, she will never, never change.

But here on the sidewalk at the trattoria she bites a hangnail, and looks again at my foot. "We should get you home," she says. "You need some rest." I wonder if she will survive what will happen to her. I wonder if she will live to meet her mother. There are many things I would ask her if only we liked each other better.

One afternoon, perhaps a month after Aïda's return to Paris, I buy a bottle of inexpensive Chianti and a round loaf of bread and head down to the ancient marketplace by the Arno. There, in the shadow of a high colonnade, the tall bronze statue of Il Porcelino guards the empty butcher stalls. It's easy to move around on the crutches now,

543

although the cobbled streets provide a challenge. I wear long loose dresses to hide my cast.

At the center of the piazza the white-robed Moroccans have spread their silver and leather goods on immaculate sheets. They sing prices as I pass. Because I have some *lire* in my pocket, I buy a thin braided bracelet of leather. Perhaps I will send it to my cousin. Perhaps I will keep it for myself. Down by the river, pigeons alight on the stones and groom their feathers. I sit with my legs dangling over a stone ledge and uncork my round-bellied bottle, and the wine tastes soft and woody. It's bottled by the Cellinis. It's pretty good, certainly not bad enough to make them go broke. I drink to their health and to the health of people everywhere, in celebration of a rather bizarre occurrence. Two days ago I sold a painting. The man who bought it laughed aloud when I said he had made a bad choice. He is an opera patron and food critic from New York City, the god-son of my painting professor back in the States. He attended our winter exhibition last January, and happened to be visiting Rome when the Del Reggio Gallery was showing our work.

It is not a painting of Aïda dancing in the grapevines, her hair full of leaves. It is not an unapologetic self-portrait, nor a glowing Tuscan landscape. It is a large sky-blue square canvas with two Chagall-style seraphim in the foreground, holding a house and a tree and a child in their cupped hands. It is called *Above the Farm.* In slightly darker blue, down below, you can make out the shadow of a tornado. Why he bought this painting, I do not know. But there's one thing I can tell you: those angels have no feet.

Although it's interesting to think of my painting hanging in this man's soaring loft in Manhattan, it makes me sad to think I will never see it again. I always feel comforted, somehow, looking at that child standing by his house and tree, calm and resigned to residence in the air. Five hundred feet off the ground, he's still the same boy he was when he stood on the earth. I imagine myself sitting on this ledge with Aïda, when she is old and I am famous. She will look at me as if I take up too much space, and I will want to push her into the Arno. But perhaps by then we will love ourselves less fiercely. Perhaps the edges of our mutual hate will have worn away, and we will have already said the things that need to be said.

Nominated by D. R. MacDonald, Elizabeth Gaffney, Daniel Orozco

TO GRASP THE NETTLE

by EAMON GRENNAN

from THE KENYON REVIEW

Empty your hands. Shake off even the sweat
of memory, the way they burned

to find the cool indented shell of flesh
at the base of her spine, how they cupped themselves

to hold her head, feeling the weight and bones of it,
every angle of her face and the curve of each earlobe

finding its place in your palm or at your fingertips,
flesh whispering to flesh in its own dialect; or the way

one of them would creep through the breathlessness
of sleep—the sheer unlikely fact of being there, and there

when the light came back—to come to rest on a breast
or claim a hand or settle a warm spot on her belly

or between stilled thighs. Shake it all off:
for as long as they bear the faintest trace

of such hard evidence against you, your hands
will not be steady and the thing will sting you.

Nominated by Philip Levine, Ted Deppe, Susan Wheeler, David Wojahn, Gibbons Ruark

SESTINA: BOB

by JONAH WINTER

from PLOUGHSHARES

According to her housemate, she is out with Bob
tonight, and when she's out with Bob
you never know *when* she'll get in. Bob
is an English professor. Bob
used to be in a motorcycle gang, or something, or maybe Bob
rides a motorcycle now. How radical of you, Bob—

I wish I could ride a motorcycle, Bob,
and also talk about Chaucer intelligently. Bob
is very tall, bearded, reserved. I saw Bob
at a poetry reading last week—he had such a Bob-
like poise—so quintessentially Bob!
The leather jacket, the granny glasses, the beard—Bob!

and you were with my ex-girlfriend, Bob!
And you're a professor, and I'm nobody, Bob,
nobody, just a flower-deliverer, Bob,
and a skinny one at that, Bob—
and you are a large person, and I am small, Bob,
and I hate my legs, Bob,

but why am I talking to you as if you were here, Bob?
I'll try to be more objective. Bob
is probably a nice guy. Or that's what one hears. Bob
is not, however, the most passionate person named Bob

you'll ever meet. Quiet, polite, succinct, Bob
opens doors for people, is reticent in grocery stores. Bob

does not talk about himself excessively to girlfriends. Bob
does not have a drinking problem. Bob
does not worry about his body, even though he's a little heavy. Bob
has never been in therapy. Bob,
also, though, does not have tenure—ha ha ha—*and* Bob
cannot cook as well as I can. Bob

never even heard of paella, and if he had, Bob
would not have changed his facial expression at all. Bob
is just so boring, and what I can't understand, Bob—
yes I'm talking to you again, is why you, Bob,
could be more desirable than me. Granted, Bob,
you're more stable, you're older, more mature *maybe* but Bob . . .

(Months later, on the Bob-front: My former girlfriend finally mar-
    ried Bob.
Of Bob, she says, "No one has taken me higher or lower than Bob."
Me? On a dark and stormy sea of Bob-thoughts, desperately, I bob.)

Nominated by Edward Falco, Tony Hoagland, David Baker, Lucia Perillo, Ploughshares

MILTON AT THE BAT

essay by JEFFREY HAMMOND

from THE ANTIOCH REVIEW

IN MY LATE FORTIES I finally acquired a skill that all college teachers dread: an ability to see myself through my students' eyes. Glimpsing my reflection in glazed stares issuing from beneath the brims of baseball caps, I was suddenly transformed from hipster to saurian. Instantly and irrevocably, I was old.

Midlife crises are murder on English professors, most of whom went into the profession because we wanted to "work with young people"—meaning, of course, ourselves. We figured that their vigor would keep us from turning into "old people," meaning our parents. Literature seemed a perfect medium for occupational self-pickling: it was a "young" topic—artsy, rebellious, and romantic. But sooner or later, the literature-as-formaldehyde gambit backfires. The people sitting in your classes are always the same age, and as year fades into year, *you're* the only person who's getting old.

We fight this, of course. The Dorian Grays of campus (sociologists sometimes offer stiff competition), English professors of a certain age tend to act and dress too young, fossilizing the sixties both in our look and in our "special topics" courses: The Literature of Zen, The Poetry of Rock (Dylan and the Beatles, of course), Woodstock as Cultural Event. You can spot us a mile away: denim dresses, ribbed turtlenecks, Paul McCartney or Mary Travers hair, now salt-and-pepper. My own bid for hipness emerges in a graying beard and black jeans, though I've come to see the limits of both. On bad days my particular burden seems especially heavy: how can a guy keep time at bay if his field is seventeenth-century poetry? Even worse, what if it's seventeenth-century *religious* poetry? Not even paisley and ponytails can save him then.

Not long ago I taught a course in Milton, the deadest, whitest, male-est poet of them all. Nobody ages you faster than Milton, and if you like him enough to teach him (God forbid you have to teach him if you don't), you'll be marked as a geezer no matter how long that ponytail gets. What's worse, you'll find yourself *feeling* like a geezer, as I did by the time the course was over. I blame Milton for finally bursting the Young Turk bubble that I hoped was sheltering me. It doesn't help that fellow geezers more in tune with the times have turned on me, adding their deft blows to the shakier assaults of the young. Peter Ackroyd's recent novel, *Milton in America,* is a case in point. Beneath a patina of historicity, the book spins a dark fantasy worthy of a junior high Dungeons 'n' Dragons fan who has just been forced to read "Lycidas": Ackroyd's Milton, dazed by the chaotic formlessness of the New World, goes berserk and wreaks bloody horror on the pristine land. In the jacket photo Ackroyd, bony-faced and intense, is dressed in SoHo black with hair greased back Steven Seagal style. The crinkles around his eyes tell me that this man is my contemporary, but he knows the score: this is an era that does not love geezers.

You'll see a lot of compensating in a Milton class. Like Avis, Milton teachers try harder: pedagogical wheels groan as we try to make our guy relevant by exposing the structures of race, class, and gender embedded in his seductively beautiful language. In the process, of course, we unwittingly reveal how reactionary we are to find his language seductively beautiful in the first place. "Beauty" is a hard sell nowadays—a poor second to politics in the literature classroom. Aesthetic pleasure has even been equated, in some circles, with an unforgivable indifference to politics, an elitist elevation of "art" over human suffering. To "enjoy" a poem is, by definition, to be distracted from worthier causes.

Milton teachers find ourselves constantly moving against the grain of modern morality. With his maddening propensity to package now-suspect ideas in lovely words, Milton exposes our antiquated selves as we try to introduce the Nintendo Generation to the hard satisfactions of his language. This last class seemed to pose more problems than usual. I smiled pleasantly as young men argued that Milton is unfair to Satan, a misunderstood slacker badgered by the biggest, baddest Dad of all. Perhaps, I replied, but what about the language? I nodded thoughtfully as young women denounced Milton's piggery because the sonnet to his dead wife, his "late espoused saint," fails to mention the color of her eyes. The sexist bastard was obviously too self-absorbed to notice her eyes—proof that he didn't really love her. Well, maybe—but again, what about that language?

If you forget that poetry is composed of words and instead find yourself wanting to cut to the political chase, there's a lot not to love in Milton, especially given the "Hard Copy" mentality of our post-Watergate era. No whipping boy of the old canon attracts more eager flagellants, and naturally, the students who hate him most have never read him. Their sullen anger is the point from which I must start, step one of the frantic dance—the affable soft sell—that constitutes my Milton course.

"Why are you taking this class?" When I ask this question on the first day, the answers usually invoke necessity in one form or another: "I heard that Milton is someone I should read." "They say that Milton is always on the GREs." "This is the only upper-level class that fits my schedule." Rare is the student who comes in actually *wanting* to read him. Students have heard that Milton was a Christian propagandist, which is true enough, but his religious absolutism is hardly a selling point. Teachers of the humanities on all levels have been preaching a variety of relativisms for some time now, usually with the best of intentions. Now, though, we're facing an unexpected and rather nasty payoff: our bracing affirmations of the positioned nature of all truths have made many students adopt a cool distance from *any* truth and from any facts that might support it. They figure it's better to keep things loose than to chase epistemological phantoms. As one student told me, the mind is like a computer's hard drive: if kept free of unneeded files, it will run faster. "Yes," replied the Old Professor, "but don't you need *some* data on that drive in order to boot up? To do anything?" The student rolled his eyes: clearly, I had missed the point.

The notion that everything is "constructed," however true it might be, is hardly a rousing call to rush out and learn something. Students capable of intuiting its impact on their education often feel guilty about how little they know. For them, the mere name "Milton" invokes a vague sense of having been cheated by well-meaning elders with Santana bass-lines still throbbing in their heads. Perceived as a personified reproach, the embodiment of What We Never Learned, Milton is the quintessential "core" writer. He comes with the stink of the remedial.

Today's students often see Milton as the worst sort of fascist: a knowledgeable one. Admittedly, Milton is a tad content-heavy, and the background necessary for reading him with a measure of understanding and appreciation has long since faded from general knowledge. If you teach him conscientiously, you'll find yourself having to supply daunting amounts of information: Renaissance and seventeenth-century literary culture, biblical sources, Protestant theology, the classical epic, the English Civil War, the history of canon-formation, the history of English poetry, and on, and on. When my students' expressions remind me how remote such matters are to them, I compensate with manic enthusiasm, chattering about Roundheads and Cavaliers like a veteran telling war stories while his pals get up from their barstools and start inching away. This tour-guide buoyancy is tiring. After class I drag myself back to my office feeling as if I personally served in Cromwell's government but had not, in 350 years, remembered to die.

In class I recount history with an energy that my students associate with personal experience, like a "bomb" party that someone threw last week. My animation must strike them as deeply strange. I'm sure they see me as a man dislodged from real time, oblivious to the compelling flash of what's happening now. They probably imagine me snatching the manuscript of the *Aeneid* from the fire, where the dying Vergil has just consigned it. "I'll need this for the Milton class," they hear me saying. Or maybe they see me in Eden, peering from behind a shrub and jotting down Freudian motifs to identify in class while Satan, assuming the form of a toad, whispers in Eve's ear. Or there I am, flushed with excitement as I break the news that Edward King's boat has gone down in the Irish Sea. "There might be a poem in this, John," the Old Professor is saying. "Write it, and I'll be able to compare it to Vergil's tenth eclogue."

This kind of rant might sound like vintage Prufrock, but I don't care about not eating peaches or wearing the bottoms of my trousers rolled: such things, I'm beginning to see, will take care of themselves. What I want to know is whether I'll ever feel up to offering the Milton course again. Do I have the stuff to introduce people for whom "get real" is a by-word to a poet who pretends to be a shepherd so he can praise a dead student tricked out as another shepherd

551

for the benefit of readers pretending to be still more shepherds? Can a middle-aged guy teach Milton again and not slide even deeper into the Hades of the un-hip? Yet once more?

It would be easy to call Milton an old person's poet, and thus chalk up my regard for him to the grim revelation of those baseball caps. But the truth is sadder and more complicated than that. I liked Milton at thirteen, when Mrs. Korliss bravely assigned brief selections from *Paradise Lost* in eighth grade. Although I didn't understand much of what we read, the word-pictures seemed magically vivid, and the speeches contained more lofty bombast than even what little I had read of Shakespeare. In eighth grade, lofty bombast was not unattractive: it was like having a Marvel comic come to life in my head. I tried reading more of *Paradise Lost* on my own but made little headway, and ended up staring for hours at the Doré engravings in a fancy edition I found in the public library.

I didn't read Milton again until college, in Professor Dolores Fetter's Survey of British Literature II. Professor Fetter was—or seemed to be—an ancient woman (she was, I realize, only about five years older than I am now) whose entire being bore witness to an era that rock 'n' roll, marijuana, and Vietnam were sweeping away forever. She was, I suppose, exactly what those baseball caps tell me I'm becoming now. When we hit Milton we started with "Lycidas," which none of us really got. We knew that this was supposed to be a moving tribute to a dead friend, but the poem struck us as patently phony. I remember a skinny kid from Cleveland saying, "For a guy who was so choked up, that shepherd sure had no problem talking." By the time we were done we'd made a pretty strong case—or at least, a loud one—that "Lycidas" was the most overrated piece of hackwork in all English literature.

Milton recovered nicely the following week, when we made our way through Books I, II, and IV of *Paradise Lost*. I could now follow the story, and was particularly impressed by how eloquent everybody was, even the devils in council. Each devil seemed perfectly reasonable—so long as he was speaking. Then there'd be another speech and another, equally attractive, perspective. That was Milton's point, of course: how things became horribly unmoored once God's Word was opposed. A postmodernist would say something here about the constructive power of discourse: didn't Satan himself say that the mind could make a heaven of hell, a hell of heaven? In college, though, it was enough to see the magic of words so forcefully demonstrated, to derive an unforgettable mental movie from these mere marks on a page. Judging from childhood nightmares, I'd always pictured evil as something wordless and uncomprehending, an alien face with no mouth. But Satan embodied it—and spoke it—so convincingly: "Which way I flie is Hell; my self am Hell."

I read all of *Paradise Lost* on my own. The theology didn't exactly thrill me, but the "special effects" were even more spectacular than in eighth grade because I could now see how they fit into the poem's cosmic picture. With Milton I could soar through Neil Armstrong's deep space; with Milton I could watch overmuscled Titans snarling and grappling on a wispy turf of clouds; with Milton I could even imagine all of time collapsing into a single plane within the cold eye of a huge God—and as I took it all in, I felt nearly as huge as that God. Although my reading of *Paradise Lost* was hardly deep, it was certainly engaged and even visceral, the response of a wide-eyed naif surprised to find that hell-fire could be so invigorating. Milton's scope impressed me, too. This one book seemed to be a treasury of classical and Christian lore, a blank-verse encyclopedia of Western culture: although I didn't come close to mastering that lore, it was exciting to know that it was all here. Even though I had gotten religion out of my system years before, I don't remember being bothered by the fact that I did not personally believe in Milton's redemptive story. It was, in fact, the fictive nature of *Paradise Lost*—Milton's creation of something out of what I thought was nothing—that I found most appealing. It seemed to me that he had taken on a far greater challenge than other writers. I could imagine Melville and Conrad on ships, Joyce walking the Dublin streets, or Stephen Crane in a cold-water flat soaking up atmosphere for *Maggie, A Girl of the Streets.* But how did Milton manage to do *his* research?

I soon learned that Satan's hissings and poutings had to remain private pleasures. Even in 1971 Milton wasn't someone to confess a taste for, at least not if you wanted to reap the chief perk of all sensitive-guy English majors: getting dates with smart girls. Kafka, Joyce, Blake, even Eliot—these were acceptable passions. You could hold forth on those guys over an Iron City and really get somewhere. Such was definitely not the case with Milton, who was beginning to acquire the elitist taint that would bring him down during the next two decades. In a time of rallies and marches and sit-ins, when we were convinced that the collusion of Anglo-American politics and Christian piety had produced little more than Vietnam, proclaiming a love for Milton was a real conversation stopper. You might as well have announced that you were a narc.

I never studied Milton again in a class, not even in grad school, where I wound up specializing in Milton's grimmer brethren, the New England Puritans. Still, I remained a fan; Milton continued to be my poet of choice for revelling in rich words and fantastic architectures, consequences be damned. I even started teaching him by accident. Nobody in the department where I took my first teaching job wanted to teach the Milton course, a lame-duck offering earmarked for demotion as a requirement along with the other "Major Figures" courses. After a group of English majors complained that Milton hadn't been offered for several years, my chair asked if I'd be willing to do it. A shrewd academic politician would have played it cool, expressing a reluctant willingness to help the department out of a tight spot. But I was young and green: on my course request form I wrote "Any day, any time." Even then I should have heeded signs that Milton would one day age me. A feminist colleague who was slightly ahead of her time complained that it was unconscionable even to offer the Milton course in this enlightened era. Her objection puzzled me: I certainly had no great rearguard battle to fight, no ambition to restore Milton to an idealized pedestal.

In the ten years since, the moral imperatives voiced by my colleague have come to underwrite nearly every phase of literary study. For better or worse, gone is the time when English professors simply pursued their obscure interests, leaving political agendas to those who practiced what used to be called, somewhat dismissively, "advocacy" teaching. Such dreamy neutrality is no longer possible. Today *all* teaching, whether by design or not, is advocacy teaching. Thus arises an unsettling question for the midlife academic: what, exactly, is a person who teaches Milton—who actually *likes* Milton—advocating?

This is a big issue—and like all big issues, it is best handled indirectly. Besides, I must be true to my race, class, ethnicity, religion, age, and especially sex (or is it gender?). Accordingly, I cannot conceive of moral contestation without visualizing a ballpark. The stands are packed, and all the literary greats are taking a turn at bat. Led to the plate by the batboy (this nondescript figure has a beard and wears black jeans), the blind and stumbling Milton, swimming in a baggy uniform with "Cambridge" written in old-timey script across the shirt, takes his stance—I've pointed him in the right direction—and waits, his lips moving in silent patter. He knows that currency is at stake, a continued spot on the canonical roster. The pitcher's name is Youth; she's a left-hander who throws heat with a side-armed delivery. His stomach roiling from swallowing juice from a plug of tobacco that some jokester gave him in the dugout, Milton appears dizzy and disoriented. His head bends down in deep concentration. As Youth delivers her first pitch and the crowd roars, he tries to block out the noise so he can pick up on the hiss of the ball and get his bat in front of it. At the critical moment his mouth pops open and the bat flails outward with a jerk.

Baseball riffs are about as hip as I can manage. Since I invoke them in class in my own bid for currency (soccer analogies would work better these days), I might as well use them here. Hardly a poet who "teaches himself," Milton's first strike is his personality—or rather, how his personality is popularly seen. Modern taste in heroes runs toward action figures, and when viewed through these lenses, Milton looks like a man who only stood and waited. He had absorbed too much classical balance—he'd irritate us by calling it *nihil nimis*—to be a wild-eyed zealot of the moment. Not for him that species of fervor which makes people uproot their lives and sail to the ends of the earth, like his New England co-religionists. Known at Cambridge as the "Lady" of Christ's College, this was not a guy to pilot a codboat, clear a forest, or sing Psalms a capella in a clapboard-sheathed meeting house in the middle of a howling wilderness.

Besides, the Puritan government needed all the cooler heads it could muster: now was no time for moderates to bail out. Almost immediately after throwing himself into political life as a translator of diplomatic correspondence, Milton watched his dream of Puritan rule begin to go south. His eyesight began to fail in the 1650s, and when the divided nation recalled Charles II from exile and the more rabid Dissenters headed for the hills, including hills in Massachusetts and Connecticut, he was stone blind and too old to start a new life.

I suppose there is something pathetic about Milton's career, especially to young people demanding unambiguous action. Nike, after all, tells them to "Just Do It," not "Just Write It." Maybe it is true that a middle-aged sense of limitations is necessary for finding something gutsy about the man, toiling away on the great Puritan epic af-

555

ter the cause was hopelessly lost. Politically and theologically, *Paradise Lost* was a poem too late, proclaiming the cosmic order that should have served as the Cromwellians' political blueprint when they had the chance. But if the possibilities for collective action were dead, individuals could still watch and pray, working out their own salvation in fear and trembling. A poem lining out God's mysterious ways might help.

Writing a Protestant epic may have seemed like a good idea at the time, but from today's perspective, Milton's decision produces only the loud whiff of strike two. Religion does not rank high on the scale of currently acceptable activisms, and Christianity, both as a religion and as a cultural system, has never held lower standing in academia. Issues that defined Milton's very identity have become campus yawners, and even those students with religious inclinations are less than pleased with Milton's theology. Their God reflects a late-twentieth-century version of Romanticized Deism; he is a benign watchmaker with unconditional love in his heart. A God like Milton's stern Covenant-keeper, who imposes strictures and then has the audacity to enforce them, makes many of my students positively livid. They take this God personally, as if remembering Dad's claw-like grip on the car keys when they were unjustly grounded. I do my best to explain Milton's theology, which was based on the now-radical notion that humanity was flawed but divinity was not. "It's just not fair," they reply.

"Life isn't either," I could add—but I don't. Why visit middle-aged cynicism on a roomful of kids? Instead, I fall back on history. This was what Milton thought: should he have lied about his beliefs in order to please readers who wouldn't be born for another three centuries? The students' answer, when I press them, is often yes. At root, a good poem says what they think, while a bad poem says something else. "I can relate to it" is the supreme aesthetic compliment, nearly synonymous with "It flows well." Here's another current aesthetic dictum: a good poem can be responded to immediately, while a bad poem makes you look something up, thereby shattering your "enjoyment." Guess how Milton fares on this one. Those constant jumps between text and explanatory notes make my students less than patient with the density of Milton's allusions. For children of Madison Avenue, network programming, and the in-crowd smarminess of MTV, tradition is something to sweep away prior to drawing breath. Believers in the New and—a minute later—the Newer, they have trouble understanding that tradition once helped writers connect with readers rather than excluding them. For them, a tradition cannot be a site of personal authenticity, a place where individual identities situate themselves and individual voices emerge. Milton, they conclude, must have larded his poems with obscure references in order to show off.

That's strike three, and technically, the Big Guy should be sitting down. But so revered a figure surely deserves more than three strikes, so Youth indulgently throws a few more. A devotee of order in all things sacred and profane, Milton based the social fabric of *Paradise Lost* on a pervasive symbiosis of unequal parties: divine and human, Christ and Satan, saved and damned, and yes, male and female. Milton's assumptions about gender are real sticking points—so real, in fact, that many students can't get beyond them. I find myself explaining the same hard truth that has been dogging me so much lately: times have changed. Students grasp the concept in the abstract, but if Milton was so great, why didn't he see which way they would change and get with the program? I tell them that compared with most thinkers of his day, he *did*; he wrote, for instance, in defense of women's education and liberalized divorce laws. But time and place allowed his thinking to go only so far. For young people, who often don't consider themselves to be constrained by anything, this is a hard lesson, and it stinks of excuse. *They've* made correct moral choices, and anyone who hasn't—or didn't—is culpable, a sellout to stale custom. Despite the historical anachronism of this argument, it has the snap of a split-fingered fastball. With strike four, the crowd is growing impatient.

Strike five—the last one Milton gets—stems not so much from who he was as from what he became. As Harold Bloom long ago pointed out, subsequent poets in English could scarcely have had a more intimidating father. Even if most undergrads are unaware of Bloom's overwrought "ephebes," sufficient authority can be detected in Milton's voice to keep a class of youngbloods sulking for an entire semester. This is no poet of affability, no gentle promoter of finding your private bliss. There are no market surveys or pauses for feedback, no lines like "So spake the Son unto the Throne Divine,/But now, dear Reader, tell me how *Thou* feelst." Add to Milton's magisterial surety his rigorous theology and didactic aims and you've got a poet who really *is*, in some ways, everybody's Dad, though eloquent and thus an especially frustrating adversary. Try generating sympathy

557

for such a figure in a roomful of post-adolescents. On bad days try sympathizing with him yourself. When the old man nearly falls down on his final swing, I find myself coming very close to not caring. It would be easy to lose sympathy for this man who made things so hard for himself, so hard for me.

Eight years ago I moved to a small college with no seventeenth-century specialist in the English department, and once again, I can offer Milton as often as I want. But *do* I want? A younger colleague recently told me that after she read some Milton in junior high, she never saw any reason to read him again. I tried to smile indulgently, embarrassed at being made to feel as old as a Moon rock. Even more disturbing was my colleague's bright certainty, her enviable sense that the Milton Question had been settled. A little miffed, as I usually am when faced with dogmatisms of any kind, I couldn't resist a dinosaur's retort: "Milton has gotten better since you were in junior high." If a fellow English professor can dismiss our guy so easily, what about the young charges sitting in my class? Is it worth the trouble to keep Milton alive? What, exactly, *is* at stake?

That last question, embarrassingly self-important, threatens to turn the teaching of Milton into a mission. That's a trap that the old unwittingly allow the young to put them in, a slippery slope toward pomposity and counter-dogmatisms—and who needs more of that? I'm perfectly willing to trash the traditional justifications for Milton's place in the canon. I never believed that reading him would make you a better person; a glance at some of the older denizens of any English department, who received their Milton in full measure somewhere along the line, gives the lie to that. As for collective betterment, the genteel liberalism that Milton was supposed to foster in the education of responsible citizens was wrongheaded from the start. Liberal openness wasn't exactly what he stood for, and try as we might, he can't be bent into an apostle of tolerance in any modern sense of the word. One glance at the Papal-like trappings he gave to the infernal palace of Pandaemonium will tell you that he was a moderate only in seventeenth-century terms, not in ours.

Nor do I believe that Milton remains essential to "cultural literacy," that bag of stuff that every educated person should supposedly know. He still appears on lists of Great Writers, but such lists are patronizing at best: "These are the books *I've* read," they suggest, "and if you want to turn out like me, you should read them too." What's more, it pains me to see someone whose writing I love being touted as a shill for good old days that never were. Students can live full lives without ever having struggled through Milton—and so, for better or worse, can faculty. The days are long past when someone could get snubbed at a dinner party—even an English department party—for missing a joking allusion to *Areopagitica*. Nowadays you can get snubbed for *making* one.

So much for better living through Milton, as reflected in a well-informed and morally upright citizenry. But what about taste and refinement? Can one's sense of beauty survive a neglect of Milton? Is a person who has read *Samson Agonistes* capable of mixing stripes and plaids? You bet. In fact, Milton's propensity to hold nothing back, if taken seriously as a model of taste, might well propel you into that aquamarine Hawaiian shirt with red and gold squid embroidered all over it. You may find yourself mesmerized by Milton's language, as I do, but that will have as much bearing on your day-to-day aesthetic life as having a taste for medieval cathedrals—nice places to visit, but terrible to live in. If anyone went around talking like Milton writes, he'd deserve—and yes, it would surely *be* a he—to be gagged and chained to protect us from his officious self. The inversions alone would drive you crazy, would they not?

I keep wanting to make a case for Milton, but the old arguments don't hold up anymore. No longer the great standard against which poetry must be judged, Milton has become the quintessential poet of our *un*ease, of all the things that we are not and probably never were. His brand of Christianity, if practiced today, would be a sure-fire ticket to extended therapy. And few would defend the class assumptions implicit in his aristocratic education, in the leisure necessary for feeling at home in the biblical and classical world in which he immersed himself. As a lower-middle-class kid from small-town Ohio, I had no natural birthright to that world, and would surely have been given the bum's rush from every chamber in Milton's Cambridge. Or consider the individualism we cherish: whenever someone tries to justify the ways of God to you, whether in an epic poem or on a streetcorner, there's not going to be much room for you to assert your particular self. As for gender, you might feel yours being either elevated to embarrassing dignity or effaced altogether in the crush of the neobiblical patriarchy that Milton promotes. And let's not even get into how "white" Milton is: as they say in the comedy clubs, forget about it.

There must be another way. If Milton is to be defended at all, he's going to have to be defended for his very weirdness, for the full consummation of his demotion from an imagined Us to a very real Other. There's rich irony—some would say comeuppance—in his transformation from Great Poet to curricular underdog. But underdog he is, and to claim otherwise is to cling to an elitist projection that has long since unravelled, with little to mourn about it. Milton is long past saving as a normative figure, as an icon of artistic and ethical standards once trumpeted in him, and while I'm grateful for that, I'm *not* grateful that we've tossed out the verbal baby with the politically dingy bathwater. Besides, isn't this particular battle over? The repeated attacks at MLA on an elitist fantasy in which Milton is central have become collective thwacks at the deadest of horses. If we want to tell the truth, we'd better start admitting that Milton has become the literary equivalent of the snail darter.

Milton has become magnificent in his irrelevance, in his alienation from our words and music. It might be time to save him for his *ab*normality, for his unyielding alterity. When the Bastille was razed Paris was left with only a vast, lackluster plaza. A midlife academic, perhaps grasping for straws, might make a similar case for preserving Milton and even for guiding the occasional tour. Such an academic might even insist that we run terrible risks whenever we throw something human away. Consider the snail darters of the air—or is it the sea? Is not a once-great writer, however impugned or antiquated, worth more than these?

Whenever I try to justify Milton's ways, whether to students or to myself, I realize that Milton fascinates me precisely because I never *could* "relate" to him. He was unlike me and anyone I ever knew. He didn't even *talk* like regular people, and seemingly made no attempt to do so. It was, in fact, the august rhythms of his voice that hooked me—the words spun out and piled up and interlocked to create a vast picture from another world. A case could be made, I suppose, that he has been rightly punished for his obsession with classical order and Protestant zeal, driven off into the desert as a subjective scapegoat for the worst extremes of Anglo-American culture. But then there is still that magnificent language, those stately words, and the fiery images they create.

When did we start insisting that writers are unworthy unless they articulate our own beliefs? Does a poem have to be "true" to be great? If our answer is yes, then we'd better be prepared to relinquish the "fictive" core of all literature, the power of language to create realities that we can experience without accepting. Milton certainly didn't see his epic as a work of fiction, but that should not obscure the fictive quality it shares with other forms of writing that we happily accept as "made up." We don't have to accede to Milton's belief that what he was writing was the truth. Like any other artist, he made something and then walked away from it, leaving us alone with the work. The words on the page remain as language shaped in accordance with the poet's truth, and we are free to reject that truth even as we recognize how beautifully he conveyed it. This is perhaps the one unassailable part of Milton's legacy. Even though I don't buy Milton's causes, I find myself incapable of dismissing anyone who can use words the way he did. Surely the strength of anti-Milton sentiment, even among those who *have* read him, is testimony to the power of those words. People cannot hate what they don't feel.

I would like to have issued a pep-talk for Miltonists, but nothing that I've said will translate into anyone's lesson plans. These pulings are too subjective for *The Milton Quarterly* or one of those "Teaching Milton" panels at MLA, and it may be that I can articulate them only because I've reached that stage in life which brings natural sympathy for lost causes and abandoned paths. There's nothing particularly edifying about a middle-aged English professor catching up with himself, confronting a vague sense of loss that could assume no clear form until Milton's irrelevance finally made him face his own.

Maybe I've *always* liked Milton for his monumental untimeliness, his stubborn allegiance to things that are no more. His poetry invokes an entire world, but that world is not ours. Although it felt spacious enough to him, it would not afford us sufficient room to move, impossible as it is for most of us to conceive of an identity based on submission to a perfect God. Millions of people once took comfort in feeling so encompassed, but they are gone, too. Even Milton's dazzlingly austere God has crept sullenly away, reduced to a bad dream by Rationalism and Romanticism and Marxism and Freudianism and Modernism and Postmodernism and everything else that has made us who we are. We keep forgetting that the God of *Paradise Lost* simply cannot harm us anymore: to get angry or run off screaming at his depiction is to overreact badly, like Elvis shooting out a TV screen because he has chanced upon a PBS documentary about hummingbirds.

Still, Milton's stern countenance keeps peering down through the ages, challenging our fitful attempts at peace. In this he *is* a reproach, as he certainly intended to be. But as I keep telling my students in that endless mantra of my Milton course, times have changed. Milton can't get to us any more than his God can. Indeed, it may be supreme testimony to his power as a writer that we still keep expecting him to leap off the page and reduce us to sheep-like believers. Once you get past this fear and realize that you don't have to accept his religion, you just might find yourself admiring his integrity in sticking his neck out for it, in dedicating his talents to something that he thought was larger than himself. Admittedly, selflessness is not a frequently recognized trait in Milton, but behind the lofty bombast I loved at thirteen was a frighteningly gifted artist laboring to efface his own presence and to keep the spotlight on what he thought would get people into heaven. He was trying to do good in his world—and in his view, it was the greatest possible good. In this lies yet another irony: Milton, so long championed by advocates of "pure" aesthetic experience unsullied by the temporal pull of politics, placed himself squarely in the "advocacy" camp. For him and his postmodern deconstructors alike, moral improvement was what literature should be all about.

A final irony emerges in the contrast between Milton's traditionally intimidating presence and his own desire to subsume himself and his art within a larger purpose. His first readers wanted to experience this kind of selflessness, too, which is why *Paradise Lost* was an instant sensation. Later readers got swept up in the grandeur of the poem as a poem, savoring beautiful frames from a movie that they did not especially want to see. Even though we moderns, masters of self-absorption, find it hard to appreciate movies that we didn't make, here's a poet who forces us to do just that, line after line and speech after speech. In the degree to which Milton has become our Other, hating him might simply be yet another expression of the public incivility that we read about in the papers, an intellectual version of road rage.

A defense of Milton in modern times might reduce to platitudes, but at least they're true platitudes. The first is a lesson in charity: there's value in listening to people who differ from us, even if history has judged them to be losers. On this Milton's loudest critics would surely agree in principle, if not always in practice. The second is a lesson in self-confidence sorely needed by us moderns, who talk big but walk with appalling timidity: confronting another species of mind—another set of assumptions altogether—need not compel us to assume that our frail selves will melt into goo from the contact. These lessons in selfhood and otherness still seem worth conveying to young people. They might even serve as bracing counters to group-think, to feeling safe only in a crowd even when it is a crowd of rebels, baseball caps in a row. If obsolescence is the curse of aging professors, conformity is the curse of our young charges, and the obsession to fit in requires every opposing force we can muster.

We can learn something from Milton's daunting otherness, from the fruits of his disobedience to us and our needs. In this, too, lies the chief mantra of my Milton course. Times change, kids, and sometimes they change a lot. Whether you're a seventeenth-century Puritan or someone who teaches a seventeenth-century Puritan, the price you pay for odd enthusiasms is obsolescence. To accept this gracefully is, it seems to me, a lesson that middle-aged academics might demonstrate as well as teach, even if it means taking up voluntary residence on the dinosaur farm, tethered and toothless in quiet pasturage along with other English professors whose classes are to be avoided. An inevitable fate need not be without purpose. If middle-aged academics refuse to serve as foils for the young, as stodgy counterpoints to their airiness, who will? The midlife sense of being out of step might even prove a real plus for the teacher of so notorious an underdog. An open-eyed embracing of irrelevance might even result in an advocacy pedagogy of one's own, a version of identity politics suitable for those of us whose beards are graying, whose black jeans are sagging, and whose popculture references are drawing increasingly blank stares.

The political is the personal after all, even for a Milton teacher. There won't be any mermaids singing; they'll more likely be exchanging frowns or, at best, puzzled looks. But there are compensations in remembering that there's no shame in striking out, especially for a blind man whose sensitive ear has been rendered useless by a roaring crowd. There might even be a measure of redemption—that standing-and-waiting kind of service which Milton praised—in helping an old man back to the dugout, bringing him some Gatorade, and carefully replacing his unmarked bat in the rack. Naturally, Milton would be smart enough to see through any encouraging chatter, but I imagine myself offering it anyway: "We'll get 'em next time, John."

We probably won't. Still, I picture the old man asking when the next game is scheduled so he can by God *be* there. This part of the fantasy, at least, is accurate: love him or hate him, nobody can say that Milton didn't give it his best. Commitments to lost causes are sometimes worth preserving, and those who do so might permit themselves the quiet satisfaction of all unsung tasks. A Milton teacher might feel, at times, like a fence-rider on the King Ranch, a twister and cutter of barbed wire miles from the press and heat of living souls. Younger faculty may roll their eyes, the baseball hats in the back rows may get pulled down even lower, and enrollments may be less than cost-effective, but there's consolation in remembering that dutiful batboys learn humility—not a bad lesson for young and old alike.

Besides, as long as I have Milton to serve as *my* crotchety foil, I'll have room in which to age—and maybe even to act my age. A middle-aged academic, inspired by Milton's intractable hoariness, might learn to shed his own rabbit-ears and to ignore cat-calls echoing from the stands. A middle-aged academic might stop whining and accept with grace the untrodden paths he once chose, even if those paths mean standing up for bastards: the incorrect, the antiquated, or the just plain weird. A middle-aged academic might even recover a measure of hipness, however oblique and unrecognized it may be. If you're really into marginalized voices, have I got a poet for you! If you don't yet feel old enough to teach him, I just might be willing to take him off your hands. Any day, any time.

Nominated by The Antioch Review

SPECIAL MENTION

(The editors also wish to mention the following important works published by small presses last year. Listings are in no particular order.)

POETRY

The Rubber Ball—Regan Good (Fence)

St. Peregrinus Cancer—Judith Hall (Persea)

The Syphilis Diaries—Pamela Moore (Missouri Review)

Buffalo—Laura Kasischke (Missouri Review)

The Swarm—Maxine Scates (Prairie Schooner)

The Changing Face of AIDS—Rafael Campo (Massachusetts Review)

My First Yiddish Poem—Maggie Anderson (Women's Review of Books)

Parsing Hurricane—David Ray (Chariton Review)

Brown's Farm—Jim Daniels (Quarterly West)

Wind—Dana Levin (*In the Surgical Theater,* Copper Canyon)

Triptych, Circa 1492—Susan Tichy (Luna)

The Pillar—Mairead Byrne (Seneca Review)

The Tree—Peter Sacks (Denver Quarterly)

Composition for Violin—Melanie Carter (Antioch Review)

Home—Paul Breslin (TriQuarterly)

For My Wife on Our Sixth Anniversary—Tim Skeen (Pikeville Review)

Tavern Puzzles—R.T. Smith (Southern Humanities Review)

The Philistine—Jim Simmerman (*Kingdom Come,* Miami University Press)

Red String—Minnie Bruce Pratt (*Walking Up Depot Street,* University of Pittsburgh Press)

The Many Uses of Camouflage—Karen Donovan (*Fugitive Red*, University of Massachusetts Press)
December 14—David Lehman (Boston Review)
Love Poems to Amy—Ricky Garni (Oyster Boy Review)
Nainital—Tanuja Mehrotra (APA Journal)
There's Raspberries—Tomaz Salamun (Black Warrior Review)
The OED—Gabriel Gudding (American Poetry Review)

NONFICTION

The Year of the 49-Star Flag—Floyd Skloot (Boulevard)
Lessons In Fire—Mary Slowik (Iowa Review)
Kafka and Me—Emily Fox Gordon (Boulevard)
Guatemala—Sharman Apt Russell (Puerto del Sol)
Blind Spots—Norma Marder (Gettysburg Review)
Not At This Address—Lee Martin (Sun)
Seeking Evil, Finding Only Good—Melody Ermachild Chavis (Turning Wheel)
In Faculty Block Number Five—Julie Rold (Missouri Review)
A Eulogy of Sorts—Amy Gerstler (Seneca Review)
from Tumbling After—Susan Parker (Chattahoochee Review)
Wapiti School—Mark Spragg (High Plains Literary Review)
Jay Gatsby, Shane, Nevada Smith—Jonathan Veitch (Southwest Review)
My Last Therapist—Emily Fox Gordon (Salmagundi)
Shame and Forgetting in the Information Age—Charles Baxter (Graywolf Forum Three)
What Is Poetry To Do?—Reginald Gibbons (To Be: 2B)
Field Trips—Stuart Dybek (Bomb)
The Catcher—Paul Zimmer (Gettysburg Review)
Sleet—Tony Whedon (Western Humanities Review)
Temp: = @ Text . . . Rick Moody (Tin House)
On Rhyme—Anthony Hecht (Yale Review)
Ersatz Thoughts—Louise Glück (Threepenny Review)
W.G. Sebald: A Profile—James Atlas (Paris Review)
Leaving Latitude: Emily Dickinson and Indian Pipes—Barbara C. Mallonee (Georgia Review)
Poetcraft—John Balaban (Spillway Nine)
The Essayist Is Sorry For Your Loss—Sara Levine (Puerto del Sol)
Hart and Fangs—Eric Ormsby (Parnassus: Poetry In Review)

Sargent and James—Millicent Bell (Raritan Review)

Art—Rick Bass (*Brown Dog of the Yaak,* Milkweed Editions)

Covering the Mirror—John Berger (Threepenny Review)

Jerzy Kosinski at Columbia—Erich Goode (Raritan Review)

A Brief for the Epigram—David Barber (Parnassus: Poetry In Review)

FICTION

Whitey—Pamela Diamond (Southwest Review)

Theories of Rain—Andrea Barrett (Southern Review)

Milk—Racelle Rosett Schaefer (Lilth)

Pagan Days—Michael Rumaker (Oyster Boy Review)

Postwar—Joyce Johnson (Open City)

Tunnel Rat—H. Lee Barnes (Clackamas Literary Review)

Planet Balls—David Mangum (Oasis)

The Soul of the Gorilla—David Borofka (Idaho Review)

The Trouble With The Truth—Jonis Agee (Nebraska Review)

Greyhound—Jean Ryan (Pleiades)

Still Life With Shotgun and Oranges—Cynthia Shearer (Oxford American)

In The Shadow of Our House—Scott Blackwood (Boston Review)

Occam's Razor—Stephen Gibson (Georgia Review)

The Shoulder Season—Martha Hurwitz (Flyway)

from Leaving Pico—Frank X. Gaspar (University Press of New England)

The Photographer—Robert Coover (Fence)

My Brother Hansel—Diana Hartog (The American Voice)

Box—A. Manette Ansay (Nebraska Review)

The Most Honest Person—Richard Burgin (Shenandoah)

Detours—Stephen Dixon (Idaho Review)

Fondue—T.C. Boyle (Antioch Review)

Lycanthropy—Kermit Moyer (Hudson Review)

Body and Soul—Jean McGarry (Boulevard)

Somebody's Son—Thomas Barbash (Press)

Owl—Elizabeth Spencer (Ontario Review)

For A Long Time, This Was Griselda's Story—Anthony Doerr (North American Review)

Leaving Algiers—Claire Messud (News from The Republic of Letters)

Palisades—Antonya Nelson (Ploughshares)
Poor Millie—Debra Spark (Green Mountains Review)
The Gleaners—Pinckney Benedict (Story)
The Meeting—Lydia Davis (Joe)
Cavadduzzo's of Cicero—Tony Ardizzone (Agni)
The Persistence of Memory—Sharon Solwitz (Crazyhorse)
Moon People—Wendy Miyake (Bamboo Ridge)
Harriet Westbrook—Tim Lockette (WordWrights)
Indians—Jon Billman (Paris Review)
Boy At the Piano—Annie Dawid (American Fiction)
Nirvana—Harold Jaffe (Two Girls Review)
How In A Lifetime?—Sydney Lea (New England Review)
Boss Man—Cathy Day (American Fiction)
Pesthouse—Anthony Bukoski (*Polonaise*, Southern Methodist University Press)
Leadbelly In Paris—Madison Smartt Bell (Oxford American)
St. Jude In Persia—Lucia Perillo (The American Voice)
Nobile's Airship—Marshall Klimasewski (Yale Review)
The Sound Is So Shallow Here—Teresa S. Mathes (Georgia Review)
Back East—Emily Hammond (Ploughshares)
The Witness—Clifford Browder (Third Coast)
New People—Ann Hood (Gulf Coast)
No Place for Me, My Love—Naomi Myrvaagnes (Harvard Review)
Fulcrum—Andrea Louie (APA Journal)
Soy Paco—Julia MacDonnell (Heart)
Kwek—Sharon May Brown (Mānoa)
Desire Lines—Jacob Molyneux (Enoch)
These Hands—Kevin Brockmeier (Georgia Review)
Obituaries—Stephen Schottenfeld (Iowa Review)
Grasp Special Comb—Stephanie Rosenfeld (Missouri Review)
Vacation—Hal Herring (Ontario Review)
Stop Breaking Down—John McManus (Ploughshares)
Mannequin—Gordon Weaver (Agni)
Leopold's Daughter—Jodee Stanley Rubins (North Atlantic Review)
Radio Skip—Stephen Marion (Epoch)
Life During Wartime—Ellie Forgotson (Literal Latté)
The Lodger In 726—Meera Nair (Threepenny Review)
White Dwarfs—Lee Martin (Another Chicago Magazine)
Deacon—Atar Hadari (Larcom Review)
Minding Nellie—Andrew Weinstein (Boulevard)

Since My House Burned Down—Mary Yukari Waters (Glimmer Train)
Orchids—Stuart Dybek (Doubletake)
After The Beep—Cornelia Nixon (Gettysburg Review)
December Birthday—Barbara Klein Moss (New England Review)
Stalky the Clown—Ira Sadoff (TriQuarterly)
Please Help Find—Stewart O'Nan (Ploughshares)
This Is Your Life—Heidi Bell (Third Coast)
The Funeral Side—Bobbie Ann Mason (The Southern Review)
The Yearbook—Ron Nyren (Paris Review)
Centrifugal Force—Susan Neville (Louisville Review)
Ursula In Uruguay—Ingrid Hill (Black Warrior Review)
Spilling the Beans: A Letter to Linda Evangelista—George Garrett (Witness)
How Aliens Think—Judith Grossman (Ploughshares)
Eclipse—Latha Viswanathan (Shenandoah)
Gambling Therapy—Danny Cook (Greensboro Review)
Gunchers—Russ Franklin (Willow Springs)
This Is How The Worst Things Can Be Remembered—G.K. Wuori (Other Voices)
This Day With You—Leslie Pietrzyk (Natural Bridge)
An In-Between Season—Phyllis Sanchez Gussler (Prairie Schooner)
Blood On A Spear—Javier Marías (Zoetrope: All Story)
Goddess Love—Trudy Lewis (Five Points)
A Gem Squash—Rose Moss (Agni)
The Widow—Romulus Linney (Missouri Review)
The Coroner's Report—Jason Brown (TriQuarterly)
Stealing the Llama Farm—Nancy Zafris (Kenyon Review)
Sorrow—Janko Polić Kamov (Partisan Review)
Grace—Eileen Bartos (Georgia Review)
Spring—Elizabeth Tippens (Ploughshares)
The Hull Case—Peter Ho Davis (Ploughshares)
Happy Birthday, Gabriella—Joanna Scott (Southern Review)
My Grandmother's Tale of How Crab-o Lost His Head—Robert Antoni (Paris Review)
Crane's Grace—Maija Rhee Devine (Kenyon Review)
Jerusalem—Elizabeth Gaffney (North American Review)
The Bartender—Andre Dubus III (Glimmer Train)
The Solid Truth—Mark Wisniewski (Nebraska Review)
Remaining In Favor—Jill Bossert (Ploughshares)

In The Country of the Young—Daniel Stern (Boulevard)
Notes to My Biographer—Adam Haslett (Zoetrope: All Story)
A Doctor's Story—Peter Baida (Missouri Review)
The Bench—Mary Ruefle (Threepenny Review)
Dividing by Zero—Ron Nyren (North American Review)
The Saint and the Magician—Romulus Linney (Image)
Pimping the Wheel—Simone Spearman (ZYZZYVA)
The Naming of Parts—Gerald Shapiro (Witness)
Rapture—Andrea Bewick (Epoch)
A Tongue in Every Wound—Robert Boswell (Harvard Review)

PRESSES FEATURED IN THE PUSHCART PRIZE EDITIONS SINCE 1976

Acts
Agni Review
Ahsahta Press
Ailanthus Press
Alaska Quarterly Review
Alcheringa/Ethnopoetics
Alice James Books
Ambergris
Amelia
American Letters and Commentary
American Literature
American PEN
American Poetry Review
American Scholar
American Short Fiction
The American Voice
Amicus Journal
Amnesty International
Anaesthesia Review
Another Chicago Magazine
Antaeus
Antietam Review
Antioch Review
Apalachee Quarterly
Aphra
Aralia Press

The Ark
Art and Understanding
Arts and Letters
Artword Quarterly
Ascensius Press
Ascent
Aspen Leaves
Aspen Poetry Anthology
Assembling
Atlanta Review
Autonomedia
Avocet Press
The Baffler
Bakunin
Bamboo Ridge
Barlenmir House
Barnwood Press
The Bellingham Review
Bellowing Ark
Beloit Poetry Journal
Bennington Review
Bilingual Review
Black American Literature Forum
Black Rooster
Black Scholar
Black Sparrow

Black Warrior Review
Blackwells Press
Bloomsbury Review
Blue Cloud Quarterly
Blue Unicorn
Blue Wind Press
Bluefish
BOA Editions
Bomb
Bookslinger Editions
Boston Review
Boulevard
Boxspring
Bridges
Brown Journal of Arts
Burning Deck Press
Caliban
California Quarterly
Callaloo
Calliope
Calliopea Press
Calyx
Canto
Capra Press
Caribbean Writer
Carolina Quarterly
Cedar Rock
Center
Chariton Review
Charnel House
Chattahoochee Review
Chelsea
Chicago Review
Chouteau Review
Chowder Review
Cimarron Review
Cincinnati Poetry Review
City Lights Books
Clown War
CoEvolution Quarterly
Cold Mountain Press
Colorado Review

Columbia: A Magazine of Poetry and
    Prose
Confluence Press
Confrontation
Conjunctions
Connecticut Review
Copper Canyon Press
Cosmic Information Agency
Countermeasures
Counterpoint
Crawl Out Your Window
Crazyhorse
Crescent Review
Cross Cultural Communications
Cross Currents
Crosstown Books
Cumberland Poetry Review
Curbstone Press
Cutbank
Dacotah Territory
Daedalus
Dalkey Archive Press
Decatur House
December
Denver Quarterly
Domestic Crude
Doubletake
Dragon Gate Inc.
Dreamworks
Dryad Press
Duck Down Press
Durak
East River Anthology
Eastern Washington University Press
Ellis Press
Empty Bowl
Epoch
Ergo!
Exquisite Corpse
Faultline
Fiction
Fiction Collective

Fiction International
Field
Fine Madness
Firebrand Books
Firelands Art Review
First Intensity
Five Fingers Review
Five Points Press
Five Trees Press
The Formalist
Fourth Genre
Frontiers: A Journal of Women Studies
Gallimaufry
Genre
The Georgia Review
Gettysburg Review
Ghost Dance
Gibbs-Smith
Glimmer Train
Goddard Journal
David Godine, Publisher
Graham House Press
Grand Street
Granta
Graywolf Press
Green Mountains Review
Greenfield Review
Greensboro Review
Guardian Press
Gulf Coast
Hanging Loose
Hard Pressed
Harvard Review
Hayden's Ferry Review
Hermitage Press
Hills
Holmgangers Press
Holy Cow!
Home Planet News
Hudson Review
Hungry Mind Review
Icarus

Icon
Iguana Press
Indiana Review
Indiana Writes
Intermedia
Intro
Invisible City
Inwood Press
Iowa Review
Ironwood
Jam To-day
The Journal
The Kanchenjuga Press
Kansas Quarterly
Kayak
Kelsey Street Press
Kenyon Review
Kestrel
Latitudes Press
Laughing Waters Press
Laurel Review
L'Epervier Press
Liberation
Linquis
Literal Latté
The Literary Review
The Little Magazine
Living Hand Press
Living Poets Press
Logbridge-Rhodes
Louisville Review
Lowlands Review
Lucille
Lynx House Press
The MacGuffin
Magic Circle Press
Malahat Review
Mānoa
Manroot
Many Mountains Moving
Marlboro Review
Massachusetts Review

McSweeney's
Meridian
Mho & Mho Works
Micah Publications
Michigan Quarterly
Mid-American Review
Milkweed Editions
Milkweed Quarterly
The Minnesota Review
Mississippi Review
Mississippi Valley Review
Missouri Review
Montana Gothic
Montana Review
Montemora
Moon Pony Press
Mount Voices
Mr. Cogito Press
MSS
Mudfish
Mulch Press
Nada Press
New America
New American Review
New American Writing
The New Criterion
New Delta Review
New Directions
New England Review
New England Review and Bread Loaf
    Quarterly
New Letters
New Virginia Review
New York Quarterly
New York University Press
News from The Republic of Letters
Nimrod
9 × 9 Industries
North American Review
North Atlantic Books
North Dakota Quarterly
North Point Press
Northern Lights

Northwest Review
Notre Dame Review
O. ARS
O. Blēk
Obsidian
Obsidian II
Oconee Review
October
Ohio Review
Old Crow Review
Ontario Review
Open City
Open Places
Orca Press
Orchises Press
Orion
Other Voices
Oxford American
Oxford Press
Oyez Press
Oyster Boy Review
Painted Bride Quarterly
Painted Hills Review
Paris Press
Paris Review
Parnassus: Poetry in Review
Partisan Review
Passages North
Penca Books
Pentagram
Penumbra Press
Pequod
Persea: An International Review
Pipedream Press
Pitcairn Press
Pitt Magazine
Pleiades
Ploughshares
Poet and Critic
Poet Lore
Poetry
Poetry East
Poetry Ireland Review

Poetry Northwest
Poetry Now
Prairie Schooner
Prescott Street Press
Press
Promise of Learnings
Provincetown Arts
Puerto Del Sol
Quarry West
The Quarterly
Quarterly West
Raccoon
Rainbow Press
Raritan: A Quarterly Review
Red Cedar Review
Red Clay Books
Red Dust Press
Red Earth Press
Red Hen Press
Release Press
Review of Contemporary Fiction
Revista Chicano-Riquena
Rhetoric Review
River Styx
Rowan Tree Press
Russian *Samizdat*
Salmagundi
San Marcos Press
Sarabande Books
Sea Pen Press and Paper Mill
Seal Press
Seamark Press
Seattle Review
Second Coming Press
Semiotext(e)
Seneca Review
Seven Days
The Seventies Press
Sewanee Review
Shankpainter
Shantih
Sheep Meadow Press
Shenandoah

A Shout In the Street
Sibyl-Child Press
Side Show
Small Moon
The Smith
Solo
Solo 2
Some
The Sonora Review
Southern Poetry Review
Southern Review
Southwest Review
Spectrum
The Spirit That Moves Us
St. Andrews Press
Story
Story Quarterly
Streetfare Journal
Stuart Wright, Publisher
Sulfur
The Sun
Sun & Moon Press
Sun Press
Sunstone
Sycamore Review
Tamagwa
Tar River Poetry
Teal Press
Telephone Books
Telescope
Temblor
The Temple
Tendril
Texas Slough
Third Coast
13th Moon
THIS
Thorp Springs Press
Three Rivers Press
Threepenny Review
Thunder City Press
Thunder's Mouth Press
Tia Chucha Press

Tikkun
Tombouctou Books
Toothpaste Press
Transatlantic Review
TriQuarterly
Truck Press
Undine
Unicorn Press
University of Georgia Press
University of Illinois Press
University of Iowa Press
University of Massachusetts Press
University of North Texas Press
University of Pittsburgh Press
University of Wisconsin Press
Unmuzzled Ox
Unspeakable Visions of the
    Individual
Vagabond
Vignette
Virginia Quarterly
Volt

Wampeter Press
Washington Writers Workshop
Water Table
Western Humanities Review
Westigan Review
White Pine Press
Wickwire Press
Willow Springs
Wilmore City
Witness
Word Beat Press
Word-Smith
Wormwood Review
Writers Forum
Xanadu
Yale Review
Yardbird Reader
Yarrow
Y'Bird
Zeitgeist Press
Zoetrope: All-Story
ZYZZYVA

CONTRIBUTING SMALL PRESSES FOR PUSHCART PRIZE XXV

A

Acorn Whistle—907 Brewster Ave., Beloit, WI 53511
Agni—236 Bay State Rd., Boston, MA 02215
Alaska Quarterly Review—3211 Providence Dr., Anchorage, AK 99508
Always in Season—P.O. Box 380403, Brooklyn, NY 11238
American Letters & Commentary—850 Park Ave., New York, NY 10021
American Literary Review—Univ. of North Texas, Denton, TX 76203
Antietam Review—41 S. Potomac St., Hagerstown, MD 21740
Antioch Review—P.O. Box 148, Yellow Springs, OH 45387
Apogee Press—P.O. Box 8177, Berkeley, CA 94707
Arctos Press—P.O. Box 401, Sausalito, CA 94966
Artful Dodge—Eng. Dept., College of Wooster, Wooster, OH 44691
Artword Quarterly—5273 Portland Ave., White Bear Lake, MN 55110
Ascent—Concordia College, 901 8th St. S, Moorhead, MN 56562
Asian American Writers' Workshop—37 St. Mark's Pl., New York, NY 10003
Atheneum Press—P.O. Box 600793, Jacksonville, FL 32260
Atlanta Review—P.O. Box 8248, Atlanta, GA 31106
The Aurorean—P.O. Box 519, Sagamore Beach, MA 02562
Axe Factory Review—P.O. Box 40691, Philadelphia, PA 19107

B

Baacchor—2555 Huntington Dr., ste. 235, San Marino, CA 91108
The Baffler—P.O. Box 278293, Chicago, IL 60637
Quentin Baker, Publisher—678 Atherton Pl., Hayward, CA 94541
The Baltimore Review—P.O. Box 410, Riderwood, MD 21139
Bamboo Ridge Press—P.O. Box 61781, Honolulu, HI 96839
Bananafish—P.O. Box 381332, Cambridge, MA 02238
Barrow Street—P.O. Box 2017, Old Chelsea Sta., New York, NY 10113
The Battery Review—2466 Hilgard Ave., #205, Berkeley, CA 94709
Baybury Review—40 High St., Highwood, IL 60040
Beloit Poetry Journal—24 Berry Cove Rd., Lemoine, ME 04605
Bellingham Review—Western Washington Univ., Bellingham, WA 98228
Bellowing Ark Press—P.O. Box 55564, Shoreline, WA 98155

Berkeley Fiction Review—201 Heller Lounge, UC, Berkeley, CA 94720
Binx Street—131 Felix St., Box #1, Santa Cruz, CA 95060
Bitter Oleander Press—4983 Tall Oaks Dr., Fayetteville, NY 13066
BkMk Press—Univ. of Missouri, Kansas City, MO 64110
Black Hat Press—508 2nd Ave., Goodhue, MN 55027
Black Warrior Review—P.O. Box 862936, Tuscaloosa, AL 35486
Blue Begonia Press—225 S. 15th Ave., Yakima, WA 98902
Blue Collar Review—P.O. Box 11417, Norfolk, VA 23517
BOA Editions, Ltd.—260 East Ave., Rochester, NY 14604
Boston Review—E53-407 MIT, Cambridge, MA 02139
Bottomfish Magazine—21250 Stevens Creek Blvd., Cupertino, CA 95014
Boulevard—508 N. Plum Pt. Dr., Exton, PA 19341
The Briarcliff Review—P.O. Box 2100, Sioux City, IA 51104
Bright Hill Press—P.O. Box 193, Treadwell, NY 13846
Brilliant Corners—Lycoming College, Williamsport, PA 17701
Broken Boulder Press—P.O. Box 172, Lawrence, KS 66044
Byline—P.O. Box 130596, Edmond, OK 73018

C

Calyx—216 SW Madison, Corvallis, OR 97339
The Caribbean Writer—Univ. of Virgin Islands, RR-2, 10000 Kingshill, St. Croix, U.S. Virgin Islands, 00850
Carolina Quarterly—Univ. of North Carolina, Chapel Hill, NC 27599
Cassowary Press—P.O. Box 10312, Burbank, CA 91510
Cedar Hill Review—3722 Hwy. 8, West, Mesa, AZ 71953
The Chariton Review—Truman State Univ., Kirksville, MO 63501
Chapiteau Press—24 Blue Moon Rd., South Stafford, VT 05070
The Chattahoochee Review—2101 Womack Rd., Dunwoody, GA 30338
Chelsea—Box 773, Cooper Sta., New York, NY 10276
Chicago Review—Univ. of Chicago, 5801 S. Kenwood Ave., Chicago, IL 60637
Chiron Review—702 N. Prairie, Saint John, KS 67576
City Lights—261 Columbus Ave., San Francisco, CA 94133
Clackamas Literary Review—19600 S. Molalla Ave., Oregon City, OR 97045
Cleveland State University Poetry Center—Eng. Dept., Cleveland, OH 44114
Coastwise Press—56 Green St., Thomaston, ME 04861
Colorado Review—Colorado State Univ., Fort Collins, CO 80523
Columbia—Dodge Hall, Columbia Univ., 2960 Broadway, New York, NY 10027
The Comstock Review—4958 St. John Dr., Syracuse, NY 13215
Confrontation—Eng. Dept., C.W. Post Campus, L.I.U., Brookville, NY 11548
Conjunctions—Bard College, Annandale-on-Hudson, NY 12504
Connecticut Review—Southern Connecticut State Univ., New Haven, CT 06515
Conspire—201 Astor, Lansing, MI 48910
Crab Orchard Review—Southern Illinois Univ., Carbondale, IL 62901
Cream City Review—English Dept., Univ. of Wisconsin, Milwaukee, WI 53201
Creative Nonfiction—5501 Walnut St., Ste. 202, Pittsburgh, PA 15232
Curbstone Press—321 Jackson St., Willimantic, CT 06226
CutBank—Univ. of Montana, Missoula, MT 59802

D

Dalkey Archive Press—ISU Campus Box 4241, Normal, IL 61790
Dancing Moon Press—P.O. Box 832, Newport, OR 97365

John Daniel & Co.—P.O. Box 21922, Santa Barbara, CA 93121
Daybreak—P.O. Box 33952, Granada Hills, CA 91394
DeeMar Communications—6325-9 Falls of Neuse Rd., Ste. 320, Raleigh, NC 27615
Defined Providence—34A Wawayanda Rd., Warwick, NY 10990
Devil Blossoms—P.O. Box 5122, Seabrook, NJ 08302
The Distillery—Motlow College, P.O. Box 8500, Lynchburg, TN 37352
DoubleTake—55 Davis Sq., Somerville, MA 02144
Downtown Brooklyn—Long Island Univ., One Univ. Plaza, Brooklyn, NY 11201
Dream Horse Press—P.O. Box 640746, San Jose, CA 95134

E

The East Village.com—185 Suffolk St., Cambridge, MA 02139
Eastern Washington University Press—Cheney, WA 99201
Ekphrasis—P.O. Box 161236, Sacramento, CA 95816
Enterzone—1017 Bayview Ave., Oakland, CA 94610
Epoch—Cornell Univ., 251 Goldwin Smith, Ithaca, NY 14853
Eureka Literary Magazine—Eureka College, Eureka, IL 61530
Event—P.O. Box 2503, New Westminster, B.C., *CANADA* V3L 5B2

F

F Magazine—600 S. Michigan Ave., Chicago, IL 60605
Faultline—English Dept., UC, Irvine, CA 92697
Fence—14 Fifth Ave., #1A, New York, NY 10011
Field—Oberlin College, 10 N. Professor St., Oberlin, OH 44074
51%—3002 Elmira Bay, Costa Mesa, CA 92626
Finishing Line Press—P.O. Box 1016, Cincinnati, OH 45201
First Intensity Magazine—P.O. Box 665, Lawrence, KS 66044
Fithian Press—P.O. Box 1525, Santa Barbara, CA 93102
580 SPLIT—P.O. Box 9982, Mills College, Oakland, CA 94613
Five Points—Georgia State Univ., Univ. Plaza, Atlanta, GA 30303
Floating Bridge Press—P.O. Box 18814, Seattle, WA 98118
The Florida Review—Univ. of Central Florida, Orlando, FL 32816
Flyway—Iowa State University, Ames, IA 50011
Foliage—P.O. Box 687, Yarmouth, ME 04096
Folly Cove Books—P.O. Box 7116, Gloucester, MA 01930
The Formalist—320 Hunter Dr., Evansville, IN 47711
Fourth Genre—229 Bessey Hall, Michigan State Univ., E. Lansing, MI 48824
Free Lunch—P.O. Box 7647, Laguna Niguel, CA 92607
Frith Press—P.O. Box 161236, Sacramento, CA 95816
Fugue—Univ. of Idaho, Moscow, ID 83844
Future of Freedom Foundation—11350 Random Hills Rd, Ste. 800, Fairfax, VA 22030
Futures Magazine—3039 38th Ave. S, Minneapolis, MN 55406

G

Gargoyle Magazine—2308 Mt. Vernon Ave., Alexandria, VA 22301
A Gathering of the Tribes—P.O. Box 20693, Tompkins Sq. Sta., NY, NY 10009
George & Mertie's Place—P.O. Box 10335, Spokane, WA 99209

The Georgia Review—Univ, of Georgia, Athens, GA 30602
The Germ—P.O. Box 2543, Providence, RI 02906
Gettysburg Review—Gettysburg College, Gettysburg, PA 17325
GGM Press—206 E.4th St., Deer Park, NY 11729
Glimmer Train—710 SW Madison St., Ste. 504, Portland, OR 97205
Global City Review—CCNY, 138 & Convent Aves., New York, NY 10031
Gorrión Press—P.O. Box 1013, New York, NY 10040
Gravity Presses—27030 Havelock, Dearborn Heights, MI 48127
Green Bean Press—P.O. Box 237, New York, NY 10013
Green Boat Press—P.O. Box 135, Manlius, NY 13104
Green Hills Literary Lantern—P.O. Box 375, Trenton, MO 64683
Green Mountains Review—Johnson State College, Johnson, VT 05656
The Greensboro Review—P.O. Box 26170, Greensboro, NC 27402
Guernica—P.O. Box 117, Sta. P, Toronto, Ont., *CANADA* M5S 2S6
Gulf Coast—English Dept., Univ. of Houston, Houston, TX 77204

H

Haight Ashbury Literary Journal—558 Joost Ave., San Francisco, CA 94127
Halemary Press—423 E. Ellis St., East Syracuse, NY 13057
Hampton Shorts—P.O. Box 1229, Watermill, NY 11976
Hanover Press, Ltd.,—P.O. Box 596, Newtown, CT 06470
HAPPY—240 E. 35th St., 11A, New York, NY 10016
Hard Row to Ho—P.O. Box 541-1, Healdsburg, CA 95448
Harvard Review—Harvard College Library, Cambridge, MA 02138
Hayden's Ferry Review—Arizona State Univ., Tempe, AZ 85287
Hawaii Pacific Review—1060 Bishop St., Honolulu, HI 96813
Heart—P.O. Box 81308, Pittsburgh, PA 15217
Helicon Nine Editions—P.O. Box 22412, Kansas City, MO 64113
Heliotrope—Box 20037, Spokane, WA 99204
The Higginsville Reader—P.O. Box 141, Three Bridges, NJ 08887
High Plains Literary Review—180 Adams St., #250, Denver, CO 80206
Howlin' Wolf Press—P.O. Box 2183, Gaithersburg, MD 20886
Hubbub—Reed College, 3203 SE Woodstock Blvd, Portland, OR 97202
The Hudson Review—684 Park Avenue, New York, NY 10021
Hutton Publications—P.O. Box 2907, Decatur, IL 62524

I

The Iconoclast—1675 Amazon Rd., Mohegan Lake, NY 10547
The Idaho Review—1910 University Dr., Boise, ID 83725
Illumination Arts Publ. Co—P.O. Box 1865, Bellevue, WA 98005
Image—323 S. Broad St., P.O. Box 674, Kennett Square, PA 19348
Indiana Review—Indiana Univ., Bloomington, IN 47405
The Iowa Review—Univ. of Iowa, Iowa City, IA 52242
Italian Americana—Univ. of Rhode Island, 80 Washington St., Providence, RI 02903

J

Jewish Currents—22 E. 17th St., Ste. 601, New York, NY 10003
The Journal—English Dept., Ohio State Univ., Columbus, OH 43210
Journal of African Travel-Writing—P.O. Box 346, Chapel Hill, NC 27514
Journal of New Jersey Poets—214 Center Grove Rd., Randolph, NJ 07869

K

Kalliope—Florida Community College, 3939 Roosevelt Blvd., Jacksonville, FL 32205
Kelsey Review—Mercer County College, P.O. Box B, Trenton, NJ 08690
The Kenyon Review—Kenyon College, Gambier, OH 43022
Kimera—N. 1316 Hollis St., Spokane, WA 99201

L

The Lantern—Westover School, Middlebury, CT 06762
The Larcom Review—P.O. Box 161, Prides Crossing, MA 01965
Laurel Review—Northwest Missouri State Univ., Maryville, MO 64468
Licking River Review—Nunn Drive, Highland Heights, KY 41099
Literal Latte—61 East 8th St., Ste. 240, New York, NY 10003
Livingston Press—Station 22, UWA, Livingston, AL 35470
Loess Hills Books, RR1, Box 189, Farragut, IA 51639
Long Island Quarterly—P.O. Box 114, Northport, NY 11768
Lost Coast—155 Cypress St., Fort Bragg, CA 95437
Lynx Eye—1880 Hill Dr., Los Angeles, CA 90041

M

The MacGuffin—Schoolcraft College, 18600 Haggerty Rd., Livonia, MI 48152
Mammoth Books—7 S. Juniata St., DuBois, PA 15801
Mandrake—P.O. Box 792, Larkspur, CA 94977
Manoa—Univ. of Hawaii, 1733 Donaghho Rd., Honolulu, HI 96822
Many Beaches Press—1527 N. 36th St., Sheboygan, WI 53081
The Marlboro Review—P.O. Box 243, Marlboro, VT 05344
Mars Hill Review—P.O. Box 10506, Bainbridge Island, WA 98110
Martin House—2003 Corral Dr., Houston, TX 77090
Medicinal Purposes—86-37 120th St., #2D, Richmond Hill, NY 11418
Meridian—Univ. of Virginia, P.O. Box 400121, Charlottesville, VA 22904
MHO & MHO Works—Box 33135, San Diego, CA 92103
Michigan Quarterly Review—Univ. of Michigan, Ann Arbor, MI 48109
Mid-American Review—Bowling Green State Univ., Bowling Green, OH 43403
Middlemarch Publishing—P.O. Box 3605, Alpine, WY 83128
Mid-List Press—4324 12th Ave. S, Minneapolis, MN 55407
Milkweed Editions—430 First Ave. N, Ste. 668, Minneapolis, MN 55401
Mind in Motion Publications—P.O. Box 1701, Bishop, CA 93515
Mind the Gap—19 N. 11th St., C-A, Brooklyn, NY 11211
Mississippi Review—Univ. of Southern Mississippi, Hattiesburg, MS 39406
The Missouri Review—Univ. of Missouri, Columbia, MO 65211
Mount Voices—c/o Harrison, 620 W. 34th St., Baltimore, MD 21211

N

Nassau Literary Review—Princeton Univ., Princeton, NJ 08544
Natural Bridge—Univ. of Missouri, 8001 Natural Bridge Rd., St. Louis, MO 63121
The Nebraska Review—Univ. of Nebraska, Omaha, NE 68182
New England Review, Middlebury College, Middlebury, VT 05753
New England Writers/Vermont Poets Assoc.—P.O. Box 483, Windsor, VT 05089
New Letters—Univ. of Missouri, 5101 Rockhill Rd., Kansas City, MO 64110
The New Orphic Review—1095 Victoria Dr., Vancouver, B.C., *CANADA* V5L 4G3
The New Renaissance—26 Hector Rd., Arlington, MA 02474
News from The Republic of Letters—120 Cushing Ave., Boston, MA 02125
New Rivers Press—420 N. 5th St., Ste. 938, Minneapolis, MN 55401
New Zoo Poetry Review—P.O. Box 36760, Richmond, VA 23235
Newcomb Publishers, Inc.—4812 N. Fairfax Dr., Arlington, VA 22203
Newton's Baby—788 Murphey St., Scottdale, GA 30079
Night Horn Books—P.O. Box 424906, San Francisco, CA 94142
Nightgaunt Press—P.O. Box 29-1991, Hollywood, CA 90029
Nightshade Press—P.O. Box 76, Troy, ME 04987
Nightsun—Frostburg State Univ., Frostburg, MD 21532
Nimrod International Journal—Univ. of Tulsa, 600 S. College Ave., Tulsa, OK 74104
The North American Review—Univ. of Northern Iowa, Cedar Falls, IA 50614
Northern Lights—P.O. Box 8084, Missouri, MT 59807
Northwest Review—Univ. of Oregon, Eugene, OR 97403
Notre Dame Review—Univ. of Notre Dame, Notre Dame, IN 46556

O

Oasis—P.O. Box 626, Largo, FL 33779
The Ohio Review—Ohio University, Athens, OH 45701
Old Crow—P.O. Box 403, Easthampton, MA 01027
Ontario Review—9 Honey Brook Dr., Princeton, NJ 08540
Open City—225 Lafayette St., Ste. 1114, New York, NY 10012
Orchises Press—P.O. Box 20602, Alexandria, VA 22320
Osiris—P.O. Box 297, Deerfield, MA 01342
Other Voices—Univ. of Illinois, 601 S. Morgan St., Chicago, IL 60607
Otter Bay Books—3507 Newland Rd., Baltimore, MD 21218
Oxford Magazine—Miami Univ., 356 Bachelor Hall, Oxford, OH 45056
Oyster Boy Review—P.O. Box 77842, San Francisco, CA 94107
O!!Zone—1266 Fountain View, Houston, TX 77057

P

Palo Alto Review—Palo Alto College, 1400 W. Villaret Blvd., San Antonio, TX 78224
Pangborn Books, Ltd.—2531 Ohio Ave., Youngstown, OH 44504
Pangolin Papers—P.O. Box 241, Nordland, WA 98358
Papyrus Publishing—P.O. Box 7144, Victoria, 3156, *AUSTRALIA*
Paris Press—P.O. Box 487, Ashfield, MA 01330
The Paris Review—541 E. 72nd St., New York, NY 10021
Parnassus—205 W. 89th St., Apt. 8F, New York, NY 10024
Partisan Review—236 Bay State Rd., Boston, MA 02215
Paterson Literary Review—Passaic Co. Community College, Passaic, NJ 07505

Pearl—3030 E. Second St., Long Beach, CA 90803
Penny Dreadful—P.O. Box 719, Radio City Sta., Hell's Kitchen, NY 10101
Peregrine—P.O. Box 1076, Amherst, MA 01004
The Permanent Press—4170 Novac Rd., Sag Harbor, NY 11963
Perugia Press—P.O. Box 108, Shutesbury, MA 01072
Phoebe—George Mason Univ., Fairfax, VA 22030
Pif Magazine—PMB 248, 4820 Yelm Hwy, SE, Ste. B, Lacey, WA 98503
The Pikeville Review—214 Sycamore St., Pikeville, KY 41501
Pine Grove Press—P.O. Box 85, Jamesville, NY 13078
Pleiades—English Dept., Central Missouri State Univ., Warrensburg, MO 64093
Ploughshares—Emerson College, 100 Beacon St., Boston, MA 02116
Poems & Plays—Middle Tennessee State Univ., Murfreesboro, TN 37132
Poet Lore—The Writer's Center, 4508 Walsh St., Bethesda, MD 20815
The Poetry Project—St. Mark's Church-in-the-Bowery, 131 E. 10th ST., New York, NY 10003
Polyphony Press—PMB 317, 207 E. Ohio St., Chicago, IL 60611
Porcupine Literary Arts Magazine—P.O. Box 259, Cedarburg, WI 53012
Pot Shard Press—P.O. Box 1363, Mendocino, CA 95460
Potomac Review—P.O. Box 354, Port Tobacco, MD 20677
Potpourri Publications—P.O. Box 8278, Prairie Village, KS 66208
Prairie Schooner—P.O. Box 880334, Lincoln, NE 68588
The Prairie Star—P.O. Box 923, Fort Collins, CO 80522
Primavera—Box 37—7547, Chicago, IL 60637
Puerto del Sol—New Mexico State Univ., Las Cruces, NM 88003

Q

QECE—406 Main St., #3C, Collegeville, PA 19426
Quarterly West—Univ. of Utah, Salt Lake City, UT 84112
Quaternity Press—255 Lafayette Ave., Staten Island, NY 10301

R

Rain Taxi—P.O. Box 3840, Minneapolis, MN 55403
Raritan—31 Mine St., New Brunswick, NJ 08903
Rattapallax—532 LaGuardia Pl., Ste. 353, New York, NY 10012
Rattle—13440 Ventura Blvd, #200, Sherman Oaks, CA 91423
RE:AL—Stephen F. Austin State Univ., P.O. Box 13007, SFA Sta., Nacogdoches, TX 75962
Reader's Break, see Pine Grove Press
Red Moon Press—P.O. Box 2461, Winchester, VA 22604
Red Raven Review—3808 Coronado Dr., Sarasota, FL 34231
Red Rock Review—Community College of So. Nevada, Las Vegas, NV 89102
Redfruit Press—P.O. Box 1549, Boyes Hot Springs, CA 95416
Ridgeway Press of Michigan—P.O. Box 120, Roseville, MI 48066
Riding the Meridian—7 Ernst Ave., Bloomfield, NJ 07003
River City—English Dept., Univ. of Memphis, Memphis, TN 38152
River King—P.O. Box 122, Freeburg, IL 62243
River Styx—634 N. Grand Blvd., St. Louis, MO 63103
Rosebud—P.O. Box 459, Cambridge, WI 53523

S

The Sacred Beverage Press—P.O. Box 10312, Burbank, CA 91510
Salt Hill—English Dept., Syracuse Univ., Syracuse, NY 13244
San Saba Press—9739 Denton Dr., Dallas, TX 75220
Santa Barbara Review—P.O. Box 808, Summerland, CA 93067
Santa Monica Review—Santa Monica College, 1900 Pico Blvd., Santa Monica, CA 90405
Sarabande Books—2234 Dundee Rd., Ste. 200, Louisville, KY 40205
Scrivener Creative Review—853 Sherbrooke St. W, Montreal, Que., *CANADA* H3A 2T6
Seal Press—3131 Western Ave., #410, Seattle, WA 98121
Seeking the Muse—P.O. Box 650, Cerro Gordo, IL 61818
Seneca Review—Hobart & William Colleges, Geneva, NY 14456
Sensations Magazine—2 Radio Ave., A-5, Secaucus, NJ 07094
SERA Publishing—P.O. Box 284, Los Gatos, CA 95031
Shenandoah—Washington & Lee Univ., Lexington, VA 24450
Sightings—190-15 Merrick Rd., Amityville, NY 11701
Skylark—2200 169th St., Hammond, IN 46323
Slipstream—P.O. Box 2071, Niagara Falls, NY 14301
Slugfest, Ltd.—P.O. Box 1238, Simpsonville, SC 29681
Somersault Press—404 Vista Heights Rd., Richmond, CA 94805
Songs of Innocence—P.O. Box 719, Radio City Sta., Hell's Kitchen, NY 10101
Southern Humanities Review—9088 Haley Center, Auburn Univ., AL 36849
The Southern Review—43 Allen Hall, LSU, Baton Rouge, LA 70803
Southwest Review—Southern Methodist Univ., Dallas, TX 75275
Sou'Wester—English Dept., Southern Illinois Univ., Edwardsville, IL 62026
The Sow's Ear Press—19535 Pleasant View Dr., Abingdon, VA 24211
Spectacle—PMB 155, 101 Middlesex Trnpke, Ste. 6, Burlington, MA 01803
Spillway—20592 Minerva Lane, Huntington Beach, CA 92646
Spinning Jenny—P.O. Box 213, New York, NY 10014
Sport Literate—P.O. Box 577166, Chicago, IL 60657
Spuyten Duyvil—P.O. Box 1852, Cathedral Sta., New York, NY 10025
Story Quarterly Magazine—P.O. Box 1416, Northbrook, IL 60065
Sufiwarrior—4200 Park Blvd., Ste. 138, Oakland, CA 94602
Sulphur River Literary Review—P.O. Box 19228, Austin, TX 78760
The Sun—107 N. Roberson St., Chapel Hill, NC 27516
Sweet Annie Press—7750 Hwy. F-24, W, Baxter, IA 50028

T

Talking River Review—Lewis-Clark State College, Lewiston, ID 83501
Talus & Scree, see Dancing Moon Press
Tebot Bach, Publisher, see Spillway
The Temple, Gu Si, El Templo—P.O. Box 100, Walla Walla, WA 99362
Thema Literary Society—Box 8747, Metairie, LA 70011
Third Coast—Western Michigan Univ., Kalamazoo, MI 49008
Threepenny Review—P.O. Box 9131, Berkeley, CA 94709
Tia Chucha Press—P.O. Box 476969, Chicago, IL 60647
Tin House—120 East End Ave., Ste. 68, New York, NY 10028
Towers & Rushing, Ltd.—P.O. Box 691745, San Antonio, TX 78269
TriQuarterly—Northwestern Univ., 2020 Ridge Ave., Evanston, IL 60208
Tsunami, Inc.—P.O. Box 100, Walla Walla, WA 99362

U

Union Co. Writers Press—P.O. Box 527, Monroe, NC 28111
Univ. of Georgia Press—330 Research Dr., Athens, GA 30602
Univ. of Massachusetts Press—P.O. Box 429, Amherst, MA 01004
Univ. of Nevada Press—MS 166, Reno, NV 89557
Univ. of North Texas Press—P.O. Box 311336, Denton, TX 76203
Univ. of Pittsburgh Press—3347 Forbes Ave., Pittsburgh, PA 15261
Univ. of Wisconsin Press—2537 Daniels St., Madison, WI 53718
University Press of Colorado—4699 Nautilus Ct., S, Boulder, CO 80301
University Press of Florida—15 NW 15th St., Gainesville, FL 32611
University Press of New England—23 S. Main St., Fl. 3, Hanover, NH 03755
The Urbanite—P.O. Box 4737, Davenport, IA 52808

V

Verse—Plymouth State College, Plymouth, NH 03264
Vice & Verse—P.O. Box 27635, Los Angeles, CA 90027
Victory Park—148 Concord St., Manchester, NH 03104
Vincent Brothers Review—4566 Northern Circle, Riverside, OH 45424

W

Wake up Heavy—P.O. Box 4668, Fresno, CA 93744
Washington Review—Box 50132, Washington, DC 20091
West Anglia Publications—P.O. Box 2683, LaJolla, CA 92038
West End Review—1250 Siskiyou Blvd., Ashland, OR 97520
Whelks Walk Press—37 Harvest Lane, Southampton, NY 11968
Whetstone—P.O. Box 1266, Barrington, IL 60011
White Eagle Coffee Store Press—P.O. Box 383, Fox River Grove, IL 60021
White Pine Press—617 Main St., Ste. 202, Buffalo, NY 14203
Willow Springs—EWU 705 West 1st Ave., Spokane, WA 99201
Wired Art from Wired Hearts—P.O. Box 1012, W. Palm Beach, FL 33402
Witness—27055 Orchard Lake Rd., Farmington Hills, MI 48334
The Word Works, Inc.—P.O. Box 42164, Washington, DC 20015
Word Wrights Magazine—1620 Argonne Pl., NW, Washington, DC 2009
Wordcraft of Oregon—P.O. Box 3235, La Grande, OR 97850
WORDS—209 East 23rd St., New York, NY 10010
Writer to Writer—P.O. Box 2336, Oak Park, IL 60303
The Writer's Garret—P.O. Box 140530, Dallas, TX 75214
Writers Ink Press—233 Mooney Pond, P.O. Box 2344, Selden, NY 11968
Writers' International Forum—P.O. Box 2109, Sequim, WA 98382

Y

Yemassee—Univ. of South Carolina, Columbia, SC 29208
Young Chicago Authors—2049 W. Division St., Chicago, IL 60622

Z

Zeropanik Press—P.O. Box 1565, Trenton, NJ 08607
Zoetrope—260 Fith Ave., Ste. 1200, New York, NY 10001
ZYZZYVA—P.O. Box 590069, San Francisco, CA 94159

CONTRIBUTORS' NOTES

BETTY ADCOCK is the author of four poetry collections from LSU Press. She is writer-in-residence at Meredith College, Raleigh, North Carolina.

BAY ANAPOL lives in Santa Fe and is completing her first novel, which includes a version of this story. She won a Rona Jaffee Grant, and a Stegner Fellowship.

JOHN ASHBERY is a past winner of The Pushcart Prize and many other awards. He lives in New York City.

GLEN CHAMBERLAIN BARRETT lives in Bozeman, Montana and teaches at Montana State University.

CLAIRE BATEMAN lives in Greenville, South Carolina. Her books include *The Bicycle Slow Race* (Wesleyan), *Friction* (Ace Mountain) and *At The Funeral of The Ether* (Furman).

MICHAEL BLUMENTHAL lives in Berlin. His work was featured in PPV and PPIX.

JANE BROX's essay is included in her collection *Five Thousand Days Like This One*, just published by Beacon Press.

E.S. BUMAS is the author of *The Price of Tea in China*, which won the Associated Writing Programs Award for a short story collection.

CATHLEEN CALBERT received the Discover/The Nation Prize. She is the author of two poetry collections, *Lessons In Space* and *Bad Judgment*.

BONNIE JO CAMPBELL lives in Kalamazoo. Her novel is due out from Scribner. Her collection, *Women & Other Animals*, which includes this story, is just out from the University of Massachusetts Press.

RON CARLSON lives in Scottsdale, Arizona and is published by W.W. Norton & Co. He last appeared in PPXXII.

MARIANNA CHERRY lives in San Francisco and is at work on her first novel. She has traveled frequently to Bali and Java.

LUCILLE CLIFTON teaches at St. Mary's College in Maryland, and is the author of many books. Her poem reprinted here appeared at the same time in *Ploughshares* and *Kestrel*.

PHILIP DACEY's books have been published by Johns Hopkins, Milkweed, Black Dirt Press and others. He teaches at Minnesota State University in Marshall.

OLENA KALYTIAK DAVIS resides in San Francisco where she is working on her second collection of poems. Her first is *And Her Soul Out of Nothing* (University of Wisconsin Press).

SHARON DOUBIAGO is the author of the just-published *Body and Soul* (Cedar Hill) which includes this poem, and also of *Hard Country* (West End).

KARL ELDER's fifth book of poems is just out from Prickly Pear Press. He teaches at Lakeland College, Sheboygan, Wisconsin.

LYNN EMANUEL's previous books of poetry are *Hotel Fiesta* and *The Dig*, which received the National Poetry Series Award. She was a poetry co-editor of *The Pushcart Prize*.

BETH ANN FENNELLY has published poems in *Shenandoah*, *Michigan Quarterly Review*, *Poetry Ireland Review* and *Best American Poetry 1996*.

GARY FINCKE has work forthcoming in *Southern Review*, *Paris Review* and *Iowa Review*. His poetry collection is just out from BkMk Press.

FRANK X. GASPAR's *A Field Guide to the Heavens* is just out from the University of Wisconsin Press, and won the Brittingham Prize. His first novel, *Leaving Pico*, just arrived from Hardscrabble Books.

ROBERT GIBB's most recent book is *The Origins of Evening* (Norton). He lives in Homestead, Pennsylvania.

ALBERT GOLDBARTH's two latest books are a volume of poetry and of essays. He won the National Book Critics Circle Award in 1991.

EAMON GRENNAN's poetry is published by Graywolf. He teaches at Vassar. His translations of Leopardi were published by Princeton University Press.

PATRICIA HAMPL last appeared in this series in PPXXIII with the story "The Bill Collector's Vacation." She lives in St. Paul.

JEFFREY HAMMOND has published three books of criticism. His work has been featured in *River Teeth*, *Salmagundi*, *Sport Literate*, *The Missouri Review* and elsewhere.

JANA HARRIS lives on a farm in Sultan, Washington. Her books are *Oh How Can I Keep On Singing?* (Ontario Review) *The Dust of Everyday Life* (Sasquatch) and *The Pearl of Ruby City* (St. Martins).

KARRI LYNN HARRISON is a writer, papermaker and printer from Tennessee. She now teaches in Baltimore.

SEAMUS HEANEY won the Nobel Prize for Literature in 1995. He lives in Dublin. His essay was originally a talk on BBC Radio 4.

MICHAEL HEFFERNAN has published six books of poetry, most recently from Salmon Poetry, Ireland. He has received three NEA grants.

WILLIAM HEYEN is Professor of English and Poet in Residence at SUNY Brockport. He is a past poetry co-editor of *The Pushcart Prize* and the author of many books, most recently from BOA Editions.

BOB HICOK's books are *The Legend of Light*, *Plus Shipping*, and the forthcoming *Animal Soul*.

KATHLEEN HILL's novel, *Still Waters in Niger*, was published in 1999 and named a "Notable Book of the Year" by the *New York Times* and *Michigan Quarterly Review*.

GLENNA HOLLOWAY is a silversmith and enamelist. Her work has been published in *Western Humanities Review*, *Notre Dame Review*, *Spoon River Poetry Review*, *The Fomalist*, *The Hollins Critic* and *Christian Century*.

VIRGINIA HOLMAN runs the literary arts program at Duke University Medical Center, where she works with long term patients, their families and medical staff. Her work has appeared in *Crescent Review*, *The Independent Weekly* and elsewhere.

FANNY HOWE is the author of several books of poetry and fiction, including *Saving History*, and *Nod*. She teaches in San Diego.

ANDREW HUDGINS teaches at the University of Cincinnati and is the author of five books of poetry, including most recently, *Babylon In A Jar*.

JONATHAN DAVID JACKSON is a poet, dancer, and choreographer. He teaches at Temple University.

KEN KALFUS lived in Russia from 1994 to 1998. His most recent book is *PU-239 and Other Russian Fantasies* (Milkweed), which includes this story. He lives in Philadelphia.

DAVID KIRBY's poetry appeared in *Best American Poetry 2000* and his *The House of Blue Light* was published by Louisiana State University.

FRED LEEBRON's novels are *Six Figures* (Knopf, 2000) and *Outwest* (Doubleday, 1996). His work has been featured in *Tin House*, *Grand Street*, *North American Review* and elsewhere.

DANIEL LIBMAN lives in Northern Illinois. His stories have appeared in *The Baffler*, *Paris Review*, *The Santa Monica Review* and *Columbia*.

BRET LOTT is the author of five novels, two story collections and a memoir. He is working on a collection of essays.

PAUL MALISZEWSKI's writing appears in *The Baffler*, *Conjunctions*, *Gettysburg Review* and elsewhere.

BEN MARCUS teaches at Columbia University. He also appeared in *Pushcart Prize XX* with "False Water Society."

CHARLES MARTIN is the author of four books of poems, including *Steal the Bacon* and *What the Darkness Proposes*, both published by Johns Hopkins Press. He is at work on a new verse translation of Ovid's *Metamorphosis* for W.W. Norton.

NANCY McCABE's work appears in *Prairier Schooner*, *Puetro del Sol*, and *Writing on the Edge*. She teaches at Presbyterian College, Clinton, South Carolina.

JANE McCAFFERTY won the Drue Heinz Prize for Literature in 1992. Her first novel, *One Heart*, is just out.

HEATHER McHUGH is a past poetry co-editor of *The Pushcart Prize*. She lives in Maine and Seattle, where she teaches at the University of Washington.

ELIZABETH McKENZIE lives in Santa Cruz, California. Her fiction has appeared in *TriQuarterly*, *Shenandoah*, and *George Mason Review*.

LYNNE McMAHON teaches at the University of Missouri. She lives in Columbia, Missouri.

ANA MENENDEZ won a *New York Times* fellowship and now divides her time between Miami and India. She is at work on a short story collection and a novel.

JOYCE CAROL OATES is the author most recently of *Blonde*. She is a Founding Editor of this series.

SHARON OLDS' sixth book of poems, *Blood, Tin, Straw* was published by Knopf in 1999. She has been the Poet Laureate of New York State.

JULIE ORRINGER is a Truman Capote Fellow in the Stegner Program at Stanford University. She won the Paris Review Discovery Prize.

JACQUELINE OSHEROW's *Dead Men's Praise* was published by Grove last year. She lives in Salt Lake City.

EDITH PEARLMAN's *Vaquita and Other Stories* won a Drue Heinz Prize and was published by the University of Pittsburgh Press in 1996. Her work has also been reprinted in *Best American Short Stories* and *O'Henry* collections.

AMUDHA RAJENDRAN has published in *The Cimarron Review*, *Lit.*, *Barrow Street* and *Verse*. She lives in New York City.

GREG RAPPLEYE is the winner of the 1999 Mississippi Review poetry prize. His book *A Path Between Houses* is just out from the University of Wisconsin Press.

ALBERTO RIOS is the author of the memoir *Capirotada* and other books. He is Professor of English at Arizona State University.

SHEROD SANTOS is the author of a collection of essays *A Poetry of Two Minds* (University of Georgia) and *The Pilot Star Elegies* (Norton), his most recent gathering of poetry.

SALVATORE SCIBONA lives in Berea, Ohio. This is his first appearance in this series, and also the first for *News From the Republic of Letters*.

RICHARD SIKEN lives in Tucson. His poems have been published in *Chelsea*, *The James White Review*, *Many Mountains Moving*, *Sonora Review* and elsewhere.

JOAN SILBER's *In My Other Life* was recently published by Sarabande Books. She is the author of the novels *In The City* and *Household Words*. She won the PEN/Hemingway Award and a Guggenheim grant.

A.A. SRINIVASAN lives in Los Angeles. "Tusk" is her first published story.

GERALD STERN was a poetry co-editor of *The Pushcart Prize*. He won a National Book Award in 1998.

JAMES TATE won the Pulitzer Prize and the William Carlos Williams Award. His latest book is *Shroud of the Gnome* (Ecco).

PAULS TOUTONGHI received an NEA grant recently. He lives in Seattle. "Regeneration" is his first published story.

PAUL VIOLI's most recent books are *Fracas* (Hanging Loose) and *Breaker* (Coffee House). His first prose collection will appear soon from Hanging Loose.

CHARLES HARPER WEBB is the author of a novel, *The Wilderness Effect*, and a book of poems, *Reading the Water*. He won the 1999 Felix Pollak Prize in Poetry.

EUDORA WELTY has published five volumes of short stories. She lives in Jackson, Mississippi in the house where she was born in 1909.

WILLIAM WENTHE's first book of poems is *Birds of Hoboken* (Orchises Press). He teaches at Texas Tech University.

JONAH WINTER writes and illustrates children's books. His most recent volume is *Fair Ball: 14 Great Stars from Baseball's Negro Leagues*.

STEPHEN YENSER lives in Los Angeles. He is the author of *The Fire in All Things* (LSU Press).

INDEX

The following is a listing in alphabetical order by author's last name of works reprinted in the *Pushcart Prize* editions.

594

597

601

603

605

608

609

611

613

616

617

619

620